FROM THE PAGES OF THE *HISTORY OF THE PELOPONNESIAN WAR*

The absence of romance in my history will, I fear, detract somewhat from its interest; but if it be judged useful by those inquirers who desire an exact knowledge of the past as an aid to the interpretation of the future, which in the course of human things must resemble if it does not reflect it, I shall be content. In fine, I have written my work, not as an essay which is to win the applause of the moment, but as a possession for all time. (Book 1, chapter 22; page 19)

'Neither are we beginning war, Peloponnesians, nor are we breaking the treaty; but these Corcyræans are our allies, and we are come to help them. So if you want to sail anywhere else, we place no obstacle in your way; but if you are going to sail against Corcyra, or any of her possessions, we shall do our best to stop you.'
(Book 1, chapter 53; pages 36–37)

'In short, I say that as a city we are the school of Hellas; while I doubt if the world can produce a man, who where he has only himself to depend upon, is equal to so many emergencies, and graced by so happy a versatility as the Athenian.' (Book 2, chapter 41; page 118)

Words had to change their ordinary meaning and to take that which was now given them. Reckless audacity came to be considered the courage of a loyal ally; prudent hesitation, specious cowardice; moderation was held to be a cloak for unmanliness; ability to see all sides of a question inaptness to act on any.
(Book 3, chapter 82; pages 198–199)

An Athenian ally, who some time after insultingly asked one of the prisoners from the island if those that had fallen were men of honour, received for answer that the *atraktos*—that is, the arrow—would be worth a great deal if it could tell men of honour from the rest.
(Book 4, chapter 40; page 241)

I lived through the whole of it, being of an age to comprehend events, and giving my attention to them in order to know the exact truth about them. It was also my fate to be an exile from my country for twenty years after my command at Amphipolis; and being present with both parties, and more especially with the Peloponnesians by reason of my exile, I had leisure to observe affairs somewhat particularly. (Book 5, chapter 26; page 307)

The siege was now pressed vigorously; and some treachery taking place inside, the Melians surrendered at discretion to the Athenians, who put to death all the grown men whom they took, and sold the women and children for slaves, and subsequently sent out five hundred colonists and inhabited the place themselves.
(Book 5, chapter 116; page 346)

The ships being now manned, and everything put on board with which they meant to sail, the trumpet commanded silence, and the prayers customary before putting out to sea were offered, not in each ship by itself, but by all together to the voice of a herald; and bowls of wine were mixed through all the armament, and libations made by the soldiers and their officers in gold and silver goblets.
(Book 6, chapter 32; page 366)

This was the greatest Hellenic achievement of any in this war, or, in my opinion, in Hellenic history; at once most glorious to the victors, and most calamitous to the conquered. They were beaten at all points and altogether; all that they suffered was great; they were destroyed, as the saying is, with a total destruction, their fleet, their army—everything was destroyed, and few out of many returned home.
(Book 7, chapter 87; page 459)

When the news was brought to Athens, for a long while they disbelieved even the most respectable of the soldiers who had themselves escaped from the scene of action and clearly reported the matter, a destruction so complete not being thought credible.
(Book 8, chapter 1; page 461)

THE HISTORY OF THE PELOPONNESIAN WAR

*Translated by Richard Crawley
and Revised by Donald Lateiner*

With an Introduction and Notes by Donald Lateiner

George Stade
Consulting Editorial Director

𝒥𝒷

BARNES & NOBLE CLASSICS
NEW YORK

ℳℬ
BARNES & NOBLE CLASSICS

NEW YORK

Published by Barnes & Noble Books
122 Fifth Avenue
New York, NY 10011

www.barnesandnoble.com/classics

Thucydides is thought to have written *The History of the
Peloponnesian War* between 431 and 400 B.C.E. Richard Crawley's
translation first appeared in 1876.

Published in 2006 by Barnes & Noble Classics with new Introduction, Note on the
Translation, Notes, Biography, Chronology, Inspired By, Comments & Questions,
and For Further Reading.

Introduction, Note on the Translation, Notes, and For Further Reading
Copyright © 2006 by Donald Lateiner.

Note on Thucydides, The World of Thucydides and the Peloponnesian War, Inspired
by *The History of the Peloponnesian War*, and Comments & Questions
Copyright © 2006 by Barnes & Noble, Inc.

Maps 2, 3, 7, and 12 are reprinted from *Ancient History: From Prehistoric Times to the
Death of Justinian, 2nd edition* by Charles Alexander Robinson, Jr.
(New York: Macmillan Company, 1967). Maps copyright © by Erwin Raisz.
Reprinted by permission of Raisz Landform Maps, Brookline, MA.

Maps 1, 4-6, and 8-11 are reprinted from *A History of Greece to 322 B.C., 2nd edition* by
H. G. Hammond (Oxford: Clarendon Press, 1967). Copyright © by Oxford University
Press. Reprinted by permission of Oxford University Press.

The History of the Peloponnesian War
ISBN-13: 978-1-59308-091-4
ISBN-10: 1-59308-091-3
LC Control Number 2005935855

Produced and published in conjunction with:
Fine Creative Media, Inc.
322 Eighth Avenue
New York, NY 10001
Michael J. Fine, President & Publisher

Printed in the United States of America

QM

3 5 7 9 10 8 6 4 2

THUCYDIDES

The author of *History of the Peloponnesian War* was born in ancient Greece into Athens' Golden Age—the era of Athenian democracy, when seminal thinkers of every kind redefined the sciences, history, mathematics, philosophy, and the arts. Socrates, Herodotus, Sophocles, Aristophanes, and Euripides flourished during Thucydides' lifetime.

The *History of the Peloponnesian War* is the only existing record for much of the activity it documents, including the life of its author. Of Thucydides we know very little. Many legends abound, such as his relationships with various luminaries of the day. Most of the accounts of his life were written centuries after his death and are not reliable.

Scholars agree on a few facts. About 460 B.C.E. Thucydides was born at Halimous, a *deme* (township) of Attica on the coast of the Saronic Gulf, southwest of Athens; he was a member of an apparently respected family whose wealth came from Thracian gold mines. As a young man Thucydides was schooled among sophists and rhetoricians, and when war between Athens and Sparta broke out in 431, he began recording its history.

He barely survived the outbreak of the plague in Athens around 430 and later took part in the war he documented. Elected a general in 424, he went to the defense of the northern city of Amphipolis, but Athens lost the city to the Spartans, and Thucydides was banished from Athens, spending twenty years in exile. Many scholars say that writing from his home in Thrace afforded him a more impartial view of the war than he might otherwise have had. Indeed, one of Thucydides' chief achievements may be his search for historical truth rather than an attempt to promote the interests of one side or the other.

Thucydides' great history remains unfinished; the events recorded extend only through the year 411. Although we do not know the circumstances of the historian's death, he returned to Athens shortly after the war ended in 404 and then labored to complete his masterwork. Thucydides died around 400 B.C.E.

TABLE OF CONTENTS

LIST OF MAPS

THE WORLD OF THUCYDIDES AND THE
HISTORY OF THE PELOPONNESIAN WAR

c.460 B.C.E. Thucydides, an Athenian, is born at Halimous, a *deme* (township) of Attica on the coast of the Saronic Gulf, southwest of Athens; he is the son of Olorus, a wealthy aristocrat. As a young man, Thucydides studies with sophists and rhetoricians.

446 Athens, a rich imperial city, has enjoyed for fifty years a democratic government and a strong navy; Attica is the territory surrounding and controlled by Athens. Less wealthy Sparta, the chief city of the Peloponnese and one ruled by a unique oligarchy (a privileged soldier class), has a strong land army. Rivals for dominance in Greece, Athens and Sparta have been engaged for some fifteen years in what is sometimes called the First Peloponnesian War. This year they sign a peace pact known as the Thirty Years' Treaty.

433 Athens strikes an alliance with Corcyra, a colony of the city of Corinth.

432 Athens attacks Potidaea, another Corinthian colony. Corinth appeals to Sparta for help. Sparta and its allies believe Athens has broken the truce of 446, and the cities renew their hostility.

431 The Peloponnesian War begins with a sneak attack by an expeditionary force of Thebes (an ally of Sparta) into the city of Plataea (an ally of Athens); the attack is defeated. Thucydides begins recording the history of the war. The Spartans, under their king, Archidamus, tentatively invade Attica. Athens goes on the offensive, attacking the Peloponnesian coasts, destroying the city of Megara and taking control and colonizing the island of Aegina. Following these military actions, Pericles, the Athenian leader, delivers a memorable funeral oration for those who have died in the battles.

430 Archidamus leads the Spartans in a determined forty-day invasion of Attica. In Athens, plague spreads virulently in the city, densely populated because the people of Attica have congregated there for safety during the war. Thucydides becomes deathly ill.

430– 429 The Spartans are repulsed when they attack cities in western Greece that are allied with Athens.

429 Pericles dies, a victim of plague, and Cleon becomes the leader of Athens.

428 Sparta again invades Attica. The cities of the island of Lesbos try to break off from Athenian rule, leading the Athenians to launch a siege of the island's great city, Mytilene.

427 Mytilene falls to Athens, and Plataea falls to Sparta. Plague hits Athens again. Cleon refuses offers of peace from the Spartans.

426 Earthquakes keep the Spartans from invading Attica, and Athens has further victories.

425 Sparta again invades Attica. Athens sends a fleet to Syracuse, on Sicily, and succeeds in capturing the island Cythera, located off the southern Peloponnese.

424 After several defeats, Athens abandons the expedition to Sicily. Thucydides is elected a general and leads a defense of Amphipolis against Spartan forces commanded by Brasidas. Thucydides' failure to save the city results in his banishment from Athens, which will last more than twenty years; during his exile, Thucydides will strengthen his resolve to portray the two sides accurately and will develop his history of the war.

423 Athens and Sparta strike a year's truce.

422 When hostilities are renewed, Cleon and Brasidas are killed in battle outside the walls of Amphipolis. Nicias replaces Cleon as the dominant leader in Athens and accepts overtures for peace from the Spartans.

421 During the six years of the shaky Peace of Nicias, there is intermittent fighting between the two powerful city-states.

418 Sparta defeats Athens and Argos at Mantinea.

416 Athens takes the island of Melos.

415 Encouraged by the brilliant general Alcibiades, Athens brings an end to the Peace of Nicias by attacking Syracuse in Sicily. Accused of parodying Demeter's rites, Alcibiades is called to trial; he escapes and defects to join the Spartans against Athens. Sparta mounts a resurgence of attacks on Athens.

413 Spartan military leadership helps Syracuse overturn an Athenian blockade, and the Athenian army and navy are defeated and enslaved trying to flee Syracuse.

412 At Sparta's instigation, the Athenian subject cities along the coast of Ionia are rocked by revolution. Alcibiades, now a traitor to the Spartan cause, wants to return to Athens, and the Athenians reluctantly accept him as a commander.

411 Oligarchic revolution by "the Four Hundred" throws Athens into turmoil and violence. Thucydides' narrative breaks off in the winter of this year.

410   Alcibiades again leads Athenian troops. In Athens, democracy is restored.

408   In retaking Byzantium for Athens, Alcibiades regains control of Black Sea trade routes.

407   Celebrated in Athens on his return, Alcibiades is given full command of the Athenian forces.

406   Alcibiades is defeated at Notium; he loses his position and retires to his estate. Athens vanquishes Sparta at Arginusae, but in Athens the Athenians' own generals are tried and executed.

405   The Athenians are severely defeated and their navy destroyed by the Spartans at Aegospotami.

404   Athens, suffering under an unbreakable Spartan blockade, surrenders; thus begins the decline of Athens as the culturally and politically dominant Greek city-state. In Athens, now a subject-ally of Sparta, a Sparta-sponsored oligarchy of the "Thirty" seizes power, and a bloody reign ensues. Plague and starvation cripple the city. Shortly after the end of the war, Thucydides returns to Athens.

403   Following battles between oligarchs and democrats for control of Athens, the traditional institutions of democracy are restored.

c.400   Thucydides dies, leaving his history unfinished.

Introduction to Thucydides
and His History

Thucydides the Athenian: Man, Citizen, General, and Historian

Thucydides has a self-effacing character. We learn little about his life from him (and less from anyone else, since the next century largely ignores his work) beyond his Athenian citizenship, the fact that he suffered from the plague, his military command, and his loss of that command after his failure to hold and secure Thracian Amphipolis. Thucydides, the son of a man named Olorus, was born into high rank and wealth at Halimous, a *deme* (township) of Attica on the coast of the Saronic Gulf, southwest of Athens (see 4.105 for mention of his right to work gold mines in Thrace). Early in the twenty-seven-year (5.26) Peloponnesian War (431–404 B.C.E.), as we call it, he was a victim of the great Athenian plague (2.47–50), a disease now unidentifiable. Thucydides was elected *strategos* (general), one of a board of ten land and sea commanders, the highest elective office that the Athenian *polis* (city-state) offered, for the Athenian year 424/423 (twelve months beginning in late June). He may have held military rank or political office before this time, since the office of *strategos* was the culmination of a military or political career; but we know nothing further. Pericles (c.495–429) held this office, elected by the sovereign people, nearly every year for thirty years, beginning around 460. Thucydides commanded Athenian ships in the North Aegean, but failed to stop the Spartan commander Brasidas from capturing a vital dependency, Amphipolis, the gateway to the North. The Athenian demos consequently deposed Thucydides from office and exiled him for twenty years, until the oligarchic *putsch* of the "Thirty" or the post-war democratic amnesty (5.26) allowed him to return home. In exile, he came to understand and appreciate the Peloponnesian view of the war. He was old enough to understand the beginnings of the fighting, he asserts (and so probably was not much older than thirty then), and the machinations before, and lived to see the disastrous end in defeat for Athens, but not to write it up in detail (5.26; 2.65). His extant *History* breaks off disconcertingly in mid-sentence in 411 (8.109; for an explanation of the sudden ending, see Canfora, *Tucidide continuato*, listed in the "For Further Reading" section).

Thucydides must have had independent means that allowed him to write. Did his Thracian mining investments and licenses hold good for the twenty years during which Athens exiled him from its empire? This speculation leads one to ask whether warfare in Thrace disturbed the mining industry. Did the cash-starved Athenians not take over the banished politician's mining "rights"?

Thucydides' banishment—the Athenians expelled him from Athens and its dependencies, including parts of Thrace—had the unexpected benefit of granting him access to enemy Spartan sources. Thucydides surely queried soldiers and officers, though he and his enemy Brasidas probably did not compare notes. The scholar G. B. Grundy (*Thucydides and the History of His Age*, vol. 2) wrote twenty-two quatrains about Thucydides' oeuvre: "He told of Brasidas the brave; / And at the great magician's touch / He rises once more from the grave, / The knight *sans peur et sans reproche*." Thucydides had Spartan sources, however, for some of the policies and thoughts attributed to Athens' enemies.

Though a highly idiosyncratic writer and thinker, like any author Thucydides betrays the influences of the literature and research of his day. Books have traced his connections to contemporary medicine, sophistic rhetoric and argumentation, philosophy, and drama (Cochrane, Finley, Solmsen, Cornford, Hunter, etc.), as well as to his historical predecessor, Herodotus (484–414). Thucydides' polemical historiographical strictures on the methods of historical research and presentation are not necessarily directed against Herodotus, since other authors, in poetry and in prose, treated the same prior events that Herodotus also mentions. For instance, in the case of the comments on the notorious Delian earthquake, the two authors seem to pass each other in the night—oblivious to the specifics that the other has mentioned. But then why is it that Thucydides' speeches rarely refer to any past event not found in Herodotus' text (Hornblower, *A Commentary on Thucydides*, vol. 2, p. 123)? When did Thucydides obtain the text of the Ionian historian? Around 424 or a decade later? Did either or both of these historians publish their histories in chunks rather than as the full text that we have today? Some have argued for independent publication of Thucydides' book 1, or 1 through 5.24 (the events leading to the war and the course of the Ten Years' War) or books 6 and 7 (the Sicilian *Expedition*, as Athenian sympathizers call it, rather than the *Invasion*).[1] Thucydides' awareness of his predecessor appears in his inclusions (for example, important battles and pre-battle harangues) and exclusions (such as ominous names). The two historians share many qualities, but they differently characterize prominent individuals and events. Their accounts of pivotal battles differ not least because of Thucydides' superior field experience as Athenian soldier and commander. Thucydides' debt to Herodotus, nevertheless, involves much more than the existence of speeches and battles—for example, inclusions of colonization, myth, and geography (see Pearson, "Thucydides and the Geographical Tradition"). Thucydides never mentions Herodotus by name, although he names the less important fifth-century historian Hellanicus (the citation is isolated, and perhaps to be excised; see Parke, "Citation and Recitation"). Is this a slight to Herodotus or a compliment? In the fifth century, no one memorized prose authors or had a wish to look up a reference. Thucydides, unlike Herodotus, does not cite the poets; as with many of his contributions, he excluded materials that others previously included.

Thucydides shares many of Herodotus' interests. They both focus on military history. They both want to report names of places and people, although the Athenian shows less interest in "coincidences" such as *nomen-omen*—for example, Hegesistratus, a name that a Spartan king identified as meaningful, when looking for a guide, because it translates as "Leader of the Expedition." Both also suppress names and make explicit or implicit decisions not to specify individuals—for example, the Spartan commander and the five Spartan judges at Plataea (3.52)—and other officers and speakers are left anonymous.

Thucydides is likely to have known several sophists, and his antithetical writing style shows the influence of the Sicilian Gorgias, whose interests included epistemology and rhetoric. He is also likely to have known Sophocles, a general as well as a tragedian. He mentions neither these two nor Socrates, a notorious Attic gadfly of Pericles and the next generation.

Thucydides states his objective in his *History* for practicing "history." He wants to be useful (1.22) to those interested in how humans behave and in what will happen repeatedly, given certain constants of human nature (compare 3.83). He makes no claim to prophecy, but, clearly, he saw "his" war as the negative exemplar for inter- and intrastate conflict. He sardonically presents orators' high-flown words that often contrast with the facts of historical events that they report, or with their predictions for the future, or with many speakers who decried fancy rhetorics (for example, 1.73; 2.41; 5.89). Nevertheless, the funeral oration that he puts in the mouth of Pericles, at a moment just before plague strikes, surpasses all possible competition in patriotic oratory. The Greeks believed not in historical cyclicity but in patterns of human behavior. Both Plato, the idealist, and Aristotle, the realist, belittle finding any universal message in specific events (see Aristotle's *Poetics* 9.1451b, with specific reference to what Alcibiades did and said),[2] but Thucydides (and Hobbes in his wake) thought otherwise. Thucydides, like Machiavelli later, was a historian as well as a political theorist.

The Athenian Empire and the Peloponnesian Wars

Soon after the Hellenes defeated the Persian invasions at Marathon, Salamis, Plataea, and Mycale early in the fifth century, the Spartans and their mainland allies went home to enjoy some well-earned peace and quiet. The Ionians on the frontier abutting Persian power, however, asked the Athenians to continue to lead an alliance to protect them from further Persian attempts to return them to Persian control as satellites or to bring them under Persian autocracy. The Athenians gladly acceded, and with their fleet enlarged for the Persian War, they quickly brought into this defensive league the willing and the unwilling. Each city-state had to pay for protection, either by means of men with ships or by cash. Many small communities quickly chose the latter, less dangerous method (1.97–99). This left them, however, at the mercy of the Delian League (also called the Hellenic League), founded in 478 and headquartered in Delos—a body, perhaps *de jure* representative and bicameral, but *de facto* under Athenian control. Spartan attitudes, initially friendly toward their recent ally, became more fearful as Athenian power grew and the league became an arm of Athenian expansion abroad and power on the mainland. The first Peloponnesian War (461–445), fought between Athens and the Delian League and Sparta and the Peloponnesian League, ended in a stalemate, since on land the latter were stronger in numbers and discipline than Athenian hoplite forces (infantrymen), while Athens and her "allies" ruled the Aegean Sea and beyond.

Diplomatic maneuvering for resources and allies marked the following fifteen years in preparation for what looked like an inevitable war. Realms outside the Aegean such as Persia, Macedon, Thrace, the Black Sea cities, and Sicily were not immediately involved but were among the prizes and potential allies. While Thucydides may have exaggerated (1.1, 23) the magnitude of the long war (there were many months of uneasy peace), he seems to have been right about the catastrophic suffering it inflicted and the permanent damage it did to Hellenic morality, civility, and interstate relations.

Thucydides included some material that one would not expect from so parsimonious a talent. He obviously felt a need to segue from the Persian Wars (detailed by Herodotus) to his own war; his account of the roughly fifty years in between (479–431), brief though it be (1.89–118), provides our best record of how the power of Athens arose and grew until it was perceived as a formidable, indeed an unendurable, threat.[3] We have the unusual biographical sketches of Themistocles and Pausanias, two heroes of the Persian Wars whom the Greeks came to view as villains. But for the most part, Thucydides discusses only geography and events in distant history (such as the

Athenian tyrants' deposition) that seem germane, misunderstood, or necessary to him.

Primarily, he reports battles, Athenian and other cities' political maneuvers, and speeches, often in pairs on opposite sides of a question. Nameless Athenians debate nameless Corinthians about Spartan policy; Diodotus debates Cleon about the fate of the Mytileneans who rebelled against Athenian rule.

In discussing the war, Thucydides left out many elements that modern students consider essential. For instance, he almost never mentions his predecessors (such as Antiochus of Syracuse, probably an eyewitness to the Athenian invasion). He seems to assume we know what we need to know, or that practices for warfare and constitutional or administrative procedure do not change. In Sparta, these procedures were hard to discover, as he comments more than once (1.79; 2.39; 4.80; 5.68). Economic procedures and conditions were not an interest of any ancient historian, but Thucydides seems to recognize the importance of imperial revenue for Athenian power, so we cannot say whether he could not obtain meaningful fiscal numbers or chose not to include such boring and distracting data in his primarily political study.

The Athenian Tribute Lists, epigraphical inscribed stone records of imperial income, are useful for supplementing Thucydides' sparse economic data, for his minimalist fiscal information leaves economic issues in the gloaming. For example, the reassessment decree of 425/424 (Fornara #136) was important psychologically and financially. Even if the legislated increase in Athenian revenues had been a flop, he probably would have included it; Thucydides is as much interested in spectacular imperial and military failures as in success, as one sees in his attention to the catastrophic Athenian expedition against Syracuse or the earlier aborted Peloponnesian attack on Piraeus (7.87; 2.93–94). How then can one explain Thucydides' blind spot for the imperial purse? Perhaps Thucydides realized that a ledger-book economic history would not hold the reader's attention "forever."

More irritating yet to an epoch of cultural historians is Thucydides' lack of attention to the sophistic movement, medicine (except for the account of the plague), the theater, the fine arts, literature, and architecture. He does attend to race (as he knew it: Greeks and Barbarians, Ionian and Dorian Greeks) and to class, at times (slave and helot [state-owned serf] revolts, the conflicts of the rich and the poor, of democrats and oligarchs). "The glory that was Greece" for Thucydides, nevertheless, was military power and political control and effectiveness; it was not marble, not drama, and not painting—certainly not child's play or gender conflicts.[4]

A general introduction to Thucydides' "intellectual setting," personal history, and idiosyncrasies requires immersion in a tiny and an alien world. Thucydides' peculiar and disturbing record of a devastating war, an uncivil war, requires knowledge of the ancient *polis*—its poetics, historiography, archaeology, and linguistics—and a willingness to wrestle with a challenging mind. Thucydides assumes his reader already possesses adequate knowledge of Aegean topography, ancient Hellenic finance, and contemporary religious procedures. Battle sacrifices, sanctuary layout, and inscriptions concerning cults intermittently appear in the ancient text only when those events impinge on politics or war. Thucydides does not explain many puzzling items—they are seemingly too elementary—although he sought an audience far off from his own time and place, and sometimes annotates the obvious, like the fact that Piraeus is Athens' port.

This frequent problem of Thucydides' silences compounds the quandary of deciding what Thucydides "takes for granted" (Gomme's phrase in *A Historical Commentary on Thucydides*). Thucydides suppresses, ignores, or takes for granted details of finance, evidence from inscriptions (for the most part), contemporary scandals, seventh-century history, the Ionian revolt, and the First Peloponnesian War. In addition to this information, Thucydides remains silent about many other topics for reasons (we can only guess) of relevance or seemliness, and geographical or chronological inaccessibility. Some of this haughty disregard seems a defect by standards of modern relevance (women, finance, contemporary sexual or bribery scandals; the Ionian revolt from Persia; most cults and oracles). Hans Müller-Strübing, a vociferous critic of Thucydides in the later nineteenth century, observed: "Thukydides ist gross im Verschweigen" ("Thucydides is big in silence"). Yet we encounter unexpected mention of dances and sacrifices celebrated at Sparta for the return of Pleistoanax (5.16).

Organization and Research in the History: Time and Space

We can briefly examine Thucydides' sources, evidence, and selectivity. Thucydides tells us that he tried to speak to as many participants as possible, not just accepting what one or another person saw, much less heard (1.22). He is hard on inaccurate (and unnamed) historians who do just that (1.20; 6.55–60; etc.). He does refer to and quote inscriptions that he has examined (6.54, 59), but not the Tribute Lists.

The attempted subjugations of the island Melos pose interesting questions. An inscriptional (and contemporary, early in the war) source (Fornara #132) records "contributions" to the Spartan war effort, and Melos is one island named. Since Melos contributed to the Peloponnesian War Fund and had been on a war footing with Athens at least since 426 (3.91), when it rejected an "invitation" to join

Athens' league, why does Thucydides imply (5.84) that it was a neutral state when the imperial Athenian navy attacked it again in 416? He provides an elaborate and frank dialogue between unnamed Melians and Athenians (5.85–116)—rather than the usual consecutive set speeches—before the barely noted fighting begins. This time the Athenians reduced and erased the old community. The paradigmatic expression of the recently theorized issue of might versus customary right appears just prior to the Sicilian Expedition. Thucydides starkly contrasts the arguments for freedom and power. Some critics have thought that here Thucydides has sacrificed some accuracy to dramatic opportunities for chronologically juxtaposing sharp antitheses and contrasting hubristic power and rapid comeuppance (compare Meiggs, *The Athenian Empire*, pp. 382–390).

For events that had occurred before his lifetime, he doubts the dependability of the history that has come down to him, but in his account of early days and the rise of previous Hellenic powers (1.1–19) he claims careful research and reasonable confidence for his inferences and explanations. Like any historian, Thucydides knows more than he tells us. The lack of competing accounts in part explains his sovereign reputation. There is no doubt that he was selective, that he gives only some speeches, although he mentions that more were delivered and reports certain incidents of siege or battle while he refers to others only in passing. Whereas Herodotus often gives alternative versions of one event, Thucydides nearly always chooses the account or reconstruction that seems best to him and ignores other versions (as for the Plataeans and Thebans at 2.5) or divergent explanations. A rare exception (5.65 provides another) appears in his account of why the Phoenician fleet never got involved in the last phase of the war (8.87; compare Lateiner, "Tissaphernes and the Phoenician Fleet," and Connor, *Thucydides*, pp. 215–217, on an innovative "open methodology") in which Thucydides provides four explanations. Thucydides does not imitate Herodotus' distancing phrases, such as "it is said" or "the Samians claim." The earlier historian felt an obligation to report events and accounts even when he knew they were false or at least contradictory. Thucydides removes both accretions and unacceptable explanations, as he consciously distances himself from Herodotus' techniques of reportage and subject matter.

The chronology (annalism) to some extent determined the structure of the work. Thucydides saw a unity to the quarter-century of conflict, a view that was not everyone's. He divides the twenty-seven-year war into three parts (5.25–26): the Ten Years' War (431–421), the six-year, ten-month peace or armistice (421–415), and the renewed war, both in Sicily (415–413) and in the Aegean (413–404). Some events, especially when the first of their kind, obtain "headline" extended coverage with speeches that underline their significance.

Book 3 alone offers the debate in Athens over how to treat surrendered rebels in Lesbos (3.26–50), the Spartans' "mock trial for Spartans" and mass executions after the siege of Plataea (3.51–68), and the lethal civil war in Corcyra (3.69–85). Book 5, after much miscellany, closes with the reduction of weak "neutrals" into dependents or their annihilation (the siege of Melos, 5.84–116).

The division into eight books is probably not the author's doing. His clearest division is into years, with years divided into winters and the longer Greek campaigning season of spring and summer and early fall. Year One begins with the present book 2, after an account of the preceding ages and the diplomatic affairs of Corcyra and Potidaea. The years 415–413 in Sicily occupy two full books, but other years receive very brief coverage. Thucydides uses formulas to begin and end a year such as (3.116–4.1; compare 4.135–5.1): "Such were the events of this winter; and with it ended the sixth year of this war, of which Thucydides was the historian. Next summer, about the time of the grain's coming into ear, ten Syracusan ... vessels sailed to Messina."

This annalism breaks up units, since Thucydides will refer to events in different theaters of the war even when it breaks up continuity within a campaign. Dionysius of Halicarnassus criticizes him bitterly for this choppy result. In an age, however, without a common calendar or even counting of years (such as the Christian calendar now provides in much of the world), Thucydides' strict organization by year ameliorated a general confusion about dates and synchronies.

Thucydides sets up a dominant and overriding system of temporal markers—summers and winters (2.1), and "meanwhile," and "right after this" (4.2, 5, 7–9)—but no one could stick to such a rigid plan without making exceptions. Even as he followed it, the method produces the "bittiness" of reporting a series of events that Dionysius complained about (Dionysius of Halicarnassus, *On Thucydides*, 9; Rood, *Thucydides*, p. 114). Displacement in time of some incidents is essential to representing the "cussedness of reality" (Rood, p. 111). For example, many events are foreshadowed by explicit anticipatory references (early Athenian intervention in Sicily: 3.90; the later Sicilian debacle: 2.8, 65; 4.81, 108; 6.15, 31; 7.28), and the decline of Athens from its acme at the start of the war (1.1; 2.20, 31, 49) to its defeat and surrender (2.65; 5.26). Fewer references take us to long past events (for example, 1.2–19, 89–118; 6.2–5). Less explicitly, Themistocles prefigures Pericles positively by his intelligence and political savvy, and Pericles prefigures his inadequate political successors negatively (1.138; 2.60, 65).

Thucydides argues at times with the way that the Greeks of his day thought about past discoveries and Hellenic settlements (for example, 4.120; compare both Westlake, *Essays on the Greek Historians and Greek History*, pp. 1–38, and Pearson). Thucydides can be universalist ("possession for ever") or assume his audience is parochial (as when he informs the reader [2.93] that Piraeus is the port of Athens). But when and why does he give or withhold basic information? Racial origin and descent, both real and fictitious, were important to the decision-making processes of the *polis*. But Thucydides usually does not indulge these approaches, and it is uncharacteristic when he mentions that Achaeans returning from the Trojan War settled Scione (4.120)—a hint of legend that is suggestive (compare 6.2) of Herodotean filiations.

The unprecedented quoted texts of treaties and the negotiations for Melos (including complications arising from extant inscriptions) have brought up questions of compositional methods for contemporary scholars. Analyst critics cheerfully set aside literary issues after pointing out the compositional problems of different sections and books: Were they early, late, finished, unrevised? Archaeologists and historians who are not conversant with recent developments in Thucydidean studies show "alarming deference to Thucydides' authority" (Hornblower, *Commentary*, vol. 2, p. 125, note 6), unlike the scathing indictments of Herodotus' allegedly sloppy research. The positivist approach believes some facts—like some rocks—are demonstrably real, and that we can turn to Thucydides to recover as much of the history of the preliminary and determinative "Fifty Years" (479–431) and the twenty-seven years of the war (431–404). Books 6 and 7 form a quasi-independent unit that recollects both Homer's Trojan expedition and contemporary Attic tragedy. Book 8 has not yet received the literary analysis that its unmined riches demand.

Another problem bedeviling Thucydidean scholarship is whether the whole work and its various sections are a "finished and experimental work of art" (the "unitarian" view) or a "fragment needing further work" (the "analytical" view; Hornblower, *Commentary*, vol. 2 [2003], p. 19). The point of view from which an action is reported, authorial intrusions, and other aids for determining the degree of completion require a sharp scalpel. We can only conjecture the physical form of the original Thucydidean "books." Perhaps he planned twenty-seven papyrus rolls for twenty-seven years. Yet each year differs in diplomatic and military activities, not to mention Thucydides' emphasis and interest in a particular occurrence (whether it is paradigmatic, fortuitous, unique). His pace varies with his materials; he packs five years into fewer than forty pages in book 5, but devotes more pages to each of years 5, 8, 17, and 19 (as Luschnat lays out in "Thukydides der Historiker," cols. 1117–1118). Finally, writing materials were expensive, even for a wealthy exile.

Presentations (Techniques)

Contextualization

Events are wayward, sudden, and unexpected, even contrary to sound reason, Thucydides comments more than once—with a general's fury or a historian's satisfaction (*aprosdokèton*, 2.91, *amathès*, 1.140; *alogos*, 1.32, 2.65—three words that can be translated as "unexpected," "unlearnable," and "unreasonable"; compare Stahl, *Thucydides*, pp. 75–99, on the disjunction between plans and events). His historical participants rarely perceive what is going on, much less correctly anticipate diplomatic affairs, internal assembly debates, and military confrontations. Using general Demosthenes as an example, Stahl and Hornblower (*Commentary*, vol. 2, p. 188) observe that few men in Thucydides' *History* ever learn anything. "Control of events" seems ludicrous to a commander or a careful reader, an unduly romantic concept (compare Hanson, *Hoplites*, on unpredictability in hoplite warfare). Speeches may be sparse or nonexistent in the *History* when talk was unproductive in assemblies or on battlefields, because it was hypocritical or fruitless (Rood, p. 91). In some speeches Thucydides offers, predictions are fulfilled; in others, expectations are thoroughly disappointed. Books 5 and 8 have few speeches. Many have thought these books less finished for that very reason, but Thucydides was an experimental artist, and his intentions may have been otherwise. He may have completed books 6 and 7 before book 5, and then, we could say, changed his technique, having decided his speeches were skewing his presentation. The dominance of speeches in his work, a factor also of Homer's *Iliad* and *Odyssey*, affected later historians, often not for the better. Books 5 and 8 reveal many plans that led to no positive results (for example, Athens' alliance with Argos; Spartan and Bœotian expectations for the Peace of Nicias in 421).

Thucydidean invention could be said to include the way in which he structures his speeches and collocates events. We would regard the latter as the privilege of the historian, who can select and omit what s/he thinks important, but presumably Thucydides does not invent his nick-o'-time salvations, popular since beggar Odysseus' return to his estate in Homer. At 3.49, the Mytileneans narrowly escape mass execution, and at 7.2 Athenian soldiers and siege engineers in a successful frenzy are just short of walling in the Syracusans. He describes all these "close-call" salvations with the same phrase: "The danger of X had indeed been great."

Battle Accounts

Thucydides was a *strategos* before he was a historian, so his battlefield accounts make more sense than those of Herodotus, his inexperienced predecessor, or many of his successors'. He knew the battlefields; he knew what kept hoplites and triremes in line. Morale is a constant concern. He knew the importance of persuasive politicians and morale-building generals; personality was decisive, with Themistocles and Pericles, and later too with Brasidas and Gylippus on the Spartan side, and Nicias and Alcibiades on the Athenian. Being right was not enough. Teutiaplus failed to convince Alcidas; his little speech (3.29–30) supplies the paradigm of a good idea that failed. Thucydides the general is interested in military ruses such as are reported at 3.108–113 (Demosthenes in Ambracia) or 4.120 (Brasidas at Scione). Phormio's strategy and naval skill with his fleet off Naupactus (2.83–92) provide the paradigm of Peloponnesian War trireme conflict at sea, including his success with the difficult tactic of the *diecplous*—sailing around and into (or into and around) your enemy's flotilla, probably shearing off most of his oars.

Assemblies

The Athenians elected Thucydides to command troops and maintain Athenian authority in war zones. The Spartans notoriously kept strangers out of their citizen-soldier assemblies and wrote down little, but the Athenians held open meetings and "published," often on Pentelic marble slabs, their decrees and judicial decisions. Thucydides must have attended many assemblies, and he reports the debates and decisions of many. According to the rules, anyone who wished could speak, but most of his speakers were also elected officials or unofficial faction leaders (such as Cleon and Hyperbolus, neither of whom he admired).

Other Events

Thucydides mentions some religious ceremonies and athletic contests, but only if they are somehow connected with the conduct of war. In book 5, pretexts arise for interfering with contests (5.30, 42, 49–50, 53–54; compare 6.16). Religion is exploited for earthly ends in various places—for example, 1.126; 3.3 and 56; 4.97–99; and the affair of the profanation of the Eleusinian Mysteries (6.27–29, 52–61), which brought down Alcibiades. Social and economic history is not in Thucydides' purview.

Calamities are in his scope, so the savage destruction of little Mycalessos, with its schoolchildren, comes in for extended note and evaluation (7.29–30; compare Lateiner, "Pathos in Thucydides"): "The disaster falling upon the whole town was unsurpassed in magnitude, and unapproached by any in suddenness and in horror." The grimmer events of war that show intensity of pathos often evoke his superlatives, especially to close an incident. For example, the stunned citizen, a stultified and wailing herald, who hears of his city's disaster in Ambracia and leaves with his task incomplete calls it (3.113) "by far the greatest disaster that befell any one Hellenic city in an equal number of days during this war."

Reversals also interest Thucydides, not for their paradoxical nature alone, but as reminders of the limited influence that humans can exert, even ones as smart as Themistocles and Pericles, Thucydides' two political-intellectual "heroes." At Pylos, the Athenians became land troops and the Spartans became seamen (4.14), and the Spartans—who, according to the Thermopylae ideology, never give up—surrendered, the biggest surprise of the war (4.12, 40). Just in the course of book 4, the buoyant Athenians slip from unexpected success at Pylos to unexpected disaster and deflation in Thrace. The Spartans, despondent after Pylos, will make nearly any peace to recover their men in Athenian prisons. In Syracuse, the defenders gave way to despair at Athenian energy and successes, but soon, with Gylippus the Spartan's arrival, the sandal was on the other foot (6.98–104; and 7.2, 11, and 71). The Athenian defeat in Sicily was the greatest reversal of all (7.87), while the commander Nicias least deserved the end he met (for reasons that remained obscure to the families of the dead).

Speeches and Other Quotations

How does one translate the problematic phrases describing Thucydides' treatment of formal and informal verbal events?—"Some I heard myself, others I got from various quarters; it was in all cases difficult to carry them word for word in one's memory, so my habit has been to make the speakers say what was in my opinion demanded of them by the various occasions." (1.22) Crawley's English represents Thucydides as adding, "of course adhering as closely as possible to the general sense of what they really said." That reassuring "of course" does not surface in the Greek. The speeches re-enact attempts at persuasion. They are not verbatim transcripts and they contain verbal echoes, responses not only to each other at one event but to speeches delivered at a far distance in time and space. Thucydides' explicit description of his method is contradictory, as I read the Greek text: What politicians really say will rarely be identical to what the occasion demands (itself a phrase capable of several interpretations).

At the Gela conference (4.58), Thucydides reports "many expressions of opinion on one side and the other," but he chose not to report the rest of them. A more serious problem emerges when we consider the element of invention in Thucydides' speeches. No one maintains that all the speeches contain only words actually spoken. Thucydides never claims to report every speech delivered in public during the Ten Years' War. It is likely, indeed necessary, that some speeches are more authentic than others. For example, who reported the Melian conference to him and at what time? The dead losers did not leave reliable notes, while the exile could not consult the conquering Athenians for more than another decade. This elementary observation encourages discussion of authenticity and individuality (4.85–87, the uniquely negative judgment of Brasidas' persuasive words). Some scholars think that all parts of all Thucydides' speeches are entirely invented—for example, Hunter, in *Thucydides: The Artful Reporter*, provocatively labels Thucydides "the least objective historian." Certainly, the speakers address their crowds with very similar syntax and rhetoric.

Only Brasidas (see Westlake, *Individuals in Thucydides*, pp. 148–165) in the *History* makes the same case in different speeches, although some other commanders certainly found themselves in a similar quandary. Spartans must have frequently tried to persuade reluctant, frightened, and terrorized Ionians to revolt from the Athenian empire (Debnar, *Speaking the Same Language*). Speeches, both direct (in quotation marks in modern editions) and indirect, are an old problem. Were they authentic constructs in the absence of hard evidence or transcripts, or are they constructed to respond to each other without regard to actual words? I reject the speculation that Thucydides provided words in situations and moments where no one spoke them. Readers, however, must realize that hardly more than a phrase here and there in any ancient historian can be actual "transcription."

Commanders presented speeches to entire armies before battle, but the pre-battle exhortations (*Feldherrnreden*; see Luschnat) may not have always consisted of one extended speech at the battle-site, delivered at one time to all soldiers, assembled and marshaled for battle. The Hellenes experienced brief, repeated clichés as the commander moved down the line, and speeches to the army, assembled prior to battlefield deployment (compare 7.69; and see Lateiner, "Nicias' Inadequate Encouragement"). Smart leaders spoke brief harangues in combat contexts.

Pagondas does not conform to the notorious formulation at 1.22: "My habit has been to make the speakers say what was in my opinion demanded of them by the various occasions," as Crawley renders it. If one believes that Thucydides is not a bare-faced liar or purveyor of whole-cloth fictions, Pagondas' words make satisfactory rhetorical sense. At 4.91 Pagondas speaks at Tanagra to the Bœotian army, in its constituent units (*lochoi*) of the Bœotian league, before proceeding to the battlefield, and scathingly criticizes the Bœotian high command. This sign of authenticity, this attempt to win goodwill, unexpectedly indicates strategic controversy in the upper echelons. Arguably (and logically) the historian is less likely to freely compose such orations (in his "library-study," working on one of his 141 speeches) than to include some words precisely because the actual exhortation surprised the original audience. The improbability of this officer's remarks forms a contrast to normal last-minute attempts to marshal hoplite courage. The sign of unexpected but refreshing candor may accurately characterize another backward Bœotian speaker bumbling through clumsy opening gambits. To his Bœotian credit, however slim his knowledge of sophistic, Gorgianic, and other Attic figures of thought and language, Pagondas won this victory near Delion after the exhortation. Thucydides hoped to find a post- or non-Athenian readership, in any case.

"Digressions"

The term "digression" suggests agreement about what indubitably suits a historical text. The perennial disagreement among historiographers about historical relevance and propriety downgrades Herodotus' more than Thucydides' selection of "includables," but even the latter writer includes passages on myth and legend that no scholar would have predicted (for example, accounts of Minos, Theseus, and Tereus: 1.4; 1.8; 2.15; 2.29). Thucydides offers at least six obviously relevant digressions on morale, each one noteworthy for rhetorical, structural, and dramatic techniques. At 2.94 and 8.96, Thucydides pauses to ponder psychological surprise. The formula "as usually happens" (4.125; compare 2.65), applied to crowd reactions, provides an authorial intrusion indicative of executive observation. He describes for us how intelligent leadership might still salvage haste and passion in assemblies, and anger and counter-productive fear in armies (3.36; 5.70; 6.63). Such phrases (compare 3.42 and 7.80) often describe politically unfortunate, because irrational, behaviors. They invite us to examine one or more of Thucydides' subtexts or his agenda. One may observe his concern for polities that have no clear and consistent strategies, in comparison with, say, Pericles at 1.141 or his curious echo, the anti-intellectual Cleon, at 3.38. Thucydides rarely adjudicates, an attitude that distinguishes his method from Herodotus' (compare Lateiner, "Tissaphernes and the Phoenician Fleet"), but when he does, we should ask what attracted his judgments.

Experimental Rhetoric, including Superlatives

Thucydides' innovations in his *History* deserve comment. Critics can never predict what Thucydides might do next. Some loose ends tucked in at the end of book 4 and at the beginning of book 5 are arguably instances of a Thucydidean habit. The inclusion of diplomatic documents seems an important intentional innovation. Thucydides' style and narrative are not homogeneous in different parts of his *History* or in treating different issues. Considerations of geography, topography, federalism, word forms and origins, place names, lists of personnel (for example, at 4.3 and 5.19), and inscriptions require different approaches. The point of view from which an action is reported (for example, Cleon's at 5.7) and the narrative line (4.50) sometimes stray from the year-by-year organization of our author (Connor, *Thucydides*; Hornblower, *Oxford Classical Dictionary*, 1996). While one scholar mirroring contemporary taste or different historical standards may find imperfections, another will admire the historian's courageous idiosyncrasies.

Thucydides gives us more in some respects than we might have expected, such as frequent superlatives of the best and the worst—a pile at 1.23 (compare 1.1; 2.31; 3.98, 113; 5.60; 7.86, 87). Sometimes these are statistical—the first trireme, the biggest army or disaster, the shortest time, etc. (for example, 1.50; 3.19, 113; 7.30, 87).

Thucydides revels in what we (misleadingly) call wordplay. For example, antithesis, false antithesis, alliteration, echoes, and rhyming sounds abound, as one expects from a writer who heard and learned much from Gorgias, the rhetorician from Leontini. The antithesis of word and deed (*logos* and *ergon*) appears eighteen times in the *epitaphios*, Pericles' funeral oration for the fallen Attic troops of one year (2.34–46). Irony and paradox in Thucydides' thought and word order give the prose of the ancient syntax-shifter a breath-taking texture. The intellectual relation of Thucydides to Gorgias the rhetorician needs as much elucidation as the rhetorical. For example, the reader should compare the point of view from which an action is reported, paradox and irony, explication of authorial bias, and structure in both. Gorgias appears to have had a strong, even determinative influence in his style and rhetoric, intentional ambiguity, and analysis of motives. See, for example, the Syracusan Hermocrates' speech (4.61) jingles, alliterates, and juggles words a la Gorgias (see Finley, *Thucydides*).

Thucydides boldly coined new words, especially abstractions. He admired, without necessarily approving, new forms of rational political analysis of the concentration of power. He treasured many traditional expressions of values, the glue of society. His neologisms include -*sis* verbal nouns that indicate an action in process (compare Patwell, *Grammar, Discourse, and Style in Thucydides Book 8*) and other abstract verbal nouns. Hornblower (*Commentary*, vol. 2) suggests that certain phrases in the general's prose might be "reminiscent of the language of Athenian official decrees." We could expect the elected Athenian official to echo vestigial formulas of his former career.

Cross-References: Retrospective and Prospective

Few explicit, self-referential internal cross-references appear in Thucydides' narrative, as compared to his speeches. Cross-references were unwieldy in the hard-to-consult ancient papyrus rolls, but some do occur (see 4.99 and 3.113 [both concerning heralds]; 5.1 and 6.94 [explicit mention of previous passage]; 4.120).

Do echoes of narrative in speeches or echoes of speeches in other speeches "weaken belief in the[ir] authenticity" (Hornblower, *Commentary*, vol. 2, on 4.95)? Echoes of the first sort are attested in all periods of history (politicians refer to the past), and echoes of the second sort (two generals or politicians simultaneously referring to the same fact or situation) are not surprising. If the historian possesses any "professional" integrity, as we think the Greeks conceived it, historical decency demands that his speeches represent the speeches delivered, and it demands that Thucydides heard them or heard reliable reports of them, and that his *History* preserves substantial elements.

Banal references to earlier events, with verbal echoes, argue only for Thucydides' use of historically appropriate battle encouragements. Echoes suggest that Thucydides paraphrases speakers' actual words, but even quasi-fundamentalists (on the issue of the veracity of his speeches), such as I, accept this degree of "creativity." Thucydides anticipates and pre-echoes, or echoes and resonantly confirms. Only sloppy logic argues that similarities between an author's and a speaker's statements prove that the historical speaker did not speak as Thucydides reports.

Literary issues have fruitfully complicated our reading of a distant mind. We want to understand Thucydides' allusions, deliberate echoes, and pre-echoes that refer back and forth in his text (beyond the few explicit ones), as well as contemporary developments in rhetorical ornament, argumentation, organization and presentation of material (structuralist studies), and Thucydides' personal intrusions and focus on events from one or more perspectives (narratology).

Evaluations/Interpretations/Analysis

Men, Groups, and Cities

Thucydides admired the achievements of the Athenian democracy (before Cleon, anyway). He considered the Athenian tyrants and the

Spartan, Corinthian, and Theban oligarchies less efficient, less inspiring, and less effective forms of government—both internally and externally. Thucydides sometimes shows the imperfections of constitutional procedures, but he does not yearn for illegal methods of government.

Historiographers in recent decades have examined interesting hypothetical issues—"what if X had happened?" or "what if Y had not occurred?" The previously unusual consideration of an unrealized hypothetical event, a "might have been," becomes a popular historiographical commonplace, called in rhetoric a *topos*. In a characteristic dramatic technique, Thucydides describes the unexpected deliverance of someone as "a narrow escape"; see 3.49; 4.129; and 7.2. The related "if . . . not" hypothetical historical narrative formula for lost chances (1.101; 2.18; 2.93–94; compare 4.106; 8.96; the strategy explained at 3.30–31) allows Thucydides to muse on what might have been decisive, if events had not developed as they did. However, rarely does Thucydides offer a decisive evaluation of competing truths (1.135; 8.48). Usually there is only his "bottom line."

The point of view from which an action is reported intensifies the drama in Thucydides, whether an event is seen from Athenian Cleon's or Spartan Brasidas' point of view. Thucydides' knowledge of his protagonists' hearts and minds presented a complex problem. More often than we might expect from his restricted access, he inferred the motives of a figure that he is unlikely to have questioned, one hostile to him or shortly to die. He often points to mistaken expectations of success, perhaps with relish. It is Hellenic to find failure more revealing than success.

Dealing justly may be part of the portfolio and toolkit of diplomats and commanders in war. Like threats, which Brasidas also brandished, and deceit (another tool in his armory), solemn declarations of truthfulness and fidelity are useful weapons in the warfare off the battlefields. In Thucydides' history, men often abandon fair promises when another approach seems more effective or cheaper. The historian may regret this being the case, but he does not ignore it. Thucydides presents Brasidas both positively and negatively (with due respect to Hornblower; see his *Commentary*, vol. 2, p. 60). Brasidas is different in Thucydides because he was different in fact from other commanders, not like the fumbling and dilatory Alcidas or some other Spartans who had no strategy for winning the hearts and minds of neutrals and the Athenians' former allies. Brasidas gets a fascinating post-mortem treatment in Thrace (5.11)—public burial and heroic honors.

Thucydides describes the deformation of civic discourse in his account of civil war (*stasis*) in Corcyra. Language perversion occurs elsewhere, notably at 4.97–99 (the debate over the dead at the battle of Delion) and at 4.108 (in Thrace), as in the prior Corcyrean *stasis* and the Athenians' subsequent arguments at Melos; but Thucydides does not mark these moments as travesties of [mis-]communication (Cogan, Orwin, Crane).

His focus is on the dynamics of major political decisions and the factors that led to them. He leaves unmentioned the quotidian events of individual and city. The silences deny historical status to many events, some of which we know from other sources, such as Aristophanes and Plutarch. Paches, commander at Mytilene, committed suicide; but Thucydides does not mention the event, although he does note the nervous admiral's referral of final judicial decision to the demos (3.28; compare 2.70; 3.98; 4.65; 5.26; 7.48, other commanders who carefully avoid assuming the assembly's privileges). Phormio, another naval achiever, disappears (3.7), and while ancient gossip records a condemnation, Thucydides provides none. Although the collection and shortfalls of tribute and other taxes (7.28; 8.15) are mentioned often enough (1.96; 2.13, 70; 4.87; 6.26; 7.48; etc.), the reassessment of the tribute, known from inscriptional evidence to have taken place in 425, receives no mention. He is silent about the alleged Peace of Callias of 449 (see Fornara #95; Stadter, "The Form and Content of Thucydides' Pentacontaetia"), and in general, before book 8 Persian interference is conspicuous by its absence.

Thucydides' politics remain debated. He makes negative comments on crowd psychology and passion. For instance, he refers to the Athenian demos' inclination for war (2.8) and against compromise (2.65), general rowdiness (4.28), and military overconfidence against the Syracusans (6.63), and its sudden fury with leaders (8.1). He and some of his speakers lament the fact that passion (*orgê*) and not reason (*gnome*) sometimes determines national policy (2.21; 4.65).

His lurking sympathy for Athens might compromise his stance of objectivity for some, had they noticed it. He does not approve of many Athenian decisions in the war, but he admires the city-state's daring and energy up to and through the leadership of Pericles, who could control the people's temper (Westlake, *Individuals in Thucydides*, pp. 23–42). Pericles himself, however, seems to think that empires must expand or die, so one lesson from the *History* is that the Athenian achievement was not possible without a willingness to exploit the weaker states and peoples. The achievement was the unification of much of the Greek world—under Athenian control, to be sure—but political disunity at home, a factor inherent in democracy, doomed that enterprise.

One cannot, I repeat, predict the appearances of Thucydides' interventions and opinions. The judgments passed on men and cities may appear in a brief summary notice, in a paragraph, epigraph, or epitaph (for example, at 2.65 on Pericles; 7.86 on Nicias), but others pop up when a man first becomes important (for instance, at 6.72 on Hermocrates). The views held by the author ought not be confused with those espoused by his speakers, not even Pericles, unless there is supporting evidence. Thucydides meditates on what constitutes political power in a state, what justifies or condemns imperialism, the rule of the powerful over the weak. He deplores violence, especially when unnecessary. He anatomizes the dynamics of collective judgment. While he condemns some democratic decisions, he is just as negative about some oligarchic policies of small and great powers. He allows speakers to express their views of various ethnic groups, although his narrative usually shows such judgments to be more facile and self-serving than analytical. He deplores the self-destructiveness of Athenian democratic power, while recognizing that Athens' brief non-democratic governments showed many of the same imploding forces.

He avoids some uncritical simplification of traditions seductively attractive to an uncritical public (1.20; 6.54), but his mind inclines to unflattering generalizations on public behavior. Imperialists have found succor in his glorification of the Athenian achievement (Pericles' funeral oration) and his *realpolitik* account of the unprovoked and unjustified attack and massacre at Melos (perhaps; see, above, the section of this essay called "Organization and Research in the *History*: Time and Space"). Anti-imperialists find a contrary endorsement in his bitter, bloody account of Athens' overreaching failure in the invasion of distant Sicily. The many achievements of Sparta demolish clichés about its slowness and inarticulateness (1.70, 84; 8.96). The Spartan's "campaign" spiel to a sequence of Athenian allies in the North Aegean appears in various formats. The procedure echoes Thucydides' own method, variations on a theme, adumbrated in the difficult chapter on how he presents speeches (1.22; compare Wilson, "What Does Thucydides Claim for His Speeches?").

The term for "leader of the people" (demagogue) was not yet the derogatory label that Plato made of it. The word *demagogos* (4.21), however, occurs in the *History* but once and is applied to Cleon, the man identified as inciting the people to exercise their imperial tyranny. The same passage's suspicious superlative *pithanotatos* ("most persuasive") occurs only thrice, applied to Cleon twice and once to the Syracusan demagogue Athenagoras, arguably a Sicilian clone of Cleon in Thucydides' slit-eyed view (6.35). Any wish for "good guys and bad guys" crashes against Thucydides' zigging and zagging. Connor's *Thucydides* (an application of Wolfgang Iser's "reader-response criticism") follows the ambivalent path that the Athenian historian cut, although he conceivably could have hacked others through the war's ideological and material jungles. The undoubted intelligence, energy, and acuity of Thucydides shaped his materials in an unprecedented and inimitable way.

Thucydides perhaps overrates some few Athenian and Spartan commanders' military genius. Thucydides' preoccupations include Brasidas, the sometimes obedient and successful appointed general of the highly regimented, classical Spartan army. That the Spartan commander is a doer of deeds and a fully competent speaker (see 4.81 and 4.84) may have warped Thucydides' judgment (Woodhead, "Thucydides' Portrait of Cleon"). Brasidas, who dominates the middle section of the war in Thucydides' account, was a liar and a singular word-twister when strategy called for it (4.108). This was Thucydides' considered judgment of a Spartan leader whose promises he accurately reported. Consequently, since Brasidas misrepresents situations for gain, his admirable skills do not concern justice, ethics, or honor in conduct—except as they achieve his devious goals. He abandons communities whose trust he had gained in such a way that they suffer terrible consequences. Campaigning generals in vicious wars sometimes must do so, it seems. He, like Themistocles, gains commendation for "brains" (*xunesis*), because both men brought friends and enemies around to their intelligent political and strategic perceptions, and because of his ability to carry out those perceptions and related policies. When Brasidas commends a line of action to his lieutenant Clearidas ("Show yourself a brave man" [5.9]), he means: "Be good at what you are trained for"—namely, threatening, capturing, and killing, not Socratic ethics. Thucydides admired this Spartan for his atypical Spartan skills and his service to a regime that seemed both unsympathetic to him (4.108) and inept to the historian.

Cleon, Brasidas' and Thucydides' enemy, may have sponsored Thucydides' exile and certainly pursued a war policy more aggressive than Pericles' (see 1.143–144; 2.13). This does not make him into the narrative's negative exemplar in all matters, or a tragic or epic hero. Cleon represents one perennial concern. Democracies and other imperial powers cannot restrain themselves in success and often overreach their prosperity, thus becoming entangled in ventures beyond their capacities (*pleonexia*). Thucydides found that what happened to Persian Xerxes in Greece happened to the Athenian empire in Sicily. Themistocles and Pericles are enthusiastically praised for their intelligence and abilities, Alcibiades for his political acumen (1.138; 2.65; 6.15; 8.86). Pericles judged this problem of empire correctly, but could not predict the great plague and did not realize that no hand but his could restrain the competition among his successors. Aristocratic and idiosyncratic Alcibiades sometimes fits the ambivalent Homeric character mold of Achilles or even that of Pericles. Did Thucydides intend these parallels? His *History* does not tell. Thucydides observed democratic and oligarchic individuals, but political theory, beyond ideology deduced from practice, hardly yet existed. The anti-imperial, anti-democratic pamphlet written by the so-called Old Oligarch (excerpts in Fornara #107) was not a work of a theoretician, but he provides some tantalizing evidence of pre-Platonic objections to the Athenian imperial and democratic internal systems. Hornblower notes (*Commentary*, vol. 2, with reference to 4.30) that "Demosthenes is one of the few men in Thucydides who is said to profit from previous mistakes." Thucydides' political optimism and pessimism lurk in many passages devoid of explicit praise or blame.

Human Limits: The Family, the *Polis*, and Military Collectives

Thucydides describes war as a hard teacher or "master" (3.82). His account of the epidemic of plague, seemingly a consequence of crowding due to the war in Athens, details the breakdown of order, of customs secular and religious. The physical disease lays out grids for the communal dis-ease. During the decades-long war, armies exterminated cities and repopulated their sites with friendlier groups. The victors killed the men and sold the women and children into slavery. This was the convention of the day. Thucydides tracks the gradual breakdown of good sense, of planning, of common courtesy and morality, what he calls the old way of life, both between city-states and within single ones. Betrayal of the fatherland for the sake of personal aggrandizement or group power marks the first major incident at tiny Plataea, and many more. Thucydides describes with calm language but clear sympathy the disintegration of army discipline during the Athenian retreat from Syracuse and the decimation—and worse—of that once proud and imperialistic force. In the Syracusan quarries, many Athenians died, and the Sicilians sold the remainder into slavery. Some bought their way out by reciting memorized dramas of Euripides, but this is Plutarch's favorite type of literary anecdote, literature put to a practical use (see, for example, *Life of Nicias* 29), not one likely to be found in Thucydides. Here is his conclusion to book 7: "This was the greatest Hellenic achievement of any in this war, or, in my opinion, in Hellenic history; at once most glorious to the victors, and most calamitous to the conquered. They were beaten at all points and altogether . . . everything was destroyed, and few out of many returned home."

Morality and Religion: Declining Decency, Breakdown of Constraints, Distant Gods

Thucydides does not consider the gods (theological issues) part of his historical topic, but the worship of the gods and other public attitudes toward oracles, earthquakes, plagues, and eclipses constitute historical events and cause morale to change and armies to die. Religious institutions and issues serve as pawns in propaganda games—for example, the curse of the Athenian goddess, the curse of Lacedæmonian Taenaron (the mutilation of the pillars of Hermes, and the parody of the Eleusinian rituals called the "mysteries" (1.125; 1.128; 6.26–28). During the plague, the power of religious ceremonies and norms disappeared in Athens (2.53), and the Corcyrean political chaos produced similar devastating and abnormal results in social life (3.81–82). Thucydides notes with disapproval attention to oracles (2.8, 17; 5.26) and faults Nicias and the Athenian troops for their fatal inclination to superstition (7.50). Activities that some attribute to religion, he assigns to military discipline, such as Spartan marching methods (5.70). He strictly excludes divine interference from historical causation, a position toward which Herodotus was moving rapidly. There is no religious or literary language of divine compensation or revenge or leveling in Thucydides' text, at least not from the historian himself (compare the pious Nicias or the desperate Melians at 7.77 and 5.104–105).

Significance

Eschewing the already suspect word "historian" and others of similar ilk, the *syngrapheus* ("data-collecting composer")—an unpretentious and misleading neologistic misnomer for the author of what is shortly to come—has become an important thinker, for historians, for philologists, for political philosophers, and for students of literature. Thucydides was insightful, methodical, and unique in his challenging idiom. The complexities of his austere syntax and thinking deliberately lead to further complexities, and every happy discovery leads to two or more new problems. The details of Thucydides' thought sometimes defeat the assumed transparency of translation. Detached stones—independent narratives in the edifice—and odd, poetic phrases contribute to an unexpected and intricate, but still comprehensible, architecture. Justus Lipsius, the Renaissance preserver and editor of many Greek texts, said: "Our opinion of Thucydides is that although he wrote up events neither many nor very great he perhaps stole in advance the palm from all who did write up great and many events. The more often you read him, the more you gain; and never does he send you off without thirst for more."[5]

Merits

Thucydides knew what he was talking about, since he had participated in Athenian assemblies and elections and had trained and fought in her military engagements. The critical approaches that envision Thucydides as engaged, passionate, or partisan necessarily apply a line-by-line reconsideration of the text. Robert Connor (1977 and *Thucydides*) first recognized the emergence of a "post-Modernist Thucydides." The shift in Thucydidean studies, a development that Cornford (*Thucydides Mythistoricus*) erratically anticipated in his discussion of tragic form and personal biases, has produced since the 1960s a "new" Thucydides, our Thucydides. This writer rarely is wholly objective, infallible, much less Olympian. His narratological persona, nevertheless, suggests cool detachment, from the choice of a third-person narrator on, but the narrator's construction of the Athenian disaster (as we philo-Athenians choose to view it) and the regretful asides on the decline of political civility inside and outside the *polis* suggest emotional and moral engagement. Jacqueline de Romilly (*Thucydides and Athenian Imperialism*) and Hans-Peter Stahl (*Thucydides: Man's Place in History*) influentially reconsider the role of reason and strategy. Their scholarship has also promoted a unitarian awareness of echoes and resonances across speeches, events, books, etc. (see Dewald, Edmunds, Hornblower [*Thucydides*], Lateiner ["Pathos in Thucydides"], Tompkins).

In recent decades, Thucydides' dramatic tactics have drawn closer attention—on the level of the word, the sentence, the section, and the entire work. Thucydides is a good organizer and suspenseful writer, a deliberately disconcerting one, shifting unevenly and unexpectedly the point of view from which an action is reported, as well as tenses, assignation of responsibility for specific acts or consequences, and his readers' sympathies. Intelligent readers modify repeatedly their views of individuals, groups, emerging tendencies, and even single events as Thucydides recounts them. Vivid details, such as the feet of men and horses under Amphipolis' gate (see 5.10), present dramatic visualizations—for example, of nonverbal behaviors, such as shaking bodies, gait and pace, unexpected silences, and stupefaction. These all occur in Thucydides, despite a tendency to downplay them on the part of scholars who compare him favorably to the more frequently dramatic Herodotus.

Thucydides' experience—military, political, and personal (the plague)—contributes to his "you are there" (autoptic) principle: Only a person living through an epoch can write its history. While few today endorse this program, it certainly adds to Thucydides' credibility. Vividness (*enargeia*) is characteristic. Thucydides pitches many scenes in a cinematic way; his vivid crosscutting, for instance, at the last battle in Syracuse harbor leaves us hanging. His foreshadowing does not destroy suspense. His nameless characters embody national characteristics, an idea with which this hopefully post-racist generation is uncomfortable. Surely, however, Spartans were different from Corinthians, and Athenians from Thebans. It is hard to refute Thucydides' contention that the Syracusans were best at fighting the Athenians because they were most like them in institutions and manners (8.96).

His originality lies in the analyses contained in his speeches and his dedication to ferreting out facts. He has definitively removed divine interference and the gods from serious secular history and made military policy and execution the central subject matter of historians. The connectivity he finds between events supplies critics with ammunition to attack his fidelity to fact or his allegiance to false analogies.

Impartiality and objectivity are always relative to opportunities. Thucydides' *History* is not patriotic toward the Athenians or the Greeks in the patent way that Livy's *History from Rome's Beginnings to the Present* clearly is and was meant to be for the Romans. Nor does he find his grand subject inspirational, as so many historians in antiquity did and now still do. His account reports a series of military defeats and degradations of the social order—a setback for a promising civilization, the erasure of mankind's best hope. The final victory of Sparta, whether he lived to recognize this, was a defeat for Greek civilization and even for Greek freedom, for the Spartans betrayed their Ionian Greek allies to their Persian paymasters. The victory of Athens would have been different—but still a blow against local liberties and autonomy. Thucydides' high perspective gave him insight into the follies and successes of both sides. Both had achievements and fatal flaws, as all political systems do, and few patriots realize. Thucydides funneled his angry dismay into the coolest narrative and analysis that a human has yet conceptualized.

Defects

We may speculate that Thucydides had little diplomatic experience. We do not have evidence one way or the other. Where we can check him, he is usually right, but often we have no other sources for his statements. He had no encyclopedias, much less the worldwide web of information and gobbledygook. So we can occasionally convict him of ignorance or even credulity (the mythical sea-ruler Minos was convenient for his thesis concerning the importance of sea power: 1.4, 8). His lack of sources, and the conflicts among the few he had, forced him to make choices and offer explanations that we may improve upon. Archaeologists have taught recent generations more about the Greek prehistoric and Archaic periods than he could possibly know.

Ernst Badian (*From Plataea to Potidaea*) argues against Thucydides' historical objectivity, allegedly exposing his pro-Athenian and anti-Spartan rhetoric, omissions, inventions, and tendencies. In his smart discussion, Badian favors descriptions such as "desperate suppression, plausible fiction, disinformation, misleading interpretations foisted upon the reader, activist journalism," etc. More than a century ago, the grumpy and now mostly forgotten Reverend Sir J. P. Mahaffy likewise objected to idolatrous modern confidence in this ancient historian's statements and judgments. Banker and historian George Grote, a liberal friend of John Mill, resented this aristocratic historian's alleged anti-democratic prejudices, betrayed in, for instance, the praise given to the incompetent Nicias, while the death of the military genius Demosthenes remains unmarked (Grote, *History* [1871], vol. 7, pp. 350–351).

Does Thucydides encourage his readers to discover heroes and villains in his text? Thucydides admired certain statesmen and generals, such as Pericles, Antiphon, and Brasidas. He puts good arguments into the mouths of others, such as King Archidamus (Wasserman, "The Speeches of King Archidamus in Thucydides") and the otherwise unknown Diodotus. He despised the glory-seeking Cleon, as the savage satirist Aristophanes did, and perhaps gives him less credit than he was due. He recognizes the military skill of the Athenian generals Phormio and Demosthenes, although they receive no summary evaluations as Pericles and Nicias do. Alcibiades, another aristocratic eccentric genius, obtains a mixed judgment—positive on his leadership acumen, negative on his loyalty to Athens (6.15; 8.48, 86). Thucydides is willing to pass judgments, but he is not a moralist when dealing with political persons and policies. There, effectiveness and long-term political consequences are his proper concern. When we turn to cities, he does not judge foreign policy on moral grounds, but he does praise and condemn particular actions for their attention to or ignoring of bedrock principles of right and wrong. For instance, the Bœotian selfish sophistry after the fall of Plataea and the Spartan condemnation of the Plataean prisoners plainly gains his disapprobation. While the Athenian condemnation of the Mytileneans, at the urging of Cleon, the leatherworks industrialist turned politician, seems "savage" to him (3.36), the subsequent (partial) reversal of the blanket death-sentence on the males affords an example of democratic inconstancy, although he also notes the masses' praiseworthy inclination to pity and rational reconsideration.

His speakers oddly share one convoluted and packed style, and that compressed, bold, and abstract idiom (see Denniston, *Greek*

Prose Style) does not match any one that we can imagine was ever used by someone hoping to be understood and persuasive in a single hearing (as Collingwood angrily argues in *The Idea of History*). Their contorted Greek lacks the individual characterization that even historians expect, wherever each is from and for whatever purpose they are pleading. The vocabulary, style, structure, and form of these speeches do not seem in any way "realistic." At best we can believe that they conform to some criteria that we have not fully understood.

Thucydides excludes many aspects of history that we anticipate, require, and enjoy. Not only do women rarely appear; also one cannot infer the scope of cultural and artistic achievements of Athens—although both Thucydides and Pericles hint at some of them (1.10; 2.38). He suppresses revealing personal anecdotes that he surely knew, a feature that is so prominent in Herodotus and in the *Lives* of the Roman imperial biographer Plutarch.

Translation

Thucydides resists readers' expectations, and he demands that you sit up, pay attention, and make every effort to connect his infrequent dots. This appears to have been conscious on his part. Thucydides wanted to make his reader take part in thinking about puzzling political sequences and barely conceivable military disasters, such as the fiasco in Sicily that debilitated an unprecedented empire. The historiography replicates the history by not re-presenting the path as clear, even after the fact. One suffering ancient or Byzantine annotator, called a scholiast, upon reaching the dramatic and unexpectedly grammatically straightforward narrative of Cylon, Pausanias, and Themistocles at 1.126–138, seems stunned. He has found that Greeks like him could read this passage as if it were (ordinary) classical Greek. He comments happily in the margin of Thucydides' text at 1.126 on its evanescent clarity (*sapheneia*), noting that "here the lion smiled."

Thucydides cherished certain old-fashioned ways, words, spellings, and cultural assumptions. Translating Attic Greek and its culture into contemporary comprehensible English for today's generation is no easy task. Translating an author whose eccentric Greek gave headaches to his ancient readers poses additional hurdles. The muscular, angular, and elliptical prose regularly baffles the best-trained Hellenists. Pericles' funeral oration for the fallen Athenians, the description of the barbaric civil war (*stasis*) in Corcyra, the experimental "Melian Dialogue" repeatedly confound the usual protocols of Attic syntax. No translation dares to preserve all the heart-stopping angularities. "Difficult animals to drive is a sheep; one man, many of them, very"; this unknown wit's profound parody of Thucydides' style captures his elliptical style. An acerbic, anonymous (and racist) British quotation appears in Grundy (*Thucydides and the History of his Age*, p. 52, note 1), who reports a lecturer's remark that Thucydides' corrupt Greek "at its best was only good Thracian"; the comment refers to Thucydides' northern Aegean connections and suggests he did not learn Greek properly. Dionysius of Halicarnassus, no dummy or slouch in trying to understand Thucydides' locutions (see Pritchett, *Dionysius of Halicarnassus*), said (*On Thucydides' Peculiar Style* 51 [my translation]): "You can count on one hand those few who are able to understand all of Thucydides, and not even these can do so without some grammatical explanation."

Arguments about meaning based on Greek word order or idiom require a translation imitating the original's difficulty. Many translations mislead the reader about the historian's craggy style and train of thought. Crawley's translation preserves the "broken symmetry" and dramatic syntax, also the intense, sublime, and enigmatic simplicity (compare Parry's comments on translations in "Herodotus and Thucydides"). Thomas Hobbes, observer of the life of men as "nasty, brutish, and short," thought Thucydides' thinking important enough to be worth struggling with his stylistic peculiarities, his gnarly prose. Rough-hewn sentences retain that frustrating, indeed irritating, texture. Thucydides exhibits an absence of humor—he is the "least ludic [playful] of writers," as Hornblower remarked (*Commentary*, vol. 2, on 4.92), discussing Thucydides' "humourlessness" and other defects. One of Thucydides' longer sentences (5.16, in twenty lines) became four sentences in Benjamin Jowett's Victorian English version—reasonably so, but the text has lost in flavor what it gained in simplified lucidity. Other translations have followed reasonable policies in translating substance as well as style, but the practice of dumbing down Thucydides' antitheses and tidying up his sudden transitions is dangerously close to the popular mistake of improving (that is, bowdlerizing) Shakespeare. Most translators lose the wonderful rhetorical contortion and avoidance of reality confected by various Spartan ambassadors (for example, 4.18). The diplomats' euphemisms in their doublespeak about error, prudence, fortune, and accidents avoids terms for conquest, extortion, and the systematic exploitation of oppressed satellites.

Reading Thucydides, the late fifth-century historian from the Attic *deme* (township) of Halimous, southwest of Athens, produced in Friedrich Nietzsche, a classicist before he slipped into philosophy and madness, "the agreeable feeling as of turning a lock with a key: a gradual, reluctant giving way, but always functional, always achieving its end" (*Wir Philologen*, p. 347). The right key for this complex lock has been lost. Intellectual politicians and politic intellectuals, Cicero in antiquity and Lorenzo Valla in the Renaissance (see the "Inspired by Thucydides" section of this edition), and the late American Senator J. William Fulbright of Vietnam War fame, have struggled with this dependably difficult author. Translators are the underappreciated preservers of history and civilization for most educated adults today. Translators can be traitors, too, sometimes trying to "modernize" a resisting text like this. (For more on the preeminence of Richard Crawley's rendering of Thucydides's *History*, see "Note on the Translation," on page xlv).

Achievement and Influence on Posterity

No author in the fourth century B.C.E. mentions Thucydides, except one anonymous but perceptive historian (the so-called Oxyrhynchus Historian). Xenophon and others picked up in the odd place where Thucydides stopped, incidentally proving to us that we have not lost once "published" parts. Neither Plato nor Aristotle mentions Thucydides, although some oblique references (for example, in the *Menexenus*, Plato's spoof funeral oration for Socrates (allegedly composed by Aspasia, Pericles' mistress) may allude to his work. Later writers, such as Lucian in his satire "How to Write History," speak of him with respect. Plutarch in his *Greek and Roman Lives*, by frequent quotation, honors his achievement. While historians generally praised his method as superior to Herodotus', most successors followed neither his structure nor his syntax. The resurrection of his authority had to wait for the resurrection of enthusiasm for the Greeks and for democracy, both rather recent. The opening up of Greece to northern European travelers, first by the Ottoman Turks and then by the Greeks' own violent revolution and independence (1821), and then the success of George Grote's liberal *History of Greece* (first edition 1846–1856; compare Roberts, *Athens on Trial*, chapter 11) encouraged the enthronement of Thucydides as the paradigm of the historian. Mahaffy complains about the apotheosis of a historian who, he thinks, grossly exaggerates the importance and magnitude of the Peloponnesian War.

One may summarize Thucydides' achievements thus:

- He freed history from divine causes, explaining ordinary and extraordinary events by observation.

- He distinguished necessary and essential causes from fortuitous and contributing factors.

- He sought evidence from all camps and compared the reports for probability and independent support, a task as difficult as it is admirable.

- He analyzed personal and communal motives to make events intelligible.

- He isolated recurring factors in human relations and in negotiation and conflict between states.

- He eliminated events that were interesting but (to him) irrelevant for the understanding of military and political history.

More people than ever before, most perhaps with no experience of the demands of ancient Greek, are hefting and praising Thucydides as a political philosopher. Thomas Hobbes had a serious dedication to Greek studies. In 1629 Hobbes' virile, if sometimes inaccurate, translation of our author claimed:

> For the principal and proper work of history being to instruct and enable men, by the knowledge of actions past, to bear themselves prudently in the present and providently towards the future: there is not extant any other (merely human) that doth more naturally and fully perform it, than this of my author. . . . Thucydides is one who, though he never digress to read a lecture, moral or political, upon his own text, nor enter into men's hearts further than the acts themselves evidently guide him, is yet accounted the most politic historiographer that ever writ.

Hiccoughing, self-promoting dandies, and name-calling hoplites, hip-wagging flute-girls, and pitcher-boys, and the generality of slumping heads—not to mention wine-flicking party games, lollygagging, throwing up, kraters of wine extended by boys and girls in deshabillé, and the raucous clamor of non-Platonic venues in Corinth, Miletus, up-scale Athens, and down-home Thrace then and now provided the serious writer of history with tough competition for attention. Even dedicated friends of Thucydides, if he had any, with tolerance for his agonized syntax and labyrinthine reasoning and analysis, such as the domestic untranquillity of Corcyra reported at 3.82–83, must sometimes pause and groan in wonder and frustration. The mental pleasures, nevertheless, of grappling with his razor-sharp intelligence and of learning from his understated narratives keep us reading and hungering for more.

Donald Lateiner teaches humanities, history, and classics courses at Ohio Wesleyan University in Delaware, Ohio, where he occupies the John Wright Chair of Humanities and Greek. He holds degrees from the University of Chicago, Cornell University, and Stanford University. He was the Thomas Day Seymour fellow for a year at the American School of Classical Studies at Athens. He has taught the ancient Greek and Roman world at the University of Pennsylvania; for Syracuse University in Florence, Italy; for Carleton College; and principally at Ohio Wesleyan. He has guided student and alumni expeditions to Etruria and Rome, and to Greece, Crete, and coastal Turkey. Lateiner teaches ancient languages, archaeology, ancient history, ancient literatures in translation, and world folklore. He has published articles on Greek history, historiography, Attic oratory, Latin lyric poetry, and Greek and Latin epic poetry and prose fiction. His published scholarly books include *The Historical Method of Herodotus* (1989) and *Sardonic Smile: Nonverbal Behavior in Homeric Epic* (1995). The Ohio Humanities Council awarded him the 2003 Bjornson Prize for his work in promoting appreciation of the cultural achievements of the ancient past.

Notes

1. Similarly, despite the modern Athenocentric name of the Peloponnesian War, Thucydides left traces of another (in fact Peloponnesian) name: "The War against the Athenians" (5.28, 31).

2. "Poetry is more philosophical and serious than history because poetry speaks more to the general truth, history to the one-by-one facts" (D. Lateiner, translator).

3. Charles Fornara's collection of translated inscriptions, papyri, scholia (ancient annotations), and obscure lexical information—*Archaic Times to the End of the Peloponnesian War*—provides a necessary and welcome supplement to Thucydides' often pithy narratives. Therefore, I cite the relevant texts in my annotations. Fornara, on pp. 203–216 of *Archaic Times*, supplies a useful glossary of Athenian and other Hellenic governmental terms, such as "archons."

4. He notoriously has Pericles comment that that woman's reputation will be best about whom the Athenians hear the least—whether for praise or blame (2.45). This seems to have been true, however much we may despise it.

5. *De Thucydidis sententia nostra: Thucydides, qui res nec multas nec magnas nimis scripsit palmam fortasse praeripit omnibus qui multas et magnas. Quem quo saepius legas, plus auferas; et numquam tamen dimittat te sine siti.*

NOTE ON THE TRANSLATION

Richard Crawley's translation of Thucydides excels in its general accuracy and scrupulous fidelity to Thucydides' tone, idiom, and rhythm. Crawley knows what his author emphasized sentence by sentence, and he does not insert unnecessary or flat words. Thomas Hobbes' famous translation (1629), his first publication, exhibits the very lively diction and style of the philosopher and his generation. Hobbes was a serious Greek scholar, but the work exhibits some queer errors. It has vigor, pith, charm, and an often literal accuracy, but today it reads awkwardly, impeded often by an unintended archaism ("what we spake hath proceeded from . . ."). Thucydides' Greek was innovative, and not archaic or archaizing, as Hobbes knew.

Benjamin Jowett's translation (1881) reads to me as primly Victorian, often excessively wordy and Latinate for service to an author who compressed much thought into few syllables. He thus translates fourteen of Thucydides' Greek words: "Wherefore I do not now commiserate the parents of the dead who stand here; I would rather comfort them." Crawley's version (1876) employs as many words but chooses more succinct syllables; his word order also catches the abrupt and crucial word play: "Comfort, therefore, not condolence, is what I have to offer to the parents of the dead who may be here." Here we have dignity, rhythm, muscle, and passion—elements of a sublime, living English rhetoric. Other more recent translations, such as Rex Warner's successful version for the Penguin series of translations (1954), employ a more casual and accessible English for the rapid modern reader, but Thucydides' concern never was popularity or easy comprehension, so Crawley's version better serves the contemporary intelligent reader who first approaches this giant of Western historiography and political analysis.

I have lightly revised the translation in places, occasionally dividing sentences in two or otherwise repunctuating them. I have systematically replaced British "corn" with American "grain," obsolete "galley" with "trireme," and the quaintly literal Athenian "council of the bean" with "council chosen by lot," the *boule* or senate.

Thucydides' history today requires the supplement of good maps and explanations of unfamiliar persons, places, institutions, technology, and ways of thinking that are no longer obvious. I have tried to elucidate these obscurities with annotations that inform students of Greek thought with factual information that the ancient reader might not have needed, with some useful cross-references, and sometimes with notice of an unusual feature in the writing of history (for Thucydides, or for ancient historiography in general). I trust they will answer readers' questions and enhance the experience of penetrating an intense mind's life work.

Richard Crawley (1840–1893) attended Oxford University, where he became an Exhibitioner (an undergraduate distinction, although not the highest) at University College and a fellow of Worcester College from 1866 to 1880. He was an outstanding student of Greek and Latin, and an athlete. He wrote a play, a satire, and various other poems, all of them forgotten today. He was called to the bar in 1869 but never practiced law. He spent most of his working years after 1873 in the life insurance business. (I thank Edward Wilson, archivist of Worcester College, for help in assembling obscure information about a man whose name lives on today only because of this unprofitable but enduring labor of love.)

In this edition of Crawley's translation of Thucydides, I have added (with the assistance of my student Michael Manner) modern chapter or paragraph numbers supplied by scholars to the ancient text. (Crawley himself divided the *History* into twenty-six chapters or episodes of modern length, but no one now refers to these divisions.)

—Donald Lateiner

HISTORY OF THE
PELOPONNESIAN WAR

CONTENTS

BOOK 5

BOOK 6

BOOK 7

BOOK 8

BOOK 1

The State of Greece from the Earliest Times to the Commencement of the Peloponnesian War

1. Thucydides, an Athenian, wrote the history of the war between the Peloponnesians* and the Athenians, beginning at the moment that it broke out,† and believing that it would be a great war, and more worthy of relation than any that had preceded it.‡ The preparations of both the combatants were in every department in the last state of perfection; and he could see the rest of the Hellenic race taking sides in the quarrel; those who delayed doing so at once having it in contemplation. Indeed this was the greatest movement yet known in history, not only of the Hellenes, but of a large part of the barbarian world§—almost of mankind. For though the events of remote antiquity, and even those that more immediately precede the war, could not from lapse of time be clearly ascertained, yet the evidences which an inquiry carried as far back as was practicable leads me to trust, all point to the conclusion that there was nothing on a great scale, either in war or in other matters.

2. For instance, it is evident that the country now called Hellas had in ancient times no settled population; on the contrary, migrations were of frequent occurrence, the several tribes readily abandoning their homes under the pressure of superior numbers. Without commerce, without freedom of communication either by land or sea, cultivating no more of their territory than the exigencies of life required,

---

*"The Peloponnese" is a geographical term for the peninsula of southwestern mainland Greece (map 4); the Peloponnesian League was the alliance of states therein led by the Spartans (named for their *polis* (city-state); they were also known as Lacedaemonians for their large district or territory).

†Thucydides wished to determine the calendrical and factual start (and end) of the war that he recorded. By our system, it was initiated in early 431 B.C.E. (All dates in these notes occurred B.C.E.—Before the Common, or Christian, Era—unless otherwise specified.)

‡Greek historians, including Thucydides, are determined to prove that the greatest significance attaches to the war that each of them commemorated.

§Greeks (or Hellenes) are those who speak Greek and conform to Greek customs (in their religion, oral ethnic history, marriage, political forms, etc.). Barbarians apparently make "bar-bar" sounds and follow different traditions, not necessarily inferior ones. Such peoples include the civilized Egyptians and Persians and the uncivilized Thracians, Illyrians, etc.

destitute of capital, never planting their land (for they could not tell when an invader might not come and take it all away, and when he did come they had no walls to stop him), thinking that the necessities of daily sustenance could be supplied at one place as well as another, they cared little for shifting their habitation, and consequently neither built large cities nor attained to any other form of greatness.* The richest soils were always most subject to this change of masters; such as the district now called Thessaly, Bœotia, most of the Peloponnese, Arcadia excepted, and the most fertile parts of the rest of Hellas. The goodness of the land favoured the aggrandisement of particular individuals, and thus created faction which proved a fertile source of ruin. It also invited invasion. Accordingly Attica, from the poverty of its soil enjoying from a very remote period freedom from faction, never changed its inhabitants. And here is no inconsiderable exemplification of my assertion, that the migrations were the cause of there being no correspondent growth in other parts. The most powerful victims of war or faction from the rest of Hellas took refuge with the Athenians as a safe retreat; and at an early period, becoming naturalised, swelled the already large population of the city to such a height that Attica became at last too small to hold them, and they had to send out colonies to Ionia.†

3. There is also another circumstance that contributes not a little to my conviction of the weakness of ancient times. Before the Trojan war‡ there is no indication of any common action in Hellas, nor indeed of the universal prevalence of the name; on the contrary, before the time of Hellen,§ son of Deucalion, no such appellation existed, but the country went by the names of the different tribes, in particular of the Pelasgian. It was not till Hellen and his sons grew strong in Phthiotis,‖ and were invited as allies into the other cities, that one by one they gradually acquired from the connection the name of Hel-

---

*Thucydides' introduction stresses achievements in political power and imperial design. Populous cities, accumulation of wealth, and creation of navies present three interrelated causes and results of great political power.

†Ionia was the western coast of central Asia Minor, now Turkey (map 12). This migration from the Hellenic mainland (map 1) occurred in the eleventh and tenth centuries, after existing political structures in Mycenean, Bronze Age Greece were disturbed by the so-called Dorian Invasions or internal upheaval.

‡This greatest conflict of Greek legend may well have occurred historically in some more complex form beyond the typical raiding of neighbors. Thucydides, who disbelieves many commonly accepted events of the Greek legendary past, accepts this one, as it helps him prove a thesis: the minor nature of imperial conflicts before the recent war that he records.

§Eponymous founder of the Hellenic race. "Hellas" and "Hellene" have served as the Greek names for "Greece" and "Greek" from the archaic period until the present.

‖Region in southern Thessaly, in central Greece (map 9).

lenes; though a long time elapsed before that name could fasten itself upon all. The best proof of this is furnished by Homer.* Born long after the Trojan war, he nowhere calls all of them by that name, nor indeed any of them except the followers of Achilles from Phthiotis, who were the original Hellenes: in his poems they are called Danaans, Argives, and Achæans. He does not even use the term barbarian, probably because the Hellenes had not yet been marked off from the rest of the world by one distinctive appellation. It appears therefore that the several Hellenic communities, comprising not only those who first acquired the name, city by city, as they came to understand each other, but also those who assumed it afterwards as the name of the whole people, were before the Trojan war prevented by their want of strength and the absence of mutual intercourse from displaying any collective action.†

Indeed, they could not unite for this expedition till they had gained increased familiarity with the sea.‡

4. And the first person known to us by tradition as having established a navy is Minos.§ He made himself master of what is now called the Hellenic sea, and ruled over the Cyclades, into most of which he sent the first colonies, expelling the Carians and appointing his own sons governors; and thus did his best to put down piracy in those waters, a necessary step to secure the revenues for his own use.

5. For in early times the Hellenes and the barbarians of the coast and islands, as communication by sea became more common, were tempted to turn pirates, under the conduct of their most powerful men; the motives being to serve their own cupidity and to support the needy. They would fall upon a town unprotected by walls, and consisting of a mere collection of villages, and would plunder it; indeed, this came to be the main source of their livelihood, no disgrace being yet attached to such an achievement, but even some glory.‖ An illustration of this is

---

*Legendary authority in all matters Greek, the nearest text to revealed truth, and therefore almost "the Bible" for Greeks even down to Thucydides' era. For us, Homer serves as a convenient name for the author(s) of the canonical *Iliad* and *Odyssey*. Following Herodotus' skepticism, Thucydides often disputes the authority of Homer as an historian as well as inspired poet, examples of historical revisionism.

†Thucydides' opening chapter (1–23) is largely a polemic focused on Greek *polis* particularism and lack of interstate cooperation.

‡Thucydides thought Athens' success was predicated on sea power, so he examines earlier thalassocracies, imperial powers that were sea-based.

§Legendary king of Crete, who ruled from the Labyrinth at Cnossus on the central northern coast (map 1). Herodotus (3.122) doubts that Minos was historical, but the usually more skeptical Thucydides wants him for a prototype of imperial sea power.

‖A student of the morally relativistic sophists, Thucydides enjoys indicating that moral values have changed, and that piracy, now illegitimate, was once for Hellenes a legitimate business and even gained kudos.

furnished by the honour with which some of the inhabitants of the continent still regard a successful marauder, and by the question we find the old poets everywhere representing the people as asking of voyagers—'Are they pirates?'—as if those who are asked the question would have no idea of disclaiming the imputation, or their interrogators of reproaching them for it. The same rapine prevailed also by land.

And even at the present day many parts of Hellas still follow the old fashion, the Ozolian Locrians for instance, the Ætolians, the Acarnanians, and that region of the continent; and the custom of carrying arms is still kept up among these continentals, from the old piratical habits.*

6. The whole of Hellas used once to carry arms, their habitations being unprotected, and their communication with each other unsafe; indeed, to wear arms was as much a part of everyday life with them as with the barbarians. And the fact that the people in these parts of Hellas are still living in the old way points to a time when the same mode of life was once equally common to all.† The Athenians were the first to lay aside their weapons, and to adopt an easier and more luxurious mode of life; indeed, it is only lately that their rich old men left off the luxury of wearing undergarments of linen, and fastening a knot of their hair with a tie of golden grasshoppers, a fashion which spread to their Ionian kindred, and long prevailed among the old men there. On the contrary a modest style of dressing, more in conformity with modern ideas, was first adopted by the Lacedæmonians,‡ the rich doing their best to assimilate their way of life to that of the common people. They also set the example of contending naked, publicly stripping and anointing themselves with oil in their gymnastic exercises. Formerly, even in the Olympic contests, the athletes who contended wore belts across their middles; and it is but a few years since that the practice ceased. To this day among some of the barbarians, especially in Asia, when prizes for boxing and wrestling are offered, belts are worn by the combatants. And there are many other points in which a likeness might be shown between the life of the Hellenic world of old and the barbarian of to-day.

---

*Thucydides brilliantly shows how economic and social differences reveal different stages of civic evolution. Backward areas to the north, such as Aetolia (map 1), still follow customs that more developed Greeks have long abandoned.

†Thucydides' evolutionary awareness was radically different from the more static, ahistorical expectations of most educated people of his generation.

‡Sparta was the chief city of the large territory of Laconia (officially known as Lacedaemon), and Messenia—two-fifths of the Peloponnese (map 1). Ancient Greeks used the names "Spartan" and "Lacedaemonian" synonymously, although the full-citizen Spartiate "equals" were only a small fraction of the population of Laconia, the more numerous inhabitants comprising the enserfed original natives, the Messenians, now called "helots," and the outlying *perioeci* (the "dwellers round").

7. With respect to their towns, later on, at an era of increased facilities of navigation and a greater supply of capital,* we find the shores becoming the site of walled towns, and the isthmuses being occupied for the purposes of commerce, and defence against a neighbour. But the old towns, on account of the great prevalence of piracy, were built away from the sea, whether on the islands or the continent, and still remain in their old sites. For the pirates used to plunder one another, and indeed all coast populations, whether seafaring or not.

8. The islanders, too, were great pirates. These islanders were Carians and Phœnicians, by whom most of the islands were colonised, as was proved by the following fact.† During the purification of Delos by Athens in this war all the graves in the island were taken up, and it was found that above half their inmates were Carians: they were identified by the fashion of the arms buried with them, and by the method of interment, which was the same as the Carians still follow.‡ But as soon as Minos had formed his navy, communication by sea became easier, as he colonised most of the islands, and thus expelled the malefactors. The coast populations now began to apply themselves more closely to the acquisition of wealth, and their life became more settled; some even began to build themselves walls§ on the strength of their newly-acquired riches. For the love of gain would reconcile the weaker to the dominion of the stronger, and the possession of capital enabled the more powerful to reduce the smaller towns to subjection. And it was at a somewhat later stage of this development that they went on the expedition against Troy.‖

9. What enabled Agamemnon to raise the armament was more, in my opinion, his superiority in strength, than the oaths of Tyndareus, which bound the suitors to follow him.# Indeed, the account given by

---

*Thucydides, as noted in the introduction to this edition, is no economic historian, but he appreciates the military and imperial need for accumulations of monetary reserves, gold and silver.

†This introduction shows the historian's unprecedented ability to infer and deduce history. From available archaeological evidence, he here argues intelligently about the culture of the former inhabitants.

‡Using analogy and interment data, Thucydides perhaps correctly identifies the former inhabitants (see map 1).

§Ancient Greek cities, except Sparta, generally walled their residential and commercial areas, if they could afford it, for defense from pirates, neighbors, and other potential enemies. This was true of Athens, Troy, and other cities, of which some, such as Corinth, also had separate elevated citadels.

‖Small but strategically placed coastal town in northwestern Troad in Asia Minor. Thucydides assumes that a Trojan war took place, an issue that is still under debate.

#In the Trojan backstory, but not in the *Iliad*, the suitors of Helen swore to make common cause in military pursuit and war, should anyone deprive the contest winner of her hand.

those Peloponnesians who have been the recipients of the most credible tradition is this. First of all Pelops, arriving among a needy population from Asia with vast wealth, acquired such power that, stranger though he was, the country was called after him; and this power fortune saw fit materially to increase in the hands of his descendants. Eurystheus had been killed in Attica by the Heraclids. Atreus was his mother's brother; and to the hands of his relation, who had left his father on account of the death of Chrysippus, Eurystheus, when he set out on his expedition, had committed Mycenæ and the government. As time went on and Eurystheus did not return, Atreus complied with the wishes of the Mycenæans, who were influenced by fear* of the Heraclids,—besides, his power seemed considerable, and he had not neglected to court the favour of the populace,†—and assumed the sceptre of Mycenæ and the rest of the dominions of Eurystheus. And so the power of the descendants of Pelops came to be greater than that of the descendants of Perseus. To all this Agamemnon succeeded. He had also a navy‡ far stronger than his contemporaries, so that, in my opinion, fear was quite as strong an element as love in the formation of the confederate expedition. The strength of his navy is shown by the fact that his own was the largest contingent, and that of the Arcadians was furnished by him; this at least is what Homer says, if his testimony is deemed sufficient.§ Besides, in his account of the transmission of the sceptre, he calls him

> 'Of many an isle, and of all Argos king.'

Now Agamemnon's was a continental power; and he could not have been master of any except the adjacent islands (and these would not be many), but through the possession of a fleet.

And from this expedition we may infer the character of earlier enterprises.

10. Now Mycenæ may have been a small place, and many of the towns of that age may appear comparatively insignificant, but no exact observer would therefore feel justified in rejecting the estimate

---

*Throughout his work Thucydides disdains the usual rhetoric of patriotism and emphasizes the power of fear, need, greed, and the pleasures of rule.

†Thucydides here makes Agamemnon analogous both to archaic tyrants such as Peisistratus and to fifth-century demagogues, leaders of the people commonly suspected or accused of selfish motives by their political competitors, especially those of more noble birth.

‡Thucydides analogizes backward from fifth-century naval significance to the source of prehistoric Agamemnon's broad influence, widely based in the Argolid (map 4).

§Thucydides sarcastically appeals to the authority of Homer, for lack of better. He often elsewhere minimizes or denies the poet's credibility.

given by the poets and by tradition of the magnitude of the armament. For I suppose* if Lacedæmon were to become desolate, and
the temples and the foundations of the public buildings were left,
that as time went on there would be a strong disposition with posterity to refuse to accept her fame as a true exponent of her power.†
And yet they occupy two-fifths of Peloponnese and lead the whole,
not to speak of their numerous allies without. Still, as the city is neither built in a compact form nor adorned with magnificent temples
and public edifices, but composed of villages after the old fashion of
Hellas, there would be an impression of inadequacy. Whereas, if
Athens were to suffer the same misfortune, I suppose that any infer-
ence from the appearance presented to the eye would make her
power to have been twice as great as it is.‡ We have therefore no
right to be sceptical, nor to content ourselves with an inspection of a
town to the exclusion of a consideration of its power; but we may
safely conclude that the armament in question surpassed all before
it, as it fell short of modern efforts;§ if we can here also accept the
testimony of Homer's poems, in which, without allowing for the exaggeration which a poet‖ would feel himself licensed to employ, we
can see that it was far from equalling ours. He has represented it as
consisting of twelve hundred vessels; the Bœotian complement of
each ship being a hundred and twenty men, that of the ships of
Philoctetes fifty. By this, I conceive, he meant to convey the maxi-
mum and the minimum complement: at any rate he does not specify
the amount of any others in his catalogue of the ships. That they were
all rowers as well as warriors we see from his account of the ships of
Philoctetes, in which all the men at the oar are bowmen. Now it is
improbable that many supernumeraries sailed if we except the kings
and high officers; especially as they had to cross the open sea with
munitions of war, in ships, moreover, that had no decks, but were

---

*Thucydides offers a hypothetical forecast about future historians, in which he indi-
cates that material remains cannot sufficiently gauge one-time political power.

†Thucydides believes that Sparta put her resources into perishable, non-material assets. The consequence is that there are no marble temples—no Parthenons, no theaters,
no personal memorials that indicate the wealth and war achievements of her citizens.

‡Athens, on the other hand, has put so many resources into permanent, or at least
durable marble, monuments that her power might later appear greater than it actually
ever was, although, as we shall see, it was more than any other Hellenic state had yet
acquired.

§Thucydides wishes to undermine the Greek belief that the Achaean armada that
sailed and rowed to Troy was greater than any ever since. Aggrandizements of the past
contradict his thesis of the progress of military and imperial powers.

‖Again, Thucydides argues, to revise common views, that historians are more informa-
tive and trustworthy than poets. Pericles makes this point in his funeral oration (2.41),
when speaking over the dead of the first year.

equipped in the old piratical fashion.* So that if we strike the average of the largest and smallest ships, the number of those who sailed will appear inconsiderable, representing, as they did, the whole force of Hellas.

11. And this was due not so much to scarcity of men as of money. Difficulty of subsistence made the invaders reduce the numbers of the army to a point at which it might live on the country during the prosecution of the war. Even after the victory they obtained on their arrival—and a victory there must have been, or the fortifications of the naval camp could never have been built—there is no indication of their whole force having been employed; on the contrary, they seem to have turned to cultivation of the Chersonese and to piracy from want of supplies. This was what really enabled the Trojans to keep the field for ten years against them;† the dispersion of the enemy making them always a match for the detachment left behind. If they had brought plenty of supplies‡ with them, and had persevered in the war without scattering for piracy and agriculture, they would have easily defeated the Trojans in the field; since they could hold their own against them with the division on service. In short, if they had stuck to the siege, the capture of Troy would have cost them less time and less trouble. But as want of money proved the weakness of earlier expeditions, so from the same cause even the one in question, more famous than its predecessors, may be pronounced on the evidence of what it effected to have been inferior to its renown and to the current opinion about it formed under the instruction of the poets.

12. Even after the Trojan war Hellas was still engaged in removing and settling, and thus could not attain to the quiet which must precede growth. The late return of the Hellenes from Ilium caused many revolutions, and factions§ ensued almost everywhere; and it was the citizens thus driven into exile who founded the cities. Sixty years after the capture of Ilium the modern Bœotians were driven out of Arne by the Thessalians, and settled in the present Bœotia, the former Cadmeis; though there was a division of them there before, some of whom joined the expedition to Ilium. Twenty years later the Dorians and the

---

*Progress includes naval design as well as political organization.

†Thucydides accepts the duration recorded by Homer for the Trojan War, but points out that not only was this a shorter period than the Peloponnesian War's twenty-seven years, but also that the earlier Greeks could have finished the war sooner had they been able to focus all their energies on it. Provisioning and other logistic problems prevented that.

‡Thucydides emphasizes the planning that went into overseas expeditions in his war and, by contraries, the lack of such planning in earlier overseas expeditions.

§Internecine economic and political differences have always riven Greek states (*poleis*). We often translate this situation (in Greek, *stasis*) into English as "civil war."

Heraclids became masters of Peloponnese; so that much had to be done and many years had to elapse before Hellas could attain to a durable tranquillity undisturbed by removals, and could begin to send out colonies, as Athens did to Ionia and most of the islands, and the Peloponnesians to most of Italy and Sicily and some places in the rest of Hellas. All these places were founded subsequently to the war with Troy.

13. But as the power of Hellas grew, and the acquisition of wealth became more an object, the revenues of the states increasing, tyrannies* were by their means established almost everywhere,—the old form of government being hereditary monarchy with definite prerogatives,—and Hellas began to fit out fleets and apply herself more closely to the sea.† It is said that the Corinthians were the first to approach the modern style of naval architecture, and that Corinth was the first place in Hellas where triremes‡ were built; and we have Ameinocles, a Corinthian shipwright, making four ships for the Samians. Dating from the end of this war,§ it is nearly three hundred years ago that Ameinocles went to Samos. Again, the earliest sea-fight in history was between the Corinthians and Corcyræans; this was about two hundred and sixty years ago, dating from the same time. Planted on an isthmus, Corinth had from time out of mind been a commercial emporium; as formerly almost all communication between the Hellenes within and without Peloponnese was carried on overland, and the Corinthian territory was the highway through which it travelled. She had consequently great money resources, as is shown by the epithet 'wealthy' bestowed by the old poets on the place, and this enabled her, when traffic by sea became more common, to procure her navy and put down piracy; and as she could offer a mart for both branches of the trade, she acquired for herself all the power which a large revenue affords. Subsequently the Ionians attained to great

---

*This term in Greek refers to governments by marginally elite individuals who achieve power by irregular means and continue to hold autocratic control indefinitely with their family supporters. It does not mean, as in contemporary English, a government that takes away civil liberties and rules irrationally (although some Greek tyrannies certainly did so).

†An important step in Hellenic military and economic advances was the turn from simple subsistence farming and pasturage to overseas, interstate commerce, especially in wine, olives, and fine manufactures (metalwork, painted pottery).

‡Triremes were the swift (up to 9 knots), ramming warships, about 120 feet long and 20 feet wide, with 170 oarsmen in groups of three at different levels, one man per oar. This bronze-beaked sinking missile dominated the seas in the fifth and early fourth centuries.

§Does Thucydides mean the year 421, the end of phase I of his war, or 404, the end of the Peloponnesian War as a whole in his opinion (as he argues in 5.25–26)?

naval strength in the reign of Cyrus,* the first king of the Persians, and of his son Cambyses,† and while they were at war with the former commanded for a while the Ionian sea. Polycrates‡ also, the tyrant of Samos, had a powerful navy in the reign of Cambyses with which he reduced many of the islands, and among them Rhenea, which he consecrated to the Delian Apollo. About this time also the Phocæans, while they were founding Marseilles, defeated the Carthaginians in a sea-fight.§

14. These were the most powerful navies. And even these, although so many generations had elapsed since the Trojan war, seem to have been principally composed of the old fifty-oars and long-boats, and to have counted few triremes among their ranks. Indeed it was only shortly before the Persian war and the death of Darius‖ the successor of Cambyses, that the Sicilian tyrants and the Corcyræans acquired any large number of triremes. For after these there were no navies of any account in Hellas till the expedition of Xerxes;# Ægina, Athens, and others may have possessed a few vessels, but they were principally fifty-oars.** It was quite at the end of this period that the war with Ægina and the prospect of the barbarian invasion enabled Themistocles†† to persuade the Athenians to build the fleet with which they fought at Salamis;‡‡ and even these vessels had not complete decks.

15. The navies, then, of the Hellenes during the period we have traversed were what I have described. All their insignificance did not prevent their being an element of the greatest power to those who cultivated them, alike in revenue and in dominion. They were the

---

*Founder of the Persian Achaemenid dynasty who put down the Medes' empire around 559 (recounted in Herodotus 1.99 and following).

†This son ruled 530–522 and conquered Egypt (see Herodotus 3).

‡Tyrant of Samos (map 12) in the years 540–522. He ruled much of the Aegean Sea but failed to ally himself with Egypt against Persia.

§The Phocaeans won the battle of Alalia, fought off Carthaginian-controlled Sardinia around 535, but had to retreat to southern Italy (see Herodotus 1.164–165).

‖Successor to Cambyses, of questionable legitimacy, but a ruler (521–486) who expanded the Persian Empire in every direction (see Herodotus 3–6).

#Son of Darius, ruler from 486–465. He organized the second invasion of Greece. His forces were victorious at Thermopylae and Artemisium, but the Hellenes defeated him decisively at sea and on land at Salamis and Plataea (map 5).

**Such "penteconters" were smaller battleships used before the development of triremes in the mid-sixth century.

††This non-aristocratic leader promoted naval ship-building and a forward-looking naval policy in Athens in the last years of the 490s. He realized that the Persians planned to attack and to try to subjugate the disunited Hellenic city-states. He was a strategist of Hellenic victory in the Persian (here called Median) War of 480–479.

‡‡The decisive naval battle of autumn 480 was fought in the Salamis straits opposite Athens' harbor, Piraeus (map 3).

means by which the islands were reached and reduced, those of the smallest area falling the easiest prey. Wars by land there were none, none at least by which power was acquired; we have the usual border contests, but of distant expeditions with conquest for object we hear nothing among the Hellenes.* There was no union of subject cities round a great state,† no spontaneous combination of equals for confederate expeditions; what fighting there was consisted merely of local warfare between rival neighbours. The nearest approach to a coalition took place in the old war between Chalcis and Eretria;‡ this was a quarrel in which the rest of the Hellenic name did to some extent take sides.

16. Various, too, were the obstacles which the national growth encountered in various localities. The power of the Ionians was advancing with rapid strides, when it came into collision with Persia, under King Cyrus, who, after having dethroned Crœsus§ and overrun everything between the Halys and the sea, stopped not till he had reduced the cities of the coast; the islands being only left to be subdued by Darius and the Phœnician navy.

17. Again, wherever there were tyrants, their habit of providing simply for themselves, of looking solely to their personal comfort and family aggrandisement, made safety the great aim of their policy, and prevented anything great proceeding from them;‖ though they would each have their affairs with their immediate neighbours. All this is only true of the mother country, for in Sicily they attained to very great power. Thus for a long time everywhere in Hellas do we find causes which make the states alike incapable of combination for great and national ends, or of any vigorous action of their own.

18. But at last a time came when the tyrants of Athens and the far older tyrannies of the rest of Hellas were, with the exception of those in Sicily, once and for all put down by Lacedæmon; for this city, though after the settlement of the Dorians, its present inhabitants, it

---

*The Greeks' umbrella name, now and then, for their varied populations, divided by dialect into Dorians, Ionians, and Aeolians.

†Thucydides contrasts old, enfeebling separatism with the more recent agglomerating leagues of the Peloponnesians and the Athenians.

‡These two cities on the large island of Euboea (map 5) were important early (late seventh century) colonizing states in the northern Aegean and Sicily. Before that, around 725, each, with many allies, fought a war over the fertile Lelantine plain lying between them.

§King of Lydia (map 1) in the mid-sixth century (reigned 560–546), he was an imperialist who conquered much of Greek Ionia (western coast of Asia Minor) and tried to stop the rising Persian king Cyrus before it was too late, but failed.

‖Thucydides respects tyrants for internal achievements and primitive imperial forays but regards them as old-fashioned in their priorities. He argues that the different polities of Athens and Sparta led to greater agglomerations of wealth and power.

suffered from factions for an unparalleled length of time, still at a
very early period obtained good laws,* and enjoyed a freedom from
tyrants which was unbroken; it has possessed the same form of government for more than four hundred years, reckoning to the end of
the late war, and has thus been in a position to arrange the affairs of
the other states. Not many years after the deposition of the tyrants,
the battle of Marathon was fought between the Medes and the
Athenians.† Ten years afterwards the barbarian returned with the
armada for the subjugation of Hellas. In the face of this great danger the command of the confederate Hellenes was assumed by the
Lacedæmonians in virtue of their superior power; and the Athenians having made up their minds to abandon their city, broke up
their homes, threw themselves into their ships, and became a naval
people.‡ This coalition, after repulsing the barbarian, soon afterwards split into two sections, which included the Hellenes who had
revolted from the king, as well as those who had aided him in the
war. At the head of the one stood Athens, at the head of the other
Lacedæmon, one the first naval, the other the first military power on
land in Hellas. For a short time the league held together, till the
Lacedæmonians and Athenians quarrelled, and made war upon
each other with their allies, a duel into which all the Hellenes sooner
or later were drawn, though some might at first remain neutral. So
that the whole period from the Median war to this,§ with some
peaceful intervals, was spent by each power in war, either with its
rival, or with its own revolted allies, and consequently afforded
them constant practice in military matters, and that experience
which is learnt in the school of danger.

19. The policy of Lacedæmon was not to exact tribute from her allies, but merely to secure their subservience to her interests by establishing oligarchies among them; Athens, on the contrary, had by
degrees deprived hers of their ships, and imposed instead contribu-

---

*The Spartans were famous for the stability of their laws (devised by the legendary
king Lycurgus; Fornara #2) and their fairness—fair at least for the elite Spartiates. The
Spartan community did not experience an individual's tyranny, as so many other cities
did (compare 8.24, 96).

†In 490 the Athenians, with their Plataean allies, routed the first amphibious Persian
invaders, an achievement that cemented many citizens' attachment to the young, still
emerging democracy.

‡The Athenians' decision (480) to abandon their city and meet the enemy with their
navy (see Fornara #55) was a source of great pride.

§The period—called the Fifty Years, or Pentacontaëtia—extends approximately from
479, the end of the Persian Wars, to 431, the beginning of the Peloponnesian War (or
Wars).

tions in money on all except Chios and Lesbos.* Both found their resources for this war separately to exceed the sum of their strength when the alliance flourished intact.

20. Having now given the result of my inquiries into early times, I grant that there will be a difficulty in believing every particular detail.† The way that most men deal with traditions, even traditions of their own country, is to receive them all alike as they are delivered, without applying any critical test whatever.‡ The general Athenian public fancy that Hipparchus was tyrant when he fell by the hands of Harmodius and Aristogiton; not knowing that Hippias, the eldest of the sons of Pisistratus,§ was really supreme, and that Hipparchus and Thessalus were his brothers; and that Harmodius and Aristogiton suspecting, on the very day, nay at the very moment fixed on for the deed, that information had been conveyed to Hippias by their accomplices, concluded that he had been warned, and did not attack him, yet, not liking to be apprehended and risk their lives for nothing, fell upon Hipparchus near the temple of the daughters of Leos, and slew him as he was arranging the Panathenaic‖ procession.

There are many other unfounded ideas current among the rest of the Hellenes, even on matters of contemporary history which have not been obscured by time. For instance, there is the notion that the Lacedæmonian kings have two votes each, the fact being that they have only one; and that there is a company of Pitane, there being simply no such thing.# So little pains do the vulgar take in the investigation of truth, accepting readily the first story that comes to hand.

21. On the whole, however, the conclusions I have drawn from the

---

*These large islands west of the Ionian mainland (map 12) continued to supply men and ships, while the other states now supplied money through a tax that went back to Aristides' admirably fair assessment of 478.

†Thucydides has sketched out patterns of accumulation of power, subjection, and wealth. He has not provided a history with dates and names. He is laying down principles that he applies to his war.

‡Thucydides rejects common and lax standards of truth for past events. He supplies some specific examples.

§This middling aristocrat and his eldest son, Hippias, ruled Athens as tyrants from approximately 565 to 514. Thucydides is correcting a common misconception, replacing jingoistic rhetoric, clan aggrandizement, and fuzzy memories with his exposé of a homosexual attraction and revenge gone astray. He returns to this topic at 6.54–59.

‖The Athenians had their local contests (compare the Panhellenic Delphic and Olympic contests) in music, athletics, poetry, etc. Pisistratus first organized such contests to promote the unity of Attica, the territory (about the size of South Carolina) in which Athens was the chief city.

#The Spartans had a small military unit called the *lochos*; Thucydides is tilting at popular misconceptions about the secretive Spartan organization. His goal is to reveal the lack of research and method used by previous chroniclers.

proofs quoted may, I believe, safely be relied on. Assuredly they will not be disturbed either by the lays of a poet displaying the exaggeration of his craft, or by the compositions of the chroniclers that are attractive at truth's expense;* the subjects they treat of being out of the reach of evidence, and time having robbed most of them of historical value by enthroning them in the region of legend.† Turning from these, we can rest satisfied with having proceeded upon the clearest data, and having arrived at conclusions as exact as can be expected in matters of such antiquity. To come to this war; despite the known disposition of the actors in a struggle to overrate its importance, and when it is over to return to their admiration of earlier events, yet an examination of the facts will show that it was much greater than the wars which preceded it.‡

22. With reference to the speeches in this history, some were delivered before the war began, others while it was going on; some I heard myself, others I got from various quarters; it was in all cases difficult to carry them word for word in one's memory,§ so my habit has been to make the speakers say what was in my opinion demanded of them by the various occasions, of course adhering as closely as possible to the general sense of what they really said.‖

And with reference to the narrative of events, far from permitting myself to derive it from the first source that came to hand, I did not even trust my own impressions, but it rests partly on what I saw myself, partly on what others saw for me, the accuracy of the report being always tried by the most severe and detailed tests possible.# My conclusions have cost me some labour from the want of coincidence

---

*Thucydides lived in an oral culture, in which inspired poets had the most prestige. He is arguing for the preferable analytical and evidence-based standards of written history.

†Herodotus and others, sometimes working only from living legends, had produced history for which confirming evidence was lacking. Thucydides rejects their looser and unverifiable standards for determining the nature of events that actually happened in the past.

‡Thucydides' chief competition for the greatest conflict in numbers and significance is the Persian attack of 480–479; it is known today from Herodotus' account, but other reports existed.

§Thucydides discusses the method of reporting his orations in one of the most controversial chapters of the book. The controversy includes what he actually says here and whether such a method is suitable for historians. Even when the historian attended a conference or assembly, he had no recording machine, and the speakers neither wrote nor later left a detailed text.

‖Does Thucydides here claim—in an apparently contradictory sentence—that he put into others' mouths what they should in their ignorant circumstances have said, or what they must have said (in the sense of audience expectations), or what they ought (as perceptive political analysts) to have said? All these conjectures are compatible with what "was in my opinion demanded of them" but less suited to that which they "really said." Both summary and invention seem to have played some unrecoverable part.

#We do not know what these tests were beyond probability and cross-checks with other sources.

between accounts of the same occurrences by different eye-witnesses, arising sometimes from imperfect memory, sometimes from undue partiality for one side or the other.*

The absence of romance in my history will, I fear, detract somewhat from its interest; but if it be judged useful by those inquirers who desire an exact knowledge of the past as an aid to the interpretation of the future, which in the course of human things must resemble if it does not reflect it,[†] I shall be content. In fine, I have written my work, not as an essay which is to win the applause of the moment, but as a possession for all time.

23. The Median war, the greatest achievement of past times, yet found a speedy decision in two actions by sea and two by land.[‡] The Peloponnesian war was prolonged to an immense length, and long as it was it was short without parallel for the misfortunes that it brought upon Hellas. Never had so many cities been taken and laid desolate, here by the barbarians, here by the parties contending (the old inhabitants being sometimes removed to make room for others); never was there so much banishing and blood-shedding, now on the field of battle, now in the strife of faction.[§] Old stories of occurrences handed down by tradition, but scantily confirmed by experience, suddenly ceased to be incredible; there were earthquakes[||] of unparalleled extent and violence; eclipses of the sun occurred with a frequency unrecorded in previous history; there were great droughts in sundry places and consequent famines, and that most calamitous and awfully fatal visitation, the plague.[#]

All this came upon them with the late war, which was begun by the Athenians and Peloponnesians by the dissolution of the thirty years'

---

*Thucydides recognizes that loyalty or dislike will affect perceptions.

†Thucydides believes future events will resemble past ones, insofar as fear, profit, greed, honor, and competitive "values" continue to govern human nature.

‡Thucydides intentionally undervalues the tremendous strategic and logistic problems of the Persian Wars. Nor was the decision he mentions necessarily "speedy," although he includes Thermopylae and Plataea, Artemisium and Salamis, a period of well over a year. By not including the earlier battle of Marathon or the later battle at the river Eurymedon, he has shortened that war and the number of engagements by more than a decade, at the least. As with his own account of an uneasy peace of 421–415, one could have predicted renewed hostilities after the Marathon repulse of the Persians or after Plataea and considered all those campaigns to be but one war.

§*Stasis* is the Greek word for internal conflict—economic, political, and social divisions that could and often did result in civil wars.

||Thucydides the rationalist unexpectedly here mentions various natural phenomena that are not strictly war-related.

#Nothing caused more harm to the Athenians than the disease that decimated their population several times over. No one has convincingly identified the actual malady, although many candidates have been eliminated (see book 2).

truce made after the conquest of Eubœa. To the question why they broke the treaty, I answer by placing first an account of their grounds of complaint and points of difference,* that no one may ever have to ask the cause which plunged the Hellenes into a war of such magnitude.† The truest cause,‡ but the one least spoken about openly, I consider to be the Athenians' growing power and the fear they caused [by this growth] to the Lacedæmonians. [This situation] pressured them into fighting the war. The two sides, in any case, publicly alleged the following grounds; these induced them, once they dissolved the treaty, to begin open war.

Causes of the War — Epidamnus — Potidæa

24. The city of Epidamnus stands on the right of the entrance of the Ionic gulf.§ Its vicinity is inhabited by the Taulantians, an Illyrian people. The place is a colony from Corcyra,‖ founded by Phalius, son of Eratocleides, of the family of the Heraclids, who had according to ancient usage been summoned for the purpose from Corinth, the mother country. The colonists were joined by some Corinthians,# and others of the Dorian race. Now, as time went on, the city of Epidamnus became great and populous; but falling a prey to factions arising, it is said, from a war with her neighbours the barbarians, she became much enfeebled, and lost a considerable amount of her power. The last act before the war was the expulsion of the nobles by the people.** The exiled party

---

*Thucydides will treat the announced causes of the war before examining the less openly discussed but more important one.

†It is ironic that the precipitating cause remains debatable: Was it the aggressiveness of the desperate Corinthians, the anxiety to seize a disappearing chance by the Spartans, or the unwillingness to compromise of the Athenians—or all three?

‡Thucydides devotes a long excursus to the growth of Athenian power (1.89–117). He may be right that Athenian power and imperial intentions reached such intensity that the Spartans in fear thought they had to stop them soon—or never. Thucydides is not a determinist. Nowhere does he assert that the war was "inevitable," a dangerous word for cool heads. (In "For Further Reading," see Arthur M. Eckstein's article for further clarification.)

§The waters west of Albania (map 8) below the Adriatic Sea.

‖This large island (later called Corfu, map 8), originally colonized by Corinth, was an important way station in east–west trade. Corcyra in turn colonized the city of Epidamnus, about 120 miles north on the mainland (map 1).

#Corinth was the single most prolific colonizing power in old Greece. Her colonies (for example, Syracuse, Ambracia, Potidaea) tended to remain closer to her than those of other cities.

**The few and the many often were in conflict over limited land and political power in the cities of late fifth-century Greece.

joined the barbarians, and proceeded to plunder those in the city by sea and land; and the Epidamnians finding themselves hard pressed, sent ambassadors to Corcyra beseeching their mother country not to allow them to perish, but to make up matters between them and the exiles, and to rid them of the war with the barbarians. The ambassadors seated themselves in the temple of Hera as suppliants,* and made the above requests to the Corcyræans. But the Corcyræans refused to accept their supplication, and they were dismissed without having effected anything.

25. When the Epidamnians found that no help could be expected from Corcyra, they were in a strait what to do next. So they sent to Delphi and inquired of the god,† whether they should deliver their city to the Corinthians, and endeavour to obtain some assistance from their founders. The answer he gave them was to deliver the city, and place themselves under Corinthian protection. So the Epidamnians went to Corinth, and delivered over the colony in obedience to the commands of the oracle. They showed that their founder came from Corinth, and revealed the answer of the god; and they begged them not to allow them to perish, but to assist them. This the Corinthians consented to do. Believing the colony to belong as much to themselves as to the Corcyræans, they felt it to be a kind of duty to undertake their protection. Besides, they hated the Corcyræans for their contempt of the mother country. Instead of meeting with the usual honours accorded to the present city by every other colony‡ at public assemblies, such as precedence at sacrifices, Corinth found herself treated with contempt by a power, which in point of wealth could stand comparison with any even of the richest communities in Hellas,§ which possessed great military strength, and which sometimes could not repress a pride in the high naval position of an island whose

---

*All Greeks worshiped the same gods, at least nominally. (Think of Socrates, for the rule and for an exception; he sacrificed and attended processions like his compatriots, but he developed a different concept of divine ethics.) Altars and temples were recognized as places of refuge from private and public menace in times of trouble.

†The oracle of Apollo at his shrine in Delphi, on the slopes of Mount Parnassus, was a Panhellenic shrine where private individuals and public representatives asked the god for answers. They put their questions to a priestess in the principal temple. The entire sanctuary provided visiting and curious Greeks with a place for sharing information.

‡An ancient Greek colony's population was gathered and organized by a mother-city but then became an independent *polis*. Exceptions such as Potidaea (map 7) were usually Corinthian colonies. The Spartans and Athenians sent abroad very few colonies because of their vast lands for internal colonization, but several cities with smaller territories sent out many. Ties of loyalty and tradition bound the new city to the originating *polis*. Once established, however, the colony could follow an unrelated foreign and domestic policy. It owed little continued return beyond annual religious rituals, a spiritual and ethnic recognition of original connections.

§Corcyra had a wealth that rivaled the resources of its founding metropolis.

nautical renown dated from the days of its old inhabitants, the Phæacians. This was one reason of the care that they lavished on their fleet, which became very efficient; indeed they began the war with a force of a hundred and twenty triremes.

26. All these grievances made Corinth eager to send the promised aid to Epidamnus. Advertisement was made for volunteer settlers, and a force of Ambraciots, Leucadians, and Corinthians was despatched. They marched by land to Apollonia, a Corinthian colony, the route by sea being avoided from fear of Corcyræan interruption. When the Corcyræans heard of the arrival of the settlers and troops in Epidamnus, and the surrender of the colony to Corinth, they took fire. Instantly putting to sea with five-and-twenty ships, which were quickly followed by others, they insolently commanded the Epidamnians to receive back the banished* nobles—(it must be premised that the Epidamnian exiles had come to Corcyra and, pointing to the sepulchres of their ancestors, had appealed to their kindred to restore them)—and to dismiss the Corinthian garrison and settlers. But to all this the Epidamnians turned a deaf ear. Upon this the Corcyræans commenced operations against them with a fleet of forty sail. They took with them the exiles, with a view to their restoration, and also secured the services of the Illyrians. Sitting down before the city, they issued a proclamation to the effect that any of the natives that chose, and the foreigners, might depart unharmed, with the alternative of being treated as enemies.† On their refusal the Corcyræans proceeded to besiege the city, which stands on an isthmus.

27. The Corinthians, receiving intelligence of the investment of Epidamnus, got together an armament and proclaimed a colony to Epidamnus, perfect political equality being guaranteed to all who chose to go. Any who were not prepared to sail at once, might by paying down the sum of fifty Corinthian drachmæ‡ have a share in the colony without leaving Corinth. Great numbers took advantage of this proclamation, some being ready to start directly, others paying the requisite forfeit. In case of their passage being disputed by the Cor

---

*When *stasis* reached the level of physical threat and harm, which was often, the weaker side might wisely choose to leave the *polis* rather than die. Alternatively, the stronger side might "legally" banish their opponents and confiscate their property. Athenian ostracism was devised, it seems, to rid a community for ten years of dangerous faction leaders without confiscating their property. It served as a non-lethal, political safety valve.

†When one force besieged another situated in a walled community, the attackers often tried psychological warfare before resorting to expensive and chancy sieges. Many Greek armies, equipped with little in the way of engineers or sanitary facilities, lost more men to disease than to wounds and killing in battle.

‡The drachma was the unit of currency in Greek cities, but each city minted its own coins, and there were several different weight standards. This sum represents close to two months' work (at a drachma per day).

cyræans, several cities were asked to lend them a convoy.* Megara prepared to accompany them with eight ships, Pale in Cephallonia with four; Epidaurus furnished five, Hermione one, Trœzen two, Leucas ten, and Ambracia eight. The Thebans and Phliasians were asked for money,† the Eleans for hulls as well; while Corinth herself furnished thirty ships and three thousand heavy infantry.‡

28. When the Corcyræans heard of their preparations they came to Corinth with envoys from Lacedæmon and Sicyon, whom they persuaded to accompany them, and bade her recall the garrison and settlers, as she had nothing to do with Epidamnus. If, however, she had any claims to make, they were willing to submit the matter to the arbitration of such of the cities in Peloponnese as should be chosen by mutual agreement, and that the colony should remain with the city to whom the arbitrators might assign it. They were also willing to refer the matter to the oracle at Delphi.§ If, in defiance of their protestations, war was appealed to, they should be themselves compelled by this violence to seek friends in quarters where they had no desire to seek them, and to make even old ties give way to the necessity of assistance. The answer they got from Corinth was, that if they would withdraw their fleet and the barbarians from Epidamnus negotiation might be possible; but, while the town was still being besieged, going before arbitrators was out of the question. The Corcyræans retorted that if Corinth would withdraw her troops from Epidamnus they would withdraw theirs, or they were ready to let both parties remain *in statu quo*, an armistice being concluded till judgment could be given.‖

29. Turning a deaf ear to all these proposals, when their ships were manned and their allies had come in, the Corinthians sent a herald before them to declare war,# and getting under weigh with seventy-

---

*The Corcyreans had the third-largest navy after the Athenians and the Corinthians. The Corinthians wanted to guard their troop and supply ships against sudden devastation in Corcyrean waters.

†Then as now, war was understandably the most expensive undertaking of a political entity. Corinth had cultivated many allies, and this moment seemed a good occasion to demand their assistance.

‡The Greek word is *hoplite*, a man equipped with heavy defensive armor, a spear, short sword, dagger, and shield.

§The oracular shrine at Delphi, in the territory called Phocis, was the center of the Hellenic informational network and a more or less dependably neutral source for arbitrators. Herodotus reports several situations in which various parties shamelessly bribed the religious authorities.

‖Greek rules of war had developed no equivalents to the modern Geneva Conventions, although there were recognized protocols for negotiation, engagement, and battlefield etiquette.

#The herald was sacrosanct as a messenger; a declaration of war was expected but not universally observed.

five ships and two thousand heavy infantry, sailed for Epidamnus to give battle to the Corcyræans. The fleet was under the command of Aristeus, son of Pellichas, Callicrates, son of Callias, and Timanor, son of Timanthes; the troops under that of Archetimus, son of Eurytimus, and Isarchidas, son of Isarchus.* When they had reached Actium in the territory of Anactorium, at the mouth of the gulf of Ambracia, where the temple of Apollo stands, the Corcyræans sent on a herald in a light boat to warn them not to sail against them. Meanwhile they proceeded to man their ships, all of which had been equipped for action, the old vessels being undergirded to make them seaworthy. On the return of the herald without any peaceful answer from the Corinthians, their ships being now manned, they put out to sea to meet the enemy with a fleet of eighty sail (forty were engaged in the siege of Epidamnus), formed line and went into action, and gained a decisive victory, and destroyed fifteen of the Corinthian vessels. The same day had seen Epidamnus compelled by its besiegers to capitulate; the conditions being that the foreigners should be sold, and the Corinthians kept as prisoners of war, till their fate should be otherwise decided.

30. After the engagement the Corcyræans set up a trophy† on Leukimme, a headland of Corcyra, and slew all their captives‡ except the Corinthians, whom they kept as prisoners of war.§ Defeated at sea, the Corinthians and their allies repaired home, and left the Corcyræans masters of all the sea about those parts. Sailing to Leucas, a Corinthian colony, they ravaged their territory, and burnt Cyllene, the harbour of the Eleans, because they had furnished ships and money to Corinth. For almost the whole of the period that followed the battle they remained masters of the sea, and the allies of Corinth were harassed by Corcyræan cruisers. At last Corinth, roused by the sufferings of her allies, sent out ships and troops in the fall of the summer, who formed an encampment at Actium and about Chimerium, in Thesprotis, for the protection of Leucas and the rest of the friendly cities. The Corcyræans on their part formed a similar station on Leukimme. Neither party made any movement, but they remained

---

*Thucydides usually makes every effort to supply names that include the patronymic (the name of the father of the person in question); it was part of his obsession with accuracy.

†Victory in battle was affirmed by he who controlled the battlefield. The victors typically created a trophy, a post decorated with the arms and armor of the defeated.

‡The rules of war permitted the killing of the losing soldiers, but it was more profitable to ransom them to their families or sell them as slaves.

§The Corinthian combatants were spared as valuable pawns in the diplomatic negotiations before, during, and after the conflict.

confronting each other till the end of the summer, and winter was at hand before either of them returned home.*

31. Corinth, exasperated by the war with the Corcyræans, spent the whole of the year after the engagement and that succeeding it in building ships, and in straining every nerve to form an efficient fleet; rowers being drawn from Peloponnese and the rest of Hellas by the inducement of large bounties. The Corcyræans, alarmed at the news of their preparations, being without a single ally in Hellas (for they had not enrolled themselves either in the Athenian or in the Lacedæmonian confederacy), decided to repair to Athens in order to enter into alliance, and to endeavour to procure support from her. Corinth also, hearing of their intentions, sent an embassy to Athens to prevent the Corcyræan navy being joined by the Athenian, and her prospect of ordering the war according to her wishes being thus impeded. An assembly was convoked, and the rival advocates appeared: the Corcyræans spoke as follows:—†

32. 'Athenians! when a people that have not rendered any important service or support to their neighbours in times past, for which they might claim to be repaid, appear before them as we now appear before you to solicit their assistance, they may fairly be required to satisfy certain preliminary conditions. They should show, first, that it is expedient or at least safe to grant their request;‡ next, that they will retain a lasting sense of the kindness. But if they cannot clearly establish any of these points, they must not be annoyed if they meet with a rebuff. Now the Corcyræans believe that with their petition for assistance they can also give you a satisfactory answer on these points, and they have therefore despatched us hither. It has so happened that our policy as regards you with respect to this request, turns out to be inconsistent, and as regards our interests, to be at the present crisis inexpedient. We say inconsistent, because a power which has never in the whole of her past history been willing to ally herself with any of her neighbours, is now found asking them to ally themselves with her. And we say inexpedient, because in our present

---

*Thucydides' dating system, accurate but difficult to follow in the narrative, divides the year into winter and summer, with summer including a spring and summer campaigning season. He did not want to depend on the names of parochial magistrates. The Greeks had no mutually agreed-upon calendar at this time.

†Thucydides' speeches—of which this is the first, and an astonishing piece of rhetoric—favor balanced clauses with imbalanced phrasing; even the antitheses and the parallels often do not exactly match. There are approximately 140 speeches in all—long and short, domestic and international, military and legislative—reported in discourse either direct (noted by quotation marks) or indirect.

‡Expedience (profit) and security (or safety, absence of fear) are the two essential motivations for states in this author's view.

war with Corinth it has left us in a position of entire isolation, and what once seemed the wise precaution of refusing to involve ourselves in alliances with other powers, lest we should also involve ourselves in risks of their choosing, has now proved to be folly and weakness. It is true that in the late naval engagement we drove back the Corinthians from our shores single-handed. But they have now got together a still larger armament from Peloponnese and the rest of Hellas; and we, seeing our utter inability to cope with them without foreign aid, and the magnitude of the danger which subjection to them implies, find it necessary to ask help from you and from every other power. And we hope to be excused if we forswear our old principle of complete political isolation,* a principle which was not adopted with any sinister intention, but was rather the consequence of an error in judgment.

33. 'Now there are many reasons why in the event of your compliance you will congratulate yourselves on this request having been made to you. First, because your assistance will be rendered to a power which, herself inoffensive, is a victim to the injustice of others. Secondly, because all that we most value is at stake in the present contest, and your welcome of us under these circumstances will be a proof of good will which will ever keep alive the gratitude you will lay up in our hearts. Thirdly, yourselves excepted, we are the greatest naval power in Hellas. Moreover, can you conceive a stroke of good fortune more rare in itself, or more disheartening to your enemies, than that the power whose adhesion you would have valued above much material and moral strength, should present herself self-invited, should deliver herself into your hands without danger and without expense, and should lastly put you in the way of gaining a high character in the eyes of the world, the gratitude of those whom you shall assist, and a great accession of strength for yourselves?† You may search all history without finding many instances of a people gaining all these advantages at once, or many instances of a power that comes in quest of assistance being in a position to give to the people whose alliance she solicits as much safety and honour as she will receive. But it will be urged that it is only in the case of a war that we shall be found useful. To this we answer that if any of you imagine that that war is far off, he is grievously mistaken, and is blind to the fact that Lacedæmon regards you with jealousy and desires war, and that Corinth is powerful there,—the same, remember, that

---

*The Corcyreans occupied the northwest corner of old Greece. An ancient colony, founded around 733, they now rivaled their founding metropolis in their armed forces and trade.

†This long sentence suggests the compact complexity of arguments used by Thucydidean speakers.

is your enemy,* and is even now trying to subdue us as a preliminary to attacking you. And this she does to prevent our becoming united by a common enmity, and her having us both on her hands, and also to insure getting the start of you in one of two ways, either by crippling our power or by making its strength her own. Now it is our policy to be beforehand with her—that is, for Corcyra to make an offer of alliance and for you to accept it; in fact, we ought to form plans against her instead of waiting to defeat the plans she forms against us.

34. 'If she asserts that for you to receive a colony of hers into alliance is not right, let her know that every colony that is well treated honours its parent state, but becomes estranged from it by injustice. For colonists are not sent forth on the understanding that they are to be the slaves of those that remain behind, but that they are to be their equals.† And that Corinth was injuring us is clear. Invited to refer the dispute about Epidamnus to arbitration, they chose to prosecute their complaints by war rather than by a fair trial. And let their conduct towards us who are their kindred be a warning to you not to be misled by their deceit, nor to yield to their direct requests; concessions to adversaries only end in self-reproach, and the more strictly they are avoided the greater will be the chance of security.

35. 'If it be urged that your reception of us will be a breach of the treaty existing between you and Lacedæmon, the answer is that we are a neutral state, and that one of the express provisions of that treaty is that it shall be competent for any Hellenic state that is neutral to join whichever side it pleases.‡ And it is intolerable for Corinth to be allowed to obtain men for her navy not only from her allies, but also from the rest of Hellas, no small number being furnished by your own subjects; while we are to be excluded both from the alliance left open to us by treaty, and from any assistance that we might get from other quarters, and you are to be accused of political immorality if you comply with our request. On the other hand, we shall have much greater cause to complain of you, if you do not comply with it; if we, who are in peril, and are no enemies of yours, meet with a repulse at

---

*Commercial competitors Corinth and Athens were barely separated geographically by the weak state of Megara. They had cooperated in the past, however, and would do so in the future.

†Hellenic colonies were not dependencies, but Corinth's colonies often maintained close symbolic relations with their metropolis—accepting priests and sometimes magistrates, and participating in the mother city's festivals.

‡They mention the treaty of 445. It seems to have allowed, as the Corcyreans state, *poleis* (Greek city-states) not otherwise engaged to join the alliances of the Athenians (the Delian League, also called the Hellenic League) or the Spartans (the Peloponnesian League).

your hands, while Corinth, who is the aggressor and your enemy, not only meets with no hindrance from you, but is even allowed to draw material for war from your dependencies. This ought not to be, but you should either forbid her enlisting men in your dominions, or you should lend us too what help you may think advisable.

'But your real policy is to afford us avowed countenance and support. The advantages of this course, as we premised in the beginning of our speech, are many. We mention one that is perhaps the chief. Could there be a clearer guarantee of our good faith than is offered by the fact that the power which is at enmity with you, is also at enmity with us, and that that power is fully able to punish defection. And there is a wide difference between declining the alliance of an inland and of a maritime power. For your first endeavour should be to prevent, if possible, the existence of any naval power except your own; failing this, to secure the friendship of the strongest that does exist.*

36. 'And if any of you believe that what we urge is expedient, but fear to act upon this belief, lest it should lead to a breach of the treaty, you must remember that on the one hand, whatever your fears, your strength will be formidable to your antagonists; on the other, whatever the confidence you derive from refusing to receive us, your weakness will have no terrors for a strong enemy. You must also remember that your decision is for Athens no less than for Corcyra, and that you are not making the best provision for her interests, if at a time when you are anxiously scanning the horizon that you may be in readiness for the breaking out of the war which is all but upon you, you hesitate to attach to your side a place whose adhesion or estrangement is alike pregnant with the most vital consequences. For it lies conveniently for the coast-navigation in the direction of Italy and Sicily,† being able to bar the passage of naval reinforcements from thence to Peloponnese, and from Peloponnese thither; and it is in other respects a most desirable station. To sum up as shortly as possible, embracing both general and particular considerations, let this show you the folly of sacrificing us. Remember that there are but three considerable naval powers in Hellas, Athens, Corcyra, and Corinth, and that if you allow two of these three to become one, and Corinth to secure us for herself, you will have to hold the sea against the united fleets of Corcyra and Peloponnese. But if you receive us, you will have our ships to reinforce you in the struggle.'

---

*The Corcyreans emphasize the importance of their large naval forces, but, in fact, they were to give the Athenians little help because of their internal conflicts.

†This strategic location was on the safest sea route to the rich Greek cities of the West. It was thus important to the Athenians who were already thinking of a Sicilian campaign (see books 3, 6, and 7).

Such were the words of the Corcyræans. After they had finished, the Corinthians* spoke as follows:—

37. 'These Corcyræans in the speech we have just heard do not confine themselves to the question of their reception into your alliance. They also talk of our being guilty of injustice, and their being the victims of an unjustifiable war. It becomes necessary for us to touch upon both these points before we proceed to the rest of what we have to say, that you may have a more correct idea of the grounds of our claim, and have good cause to reject their petition. According to them, their old policy of refusing all offers of alliance was a policy of moderation. It was in fact adopted for bad ends, not for good; indeed their conduct is such as to make them by no means desirous of having allies present to witness it, or of having the shame of asking their concurrence. Besides, their geographical situation makes them independent of others, and consequently the decision in cases where they injure any lies not with judges appointed by mutual agreement, but with themselves, because while they seldom make voyages to their neighbours, they are constantly being visited by foreign vessels which are compelled to put in to Corcyra. In short, the object that they propose to themselves in their specious policy of complete isolation, is not to avoid sharing in the crimes of others, but to secure a monopoly of crime to themselves,—the license of outrage wherever they can compel, of fraud wherever they can elude, and the enjoyment of their gains without shame. And yet if they were the honest men they pretend to be, the less hold that others had upon them, the stronger would be the light in which they might have put their honesty by giving and taking what was just.

38. 'But such has not been their conduct either towards others or towards us. The attitude of our colony towards us has always been one of estrangement, and is now one of hostility; for, say they, "We were not sent out to be ill-treated." We rejoin that we did not found the colony to be insulted by them, but to be their head,† and to be regarded with a proper respect. At any rate our other colonies honour us, and we are very much beloved by our colonists;‡ and clearly, if the majority are satisfied with us, these can have no good reason for a dissatisfaction in which they stand alone, and we are not acting improperly in making war against them, nor are we making war against them

---

*Thucydides usually provides speeches in pairs (antilogies, or opposing arguments); this first set, delivered to the Athenian assembly, sets the expectation and paradigm.

†The Corinthians claim their traditional privileges, but the Hellenic model does not resemble the totally controlled English, French, or Spanish colonies of the early modern period. No founded city had to show continued deference to its founding metropolis.

‡Although this remark may be true, it does not establish legal rights for the Corinthians over the Corcyreans.

without having received signal provocation. Besides, if we were in the wrong, it would be honourable in them to give way to our wishes, and disgraceful for us to trample on their moderation; but in the pride and license of wealth they have sinned again and again against us, and never more deeply than when Epidamnus, our dependency, which they took no steps to claim in its distress, upon our coming to relieve it, was by them seized, and is now held by force of arms.

39. 'As to their allegation that they wished the question to be first submitted to arbitration, it is obvious that a challenge coming from the party who is safe in a commanding position, cannot gain the credit due only to him who, before appealing to arms, in deeds as well as words, places himself on a level with his adversary. In their case, it was not before they laid siege to the place, but after they at length understood that we should not tamely suffer it, that they thought of the specious word arbitration. And not satisfied with their own misconduct there, they appear here now requiring you to join with them not in alliance, but in crime, and to receive them in spite of their being at enmity with us. But it was when they stood firmest, that they should have made overtures to you, and not at a time when we have been wronged, and they are in peril; nor yet at a time when you will be admitting to a share in your protection those who never admitted you to a share in their power, and will be incurring an equal amount of blame from us with those in whose offences you had no hand. No, they should have shared their power with you before they asked you to share your fortunes with them.

40. 'So then the reality of the grievances we come to complain of, and the violence and rapacity of our opponents, have both been proved. But that you cannot equitably receive them, this you have still to learn. It may be true that one of the provisions of the treaty is that it shall be competent for any state, whose name was not down on the list, to join whichever side it pleases.* But this agreement is not meant for those whose object in joining is the injury of other powers, but for those whose need of support does not arise from the fact of defection, and whose adhesion will not bring to the power that is mad enough to receive them war instead of peace;† which will be the case with you, if you refuse to listen to us. For you cannot become their auxiliary and remain our friend; if you join in their attack, you must share the punishment which the defenders inflict on them. And yet you have the best possible right to be neutral, or failing this, you should on the contrary join us against them. Corinth is at least in

---

*The Corinthians cannot disprove this irritating fact, so they proceed to argue it away.
†The Corinthians are threatening the Athenians with war if they jump at this golden opportunity for alliance.

treaty with you; with Corcyra you were never even in truce. But do not lay down the principle that defection is to be patronised. Did we on the defection of the Samians record our vote against you, when the rest of the Peloponnesian powers were equally divided on the question whether they should assist them?* No, we told them to their face that every power has a right to punish its own allies. Why, if you make it your policy to receive and assist all offenders, you will find that just as many of your dependencies will come over to us, and the principle that you establish will press less heavily on us than on yourselves.

41. 'This then is what Hellenic law† entitles us to demand as a right. But we have also advice to offer and claims on your gratitude, which, since there is no danger of our injuring you, as we are not enemies, and since our friendship does not amount to very frequent intercourse, we say ought to be liquidated at the present juncture. When you were in want of ships of war for the war against the Æginetans, before the Persian invasion, Corinth supplied you with twenty vessels.‡ That good turn, and the line we took on the Samian question, when we were the cause of the Peloponnesians refusing to assist them, enabled you to conquer Ægina, and to punish Samos. And we acted thus at crises when, if ever, men are wont in their efforts against their enemies to forget everything for the sake of victory, regarding him who assists them then as a friend, even if thus far he has been a foe, and him who opposes them then as a foe, even if he has thus far been a friend; indeed they allow their real interests to suffer from their absorbing preoccupation in the struggle.

42. 'Weigh well these considerations, and let your youth learn what they are from their elders,§ and let them determine to do unto us as we have done unto you. And let them not acknowledge the justice of what we say, but dispute its wisdom in the contingency of war. Not only is the straightest path generally speaking the wisest; but the coming of the war

---

*The Corinthians claim that the Athenians owe them a favor for not stepping in to oppose Athenian imperial interests when the Samians had revolted from their league in 440. It remains unclear why the Corinthians opposed Peloponnesian intervention, if in fact they did.

†There was no United States of Greece, and no international court, but there were traditional standards of state behavior, many of which collapsed in this war. The standards arose from common language, religion, "history" (that is, popular conceptions of past common actions, interests, and differences), and perceived "blood."

‡Corinth and Aegina were even closer neighbors and trading rivals, especially in the Archaic period (c.730–480 B.C.E.). "The enemy of my enemy is my friend" was a maxim in practice, if not phrase, in ancient Greek international relations. In the tiny world of the *poleis* there were many of these fluid alliances.

§Many Thucydidean speakers in many cities urge elders to inform younger men of the rigors and dangers of war. Rarely do they succeed.

which the Corcyræans have used as a bugbear to persuade you to do wrong, is still uncertain, and it is not worth while to be carried away by it into gaining the instant and declared enmity of Corinth. It were, rather, wise to try and counteract the unfavourable impression which your conduct to Megara* has created. For kindness opportunely shown has a greater power of removing old grievances than the facts of the case may warrant. And do not be seduced by the prospect of a great naval alliance. Abstinence from all injustice to other first-rate powers is a greater tower of strength, than anything that can be gained by the sacrifice of permanent tranquillity for an apparent temporary advantage.

43. 'It is now our turn to benefit by the principle that we laid down at Lacedæmon, that every power has a right to punish her own allies. We now claim to receive the same from you, and protest against your rewarding us for benefiting you by our vote by injuring us by yours. On the contrary, return us like for like, remembering that this is that very crisis in which he who lends aid is most a friend, and he who opposes is most a foe. And for these Corcyræans—neither receive them into alliance in our despite, nor be their abettors in crime. So do, and you will act as we have a right to expect of you, and at the same time best consult your own interests.'

44. Such were the words of the Corinthians.

When the Athenians had heard both out, two assemblies were held. In the first there was a manifest disposition to listen to the representations of Corinth; in the second, public feeling had changed,† and an alliance with Corcyra was decided on, with certain reservations. It was to be a defensive, not an offensive alliance. It did not involve a breach of the treaty with Peloponnese: Athens could not be required to join Corcyra in any attack upon Corinth. But each of the contracting parties had a right to the other's assistance against invasion, whether of his own territory, or that of an ally. For it began now to be felt that the coming of the Peloponnesian war was only a question of time, and no one was willing to see a naval power of such magnitude as Corcyra sacrificed to Corinth; though if they could let them weaken each other by mutual conflict,‡ it would be no bad prepara-

---

*The Athenians had banned Megarian goods and vessels from the harbors of Athens and its allies. This embargo had seriously damaged the Megarian commercial economy. Plutarch provides more information (in his biography of *Pericles*) than does Thucydides, who alludes to such a decree (passed at Pericles' behest) but oddly does not give any details of it.

†Thucydides notes the lability of the democracy, for better and for worse.

‡Corcyra had not been friendly before, and Corinth had long been a problem for Athens' expansion into Corinth's sphere of influence, so the Athenians figure they have nothing to lose, if the two cities wear each other down. (Fornara #126 offers inscriptional information about the Athenian squadron.)

tion for the struggle which Athens might one day have to wage with Corinth and the other naval powers. At the same time the island seemed to lie conveniently on the coasting passage to Italy and Sicily.

45. With these views, Athens received Corcyra into alliance, and on the departure of the Corinthians not long afterwards, sent ten ships to their assistance. They were commanded by Lacedæmonius,* the son of Cimon, Diotimus, the son of Strombichus, and Proteas, the son of Epicles. Their instructions were to avoid collision with the Corinthian fleet except under certain circumstances. If it sailed to Corcyra and threatened a landing on her coast, or in any of her possessions, they were to do their utmost to prevent it. These instructions were prompted by an anxiety to avoid a breach of the treaty.

46. Meanwhile the Corinthians completed their preparations, and sailed for Corcyra with a hundred and fifty ships. Of these Elis furnished ten, Megara twelve, Leucas ten, Ambracia twenty-seven, Anactorium one, and Corinth herself ninety. Each of these contingents had its own admiral, the Corinthian being under the command of Xenoclides, son of Euthycles, with four colleagues. Sailing from Leucas, they made land at the part of the continent opposite Corcyra. They anchored in the harbour of Chimerium, in the territory of Thesprotis, above which, at some distance from the sea, lies the city of Ephyre, in the Elean district. By this city the Acherusian lake pours its waters into the sea. It gets its name from the river Acheron, which flows through Thesprotis, and falls into the lake. There also the river Thyamis flows, forming the boundary between Thesprotis and Kestrine; and between these rivers rises the point of Chimerium. In this part of the continent the Corinthians now came to anchor, and formed an encampment.

47. When the Corcyræans saw them coming, they manned a hundred and ten ships, commanded by Meikiades, Aisimides, and Eurybatus, and stationed themselves at one of the Sybota isles; the ten Athenian ships being present. On point Leukimme they posted their land forces, and a thousand heavy infantry who had come from Zacynthus to their assistance. Nor were the Corinthians on the mainland without their allies. The barbarians flocked in large numbers to their assistance, the inhabitants of this part of the continent being old allies of theirs.

48. When the Corinthian preparations were completed they took three days' provisions, and put out from Chimerium by night, ready for action. Sailing with the dawn, they sighted the Corcyræan fleet out

---

*The strange Athenian name belongs to the son of Cimon, an aristocratic competitor of the aristocrat Pericles, friend of the *demos* (populace). Cimon was close to the Lacedaemonians and represented their interests in Athens (as a *proxenos*, a kind of consular representative).

at sea, and coming towards them. When they perceived each other, both sides formed in order of battle. On the Corcyræan right wing* lay the Athenian ships, the rest of the line being occupied by their own vessels formed in three squadrons, each of which was commanded by one of the three admirals. Such was the Corcyræan formation. The Corinthian was as follows: on the right wing lay the Megarian and Ambraciot ships, in the centre the rest of the allies in order. But the left was composed of the best sailers† in the Corinthian navy, to encounter the Athenians and the right wing of the Corcyræans.

49. As soon as the signals were raised on either side, they joined battle. Both sides had a large number of heavy infantry on their decks, and a large number of archers and darters, the old imperfect armament still prevailing.‡ The sea-fight was an obstinate one, though not remarkable for its science; indeed it was more like a battle by land.§ Whenever they charged each other, the multitude and crush of the vessels made it by no means easy to get loose; besides, their hopes of victory lay principally in the heavy infantry on the decks, who stood and fought in order, the ships remaining stationary. The manœuvre of breaking the line was not tried:‖ in short, strength and pluck had more share in the fight than science. Everywhere tumult reigned, the battle being one scene of confusion; meanwhile the Athenian ships, by coming up to the Corcyræans whenever they were pressed, served to alarm the enemy, though their commanders could not join in the battle from fear of their instructions.# The right wing of the Corinthians suffered most. The Corcyræans routed it, and chased them in disorder to the continent with twenty ships, sailed up to their camp, and burnt the tents which they found empty, and plundered the stuff. So in this quarter the Corinthians and their allies were defeated,

---

*The right wing of the front line infantry was the post of honor and greatest danger (because no additional hoplites protected the unprotected spear arm); by analogy, it is a naval post of honor.

†The naval skill of the Athenians made them formidable, and the Corinthians put their best ships against them.

‡During the Peloponnesian War, ships became faster, and naval technology, weaponry, and maneuvers developed—technological progress that was independent of the usual complement of shipboard marines.

§Thucydides notes the old-fashioned fighting techniques, common before this war, which honed new skills in naval engagements.

‖The *diecplous* required the offensive line to sail through the enemy (shearing off oars if possible) and then turn to ram them amidships. Lighter ships with more highly trained crews could do this. Athenian sailors practiced regularly; no other navy had comparable training.

#The *ecclesia*, the assembly of all citizens, could summarily dismiss Athenian commanders for not following or for exceeding specifically formulated instructions.

and the Corcyræans were victorious. But where the Corinthians themselves were, on the left, they gained a decided success; the scanty forces of the Corcyræans being further weakened by the want of the twenty ships absent on the pursuit. Seeing the Corcyræans hard pressed, the Athenians began at length to assist them more unequivocally. At first, it is true, they refrained from charging any ships; but when the rout was becoming patent, and the Corinthians were pressing on, the time at last came when every one set to, and all distinction was laid aside, and it came to this point, that the Corinthians and Athenians raised their hands against each other.

50. After the rout, the Corinthians, instead of employing themselves in lashing fast and hauling after them the hulls of the vessels which they had disabled, turned their attention to the men, whom they butchered* as they sailed through, not caring so much to make prisoners. Some even of their own friends were slain by them, by mistake,† in their ignorance of the defeat of the right wing. For the number of the ships on both sides, and the distance to which they covered the sea, made it difficult after they had once joined, to distinguish between the conquering and the conquered; this battle proving far greater than any before it, any at least between Hellenes, for the number of vessels engaged.‡ After the Corinthians had chased the Corcyræans to the land, they turned to the wrecks and their dead, most of whom they succeeded in getting hold of and conveying to Sybota, the rendezvous of the land forces furnished by their barbarian allies. Sybota, it must be known, is a desert harbour of Thesprotis. This task over, they mustered anew, and sailed against the Corcyræans, who on their part advanced to meet them with all their ships that were fit for service and remaining to them, accompanied by the Athenian vessels, fearing that they might attempt a landing in their territory. It was by this time getting late, and the pæan§ had been sung for the attack, when the Corinthians suddenly began to back water. They had observed twenty Athenian ships sailing up, which had been sent out afterwards to reinforce the ten vessels by the Athenians, who feared, as it turned out justly, the defeat of the Corcyræans and the inability of their handful of ships to protect them.

---

*On rare occasions Thucydides comments about savage behavior in war, but his choice of words makes clear that he disapproves of irrational vengeance and displays of anger.

†There is irony in killing disabled allies and fellow-citizens. Thucydides highlights ignorance and misapprehension in small and large matters (compare Stahl, *Thucydides*).

‡The historian has emphasized that his war is bigger; even the battles running up to the war have notable magnitude.

§This war-chant, nominally a prayerful song to Apollo, helped to synchronize marchers, rowers, and other bands of fighting and ceremonious groups of men and women.

51. These ships were thus seen by the Corinthians first. They suspected that they were from Athens, and that those which they saw were not all, but that there were more behind; they accordingly began to retire. The Corcyræans meanwhile had not sighted them, as they were advancing from a point which they could not so well see, and were wondering why the Corinthians were backing water, when some caught sight of them, and cried out that there were ships in sight ahead. Upon this they also retired; for it was now getting dark, and the retreat of the Corinthians had suspended hostilities. Thus they parted from each other, and the battle ceased with night. The Corcyræans were in their camp at Leukimme, when these twenty ships from Athens, under the command of Glaucon, the son of Leagrus, and Andocides, son of Leogoras, bore on through the corpses and the wrecks, and sailed up to the camp, not long after they were sighted. It was now night, and the Corcyræans feared that they might be hostile vessels; but they soon knew them, and the ships came to anchor.

52. The next day the thirty Athenian vessels put out to sea, accompanied by all the Corcyræan ships that were seaworthy, and sailed to the harbour at Sybota, where the Corinthians lay, to see if they would engage. The Corinthians put out from the land, and formed a line in the open sea, but beyond this made no further movement, having no intention of assuming the offensive. For they saw reinforcements arrived fresh from Athens, and themselves confronted by numerous difficulties, such as the necessity of guarding the prisoners whom they had on board, and the want of all means of refitting their ships in a desert place. What they were thinking more about was how their voyage home was to be effected; they feared that the Athenians might consider that the treaty was dissolved by the collision which had occurred, and forbid their departure.

53. Accordingly they resolved to put some men on board a boat, and send them without a herald's wand to the Athenians, as an experiment. Having done so, they spoke as follows: 'You do wrong, Athenians, to begin war and break the treaty. Engaged in chastising our enemies, we find you placing yourselves in our path in arms against us. Now if your intentions are to prevent us sailing to Corcyra, or anywhere else that we may wish, and if you are for breaking the treaty, first take us that are here, and treat us as enemies.' Such was what they said, and all the Corcyræan armament that were within hearing immediately called out to take them and kill them.* But the Athenians answered as follows: 'Neither are we beginning war, Pelo-

---

*The heraldless men test whether the Athenians regard the Corinthians as official enemies, in a state of war. The Corinthians presumably expected the response they got.

ponnesians, nor are we breaking the treaty; but these Corcyræans are our allies, and we are come to help them. So if you want to sail anywhere else, we place no obstacle in your way; but if you are going to sail against Corcyra, or any of her possessions, we shall do our best to stop you.'

54. Receiving this answer from the Athenians, the Corinthians commenced preparations for their voyage home, and set up a trophy* in Sybota, on the continent; while the Corcyræans took up the wrecks and dead that had been carried out to them by the current, and by a wind which rose in the night and scattered them in all directions, and set up their trophy in Sybota, on the island, as victors. The reasons each side had for claiming the victory were these. The Corinthians had been victorious in the sea-fight until night; and having thus been enabled to carry off most wrecks and dead, they were in possession of no fewer than a thousand prisoners of war, and had sunk close upon seventy vessels. The Corcyræans had destroyed about thirty ships, and after the arrival of the Athenians had taken up the wrecks and dead on their side; they had besides seen the Corinthians retire before them, backing water on sight of the Athenian vessels, and upon the arrival of the Athenians refuse to sail out against them from Sybota.

55. Thus both sides claimed the victory.

The Corinthians on the voyage home took Anactorium, which stands at the mouth of the Ambracian gulf. The place was taken by treachery,† being common ground to the Corcyræans and Corinthians. After establishing Corinthian settlers there, they retired home. Eight hundred of the Corcyræans were slaves; these they sold; two hundred and fifty they retained in captivity, and treated with great attention, in the hope that they might bring over their country to Corinth on their return; most of them being, as it happened, men of very high position in Corcyra. In this way Corcyra maintained her political existence in the war with Corinth, and the Athenian vessels left the island. This was the first cause of the war that Corinth had against the Athenians, viz. that they had fought against them with the Corcyræans in time of treaty.

56. Almost immediately after this, fresh differences arose between the Athenians and Peloponnesians, and contributed their share to the war. Corinth was forming schemes for retaliation, and Athens suspected her hostility. The Potidæans, who inhabit the isthmus of Pal-

---

*This duel of trophies reflects the uncertain nature of victory, especially in situations where one side does not fully disperse or capture the other. Both sides claimed the victory.

†Thucydides regularly notes violations of the conventions of war, even or especially between opponents who had a special bond.

lene,* being a Corinthian colony, but tributary allies of Athens,† were
ordered to raze the wall looking towards Pallene, to give hostages, to
dismiss the Corinthian magistrates,‡ and in future not to receive the
persons sent from Corinth annually to succeed them. It was feared
that they might be persuaded by Perdiccas§ and the Corinthians to revolt, and might draw the rest of the allies in the direction of Thrace to
revolt with them.

57. These precautions against the Potidæans were taken by the
Athenians immediately after the battle at Corcyra. Not only was
Corinth at length openly hostile, but Perdiccas, son of Alexander, king
of the Macedonians, had from an old friend and ally been made an
enemy. He had been made an enemy by the Athenians entering into
alliance with his brother Philip and Derdas, who were in league
against him. In his alarm he had sent to Lacedæmon to try to involve
the Athenians in a war with the Peloponnesians, and was endeavouring to win over Corinth in order to bring about the revolt of Potidæa.
He also made overtures to the Chalcidians in the direction of Thrace,
and to the Bottiæans, to persuade them to join in the revolt; for he
thought that if these places on the border could be made his allies, it
would be easier to carry on the war with their co-operation. Alive to
all this, and wishing to anticipate the revolt of the cities, the Athenians acted as follows. They were just then sending off thirty ships and
a thousand heavy infantry for his country under the command of
Archestratus, son of Lycomedes, with four colleagues. They instructed
the captains to take hostages of the Potidæans, to raze the wall, and
to be on their guard against the revolt of the neighbouring cities.

58. Meanwhile the Potidæans sent envoys to Athens on the chance
of persuading them to take no new steps in their matters; they also
went to Lacedæmon with the Corinthians to secure support in case of
need. Failing after prolonged negotiation to obtain anything satisfactory from the Athenians; being unable, for all they could say, to prevent the vessels that were destined for Macedonia from also sailing

---

*The scene of conflict changes from northwestern to northeastern Greece (map 7), but
in both situations Corinthian colonies (often defensively sited on an isthmus) cause
friction between the metropolis and Athens. The difference in the east is that the Potidaeans had maintained with interruption their close friendship with the mother city.

†The conflict between present imperial obligations arising from military weakness and
Athenian power, on the one hand, and traditional sentiments and the inclination not to
support Athens politically, on the other, was the root of many confrontations in this
war.

‡The Potidaeans, perhaps because of military weakness, had exceptionally close bonds
with Corinth, their founding city.

§This longtime king of Macedon (450–413) was not very stable on his throne or well
situated with his family or neighbors.

against them; and receiving from the Lacedæmonian government a promise to invade Attica, if the Athenians should attack Potidæa, the Potidæans, thus favoured by the moment, at last entered into league with the Chalcidians and Bottiæans, and revolted. And Perdiccas induced the Chalcidians to abandon and demolish their towns on the seaboard,* and settling inland at Olynthus, to make that one city a strong place: meanwhile to those who followed his advice he gave a part of his territory in Mygdonia round Lake Bolbe as a place of abode while the war against the Athenians should last. They accordingly demolished their towns, removed inland, and prepared for war.

59. The thirty ships of the Athenians, arriving before the Thracian places, found Potidæa and the rest in revolt. Their commanders considering it to be quite impossible with their present force to carry on war with Perdiccas, and with the confederate towns as well, turned to Macedonia, their original destination, and having established themselves there, carried on war in co-operation with Philip, and the brothers of Derdas, who had invaded the country from the interior.

60. Meanwhile the Corinthians, with Potidæa in revolt, and the Athenian ships on the coast of Macedonia, alarmed for the safety of the place, and thinking its danger theirs, sent volunteers from Corinth, and mercenaries from the rest of Peloponnese, to the number of sixteen hundred heavy infantry in all, and four hundred light troops. Aristeus, son of Adimantus, who was always a steady friend to the Potidæans, took command of the expedition, and it was principally for love of him that most of the men from Corinth volunteered. They arrived in Thrace forty days after the revolt of Potidæa.

61. The Athenians also immediately received the news of the revolt of the cities. On being informed that Aristeus and his reinforcements were on their way, they sent two thousand heavy infantry of their own citizens and forty ships against the places in revolt, under the command of Callias, son of Calliades, and four colleagues. They arrived in Macedonia first, and found the force of a thousand men that had been first sent out, just become masters of Therme and besieging Pydna. Accordingly they also joined in the investment, and besieged Pydna for a while. Subsequently they came to terms and concluded a forced alliance with Perdiccas, hastened by the calls of Potidæa, and by the arrival of Aristeus at that place. They withdrew from Macedonia, going to Berœa and thence to Strepsa, and, after a futile attempt on the latter place, they pursued by land their march to Potidæa with three thousand heavy infantry of their own citizens, besides a number of their allies, and six hundred Macedonian horsemen,

---

*Such towns were vulnerable to Athenian pressure; the further inland a town, the less it had to fear from sudden naval incursions.

the followers of Philip and Pausanias. With these sailed seventy ships along the coast. Advancing by short marches, on the third day they arrived at Gigonus, where they encamped.

62. Meanwhile the Potidæans and the Peloponnesians with Aristeus were encamped on the side looking towards Olynthus on the isthmus, in expectation of the Athenians, and had established their market outside the city. The allies had chosen Aristeus general of all the infantry; while the command of the cavalry was given to Perdiccas, who had at once left the alliance of the Athenians and gone back to that of the Potidæans,* having deputed Iolaus as his general. The plan of Aristeus was to keep his own force on the isthmus, and await the attack of the Athenians; leaving the Chalcidians and the allies outside the isthmus, and the two hundred cavalry from Perdiccas in Olynthus to act upon the Athenian rear, on the occasion of their advancing against him; and thus to place the enemy between two fires. While Callias the Athenian general and his colleagues despatched the Macedonian horse and a few of the allies to Olynthus, to prevent any movement being made from that quarter, the Athenians themselves broke up their camp and marched against Potidæa. After they had arrived at the isthmus, and saw the enemy preparing for battle, they formed against him, and soon afterwards engaged. The wing of Aristeus, with the Corinthians and other picked troops round him, routed the wing opposed to it, and followed for a considerable distance in pursuit. But the rest of the army of the Potidæans and of the Peloponnesians was defeated by the Athenians, and took refuge within the fortifications.

63. Returning from the pursuit, Aristeus perceived the defeat of the rest of the army. Being at a loss which of the two risks to choose, whether to go to Olynthus or to Potidæa, he at last determined to draw his men into as small a space as possible, and force his way with a run into Potidæa. Not without difficulty, through a storm of missiles, he passed along by the breakwater through the sea, and brought off most of his men safe, though a few were lost. Meanwhile the auxiliaries of the Potidæans from Olynthus, which is about seven miles off, and in sight of Potidæa, when the battle began and the signals were raised, advanced a little way to render assistance; and the Macedonian horse formed against them to prevent it. But on victory speedily declaring for the Athenians and the signals being taken down, they retired back within the wall; and the Macedonians returned to the

---

*Perdiccas was not a trustworthy ally of any power in the more developed parts of Greece to the south. Like other rulers of backward states, he diplomatically played the distant powers off against each other. Within seventy-five years, his state, under Philip II of Macedon, would figure out how to dishearten and demolish the old Greek leagues and powers.

Athenians. Thus there were no cavalry present on either side. After the battle the Athenians set up a trophy, and gave back their dead to the Potidæans under truce. The Potidæans and their allies had close upon three hundred killed; the Athenians a hundred and fifty of their own citizens, and Callias their general.*

64. The wall on the side of the isthmus had now works at once raised against it, and manned by the Athenians. That on the side of Pallene had no works raised against it. They did not think themselves strong enough at once to keep a garrison in the isthmus, and to cross over to Pallene and raise works there; they were afraid that the Potidæans and their allies might take advantage of their division to attack them. Meanwhile the Athenians at home learning that there were no works at Pallene, sometime afterwards sent off sixteen hundred heavy infantry of their own citizens under the command of Phormio, son of Asopius.† Arrived at Pallene, he fixed his head-quarters at Aphytis, and led his army against Potidæa by short marches, ravaging the country as he advanced. No one venturing to meet him in the field, he raised works against the wall on the side of Pallene. So at length Potidæa was strongly invested on either side, and from the sea by the ships co-operating in the blockade.

65. Aristeus, seeing its investment complete, and having no hope of its salvation, except in the event of some movement from the Peloponnese, or of some other improbable contingency, advised all except five hundred to watch for a wind, and sail out of the place, in order that their provisions might last the longer. He was willing to be himself one of those who remained. Unable to persuade them, and desirous of acting on the next alternative, and of having things outside in the best posture possible, he eluded the guardships of the Athenians and sailed out. Remaining among the Chalcidians, he continued to carry on the war; in particular he laid an ambuscade near the city of the Sermylians, and cut off many of them; he also communicated with Peloponnese, and tried to contrive some method by which help might be brought. Meanwhile, after the completion of the investment of Potidæa,‡ Phormio next employed his sixteen hundred men in ravaging Chalcidice and Bottiæa: some of the towns also were taken by him.

---

*Greek generals fought at the head of their troops on land and sea, so they were commonly wounded or killed.

†Phormio was a successful and popular (c.440–428) Athenian general (*strategos*) to whom Thucydides allots no speeches. He will be prominent in book 2 for his naval skill, prospective planning, and victories.

‡Investment, or circumvallation, is the surrounding of a walled city with another wall to keep defenders in and allies out; it was common in ancient warfare. The attack on Syracuse will fail because the invading Athenians cannot complete their land wall or entirely block the harbor.

Congress of the Peloponnesian Confederacy at Lacedæmon

66. The Athenians and Peloponnesians had these antecedent grounds of complaint against each other:* the complaint of Corinth was that her colony of Potidæa, and Corinthian and Peloponnesian citizens within it, were being besieged; that of Athens against the Peloponnesians that they had incited a town of hers, a member of her alliance and a contributor to her revenue, to revolt, and had come and were openly fighting against her on the side of the Potidæans. For all this, war had not yet broken out: there was still truce for a while; for this was a private enterprise on the part of Corinth.

67. But the siege of Potidæa put an end to her inaction; she had men inside it: besides, she feared for the place. Immediately summoning the allies to Lacedæmon, she came and loudly accused Athens of breach of the treaty and aggression on the rights of Peloponnese. With her, the Æginetans, formally unrepresented from fear of Athens, in secret proved not the least urgent of the advocates for war, asserting that they had not the independence guaranteed to them by the treaty.† After extending the summons to any of their allies and others who might have complaints to make of Athenian aggression, the Lacedæmonians held their ordinary assembly, and invited them to speak. There were many who came forward and made their several accusations; among them the Megarians, in a long list of grievances, called special attention to the fact of their exclusion from the ports of the Athenian empire and the market of Athens, in defiance of the treaty.‡ Last of all the Corinthians came forward, and having let those who preceded them inflame the Lacedæmonians, now followed with a speech to this effect:—

68. 'Lacedæmonians! the confidence which you feel in your constitution and social order, inclines you to receive any reflexions of ours on other powers with a certain scepticism. Hence springs your moderation, but hence also the rather limited knowledge which you betray in dealing with foreign politics. Time after time was our voice raised to warn you of the blows about to be dealt us by Athens, and time after time, instead of taking the trouble to ascertain the worth of our communications, you contented yourselves with suspecting the speakers of being inspired by private interest. And so, instead of call-

---

*Ancient authors often end a section with a repeated phrase of summation. Thucydides indicates that, more than the Corcyraean, the Potidaean confrontation with the Athenian empire disturbed Corinthian interests.

†The Thirty Years Treaty of 446/445 guaranteed autonomy to states not in either alliance.

‡The trading Megarians were especially damaged by the Athenians' exclusion of them from Ionian markets and from Athens itself (see Fornara #123).

ing these allies together before the blow fell, you have delayed to do so till we are smarting under it; allies among whom we have not the worst title to speak, as having the greatest complaints to make, complaints of Athenian outrage and Lacedæmonian neglect. Now if these assaults on the rights of Hellas* had been made in the dark you might be unacquainted with the facts, and it would be our duty to enlighten you. As it is, long speeches are not needed where you see servitude accomplished for some of us, meditated for others—in particular for our allies—and prolonged preparations in the aggressor against the hour of war. Or what, pray, is the meaning of their reception of Corcyra by fraud, and their holding it against us by force? what of the siege of Potidæa?—places one of which lies most conveniently for any action against the Thracian towns; while the other would have contributed a very large navy to the Peloponnesians?

69. 'For all this you are responsible. You it was who first allowed them to fortify their city after the Median war, and afterwards to erect the long walls,†—you who, then and now, are always depriving of freedom not only those whom they have enslaved,‡ but also those who have as yet been your allies. For the true author of the subjugation of a people is not so much the immediate agent, as the power which permits it having the means to prevent it; particularly if that power aspires to the glory of being the liberator of Hellas.§ We are at last assembled. It has not been easy to assemble, nor even now are our objects defined. We ought not to be still inquiring into the fact of our wrongs, but into the means of our defence. For the aggressors with matured plans to oppose to our indecision have cast threats aside and betaken themselves to action. And we know what are the paths by which Athenian aggression travels, and how insidious is its progress. A degree of confidence she may feel from the idea that your bluntness of perception prevents your noticing her; but it is nothing to the impulse which her advance will receive from the knowledge that you see, but do not care to interfere. You, Lacedæmonians, of all the Hel-

---

*The Corinthians speak of common traditions and recognized modes of interstate behaviors in an age when power had replaced custom.

†Around 460, Athens had built, in addition to its circular city wall, a set of "long" walls (first two, later three) that connected the inland city to the ports, both at Phalerum (a coastal *deme*, or township) and Piraeus, about 4 miles southwest of the city. The walls were nearly 200 yards apart and rendered the inland city a fortress nearly invulnerable to land attack (map 3).

‡"Freedom" and "slavery" were catchwords of Hellenic politics. The citizens in *poleis* reduced to paying tribute were not legally slaves, but their foreign (and sometimes domestic) policy had to follow Athens' own.

§Sparta's absence of an overseas empire allowed her, despite her long-subjected helots in conquered Messenia and absolute command of other classes, to win the initial and ongoing war of words over who protected and "spread" freedom.

lenes are alone inactive,* and defend yourselves not by doing anything but by looking as if you would do something; you alone wait till the power of an enemy is becoming twice its original size, instead of crushing it in its infancy. And yet the world used to say that you were to be depended upon; but in your case, we fear, it said more than the truth. The Mede, we ourselves know, had time to come from the ends of the earth to Peloponnese, without any force of yours worthy of the name advancing to meet him.† But this was a distant enemy. Well, Athens at all events is a near neighbour, and yet Athens you utterly disregard; against Athens you prefer to act on the defensive instead of on the offensive, and to make it an affair of chances by deferring the struggle till she has grown far stronger than at first. And yet you know that on the whole the rock on which the barbarian was wrecked was himself, and that if our present enemy Athens has not again and again annihilated us, we owe it more to her blunders than to your protection.‡ Indeed, expectations from you have before now been the ruin of some, whose faith induced them to omit preparation.

'We hope that none of you will consider these words of remonstrance to be rather words of hostility; men remonstrate with friends who are in error, accusations they reserve for enemies who have wronged them.§

70. 'Besides, we consider that we have as good a right as any one to point out a neighbour's faults, particularly when we contemplate the great contrast between the two national characters; a contrast of which, as far as we can see, you have little perception, having never yet considered what sort of antagonists you will encounter in the Athenians, how widely, how absolutely different‖ from yourselves. The Athenians are addicted to innovation, and their designs are characterised by swiftness alike in conception and execution; you have a genius for keeping what you have got, accompanied by a total want of invention, and when forced to act you never go far enough. Again, they are adventurous beyond their power, and daring beyond their

---

*The Athenians had not attacked Laconian territory or Sparta's immediate allies; the land-based Lacedaemonians remained passive as long as their allies allowed them to.

†The Lacedæmonians, with a subjected hostile population, could not stray far from home, and so awaited their enemies in their own territory or policed those nearby.

‡The Corinthians complain that a more aggressive foreign policy is necessary to meet the active Athenian threat. The Athenians over-reached at various times in various theaters of war.

§The Corinthians must defend their strong criticisms of Sparta, the hegemonic state, but there is an implied threat of defection if the Spartans ignore Corinthian interests.

‖Thucydides' Corinthians provide a useful and stinging comparison of Spartan and Athenian characteristics, especially their valor and policy initiatives. The antithesis is perhaps overdrawn.

judgment, and in danger they are sanguine; your wont is to attempt less than is justified by your power, to mistrust even what is sanctioned by your judgment, and to fancy that from danger there is no release. Further, there is promptitude on their side against procrastination on yours; they are never at home, you are never from it: for they hope by their absence to extend their acquisitions, you fear by your advance to endanger what you have left behind.* They are swift to follow up a success, and slow to recoil from a reverse. Their bodies they spend ungrudgingly in their country's cause; their intellect they jealously husband to be employed in her service. A scheme unexecuted is with them a positive loss, a successful enterprise a comparative failure. The deficiency created by the miscarriage of an undertaking is soon filled up by fresh hopes; for they alone are enabled to call a thing hoped for a thing got, by the speed with which they act upon their resolutions. Thus they toil on in trouble and danger all the days of their life, with little opportunity for enjoying,† being ever engaged in getting: their only idea of a holiday is to do what the occasion demands, and to them laborious occupation is less of a misfortune than the peace of a quiet life. To describe their character in a word, one might truly say that they were born into the world to take no rest themselves and to give none to others.

71. 'Such is Athens, your antagonist. And yet, Lacedæmonians, you still delay, and fail to see that peace stays longest with those, who are not more careful to use their power justly than to show their determination not to submit to injustice. On the contrary, your ideal of fair dealing is based on the principle that if you do not injure others, you need not risk your own fortunes in preventing others from injuring you. Now you could scarcely have succeeded in such a policy even with a neighbour like yourselves; but in the present instance, as we have just shown, your habits are old-fashioned‡ as compared with theirs. It is the law as in art, so in politics, that improvements ever prevail; and though fixed usages may be best for undisturbed communities, constant necessities of action must be accompanied by the constant improvement of methods. Thus it happens that the vast experience of Athens has carried her further than you on the path of innovation.

'Here, at least, let your procrastination end. For the present, assist

---

*A not subtle reference to Spartan anxiety over their subjected helots (community slaves tied to the land) and the *perioeci*, a class of indentured, disadvantaged "dwellers round."

†The Corinthians emphasize the determination of the Athenians not to let any opportunities for imperial aggrandizement slip by. Pericles later will emphasize their equal willingness to put toil aside and enjoy cultural opportunities for art, leisure, etc.

‡Thucydides emphasizes Athenian innovation, here and elsewhere. There never had been, especially since the Bronze Age, a Greek empire with a scope like the Athenians'.

your allies and Potidæa in particular, as you promised, by a speedy invasion of Attica,* and do not sacrifice friends and kindred to their bitterest enemies, and drive the rest of us in despair to some other alliance. Such a step would not be condemned either by the gods who received our oaths, or by the men who witnessed them. The breach of a treaty cannot be laid to the people whom desertion compels to seek new relations, but to the power that fails to assist its confederate. But if you will only act, we will stand by you; it would be unnatural for us to change, and never should we meet with such a congenial ally. For these reasons choose the right course, and endeavour not to let Peloponnese under your supremacy degenerate from the prestige that it enjoyed under that of your ancestors.'

72. Such were the words of the Corinthians. There happened to be Athenian envoys present at Lacedæmon on other business.† On hearing the speeches they thought themselves called upon to come before the Lacedæmonians. Their intention was not to offer a defence on any of the charges which the cities brought against them, but to show on a comprehensive view that it was not a matter to be hastily decided on, but one that demanded further consideration. There was also a wish to call attention to the great power of Athens, and to refresh the memory of the old and enlighten the ignorance of the young, from a notion that their words might have the effect of inducing them to prefer tranquillity to war. So they came to the Lacedæmonians and said that they too, if there was no objection, wished to speak to their assembly. They replied by inviting them to come forward. The Athenians advanced, and spoke as follows:—

73. 'The object of our mission here was not to argue with your allies, but to attend to the matters on which our State despatched us. However, the vehemence of the outcry that we hear against us has prevailed on us to come forward. It is not to combat the accusations of the cities (indeed you are not the judges before whom either we or they can plead), but to prevent your taking the wrong course on matters of great importance by yielding too readily to the persuasions of your allies. We also wish to show on a review of the whole indictment that we have a fair title to our possessions, and that our country has claims to consideration. We need not refer to remote antiquity:‡ there we could appeal

---

*The Corinthian strategy, itself old-fashioned, is to force the Athenians to defend their homeland, farms, fields, trees, and livestock (farmers' capital).

†Thucydides dislikes vagueness, but he did not know why Athenians were present then and there. Their response allows Thucydides to present an antilogy, another opposed pair of speeches. Athens lies distant, about 140 miles, from Sparta.

‡A *topos* (commonplace) of late-fifth-century speakers is to claim to avoid any lengthy appeal to traditional arguments about past achievements. The rhetorical ploy of telling people what you won't tell them is called preterition.

to the voice of tradition, but not to the experience of our audience. But to the Median war and contemporary history we must refer, although we are rather tired of continually bringing this subject forward. In our action during that war we ran great risk to obtain certain advantages: you had your share in the solid results, do not try to rob us of all share in the good that the glory may do us. However, the story shall be told not so much to deprecate hostility as to testify against it, and to show, if you are so ill-advised as to enter into a struggle with Athens, what sort of an antagonist she is likely to prove. We assert that at Marathon we were at the front, and faced the barbarian single-handed.* That when he came the second time, unable to cope with him by land we went on board our ships with all our people, and joined in the action at Salamis.† This prevented his taking the Peloponnesian states in detail, and ravaging them with his fleet; when the multitude of his vessels would have made any combination for self-defence impossible. The best proof of this was furnished by the invader himself. Defeated at sea, he considered his power to be no longer what it had been, and retired as speedily as possible with the greater part of his army.

74. 'Such, then, was the result of the matter, and it was clearly proved that it was on the fleet of Hellas that her cause depended. Well, to this result we contributed three very useful elements, viz. the largest number of ships, the ablest commander, and the most unhesitating patriotism.‡ Our contingent of ships was little less than two-thirds of the whole four hundred; the commander was Themistocles, through whom chiefly it was that the battle took place in the straits, the acknowledged salvation of our cause. Indeed, this was the reason of your receiving him with honours such as had never been accorded to any foreign visitor. While for daring patriotism we had no competitors. Receiving no reinforcements from behind, seeing everything in front of us already subjugated, we had the spirit, after abandoning our city, after sacrificing our property (instead of deserting the remainder of the league or depriving them of our services by dispersing),§ to throw ourselves into our ships and meet the danger, without

---

*The Plataeans, loyal allies in this present war, had first come to the aid of the Athenians at Marathon in 490 (see Herodotus 6 and Fornara #49, #50, and #51). Only this small contingent found time and determination to organize and provide assistance. The Spartans later claimed that soon after they would have done so.

†The Athenians were responsible for the time and place of the decisive naval battle of October 480, fought off their coast and port. After this loss, King Xerxes decided to cut his losses and retreat to Asia Minor.

‡The Athenians contributed more than 200 ships and the strategist Themistocles, and abandoned their city in order to chance everything on this battle (Fornara #55).

§The odds were strongly weighted against Hellenic victory, so various communities chose to abandon the Greek cause and join the Persians (Medes).

a thought of resenting your neglect to assist us. We assert, therefore, that we conferred on you quite as much as we received. For you had a stake to fight for; the cities which you had left were still filled with your homes, and you had the prospect of enjoying them again; and your coming was prompted quite as much by fear for yourselves as for us; at all events, you never appeared till we had nothing left to lose. But we left behind us a city that was a city no longer, and staked our lives for a city that had an existence only in desperate hope,* and so bore our full share in your deliverance and in ours. But if we had copied others, and allowed fears for our territory to make us give in our adhesion to the Mede before you came, or if we had suffered our ruin to break our spirit and prevent us embarking in our ships, your naval inferiority would have made a sea-fight unnecessary, and his objects would have been peaceably attained.

75. 'Surely, Lacedæmonians, neither by the patriotism that we displayed at that crisis, nor by the wisdom of our counsels, do we merit our extreme unpopularity with the Hellenes, not at least unpopularity for our empire. That empire we acquired by no violent means, but because you were unwilling to prosecute to its conclusion the war against the barbarian, and because the allies attached themselves to us and spontaneously asked us to assume the command.† And the nature of the case first compelled us to advance our empire to its present height; fear being our principal motive, though honour and interest afterwards came in.‡ And at last, when almost all hated us, when some had already revolted and had been subdued, when you had ceased to be the friends that you once were, and had become objects of suspicion and dislike, it appeared no longer safe to give up our empire; especially as all who left us would fall to you. And no one can quarrel with a people for making, in matters of tremendous risk, the best provision that it can for its interest.

76. 'You, at all events, Lacedæmonians, have used your supremacy to settle the states in Peloponnese as is agreeable to you. And if at the period of which we were speaking you had persevered to the end of the matter, and had incurred hatred in your command, we are sure that you would have made yourselves just as galling to the allies, and

---

*The Persians burned down much of the city. The women, children, and infirm were moved out to various other locations (the "Themistocles decree," Fornara #55).

†Spartan concerns about domestic control in Lacedaemon demanded that the Spartiate army and their other personnel return home as quickly as possible. The Athenians rightly aver that their leadership was first requested by smaller Greek states in the eastern theater; they needed immediate protection from Persian initiatives to recover lost territories and revenge.

‡Fear, honor, and interest provide a triad of motives that often motivate Thucydides' speakers' understanding of communities.

would have been forced to choose between a strong government and danger to yourselves. It follows that it was not a very wonderful action, or contrary to the common practice of mankind, if we did accept an empire that was offered to us, and refused to give it up under the pressure of three of the strongest motives, fear, honour, and interest. And it was not we who set the example, for it has always been the law that the weaker should be subject to the stronger.* Besides, we believed ourselves to be worthy of our position, and so you thought us till now, when calculations of interest have made you take up the cry of justice—a consideration which no one ever yet brought forward to hinder his ambition when he had a chance of gaining anything by might.† And praise is due to all who, if not so superior to human nature as to refuse dominion, yet respect justice more than their position compels them to do.

'We imagine that our moderation would be best demonstrated by the conduct of others who should be placed in our position; but even our equity has very unreasonably subjected us to condemnation instead of approval.

77. 'Our abatement of our rights in the contract trials with our allies, and our causing them to be decided by impartial laws at Athens, have gained us the character of being litigious. And none care to inquire why this reproach is not brought against other imperial powers, who treat their subjects with less moderation than we do; the secret being that where force can be used, law is not needed. But our subjects are so habituated to associate with us as equals, that any defeat whatever that clashes with their notions of justice, whether it proceeds from a legal judgment or from the power which our empire gives us, makes them forget to be grateful for being allowed to retain most of their possessions, and more vexed at a part being taken, than if we had from the first cast law aside and openly gratified our covetousness. If we had done so, not even would they have disputed that the weaker must give way to the stronger. Men's indignation, it seems, is more excited by legal wrong than by violent wrong; the first looks like being cheated by an equal, the second like being compelled by a superior. At all events they contrived to put up with much worse treatment than this from the Mede,‡ yet they think our rule severe, and this is to be expected, for the present always weighs heavy on the

---

*Thucydides does not say that "might makes right" but only that strength will assert itself.

†The Athenians acidly point out that justice is an argument that only weaker parties are interested in. In international affairs, dominant powers will generally do what they can.

‡The Athenians boast that they accord their subjects more autonomy and more legal rights in court than they had ever known at the hands of the barbarian Persians. And it's probably true.

conquered. This at least is certain. If you were to succeed in over-throwing us and in taking our place, you would speedily lose the popularity with which fear of us has invested you, if your policy of to-day is at all to tally with the sample that you gave of it during the brief period of your command against the Mede. Not only is your life at home regulated by rules and institutions incompatible with those of others,* but your citizens abroad act neither on these rules nor on those which are recognised by the rest of Hellas.†

78. 'Take time then in forming your resolution, as the matter is of great importance; and do not be persuaded by the opinions and complaints of others to bring trouble on yourselves, but consider the vast influence of accident in war,‡ before you are engaged in it. As it continues, it generally becomes an affair of chances, chances from which neither of us is exempt, and whose event we must risk in the dark. It is a common mistake in going to war to begin at the wrong end, to act first, and wait for disaster to discuss the matter. But we are not yet by any means so misguided, nor, so far as we can see, are you; accordingly, while it is still open to us both to choose aright, we bid you not to dissolve the treaty, or to break your oaths, but to have our differences settled by arbitration according to our agreement. Or else we take the gods who heard the oaths to witness, and if you begin hostilities, whatever line of action you choose, we will try not to be behindhand in repelling you.'

79. Such were the words of the Athenians. After the Lacedæmonians had heard the complaints of the allies against the Athenians, and the observations of the latter, they made all withdraw,§ and consulted by themselves on the question before them. The opinions of the majority all led to the same conclusion; the Athenians were open aggressors, and war must be declared at once. But Archidamus, the Lacedæmonian king,‖ came forward, who had the reputation of being at once a wise and a moderate man, and made the following speech:—

---

*The Athenians argue, and history proved them right, that only by political inaction could the Spartans remain popular in the imagination of others. Their regimented lifestyle and secretive government were incompatible with that of every other Greek state, yet they often clumsily intervened in other states' affairs.

†When abroad, as we shall see with the Spartan regent Pausanias in 1.95 and 130, Spartans tended to bully other free nationals and to have few skills in negotiation. In Sparta, men had little need of persuasive diplomatic talents.

‡Chance often defeats the best-laid plans, especially in war. This commonplace appears later in the mouths of others, before and after various catastrophes.

§The Spartans were notorious for driving out foreigners (*xenelasia*) and for not allowing foreigners to observe their assembly's political discussions, other deliberations, and ceremonies.

‖Historians sometimes call the first ten years of the war (431–421) the Archidamian War since the Spartan king directed policy for its duration. Archidamus appreciated better than many of his countrymen the difficulties of defeating the Athenians.

80. 'I have not lived so long, Lacedæmonians, without having had the experience of many wars, and I see those among you of the same age as myself, who will not fall into the common misfortune of longing for war from inexperience or from a belief in its advantage and its safety. This, the war on which you are now debating, would be one of the greatest magnitude, on a sober consideration of the matter. In a struggle with Peloponnesians and neighbours our strength is of the same character, and it is possible to move swiftly on the different points. But a struggle with a people who live in a distant land, who have also an extraordinary familiarity with the sea, and who are in the highest state of preparation in every other department; with wealth private and public, with ships, and horses, and heavy infantry, and a population such as no one other Hellenic place can equal, and lastly a number of tributary allies—what can justify us in rashly beginning such a struggle?* wherein is our trust that we should rush on it unprepared? Is it in our ships? There we are inferior; while if we are to practise and become a match for them, time must intervene. Is it in our money? There we have a far greater deficiency. We neither have it in our treasury, nor are we ready to contribute it from our private funds.

81. 'Confidence might possibly be felt in our superiority in heavy infantry and population, which will enable us to invade and devastate their lands. But the Athenians have plenty of other land in their empire, and can import what they want by sea. Again, if we are to attempt an insurrection of their allies, these will have to be supported with a fleet, most of them being islanders. What then is to be our war? For unless we can either beat them at sea, or deprive them of the revenues which feed their navy, we shall meet with little but disaster. Meanwhile our honour will be pledged to keeping on, particularly if it be the opinion that we began the quarrel. For let us never be elated by the fatal hope of the war being quickly ended by the devastation of their lands. I fear rather that we may leave it as a legacy to our children; so improbable is it that the Athenian spirit will be the slave of their land, or Athenian experience be cowed by war.

82. 'Not that I would bid you be so unfeeling as to suffer them to injure your allies, and to refrain from unmasking their intrigues; but I do bid you not to take up arms at once, but to send and remonstrate with them in a tone not too suggestive of war, nor again too suggestive of submission, and to employ the interval in perfecting our own preparations. The means will be, first, the acquisition of al-

---

*Archidamus reviews the power and flexibility of the Spartans' Athenian enemies. The Spartans favored single, pitched, decisive battles on land. Archidamus worried they would not have the opportunity for a quick return to their farms.

lies, Hellenic or barbarian* it matters not, so long as they are an accession to our strength naval or pecuniary—I say Hellenic or barbarian, because the odium of such an accession to all who like us are the objects of the designs of the Athenians is taken away by the law of self-preservation—and secondly the development of our home resources. If they listen to our embassy, so much the better; but if not, after the lapse of two or three years our position will have become materially strengthened, and we can then attack them if we think proper. Perhaps by that time the sight of our preparations, backed by language equally significant, will have disposed them to submission, while their land is still untouched, and while their counsels may be directed to the retention of advantages as yet undestroyed. For the only light in which you can view their land is that of a hostage in your hands, a hostage the more valuable the better it is cultivated. This you ought to spare as long as possible, and not make them desperate, and so increase the difficulty of dealing with them. For if while still unprepared, hurried away by the complaints of our allies, we are induced to lay it waste, have a care that we do not bring deep disgrace and deep perplexity upon Peloponnese. Complaints, whether of communities or individuals, it is possible to adjust; but war undertaken by a coalition for sectional interests, whose progress there is no means of foreseeing, does not easily admit of creditable settlement.

83. 'And none need think it cowardice for a number of confederates to pause before they attack a single city. The Athenians have allies as numerous as our own, and allies that pay tribute, and war is a matter not so much of arms as of money, which makes arms of use.† And this is more than ever true in a struggle between a continental and a maritime power. First, then, let us provide money, and not allow ourselves to be carried away by the talk of our allies before we have done so: as we shall have the largest share of responsibility for the consequences be they good or bad, we have also a right to a tranquil inquiry respecting them.

84. 'And the slowness and procrastination, the parts of our character that are most assailed by their criticism, need not make you blush. If we undertake the war without preparation, we should by hastening its commencement only delay its conclusion: further, a

---

*Both sides hoped to gain the financial and manpower support of the "deep pockets" of the Persian Empire. In addition, allies might be obtained from Thrace and Macedonia, Egypt, Italy, and Greek communities around the Black Sea.

†Archidamus knows that the Athenians have a large war chest (2.13–14) and the Peloponnesians have none. "Borrowing" from the rich Panhellenic religious shrines at Olympia and Delphi was not a diplomatic way to win foreign friends, and the *polis* had difficulty paying back seized assets.

free and a famous city has through all time been ours. The quality which they condemn is really nothing but a wise moderation; thanks to its possession, we alone do not become insolent in success and give way less than others in misfortune; we are not carried away by the pleasure of hearing ourselves cheered on to risks which our judgment condemns; nor, if annoyed, are we any the more convinced by attempts to exasperate us by accusation. We are both warlike and wise, and it is our sense of order that makes us so. We are warlike, because self-control contains honour as a chief constituent, and honour bravery. And we are wise, because we are educated with too little learning to despise the laws,* and with too severe a self-control to disobey them, and are brought up not to be too knowing in useless matters,—such as the knowledge which can give a specious criticism of an enemy's plans in theory, but fails to assail them with equal success in practice,—but are taught to consider that the schemes of our enemies are not dissimilar to our own, and that the freaks of chance are not determinable by calculation.† In practice we always base our preparations against an enemy on the assumption that his plans are good; indeed, it is right to rest our hopes not on a belief in his blunders, but on the soundness of our provisions. Nor ought we to believe that there is much difference between man and man, but to think that the superiority lies with him who is reared in the severest school.

85. 'These practices, then, which our ancestors have delivered to us, and by whose maintenance we have always profited, must not be given up. And we must not be hurried into deciding in a day's brief space a question which concerns many lives and fortunes and many cities, and in which honour is deeply involved,—but we must decide calmly. This our strength peculiarly enables us to do. As for the Athenians, send to them on the matter of Potidæa, send on the matter of the alleged wrongs of the allies, particularly as they are prepared with legal satisfaction; and to proceed against one who offers arbitration as against a wrongdoer, law forbids. Meanwhile do not omit preparation for war. This decision will be the best for yourselves, the most terrible to your opponents.'

Such were the words of Archidamus. Last came forward

---

*Spartans boast of their limited book learning and other forms of high cultural immersion. It had not always been so; in archaic times, Sparta produced lovely and significant art for more than a century.

†The king warns his countrymen of the many ways that their admittedly superior infantry might not be able to win the war for them. Stahl's book discusses the limits of calculation in Thucydides.

Sthenelaidas, one of the Ephors* for that year, and spoke to the
Lacedæmonians as follows:—

86. 'The long speech of the Athenians I do not pretend to understand. They said a good deal in praise of themselves, but nowhere denied that they are injuring our allies and Peloponnese. And yet if they
behaved well against the Mede then, but ill towards us now, they deserve double punishment for having ceased to be good and for having become bad. We meanwhile are the same then and now, and shall
not, if we are wise, disregard the wrongs of our allies, or put off till to-
morrow the duty of assisting those who must suffer to-day. Others
have much money and ships and horses, but we have good allies
whom we must not give up to the Athenians, nor by lawsuits and
words decide the matter, as it is anything but in word that we are
harmed, but render instant and powerful help. And let us not be told
that it is fitting for us to deliberate under injustice; long deliberation
is rather fitting for those who have injustice in contemplation. Vote
therefore, Lacedæmonians, for war, as the honour of Sparta demands,
and neither allow the further aggrandisement of Athens, nor betray our
allies to ruin, but with the gods let us advance against the aggressors.'

87. With these words he, as Ephor, himself put the question to the
assembly of the Lacedæmonians. He said that he could not determine
which was the loudest acclamation (their mode of decision is by acclamation not by voting);† the fact being that he wished to make them
declare their opinion openly and thus to increase their ardour for
war. Accordingly he said, 'All Lacedæmonians who are of opinion
that the treaty has been broken, and that Athens is guilty, leave your
seats and go there,' pointing out a certain place; 'all who are of the opposite opinion, there.' They accordingly stood up and divided; and
those who held that the treaty had been broken were in a decided
majority. Summoning the allies, they told them that their opinion was
that Athens had been guilty of injustice, but that they wished to con-
voke all the allies and put it to the vote; in order that they might make
war, if they decided to do so, on a common resolution. Having thus
gained their point, the delegates returned home at once; the Athenian
envoys a little later, when they had despatched the objects of their
mission. This decision of the assembly judging that the treaty had

---

*The Spartan polity recognized two hereditary kings, a *gerousia* (or senate of elders),
an *apella* (or assembly of warriors), and, later than Lycurgus (the legendary seventh-
century lawgiver), five ephors—"overseers" elected a year at a time, who limited the
kings' power (after most Greek states had abolished their monarchies) and accompanied them in the field. This crabby speech shows unusual (for Thucydides) individual
character.

†Thucydides notes the primitive (very Homeric) character of Spartan voting procedures.

been broken, was made in the fourteenth year of the thirty years' truce, which was entered into after the affair of Eubœa.*

88. The Lacedæmonians voted that the treaty had been broken, and that war must be declared, not so much because they were persuaded by the arguments of the allies, as because they feared the growth of the power of the Athenians, seeing most of Hellas already subject to them.[†]

From the End of the Persian to the Beginning of the Peloponnesian War—Athenian Progress from Supremacy to Empire

89. The way in which Athens came to be placed in the circumstances under which her power grew was this. After the Medes had returned from Europe, defeated by sea and land by the Hellenes, and after those of them who had fled with their ships to Mycale had been destroyed, Leotychides, King of the Lacedæmonians, the commander of the Hellenes at Mycale, departed home with the allies from Peloponnese. But the Athenians and the allies from Ionia and Hellespont, who had now revolted from the king,[‡] remained and laid siege to Sestos, which was still held by the Medes. After wintering before it, they became masters of the place on its evacuation by the barbarians; and after this they sailed away from Hellespont to their respective cities. Meanwhile the Athenian people, after the departure of the barbarian from their country, at once proceeded to carry over their children and wives, and such property as they had left, from the places where they had deposited them, and prepared to rebuild their city and their walls.[§] For only isolated portions of the circumference had been left standing, and most of the houses were in ruins; though a few remained, in which the Persian grandees had taken up their quarters.

---

*Around November 432, the Spartans decide to go to war. Fourteen years earlier, the Peloponnesians and the Athenian forces contested the land of Euboea (the name means "good cow-land"), as Thucydides will mention in the account of the "50 Years."

†Thucydides distinguishes the publicly alleged causes among the allies and neutrals from another, less open, source of Spartan anxiety (compare 1.23, 118). He avers that not so much justice as a tipping balance of international power moved the Spartiates to vote to declare war against the Athenians.

‡The naked word "king" refers to the imperial Persian autocrat, if not otherwise modified. Thucydides begins his account covering 478–432 of Hellenic, post–Persian Wars politics, imperialism, and interstate diplomacy.

§The old Athenian walls were ruined; without walls, no city on the mainland was safe from the threat or reality of Spartan interference. This had been the dilemma of Athens in the recent past.

MAP 1. AEGEAN BASIN

90. Perceiving what they were going to do, the Lacedæmonians sent an embassy to Athens. They would have themselves preferred to see neither her nor any other city in possession of a wall; though here they acted principally at the instigation of their allies, who were alarmed at the strength of her newly acquired navy, and the valour which she had displayed in the war with the Medes. They begged her not only to abstain from building walls for herself, but also to join them in throwing down the walls that still held together of the ultra-Peloponnesian cities. The real meaning of their advice, the suspicion that it contained against the Athenians, was not proclaimed;* it was urged that so the barbarian, in the event of a third invasion, would not have any strong place, such as he now had in Thebes, for his base of operations; and that Peloponnese would suffice for all as a base both for retreat and offence. After the Lacedæmonians had thus spoken, they were, on the advice of Themistocles, immediately dismissed by the Athenians, with the answer that ambassadors should be sent to Sparta to discuss the question. Themistocles told the Athenians to send him off with all speed to Lacedæmon, but not to despatch his colleagues as soon as they had selected them, but to wait until they had raised their wall to the height from which defence was possible.†
Meanwhile the whole population in the city was to labour at the wall, the Athenians, their wives and their children, sparing no edifice, private or public, which might be of any use to the work, but throwing all down. After giving these instructions, and adding that he would be responsible for all other matters there, he departed. Arrived at Lacedæmon he did not seek an audience with the authorities, but tried to gain time and made excuses. When any of the government asked him why he did not appear in the assembly, he would say that he was waiting for his colleagues, who had been detained in Athens by some engagement; however, that he expected their speedy arrival, and wondered that they were not yet there.

91. At first the Lacedæmonians trusted the words of Themistocles, through their friendship for him; but when others arrived, all distinctly declaring that the work was going on and already attaining some elevation, they did not know how to disbelieve it. Aware of this, he told them that rumours are deceptive, and should not be trusted; they should send some reputable persons from Sparta to inspect, whose report might be trusted. They despatched them accordingly. Concerning

---

*The policy of Sparta was for that *polis* to have the dominant army in Greece, a professional one, and for all cities (including Sparta) to be without walls. The absence of serious siege machines meant that a walled city was very hard to take. The Athenians saw no reason to subject their interests to Sparta's.

†Themistocles used guile, since force did not exist on his side. The delaying tactic of their recent ally deceived the Spartans.

these Themistocles secretly sent word to the Athenians to detain them as far as possible without putting them under open constraint, and not to let them go until they had themselves returned. For his colleagues had now joined him, Abronichus, son of Lysicles, and Aristides, son of Lysimachus,* with the news that the wall was sufficiently advanced; and he feared that when the Lacedæmonians heard the facts, they might refuse to let them go. So the Athenians detained the envoys according to his message, and Themistocles had an audience with the Lacedæmonians, and at last openly told them that Athens was now fortified sufficiently to protect its inhabitants; that any embassy which the Lacedæmonians or their allies might wish to send to them, should in future proceed on the assumption that the people to whom they were going was able to distinguish both its own and the general interests. That when the Athenians thought fit to abandon their city and to embark in their ships, they ventured on that perilous step without consulting them; and that on the other hand, wherever they had deliberated with the Lacedæmonians, they had proved themselves to be in judgment second to none. That they now thought it fit that their city should have a wall, and that this would be more for the advantage of both the citizens of Athens and the Hellenic confederacy; for without equal military strength it was impossible to contribute equal or fair counsel to the common interest. It followed, he observed, either that all the members of the confederacy should be without walls, or that the present step should be considered a right one.

92. The Lacedæmonians did not betray any open signs of anger against the Athenians at what they heard. The embassy, it seems, was prompted not by a desire to obstruct, but to guide the counsels of their government: besides Spartan feeling was at that time very friendly towards Athens on account of the patriotism which she had displayed in the struggle with the Mede. Still the defeat of their wishes could not but cause them secret annoyance. The envoys of each state departed home without complaint.

93. In this way the Athenians walled their city in a little while. To this day the building shows signs of the haste of its execution; the foundations are laid of stones of all kinds, and in some places not wrought or fitted,† but placed just in the order in which they were

---

*Plutarch wrote an extant biography of this aristocratic man known as "the just." Aristides had competed in various political venues with Themistocles. He set the original tribute levels for the allies at the formation of the Delian (or Hellenic) League in 478/477. The confederates of Athens later considered these amounts to be comparatively reasonable.

†The so-called Themistoclean wall sacrificed regularity, beauty, and respect for property to the need for speed. One can still visit parts of this 4-mile wall in the Ceramicus (map 3), the potters' quarter and cemetery district of ancient Athens.

brought by the different hands; and many columns, too, from tombs and sculptured stones were put in with the rest. For the bounds of the city were extended at every point of the circumference;* and so they laid hands on everything without exception in their haste. Themistocles also persuaded them to finish the walls of Piræus, which had been begun before, in his year of office as archon;† being influenced alike by the fineness of a locality that has three natural harbours, and by the great start which the Athenians would gain in the acquisition of power by becoming a naval people. For he first ventured to tell them to stick to the sea and forthwith began to lay the foundations of the empire. It was by his advice, too, that they built the walls of that thickness which can still be discerned round Piræus, the stones being brought up by two waggons meeting each other. Between the walls thus formed there was neither rubble nor mortar, but great stones hewn square and fitted together, cramped to each other on the outside with iron and lead. About half the height that he intended was finished. His idea was by their size and thickness to keep off the attacks of an enemy; he thought that they might be adequately defended by a small garrison of invalids, and the rest be freed for service in the fleet. For the fleet claimed most of his attention. He saw, as I think, that the approach by sea was easier for the king's army than that by land: he also thought Piræus more valuable than the upper city; indeed, he was always advising the Athenians, if a day should come when they were hard pressed by land, to go down into Piræus, and defy the world with their fleet.‡ Thus, therefore, the Athenians completed their wall, and commenced their other buildings immediately after the retreat of the Mede.

94. Meanwhile Pausanias, son of Cleombrotus, was sent out from Lacedæmon as commander-in-chief of the Hellenes, with twenty ships from Peloponnese. With him sailed the Athenians with thirty ships, and a number of the other allies. They made an expedition against Cyprus and subdued most of the island, and afterwards against Byzantium, which was in the hands of the Medes, and com-

---

*Athens' enclosed defensible space was enlarged so that it included developed urban areas and some former "suburbs."

†Probably he held this office in 482, but certainly some time before the great expedition of Xerxes. The Athenians annually appointed nine archons, the most important office before and under the tyrants but one that diminished in significance in the fifth century. The archons, once the chief magistrates, then became ceremonial officials and conveners of the courts, and the *strategoi* (generals) became the most influential democratic office-holders (compare Connor, *New Politicians of Fifth-century Athens*).

‡Themistocles enunciated the policy that Pericles endorses during the war: The Athenians' sea-based power and strike-forces would trump the limited reach of the Lacedaemonians' land-based power.

pelled it to surrender.* This event took place while the Spartans were still supreme.

95. But the violence of Pausanias had already begun to be disagreeable to the Hellenes, particularly to the Ionians and the newly liberated populations. These resorted to the Athenians and requested them as their kinsmen to become their leaders, and to stop any attempt at violence on the part of Pausanias. The Athenians accepted their overtures, and determined to put down any attempt of the kind and to settle everything else as their interests might seem to demand. In the meantime the Lacedæmonians recalled Pausanias for an investigation of the reports which had reached them. Manifold and grave accusations had been brought against him by Hellenes arriving in Sparta; and, to all appearance, there had been in him more of the mimicry of a despot than of the attitude of a general. As it happened, his recall came just at the time when the hatred which he had inspired had induced the allies to desert him, the soldiers from Peloponnese excepted, and to range themselves by the side of the Athenians.† On his arrival at Lacedæmon, he was censured for his private acts of oppression, but was acquitted on the heaviest counts and pronounced not guilty; it must be known that the charge of Medism formed one of the principal, and to all appearance one of the best founded articles against him. The Lacedæmonians did not, however, restore him to his command, but sent out Dorkis and certain others with a small force; who found the allies no longer inclined to concede to them the supremacy. Perceiving this they departed, and the Lacedæmonians did not send out any to succeed them. They feared for those who went out a deterioration similar to that observable in Pausanias;‡ besides, they desired to be rid of the Median war, and were satisfied of the competency of the Athenians for the position, and of their friendship at the time towards themselves.

96. The Athenians having thus succeeded to the supremacy by the voluntary act of the allies through their hatred of Pausanias, fixed which cities were to contribute money against the barbarian, which ships;§

---

*Thucydides describes the advance of Athenian power under the legitimate and noble banner of freeing Greeks from Persian rule. Byzantium guarded the entry into the Black Sea (map 1), an important source of many raw materials and the site of many early Greek colonies.

†The Spartan regent Pausanias' alienation of all the allies who still faced Persian pressure led them to seek out Athenian leadership or hegemony.

‡The Spartan lifestyle was poorly suited to sudden access to non-egalitarian wealth and power. Pausanias is one of many Spartan commanders who could not resist the allure of power and luxury.

§The Delian (or Hellenic) League may have been bi- or unicameral. The Athenians held the hegemony or upper hand by law, politics, or military contributions and might.

their professed object being to retaliate for their sufferings by ravaging the king's country. Now was the time that the office of 'Treasurers for Hellas' was first instituted by the Athenians.* These officers received the tribute, as the money contributed was called. The tribute was first fixed at four hundred and sixty talents.† The common treasury was at Delos, and the congresses were held in the temple.‡

97. Their supremacy commenced with independent allies who acted on the resolutions of a common congress. It was marked by the following undertakings in war and in administration during the interval between the Median and the present war, against the barbarian, against their own rebel allies, and against the Peloponnesian powers which would come in contact with them on various occasions. My excuse for relating these events, and for venturing on this digression, is that this passage of history has been omitted by all my predecessors, who have confined themselves either to Hellenic history before the Median war, or to the Median war itself.§ Hellanicus, it is true, did touch on these events in his Athenian history; but he is somewhat concise and not accurate in his dates.‖ Besides, the history of these events contains an explanation of the growth of the Athenian empire.

98. First the Athenians besieged and captured Eion on the Strymon from the Medes, and made slaves of the inhabitants, being under the command of Cimon,# son of Miltiades. Next they enslaved Scyros, the island in the Ægean, containing a Dolopian population, and colonised it themselves. This was followed by a war against Carystus,

---

*The *Hellenotamiai* were money-collectors for the newly established league, one founded to protect the autonomy of Greeks against Persian power and taxation. They were elected by and therefore answerable to the Athenians.

†Four hundred and sixty talents seemed a reasonable sum (2,760,000 drachmas) when divided equitably among the many contributing cities and islands. After the Athenians repeatedly raised tribute levels, this levy seemed to symbolize a former golden age.

‡Delos (map 1), birthplace and sanctuary of Panhellenic Apollo, provided a geographically central site as well as sacred ground for all Ionians. Placing the treasury there originally reassured the allies that Athens was not creating an empire for itself. In 454 the Athenians moved the treasury to Athens for "safekeeping." The symbolism of Athenian domination was clear, and Pericles did not pretend otherwise.

§Thucydides justifies a section on events prior to his war but after Herodotus'.

‖The prolific literary productions of Hellanicus, a chronicler from Lesbos (c.490–406) are no longer extant, but he was one of the first to write local histories, including those of his homeland Lesbos and of Athens. Such works included local myths and geography as well as pivotal military and political events—the ones that now one calls "history." Thucydides mentions no other prose writer by name in his *History* (see Parke, "Citation and Recitation").

#Cimon, scion of the Philaïd clan, descendant of Miltiades, victor at Marathon, was an aristocrat who thought Athens and Sparta should work together. His policy envisioned a dyarchy. The idea fell for lack of support in both cities. (See Plutarch's life of this influential Athenian.)

in which the rest of Eubœa remained neutral, and which was ended by surrender on conditions. After this Naxos left the confederacy,* and a war ensued, and she had to return after a siege; this was the first instance of the engagement being broken by the subjugation of an allied city, a precedent which was followed by that of the rest in the order which circumstances prescribed.

99. Of all the causes of defection, that connected with arrears of tribute and vessels, and with failure of service, was the chief; for the Athenians were very severe and exacting, and made themselves offensive by applying the screw of necessity to men who were not used to and in fact not disposed for any continuous labour.† In some other respects the Athenians were not the old popular rulers they had been at first; and if they had more than their fair share of service, it was correspondingly easy for them to reduce any that tried to leave the confederacy. For this the allies had themselves to blame;‡ the wish to get off service making most of them arrange to pay their share of the expense in money instead of in ships, and so to avoid having to leave their homes.§ Thus while Athens was increasing her navy with the funds which they contributed, a revolt always found them without resources or experience for war.

100. Next we come to the actions by land and by sea at the river Eurymedon, between the Athenians with their allies, and the Medes, when the Athenians won both battles on the same day under the conduct of Cimon, son of Miltiades, and captured and destroyed the whole Phœnician fleet, consisting of two hundred vessels. Some time afterwards occurred the defection of the Thasians,‖ caused by disagreements about the marts on the opposite coast of Thrace, and about the mine in their

---

*Naxos' reduction after its defection from the Delian League (c.468) showed that the league or its Athenian leaders did not now envision the league as a coalition of the willing. The voluntary entry and adhesion was now no longer a matter of choice. Naxos is a rich, powerful island in the Cyclades (map 1; Fornara #56 describes the services of its citizens in the Persian Wars).

†Thucydides appears to endorse the Hellenic belief that the Ionians were less suited to hard work and political activity than the Dorians or the Athenians.

‡Thucydides squarely blames the Ionian allies (and others in the league) for their plight. Given a choice between contributions in men or money, they chose to buy their way out of military training and service (and possession of ships). That choice produced a situation in which they could no longer defend their freedom.

§The Allies preferred paying tax to active service, and so paid their way into subjection and lost the ability and equipment to maintain their cities' autonomy.

‖This rich island in the northern Aegean (map 7) had mines of its own and on the Thracian mainland opposite. Their defection from the league in 465/464 was met with attack and siege, revealing once again that membership was no longer voluntary. (Fornara #62 describes Athenian settlements on the mainland opposite, and #100 contains regulations of the colonists at nearby Brea in Thrace.)

possession. Sailing with a fleet to Thasos, the Athenians defeated them at sea and effected a landing on the island. About the same time they sent ten thousand settlers of their own citizens and the allies to settle the place then called Ennea Hodoi or Nine Ways, now Amphipolis. They succeeded in gaining possession of Ennea Hodoi from the Edonians, but on advancing into the interior of Thrace were cut off in Drabescus, a town of the Edonians, by the assembled Thracians, who regarded the settlement of the place Ennea Hodoi as an act of hostility.

101. Meanwhile the Thasians being defeated in the field and suffering siege, appealed to Lacedæmon, and desired her to assist them by an invasion of Attica. Without informing Athens, she promised and intended to do so, but was prevented by the occurrence of the earthquake,* accompanied by the secession of the Helots and the Thuriats and Æthæans of the Periœci† to Ithome. Most of the Helots‡ were the descendants of the old Messenians that were enslaved in the famous war; and so all of them came to be called Messenians. So the Lacedæmonians being engaged in a war with the rebels in Ithome, the Thasians in the third year of the siege obtained terms from the Athenians by razing their walls, delivering up their ships, and arranging to pay the monies demanded at once, and tribute in future; giving up their possessions on the continent together with the mine.§

102. The Lacedæmonians meanwhile finding the war against the rebels in Ithome likely to last, invoked the aid of their allies, and especially of the Athenians, who came in some force under the command of Cimon. The reason for this pressing summons lay in their reputed skill in siege operations; a long siege had taught the Lacedæmonians their own deficiency in this art, else they would have taken the place by assault. The first open quarrel‖ between the Lacedæmo-

---

*This seismic disturbance in 464 produced a political one: The helots and some allies congregated on Mount Ithome in the western Peloponnese (map 4). Consequently, the Spartans feared the overthrow of their repressive constitution.

†This unenfranchised population, probably suppressed Messenians of the Dark Ages, identified themselves with the ruling Spartiates rather than with the bottom-rung helots, as some American "poor whites" did in post-bellum America. They fought alongside them but had no say in the making of policy, foreign or domestic.

‡This population, perhaps resident in the Peloponnese before the Spartans came in at the end of the Bronze Age, had no rights. They provided the agricultural labor that enabled the Spartiates to remain on military alert and in training most of their adult lives. (Fornara #13 and #67 offer other sources concerning this revolt.)

§Thucydides had financial interests in these mines, and political influence, according to 4.105 and such ancient biographies as that written by Marcellinus.

‖Cimon the aristocrat (father of Lacedaemonius and the subject of one of Plutarch's many Greek biographies) wished to cooperate with the Spartans; he had called the two leading cities "the yokefellows of Hellas." This repulse of the assisting Athenian troops led to a decline in his influence and popularity at home.

nians and Athenians arose out of this expedition. The Lacedæmonians, when assault failed to take the place, apprehensive of the enterprising and revolutionary character of the Athenians, and further looking upon them as of alien extraction, began to fear that if they remained, they might be tempted by the besieged in Ithome to attempt some political changes. They accordingly dismissed them alone of the allies, without declaring their suspicions, but merely saying that they had now no need of them. But the Athenians, aware that their dismissal did not proceed from the more honourable reason of the two, but from suspicions which had been conceived, went away deeply offended, and conscious of having done nothing to merit such treatment from the Lacedæmonians; and the instant that they returned home they broke off the alliance which had been made against the Mede, and allied themselves with Sparta's enemy Argos;* each of the contracting parties taking the same oaths and making the same alliance with the Thessalians.

103. Meanwhile the rebels in Ithome, unable to prolong further a ten years' resistance, surrendered to Lacedæmon; the conditions being that they should depart from Peloponnese under safe conduct, and should never set foot in it again: any one who might hereafter be found there was to be the slave of his captor. It must be known that the Lacedæmonians had an old oracle from Delphi, to the effect that they should let go the suppliant of Zeus at Ithome. So they went forth with their children and their wives, and being received by Athens from the hatred that she now felt for the Lacedæmonians, were located at Naupactus,† which she had lately taken from the Ozolian Locrians. The Athenians received another addition to their confederacy in the Megarians; who left the Lacedæmonian alliance, annoyed by a war about boundaries forced on them by Corinth. The Athenians occupied Megara and Pegæ, and built the Megarians their long walls from the city to Nisæa, in which they placed an Athenian garrison. This was the principal cause of the Corinthians conceiving such a deadly hatred against Athens.

104. Meanwhile Inaros, son of Psammetichus, a Libyan king of the Libyans on the Egyptian border, having his head-quarters at Marea, the town above Pharos, caused a revolt of almost the whole of Egypt from King Artaxerxes,‡ and placing himself at its head, invited the Athenians to his assistance. Abandoning a Cyprian expedition upon which they

---

*This neighbor of Sparta often disputed their common borderlands. Although not as powerful as the leading powers, Argos represented a present danger, a back-door entry into Laconia, inhibiting all Spartan overseas inclinations.

†This community northeast on the Corinthian Gulf (map 5) commanded a strategic position for policing peacetime shipping and warships.

‡The son and successor of Xerxes (assassinated in 464) ruled until 424.

happened to be engaged with two hundred ships of their own and their allies, they arrived in Egypt and sailed from the sea into the Nile, and making themselves masters of the river and two-thirds of Memphis, addressed themselves to the attack of the remaining third, which is called White Castle. Within it were Persians and Medes who had taken refuge there, and Egyptians who had not joined the rebellion.

105. Meanwhile the Athenians, making a descent from their fleet upon Haliæ, were engaged by a force of Corinthians and Epidaurians; and the Corinthians were victorious. Afterwards the Athenians engaged the Peloponnesian fleet off Cecruphalia; and the Athenians were victorious. Subsequently war broke out between Ægina and Athens, and there was a great battle at sea off Ægina between the Athenians and Æginetans, each being aided by their allies; in which victory remained with the Athenians, who took seventy of the enemy's ships, and landed in the country and commenced a siege under the command of Leocrates, son of Strœbus. Upon this the Peloponnesians, desirous of aiding the Æginetans, threw into Ægina a force of three hundred heavy infantry, who had before been serving with the Corinthians and Epidaurians. Meanwhile the Corinthians and their allies occupied the heights of Geraneia, and marched down into the Megarid, in the belief that with a large force absent in Ægina and Egypt, Athens would be unable to help the Megarians without raising the siege of Ægina. But the Athenians, instead of moving the army of Ægina, raised a force of the old and young men that had been left in the city, and marched into the Megarid under the command of Myronides. After a drawn battle with the Corinthians, the rival hosts parted, each with the impression that they had gained the victory. The Athenians, however, if anything, had rather the advantage, and on the departure of the Corinthians set up a trophy. Urged by the taunts of the elders in their city,* the Corinthians made their preparations, and about twelve days afterwards came and set up their trophy as victors. Sallying out from Megara, the Athenians cut off the party that was employed in erecting the trophy, and engaged and defeated the rest.

106. In the retreat of the vanquished army, a considerable division, pressed by the pursuers and mistaking the road, dashed into a field on some private property, with a deep trench all round it, and no way out. Being acquainted with the place, the Athenians hemmed their front with heavy infantry, and placing the light troops round in a circle, stoned all who had gone in. Corinth here suffered a severe blow. The bulk of her army continued its retreat home.

107. About this time the Athenians began to build the long walls

---

*The inexperienced are often more eager for battle than their parents' generation, but not in this example.

to the sea,* that towards Phalerum and that towards Piræus. Meanwhile the Phocians made an expedition against Doris, the old home of the Lacedæmonians, containing the towns of Bœum, Kitinium, and Erineum. They had taken one of these towns, when the Lacedæmonians under Nicomedes, son of Cleombrotus, commanding for King Pleistoanax, son of Pausanias, who was still a minor, came to the aid of the Dorians with fifteen hundred heavy infantry of their own, and ten thousand of their allies. After compelling the Phocians to restore the town on conditions, they began their retreat. The route by sea, across the Crissæan gulf, exposed them to the risk of being stopped by the Athenian fleet; that across Geraneia seemed scarcely safe, the Athenians holding Megara and Pegæ. For the pass was a difficult one, and was always guarded by the Athenians; and, in the present instance, the Lacedæmonians had information that they meant to dispute their passage. So they resolved to remain in Bœotia, and to consider which would be the safest line of march. They had also another reason for this resolve. Secret encouragement had been given them by a party in Athens, who hoped to put an end to the reign of democracy and the building of the long walls.† Meanwhile the Athenians marched against them with their whole levy and a thousand Argives and the respective contingents of the rest of their allies. Altogether they were fourteen thousand strong. The march was prompted by the notion that the Lacedæmonians were at a loss how to effect their passage, and also by suspicions of an attempt to overthrow the democracy. Some cavalry also joined the Athenians from their Thessalian allies; but these went over to the Lacedæmonians during the battle.

108. The battle was fought at Tanagra in Bœotia. After heavy loss on both sides victory declared for the Lacedæmonians and their allies. After entering the Megarid and cutting down the fruit trees,‡ the Lacedæmonians returned home across Geraneia and the isthmus. Sixty-two days after the battle the Athenians marched into Bœotia

---

*This initiative connecting the inland city to the port not only gave the Athenians protection against Peloponnesian superior infantry forces but allowed them to prevent a siege that would exhaust food and other vital supplies.

†Both enemies and parties in Athens ill disposed to the democracy (an evolving form of government, but no older than 511) thought such long walls would encourage Athenian self-confidence and entrench the government that provided poorer Athenians with employment opportunities. (Fornara #79 provides construction details.)

‡Grapevines take about seven years, olive trees about twenty-five, before becoming fully productive. The threat to cut down the agricultural capital "machinery" would often bring a weak state to its knees. The actual deed led to long-standing enmities. The Greeks have long memories. (Fornara #80 translates a Spartan thank-offering for their victory at Tanagra.)

under the command of Myronides, defeated the Bœotians in battle at Œnophyta, and became masters of Bœotia and Phocis. They dismantled the walls of the Tanagræans, took a hundred of the richest men of the Opuntian Locrians as hostages, and finished their own long walls. This was followed by the surrender of the Æginetans to Athens on conditions; they pulled down their walls, gave up their ships, and agreed to pay tribute in the future.* The Athenians sailed round Peloponnese under Tolmides, son of Tolmæus, burnt the arsenal of Lacedæmon, took Chalcis, a town of the Corinthians, and in a descent upon Sicyon defeated the Sicyonians in battle.

109. Meanwhile the Athenians in Egypt and their allies were still there, and encountered all the vicissitudes of war. First the Athenians were masters of Egypt, and the king sent Megabazus, a Persian, to Lacedæmon with money to bribe the Peloponnesians to invade Attica and so draw off the Athenians from Egypt. Finding that the matter made no progress, and that the money was only being wasted, he recalled Megabazus with the remainder of the money, and sent Megabazus, son of Zopyrus, a Persian, with a large army to Egypt. Arriving by land he defeated the Egyptians and their allies in a battle, and drove the Hellenes out of Memphis, and at length shut them up in the island of Prosopitis, where he besieged them for a year and six months. At last, draining the canal of its waters, which he diverted into another channel, he left their ships high and dry and joined most of the island to the mainland, and then marched over on foot and captured it.

110. Thus the enterprise of the Hellenes came to ruin after six years of war. Of all that large host a few travelling through Libya reached Cyrene in safety, but most of them perished. And thus Egypt returned to its subjection to the king,† except Amyrtæus, the king in the marshes, whom they were unable to capture from the extent of the marsh; the marshmen being also the most warlike of the Egyptians. Inaros, the Libyan king, the sole author of the Egyptian revolt, was betrayed, taken, and crucified. Meanwhile a relieving squadron of fifty vessels had sailed from Athens and the rest of the confederacy for Egypt. They put in to shore at the Mendesian mouth of the Nile, in total ignorance of what had occurred. Attacked on the land side by the troops, and from the sea by the Phœnician navy, most of the ships were destroyed; the few remaining being saved by retreat.

---

*These terms involving walls, ships, and tributes were standard demands of the expanding Athenians when they were successful. (Fornara #84 describes Tolmides.)

†Egypt had been a province of the Persian Empire since Cambyses' conquest, around 522. The Greek post–Persian War "mission" to weaken the Persian Empire had the additional virtue of strengthening the Hellenic alliance, soon in reality an Athenian empire. The Greeks interfered repeatedly with this Persian dependency (Fornara #72 and #77).

Such was the end of the great expedition of the Athenians and their allies to Egypt.

111. Meanwhile Orestes, son of Echecratidas, the Thessalian king, being an exile from Thessaly,* persuaded the Athenians to restore him. Taking with them the Bœotians and Phocians their allies, the Athenians marched to Pharsalus in Thessaly. They became masters of the country, though only in the immediate vicinity of the camp; beyond which they could not go for fear of the Thessalian cavalry. But they failed to take the city or to attain any of the other objects of their expedition, and returned home with Orestes without having effected anything. Not long after this a thousand of the Athenians embarked in the vessels that were at Pegæ (Pagæ, it must be remembered, was now theirs), and sailed along the coast to Sicyon under the command of Pericles, son of Xanthippus. Landing in Sicyon and defeating the Sicyonians who engaged them, they immediately took with them the Achæans, and sailing across, marched against and laid siege to Œniadæ in Acarnania.† Failing however to take it, they returned home.

112. Three years afterwards a truce was made between the Peloponnesians and Athenians for five years. Released from Hellenic war, the Athenians made an expedition to Cyprus with two hundred vessels of their own and their allies, under the command of Cimon.‡ Sixty of these were detached to Egypt at the instance of Amyrtæus, the king in the marshes; the rest laid siege to Kitium, from which, however, they were compelled to retire by the death of Cimon and by scarcity of provisions. Sailing off Salamis in Cyprus, they fought with the Phœnicians, Cyprians, and Cilicians by land and sea, and being victorious on both elements departed home, and with them the returned squadron from Egypt. After this the Lacedæmonians marched out on a sacred war, and becoming masters of the temple at Delphi, placed it in the hands of the Delphians. Immediately after their retreat, the Athenians marched out, became masters of the temple, and placed it in the hands of the Phocians.

113. Some time after this, Orchomenus, Chæronea, and some other places in Bœotia, being in the hands of the Bœotian exiles, the Athenians marched against the above-mentioned hostile places with a

---

*Thessaly, a politically primitive area of northeastern Greece, allowed greater powers to establish footholds in disputed territories (map 1).

†Acarnania in northwestern Greece was also often a battleground for competing powers with interests beyond their borders (map 1).

‡Cimon's expedition to Cyprus was an attempt to redirect Athenian imperialism away from competition with Dorian Greeks in Sparta and Corinth and toward barbarians, especially the Persians. Cyprus, an island entrepôt between the Near East and Greece, was another conquest of Cambyses' Persians, this one around 525. Cimon's death in 451 put an end to his policy of reconciling the major Hellenic powers.

thousand Athenian heavy infantry and the allied contingents, under the command of Tolmides, son of Tolmæus. They took Chæronea, and made slaves of the inhabitants, and leaving a garrison, commenced their return. On their road they were attacked at Coronæa, by the Bœotian exiles from Orchomenus, with some Locrians and Eubœan exiles, and others who were of the same way of thinking, were defeated in battle, and some killed, others taken captive. The Athenians evacuated all Bœotia by a treaty providing for the recovery of the men; and the exiled Bœotians returned, and with all the rest regained their independence.

114. This was soon afterwards followed by the revolt of Eubœa from Athens.* Pericles had already crossed over with an army of Athenians to the island, when news was brought to him that Megara had revolted, that the Peloponnesians were on the point of invading Attica, and that the Athenian garrison had been cut off by the Megarians, with the exception of a few who had taken refuge in Nisæa. The Megarians had introduced the Corinthians, Sicyonians, and Epidaurians into the town before they revolted. Meanwhile Pericles brought his army back in all haste from Eubœa. After this the Peloponnesians marched into Attica as far as Eleusis and Thrius, ravaging the country under the conduct of King Pleistoanax, the son of Pausanias, and without advancing further returned home. The Athenians then crossed over again to Eubœa under the command of Pericles, and subdued the whole of the island: all but Histiæa was settled by convention; the Histiæans they expelled from their homes, and occupied their territory themselves.

115. Not long after their return from Eubœa, they made a truce with the Lacedæmonians and their allies for thirty years,† giving up the posts which they occupied in Peloponnese, Nisæa, Pegæ, Trœzen, and Achaia. In the sixth year of the truce, war broke out between the Samians and Milesians about Priene. Worsted in the war, the Milesians came to Athens with loud complaints against the Samians. In this they were joined by certain private persons from Samos itself, who wished to revolutionise the government. Accordingly the Athenians sailed to Samos with forty ships and set up a democracy;‡ took

---

*Euboea is a large, rich island off the east coast of Attica and Boeotia (map 5). The Athenians established there both tributary allies and cleruchies (colonies of Athenian citizens) for the benefit of the Athenian people. The revolt continued from 445 to 440.

†The truce established by the Thirty Years Treaty began in 446. It lasted for fewer than fifteen years. (Fornara #102 and #103 offer post-war regulations governing defeated Eretria and Chalcis.)

‡The Samian people were among Athens' most loyal allies, but even there (map 1) some of the upper classes resented the loss of autonomy; they revolted in 440/439. (Fornara #110, #113, and #115 provide epigraphical evidence for this serious rebellion. Fornara's inscriptions #66 and #92 document similar Milesian political upheavals.)

hostages from the Samians, fifty boys and as many men, lodged them in Lemnos, and after leaving a garrison in the island returned home. But some of the Samians had not remained in the island, but had fled to the continent. Making an agreement with the most powerful of those in the city, and an alliance with Pissuthnes, son of Hystaspes, the then satrap of Sardis,* they got together a force of seven hundred mercenaries, and under cover of night crossed over to Samos. Their first step was to rise on the commons, most of whom they secured, their next to steal their hostages from Lemnos; after which they revolted, gave up the Athenian garrison left with them and its commanders to Pissuthnes, and instantly prepared for an expedition against Miletus. The Byzantines also revolted with them.

116. As soon as the Athenians heard the news, they sailed with sixty ships against Samos. Sixteen of these went to Caria to look out for the Phœnician fleet, and to Chios and Lesbos carrying round orders for reinforcements, and so never engaged; but forty-four ships under the command of Pericles with nine colleagues gave battle, off the island of Tragia, to seventy Samian vessels, of which twenty were transports, as they were sailing from Miletus. Victory remained with the Athenians. Reinforced afterwards by forty ships from Athens, and twenty-five Chian and Lesbian vessels, the Athenians landed, and having the superiority by land invested the city with three walls; it was also invested from the sea. Meanwhile Pericles took sixty ships from the blockading squadron, and departed in haste for Caunus and Caria, intelligence having been brought in of the approach of the Phœnician fleet to the aid of the Samians; indeed Stesagoras and others had left the island with five ships to bring them.

117. But in the meantime the Samians made a sudden sally, and fell on the camp, which they found unfortified. Destroying the look-out vessels, and engaging and defeating such as were being launched to meet them, they remained masters of their own seas for fourteen days, and carried in and carried out what they pleased. But on the arrival of Pericles, they were once more shut up. Fresh reinforcements afterwards arrived—forty ships from Athens with Thucydides,† Hagnon, and Phormio; twenty with Tlepolemus and Anticles, and thirty vessels from Chios and Lesbos. After a brief attempt at fighting, the Samians, unable to hold out, were reduced after a nine months' siege, and surrendered on conditions; they razed their walls,

---

*A satrap was a Persian governor. The Persians were as interested in undermining the expanding Athenian empire as the Athenians were in picking off chunks of theirs. More such jockeying and flip-flops occur in book 8.

†Not the author of this *History* but another general, the son of Melesias, who became the leader of the traditional, conservative, sometimes reactionary faction at Athens after Cimon's death.

gave hostages, delivered up their ships, and arranged to pay the expenses of the war by instalments. The Byzantines also agreed to be subject as before.

Second Congress at Lacedæmon — Preparations for War and Diplomatic Skirmishes — Cylon — Pausanias — Themistocles

118. After this, though not many years later, we at length come to what has been already related, the affairs of Corcyra and Potidæa, and the events that served as a pretext for the present war. All these actions of the Hellenes against each other and the barbarian occurred in the fifty years' interval between the retreat of Xerxes and the beginning of the present war.* During this interval the Athenians succeeded in placing their empire on a firmer basis, and advanced their own home power to a very great height. The Lacedæmonians, though fully aware of it, opposed it only for a little while, but remained inactive during most of the period, being of old slow to go to war except under the pressure of necessity, and in the present instance being hampered by wars at home; until the growth of the Athenian power could be no longer ignored, and their own confederacy became the object of its encroachments. They then felt that they could endure it no longer, but that the time had come for them to throw themselves heart and soul upon the hostile power, and break it, if they could, by commencing the present war. And though the Lacedæmonians had made up their own minds on the fact of the breach of the treaty and the guilt of the Athenians, yet they sent to Delphi and inquired of the god whether it would be well with them if they went to war; and, as it is reported, received from him the answer that if they put their whole strength into the war, victory would be theirs, and the promise that he himself would be with them, whether invoked or uninvoked.†

119. Still they wished to summon their allies again, and to take their vote on the propriety of making war. After the ambassadors from the confederates had arrived and a congress had been convened, they all spoke their minds, most of them denouncing the Athenians and demanding that the war should begin. In particular the Corinthians. They had before on their own account canvassed the cities in detail to induce them to vote for the war, in the fear that it might come too late

---

*The Pentacontaëtia (Fifty Years) between the Persian and the Peloponnesian Wars was predominantly a time of political conflict but not open warfare between the major Greek powers.

†Thucydides again reports a Delphic pronouncement, presumably because it swayed public opinion.

to save Potidæa; they were present also on this occasion, and came forward the last, and made the following speech:—

120. 'Fellow allies, we can no longer accuse the Lacedæmonians of having failed in their duty: they have not only voted for war themselves, but have assembled us here for that purpose.* We say their duty, for supremacy has its duties. Besides equitably administering private interests, leaders are required to show a special care for the common welfare in return for the special honours accorded to them by all in other ways. For ourselves, all who have already had dealings with the Athenians require no warning to be on their guard against them. The states more inland and out of the highway of communication should understand that if they omit to support the coast powers, the result will be to injure the transit of their produce for exportation and the reception in exchange of their imports from the sea; and they must not be careless judges of what is now said, as if it had nothing to do with them, but must expect that the sacrifice of the powers on the coast will one day be followed by the extension of the danger to the interior, and must recognise that their own interests are deeply involved in this discussion. For these reasons they should not hesitate to exchange peace for war. If wise men remain quiet, while they are not injured, brave men abandon peace for war when they are injured, returning to an understanding on a favourable opportunity: in fact, they are neither intoxicated by their success in war, nor disposed to take an injury for the sake of the delightful tranquillity of peace. Indeed, to falter for the sake of such delights is, if you remain inactive, the quickest way of losing the sweets of repose to which you cling; while to conceive extravagant pretensions from success in war is to forget how hollow is the confidence by which you are elated. For if many ill-conceived plans have succeeded through the still greater fatuity of an opponent, many more, apparently well laid, have on the contrary ended in disgrace. The confidence with which we form our schemes is never completely justified in their execution; speculation is carried on in safety, but, when it comes to action, fear causes failure.

121. 'To apply these rules to ourselves, if we are now kindling war it is under the pressure of injury, and with adequate grounds of complaint; and after we have chastised the Athenians we will in season desist. We have many reasons to expect success,—first, superiority in numbers and in military experience, and secondly our general and unvarying obedience in the execution of orders. The naval strength which they possess shall be raised by us from our respective an-

---

*The Corinthians either want the war sooner so their chances to win are better, or they fear the Spartans will never be induced to begin a war that the Corinthians cannot fight without them.

tecedent resources, and from the monies at Olympia and Delphi. A loan from these enables us to seduce their foreign sailors by the offer of higher pay. For the power of Athens is more mercenary than national; while ours will not be exposed to the same risk, as its strength lies more in men than in money. A single defeat at sea is in all likelihood their ruin:* should they hold out, in that case there will be the more time for us to exercise ourselves in naval matters; and as soon as we have arrived at an equality in science, we need scarcely ask whether we shall be their superiors in courage. For the advantages that we have by nature they cannot acquire by education; while their superiority in science must be removed by our practice. The money required for these objects shall be provided by our contributions:† nothing indeed could be more monstrous than the suggestion that, while their allies never tire of contributing for their own servitude, we should refuse to spend for vengeance and self-preservation the treasure which by such refusal we shall forfeit to Athenian rapacity, and see employed for our own ruin.

122. 'We have also other ways of carrying on the war, such as revolt of their allies, the surest method of depriving them of their revenues, which are the source of their strength, and establishment of fortified positions in their country, and various operations which cannot be foreseen at present. For war of all things proceeds least upon definite rules,‡ but draws principally upon itself for contrivances to meet an emergency; and in such cases the party who faces the struggle and keeps his temper best meets with most security, and he who loses his temper about it with correspondent disaster. Let us also reflect that if it was merely a number of disputes of territory between rival neighbours, it might be borne; but here we have an enemy in Athens, that is a match for our whole coalition, and more than a match for any of its members; so that unless as a body and as individual nationalities and individual cities we make an unanimous stand against her, she will easily conquer us divided and in detail. That conquest, terrible as it may sound, would, it must be known, have no other end than slavery§ pure and simple; a word which Peloponnese

---

*The Corinthians make many valid points, but their belief that one defeat will ruin the Athenians is repeatedly shown as wildly wrong. The same is true for their hope that they will soon equal the Athenian navy in seamanship in naval battles.

†No other Dorian city was as wealthy as Corinth or as eager for war to protect its interests. As Pericles later says, the Peloponnesians do not have the financial reserves or resources that the Athenians do.

‡Both sides were aware of the unpredictability of the outcomes of warfare. Pericles and Nicias will repeat the sentiment, here voiced by Archidamus.

§"Slavery" was a catchword of the propagandists directing the Dorian liberation "movement" in their hope of getting the allies of Athens to revolt. Sometimes it worked.

cannot even hear whispered without disgrace, or without disgrace see so many states abused by one. Meanwhile the opinion would be either that we were justly so used, or that we put up with it from cowardice, and were proving degenerate sons in not even securing for ourselves the freedom which our fathers gave to Hellas; and in allowing the establishment in Hellas of a tyrant state, though in individual states we think it our duty to put down sole rulers. And we do not know how this conduct can be held free from three of the gravest failings, want of sense, of courage, or of vigilance. For we do not suppose that you have taken refuge in that contempt of an enemy which has proved so fatal in so many instances,—a feeling which from the numbers that it has ruined has come to be called, not contemptuous but contemptible.

123. 'There is, however, no advantage in reflexions on the past further than may be of service to the present. For the future we must provide by maintaining what the present gives us and redoubling our efforts; it is hereditary to us to win virtue as the fruit of labour, and you must not change the habit, even though you should have a slight advantage in wealth and resources; for it is not right that what was won in want should be lost in plenty. No, we must boldly advance to the war for many reasons; the god has commanded it and promised to be with us, and the rest of Hellas will all join in the struggle, part from fear, part from interest.* You will not be the first to break a treaty which the god, in advising us to go to war, judges to be violated already, but rather to support a treaty that has been outraged: indeed, treaties are broken not by resistance but by aggression.

124. 'Your position, therefore, from whatever quarter you may view it, will amply justify you in going to war; and this step we recommend in the interests of all, bearing in mind that identity of interests is the surest of bonds whether between states or individuals. Delay not, therefore, to assist Potidæa, a Dorian city besieged by Ionians, which is quite a reversal of the order of things; nor to assert the freedom of the rest. It is impossible for us to wait any longer when waiting can only mean immediate disaster for some of us and, if it comes to be known that we have conferred but do not venture to protect ourselves, like disaster in the near future for the rest. Delay not, fellow allies, but convinced of the necessity of the crisis and the wisdom of this counsel, vote for the war, undeterred by its immediate terrors, but looking beyond to the lasting peace by which it will be succeeded. Out of war peace gains fresh stability, but to refuse to abandon repose for war is not so sure a method of avoiding danger.

---

*Fear and self-interest are common political motivators in this text, and the Corinthian speech whips them up.

We must believe that the tyrant city* that has been established in Hellas has been established against all alike, with a programme of universal empire, part fulfilled, part in contemplation; let us then attack and reduce it, and win future security for ourselves and freedom for the Hellenes who are now enslaved.'

Such were the words of the Corinthians.

125. The Lacedæmonians having now heard all give their opinion, took the vote of all the allied states present in order, great and small alike; and the majority voted for war. This decided it was still impossible for them to commence at once, from their want of preparation; but it was resolved that the means requisite were to be procured by the different states, and that there was to be no delay. And indeed, in spite of the time occupied with the necessary arrangements, less than a year elapsed before Attica was invaded, and the war openly begun.

126. This interval was spent in sending embassies to Athens charged with complaints, in order to obtain as good a pretext for war as possible, in the event of her paying no attention to them.† The first Lacedæmonian embassy was to order the Athenians to drive out the curse of the goddess; the history of which is as follows.‡ In former generations there was an Athenian of the name of Cylon, a victor at the Olympic games, of good birth and powerful position, who had married a daughter of Theagenes, a Megarian, at that time tyrant of Megara. Now this Cylon was inquiring at Delphi; when he was told by the god to seize the Acropolis of Athens on the grand festival of Zeus. Accordingly, procuring a force from Theagenes and persuading his friends to join him, when the Olympic festival in Peloponnese came, he seized the Acropolis, with the intention of making himself tyrant, thinking that this was the grand festival of Zeus, and also an occasion appropriate for a victor at the Olympic games. Whether the grand festival that was meant was in Attica or elsewhere was a question which he never thought of, and which the oracle did not offer to

---

*Not only enemies but some conservative Athenians such as Cimon regarded the unprecedented position of Athens as contrary to Greek customs of local autonomy. Athens' control of so many cities gave it the revenues to build the Acropolis, to hold festivals (dramatic, poetic, athletic, etc.), and to maintain armed forces that expanded Athenian power and advanced her glory.

†Both sides put the year between the Peloponnesian decision and open warfare to serious use, in both collecting material and promoting propaganda such as follows.

‡Religious pretexts for war were an old tradition. Having god on your side boosted morale, long before Christian and other doctrines of "just wars." The Romans believed and claimed that they "never" fought without a finding by their fetial priests (those associated with diplomatic negotiations) that Rome had been wronged. Their victims begged to disagree.

solve.* For the Athenians also have a festival which is called the grand festival of Zeus Meilichios or Gracious, viz. the Diasia. It is celebrated outside the city, and the whole people sacrifice not real victims but a number of bloodless offerings peculiar to the country. However, fancying he had chosen the right time, he made the attempt. As soon as the Athenians perceived it, they flocked in, one and all, from the country, and sat down, and laid siege to the citadel. But as time went on, weary of the labour of blockade, most of them departed; the responsibility of keeping guard being left to the nine archons, with plenary powers to arrange everything according to their good judgment. It must be known that at that time most political functions were discharged by the nine archons. Meanwhile Cylon and his besieged companions were distressed for want of food and water. Accordingly Cylon and his brother made their escape; but the rest being hard pressed, and some even dying of famine, seated themselves as suppliants at the altar in the Acropolis. The Athenians who were charged with the duty of keeping guard, when they saw them at the point of death in the temple, raised them up on the understanding that no harm should be done to them, led them out and slew them. Some who as they passed by took refuge at the altars of the awful goddesses were despatched on the spot. From this deed the men who killed them were called accursed and guilty against the goddess, they and their descendants. Accordingly these cursed ones were driven out by the Athenians, driven out again by Cleomenes of Lacedæmon and an Athenian faction; the living were driven out, and the bones of the dead were taken up; thus they were cast out. For all that, they came back afterwards, and their descendants are still in the city.

127. This, then, was the curse that the Lacedæmonians ordered them to drive out. They were actuated primarily, as they pretended, by a care for the honour of the gods; but they also knew that Pericles, son of Xanthippus, was connected with the curse on his mother's side,† and they thought that his banishment would materially advance their designs on Athens. Not that they really hoped to succeed in procuring this; they rather thought to create a prejudice against him in the eyes of his countrymen from the feeling that the war would be

---

*Thucydides mocks the ambiguity of the oracles. His references to the gods suggest that they did not interfere in human history, one of his advances over some previous and many subsequent chroniclers.

†Pericles was related to the Alcmaeonid clan, and therefore descended from some of those who had executed, contrary to an agreement, the supporters of the would-be tyrant Cylon (c.632). Whatever Pericles' faults, most Athenians did not take his 200-year-old curse-problem seriously. Elsewhere, the accusation may have enjoyed more traction.

partly caused by his misfortune. For being the most powerful man of his time, and the leading Athenian statesman, he opposed the Lacedæmonians in everything, and would have no concessions, but ever urged the Athenians on to war.

128. The Athenians retorted by ordering the Lacedæmonians to drive out the curse of Tænarus. The Lacedæmonians had once raised up some Helot suppliants from the temple of Poseidon at Tænarus, led them away and slain them; for which they believe the great earthquake at Sparta to have been a retribution. The Athenians also ordered them to drive out the curse of the goddess of the Brazen House; the history of which is as follows.* After Pausanias the Lacedæmonian had been recalled by the Spartans from his command in the Hellespont (this is his first recall), and had been tried by them and acquitted, not being again sent out in a public capacity, he took a galley of Hermoine on his own responsibility, without the authority of the Lacedæmonians, and arrived as a private person in the Hellespont. He came ostensibly for the Hellenic war, really to carry on his intrigues with the king, which he had begun before his recall, being ambitious of reigning over Hellas. The circumstance which first enabled him to lay the king under an obligation, and to make a beginning of the whole design was this. Some connexions and kinsmen of the king had been taken in Byzantium, on its capture from the Medes, when he was first there, after the return from Cyprus. These captives he sent off to the king without the knowledge of the rest of the allies, the account being that they had escaped from him. He managed this with the help of Gongylus, an Eretrian, whom he had placed in charge of Byzantium and the prisoners. He also gave Gongylus a letter for the king, the contents of which were as follows, as was afterwards discovered: 'Pausanias, the general of Sparta, anxious to do you a favour, sends you these his prisoners of war. I propose also, with your approval, to marry your daughter, and to make Sparta and the rest of Hellas subject to you. I may say that I think I am able to do this, with your co-operation. Accordingly if any of this please you, send a safe man to the sea through whom we may in future conduct our correspondence.'

129. This was all that was revealed in the writing, and Xerxes was pleased with the letter.† He sent off Artabazus, son of Pharnaces, to

---

*This diplomatic jockeying for the moral upper hand bizarrely sets curse shenanigan against counter-curse shenanigan.

†Thucydides' account of the dramatic adventures of Pausanias and Themistocles differs from his usual style (it is easier) and content (it resembles much more romantic biographies). For these reasons, some have thought the composition earlier than the rest of the *History*. While he never tells us why or how he thought he knew any of the thoughts of characters in his narrative, it is even less likely that he had a source for King Xerxes' ruminations. (Fornara #61 sets out additional details for Pausanias, #65 for Themistocles.)

the sea with orders to supersede Megabates, the previous governor in the satrapy of Daskylion,* and to send over as quickly as possible to Pausanias at Byzantium a letter which he entrusted to him; to show him the royal signet, and to execute any commission which he might receive from Pausanias on the king's matters, with all care and fidelity. Artabazus on his arrival carried the king's orders into effect, and sent over the letter, which contained the following answer:— 'Thus saith King Xerxes to Pausanias. For the men whom you have saved for me across sea from Byzantium, an obligation is laid up for you in our house, recorded for ever; and with your proposals I am well pleased. Let neither night nor day stop you from diligently performing any of your promises to me; neither for cost of gold nor of silver let them be hindered, nor yet for number of troops, wherever it may be that their presence is needed; but with Artabazus, an honourable man whom I send you, boldly advance my objects and yours, as may be most for the honour and interest of us both.'

130. Before held in high honour by the Hellenes as the hero of Platæa,† Pausanias, after the receipt of this letter, became prouder than ever, and could no longer live in the usual style, but went out of Byzantium in a Median dress, was attended on his march through Thrace by a bodyguard of Medes and Egyptians, kept a Persian table, and was quite unable to contain his intentions, but betrayed by his conduct in trifles what his ambition looked one day to enact on a grander scale. He also made himself difficult of access, and displayed so violent a temper to every one without exception that no one could come near him. Indeed, this was the principal reason why the confederacy went over to the Athenians.

131. The above-mentioned conduct, coming to the ears of the Lacedæmonians, occasioned his first recall. And after his second voyage out in the ship of Hermoine, without their orders, he gave proofs of similar behaviour. Besieged and expelled from Byzantium by the Athenians, he did not return to Sparta; but news came that he had settled at Colonæ in the Troad, and was intriguing with the barbarians, and that his stay there was for no good purpose; and the Ephors, now no longer hesitating, sent him a herald and a scytale‡ with orders to

---

*Daskylion is on the shore of Lake Daskylitis, near the Sea of Marmara, capital of the Persian province or satrapy of Hellespontine Phrygia. Artabazus seemed better suited than Megabates to conduct this delicate negotiation.

†Plataea, situated in southwestern Boeotia (map 2), suffered the decisive army-battle in the Persian Wars, in late 479. An alliance of Greeks under the regent Pausanias defeated the Persian armies under Masistes (see Herodotus book 9). Pausanias served as regent or surrogate king because his first cousin Pleistarchus was still a minor.

‡The Spartan authorities had a code machine, a staff (*scytale*) around which they elaborately wound a cloth on which important diplomatic messages were written.

accompany the herald or be declared a public enemy. Anxious above everything to avoid suspicion, and confident that he could quash the charge by means of money, he returned a second time to Sparta. At first thrown into prison by the Ephors (whose powers enable them to do this to the king),* he soon compromised the matter and came out again, and offered himself for trial to any who wished to institute an inquiry concerning him.

132. Now the Spartans had no tangible proof against him—neither his enemies nor the nation—of that indubitable kind required for the punishment of a member of the royal family, and at that moment in high office; he being regent for his first cousin King Pleistarchus, Leonidas' son, who was still a minor. But by his contempt of the laws and imitation of the barbarians, he gave grounds for much suspicion of his being discontented with things established; all the occasions on which he had in any way departed from the regular customs were passed in review, and it was remembered that he had taken upon himself to have inscribed on the tripod† at Delphi, which was dedicated by the Hellenes as the first-fruits of the spoil of the Medes, the following couplet:—

> 'The Mede defeated, great Pausanias raised
> This monument, that Phœbus might be praised.'

At the time the Lacedæmonians had at once erased the couplet, and inscribed the names of the cities that had aided in the overthrow of the barbarian and dedicated the offering. Yet it was considered that Pausanias had here been guilty of a grave offence, which, interpreted by the light of the attitude which he had since assumed, gained a new significance, and seemed to be quite in keeping with his present schemes.‡ Besides, they were informed that he was even intriguing with the Helots; and such indeed was the fact, for he promised them freedom and citizenship if they would join him in insurrection, and would help him to carry out his plans to the end. Even now, mis-

---

*The ephors, the board of five "overseer" magistrates, developed late in Spartan constitutional history as a check on the two kings' authority in the field or at home. The Spartan warrior-band elected these "overseers" annually.

†Tripods were three-legged metal stands that supported large bowls or pots. Awarded at athletic contests, they were considered appropriate gift-offerings to favorable gods. They were usually made of bronze or iron in kitchen dimensions, though larger stands of more precious metals (silver and gold) were also dedicated. Many of these handsome objects stood in Panhellenic and other, local sanctuaries; a small percentage survived to be excavated.

‡The corporate nature of Spartan society frowned upon the elevation of any individual, king or not. Pausanias' hubris seemed to have developed roots earlier, before his later behavior exhibited manifestly autocratic and Persian tendencies.

trusting the evidence even of the Helots themselves, the Ephors would not consent to take any decided step against him; in accordance with their regular custom towards themselves, namely, to be slow in taking any irrevocable resolve in the matter of a Spartan citizen, without indisputable proof. At last, it is said, the person who was going to carry to Artabazus the last letter for the king, a man of Argilus, once the favourite and most trusty servant of Pausanias, turned informer. Alarmed by the reflexion that none of the previous messengers had ever returned, having counterfeited the seal, in order that, if he found himself mistaken in his surmises, or if Pausanias should ask to make some correction, he might not be discovered, he undid the letter, and found the postscript that he had suspected, viz., an order to put him to death.*

133. On being shown the letter the Ephors now felt more certain. Still, they wished to hear Pausanias commit himself with their own ears. Accordingly the man went by appointment to Tænarus as a suppliant, and there built himself a hut divided into two by a partition; within which he concealed some of the Ephors and let them hear the whole matter plainly. For Pausanias came to him and asked him the reason of his suppliant position; and the man reproached him with the order that he had written concerning him, and one by one declared all the rest of the circumstances, how he who had never yet brought him into any danger, while employed as agent between him and the king, was yet just like the mass of his servants, to be rewarded with death. Admitting all this, and telling him not to be angry about the matter, Pausanias gave him the pledge of raising him up from the temple, and begged him to set off as quickly as possible, and not to hinder the business in hand.

134. The Ephors listened carefully, and then departed, taking no action for the moment, but, having at last attained to certainty, were preparing to arrest him in the city. It is reported that, as he was about to be arrested in the street, he saw from the face of one of the Ephors† what he was coming for; another, too, made him a secret signal, and betrayed it to him from kindness. Setting off with a run for the temple of the goddess of the Brazen House, the enclosure of which was near at hand, he succeeded in taking sanctuary before they took him, and entering into a small chamber, which formed part of the temple, to avoid being exposed to the weather, lay still there. The Ephors, for

---

*The sudden realization suits the anecdotal mode better than historical reality. The scholiast (ancient annotator) of these chapters reprising the biographies of Themistocles and Pausanias noted, with rare humor, "Here the lion [Thucydides] smiled."

†Thucydides mentions non-verbal behaviors rarely in comparison to his prose predecessor Herodotus or his poetic predecessor Homer.

the moment distanced in the pursuit, afterwards took off the roof of the chamber, and having made sure that he was inside, shut him in, barricaded the doors, and staying before the place, reduced him by starvation. When they found that he was on the point of expiring, just as he was, in the chamber, they brought him out of the temple, while the breath was still in him, and as soon as he was brought out he died. They were going to throw him into the Kaiadas, where they cast criminals, but finally decided to inter him somewhere near. But the god at Delphi afterwards ordered the Lacedæmonians to remove the tomb to the place of his death—where he now lies in the consecrated ground, as an inscription on a monument declares*—and, as what had been done was a curse to them, to give back two bodies instead of one to the goddess of the Brazen House. So they had two brazen statues made, and dedicated them as a substitute for Pausanias.

135. Accordingly the Athenians retorted by telling the Lacedæmonians to drive out what the god himself had pronounced to be a curse.

To return to the Medism of Pausanias. Matter was found in the course of the inquiry to implicate Themistocles; and the Lacedæmonians accordingly sent envoys to the Athenians, and required them to punish him as they had punished Pausanias. The Athenians consented to do so. But he had, as it happened, been ostracised,† and, with a residence at Argos, was in the habit of visiting other parts of Peloponnese. So they sent with the Lacedæmonians, who were ready to join in the pursuit, persons with instructions to take him wherever they found him.

136. But Themistocles got scent of their intentions, and fled from Peloponnese to Corcyra, which was under obligations towards him. But the Corcyræans alleged that they could not venture to shelter him at the cost of offending Athens and Lacedæmon, and they conveyed him over to the continent opposite. Pursued by the officers who hung on the report of his movements, at a loss where to turn, he was compelled to stop at the house of Admetus, the Molossian king,

---

*Thucydides rarely refers to existing physical monuments; the reference shows acquaintance with Spartan topography, as well as with Spartan obedience to divine messages once interpreted to their satisfaction.

†Ostracism was a formal legal mechanism to deal with political eccentrics or those thought to be a danger to the community. Rather than the assassination of a rival or the exile of a man and his family indefinitely (practices that were common elsewhere), ostracism involved a vote of the *polis* to remove one man alone for ten years, his property staying under the control of his family. Each year of the Athenian democracy, the community voted whether to hold an ostracism; if so, a minimum of 6,000 votes was required for an individual to suffer this limited disassociation from the *polis*. Aristides and Themistocles are among the fifteen or so individuals who were actually ostracized. Hyperbolus' ostracism in 415 discredited the institution.

though they were not on friendly terms. Admetus happened not to be indoors, but his wife, to whom he made himself a suppliant, instructed him to take their child in his arms and sit down by the hearth.* Soon afterwards Admetus came in, and Themistocles told him who he was, and begged him not to revenge on Themistocles in exile any opposition which his requests might have experienced from Themistocles at Athens. Indeed, he was now far too low for his revenge; retaliation was only honourable between equals. Besides, his opposition to the king had only affected the success of a request, not the safety of his person; if the king were to give him up to the pursuers that he mentioned, and the fate which they intended for him, he would just be consigning him to certain death.

137. The king listened to him and raised him up with his son, as he was sitting with him in his arms after the most effectual method of supplication, and on the arrival of the Lacedæmonians not long afterwards, refused to give him up for anything they could say, but sent him off by land to the other sea to Pydna in Alexander's dominions,† as he wished to go to the Persian king. There he met with a merchantman on the point of starting for Ionia. Going on board, he was carried by a storm to the Athenian squadron which was blockading Naxos. In his alarm—he was luckily unknown to the people in the vessel—he told the master who he was and what he was flying for, and said that, if he refused to save him, he would declare that he was taking him for a bribe.‡ Meanwhile their safety consisted in letting no one leave the ship until a favourable time for sailing should arise. If he complied with his wishes, he promised him a proper recompense. The master acted as he desired, and, after lying to for a day and a night out of the reach of the squadron, at length arrived at Ephesus.§

After having rewarded him with a present of money, as soon as he received some from his friends at Athens and from his secret hoards at Argos, Themistocles started inland with one of the Coast-Persians, and sent a letter to King Artaxerxes, Xerxes' son, who had just come

---

*Admetus respects the suppliant; the scene with the queen's help recalls Odysseus' suppliancy on Scheria in *Odyssey* 7. Possession of the child at the father's domestic hearth almost guarantees protection against any violence occurring at the sanctuary of royal power.

†From Molossia in Epirus on the west coast, Themistocles travels to Macedonia on the east (maps 8 and 9).

‡Thucydides will write in 1.138 that no one was more intellectually competent than Themistocles and no one was better in responding to the unexpected. Here we have an amoral example.

§Ephesus marks the western edge of Persian control in Asia Minor (map 10). It always combined Asiatic and Greek influences. It had been a leading city in Greek colonization and trade.

to the throne. Its contents were as follows:* 'I, Themistocles, am come to you, who did your house more harm than any of the Hellenes, when I was compelled to defend myself against your father's invasion,—harm, however, far surpassed by the good that I did him during his retreat, which brought no danger for me but much for him. For the past, you are a good turn in my debt,'—here he mentioned the warning sent to Xerxes from Salamis to retreat, as well as his finding the bridges unbroken, which, as he falsely pretended, was due to him,—'for the present, able to do you great service, I am here, pursued by the Hellenes for my friendship for you. However, I desire a year's grace, when I shall be able to declare in person the objects of my coming.'

138. It is said that the king approved his intention, and told him to do as he said. He employed the interval in making what progress he could in the study of the Persian tongue, and of the customs of the country.† Arrived at Court at the end of the year, he attained to very high consideration there, such as no Hellene has ever possessed before or since; partly from his splendid antecedents, partly from the hopes which he held out of effecting for him the subjugation of Hellas, but principally by the proof which experience daily gave of his capacity. For Themistocles was a man who exhibited the most indubitable signs of genius; indeed, in this particular he has a claim on our admiration quite extraordinary and unparalleled.‡ By his own native capacity, alike unformed and unsupplemented by study, he was at once the best judge in those sudden crises which admit of little or of no deliberation, and the best prophet of the future, even to its most distant possibilities. An able theoretical expositor of all that came within the sphere of his practice, he was not without the power of passing an adequate judgment in matters in which he had no experience. He could also excellently divine the good and evil which lay hid in the unseen future. In fine, whether we consider the extent of his natural powers, or the slightness of his application, this extraordinary

---

*Artaxerxes succeeded his murdered father in 464; Thucydides is regrettably sparing in dates in his earlier run-up to the war and in this biographical diversion. There is little likelihood that anyone would have possessed a copy of this letter to the Great King (the king of Persia) that Thucydides vouches for.

†Very few Greeks, as far as we know, bothered to learn other languages, even Latin when the Romans ruled Greece for centuries, but Themistocles was serious about gaining the goodwill of the Achaemenid royal house.

‡Book 1 provides paradigms of individuals admirable and not, states canny and not, past policies and historical trends successful and not. Thucydides often conveys evaluations indirectly, but here he is at his most explicit. Shortly afterward, Pericles will speak in "real time," and Thucydides clearly thinks he had earned and obtained the mantle of his Athenian predecessor in leading the *demos*.

man must be allowed to have surpassed all others in the faculty of intuitively meeting an emergency.* Disease was the real cause of his death; though there is a story of his having ended his life by poison, on finding himself unable to fulfil his promises to the king.† However this may be, there is a monument to him in the market-place of Asiatic Magnesia.‡ He was governor of the district, the king having given him Magnesia, which brought in fifty talents a year, for bread, Lampsacus, which was considered to be the richest wine country, for wine, and Myos for other provisions. His bones, it is said, were conveyed home by his relatives in accordance with his wishes, and interred in Attic ground. This was done without the knowledge of the Athenians; as it is against the law to bury in Attica an outlaw for treason.§ So ends the history of Pausanias and Themistocles, the Lacedæmonian and the Athenian, the most famous men of their time in Hellas.‖

139. To return to the Lacedæmonians. The history of their first embassy, the injunctions which it conveyed, and the rejoinder which it provoked, concerning the expulsion of the accursed persons, have been related already.# It was followed by a second, which ordered Athens to raise the siege of Potidæa, and to respect the independence of Ægina. Above all, it gave her most distinctly to understand that war might be prevented by the revocation of the Megara decree, excluding

---

*War causes emergencies; Themistocles' success involved anticipating crises (such as building a fleet to meet the Persians at Salamis) as well as persuading poor Athenians to divert revenues from themselves to finance a defense against a potential threat.

†Thucydides rarely offers the variant versions that are common in Herodotus. The reason here may well be his distance in time from reliable sources.

‡Two cities were named Magnesia; this one in southwestern Asia Minor on the Maeander River is about 15 miles southeast of Ephesus. We see how successful Themistocles was in his plan. Imagine a twentieth-century power putting the leader of its victorious enemies in charge of one of its own imperial possessions (for example, Ho Chi Minh as governor of Puerto Rico).

§This refers to a decree of treason subsequent to the Spartan information (real or quite likely cooked up), not to his original ostracism, which was not a result of accusations of treason.

‖Thucydides, following Herodotus' practice and exhibiting a feature of oral composition, often employs ring composition, a device in which a conclusion echoes in vocabulary and structure the opening words, a kind of chapter-making device. We find this in large units and small in book 1; this sentence forms a "ring" with 1.128.

#Cross-references are rare in Thucydides' text. Although he lacked our developed systems of volumes, chapters, pages, and footnotes, one can determine that he here refers to chapter 125. The series of Spartan embassies (diplomatic missions) makes clear that Sparta seriously hoped to avoid war but had no coherent policy to achieve that goal.

the Megarians from the use of Athenian harbours and of the market of Athens.* But Athens was not inclined either to revoke the decree, or to entertain their other proposals; she accused the Megarians of pushing their cultivation into the consecrated ground and the unenclosed land on the border, and of harbouring her runaway slaves. At last an embassy arrived with the Lacedæmonian ultimatum. The ambassadors were Ramphias, Melesippus, and Agesander. Not a word was said on any of the old subjects; there was simply this:—'Lacedæmon wishes the peace to continue, and there is no reason why it should not, if you would leave the Hellenes independent.'† Upon this the Athenians held an assembly, and laid the matter before their consideration. It was resolved to deliberate once for all on all their demands, and to give them an answer. There were many speakers‡ who came forward and gave their support to one side or the other, urging the necessity of war, or the revocation of the decree and the folly of allowing it to stand in the way of peace. Among them came forward Pericles,§ son of Xanthippus, the first man of his time at Athens, ablest alike in counsel and in action, and gave the following advice:—

140. 'There is one principle, Athenians, which I hold to through everything, and that is the principle of no concession to the Peloponnesians. I know that the spirit which inspires men while they are being persuaded to make war, is not always retained in action; that as circumstances change, resolutions change. Yet I see that now as before the same, almost literally the same, counsel is demanded of me; and I put it to those of you, who are allowing yourselves to be persuaded, to support the national resolves even in the case of reverses, or to forfeit all credit for their wisdom in the event of success. For sometimes,

---

*Plutarch and Aristophanes tell us more in anecdotes about Athenian trade policies toward Megara, Athens' commercial neighbor to the west. Pericles' policy of "no concessions" made sense if, as he argued, sooner or later the Peloponnesians would demand more than the Athenians could happily concede. The Athenians had no reason to be generous to this neighbor with whom there had been incessant border quarrels.

†Hellenic independence is a hollow plea from the Laconic state that had enslaved thousands for generations inside its own borders. Autonomy, however, resonated with undecided neutrals and appealed to those forced into Athens' imperial alliance in the previous fifty years.

‡Thucydides' imperious manner leads him to focus on the decisive speech and speaker without even naming the other speakers or describing their positions. Although he avoids many faults of other historians, many of his silences deserve some criticism.

§Pericles was the most successful democratic politician of the fifth century and the name responsible for many of its cultural as well as political achievements. He was aristocratic by his birth-relations with the Alcmaeonid clan (via his mother, Agariste, not his father, Xanthippus). Thucydides admired his mind, policies, and political capacity without explicit reservation, as one reads in his "epitaph" (2.65).

the course of things is as arbitrary as the plans of man;* indeed this is why we usually blame chance for whatever does not happen as we expected. Now it was clear before, that Lacedæmon entertained designs against us; it is still more clear now. The treaty provides that we shall mutually submit our differences to legal settlement, and that we shall meanwhile each keep what we have. Yet the Lacedæmonians never yet made us any such offer, never yet would accept from us any such offer; on the contrary, they wish complaints to be settled by war instead of by negotiation; and in the end we find them here dropping the tone of expostulation and adopting that of command.

'They order us to raise the siege of Potidæa, to let Ægina be independent, to revoke the Megara decree; and they conclude with an ultimatum warning us to leave the Hellenes independent. I hope that you will none of you think that we shall be going to war for a trifle if we refuse to revoke the Megara decree, which appears in front of their complaints, and the revocation of which is to save us from war, or let any feeling of self-reproach linger in your minds, as if you went to war for slight cause. Why, this trifle contains the whole seal and trial of your resolution. If you give way, you will instantly have to meet some greater demand, as having been frightened into obedience in the first instance; while a firm refusal will make them clearly understand that they must treat you more as equals.† Make your decision therefore at once, either to submit before you are harmed, or if we are to go to war, as I for one think we ought, to do so without caring whether the ostensible cause be great or small, resolved against making concessions or consenting to a precarious tenure of our possessions.‡ For all claims from an equal, urged upon a neighbour as commands, before any attempt at legal settlement, be they great or be they small, have only one meaning, and that is slavery.

141. 'As to the war and the resources of either party, a detailed comparison will not show you the inferiority of Athens. Personally engaged in the cultivation of their land, without funds either private or public, the Peloponnesians are also without experience in long wars across sea, from the strict limit which poverty imposes on their

---

*Pericles planned for a long war and stockpiled military and civilian goods, but he did not foresee, among other things, the savage plague that killed him and tens of thousands of others.

†Pericles summarizes Peloponnesian demands: Give up Potidaea and Aegina, let Megarians trade where they will, and provide the Hellenes with autonomy. He recognizes that each demand, not a small thing in itself, is part of a larger policy of picking off Athens' sources of wealth and power. Thus, he recommends summary rejection of all of them.

‡Pericles reconfigures the demand as a stark antithesis: submission to Peloponnesian dominance or war.

attacks upon each other.* Powers of this description are quite incapable of often manning a fleet or often sending out an army: they cannot afford the absence from their homes, the expenditure from their
own funds; and besides, they have not command of the sea. Capital, it
must be remembered, maintains a war more than forced contributions. Farmers are a class of men that are always more ready to serve
in person than in purse. Confident that the former will survive the
dangers, they are by no means so sure that the latter will not be prematurely exhausted, especially if the war last longer than they expect,
which it very likely will. In a single battle the Peloponnesians and
their allies may be able to defy all Hellas, but they are incapacitated
from carrying on a war against a power different in character from
their own, by the want of the single council-chamber requisite to
prompt and vigorous action, and the substitution of a deliberative
body composed of various races, in which every state possesses an
equal vote, and each presses its own ends, a condition of things which
generally results in no action at all.† The great wish of some is to
avenge themselves on some particular enemy, the great wish of others
to save their own pocket. Slow in assembling, they devote a very small
fraction of the time to the consideration of any public object, most of
it to the prosecution of their own objects. Meanwhile each fancies that
no harm will come of his neglect, that it is the business of somebody
else to look after this or that for him; and so, by the same notion being
entertained by all separately, the common cause imperceptibly decays.

142. 'But the principal point is the hindrance that they will experience from want of money. The slowness with which it comes in will
cause delay; but the opportunities of war wait for no man. Again, we
need not be alarmed either at the possibility of their raising fortifications in Attica, or at their navy. It would be difficult for any system of
fortifications to establish a rival city, even in time of peace, much
more, surely, in an enemy's country, with Athens just as much fortified
against it, as it against Athens;‡ while a mere post might be able to do
some harm to the country by incursions and by the facilities which it
would afford for desertion, but can never prevent our sailing into

---

*Pericles expresses scorn for the Spartan alliance's lack of imperial and martial infra-
structure.

†Pericles describes Athenian ability to determine policy without consultation of allies
as an advantage and the standing navy as another. The needs of farmers will keep the
Peloponnesian allies from persevering in the field—as they must, for victory.

‡Thucydides presented the "archaeology," or history of the distant past (whose record
is beyond dependable historical test), to support a strongly held thesis. Chapters
1.1–1.19 have emphasized the necessity of ready financial reserves (coin or coinable
silver and gold) and naval power (thalassocracy) for Mediterranean imperial success.
Pericles will soon "echo" the author.

their country and raising fortifications there, and making reprisals with our powerful fleet. For our naval skill is of more use to us for service on land, than their military skill for service at sea. Familiarity with the sea they will not find an easy acquisition.* If you who have been practising at it ever since the Median invasion have not yet brought it to perfection, is there any chance of anything considerable being effected by an agricultural, unseafaring population, who will besides be prevented from practising by the constant presence of strong squadrons of observation from Athens? With a small squadron they might hazard an engagement, encouraging their ignorance by numbers; but the restraint of a strong force will prevent their moving, and through want of practice they will grow more clumsy, and consequently more timid. It must be kept in mind that seamanship, just like anything else, is a matter of art, and will not admit of being taken up occasionally as an occupation for times of leisure; on the contrary, it is so exacting as to leave leisure for nothing else.

143. 'Even if they were to touch the moneys at Olympia or Delphi, and try to seduce our foreign sailors by the temptation of higher pay,† that would only be a serious danger if we could not still be a match for them, by embarking our own citizens and the aliens resident‡ among us. But in fact by this means we are always a match for them; and, best of all, we have a larger and higher class of native coxswains and sailors among our own citizens than all the rest of Hellas. And to say nothing of the danger of such a step, none of our foreign sailors would consent to become an outlaw from his country, and to take service with them and their hopes, for the sake of a few days' high pay.

'This, I think, is a tolerably fair account of the position of the Peloponnesians; that of Athens is free from the defects that I have criticised in them, and has other advantages of its own, which they can show nothing to equal. If they march against our country we will sail against theirs, and it will then be found that the desolation of the whole of Attica is not the same as that of even a fraction of Peloponnese; for they will not be

---

*Not only ships, but trained rowers, steersmen, and marines for boarding enemy ships, are not easily or quickly developed. That much is true, but Pericles had not expected the Peloponnesians to continue as long as they did, or other powers, such as the Persians and the Sicilians, to decide to join them.

†Pericles considered seizure of, or loans from, the large accumulations of capital metals at Panhellenic sanctuaries, but he dismisses this money as not decisive for Athenian necessities in this war. The Peloponnesians did make use of these funds at mainland sites that the Athenians could not master.

‡Athens was home to many citizens of other cities. Some of them were transient but many of them permanent—for instance, Lysias the orator, at whose father's house Plato sets his dialogue the *Republic* soon after the war's end. Such *metics* (resident aliens) were sometimes rich and educated. They freely mixed with leading Athenians, as we see in Plato's historically situated text.

able to supply the deficiency except by a battle, while we have plenty of land both on the islands and the continent. The rule of the sea is indeed a great matter. Consider for a moment. Suppose that we were islanders: can you conceive a more impregnable position? Well, this in future should, as far as possible, be our conception of our position.* Dismissing all thought of our land and houses, we must vigilantly guard the sea and the city. No irritation that we may feel for the former must provoke us to a battle with the numerical superiority of the Peloponnesians. A victory would only be succeeded by another battle against the same superiority: a reverse involves the loss of our allies, the source of our strength, who will not remain quiet a day after we become unable to march against them.† We must cry not over the loss of houses and land but of men's lives; since houses and land do not gain men, but men them. And if I had thought that I could persuade you, I would have bid you go out and lay them waste with your own hands, and show the Peloponnesians that this at any rate will not make you submit.

144. 'I have many other reasons to hope for a favourable issue, if you can consent not to combine schemes of fresh conquest with the conduct of the war, and will abstain from wilfully involving yourselves in other dangers; indeed, I am more afraid of our own blunders than of the enemy's devices.‡ But these matters shall be explained in another speech, as events require; for the present dismiss these men with the answer that we will allow Megara the use of our market and harbours, when the Lacedæmonians suspend their alien acts in favour of us and our allies, there being nothing in the treaty to prevent either one or the other: that we will leave the cities independent, if independent we found them when we made the treaty, and when the Lacedæmonians grant to their cities an independence not involving subservience to Lacedæmonian interests, but such as each severally may desire: that we are willing to give the legal satisfaction which our agreements specify, and that we shall not commence hostilities, but shall resist those who do commence them.§ This is an answer agree-

---

*Athenian sea power was the basis of the empire. The fact that Attica is a part of the Balkan peninsula meant that Athens was vulnerable to attacks from Sparta, Boeotia, and any other army that could advance to the southeast. The long walls to Piraeus were a limited insulation, but they sucked up a significant number of troops to man them.

†Pericles here recognizes, as he will in his last speech in book 2, that the Athenian empire rests on its power, not on its popularity. He is hardheaded about the so-called allies' acceptance of Athenian leadership. This is not to say that they did not reap advantages from participation in the empire—trade and naval service pay.

‡Pericles anticipates what Thucydides emphasizes at 2.65, that the Athenians lost the war more through their own mistakes than the enemies' military genius. This may be wrong, but his account supports the thesis.

§Pericles' recommended response, point by point, is part of diplomatic sparring, an attempt to render patent the self-serving nature of the Peloponnesian demands.

able at once to the rights and the dignity of Athens. It must be thoroughly understood that war is a necessity; but that the more readily we accept it, the less will be the ardour of our opponents, and that out of the greatest dangers communities and individuals acquire the greatest glory. Did not our fathers resist the Medes not only with resources far different from ours, but even when those resources had been abandoned; and more by wisdom than by fortune, more by daring than by strength, did not they beat off the barbarian and advance their affairs to their present height? We must not fall behind them, but must resist our enemies in any way and in every way, and attempt to hand down our power to our posterity unimpaired.'

145. Such were the words of Pericles. The Athenians, persuaded of the wisdom of his advice, voted as he desired, and answered the Lacedæmonians as he recommended, both on the separate points and in the general; they would do nothing on dictation, but were ready to have the complaints settled in a fair and impartial manner by the legal method, which the terms of the truce prescribed. So the envoys departed home, and did not return again.

146. These were the charges and differences existing between the rival powers before the war, arising immediately from the affair at Epidamnus and Corcyra. Still intercourse continued in spite of them, and mutual communication. It was carried on without heralds, but not without suspicion, as events were occurring which were equivalent to a breach of the treaty and matter for war.*

---

*Ring composition reminds the reader that Thucydides promised to describe the differences between Athens and its so-called allies, and Sparta with its looser coalition. These differences were both immediate, as with Epidamnus and Corcyra, and longerterm, some originating at least as early as the defeat of the Persians in 479. Recall that in 1.23 we read his view of the truest reason for this conflict, although the least commonly mentioned: the growing power of the Athenians and the growing fear of the Spartans that they would no longer be able to defeat it.

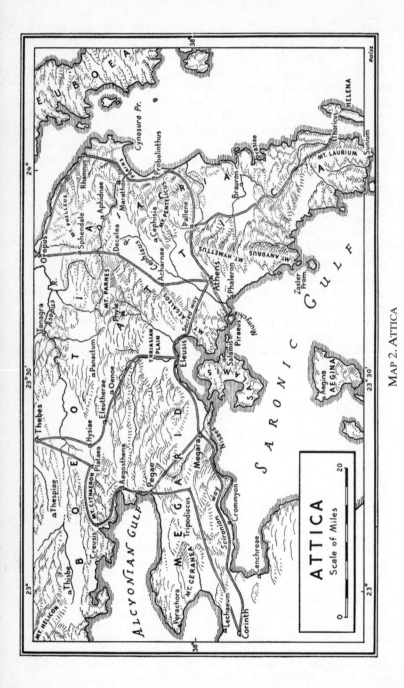

MAP 2. ATTICA

BOOK 2

Beginning of the Peloponnesian War—First Invasion of Attica—Funeral Oration of Pericles

1. The war between the Athenians and Peloponnesians and the allies on either side now really begins. For now all intercourse except through the medium of heralds ceased, and hostilities were commenced and prosecuted without intermission. The history follows the chronological order of events by summers and winters.*

2. The thirty years' truce which was entered into after the conquest of Eubœa lasted fourteen years. In the fifteenth, in the forty-eighth year of the priestess-ship of Chrysis at Argos, in the Ephorate of Ænesias at Sparta, in the last month but two of the Archonship of Pythodorus at Athens,† and six months after the battle of Potidæa, just at the beginning of spring, a Theban force a little over three hundred strong, under the command of their Bœotarchs,‡ Pythangelus, son of Phyleides, and Diemporus, son of Onetorides, about the first watch of the night, made an armed entry into Platæa, a town of Bœotia in alliance with Athens. The gates were opened to them by a Platæan called

---

*Book 1 has drawn the background to war, not battles. One now meets no further arguments and bloviating diplomacy, but the fighting. Thucydides will provide a different kind of chronology, based on seasons, in order to avoid the obscure systems of his predecessors, the logographers or city-chroniclers and geographers (such as Hecataeus and Hellanicus, the latter mentioned at 1.97) and the historian Herodotus (a monumental thinker never mentioned by name; see Parke). The logographers' systems depended on local magistrates and holders of priestly offices, dates unknown to inhabitants of other cities.

†This solemn, multi-anchored dating attempts a Panhellenic perspective, while it suggests how little the parochial dating systems of each *polis* would mean to Hellenes resident anywhere else. Local dates depended on holders of secular or religious offices. Pythodorus is significant only for giving his name (as eponymous archon) to the year in Athens, his city. No system for dating such as ours was widely recognized. The reader should develop a mental map locating Argos, Sparta, Corinth, Athens, Plataea, and Thebes (maps 4 and 5).

‡The truce becomes void by the Theban attack in early 431. The Thebans held the leading city of Boeotia, a fertile and strategic area between northern and southern Greece. The Plataeans had found their policies uncongenial to their interests. On the principle that "the enemy of my enemy is my friend," they had thrown their lot in with the Athenians—oddly enough at Spartan urging, as Herodotus (6.108) recounts. Boeotarchs are the officials of the Boeotian League, a group of nine to eleven Dorian cities banded together northwest of Attica. On the same political principle, as well as because of Dorian ethnic bias, the Boeotians allied with their distant Peloponnesian brethren.

Naucleides, who, with his party, had invited them in, meaning to put to death the citizens of the opposite party, bring over the city to Thebes, and thus obtain power for themselves.* This was arranged through Eurymachus, son of Leontiades, a person of great influence at Thebes. For Platæa had always been at variance with Thebes; and the latter, foreseeing that war was at hand, wished to surprise her old enemy in time of peace,† before hostilities had actually broken out. Indeed this was how they got in so easily without being observed, as no guard had been posted. After the soldiers had grounded arms in the market-place, those who had invited them in wished them to set to work at once and go to their enemies' houses. This, however, the Thebans refused to do, but determined to make a conciliatory proclamation, and if possible to come to a friendly understanding with the citizens. Their herald accordingly invited any who wished to resume their old place in the confederacy of their countrymen‡ to ground arms with them, for they thought that in this way the city would readily join them.

3. On becoming aware of the presence of the Thebans within their gates, and of the sudden occupation of the town, the Platæans concluded in their alarm that more had entered than was really the case, the night preventing their seeing them. They accordingly came to terms, and accepting the proposal, made no movement; especially as the Thebans offered none of them any violence. But somehow or other, during the negotiations, they discovered the scanty numbers of the Thebans,§ and decided that they could easily attack and overpower them; the mass of the Platæans being averse to revolting from Athens. At all events they resolved to attempt it. Digging through the party walls of the houses,‖ they thus managed to join each other without being seen going through the streets, in which they placed waggons without the beasts in them, to serve as a barricade, and arranged everything else as seemed convenient for the occasion. When everything had been done that circumstances permitted, they watched

---

*Naucleides' treasonous intention reveals the polarization of internal politics, even at the beginning of the war. Thucydides provides names and citizenship whenever he can, often with patronymic (the name of the father of the person in question).

†Surprise attack was not contrary to Hellenic wartime practice or principles, but the Thirty Years Treaty and the attack at night made this Plataean treason more treacherous.

‡Thucydides likes to note appeals to ethnic ties, but like appeals to the gods, they are usually cynically motivated and transparent to the target audience—as here.

§The darkness had hidden the paucity of attacking Thebans, and the provisional agreement seemed foolish—once their scant numbers became known.

‖Greek communities often built houses with shared residential walls, as one observes with the remains of urban private residences at Olynthus or Priene. Above a stone socle (base), the material was usually rammed mud-brick, a cheap material but notably enduring under a proper roof with extended eaves (see Camp, *Archaeology of Athens*, illustration 122).

their opportunity and went out of their houses against the enemy. It was still night, though daybreak was at hand: in daylight it was thought that their attack would be met by men full of courage and on equal terms with their assailants, while in darkness it would fall upon panic-stricken troops, who would also be at a disadvantage from their enemy's knowledge of the locality. So they made their assault at once, and came to close quarters as quickly as they could.

4. The Thebans, finding themselves outwitted, immediately closed up to repel all attacks made upon them. Twice or thrice they beat back their assailants. But the men shouted and charged them, the women and slaves* screamed and yelled from the houses and pelted them with stones and tiles; besides, it had been raining hard all night; and so at last their courage gave way, and they turned and fled through the town. Most of the fugitives were quite ignorant of the right ways out, and this, with the mud, and the darkness caused by the moon being in her last quarter, and the fact that their pursuers knew their way about and could easily stop their escape, proved fatal to many. The only gate open was the one by which they had entered, and this was shut by one of the Platæans driving the spike of a javelin into the bar instead of the bolt;† so that even here there was no longer any means of exit. They were now chased all over the town. Some got on the wall and threw themselves over, in most cases with a fatal result. One party managed to find a deserted gate, and obtaining an axe from a woman,‡ cut through the bar; but as they were soon observed only a few succeeded in getting out. Others were cut off in detail in different parts of the city. The most numerous and compact body rushed into a large building next to the city wall: the doors on the side of the street happened to be open, and the Thebans fancied that they were the gates of the town, and that there was a passage right through to the outside. The Platæans, seeing their enemies in a trap, now consulted whether they should set fire to the building and burn them just as they were, or whether there was anything else that they could do with them; until at length these and the rest of the Theban survivors found wandering about the town agreed to an unconditional surrender of themselves and their arms to the Platæans.

---

*The Thebans lost their advantage of unexpectedness and were now trapped in a town with which they were not familiar. Their Plataean friends do not seem to have helped much. Note how women and slaves aid in the defense of the city.

†The detail of how they secured the gate suggests an eyewitness source. Since the surviving Plataeans were eventually to remove themselves to Athens, one of them there might have told Thucydides this rousing tale of guerrilla warfare.

‡Women play a much smaller part in this historian's account than in that of Herodotus. Here a woman, perhaps a spouse or relative of one of Naucleides' supporters, aids the escaping invaders.

While such was the fate of the party in Platæa,

5. the rest of the Thebans who were to have joined them with all their forces before daybreak, in case of anything miscarrying with the body that had entered, received the news of the affair on the road, and pressed forward to their succour. Now Platæa is nearly eight miles from Thebes,* and their march was delayed by the rain that had fallen in the night, for the river Asopus had risen and was not easy of passage; and so, having to march in the rain, and being hindered in crossing the river, they arrived too late, and found the whole party either slain or captive. When they learned what had happened, they at once formed a design against the Platæans outside the city. As the attack had been made in time of peace, and was perfectly unexpected, there were of course men and livestock in the fields;† and the Thebans wished if possible to have some prisoners to exchange against their countrymen in the town, should any chance to have been taken alive. Such was their plan. But the Platæans suspected their intention almost before it was formed, and becoming alarmed for their fellow-citizens outside the town, sent a herald to the Thebans, reproaching them for their unscrupulous attempt to seize their city in time of peace, and warning them against any outrage on those outside. Should the warning be disregarded, they threatened to put to death the men they had in their hands, but added that, on the Thebans retiring from their territory, they would surrender the prisoners to their friends. This is the Theban account of the matter, and they say that they had an oath given them. The Platæans, on the other hand, do not admit any promise of an immediate surrender, but make it contingent upon subsequent negotiation: the oath they deny altogether.‡ Be this as it may, upon the Thebans retiring from their territory without committing any injury, the Platæans hastily got in whatever they had in the country and immediately put the men to death. The prisoners

---

*A simple example of unforeseeable complications in war: rain and a rising river. Most Greek streams go dry in summer but swell in winter and early spring—the time of this attack in February, 431 (2.1). The Mediterranean Greek spring begins to warm up the land when northern climes are still snowbound.

†Hellenic cities were sites of homes and public buildings, sacred and secular. The fields, orchards, and animal pastures beyond were the source of 95 percent of Greek incomes, and these were found outside the often-walled enclosures of the small cities. Many Athenians had city residences at Athens but also country houses, sometimes fortified dwellings near their fields. Their farming establishments could easily be located 25 miles away from town.

‡Thucydides rarely gives different versions, obviously not because they did not exist, and perhaps not because Herodotus often does, but because he thinks the historian should reach and offer the historically best account that he can. This story provides an exception. Another important one occurs in 8.87, where we read four accounts for the non-appearance in this war of the numerous Phoenician fleet.

were a hundred and eighty in number; Eurymachus, the person with whom the traitors had negotiated, being one.*

6. This done, the Platæans sent a messenger to Athens, gave back the dead to the Thebans under a truce,† and arranged things in the city as seemed best to meet the present emergency. The Athenians meanwhile, having had word of the affair sent them immediately after its occurrence, had instantly seized all the Bœotians in Attica, and sent a herald to the Platæans to forbid their proceeding to extremities with their Theban prisoners without instructions from Athens.‡ The news of the men's death had of course not arrived; the first messenger having left Platæa just when the Thebans entered it, the second just after their defeat and capture; so there was no later news. Thus the Athenians sent their orders in ignorance of the facts; and the herald on his arrival found the men slain. After this the Athenians marched to Platæa and brought in provisions, and left a garrison in the place, also taking away the women and children and such of the men as were least efficient.§

7. After the affair at Platæa the treaty had been broken by an overt act, and Athens at once prepared for war, as did also Lacedæmon and her allies. They resolved to send embassies to the king and to such other of the barbarian powers as either party could look to for assistance, and tried to ally themselves with the independent states at home.‖ Lacedæmon, in addition to the existing marine, gave orders to the states that had declared for her in Italy and Sicily to build vessels up to a grand total of five hundred, the quota of each city being determined by its size, and also to provide a specified sum of money. Till these were ready they were to remain neutral and to admit single Athenian ships into their harbours. Athens on her part reviewed her existing confederacy, and sent embassies to the places more immediately round Peloponnese, Corcyra, Cephallenia, Acarnania, and Za-

---

*Thucydides' numbers are accurate when one can check them, but one rarely can do that. He bluntly calls the Plataeans cooperating with the Thebans "traitors."

†The Plataeans, minor players at best, send to their dominant ally for advice but allow the Thebans their dead, a fundamental protocol of Hellenic war practice that the Hellenes will not always observe as the war grows fiercer.

‡The Athenians regard the Boeotian attackers objectively and coolly as pawns in negotiation, not hated traitors and sneak-attackers. The Plataean execution of the attackers forces the Athenians' hand; they fortify their allies' walls and bring in stores for the expected siege.

§Removal of non-combatants secures their safety and enables the warriors to hold out longer.

‖Open hostilities require the two sides to seek whatever help they can get in Greece and beyond. The scope of the two powers' search for support is bounded only by the perceived self-interest of potential allies in a world with severe limitations in travel, trade, and communication.

cynthus; perceiving that if these could be relied on she could carry the war all round Peloponnese.

8. And if both sides nourished the boldest hopes and put forth their utmost strength for the war, this was only natural. Zeal is always at its height at the commencement of an undertaking; and on this particular occasion Peloponnese and Athens were both full of young men whose inexperience made them eager to take up arms, while the rest of Hellas stood straining with excitement at the conflict of its leading cities.* Everywhere predictions were being recited and oracles being chanted by such persons as collect them, and this not only in the contending cities.† Further, some while before this, there was an earthquake at Delos, for the first time in the memory of the Hellenes. This was said and thought to be ominous of the events impending; indeed, nothing of the kind that happened was allowed to pass without remark. The good wishes of men made greatly for the Lacedæmonians, especially as they proclaimed themselves the liberators of Hellas.‡ No private or public effort that could help them in speech or action was omitted; each thinking that the cause suffered wherever he could not himself see to it. So general was the indignation felt against Athens, whether by those who wished to escape from her empire, or were apprehensive of being absorbed by it.

9. Such were the preparations and such the feelings with which the contest opened.

The allies of the two belligerents were the following. These were the allies of Lacedæmon: all the Peloponnesians within the Isthmus except the Argives and Achæans, who were neutral; Pellene being the only Achæan city that first joined in the war, though her example was afterwards followed by the rest. Outside Peloponnese the Megarians, Locrians, Bœotians, Phocians, Ambraciots, Leucadians, and Anactorians. Of these, ships were furnished by the Corinthians, Megarians, Sicyonians, Pellenians, Eleans, Ambraciots, and Leucadians; and cavalry by the Bœotians, Phocians, and Locrians. The other states sent in-

---

*Repeatedly Thucydides describes young men as eager for war because they are ignorant of it. In fact, many Hellenic wars repeated themselves at thirty-year intervals, when a new generation was available to steal, rob, pillage, burn, and rape the neighbors' holdings and families.

†Thucydides reports oracles and soothsayers' predictions, only to mock them. When they turn out true, he judged it coincidental, but Thucydides underlines the increased faith of ordinary people. Religious standards of conduct and observances were to deteriorate as the plague hit (later in this book) and war rendered traditional behaviors quaint or even ridiculous in the eyes of many.

‡Catchwords were motivators, and in the propaganda war, the Peloponnesian alliance had the advantage over the Athenian empire: the perception that they had created a coalition of the willing.

fantry.* This was the Lacedæmonian confederacy. That of Athens comprised the Chians, Lesbians, Platæans, the Messenians in Naupactus, most of the Acarnanians, the Corcyræans, Zacynthians, and some tributary cities in the following areas, viz., Caria upon the sea with her Dorian neighbours, Ionia, the Hellespont, the Thracian towns, the islands lying between Peloponnese and Crete towards the east, and all the Cyclades except Melos and Thera. Of these, ships were furnished by Chios, Lesbos, and Corcyra, infantry and money by the rest. Such were the allies of either party and their resources for the war.†

10. Immediately after the affair at Platæa, Lacedæmon sent round orders to the cities in Peloponnese and the rest of her confederacy to prepare troops and the provisions requisite for a foreign campaign, in order to invade Attica. The several states were ready at the time appointed and assembled at the Isthmus; the contingent of each city being two-thirds of its whole force. After the whole army had mustered, the Lacedæmonian king, Archidamus, the leader of the expedition,‡ called together the generals of all the states and the principal persons and officers, and exhorted them as follows:—

11. 'Peloponnesians and allies, our fathers made many campaigns both within and without Peloponnese, and the elder men among us here are not without experience in war. Yet we have never set out with a larger force than the present; and if our numbers and efficiency are remarkable, so also is the power of the state against which we march. We ought not then to show ourselves inferior to our ancestors, or unequal to our own reputation. For the hopes and attention of all Hellas are bent upon the present effort, and its sympathy is with the enemy of the hated Athens. Therefore, numerous as the invading army may appear to be, and certain as some may think it that our adversary will not meet us in the field, this is no sort of justification for the least negligence upon the march; but the officers and men of each particular city should always be prepared for the advent of danger in their own quarters. The course of war cannot be foreseen,§ and its attacks are gener-

---

*The Peloponnesian strength was on land, the Athenian on sea; this disconnect certainly lengthened the war. Homer provides a catalogue of the contingents at Ilion in the *Iliad*, book 2, so there is literary precedent as well as historical responsibility at work here.

†It is significant that only three allies supply ships (a fourth, Samos, having revolted in 440 with its navy intact, lost this privilege).

‡Field-commander exhortations, before campaigns or battles, are a Thucydidean innovation that his successors imitated. Such speeches often provide analysis, strategy, and even tactics, as well as boosting morale. Archidamus, king and commander, exhorts the allied troops but with characteristic Spartan caution. By the end of book 7, Thucydides tired of vacuous repetitions. His account of Nicias' last speeches clarifies the breakdown of the morale of commander and troops.

§Numbers never sufficiently protect an army from ambushes. Without sophisticated modern locating equipment, the problem was all the more common.

ally dictated by the impulse of the moment; and where overweening self-confidence has despised preparation, a wise apprehension has often been able to make head against superior numbers. Not that confidence is out of place in an army of invasion, but in an enemy's country it should also be accompanied by the precautions of apprehension: troops will by this combination be best inspired for dealing a blow, and best secured against receiving one. In the present instance, the city against which we are going, far from being so impotent for defence, is on the contrary most excellently equipped at all points; so that we have every reason to expect that they will take the field against us,* and that if they have not set out already before we are there, they will certainly do so when they see us in their territory wasting and destroying their property. For men are always exasperated at suffering injuries to which they are not accustomed, and on seeing them inflicted before their very eyes; and where least inclined for reflexion, rush with the greatest heat to action. The Athenians are the very people of all others to do this, as they aspire to rule the rest of the world,† and are more in the habit of invading and ravaging their neighbours' territory, than of seeing their own treated in the like fashion. Considering, therefore, the power of the state against which we are marching, and the greatness of the reputation which, according to the event, we shall win or lose for our ancestors‡ and ourselves, remember as you follow where you may be led to regard discipline and vigilance as of the first importance, and to obey with alacrity the orders transmitted to you; as nothing contributes so much to the credit and safety of an army as the union of large bodies by a single discipline.'§

12. With this brief speech, dismissing the assembly, Archidamus first sent off Melesippus, son of Diacritus, a Spartan, to Athens, in case she should be more inclined to submit on seeing the Peloponnesians actually on the march. But the Athenians did not admit him into the city or to their assembly; Pericles having already carried a motion against admitting either herald or embassy from the Lacedæmonians after they had once marched out. The herald was accordingly sent away

---

*Archidamus rationally expects the Athenians to march out to defend their capital investments: olive trees, grape vines, farm-buildings with precious wood and iron farm equipment. He is wrong. Pericles encouraged the Athenians to burn the flammable resources themselves.

†Archidamus' claim about Athenian aspirations and aggression sounds hyperbolic here, but it echoes the Corinthians' earlier speech, conforms to the expeditions in Cyprus and Egypt, and pre-echoes Athenian motivations in Sicily.

‡The ripe appeal to ancestors, found in the mouths of all parties, is another patriotic trope, one that seems to suggest lack of more dependable resources.

§Peloponnesians emphasize their own discipline and Athenian individualism. Pericles, in his funeral oration later in this book, responds to such claims.

without an audience, and ordered to be beyond the frontier that same day; in future, if those who sent him had a proposition to make they must retire to their own territory before they despatched embassies to Athens. An escort was sent with Melesippus to prevent his holding communication with any one. When he reached the frontier and was just going to be dismissed, he departed with these words: 'This day will be the beginning of great misfortunes to the Hellenes.'* As soon as he arrived at the camp, and Archidamus learnt that the Athenians had still no thoughts of submitting, he at length began his march, and advanced with his army into their territory. Meanwhile the Bœotians, sending their contingent and cavalry to join the Peloponnesian expedition, went to Platæa with the remainder and laid waste the country.

13. While the Peloponnesians were still mustering at the Isthmus, or on the march before they invaded Attica, Pericles, son of Xanthippus, one of the ten generals of the Athenians, finding that the invasion was to take place, conceived the idea that Archidamus, who happened to be his friend,† might possibly pass by his estate without ravaging it. This he might do, either from a personal wish to oblige him, or acting under instructions from Lacedæmon for the purpose of creating a prejudice against him, as had been before attempted in the demand for the expulsion of the accursed family. He accordingly took the precaution of announcing to the Athenians in the assembly that, although Archidamus was his friend, yet this friendship should not extend to the detriment of the state, and that in case the enemy should make his houses and lands an exception to the rest and not pillage them, he at once gave them up to be public property, so that they should not bring him into suspicion. He also gave the citizens some advice on their present affairs in the same strain as before.‡ They were to prepare for the war, and to carry in their property from the country. They were not to go out to battle, but to come into the city and guard it, and get ready their fleet, in which their real strength lay.§

---

*Melesippus the herald has a ceremonial role in the commencement of hostilities. His final and brief words echo both Homer and Herodotus and reflect the Hellenic interest in causation.

†Hellenic aristocrats often had inherited family friendships (*xenia*). Pericles, attacked more than once for his family, anticipates another wily propaganda ploy by the enemy to avoid the hostility of his fellow Athenians.

‡Thucydides thinks the Athenians were too prone to change their minds (Cleon too will say so in book 3). Pericles shares this disapproval, and until his early death sticks to his policy of no appeasement or compromise.

§Pericles' dependence on the fleet is rational, but his readiness to see his fellow citizens lose all their property and ancestral possessions beyond the city walls is unrealistic. It made many, especially the wealthy with the most to lose, indefinitely bitter about the democratic war strategy.

They were also to keep a tight rein on their allies—the strength of Athens being derived from the money brought in by their payments, and success in war depending principally upon conduct and capital. Here they had no reason to despond. Apart from other sources of income, an average revenue of six hundred talents of silver was drawn from the tribute of the allies;* and there were still six thousand talents of coined silver in the Acropolis, out of nine thousand seven hundred that had once been there, from which the money had been taken for the porch of the Acropolis, the other public buildings, and for Potidæa.† This did not include the uncoined gold and silver in public and private offerings, the sacred vessels for the processions and games, the Median spoils, and similar resources to the amount of five hundred talents. To this he added the treasures of the other temples. These were by no means inconsiderable, and might fairly be used. Nay, if they were ever absolutely driven to it, they might take even the gold ornaments of Athene herself; for the statue contained forty talents of pure gold and it was all removable. This might be used for self-preservation, and must every penny of it be restored. Such was their financial position—surely a satisfactory one. Then they had an army of thirteen thousand heavy infantry, besides sixteen thousand more in the garrisons and on home duty at Athens.‡ This was at first the number of men on guard in the event of an invasion: it was composed of the oldest and youngest levies and the resident aliens who had heavy armour. The Phaleric wall ran for four

---

*Thucydides recognizes the importance of financial resources, but he says rather little about economics in general (and that little is rarely as specific as this—a very valuable datum). For example, he does not mention a sweeping decree requiring use of Athenian coinage (Fornara #97; compare Meiggs, *The Athenian Empire*) or decrees reassessing (Fornara #130) and tightening tribute collection (Fornara #98, #119, #133; compare Ste. Croix, *The Origins of the Peloponnesian War*). Kallett-Marx (*Money, Expense and Na al Power in Thucydides' History 1–5.24*) analyzes Thucydides' treatment of money and war-power.

†He adds 600 silver talents average revenue to 6,000 talents in coins. The Athenians had spent 3,700 talents on public buildings and the expensive siege of Potidaea. In addition, there are about 500 talents of various gold and silver objects that the state owns and can coin, if necessary, and other resources yet. An Attic talent (there were many other standards) of anything weighs approximately 57 pounds (25.86 kg). It is comprised of 60 minae, or 6,000 drachmae, or 36,000 obols. The current equivalent of the talent is hard to compute. A skilled Athenian workman (engineer, stonemason) at this time, the Acropolis building records inform us, earned a drachma each day, so perhaps 300 each year. By this reckoning, one talent would pay for a year twenty full-time skilled workmen (free or slave). Currently (2006 C.E.), a skilled American worker might earn from about $160–$180 each day or approximately $51,000 each year. Twenty workers would receive $1,020,000.

‡Statistics are rare in ancient historians, especially numbers for a city's entire fighting force.

miles, before it joined that round the city; and of this last nearly five had a guard, although part of it was left without one, viz. that between the Long Wall and the Phaleric. Then there were the Long Walls to Piræus, a distance of some four miles and a half, the outer of which was manned. Lastly, the circumference of Piræus with Munychia was nearly seven miles and a half; only half of this, however, was guarded. Pericles also showed them that they had twelve hundred horse including mounted archers, with sixteen hundred archers unmounted, and three hundred triremes fit for service.* Such were the resources of Athens in the different departments when the Peloponnesian invasion was impending and hostilities were being commenced. Pericles also urged his usual arguments for expecting a favourable issue to the war.

14. The Athenians listened to his advice, and began to carry in their wives and children from the country, and all their household furniture, even to the woodwork of their houses which they took down. Their sheep and cattle they sent over to Eubœa and the adjacent islands.† But they found it hard to move, as most of them had been always used to live in the country.

15. From very early times this had been more the case with the Athenians than with others. Under Cecrops and the first kings, down to the reign of Theseus,‡ Attica had always consisted of a number of independent townships, each with its own town-hall and magistrates. Except in times of danger the king at Athens was not consulted; in ordinary seasons they carried on their government and settled their affairs without his interference; sometimes even they waged war against him, as in the case of the Eleusinians with Eumolpus against Erechtheus. In Theseus, however, they had a king of equal intelligence and power; and one of the chief features in his organisation of the country was to abolish the council-chambers and magistrates of the petty cities, and to merge them in the single council-chamber and town-hall of the present capital. Individuals might still enjoy their private property just as before, but they were henceforth compelled to have only one political centre, viz. Athens; which thus counted all the inhabitants of Attica among her citizens, so that when Theseus

---

*Information on the walls, the cavalry, and the bowmen for long-range fighting is also useful for archaeologists and military historians. The point intends to prove how well equipped and manned the Athenians were.

†The islands of the Athenian confederacy were deemed safe from Peloponnesian attack. Euboea at the narrowest point (the swift channel Euripus) lies only 130 feet from the eastern mainland district Boeotia (map 5).

‡The legendary Theseus, killer of the Cretan Minotaur and seducer of Ariadne, was credited with being the father of his country, Attica, comprising villages (*demes*) and towns of which Athens was by far the largest.

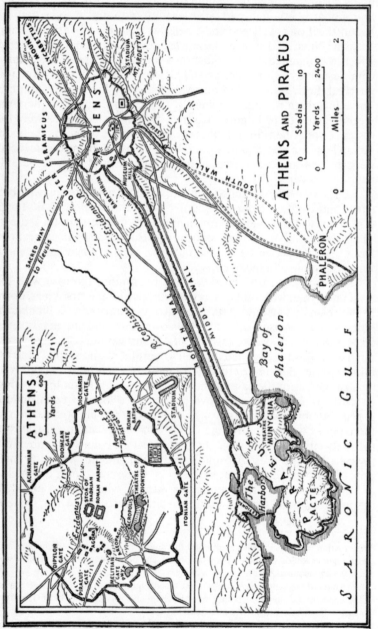

MAP 3. ATHENS AND PIRAEUS

died he left a great state behind him.* Indeed, from him dates the Synœcia, or Feast of Union; which is paid for by the state, and which the Athenians still keep in honour of the goddess. Before this the city consisted of the present citadel and the district beneath it looking rather towards the south.† This is shown by the fact that the temples of the other deities, besides that of Athene, are in the citadel; and even those that are outside it are mostly situated in this quarter of the city, as that of the Olympian Zeus, of the Pythian Apollo, of Earth, and of Dionysus in the Marshes, the same in whose honour the older Dionysia are to this day celebrated in the month of Anthesterion not only by the Athenians but also by their Ionian descendants.‡ There are also other ancient temples in this quarter. The fountain too, which, since the alteration made by the tyrants, has been called Enneacrounos, or Nine Pipes, but which, when the spring was open, went by the name of Callirhoe, or Fairwater, was in those days, from being so near, used for the most important offices.§ Indeed, the old fashion of using the water before marriage and for other sacred purposes is still kept up. Again, from their old residence in that quarter, the citadel is still known among Athenians as the *city*.

16. The Athenians thus long lived scattered over Attica in independent townships. Even after the centralisation of Theseus, old habit still prevailed; and from the early times down to the present war most Athenians still lived in the country with their families and households, and were consequently not at all inclined to move now, especially as they had only just restored their establishments after the Median invasion. Deep was their trouble and discontent at abandoning their houses and the hereditary temples of the ancient constitution, and at having to change their habits of life and to bid farewell to what each regarded as his native city.‖

17. When they arrived at Athens, though a few had houses of their own to go to, or could find an asylum with friends or relatives, by far

---

*Thucydides rarely credits myth with containing any history, but it suits his account of the growth of Attica to give Theseus credit for its unification (*synoikismos*).

†Athens now fills up the central Attic plain surrounded by low mountain ranges. From Mycenean times, the Acropolis was a fortified citadel, and, as at Troy and Mycenae, the village folk gathered their modest houses tightly around their central bastion.

‡Athens' theatrical festivals were cultural magnets and, like the Athenian 2004 Olympic games, sources of income for the local hospitality providers. The Ionian migrations of the eleventh and tenth centuries may have set out to the western coast of Turkey from Athenian ports. The Athenians, which claimed theirs was the metropolis of all the Ionian cities, celebrated in February/March the Dionysiac and Panionian Anthesteria festival.

§This public spring and fountain-house, to the north of the Acropolis on the south side of the Athenian agora, was favored for ritual ablutions (map 3).

‖Thucydides notes the local, parochial patriotism of the farmers of Attica.

the greater number had to take up their dwelling in the parts of the city that were not built over and in the temples and chapels of the heroes, except the Acropolis and the temple of the Eleusinian Demeter* and such other places as were always kept closed. The occupation of the plot of ground lying below the citadel called the Pelasgian† had been forbidden by a curse; and there was also an ominous fragment of a Pythian oracle which said—

> 'Leave the Pelasgian parcel desolate,
> Woe worth the day that men inhabit it!'

Yet this too was now built over in the necessity of the moment. And in my opinion, if the oracle proved true, it was in the opposite sense to what was expected.‡ For the misfortunes of the state did not arise from the unlawful occupation, but the necessity of the occupation from the war; and though the god did not mention this, he foresaw that it would be an evil day for Athens in which the plot came to be inhabited. Many also took up their quarters in the towers of the walls or wherever else they could. For when they were all come in, the city proved too small to hold them;§ though afterwards they divided the long walls and a great part of Piræus into lots and settled there. All this while great attention was being given to the war; the allies were being mustered, and an armament of a hundred ships equipped for Peloponnese. Such was the state of preparation at Athens.

18. Meanwhile the army of the Peloponnesians was advancing. The first town they came to in Attica was Œnoe, where they were to enter the country. Sitting down before it, they prepared to assault the wall with engines and otherwise. Œnoe, standing upon the Athenian and Bœotian border, was of course a walled town, and was used as a fortress by the Athenians in time of war.‖ So the Peloponnesians prepared for their assault, and wasted some valuable time before the place. This delay brought the gravest censure upon Archidamus. Even during the levying of the war he had gained credit for weakness and

---

*The Temple of Eleusinian Demeter, also in the Agora, has not been firmly located by the dedicated American excavators of the last seventy-five years.

†The Pelasgian area was probably located to the south of the Acropolis, near the later theater of Dionysus.

‡Thucydides, student of the sophists, twits superstitious souls who put their trust in oracles.

§Pericles miscalculated the ground suitable for habitation; the spread of the plague later this year multiplied the sufferings exponentially.

‖The Athenians built a chain of forts around the land edges of their territory of Attica. The ever-hostile Boeotians might attack outlying Attic communities on the shared frontier as they did their fellow Boeotians at Plataea.

Athenian sympathies by the half measures he had advocated; and after the army had assembled he had further injured himself in public estimation by his loitering at the Isthmus and the slowness with which the rest of the march had been conducted. But all this was as nothing to the delay at Œnoe. During this interval the Athenians were carrying in their property; and it was the belief of the Peloponnesians that a quick advance would have found everything still out, had it not been for his procrastination.* Such was the feeling of the army towards Archidamus during the siege. But he, it is said, expected that the Athenians would shrink from letting their land be wasted, and would make their submission while it was still uninjured; and this was why he waited.

19. But after he had assaulted Œnoe, and every possible attempt to take it had failed, as no herald came from Athens, he at last broke up his camp and invaded Attica. This was about eighty days after the Theban attempt upon Platæa, just in the middle of summer, when the grain was ripe, and Archidamus, son of Zeuxis, King of Lacedæmon, was in command. Encamping in Eleusis and the Thriasian plain, they began their ravages, and putting to flight some Athenian horse at a place called Rheiti, or the Brooks, they then advanced, keeping Mount Ægaleus on their right, through Cropia, until they reached Acharnæ, the largest of the Athenian demes or townships. Sitting down before it, they formed a camp there, and continued their ravages for a long while.

20. The reason why Archidamus remained in order of battle at Acharnæ during this incursion, instead of descending into the plain, is said to have been this. He hoped that the Athenians might possibly be tempted by the multitude of their youth and the unprecedented efficiency of their service to come out to battle and attempt to stop the devastation of their lands. Accordingly, as they had not met him at Eleusis or the Thriasian plain, he tried if they could be provoked to a sally by the spectacle of a camp at Acharnæ.† He thought the place itself a good position for encamping; and it seemed likely that such an important part of the state as the three thousand heavy infantry of the Acharnians would refuse to submit to the ruin of their property, and would force a battle on the rest of the citizens.‡ On the other

---

*Spartans, individually and corporately, were slow to act but hard to stop once they made up their minds. As the next sentence makes clear, Archidamus had a strategy, but it did not work.

†Acharnae was a large and populous *deme* north of central Athens (map 2), and an angry one, as one infers from Aristophanes' war comedy *Acharnians*. The play illustrates, in fact, a widely shared Athenian feeling toward the devastation of the residents' livelihoods, their farms and homesteads.

‡Pericles restrained the Athenians from fighting at Eleusis or the nearby Thriasian plain (map 2), but Archidamus thought that the 3,000 young Acharnian hoplites would not stand by while their properties suffered.

hand, should the Athenians not take the field during this incursion, he could then fearlessly ravage the plain in future invasions, and extend his advance up to the very walls of Athens. After the Acharnians had lost their own property they would be less willing to risk themselves for that of their neighbours; and so there would be division in the Athenian counsels. These were the motives of Archidamus for remaining at Acharnæ.

21. Meanwhile, as long as the army was at Eleusis and the Thriasian plain, hopes were still entertained of its not advancing any nearer. It was remembered that Pleistoanax, son of Pausanias, king of Lacedæmon, had invaded Attica with a Peloponnesian army fourteen years before, but had retreated without advancing farther than Eleusis and Thria, which indeed proved the cause of his exile from Sparta, as it was thought he had been bribed to retreat. But when they saw the army at Acharnæ,* barely seven miles from Athens, they lost all patience. The territory of Athens was being ravaged before the very eyes of the Athenians, a sight which the young men had never seen before and the old only in the Median wars; and it was naturally thought a grievous insult, and the determination was universal, especially among the young men, to sally forth and stop it. Knots were formed in the streets and engaged in hot discussion; for if the proposed sally was warmly recommended, it was also in some cases opposed. Oracles of the most various import were recited by the collectors, and found eager listeners in one or other of the disputants.† Foremost in pressing for the sally were the Acharnians, as constituting no small part of the army of the state, and as it was their land that was being ravaged. In short, the whole city was in a most excited state; Pericles was the object of general indignation; his previous counsels were totally forgotten; he was abused for not leading out the army which he commanded, and was made responsible for the whole of the public suffering.‡

22. He, meanwhile, seeing anger and infatuation just now in the ascendant, and confident of his wisdom in refusing a sally, would not call either assembly or meeting of the people, fearing the fatal results of a debate inspired by passion and not by prudence. Accordingly he addressed himself to the defence of the city, and kept it as quiet as

---

*Thucydides describes this anti-Periclean movement both to indicate the power of his personal authority and the limits of it (compare 2.65).

†Oracles, often ambiguous and never presumed to be self-evident, were good to argue with. Herodotus 7.141 reports more of them, most famously the Delphic "wooden wall" oracle delivered before the sea-battle of Salamis.

‡The power of the board of ten *strategoi* to call an assembly was significant but not absolute. Thucydides clearly was impressed with Pericles' ability to stand superior to mob psychology and popular feelings.

possible, though he constantly sent out cavalry to prevent raids on the lands near the city from flying parties of the enemy. There was a trifling affair at Phrygia between a squadron of the Athenian horse with the Thessalians and the Bœotian cavalry; in which the former had rather the best of it, until the heavy infantry advanced to the support of the Bœotians, when the Thessalians and Athenians were routed and lost a few men, whose bodies, however, were recovered the same day without a truce. The next day the Peloponnesians set up a trophy. Ancient alliance brought the Thessalians to the aid of Athens; those who came being the Larisæans, Pharsalians, Cranonians, Pyrasians, Gyrtonians, and Pheræans. The Larisæan commanders were Polymedes and Aristonus, two party leaders in Larisa; the Pharsalian general was Menon; each of the other cities had also its own commander.*

23. In the meantime the Peloponnesians, as the Athenians did not come out to engage them, broke up from Acharnæ and ravaged some of the demes† between Mount Parnes and Brilessus. While they were in Attica the Athenians sent off the hundred ships which they had been preparing round Peloponnese, with a thousand heavy infantry and four hundred archers on board, under the command of Carcinus, son of Xenotimus, Proteas, son of Epicles, and Socrates, son of Antigenes. This armament weighed anchor and started on its cruise, and the Peloponnesians, after remaining in Attica as long as their provisions lasted, retired through Bœotia by a different road to that by which they had entered. As they passed Oropus they ravaged the territory of Graea, which is held by the Oropians from Athens, and reaching Peloponnese broke up to their respective cities.

24. After they had retired the Athenians set guards by land and sea at the points at which they intended to have regular stations during the war. They also resolved to set apart a special fund of a thousand talents from the monies in the Acropolis. This was not to be spent, but the current expenses of the war were to be otherwise provided for. If any one should move or put to the vote a proposition for using the money for any purpose whatever except that of defending the city in the event of the enemy bringing a fleet to make an attack by sea, it should be a capital offence.‡ With this sum of money they also set

---

*Thessaly was good, fertile horse-raising country (map 1). The Athenians had real allies as well as pseudo-allies or subjects. In mainland territories, it was easier (or only possible) for them to support one side, the popular one, than to rule by means of Athenian magistrates and troops.

†The Peloponnesians are trying to spread pain and suffering in the community, perhaps in hopes that a revolutionary movement would seize the Athenians, something that did happen nearly twenty years later.

‡The sovereign assembly (*ecclesia*) could make or break any such rules that it wished. The goal here was to establish an untouchable reserve.

aside a special fleet of one hundred galleys, the best ships of each year, with their captains. None of these were to be used except with the money and against the same peril, should such peril arise.

25. Meanwhile the Athenians in the hundred ships round Peloponnese, reinforced by a Corcyræan squadron of fifty vessels and some others of the allies in those parts, cruised about the coasts and ravaged the country. Among other places they landed in Laconia and made an assault upon Methone; there being no garrison in the place, and the wall being weak. But it so happened that Brasidas, son of Tellis, a Spartan, was in command of a guard for the defence of the district.* Hearing of the attack, he hurried with a hundred heavy infantry to the assistance of the besieged, and dashing through the army of the Athenians, which was scattered over the country and had its attention turned to the wall, threw himself into Methone. He lost a few men in making good his entrance, but saved the place and won the thanks of Sparta by his exploit, being thus the first officer who obtained this notice during the war. The Athenians at once weighed anchor and continued their cruise. Touching at Pheia in Elis, they ravaged the country for two days and defeated a picked force of three hundred men that had come from the vale of Elis and the immediate neighbourhood to the rescue. But a stiff squall came down upon them, and not liking to face it in a place where there was no harbour, most of them got on board their ships, and doubling Point Ichthys sailed into the port of Pheia. In the meantime the Messenians, and some others who could not get on board, marched over by land and took Pheia. The fleet afterwards sailed round and picked them up and then put to sea; Pheia being evacuated, as the main army of the Eleans had now come up. The Athenians continued their cruise, and ravaged other places on the coast.

26. About the same time the Athenians sent thirty ships to cruise round Locris and also to guard Eubœa; Cleopompus, son of Clinias, being in command. Making descents from the fleet he ravaged certain places on the sea-coast, and captured Thronium and took hostages from it. He also defeated at Alope the Locrians that had assembled to resist him.

27. During the summer the Athenians also expelled the Æginetans with their wives and children from Ægina, on the ground of their having been the chief agents in bringing the war upon them. Besides, Ægina lies so near Peloponnese, that it seemed safer to send colonists of their own to hold it, and shortly afterwards the settlers were sent

---

*Brasidas will be the best general the Spartans field in the course of Thucydides' work. Toward the end of the war, Lysander (see Plutarch's biography) will match him in strategy, speed, and ruthless exploitation of political and military advantages.

out. The banished Æginetans found an asylum in Thyrea, which was given to them by Lacedæmon, not only on account of her quarrel with Athens, but also because the Æginetans had laid her under obligations at the time of the earthquake and the revolt of the Helots. The territory of Thyrea is on the frontier of Argolis and Laconia, reaching down to the sea. Those of the Æginetans who did not settle here were scattered over the rest of Hellas.

28. The same summer, at the beginning of a new lunar month, the only time by the way at which it appears possible, the sun was eclipsed after noon.* After it had assumed the form of a crescent and some of the stars had come out, it returned to its natural shape.

29. During the same summer Nymphodorus, son of Pythes, an Abderite, whose sister Sitalces had married, was made their *Proxenus* by the Athenians and sent for to Athens. They had hitherto considered him their enemy; but he had great influence with Sitalces, and they wished this prince to become their ally. Sitalces was the son of Teres and king of the Thracians. Teres, the father of Sitalces, was the first to establish the great kingdom of the Odrysians on a scale quite unknown to the rest of Thrace, a large portion of the Thracians being independent. This Teres is in no way related to Tereus who married Pandion's daughter Procne from Athens; nor indeed did they belong to the same part of Thrace.† Tereus lived in Daulis, part of what is now called Phocis, but which at that time was inhabited by Thracians. It was in this land that the women perpetrated the outrage upon Itys; and many of the poets when they mention the nightingale call it the Daulian bird. Besides, Pandion in contracting an alliance for his daughter would consider the advantages of mutual assistance, and would naturally prefer a match at the above moderate distance to the journey of many days which separates Athens from the Odrysians. Again the names are different; and this Teres was king of the Odrysians, the first by the way who attained to any power. Sitalces, his son, was now sought as an ally by the Athenians, who desired his aid in the reduction of the Thracian towns and of Perdiccas. Coming to

---

*Thucydides, like Socrates, spends little time explaining natural phenomena (compared to predecessors such as Hecataeus and Herodotus), but he will include both a phenomenon with political consequences (such as the eclipse that stalled the Athenian pull-out from Sicily, 7.50) or an occasional note such as this (1.23; 4.52; compare Pearson, "Thucydides and the Geographical Tradition").

†Similarly, Thucydides will include an occasional mythological reference, perhaps based on mythographic texts, such as this one describing the original settlers of Thrace (map 9) and the royal family's genealogical pretensions. The Athenians wanted Thracian allies to occupy or defeat the Greek colonies connected to Corinth or other Peloponnesian cities. (Athenian agreements with Methone and Perdiccas are reported in Fornara #128.)

Athens, Nymphodorus concluded the alliance with Sitalces and made his son Sadocus an Athenian citizen, and promised to finish the war in Thrace by persuading Sitalces to send the Athenians a force of Thracian horse and light infantry. He also reconciled them with Perdiccas, and induced them to restore Therme to him; upon which Perdiccas at once joined the Athenians and Phormio in an expedition against the Chalcidians. Thus Sitalces, son of Teres, king of the Thracians, and Perdiccas, son of Alexander, king of the Macedonians, became allies of Athens.*

30. Meanwhile the Athenians in the hundred vessels were still cruising round Peloponnese. After taking Sollium, a town belonging to Corinth, and presenting the city and territory to the Acarnanians of Palaira, they stormed Astacus, expelled its tyrant Evarchus, and gained the place for their confederacy. Next they sailed to the island of Cephallenia and brought it over without using force. Cephallenia lies off Acarnania and Leucas, and consists of four states, the Paleans, Cranians, Samæans, and Pronæans. Not long afterwards the fleet returned to Athens.

31. Towards the autumn of this year the Athenians invaded the Megarid with their whole levy, resident aliens† included, under the command of Pericles, son of Xanthippus. The Athenians in the hundred ships round Peloponnese on their journey home had just reached Ægina, and hearing that the citizens at home were in full force at Megara, now sailed over and joined them. This was without doubt the largest army of Athenians ever assembled, the state being still in the flower of her strength and yet unvisited by the plague.‡ Full ten thousand heavy infantry were in the field, all Athenian citizens, besides the three thousand before Potidæa. Then the resident aliens who joined in the incursion were at least three thousand strong; besides which there was a multitude of light troops.§ They ravaged the greater part of the territory, and then retired. Other incursions into the Megarid were afterwards made by the Athenians annually during

---

*The semi-barbarous kingdoms of the northern Aegean were the source of silver, timber, and hides, as well as manpower. This double alliance was a great coup.

†Resident aliens (*metics*) were landed immigrants; they generally had no or limited legal rights (needing a *proxenos*, or legal representative, to appear in court) and could not own real estate in the *polis* of their choice. Plato's *Republic* takes place at the home of Cephalus, a *metic* from Syracuse, whose sons include Lysias, later one of the canonical ten Attic orators (but still a *metic*).

‡Thucydides refers forward rarely, here to a decisive setback for the Athenian war strategy.

§Light troops, unlike hoplites, had little armor and fought at a distance from the enemy with slings, bow and arrows, and throwing spears. They often fought around the edges of a hoplite engagement.

the war, sometimes only with cavalry, sometimes with all their forces. This went on until the capture of Nisæa.*

32. Atalanta also, the desert island off the Opuntian coast, was towards the end of this summer converted into a fortified post by the Athenians, in order to prevent privateers issuing from Opus and the rest of Locris and plundering Eubœa. Such were the events of this summer after the return of the Peloponnesians from Attica.

33. In the ensuing winter the Acarnanian Evarchus, wishing to return to Astacus, persuaded the Corinthians to sail over with forty ships and fifteen hundred heavy infantry and restore him; himself also hiring some mercenaries.† In command of the force were Euphamidas, son of Aristonymus, Timoxenus, son of Timocrates, and Eumachus, son of Chrysis, who sailed over and restored him, and after failing in an attempt on some places on the Acarnanian coast which they were desirous of gaining, began their voyage home. Coasting along shore they touched at Cephallenia and made a descent on the Cranian territory, and losing some men by the treachery of the Cranians, who fell suddenly upon them after having agreed to treat, put to sea somewhat hurriedly and returned home.

34. In the same winter the Athenians gave a funeral at the public cost to those who had first fallen in this war. It was a custom of their ancestors, and the manner of it is as follows.‡ Three days before the ceremony, the bones of the dead are laid out in a tent which has been erected; and their friends bring to their relatives such offerings as they please. In the funeral procession cypress coffins are borne in cars, one for each tribe;§ the bones of the deceased being placed in the coffin of their tribe. Among these is carried one empty bier decked for the missing, that is, for those whose bodies could not be recovered. Any citizen or stranger who pleases, joins in the procession: and the female relatives are there to wail at the burial. The dead are laid in the public sepulchre in the most beautiful suburb of the city, in which

---

*Nisaea was one port of Megara, as Piraeus was the main port of Athens (map 2). Megara was a trading town, so this seizure crippled her economy.

†Thucydides reports many smaller wars in which local rivals asked for help from the main combatants. Evarchus is a tin-horn dictator whom the Athenians threw out of Astacus, but three chapters later the Corinthians restore him. And of him we hear no more.

‡Thucydides eschews Herodotus' ethnography and self-glorifying oratory, but here he limns the scene for one of three speeches by Pericles, this the *epitaphios*, or funeral oration (in patriotic mode) in which he explains what the Athenians are or should be fighting for.

§The Athenians of the fifth century had ten tribes, each with an eponymous hero. These tribes were useful units for organization of the government (the *prytanes* [see note on p. 320] of the *boule*, or political council) and for calling up drafted citizens to serve as soldiers.

those who fall in war are always buried;* with the exception of those
slain at Marathon, who for their singular and extraordinary valour
were interred on the spot where they fell.† After the bodies have been
laid in the earth, a man chosen by the state, of approved wisdom and
eminent reputation, pronounces over them an appropriate panegyric;
after which all retire. Such is the manner of the burying; and throughout the whole of the war, whenever the occasion arose, the established custom was observed. Meanwhile these were the first that had
fallen, and Pericles, Son of Xanthippus, was chosen to pronounce
their eulogy. When the proper time arrived, he advanced from the
sepulchre to an elevated platform in order to be heard by as many of
the crowd as possible, and spoke as follows:—

35. 'Most of my predecessors in this place have commended him
who made this speech part of the law, telling us that it is well that it
should be delivered at the burial of those who fall in battle. For myself, I should have thought that the worth which had displayed itself
in deeds, would be sufficiently rewarded by honours also shown by
deeds; such as you now see in this funeral prepared at the people's
cost.‡ And I could have wished that the reputations of many brave
men were not to be imperilled in the mouth of a single individual,
to stand or fall according as he spoke well or ill. For it is hard to
speak properly upon a subject where it is even difficult to convince
your hearers that you are speaking the truth. On the one hand, the
friend who is familiar with every fact of the story, may think that
some point has not been set forth with that fulness which he wishes
and knows it to deserve; on the other, he who is a stranger to the
matter may be led by envy to suspect exaggeration if he hears anything above his own nature.§ For men can endure to hear others
praised only so long as they can severally persuade themselves of
their own ability to equal the actions recounted: when this point is
passed, envy comes in and with it incredulity. However, since our
ancestors have stamped this custom with their approval, it becomes

---

*This is the part of the Ceramicus (Potters' Quarter) outside the city walls, excavated
largely by German archaeologists in the twentieth century. In 1997 the Greek Archaeological Service excavated a state burial for soldiers here.

†A mound at Marathon (map 2), excavated by Schliemann and others in the late nineteenth century and still visible, held the bodies of the Athenian dead. Thucydides marks
the exception that proves the rule.

‡Pericles' speech features the highly elaborated style of Gorgias, a Sicilian sophist who
ornamented his words in rhythmic and rhyming ways as well as with antithesis (see Finley, *Thucydides*). One favorite antithesis of Thucydides and his speaker Pericles here is
"word" and "deed" (*logos* and *ergon*; compare Parry, *Logos and Ergon in Thucydides*).

§"On the one hand, . . . on the other" articulates antitheses in Greek literature of all
periods. The contrast here between the unsatisfied and the suspicious listener is brilliantly put.

my duty to obey the law and to try to satisfy your several wishes and opinions as best I may.

36. 'I shall begin with our ancestors:* it is both just and proper that they should have the honour of the first mention on an occasion like the present. They dwelt in the country without break in the succession from generation to generation, and handed it down free to the present time by their valour.† And if our more remote ancestors deserve praise, much more do our own fathers, who added to their inheritance the empire which we now possess, and spared no pains to be able to leave their acquisitions to us of the present generation. Lastly, there are few parts of our dominions that have not been augmented by those of us here, who are still more or less in the vigour of life; while the mother country has been furnished by us with everything that can enable her to depend on her own resources whether for war or for peace. That part of our history which tells of the military achievements which gave us our several possessions, or of the ready valour with which either we or our fathers stemmed the tide of Hellenic or foreign aggression, is a theme too familiar to my hearers for me to dilate on, and I shall therefore pass it by.‡ But what was the road by which we reached our position, what the form of government under which our greatness grew, what the national habits out of which it sprang; these are questions which I may try to solve before I proceed to my panegyric upon these men; since I think this to be a subject upon which on the present occasion a speaker may properly dwell, and to which the whole assemblage, whether citizens or foreigners,§ may listen with advantage.

37. 'Our constitution does not copy the laws of neighbouring states; we are rather a pattern to others than imitators ourselves.‖ Its administration favours the many instead of the few; this is why it is called a democracy. If we look to the laws, they afford equal justice to all in their private differences; if to social standing, advancement in

---

*Thucydides employs the *topos* (commonplace) of starting from the ancestors—only to undercut it. Pericles is proud of his father's and of his own generation.

†The Athenians claimed to be autochthonous, sprung from the land and not immigrants. They were also proud of their autonomy.

‡Preterition (the rhetorical ploy of telling people what you won't tell them) is both a literary device but also homage to Herodotus, who had presented the story of the Persian invasions and other internecine wars.

§Pericles mentions the openness of Athenian rituals; the contrast to the xenophobia of the Spartans, implicit here, is later made explicit.

‖The Athenian democracy was *sui generis*, first and alone of its kind. Most contemporary and later regimes and societies considered it, as Alcibiades says at Sparta (6.89), "an acknowledged folly." A contemporary, anonymous critic, now called "the Old Oligarch," summarizes in his own words the aristocratic traditionalist's objections to egalitarian Athens (Fornara #107).

public life falls to reputation for capacity, class considerations not being allowed to interfere with merit; nor again does poverty bar the way, if a man is able to serve the state, he is not hindered by the obscurity of his condition. The freedom which we enjoy in our government extends also to our ordinary life. There, far from exercising a jealous surveillance over each other,* we do not feel called upon to be angry with our neighbour for doing what he likes, or even to indulge in those injurious looks which cannot fail to be offensive, although they inflict no positive penalty.† But all this ease in our private relations does not make us lawless as citizens. Against this fear is our chief safeguard, teaching us to obey the magistrates and the laws, particularly such as regard the protection of the injured, whether they are actually on the statute book,‡ or belong to that code which, although unwritten,§ yet cannot be broken without acknowledged disgrace.

38. 'Further, we provide plenty of means for the mind to refresh itself from business. We celebrate games and sacrifices all the year round, and the elegance of our private establishments forms a daily source of pleasure and helps to banish the spleen;‖ while the magnitude of our city draws the produce of the world into our harbour, so that to the Athenian the fruits of other countries are as familiar a luxury as those of his own.

39. 'If we turn to our military policy, there also we differ from our antagonists. We throw open our city to the world, and never by alien acts exclude foreigners from any opportunity of learning or observing, although the eyes of an enemy may occasionally profit by our liberality;# trusting less in system and policy than to the native spirit of our citizens; while in education, where our rivals from their very cra-

---

*Pericles praises *eleutheria*, freedom from constraints, in contrast here not only to the militarized Spartiate society but also to most other rigid Greek communities.

†Pericles is sensitive to non-verbal communications. Spartans silently shunned deviant members of their community—for instance, the hapless sole survivor of Thermopylae.

‡The Athenians were unusual in generally engraving laws on stone where all could see and quote them.

§Pericles distinguishes positive pieces of legislation from traditional mores, some of which, although unwritten (see Ostwald, *From Popular So ereignty to the So ereignty of Law*), are more powerful than statutes.

‖Athenian public entertainments and predominantly secular educational events had no parallel in the Hellenic world. The elegance of private homes is a more surprising claim, since Athenian houses were generally small and dark (by Roman or American standards, at least).

#Athens' open society permitted foreigners to visit nearly every nook and cranny. The Spartans, on the contrary, practiced *xenelasia* (expulsion of foreigners), and they declared war on the helots every year, in order to kill them without incurring blood pollution for homicide.

dles by a painful discipline seek after manliness, at Athens we live exactly as we please, and yet are just as ready to encounter every legitimate danger. In proof of this it may be noticed that the Lacedæmonians do not invade our country alone, but bring with them all their confederates; while we Athenians advance unsupported into the territory of a neighbour, and fighting upon a foreign soil usually vanquish with ease men who are defending their homes. Our united force was never yet encountered by any enemy, because we have at once to attend to our navy and to despatch our citizens by land upon a hundred different services; so that, wherever they engage with some such fraction of our strength, a success against a detachment is magnified into a victory over the nation, and a defeat into a reverse suffered at the hands of our entire people. And yet if with habits not of labour but of ease, and courage not of art but of nature, we are still willing to encounter danger, we have the double advantage of escaping the experience of hardships in anticipation and of facing them in the hour of need as fearlessly as those who are never free from them.

'Nor are these the only points in which our city is worthy of admiration.

40. 'We cultivate refinement without extravagance and knowledge without effeminacy;* wealth we employ more for use than for show, and place the real disgrace of poverty not in owning to the fact but in declining the struggle against it. Our public men have, besides politics, their private affairs to attend to, and our ordinary citizens, though occupied with the pursuits of industry, are still fair judges of public matters;† for, unlike any other nation, regarding him who takes no part in these duties not as unambitious but as useless,‡ we Athenians are able to judge at all events if we cannot originate, and instead of looking on discussion as a stumbling-block in the way of action, we think it an indispensable preliminary to any wise action at all. Again, in our enterprises we present the singular spectacle of daring and deliberation, each carried to its highest point, and both united in the same persons; although usually decision is the fruit of ignorance, hesitation of reflexion. But the palm of courage will surely be adjudged most justly to those, who best know the difference between hardship and pleasure and yet are never tempted to shrink from danger. In generosity

---

*Athenian artistic accomplishments were unsurpassed; Athens was the center of late-fifth-century aesthetic and intellectual activities (see Osborne, *Archaic and Classical Greek Art*). Athenians saw nothing unmanly in song, dance, literature, astronomy, scientific debates, etc.

†Athenian citizens had money-earning occupations, but they also were the sovereign authority for the passage of laws and declarations of war, and judges in court cases.

‡The Greek word *idiotes* (a "private person") spawned our English "idiot." The person not involved in public business was in a private world, "out of it."

we are equally singular, acquiring our friends by conferring, not by receiving, favours. Yet, of course, the doer of the favour is the firmer friend of the two, in order by continued kindness to keep the recipient in his debt; while the debtor feels less keenly from the very consciousness that the return he makes will be a payment, not a free gift.* And it is only the Athenians who, fearless of consequences, confer their benefits not from calculations of expediency, but in the confidence of liberality.

41. 'In short, I say that as a city we are the school of Hellas;† while I doubt if the world can produce a man, who where he has only himself to depend upon, is equal to so many emergencies, and graced by so happy a versatility as the Athenian. And that this is no mere boast thrown out for the occasion, but plain matter of fact, the power of the state acquired by these habits proves. For Athens alone of her contemporaries is found when tested to be greater than her reputation, and alone gives no occasion to her assailants to blush at the antagonist by whom they have been worsted, or to her subjects‡ to question her title by merit to rule. Rather, the admiration of the present and succeeding ages will be ours, since we have not left our power without witness, but have shown it by mighty proofs; and far from needing a Homer for our panegyrist,§ or other of his craft whose verses might charm for the moment only for the impression which they gave to melt at the touch of fact, we have forced every sea and land to be the highway of our daring, and everywhere, whether for harm or for good,‖ have left imperishable monuments behind us. Such is the Athens for which these men, in the assertion of their resolve not to lose her, nobly fought and died; and well may every one of their survivors be ready to suffer in her cause.

42. 'Indeed if I have dwelt at some length upon the character of our country, it has been to show that our stake in the struggle is not the same as theirs who have no such blessings to lose, and also that the panegyric of the men over whom I am now speaking might be by

---

*Thucydides here, like Machiavelli, notes that giving a gift entails owning a debt, while receiving another's largesse puts one in debt.

†Perhaps better translated as "education of Hellas," meaning that all Greece learns from Athens' experiments and achievements.

‡Pericles' vaunt suggests that it is an honor to be Athens' vassal. Not all the foreigners in the public burial ceremony's audience would share this view.

§Thucydides and Pericles use the exaggerations of Homer, standing for poets in general, as a foil for their factual claims.

‖Some critics doubt that any panegyrist (which Pericles certainly is here) would mention "imperishable monuments of harm." Pericles and then Cleon, aping him, describe Athens' empire as a "tyranny," however. Thucydides objects to the abuse of meaning, the epidemic of euphemisms, found in later Peloponnesian War politics (see especially 3.82–84).

definite proofs established. That panegyric is now in a great measure complete; for the Athens that I have celebrated is only what the heroism of these and their like have made her, men whose fame, unlike that of most Hellenes, will be found to be only commensurate with their deserts. And if a test of worth be wanted, it is to be found in their closing scene, and this not only in the cases in which it set the final seal upon their merit, but also in those in which it gave the first intimation of their having any.* For there is justice in the claim that stedfastness in his country's battles should be as a cloak to cover a man's other imperfections; since the good action has blotted out the bad, and his merit as a citizen more than outweighed his demerits as an individual. But none of these allowed either wealth with its prospect of future enjoyment to unnerve his spirit, or poverty with its hope of a day of freedom and riches to tempt him to shrink from danger. No, holding that vengeance upon their enemies was more to be desired than any personal blessings, and reckoning this to be the most glorious of hazards, they joyfully determined to accept the risk, to make sure of their vengeance and to let their wishes wait; and while committing to hope the uncertainty of final success, in the business before them they thought fit to act boldly and trust in themselves. Thus choosing to die resisting, rather than to live submitting,† they fled only from dishonour, but met danger face to face, and after one brief moment, while at the summit of their fortune, escaped, not from their fear, but from their glory.

43. 'So died these men as became Athenians. You, their survivors, must determine to have as unfaltering a resolution in the field, though you may pray that it may have a happier issue. And not contented with ideas derived only from words of the advantages which are bound up with the defence of your country, though these would furnish a valuable text to a speaker even before an audience so alive to them as the present, you must yourselves realise the power of Athens, and feed your eyes upon her from day to day, till love of her fills your hearts;‡ and then when all her greatness

---

*Pericles' antithesis contrasts those men who died after gaining military glory to those who died before any civic achievement, with nothing to their credit. This personal life-sacrifice for the state makes up for all prior errors or lack of achievement.

†Crawley's translation nicely captures the elegant Gorgianic oppositions of the original Greek.

‡Pericles' erotic images reinforce a political credo (compare Fornara #74), one startling novelty of this difficult but rewarding composition. We don't know how close the historian's words hew to the speech the politician actually gave, a problem discussed in the introduction. For example, Thucydides' Pericles only obliquely refers to the great architectural monuments on the Athenian acropolis, the ones that tourists still dutifully visit the Nike temple, the Propylaea gateway, and the Parthenon (both temple and state treasury; on these structures, see Fornara #93, #118, #120; Camp, pp. 74–137; map 3, insert).

shall break upon you, you must reflect that it was by courage, sense of duty, and a keen feeling of honour in action that men were enabled to win all this, and that no personal failure in an enterprise could make them consent to deprive their country of their valour, but they laid it at her feet as the most glorious contribution that they could offer. For this offering of their lives made in common by them all they each of them individually received that renown which never grows old, and for a sepulchre, not so much that in which their bones have been deposited, but that noblest of shrines wherein their glory is laid up to be eternally remembered upon every occasion on which deed or story shall call for its commemoration. For heroes have the whole earth for their tomb;* and in lands far from their own, where the column with its epitaph declares it, there is enshrined in every breast a record unwritten with no tablet to preserve it, except that of the heart. These take as your model, and judging happiness to be the fruit of freedom and freedom of valour, never decline the dangers of war. For it is not the miserable that would most justly be unsparing of their lives; these have nothing to hope for: it is rather they to whom continued life may bring reverses as yet unknown, and to whom a fall, if it came, would be most tremendous in its consequences. And surely, to a man of spirit, the degradation of cowardice must be immeasurably more grievous than the unfelt death which strikes him in the midst of his strength and patriotism!

44. 'Comfort, therefore, not condolence, is what I have to offer to the parents of the dead who may be here. Numberless are the chances to which, as they know, the life of man is subject; but fortunate indeed are they who draw for their lot a death so glorious as that which has caused your mourning, and to whom life has been so exactly measured as to terminate in the happiness in which it has been passed. Still I know that this is a hard saying,† especially when those are in question of whom you will constantly be reminded by seeing in the homes of others blessings of which once you also boasted: for grief is felt not so much for the want of what we have never known, as for the loss of that to which we have been long accustomed. Yet you who are still of an age to beget children must bear up in the hope of having others in their stead; not only will they help you to forget those whom you have lost, but will be to the state at once a reinforcement and a security; for never can a fair or just pol-

---

*The hyperbole here honors the dead and comforts the survivors. (Fornara #78 translates an earlier example of an Athenian casualty list.)

†Pericles acknowledges that his comfort will be cold to some of the bereaved, but he has used an emotional moment to make a rational case.

icy be expected of the citizen who does not, like his fellows, bring to the decision the interests and apprehensions of a father.* While those of you who have passed your prime must congratulate yourselves with the thought that the best part of your life was fortunate, and that the brief span that remains will be cheered by the fame of the departed. For it is only the love of honour that never grows old; and honour it is, not gain, as some would have it, that rejoices the heart of age and helplessness.

45. 'Turning to the sons or brothers of the dead, I see an arduous struggle before you. When a man is gone, all are wont to praise him, and should your merit be ever so transcendent, you will still find it difficult not merely to overtake, but even to approach their renown. The living have envy to contend with, while those who are no longer in our path are honoured with a goodwill into which rivalry does not enter. On the other hand, if I must say anything on the subject of female excellence to those of you who will not be in widowhood, it will be all comprised in this brief exhortation. Great will be your glory in not falling short of your natural character; and greatest will be hers who is least talked of among the men whether for good or for bad.†

46. 'My task is now finished. I have performed it to the best of my ability, and in word, at least, the requirements of the law are now satisfied. If deeds be in question, those who are here interred have received part of their honours already, and for the rest, their children will be brought up till manhood at the public expense:‡ the state thus offers a valuable prize, as the garland of victory in this race of valour, for the reward both of those who have fallen and their survivors. And where the rewards for merit are greatest, there are found the best citizens.

'And now that you have brought to a close your lamentations for your relatives, you may depart.'

---

*All Athenian males from the age of eighteen to sixty were liable for military duty. Pericles here declares that those who vote on going to war should be those who have a stake in the men who risk their lives in the military.

†This infamous dismissal of women reflects an unexpectedly traditional view held in patriarchal Athens, though in a speech over war casualties, it might be less surprising than in a sophist's discussion group. While the statement reflects the idea that a house's honor depends on its women's social invisibility (Loraux, *The In ention of Athens*), most Athenian women were not so secluded.

‡The Athenians took care of war orphans with a stipend. Many Athenian families had only one or two children.

Second Year of the War — The Plague at Athens — Position
and Policy of Pericles — Fall of Potidœa

47. Such was the funeral that took place during this winter, with which the first year of the war came to an end.* In the first days of summer the Lacedæmonians and their allies, with two-thirds of their forces as before, invaded Attica, under the command of Archidamus, son of Zeuxidamus, king of Lacedæmon, and sat down and laid waste the country. Not many days after their arrival in Attica the plague first began to show itself among the Athenians. It was said that it had broken out in many places previously in the neighbourhood of Lemnos and elsewhere; but a pestilence of such extent and mortality was nowhere remembered. Neither were the physicians† at first of any service, ignorant as they were of the proper way to treat it, but they died themselves the most thickly, as they visited the sick most often; nor did any other human art succeed any better. Supplications in the temples, divinations, and so forth were found equally futile,‡ till the overwhelming nature of the disaster at last put a stop to them altogether.

48. It first began, it is said, in the parts of Ethiopia above Egypt, and thence descended into Egypt and Libya and into most of the king's country. Suddenly falling upon Athens, it first attacked§ the population in Piræus,—which was the occasion of their saying that the Peloponnesians had poisoned the reservoirs, there being as yet no wells there—and afterwards appeared in the upper city, when the deaths became much more frequent. All speculation as to its origin and its causes, if causes can be found adequate to produce so great a disturbance, I leave to other writers, whether lay or professional;‖ for my-

---

*Thucydides marks the end of the first year. We have advanced, however, through almost one-fourth of the extant text, indicating Thucydides' interest in causation. There is no chapter heading or other break in the text between the proud funeral oration and the description of the humbling and devastating plague of 430. This juxtaposition or collocation of opposites is a characteristic method of the "poetic" historian. We shall meet it again, for instance, in the seemingly pointless Athenian destruction of tiny Melos and the immediately subsequent pride and destruction of the Athenian expeditionary armament in Sicily.

†Medical and historical scholars have variously identified this affliction as typhus, typhoid, smallpox, and other diseases that have disappeared or mutated into another form with other symptoms. Thucydides describes the disease in detail, much as the contemporary Hippocratic physicians would have, but he devotes more space to the social and political consequences, as a historian must do. (See Cochrane, *Thucydides and the Science of History*, and Hornblower's *Commentary* for hypotheses.)

‡Human and divine arts were equally ineffective. Thucydides marks the decline in religious belief and the growth in pessimism.

§The description of the path of the disease shows an awareness of contagion.

‖Thucydides, like Socrates, prefers to discuss what humans can know rather than speculate on issues beyond verification or logical refutation.

self, I shall simply set down its nature, and explain the symptoms by which perhaps it may be recognised by the student, if it should ever break out again. This I can the better do, as I had the disease myself,* and watched its operation in the case of others.

49. That year then is admitted to have been otherwise unprecedentedly free from sickness; and such few cases as occurred all eventuated in this. As a rule, however, there was no ostensible cause; but people in good health were all of a sudden attacked by violent heats in the head, and redness and inflammation in the eyes, the inward parts, such as the throat or tongue, becoming bloody and emitting an unnatural and fetid breath. These symptoms were followed by sneezing and hoarseness, after which the pain soon reached the chest, and produced a hard cough.† When it fixed in the stomach, it upset it; and discharges of bile of every kind named by physicians ensued, accompanied by very great distress. In most cases also an ineffectual retching followed, producing violent spasms, which in some cases ceased soon after, in others much later. Externally the body was not very hot to the touch, nor pale in its appearance, but reddish, livid, and breaking out into small pustules and ulcers. But internally it burned so that the patient could not bear to have on him clothing or linen even of the very lightest description; or indeed to be otherwise than stark naked. What they would have liked best would have been to throw themselves into cold water; as indeed was done by some of the neglected sick, who plunged into the rain-tanks in their agonies of unquenchable thirst; though it made no difference whether they drank little or much. Besides this, the miserable feeling of not being able to rest or sleep never ceased to torment them. The body meanwhile did not waste away so long as the distemper was at its height, but held out to a marvel against its ravages; so that when they succumbed, as in most cases, on the seventh or eighth day to the internal inflammation, they had still some strength in them.‡ But if they passed this stage, and the disease descended further into the bowels, inducing a violent ulceration there accompanied by severe diarrhœa, this brought on a weakness which was generally fatal. For the disorder first settled in the head, ran its course from thence through the whole of the body, and even where it did not prove mortal, it still left its mark on the extremities; for it settled in the privy parts, the fingers and the toes, and

---

*The author provides a rare personal reference to himself, generally noted only in the third person. This fact enables us to place him in Athens at the time of the plague. Thucydides again mentions "usefulness" as a criterion by which to judge his work.

†Fifth-century Hippocratic essays on medicine such as *Epidemics* provide similar diagnoses.

‡Thucydides reports the sequence of parts of the body affected and the length of the course of the disease.

many escaped with the loss of these, some too with that of their eyes. Others again were seized with an entire loss of memory on their first recovery, and did not know either themselves or their friends.

50. But while the nature of the distemper was such as to baffle all description, and its attacks almost too grievous for human nature to endure, it was still in the following circumstance that its difference from all ordinary disorders was most clearly shown. All the birds and beasts that prey upon human bodies, either abstained from touching them (though there were many lying unburied), or died after tasting them. In proof of this, it was noticed that birds of this kind actually disappeared; they were not about the bodies, or indeed to be seen at all. But of course the effects which I have mentioned could best be studied in a domestic animal like the dog.

51. Such then, if we pass over the varieties of particular cases, which were many and peculiar, were the general features of the distemper.* Meanwhile the town enjoyed an immunity from all the ordinary disorders; or if any case occurred, it ended in this. Some died in neglect, others in the midst of every attention. No remedy was found that could be used as a specific; for what did good in one case, did harm in another. Strong and weak constitutions proved equally incapable of resistance, all alike being swept away, although dieted† with the utmost precaution. By far the most terrible feature in the malady was the dejection which ensued when any one felt himself sickening, for the despair‡ into which they instantly fell took away their power of resistance, and left them a much easier prey to the disorder; besides which, there was the awful spectacle of men dying like sheep, through having caught the infection in nursing each other. This caused the greatest mortality. On the one hand, if they were afraid to visit each other, they perished from neglect; indeed many houses were emptied of their inmates for want of a nurse: on the other, if they ventured to do so, death was the consequence. This was especially the case with such as made any pretensions to goodness:§ honour made them unsparing of themselves in their attendance in their friends' houses, where even the members of the family were at last worn out by the moans of the dying, and succumbed to the force of the disaster. Yet it was with those who had recovered from the disease that the sick and the dying found most compassion. These knew

---

*Having described the symptoms, Thucydides advances to the social consequences.

†Diet was one of the chief available responses of the Hippocratic physicians; also included were bleeding, rest, and exercise, along with the limited medicinal preparations of the day.

‡Psychological factors and consequences contributed to the city's severe malaise.

§Moral character affected people's behavior; often the good assisted the sick to their own disadvantage.

what it was from experience, and had now no fear for themselves; for the same man was never attacked twice—never at least fatally. And such persons not only received the congratulations of others, but themselves also, in the elation of the moment,* half entertained the vain hope that they were for the future safe from any disease whatsoever.

52. An aggravation of the existing calamity was the influx from the country into the city, and this was especially felt by the new arrivals.† As there were no houses to receive them, they had to be lodged at the hot season of the year in stifling cabins, where the mortality raged without restraint. The bodies of dying men lay one upon another, and, half-dead creatures reeled about the streets and gathered round all the fountains in their longing for water.‡ The sacred places also in which they had quartered themselves were full of corpses of persons that had died there, just as they were; for as the disaster passed all bounds, men, not knowing what was to become of them, became utterly careless of everything, whether sacred or profane. All the burial rites before in use were entirely upset, and they buried the bodies as best they could.§ Many from want of the proper appliances, through so many of their friends having died already, had recourse to the most shameless sepultures: sometimes getting the start of those who had raised a pile, they threw their own dead body upon the stranger's pyre and ignited it; sometimes they tossed the corpse which they were carrying on the top of another that was burning, and so went off.

53. Nor was this the only form of lawless extravagance which owed its origin to the plague. Men now coolly ventured on what they had formerly done in a corner, and not just as they pleased, seeing the rapid transitions produced by persons in prosperity suddenly dying and those who before had nothing succeeding to their property. So they resolved to spend quickly and enjoy themselves, regarding their lives and riches as alike things of a day. Perseverance in what men called honour was popular with none, it was so uncertain whether they would be spared to attain the object; but it was settled that present enjoyment, and all that contributed to it, was both honourable and useful. Fear of gods or law of man there was none to restrain

---

*Irrational elation caught the historian's attention.

†The city, already crowded by wartime refugees from the country, became, because of the epidemic, even less suitable for the heavy influx of refugees.

‡The macabre picture here belies Thucydides' reputation for plain facts.

§The disturbance of traditional ways—*nomoi* (translatable as habits, customs, rites, and laws)—is a central concern of this historian. This passage does not prove any religiosity on the author's part but provides evidence for the general violation of deeply held beliefs about burial, which was central in Greek worship and in particular focus in Homer's *Iliad* and Sophocles' *Antigone*.

them.* As for the first, they judged it to be just the same whether they worshipped them or not, as they saw all alike perishing; and for the last, no one expected to live to be brought to trial for his offences, but each felt that a far severer sentence had been already passed upon them all and hung ever over their heads, and before this fell it was only reasonable to enjoy life a little.

54. Such was the nature of the calamity, and heavily did it weigh on the Athenians; death raging within the city and devastation without. Among other things which they remembered in their distress was, very naturally, the following verse which the old men said had long ago been uttered:†

> *'A Dorian war shall come and with it death.'*

So a dispute arose as to whether "dearth" and not "death" had not been the word in the verse; but at the present juncture, it was of course decided in favour of the latter; for the people made their recollection fit in with their sufferings. I fancy, however, that if another Dorian war should ever afterwards come upon us, and a dearth should happen to accompany it, the verse will probably be read accordingly. The oracle also which had been given to the Lacedæmonians was now remembered by those who knew of it. When the God was asked whether they should go to war, he answered that if they put their might into it, victory would be theirs, and that he would himself be with them. With this oracle events were supposed to tally.‡ For the plague broke out so soon as the Peloponnesians invaded Attica, and never entering Peloponnese (not at least to an extent worth noticing), committed its worst ravages at Athens, and next to Athens, at the most populous of the other towns. Such the history of the plague.

55. After ravaging the plain the Peloponnesians advanced into the Paralian region as far as Laurium, where the Athenian silver mines are, and first laid waste the side looking towards Peloponnese, next that which faces Eubœa and Andros. But Pericles, who was still general, held the same opinion as in the former invasion, and would not let the Athenians march out against them.

56. However, while they were still in the plain, and had not yet en-

---

*The breakdown of customary acts and beliefs would eventually corrupt all Hellenic society, but we find it first in Athens, the "education of Hellas," near the beginning of the war.

†The Greek words *limos* and *loimos* ("hunger" and "pestilential disease") are close enough in sound and spelling to provide certainty for those who happily looked for accurate predictions in ancient prophecies. Crawley translated into English words of appropriately similar sound: "dearth" and "death."

‡The Peloponnesian prophecy provided aid and comfort to the Athenians' enemies.

tered the Paralian land, he had prepared an armament of a hundred ships for Peloponnese, and when all was ready put out to sea. On board the ships he took four thousand Athenian heavy infantry, and three hundred cavalry in horse transports, then for the first time made out of old galleys; fifty Chian and Lesbian vessels also joining in the expedition.* When this Athenian armament put out to sea, they left the Peloponnesians in Attica in the Paralian region. Arriving at Epidaurus in Peloponnese they ravaged most of the territory, and even had hopes of taking the town by an assault: in this however they were not successful. Putting out from Epidaurus, they laid waste the territory of Trœzen, Halieis, and Hermione, all towns on the coast of Peloponnese, and thence sailing to Prasiai, a maritime town in Laconia, ravaged part of its territory, and took and sacked the place itself; after which they returned home, but found the Peloponnesians gone and no longer in Attica.

57. During the whole time that the Peloponnesians were in Attica and the Athenians on the expedition in their ships, men kept dying of the plague both in the armament and in Athens. Indeed it was actually asserted that the departure of the Peloponnesians was hastened by fear of the disorder; as they heard from deserters that it was in the city, and also could see the burials going on. Yet in this invasion they remained longer than in any other, and ravaged the whole country, for they were about forty days in Attica.

58. The same summer Hagnon, son of Nicias, and Cleopompus, son of Clinias, the colleagues of Pericles, took the armament of which he had lately made use, and went off upon an expedition against the Chalcidians in the direction of Thrace and Potidæa, which was still under siege. As soon as they arrived, they brought up their engines against Potidæa and tried every means of taking it, but did not succeed either in capturing the city or in doing anything else worthy of their preparations. For the plague attacked them here also, and committed such havoc as to cripple them completely, even the previously healthy soldiers of the former expedition catching the infection from Hagnon's troops; while Phormio and the sixteen hundred men whom he commanded only escaped by being no longer in the neighbourhood of the Chalcidians. The end of it was that Hagnon returned with his ships to Athens, having lost one thousand and fifty out of four thousand heavy infantry in about forty days; though the soldiers stationed there before remained in the country and carried on the siege of Potidæa.

59. After the second invasion of the Peloponnesians a change

---

*These were the last allies with their own fleets and military equipment. Lesbos will revolt in book 3, Chios in book 8.

came over the spirit of the Athenians. Their land had now been twice laid waste; and war and pestilence at once pressed heavy upon them. They began to find fault with Pericles, as the author of the war and the cause of all their misfortunes, and became eager to come to terms with Lacedæmon, and actually sent ambassadors thither, who did not however succeed in their mission. Their despair was now complete and all vented itself upon Pericles. When he saw them exasperated at the present turn of affairs and acting exactly as he had anticipated, he called an assembly, being (it must be remembered) still general,* with the double object of restoring confidence and of leading them from these angry feelings to a calmer and more hopeful state of mind. He accordingly came forward and spoke as follows:†

60. 'I was not unprepared for the indignation of which I have been the object, as I know its causes; and I have called an assembly for the purpose of reminding you upon certain points, and of protesting against your being unreasonably irritated with me, or cowed by your sufferings. I am of opinion that national greatness is more for the advantage of private citizens, than any individual well-being coupled with public humiliation. A man may be personally ever so well off, and yet if his country be ruined he must be ruined with it; whereas a flourishing commonwealth always affords chances of salvation to unfortunate individuals. Since then a state can support the misfortunes of private citizens, while they cannot support hers, it is surely the duty of every one to be forward in her defence, and not like you to be so confounded with your domestic afflictions as to give up all thoughts of the common safety, and to blame me for having counselled war and yourselves for having voted it. And yet if you are angry with me, it is with one who, as I believe, is second to no man either in knowledge of the proper policy, or in the ability to expound it, and who is moreover not only a patriot but an honest one. A man possessing that knowledge without that faculty of exposition might as well have no idea at all on the matter: if he had both these gifts, but no love for his country, he would be but a cold advocate for her interests; while were his patriotism not proof against bribery, everything would go for a price. So that if you thought that I was even moderately distinguished for these qualities when you took my advice and went to war, there is

---

*Pericles' legal power as *strategos* enabled him to call extraordinary meetings of the assembly as well as to command armies, but the assembly could fine or depose him any day at will.

†This is Pericles' third and last speech. It conveys his intransigence and conviction that the Athenians could win only by persevering without compromise. It illustrates Thucydides' contention that he led without pandering to the *demos* (populace).

certainly no reason now why I should be charged with having done wrong.*

61. 'For those of course who have a free choice in the matter and whose fortunes are not at stake, war is the greatest of follies. But if the only choice was between submission with loss of independence, and danger with the hope of preserving that independence,—in such a case it is he who will not accept the risk that deserves blame, not he who will. I am the same man and do not alter,† it is you who change, since in fact you took my advice while unhurt, and waited for misfortune to repent of it; and the apparent error of my policy lies in the infirmity of your resolution, since the suffering that it entails is being felt by every one among you, while its advantage is still remote and obscure to all, and a great and sudden reverse having befallen you, your mind is too much depressed to persevere in your resolves. For before what is sudden, unexpected, and least within calculation the spirit quails; and putting all else aside, the plague has certainly been an emergency of this kind. Born, however, as you are, citizens of a great state, and brought up, as you have been, with habits equal to your birth, you should be ready to face the greatest disasters and still to keep unimpaired the lustre of your name. For the judgment of mankind is as relentless to the weakness that falls short of a recognised renown, as it is jealous of the arrogance that aspires higher than its due. Cease then to grieve for your private afflictions, and address yourselves instead to the safety of the commonwealth.

62. 'If you shrink before the exertions which the war makes necessary, and fear that after all they may not have a happy result, you know the reasons by which I have often demonstrated to you the groundlessness of your apprehensions. If those are not enough, I will now reveal an advantage arising from the greatness of your dominion, which I think has never yet suggested itself to you, which I never mentioned in my previous speeches, and which has so bold a sound that I should scarce adventure it now, were it not for the unnatural depression which I see around me. You perhaps think that your empire extends only over your allies; I will declare to you the truth. The visible field of action has two parts, land and sea. In the whole of one of these you are completely supreme, not merely as far as you use it at present, but also to what further extent you may think fit: in fine, your naval resources are such that your vessels may go where they please, without the king or any other nation on earth being able to

---

*The strategist's defensive tone is understandable amid the terrible suffering of the people.

†Pericles boldly condemns the electorate for inconsistency, something unexpected in the Greek world that condemned democratic leaders for listing in the wind.

stop them.* So that although you may think it a great privation to lose the use of your land and houses, still you must see that this power is something widely different; and instead of fretting on their account, you should really regard them in the light of the gardens and other accessories that embellish a great fortune, and as, in comparison, of little moment. You should know too that liberty preserved by your efforts will easily recover for us what we have lost, while, the knee once bowed, even what you have will pass from you. Your fathers receiving these possessions not from others, but from themselves, did not let slip what their labour had acquired, but delivered them safe to you; and in this respect at least you must prove yourselves their equals, remembering that to lose what one has got is more disgraceful than to be baulked in getting, and you must confront your enemies not merely with spirit but with disdain. Confidence indeed a blissful ignorance can impart, ay, even to a coward's breast, but disdain is the privilege of those who, like us, have been assured by reflexion of their superiority to their adversary. And where the chances are the same, knowledge fortifies courage by the contempt which is its consequence, its trust being placed, not in hope, which is the prop of the desperate,† but in a judgment grounded upon existing resources, whose anticipations are more to be depended upon.

63. 'Again, your country has a right to your services in sustaining the glories of her position. These are a common source of pride to you all, and you cannot decline the burdens of empire and still expect to share its honours. You should remember also that what you are fighting against is not merely slavery as an exchange for independence, but also loss of empire and danger from the animosities incurred in its exercise. Besides, to recede is no longer possible, if indeed any of you in the alarm of the moment has become enamoured of the honesty of such an unambitious part. For what you hold is, to speak somewhat plainly, a tyranny;‡ to take it perhaps was wrong, but to let it go is unsafe. And men of these retiring views, making converts of others, would quickly ruin a state; indeed the result would be the same if they could live independent by themselves; for the retiring and unambitious are never secure without vigorous protectors at their side; in

---

*The claim exaggerates Athenian power. Although no fleet was superior, the number of opponents of Athens made it unwise for the city's fleets to sail too deeply into Persian-controlled waters. There were also dangers of capture and defeat to face in landing expeditionary forces on the Peloponnesian coasts.

†The strategist still remains confident in the accumulated Athenian resources set aside for fighting this war.

‡Pericles does not gloss over the hostile reactions that the Athenians' power has aroused. His successor Cleon and others will echo his words.

fine, such qualities are useless to an imperial city, though they may help a dependency to an unmolested servitude.

64. 'But you must not be seduced by citizens like these or angry with me,—who, if I voted for war, only did as you did yourselves,—in spite of the enemy having invaded your country and done what you could be certain that he would do, if you refused to comply with his demands; and although besides what we counted for, the plague has come upon us—the only point indeed at which our calculation has been at fault.* It is this, I know, that has had a large share in making me more unpopular than I should otherwise have been,—quite undeservedly, unless you are also prepared to give me the credit of any success with which chance may present you. Besides, the hand of Heaven must be borne with resignation, that of the enemy with fortitude; this was the old way at Athens, and do not you prevent it being so still. Remember, too, that if your country has the greatest name in all the world, it is because she never bent before disaster; because she has expended more life and effort in war than any other city, and has won for herself a power greater than any hitherto known, the memory of which will descend to the latest posterity; even if now, in obedience to the general law of decay,† we should ever be forced to yield, still it will be remembered that we held rule over more Hellenes than any other Hellenic state, that we sustained the greatest wars against their united or separate powers, and inhabited a city unrivalled by any other in resources or magnitude. These glories may incur the censure of the slow and unambitious; but in the breast of energy they will awake emulation, and in those who must remain without them an envious regret. Hatred and unpopularity at the moment have fallen to the lot of all who have aspired to rule others; but where odium must be incurred, true wisdom incurs it for the highest objects. Hatred also is short lived; but that which makes the splendour of the present and the glory of the future remains for ever unforgotten. Make your decision, therefore, for glory then and honour now, and attain both objects by instant and zealous effort: do not send heralds to Lacedæmon, and do not betray any sign of being oppressed by your present sufferings, since they whose minds are least sensitive to calamity, and whose hands are most quick to meet it, are the greatest men and the greatest communities.'

65. Such were the arguments by which Pericles tried to cure the

---

*Thucydides' Pericles emphasizes a point that Thucydides has already made: The plague went beyond human calculation (compare Stahl, then Rood, *Thucydides: Narrati e and Explanation*, on the limits of human prediction).

†Thucydides occasionally hypostatizes grand theories, and his most admired politician here recognizes that Athens will one day lose its hegemony—an echo of the final statement in Herodotus' preface (1.5) about the instability of human and imperial fortunes.

Athenians of their anger against him and to divert their thoughts from their immediate afflictions. As a community he succeeded in convincing them; they not only gave up all idea of sending to Lacedæmon, but applied themselves with increased energy to the war; still as private individuals they could not help smarting under their sufferings, the common people having been deprived of the little that they ever possessed, while the higher classes had lost fine properties with costly establishments and buildings in the country, and, worst of all, had war instead of peace. In fact, the public feeling against him did not subside until he had been fined. Not long afterwards, however, according to the way of the multitude,* they again elected him general and committed all their affairs to his hands, having now become less sensitive to their private and domestic afflictions, and understanding that he was the best man of all for the public necessities. For as long as he was at the head of the state during the peace, he pursued a moderate and conservative policy; and in his time its greatness was at its height.

When the war broke out, here also he seems to have rightly gauged the power of his country. He outlived its commencement two years and six months, and the correctness of his previsions respecting it became better known by his death. He told them to wait quietly, to pay attention to their navy, to attempt no new conquests, and to expose the city to no hazards during the war, and doing this, promised them a favourable result. What they did was the very contrary,† allowing private ambitions and private interests, in matters apparently quite foreign to the war, to lead them into projects unjust both to themselves and to their allies—projects whose success would only conduce to the honour and advantage of private persons, and whose failure entailed certain disaster on the country in the war.

The causes of this are not far to seek. Pericles indeed, by his rank, ability, and known integrity, was enabled to exercise an independent control over the multitude—in short, to lead them instead of being led by them;‡ for as he never sought power by improper means, he was never compelled to flatter them, but, on the contrary, enjoyed so high an estimation that he could afford to anger them by contradiction. Whenever he saw them unseasonably and insolently elated, he

---

*Thucydides—an elitist, like all ancient Greeks, including democratic Athenians—in his own person here condemns the fickleness of the multitude.

†This encomium of Pericles' leadership is just as much a condemnation of his successors, both the leaders and the voting population.

‡Some read this sentence as a condemnation of democracy—the form of government. Thucydides' politics are obscure, but one can easily argue that, once elected, a democratic leader must lead his people.

would with a word reduce them to alarm; on the other hand, if they fell victims to a panic, he could at once restore them to confidence.

In short, what was nominally a democracy became in his hands government by the first citizen.* With his successors it was different. More on a level with one another, and each grasping at supremacy, they ended by committing even the conduct of state affairs to the whims of the multitude. This, as might have been expected in a great and sovereign state, produced a host of blunders, and amongst them the Sicilian expedition;† though this failed not so much through a miscalculation of the power of those against whom it was sent, as through a fault in the senders in not taking the best measures afterwards to assist those who had gone out, but choosing rather to occupy themselves with private cabals for the leadership of the commons, by which they not only paralysed operations in the field, but also first introduced civil discord at home.‡

Yet after losing most of their fleet besides other forces in Sicily, and with faction already dominant in the city, they could still for eight years§ make head against their original adversaries, joined not only by the Sicilians, but also by their own allies nearly all in revolt, and at last by the king's son, Cyrus, who furnished the funds for the Peloponnesian navy. Nor did they finally succumb till they fell the victims of their own intestine disorders. So superfluously abundant were the resources from which the genius of Pericles foresaw an easy triumph‖ in the war over the unaided forces of the Peloponnesians.

66. During the same summer the Lacedæmonians and their allies made an expedition with a hundred ships against Zacynthus, an island lying off the coast of Elis, peopled by a colony of Achæans from Peloponnese, and in alliance with Athens. There were a thousand Lacedæmonian heavy infantry on board, and Cnemus, a Spartan, as admiral. They made a descent from their ships, and ravaged most of the country; but as the inhabitants would not submit, they sailed back home.

---

*Pericles was unique in his capacity to draw the *demos* into agreement with him. Thucydides does not here endorse monarchy, tyranny, or disguised autocracy.

†This forward reference to the subject of books 6 and 7, the Athenian aggression and defeat in Sicily, dates this important evaluative paragraph to sometime after 413. Even later material in it dates this unique comprehensive discussion to after 404, the end of the Peloponnesian War.

‡Thucydides implies here and states below that for Athens internal conflict was more debilitating than external enemies and hostile alliances.

§Here Thucydides betrays his patriotic admiration for Athens, the military machine. The number needs to be emended to "eight" years (from "three") since Thucydides refers to 411–404, the date of the Athenians' unconditional surrender.

‖Thucydides clearly states that the Athenians could have won, had not the plague, Pericles' death, and internal disorder disrupted an intelligent strategy. The concluding remark reveals Thucydides' belief in Pericles' calculations.

67. At the end of the same summer the Corinthian Aristeus, Aneristus, Nicolaus, and Pratodamus, envoys from Lacedæmon, Timagoras, a Tegean, and a private individual named Pollis from Argos, on their way to Asia to persuade the king to supply funds and join in the war, came to Sitalces, son of Teres in Thrace, with the idea of inducing him, if possible, to forsake the alliance of Athens and to march on Potidæa then besieged by an Athenian force, and also of getting conveyed by his means to their destination across the Hellespont to Pharnabazus, who was to send them up the country to the king.* But there chanced to be with Sitalces some Athenian ambassadors, Learchus, son of Callimachus, and Ameiniades, son of Philemon, who persuaded Sitalces' son, Sadocus, the new Athenian citizen, to put the men into their hands and thus prevent their crossing over to the king and doing their part to injure the country of his choice. He accordingly had them seized, as they were travelling through Thrace to the vessel in which they were to cross the Hellespont, by a party whom he had sent on with Learchus and Ameiniades, and gave orders for their delivery to the Athenian ambassadors, by whom they were brought to Athens. On their arrival, the Athenians, afraid that Aristeus, who had been notably the prime mover in the previous affairs of Potidæa and their Thracian possessions, might live to do them still more mischief if he escaped, slew them all the same day,† without giving them a trial or hearing the defence which they wished to offer, and cast their bodies into a pit; thinking themselves justified in using in retaliation the same mode of warfare which the Lacedæmonians had begun, when they slew and cast into pits all the Athenian and allied traders whom they caught on board the merchantmen round Peloponnese. Indeed, at the outset of the war, the Lacedæmonians butchered as enemies all whom they took on the sea, whether allies of Athens or neutrals.

68. About the same time towards the close of the summer, the Ambraciot forces, with a number of barbarians that they had raised, marched against the Amphilochian Argos and the rest of that country. The origin of their enmity against the Argives was this. This Argos and the rest of Amphilochia were colonised by Amphilochus, son of Amphiaraus. Dissatisfied with the state of affairs at home on his return thither after the Trojan war, he built this city in the Ambracian gulf, and

---

*The Corinthians, who had much to lose in this war, saw the need, in the face of Athenian resources and material, to gain alliances beyond Greece itself. Pharnabazus was the Persian satrap most convenient to Corinthian northern Aegean bases.

†The note informs us of the breakdown of judicial procedures in Athens. The horrifying Athenian breach of Hellenic rules of war is balanced immediately by the Lacedæmonians' prior actions. Both acts support Thucydides' opening statements (and several later in the civil war in Corcyra) about how the progress of this war degraded Hellenic standards of behavior.

named it Argos after his own country. This was the largest town in Amphilochia, and its inhabitants the most powerful. Under the pressure of misfortune many generations afterwards, they called in the Ambraciots, their neighbours on the Amphilochian border, to join their colony; and it was by this union with the Ambraciots that they learnt their present Hellenic speech, the rest of the Amphilochians being barbarians. After a time the Ambraciots expelled the Argives and held the city themselves. Upon this the Amphilochians gave themselves over to the Acarnanians; and the two together called the Athenians, who sent them Phormio as general and thirty ships; upon whose arrival they took Argos by storm, and made slaves of the Ambraciots; and the Amphilochians and Acarnanians inhabited the town in common. After this began the alliance between the Athenians and Acarnanians. The enmity of the Ambraciots against the Argives thus commenced with the enslavement of their citizens; and afterwards during the war they collected this armament among themselves and the Chaonians, and other of the neighbouring barbarians. Arrived before Argos, they became masters of the country; but not being successful in their attacks upon the town, returned home and dispersed among their different peoples.

Such were the events of the summer.

69. The ensuing winter the Athenians sent twenty ships round Peloponnese, under the command of Phormio, who stationed himself at Naupactus and kept watch against any one sailing in or out of Corinth and the Crissæan gulf.* Six others went to Caria and Lycia under Melesander, to collect tribute in those parts, and also to prevent the Peloponnesian privateers from taking up their station in those waters and molesting the passage of the merchantmen from Phaselis and Phœnicia and the adjoining continent. However, Melesander, going up the country into Lycia with a force of Athenians from the ships and the allies, was defeated and killed in battle, with the loss of a number of his troops.

70. The same winter the Potidæans at length found themselves no longer able to hold out against their besiegers. The inroads of the Peloponnesians into Attica had not had the desired effect of making the Athenians raise the siege. Provisions there were none left; and so far had distress for food gone in Potidæa that, besides a number of other horrors, instances had even occurred of the people having eaten one another.† So in this extremity they at last made proposals for capitulating to the Athenian generals in command against them,

---

*This brief note on Phormio's naval posting in late 430 soon leads to one of the great battle accounts of the war, a paradigm of Athenian nautical skill.

†Potidaea's tenacity is remarkable; cannibalism is recorded for several ancient sieges (for instance, Saguntum in Livy's narrative of the Hannibalic wars), but we have no confirmation.

Xenophon, son of Euripides, Hestiodorus, son of Aristocleides, and Phanomachus, son of Callimachus. The generals accepted their proposals, seeing the sufferings of the army in so exposed a position; besides which the state had already spent two thousand talents upon the siege.* The terms of the capitulation were as follows: a free passage out for themselves, their children, wives and auxiliaries, with one garment apiece, the women with two, and a fixed sum of money for their journey. Under this treaty they went out to Chalcidice and other places, according as was in their power. The Athenians, however, blamed the generals for granting terms without instructions from home,[†] being of opinion that the place would have had to surrender at discretion. They afterwards sent settlers of their own to Potidæa, and colonised it. Such were the events of the winter, and so ended the second year of this war of which Thucydides was the historian.[‡]

Third Year of the War—Investment (Siege) of Platæa— Naval Victories of Phormio—Thracian Irruption into Macedonia under Sitalces

71. The next summer the Peloponnesians and their allies, instead of invading Attica, marched against Platæa, under the command of Archidamus, son of Zeuxidamus, king of the Lacedæmonians. He had encamped his army and was about to lay waste the country, when the Platæans hastened to send envoys to him, and spoke as follows:—

'Archidamus and Lacedæmonians, in invading the Platæan territory, you do what is wrong in itself, and worthy neither of yourselves nor of the fathers[§] who begot you. Pausanias, son of Cleombrotus, your countryman, after freeing Hellas from the Medes with the help of those Hellenes who were willing to undertake the risk of the battle fought near our city, offered sacrifice to Zeus the Liberator in the

---

*The siege of Potidaea (map 6) swallowed much of Pericles' war reserve. The plague brought from home and the rigors of winter in Thrace made peace on terms welcome.

[†]Thucydides regularly records conflict between generals in the field and the assembly back in Athens. Given the primitive state of ancient long-distance communications, a general must make many decisions without opportunity to refer matters to the sovereign people. The people could retaliate, as *strategoi* rightly fear.

[‡]Thucydides stamps the work as his own, something necessary in a world without copyright. Separate papyrus scrolls (volumes) need authorial identification more frequently than do printed books. The year 429 begins.

[§]The Plataean campaigns, culminating in betrayal and tragedy, offer frequent reference to the days of yore, when tiny Plataea stood with the Athenians at Marathon and became the site of the last Persian campaign, in which the Hellenes defeated the army of Mardonius in 479 (Herodotus book 9).

market-place of Platæa, and calling all the allies together restored to the Platæans their city and territory, and declared it independent and inviolate against aggression or conquest. Should any such be attempted, the allies present were to help according to their power. Your fathers rewarded us thus for the courage and patriotism that we displayed at that perilous epoch; but you do just the contrary, coming with our bitterest enemies, the Thebans, to enslave us. We appeal, therefore, to the gods to whom the oaths* were then made, to the gods of your ancestors, and lastly to those of our country, and call upon you to refrain from violating our territory or transgressing the oaths, and to let us live independent, as Pausanias decreed.'

72. The Platæans had got thus far when they were cut short by Archidamus saying, 'There is justice, Platæans, in what you say, if you act up to your words. According to the grant of Pausanias, continue to be independent yourselves, and join in freeing those of your fellow-countrymen who, after sharing in the perils of that period, joined in the oaths to you, and are now subject to the Athenians; for it is to free them and the rest that all this provision and war has been made. I could wish that you would share our labours and abide by the oaths yourselves; if this is impossible, do what we have already required of you—remain neutral, enjoying your own; join neither side, but receive both as friends, neither as allies for the war. With this we shall be satisfied.' Such were the words of Archidamus. The Platæans, after hearing what he had to say, went into the city and acquainted the people with what had passed, and presently returned for answer that it was impossible for them to do what he proposed without consulting the Athenians, with whom their children and wives now were; besides which they had their fears for the town. After his departure, what was to prevent the Athenians from coming and taking it out of their hands, or the Thebans, who would be included in the oaths, from taking advantage of the proposed neutrality to make a second attempt to seize the city? Upon these points he tried to reassure them by saying: 'You have only to deliver over the city and houses to us Lacedæmonians, to point out the boundaries of your land, the number of your fruit-trees, and whatever else can be numerically stated, and yourselves to withdraw wherever you like as long as the war shall last. When it is over we will restore to you whatever we received, and in the interim hold it in trust and keep it in cultivation, paying you a sufficient allowance.'†

---

*Appeals to the gods, anyone's divinity, always fail in Thucydides. The Plataeans, the Melians, and Nicias all die after such entreaties.

†The Spartans' terms are speciously attractive, but the Plataeans have reason not to trust them, as becomes uncomfortably clear when they do surrender and the Spartans yield to the Theban desire for revenge.

73. When they had heard what he had to say, they re-entered the city, and after consulting with the people said that they wished first to acquaint the Athenians with this proposal, and in the event of their approving to accede to it; in the meantime they asked him to grant them a truce and not to lay waste their territory. He accordingly granted a truce for the number of days requisite for the journey, and meanwhile abstained from ravaging their territory. The Platæan envoys went to Athens, and consulted with the Athenians, and returned with the following message to those in the city: 'The Athenians say, Platæans, that they never hitherto, since we became their allies, on any occasion abandoned us to an enemy, nor will they now neglect us, but will help us according to their ability; and they adjure you by the oaths which your fathers swore, to keep the alliance unaltered.'

74. On the delivery of this message by the envoys, the Platæans resolved not to be unfaithful to the Athenians but to endure, if it must be, seeing their lands laid waste and any other trials that might come to them, and not to send out again, but to answer from the wall that it was impossible for them to do as the Lacedæmonians proposed. As soon as he had received this answer, King Archidamus proceeded first to make a solemn appeal to the gods and heroes of the country in words following:—'Gods and heroes of the Platæan territory, be my witnesses that not as aggressors originally, nor until these had first departed from the common oath, did we invade this land, in which our fathers offered you their prayers before defeating the Medes, and which you made auspicious to the Hellenic arms; nor shall we be aggressors in the measures to which we may now resort, since we have made many fair proposals but have not been successful. Graciously accord that those who were the first to offend may be punished for it, and that vengeance may be attained by those who would righteously inflict it.'

75. After this appeal to the gods Archidamus put his army in motion. First he enclosed the town with a palisade formed of the fruit-trees which they cut down,* to prevent further egress from Platæa; next they threw up a mound against the city, hoping that the largeness of the force employed would insure the speedy reduction of the place. They accordingly cut down timber from Cithæron, and built it up on either side, laying it like lattice-work to serve as a wall to keep the mound from spreading abroad, and carried to it wood and stones and

---

*Sieges, in the absence of effective engines, were rarely successful in antiquity until the fourth century. Cutting down the trees (Thucydides does not specify any kind) serves several purposes—for example, it permanently disrupts the defenders' economy, while providing firewood and defensive equipment for the besiegers. Thucydides the soldier offers rich detail of this paradigmatic land-siege, this description standing duty for many others, but it was also an example of military innovation.

earth and whatever other material might help to complete it. They continued to work at the mound for seventy days and nights without intermission, being divided into relief parties to allow of some being employed in carrying while others took sleep and refreshment; the Lacedæmonian officer attached to each contingent keeping the men to the work.

But the Platæans, observing the progress of the mound, constructed a wall of wood and fixed it upon that part of the city wall against which the mound was being erected, and built up bricks inside it which they took from the neighbouring houses. The timbers served to bind the building together, and to prevent its becoming weak as it advanced in height; it had also a covering of skins and hides, which protected the woodwork against the attacks of burning missiles and allowed the men to work in safety. Thus the wall was raised to a great height, and the mound opposite made no less rapid progress. The Platæans also thought of another expedient; they pulled out part of the wall upon which the mound abutted, and carried the earth into the city.*

76. Discovering this the Peloponnesians twisted up clay in wattles of reed and threw it into the breach formed in the mound, in order to give it consistency and prevent its being carried away like the soil. Stopped in this way the Platæans changed their mode of operation, and digging a mine from the town calculated their way under the mound, and began to carry off its material as before. This went on for a long while without the enemy outside finding it out, so that for all they threw on the top their mound made no progress in proportion, being carried away from beneath and constantly settling down in the vacuum.

But the Platæans, fearing that even thus they might not be able to hold out against the superior numbers of the enemy, had yet another invention. They stopped working at the large building in front of the mound, and starting at either end of it inside from the old low wall, built a new one in the form or a crescent running in towards the town; in order that in the event of the great wall being taken this might remain, and the enemy have to throw up a fresh mound against it, and as they advanced within might not only have their trouble over again, but also be exposed to missiles on their flanks.† While raising the mound the Peloponnesians also brought up engines against the city,

---

*This defensive innovation caught the general's eye. Aeneas Tacticus, active in the next century, wrote an extant handbook on siege warfare.

†Punching a hole in a besieged city's wall only enabled one to address the next step, penetrating a city of mostly hostile inhabitants. As the U.S. Army again realized in the second Iraq war of 2003 C.E., entering a warren of buildings can expose you to more lethal fire than fighting on an open battlefield.

one of which was brought up upon the mound against the great building and shook down a good piece of it, to the no small alarm of the Platæans. Others were advanced against different parts of the wall but were lassoed and broken by the Platæans; who also hung up great beams by long iron chains from either extremity of two poles laid on the wall and projecting over it, and drew them up at an angle whenever any point was threatened by the engine, and loosing their hold let the beam go with its chains slack, so that it fell with a run and snapped off the nose of the battering ram.

77. After this the Peloponnesians, finding that their engines effected nothing, and that their mound was met by the counterwork, concluded that their present means of offence were unequal to the taking of the city,* and prepared for its circumvallation. First, however, they determined to try the effects of fire and see whether they could not, with the help of a wind, burn the town as it was not a large one; indeed they thought of every possible expedient by which the place might be reduced without the expense of a blockade. They accordingly brought faggots of brush-wood and threw them from the mound, first into the space between it and the wall; and this soon becoming full from the number of hands at work, they next heaped the faggots up as far into the town as they could reach from the top, and then lighted the wood by setting fire to it with sulphur and pitch. The consequence was a fire greater than any one had ever yet seen produced by human agency, though it could not of course be compared to the spontaneous conflagrations sometimes known to occur through the wind rubbing the branches of a mountain forest together. And this fire was not only remarkable for its magnitude, but was also, at the end of so many perils, within an ace† of proving fatal to the Platæans; a great part of the town became entirely inaccessible, and had a wind blown upon it, in accordance with the hopes of the enemy, nothing could have saved them. As it was, there is also a story‡ of heavy rain and thunder having come on by which the fire was put out and the danger averted.

78. Failing in this last attempt the Peloponnesians left a portion of their forces on the spot, dismissing the rest, and built a wall of circumvallation round the town, dividing the ground among the various cities present; a ditch being made within and without the lines, from which they got their bricks. All being finished by about the rising of

---

*Attempts to penetrate Plataea having been unsuccessful, the Peloponnesians decide to starve the enemy by surrounding the city with a wall and a ditch.

†Thucydides likes to note close calls to disaster. He will do the same with Mytilene (3.49) and Syracuse (7.2).

‡This is another rare example of alternative versions in Thucydides, here as usual delivered without attribution to any sources.

Arcturus,* they left men enough to man half the wall, the rest being manned by the Bœotians, and drawing off their army dispersed to their several cities. The Platæans had before sent off their wives and children and oldest men and the mass of the non-combatants to Athens; so that the number of the besieged left in the place comprised four hundred of their own citizens, eighty Athenians, and a hundred and ten women to bake their bread. This was the sum total at the commencement of the siege; and there was no one else within the walls, bond or free. Such were the arrangements made for the blockade of Platæa.

79. The same summer and simultaneously with the expedition against Platæa, the Athenians marched with two thousand heavy infantry and two hundred horse against the Chalcidians in the direction of Thrace and the Bottiæans, just as the grain was getting ripe, under the command of Xenophon, son of Euripides, with two colleagues. Arriving before Spartolus in Bottiæa, they destroyed the grain and had some hopes of the city coming over through the intrigues of a faction within. But those of a different way of thinking had sent to Olynthus; and a garrison of heavy infantry and other troops arrived accordingly. These issuing from Spartolus were engaged by the Athenians in front of the town: the Chalcidian heavy infantry, and some auxiliaries with them, were beaten and retreated into Spartolus; but the Chalcidian horse and light troops defeated the horse and light troops of the Athenians. The Chalcidians had already a few peltasts† from Crusis, and presently after the battle were joined by some others from Olynthus; upon seeing whom the light troops from Spartolus, emboldened by this accession and by their previous success, with the help of the Chalcidian horse and the reinforcement just arrived again attacked the Athenians, who retired upon the two divisions which they had left with their baggage. Whenever the Athenians advanced, their adversary gave way, pressing them with missiles the instant they began to retire. The Chalcidian horse also, riding up and charging them just as they pleased, at last caused a panic amongst them and routed and pursued them to a great distance. The Athenians took refuge in Potidæa, and afterwards recovered their dead under truce, and returned to Athens with the remnant of their army; four hundred and thirty men and all the generals having fallen.‡ The Chalcidians and Bottiæans set up a trophy, took up their dead, and dispersed to their several cities.

80. The same summer, not long after this, the Ambraciots and

---

*The astronomical notation marks the middle of our September 429.

†Light-armed infantry scouts and skirmishers.

‡The Chalcidians defeat the Athenians and three of their ten generals without aid from Sparta, a notable setback for Athens.

Chaonians, being desirous of reducing the whole of Acarnania and detaching it from Athens, persuaded the Lacedæmonians to equip a fleet from their confederacy and send a thousand heavy infantry to Acarnania, representing that if a combined movement were made by land and sea, the coast Acarnanians would be unable to march, and the conquest of Zacynthus and Cephallenia easily following on the possession of Acarnania, the cruise round Peloponnese would be no longer so convenient for the Athenians. Besides which there was a hope of taking Naupactus.* The Lacedæmonians accordingly at once sent off a few vessels with Cnemus, who was still high admiral, and the heavy infantry on board; and sent round orders for the fleet to equip as quickly as possible and sail to Leucas. The Corinthians were the most forward in the business; the Ambraciots being a colony of theirs. While the ships from Corinth, Sicyon, and the neighbourhood were getting ready, and those from Leucas, Anactorium, and Ambracia, which had arrived before, were waiting for them at Leucas, Cnemus and his thousand heavy infantry had run into the gulf, giving the slip to Phormio, the commander of the Athenian squadron stationed off Naupactus, and began at once to prepare for the land expedition. The Hellenic troops with him consisted of the Ambraciots, Leucadians, and Anactorians, and the thousand Peloponnesians with whom he came; the barbarian of a thousand Chaonians, who, belonging to a nation that has no king, were led by Photys and Nicanor, the two members of the royal family to whom the chieftainship for that year had been confided.

With the Chaonians came also some Thesprotians, like them without a king, some Molossians and Atintanians led by Sabylinthus, the guardian of king Tharyps who was still a minor, and some Paravæans, under their King Orœdus, accompanied by a thousand Orestians, subjects of King Antiochus and placed by him under the command of Orœdus. There were also a thousand Macedonians sent by Perdiccas without the knowledge of the Athenians, but they arrived too late. With this force Cnemus set out, without waiting for the fleet from Corinth. Passing through the territory of Amphilochian Argos, and sacking the open village of Limnæa,† they advanced to Stratus the Acarnanian capital; this once taken, the rest of the country, they felt convinced, would speedily follow.

81. The Acarnanians, finding themselves invaded by a large army

---

*Those who hoped to profit from Lacedaemonian hostilities toward Athens always had a good reason for asking the Spartans to help them. Naupactus guards the critical chokepoint entrance and exit to the Corinthian Gulf (map 4). The Messenians held it, in gratitude and alliance, for the Athenians.

†The Spartan commander Cnemus valiantly sets out to dispirit and conquer the Acarnanians, the Athenians' allies. His follow-through was better here than in the Saronic Gulf incident later in this campaign season (2.93).

by land, and from the sea threatened by a hostile fleet, made no combined attempt at resistance, but remained to defend their homes, and sent for help to Phormio, who replied that when a fleet was on the point of sailing from Corinth, it was impossible for him to leave Naupactus unprotected. The Peloponnesians meanwhile and their allies advanced upon Stratus in three divisions, with the intention of encamping near it and attempting the wall by force if they failed to succeed by negotiation. The order of march was as follows: the centre was occupied by the Chaonians and the rest of the barbarians, with the Leucadians and Anactorians and their followers on the right, and Cnemus with the Peloponnesians and Ambraciots on the left; each division being a long way off from, and sometimes even out of sight of, the others. The Hellenes advanced in good order, keeping a look-out till they encamped in a good position; but the Chaonians, filled with self-confidence, and having the highest character for courage among the tribes of that part of the continent,* without waiting to occupy their camp, rushed on with the rest of the barbarians, in the idea that they should take the town by assault and obtain the sole glory of the enterprise. While they were coming on, the Stratians, becoming aware how things stood, and thinking that the defeat of this division would considerably dishearten the Hellenes behind it, occupied the environs of the town with ambuscades, and as soon as they approached engaged them at close quarters from the city and the ambuscades. A panic seizing the Chaonians, great numbers of them were slain; and as soon as they were seen to give way the rest of the barbarians turned and fled. Owing to the distance by which their allies had preceded them, neither of the Hellenic divisions knew anything of the battle, but fancied they were hastening on to encamp. However, when the flying barbarians broke in upon them, they opened their ranks to receive them, brought their divisions together, and stopped quiet where they were for the day; the Stratians not offering to engage them, as the rest of the Acarnanians had not yet arrived, but contenting themselves with slinging at them from a distance, which distressed them greatly, as there was no stirring without their armour. The Acarnanians would seem to excel in this mode of warfare.

82. As soon as night fell, Cnemus hastily drew off his army to the river Anapus, about nine miles from Stratus, recovering his dead next day under truce, and being there joined by the friendly Œniadæ, fell back upon their city before the enemy's reinforcements came up. From hence each returned home; and the Stratians set up a trophy for the battle with the barbarians.

---

*Barbarian over-confidence leads to another disaster for the Chaonians (see Stratus on map 8).

83. Meanwhile the fleet from Corinth and the rest of the confederates in the Crissæan gulf, which was to have co-operated with Cnemus and prevented the coast Acarnanians from joining their countrymen in the interior, was disabled from doing so by being compelled about the same time as the battle at Stratus to fight with Phormio and the twenty Athenian vessels stationed at Naupactus. For they were watched, as they coasted along out of the gulf, by Phormio, who wished to attack in the open sea. But the Corinthians and allies had started for Acarnania without any idea of fighting at sea, and with vessels more like transports for carrying soldiers;* besides which, they never dreamed of the twenty Athenian ships venturing to engage their forty-seven.† However, while they were coasting along their own shore, there were the Athenians sailing along in line with them; and when they tried to cross over from Patræ in Achæa to the mainland on the other side, on their way to Acarnania, they saw them again coming out from Chalcis and the river Evenus to meet them. They slipped from their moorings in the night, but were observed, and were at length compelled to fight in mid passage. Each state that contributed to the armament had its own general; the Corinthian commanders were Machaon, Isocrates, and Agatharchidas. The Peloponnesians ranged their vessels in as large a circle as possible without leaving an opening, with the prows outside and the sterns in;‡ and placed within all the small craft in company, and their five best sailers to issue out at a moment's notice and strengthen any point threatened by the enemy.

84. The Athenians, formed in line, sailed round and round them, and forced them to contract their circle, by continually brushing past and making as though they would attack at once, having been previously cautioned by Phormio not to do so till he gave the signal. His hope was that the Peloponnesians would not retain their order like a force on shore, but that the ships would fall foul of one another and the small craft cause confusion; and if the wind should blow from the gulf (in expectation of which he kept sailing round them, and which usually rose towards morning), they would not, he felt sure, remain steady an instant. He also thought that it rested with him to attack when he pleased, as his ships were better sailers, and that an attack timed by the coming of the wind would tell best. When the wind came down, the enemy's ships were now in a narrow space, and what with

---

*The Corinthians prepared for the war they wanted to fight but found themselves immersed in a naval battle, not a land one.

†The Athenians are not put off by the odds of twenty ships against forty-seven; they know their tactical superiority.

‡This defensive maneuver with ships radiating out from centralized sterns might have succeeded with sailors trained less well than the Athenians were.

the wind and the small craft dashing against them, at once fell into confusion: ship fell foul of ship, while the crews were pushing them off with poles, and by their shouting, swearing, and struggling with one another, made captains' orders and boatswains' cries alike inaudible, and through being unable for want of practice to clear their oars in the rough water, prevented the vessels from obeying their helmsmen properly. At this moment Phormio gave the signal, and the Athenians attacked. Sinking first one of the admirals, they then disabled all they came across, so that no one thought of resistance for the confusion, but fled for Patræ and Dyme in Achæa. The Athenians gave chase and captured twelve ships, and taking most of the men out of them sailed to Molycrium, and after setting up a trophy on the promontory of Rhium and dedicating a ship to Poseidon, returned to Naupactus. As for the Peloponnesians, they at once sailed with their remaining ships along the coast from Dyme and Patræ to Cyllene, the Eleian arsenal; where Cnemus and the ships from Leucas that were to have joined them, also arrived after the battle at Stratus.

85. The Lacedæmonians now sent to the fleet to Cnemus three commissioners, Timocrates, Brasidas, and Lycophron, with orders to prepare to engage again with better fortune, and not to be driven from the sea by a few vessels; for they could not at all account for their discomfiture, the less so as it was their first attempt at sea;* and they fancied that it was not that their marine was so inferior, but that there had been misconduct somewhere, not considering the long experience of the Athenians as compared with the little practice which they had had themselves.† The commissioners were accordingly sent in anger. As soon as they arrived they set to work with Cnemus to order ships from the different states, and to put those which they already had in fighting order. Meanwhile Phormio sent word to Athens of their preparations and his own victory, and desired as many ships as possible to be speedily sent to him, as he stood in daily expectation of a battle. Twenty were accordingly sent, but instructions were given to their commander to go first to Crete. For Nicias, a Cretan of Gortys, who was *Proxenus* of the Athenians,‡ had persuaded them to sail against Cydonia, promising to procure the reduction of that hostile town; his real wish being to oblige the Polichnitans, neighbours of the Cydonians. He accordingly went with the ships to Crete, and, ac-

*The Spartan government could not comprehend Phormio's victory at Stratus, so they investigated what went wrong—needing and intending to blame someone.

†Thucydides emphasizes that practice and training, not luck, accounted for the unexpected Athenian victory.

‡Another example, whether or not the name Nicias is correct for the Cretan, of local politics trying to leverage the international war for local advantage against neighbors or fellow-citizens.

companied by the Polichnitans, laid waste the lands of the Cydonians; and, what with adverse winds and stress of weather, wasted no little time there.

86. While the Athenians were thus detained in Crete, the Peloponnesians in Cyllene got ready for battle, and coasted along to Panormus in Achæa, where their land army had come to support them. Phormio also coasted along to Molycrian Rhium, and anchored outside it with twenty ships, the same as he had fought with before. This Rhium was friendly to the Athenians. The other, in Peloponnese, lies opposite to it; the sea between them is about three-quarters of a mile broad, and forms the mouth of the Crissæan gulf. At this, the Achæan Rhium, not far off Panormus, where their army lay, the Peloponnesians now cast anchor with seventy-seven ships, when they saw the Athenians do so. For six or seven days they remained opposite each other, practising and preparing for the battle; the one resolved not to sail out of the Rhia into the open sea, for fear of the disaster which had already happened to them, the other not to sail into the straits, thinking it advantageous to the enemy to fight in the narrows. At last Cnemus and Brasidas and the rest of the Peloponnesian commanders, being desirous of bringing on a battle as soon as possible, before reinforcements should arrive from Athens, and noticing that the men were most of them cowed by the previous defeat and out of heart for the business, first called them together and encouraged them as follows:*—

87. 'Peloponnesians, the late engagement which may have made some of you afraid of the one now in prospect, really gives no just ground for apprehension. Preparation for it, as you know, there was little enough; and the object of our voyage was not so much to fight at sea as an expedition by land. Besides this, the chances of war were largely against us; and perhaps also inexperience had something to do with our failure in our first naval action. It was not, therefore, cowardice that produced our defeat, nor ought the determination which force has not quelled, but which still has a word to say with its adversary, to lose its edge from the result of an accident; but admitting the possibility of a chance miscarriage, we should know that brave hearts must be always brave, and while they remain so can never put forward inexperience as an excuse for misconduct. Nor are you so behind the enemy in experience as you are ahead of him in courage; and although the science of your opponents would, if valour accompanied

---

*The battle exhortation, a common element in Thucydides and therefore in later historians, provides a convenient location for the author's analysis of factors that will determine the outcome of the coming battle. Their historicity has been questioned, especially given the length of a drawn-up battle line and the general confusion before battle. (See Pritchett, *The Greek State at War*, on elements of Greek warfare.)

it, have also the presence of mind to carry out at an emergency the lesson it has learnt, yet a faint heart will make all art powerless in the face of danger. For fear takes away presence of mind, and without valour art is useless. Against their superior experience set your superior daring, and against the fear induced by defeat the fact of your having been then unprepared; remember, too, that you have always the advantage of superior numbers, and of engaging off your own coast, supported by your heavy infantry; and as a rule, numbers and equipment give victory.* At no point, therefore, is defeat likely; and as for our previous mistakes, the very fact of their occurrence will teach us better for the future. Steersmen and sailors may, therefore, confidently attend to their several duties, none quitting the station assigned to them: as for ourselves, we promise to prepare for the engagement at least as well as your previous commanders, and to give no excuse for any one misconducting himself. Should any insist on doing so, he shall meet with the punishment he deserves, while the brave shall be honoured with the appropriate rewards of valour.'

88. The Peloponnesian commanders encouraged their men after this fashion. Phormio, meanwhile, being himself not without fears for the courage of his men, and noticing that they were forming in groups among themselves† and were alarmed at the odds against them, desired to call them together and give them confidence and counsel in the present emergency. He had before continually told them, and had accustomed their minds to the idea, that there was no numerical superiority that they could not face; and the men themselves had long been persuaded that Athenians need never retire before any quantity of Peloponnesian vessels. At the moment, however, he saw that they were dispirited by the sight before them and wishing to refresh their confidence, called them together and spoke as follows:—

89. 'I see, my men, that you are frightened by the number of the enemy, and I have accordingly called you together, not liking you to be afraid of what is not really terrible. In the first place, the Peloponnesians, already defeated, and not even themselves thinking that they are a match for us, have not ventured to meet us on equal terms, but have equipped this multitude of ships against us. Next, as to that upon which they most rely, the courage which they suppose constitutional to them, their confidence here only arises from the success which their

---

*The Peloponnesian commanders at Naupactus stress the importance of their advantages, but numbers in themselves rarely produce victory.

†Phormio, who could not have heard the enemy's exhortation, produces his own for the Athenians and their allies, responding to that speech almost point for point. This artificial responsion leads many scholars to question whether the speeches reported truly resemble what was actually said before battle (see de Romilly, *Thucydides and Athenian Imperialism*, and Hunter, *Thucydides: The Artful Reporter*).

experience in land service usually gives them, and which they fancy will do the same for them at sea. But this advantage will in all justice belong to us on this element, if to them on that; as they are not superior to us in courage, but we are each of us more confident, according to our experience in our particular department. Besides, as the Lacedæmonians use their supremacy over their allies to promote their own glory, they are most of them being brought into danger against their will, or they would never, after such a decided defeat, have ventured upon a fresh engagement. You need not, therefore, be afraid of their dash. You, on the contrary, inspire a much greater and better founded alarm, both because of your late victory and also of their belief that we should not face them unless about to do something worthy of a success so signal. An adversary numerically superior, like the one before us, comes into action trusting more to strength than to resolution; while he who voluntarily confronts tremendous odds must have very great internal resources to draw upon.

'For these reasons the Peloponnesians fear our irrational audacity more than they would ever have done a more commensurate preparation. Besides, many armaments have before now succumbed to an inferior through want of skill or sometimes of courage; neither of which defects certainly are ours. As to the battle, it shall not be, if I can help it, in the strait, nor will I sail in there at all; seeing that in a contest between a number of clumsily managed vessels and a small, fast, well-handled squadron, want of sea room is an undoubted disadvantage.* One cannot run down an enemy properly without having a sight of him a good way off, nor can one retire at need when pressed; one can neither break the line nor return upon his rear, the proper tactics for a fast sailer; but the naval action necessarily becomes a land one, in which numbers must decide the matter. For all this I will provide as far as can be. Do you stay at your posts by your ships, and be sharp at catching the word of command, the more so as we are observing one another from so short a distance; and in action think order and silence all important†—qualities useful in war generally, and in naval engagements in particular. Behave before the enemy in a manner worthy of your past exploits. The issues you will fight for are great—to destroy the naval hopes of the Peloponnesians or to bring nearer to the Athenians their fears for the sea. And I may once more remind you that you have defeated most of them already; and beaten men do not face a danger twice with the same determination.'

---

*Phormio explains his tactics. He will employ his men's superior rowing and sailing skill to outmaneuver the enemy in open seas. Morrison and Coates describe the trireme, its capacities, and its history in Greek warfare.

†His speech combines moral suasion, references to the past, and a coherent plan for victory.

90. Such was the exhortation of Phormio. The Peloponnesians finding that the Athenians did not sail into the gulf and the narrows, in
order to lead them in whether they wished it or not, put out at dawn,
and forming four abreast, sailed inside the gulf in the direction of their
own country, the right wing leading as they had lain at anchor. In this
wing were placed twenty of their best sailers; so that in the event of
Phormio thinking that their object was Naupactus, and coasting along
thither to save the place, the Athenians might not be able to escape
their onset by getting outside their wing, but might be cut off by the
vessels in question. As they expected, Phormio, in alarm for the place
at that moment emptied of its garrison, as soon as he saw them put
out, reluctantly and hurriedly embarked and sailed along shore; the
Messenian land forces moving along also to support him. The Peloponnesians seeing him coasting along with his ships in single file, and
by this inside the gulf and close in shore as they so much wished, at
one signal tacked suddenly and bore down in line at their best speed
on the Athenians, hoping to cut off the whole squadron. The eleven
leading vessels, however, escaped the Peloponnesian wing and its sudden movement, and reached the more open water; but the rest were
overtaken as they tried to run through, driven ashore and disabled;
such of the crews being slain as had not swum out of them. Some of
the ships the Peloponnesians lashed to their own, and towed off
empty; one they took with the men in it; others were just being towed
off, when they were saved by the Messenians dashing into the sea with
their armour and fighting from the decks that they had boarded.*

91. Thus far victory was with the Peloponnesians, and the Athenian
fleet destroyed; the twenty ships in the right wing being meanwhile in
chase of the eleven Athenian vessels that had escaped their sudden
movement and reached the more open water. These, with the exception of one ship, all outsailed them and got safe into Naupactus, and
forming close in shore opposite the temple of Apollo, with their
prows facing the enemy, prepared to defend themselves in case the
Peloponnesians should sail in shore against them. After a while the
Peloponnesians came up, chanting the pæan for their victory as they
sailed on; the single Athenian ship remaining being chased by a Leucadian far ahead of the rest. But there happened to be a merchantman lying at anchor in the roadstead, which the Athenian ship found
time to sail round, and struck the Leucadian in chase amidships and
sank her.† An exploit so sudden and unexpected produced a panic

---

*This odd combination of naval battle with interference from sideline supporters on
land marks the first phase of the battle in which the Athenians got the worst.

†The Athenians, however, perceive an opportunity to turn things around and do so.
Thucydides marks sudden reversals and the ensuing panic on one or both sides.

among the Peloponnesians; and having fallen out of order in the excitement of victory, some of them dropped their oars and stopped their way in order to let the main body come up—an unsafe thing to do considering how near they were to the enemy's prows; while others ran aground in the shallows, in their ignorance of the localities.

92. Elated at this incident, the Athenians at one word gave a cheer, and dashed at the enemy, who, embarrassed by his mistakes and the disorder in which he found himself, only stood for an instant, and then fled for Panormus, whence he had put out. The Athenians following on his heels took the six vessels nearest them, and recovered those of their own which had been disabled close in shore and taken in tow at the beginning of the action; they killed some of the crews and took some prisoners. On board the Leucadian which went down off the merchantman, was the Lacedæmonian Timocrates, who killed himself when the ship was sunk, and was cast up in the harbour of Naupactus. The Athenians on their return set up a trophy on the spot from which they had put out and turned the day, and picking up the wrecks and dead that were on their shore, gave back to the enemy their dead under truce. The Peloponnesians also set up a trophy as victors for the defeat inflicted upon the ships they had disabled in shore, and dedicated the vessel which they had taken at Achæan Rhium, side by side with the trophy. After this, apprehensive of the reinforcement expected from Athens, all except the Leucadians sailed into the Crissæan gulf for Corinth. Not long after their retreat, the twenty Athenian ships, which were to have joined Phormio before the battle, arrived at Naupactus.

Thus the summer ended.

93. Winter was now at hand; but before dispersing the fleet,* which had retired to Corinth and the Crissæan gulf, Cnemus, Brasidas, and the other Peloponnesian captains allowed themselves to be persuaded by the Megarians to make an attempt upon Piræus, the port of Athens, which from her decided superiority at sea had been naturally left unguarded and open. Their plan was as follows:—The men were each to take their oar, cushion, and rowlock thong, and going overland from Corinth to the sea on the Athenian side, to get to Megara as quickly as they could, and launching forty vessels, which happened to be in the docks at Nisæa, to sail at once to Piræus. There was no fleet on the look-out in the harbour, and no one had the least idea of the enemy attempting a surprise;† while an open attack would,

---

*Fragile and small ancient warships did not sail at night or in the winter, when hostilities ceased for several months. The Lacedaemonians were looking for a major victory with a short campaign.

†The Athenians never expected to be attacked by sea and so had made insufficient preparations for homeland defense.

it was thought, never be deliberately ventured on, or, if in contemplation, would be speedily known at Athens. Their plan formed, the next step was to put it in execution. Arriving by night and launching the vessels from Nisæa, they sailed, not to Piræus as they had originally intended, being afraid of the risk, besides which there was some talk of a wind having stopped them, but to the point of Salamis that looks towards Megara; where there was a fort and a squadron of three ships to prevent anything sailing in or out of Megara. This fort they assaulted, and towed off the galleys empty, and surprising the inhabitants began to lay waste the rest of the island.

94. Meanwhile fire signals were raised to alarm Athens, and a panic ensued there as serious as any that occurred during the war.* The idea in the city was that the enemy had already sailed into Piræus: in Piræus it was thought that they had taken Salamis and might at any moment arrive in the port; as indeed might easily have been done if their hearts had been a little firmer: certainly no wind would have prevented them. As soon as day broke the Athenians assembled in full force, launched their ships, and embarking in haste and uproar went with the fleet to Salamis, while their soldiery mounted guard in Piræus. The Peloponnesians, on becoming aware of the coming relief, after they had overrun most of Salamis, hastily sailed off with their plunder and captives and the three ships from Fort Budorum to Nisæa; the state of their ships also causing them some anxiety, as it was a long while since they had been launched, and they were not water-tight. Arrived at Megara, they returned back on foot to Corinth. The Athenians finding them no longer at Salamis, sailed back themselves; and after this made arrangements for guarding Piræus more diligently in future, by closing the harbours, and by other suitable precautions.

95. About the same time, at the beginning of this winter, Sitalces, son of Teres, the Odrysian king of Thrace, made an expedition against Perdiccas, son of Alexander, king of Macedonia, and the Chalcidians in the neighbourhood of Thrace; his object being to enforce one promise and fulfil another. On the one hand Perdiccas had made him a promise, when hard pressed at the commencement of the war, upon condition that Sitalces should reconcile the Athenians to him and not attempt to restore his brother and enemy, the pretender Philip, but had not offered to fulfil his engagement; on the other he, Sitalces, on entering into alliance with the Athenians, had agreed to put an end to the Chalcidian war in Thrace. These were the two objects of his invasion. With him he brought Amyntas, the son of Philip, whom he des-

*Panic at Athens marks the unexpected presence of the enemy at nearby Salamis, opposite the port of Piraeus. But the daring plan came to very little for want of pluck.

tined for the throne of Macedonia, and some Athenian envoys then at his court on this business, and Hagnon as general; for the Athenians were to join him against the Chalcidians with a fleet and as many soldiers as they could get together.

96. Beginning with the Odrysians,* he first called out the Thracian tribes subject to him between mounts Hæmus and Rhodope and the Euxine and Hellespont; next the Getæ beyond Hæmas, and the other hordes settled south of the Danube in the neighbourhood of the Euxine, who, like the Getæ, border on the Scythians and are armed in the same manner, being all mounted archers. Besides these he summoned many of the Hill Thracian independent swordsmen, called Dii and mostly inhabiting Mount Rhodope, some of whom came as mercenaries, others as volunteers; also the Agrianes and Lææans, and the rest of the Pæonian tribes in his empire, at the confines of which these lay, extending up to the Lææan Pæonians and the river Strymon, which flows from Mount Scombrus through the country of the Agrianes and Lææans; there the empire of Sitalces ends and the territory of the independent Pæonians begins. Bordering on the Triballi, also independent, were the Treres and Tilatæans, who dwell to the north of Mount Scombrus and extend towards the setting sun as far as the river Oskius. This river rises in the same mountains as the Nestus and Hebrus, a wild and extensive range connected with Rhodope.

97. The empire of the Odrysians extended along the sea-board from Abdera to the mouth of the Danube in the Euxine. The navigation of this coast by the shortest route takes a merchantman four days and four nights with a wind astern the whole way: by land an active man, travelling by the shortest road, can get from Abdera to the Danube in eleven days. Such was the length of its coast line. Inland from Byzantium to the Lææans and the Strymon, the farthest limit of its extension into the interior, it is a journey of thirteen days for an active man. The tribute from all the barbarian districts and the Hellenic cities, taking what they brought in under Seuthes, the successor of Sitalces, who raised it to its greatest height, amounted to about four hundred talents in gold and silver.† There were also presents in gold and silver to a no less amount, besides stuff, plain and embroidered, and other articles, made not only for the king, but also for the Odrysian lords and nobles. For there was here established a custom opposite to that prevailing in the Persian kingdom, namely, of taking

---

*Sitalces, king of the Thracians, played one side off against the other. At this time, he was working with the Athenians.

†The Thracians were not politically organized or much civilized but quite wealthy, as this annual treasure of 400 talents makes clear. At Attic talent was a unit of money and of weight (about 57 pounds, or 25.86 kg); see the note at 2.13, p. 102. Other standards of weight differed; for example, the Aeginetan talent weighed 37.8 kg.

rather than giving; more disgrace being attached to not giving when asked than to asking and being refused; and although this prevailed elsewhere in Thrace, it was practised most extensively among the powerful Odrysians, it being impossible to get anything done without a present.* It was thus a very powerful kingdom; in revenue and general prosperity surpassing all in Europe between the Ionian gulf and the Euxine, and in numbers and military resources coming decidedly next to the Scythians, with whom indeed no people in Europe can bear comparison, there not being even in Asia any nation singly a match for them if unanimous, though of course they are not on a level with other races in general intelligence and the arts of civilised life.†

98. It was the master of this empire that now prepared to take the field, everything was ready, he set out on his march for Macedonia, first through his own dominions, next over the desolate range of Cercine that divides the Sintians and Pæonians, crossing by a road which he had made by felling the timber on a former campaign against the latter people. Passing over these mountains, with the Pæonians on his right and the Sintians and Mædians on the left, he finally arrived at Doberus, in Pæonia, losing none of his army on the march, except perhaps by sickness, but receiving some augmentations, many of the independent Thracians volunteering to join him in the hope of plunder; so that the whole is said to have formed a grand total of a hundred and fifty thousand. Most of this was infantry, though there was about a third cavalry, furnished principally by the Odrysians themselves and next to them by the Getæ. The most warlike of the infantry were the independent swordsmen who came down from Rhodope; the rest of the mixed multitude that followed him being chiefly formidable by their numbers.

99. Assembling in Doberus, they prepared for descending from the heights upon Lower Macedonia, where the dominions of Perdiccas lay; for the Lyncestæ, Elimiots, and other tribes more inland, though Macedonians by blood and allies and dependents of their kindred, still have their own separate governments. The country on the sea coast, now called Macedonia, was first acquired by Alexander, the father of Perdiccas, and his ancestors, originally Temenids from Argos.‡

---

*Thucydides scorns the venality and lack of self-control to be found among the primitive northern Greeks.

†The Scyths of southern Russia and the Ukraine are described as both less civilized and less intelligent (than the Greeks, of course). Thucydides, who had enjoyed extensive Thracian contacts, shared certain ethnic prejudices of his age. The Macedonians also come off as decidedly inferior to the Greeks but superior to the Thracians.

‡Thucydides includes odd ethnographic notes, part of the Greek historiographical tradition at least from the time of Hecataeus, who combined geography, mythography, anthropology, and recent history (maps 8 and 9 and Pearson, "Thucydides and the Geographical Tradition").

This was effected by the expulsion from Pieria of the Pierians, who afterwards inhabited Phagres and other places under Mount Pangæus, beyond the Strymon (indeed the country between Pangæus and the sea is still called the Pierian gulf); of the Bottiæans, at present neighbours of the Chalcidians, from Bottia, and by the acquisition in Pæonia of a narrow strip along the river Axius extending to Pella and the sea; the district of Mygdonia, between the Axius and the Strymon, being also added by the expulsion of the Edonians. From Eordia also were driven the Eordians, most of whom perished, though a few of them still live round Physca, and the Almopians from Almopia. These Macedonians also conquered places belonging to the other tribes, which are still theirs—Anthemus, Crestonia, Bisaltia, and much of Macedonia Proper. The whole is now called Macedonia, and at the time of the invasion of Sitalces, Perdiccas, Alexander's son, was the reigning king.

100. These Macedonians, unable to take the field against so numerous an invader, shut themselves up in such strong places and fortresses as the country possessed. Of these there was no great number, most of those now found in the country having been erected subsequently by Archelaus,* the son of Perdiccas, on his accession, who also cut straight roads, and otherwise put the kingdom on a better footing as regards horses, heavy infantry, and other war material than had been done by all the eight kings that preceded him. Advancing from Doberus, the Thracian host first invaded what had been once Philip's government, and took Idomene by assault, Gortynia, Atalanta, and some other places by negotiation, these last coming over for love of Philip's son, Amyntas, then with Sitalces. Laying siege to Europus, and failing to take it, he next advanced into the rest of Macedonia to the left of Pella and Cyrrhus, not proceeding beyond this into Bottia and Pieria, but staying to lay waste Mygdonia, Crestonia, and Anthemus. The Macedonians never even thought of meeting him with infantry; but the Thracian host was, as opportunity offered, attacked by handfuls of their horse, which had been reinforced from their allies in the interior. Armed with cuirasses, and excellent horsemen, wherever these charged they overthrew all before them, but ran considerable risk in entangling themselves in the masses of the enemy, and so finally desisted from these efforts, deciding that they were not strong enough to venture against numbers so superior.

101. Meanwhile Sitalces opened negotiations with Perdiccas on the objects of his expedition; and finding that the Athenians, not believing

---

*Archelaus marked a watershed in Macedonian independence and advance into the comity of civilized, bloodthirsty nations. Here Thucydides credits him with building Macedonian fortifications and roads, and improving army organization and equipment.

that he would come, did not appear with their fleet, though they sent presents and envoys, despatched a large part of his army against the Chalcidians and Bottiæans, and shutting them up inside their walls laid waste their country. While he remained in these parts, the people farther south, such as the Thessalians, Magnetes, and the other tribes subject to the Thessalians, and the Hellenes as far as Thermopylæ, all feared that the army might advance against them, and prepared accordingly. These fears were shared by the Thracians beyond the Strymon to the north, who inhabited the plains, such as the Panæans, the Odomanti, the Droi and the Dersæans, all of whom are independent. It was even matter of conversation among the Hellenes who were enemies of Athens whether he might not be invited by his ally to advance also against them. Meanwhile he held Chalcidice and Bottice and Macedonia, and was ravaging them all; but finding that he was not succeeding in any of the objects of his invasion, and that his army was without provisions and was suffering from the severity of the season, he listened to the advice of Seuthes, son of Sparadocus, his nephew and highest officer, and decided to retreat without delay. This Seuthes had been secretly gained by Perdiccas by the promise of his sister in marriage with a rich dowry.* In accordance with this advice, and after a stay of thirty days in all, eight of which were spent in Chalcidice, he retired home as quickly as he could; and Perdiccas afterwards gave his sister Stratonice to Seuthes as he had promised. Such was the history of the expedition of Sitalces.

102. In the course of this winter, after the dispersion of the Peloponnesian fleet, the Athenians in Naupactus, under Phormio, coasted along to Astacus and disembarked, and marched into the interior of Acarnania with four hundred Athenian heavy infantry and four hundred Messenians. After expelling some suspected persons from Stratus, Coronta, and other places, and restoring Cynes, son of Theolytus, to Coronta, they returned to their ships, deciding that it was impossible in the winter season to march against Œniadæ, a place which, unlike the rest of Acarnania, had been always hostile to them; for the river Achelous flowing from Mount Pindus through Dolopia and the country of the Agræans and Amphilochians and the plain of Acarnania, past the town of Stratus in the upper part of its course, forms lakes where it falls into the sea round Œniadæ, and thus makes it impracticable for an army in winter by reason of the water. Opposite to Œniadæ lie most of the islands called Echinades, so close to the mouths of the Achelous that that powerful stream is constantly forming deposits against them, and has already joined some of the islands

---

*Marriages of daughters and sisters sealed many traditional dynastic alliances in the ancient world. These marriages often brought land and cash.

to the continent, and seems likely in no long while to do the same with the rest.* For the current is strong, deep, and turbid, and the islands are so thick together that they serve to imprison the alluvial deposit and prevent its dispersing, lying, as they do, not in one line, but irregularly, so as to leave no direct passage for the water into the open sea. The islands in question are uninhabited and of no great size. There is also a story† that Alcmæon, son of Amphiraus, during his wanderings after the murder of his mother was bidden by Apollo to inhabit this spot, through an oracle which intimated that he would have no release from his terrors until he should find a country to dwell in which had not been seen by the sun, or existed as land at the time he slew his mother; all else being to him polluted ground. Perplexed at this, the story goes on to say, he at last observed this deposit of the Achelous, and considered that a place sufficient to support life upon, might have been thrown up during the long interval that had elapsed since the death of his mother and the beginning of his wanderings. Settling, therefore, in the district round Œniadæ, he founded a dominion, and left the country its name from his son Acarnan. Such is the story‡ we have received concerning Alcmæon.

103. The Athenians and Phormio putting back from Acarnania and arriving at Naupactus, sailed home to Athens in the spring, taking with them the ships that they had captured, and such of the prisoners made in the late actions as were freemen; who were exchanged, man for man.§ And so ended this winter, and the third year of this war, of which Thucydides was the historian.‖

---

*The rare mythical and geographical excursus on the Achelous River reflects the manner of Herodotus and the northern Aegean interests of Thucydides (map 4).

†The rarer mythological excursus in Thucydides more commonly appears when he describes the fringes of the Hellenic world.

‡The closing remark separates myth from history, past from present, and Thucydides' known events from reported legends.

§This is the common protocol for exchange of prisoners, a humane tradition that became rarer as the war became angrier. The same degeneration holds true for Homer's account of the tenth year of the Trojan War.

‖The formula of closure for winter of the year 429 does not include any kind of summary. The next book presents less forgiving pictures of Hellenic hatreds and killings.

BOOK 3

Fourth and Fifth Years of the War—Revolt of Mitylene

1. The next summer, just as the grain was getting ripe, the Peloponnesians and their allies invaded Attica under the command of Archidamus, son of Zeuxidamus, king of the Lacedæmonians,* and sat down and ravaged the land; the Athenian horse as usual attacking them, wherever it was practicable, and preventing the mass of the light troops from advancing from their camp and wasting the parts near the city. After staying the time for which they had taken provisions, the invaders retired and dispersed to their several cities.†

2. Immediately after the invasion of the Peloponnesians all Lesbos, except Methymna, revolted from the Athenians.‡ The Lesbians had wished to revolt even before the war, but the Lacedæmonians would not receive them; and yet now when they did revolt, they were compelled to do so sooner than they had intended. While they were waiting until the moles for their harbours and the ships and walls that they had in building should be finished, and for the arrival of archers and grain and other things that they were engaged in fetching from the Pontus, the Tenedians, with whom they were at enmity, and the Methymnians, and some persons in a private dispute in Mitylene itself, who were *Proxeni* of Athens, informed the Athenians that the Mitylenians were forcibly uniting the island under their sovereignty, and that the preparations about which they were so active, were all concerted with the Bœotians their kindred§ and the Lacedæmonians with a view to a revolt, and that unless they were immediately prevented, Athens would lose Lesbos.

3. However, the Athenians, distressed by the plague, and by the war that had recently broken out and was now raging, thought it a serious matter to add Lesbos with its fleet and untouched resources to

---

*The invasion of 428 will be this royal Spartan's last campaign; he is introduced again formally.

†The yearly incursion reestablished Spartan intentions and good faith but would not win the war, as the Lesbians soon point out.

‡One example, among many, of careful planning upset by an unforeseeable complication. The Lesbians' widely felt dissatisfaction gives the lie to Athenian claims of equity.

§The Hellenes thought of themselves as divided into three ethnic and dialectal groups: Dorians, Ionians, and Aeolians. The Aeolic-speaking people of Boeotia considered themselves to have settled the northern Aegean islands (for example, Lesbos) and the northwestern Anatolian coast.

the list of their enemies; and at first would not believe the charge, giving too much weight to their wish that it might not be true.* But when an embassy which they sent had failed to persuade the Mitylenians to give up the union and preparations complained of, they became alarmed, and resolved to strike the first blow. They accordingly suddenly sent off forty ships that had been got ready to sail round Peloponnese, under the command of Cleippides, son of Deinias, and two others; word having been brought them of a festival in honour of the Malean Apollo outside the town, which is kept by the whole people of Mitylene,† and at which, if haste were made, they might hope to take them by surprise. If this plan succeeded, well and good; if not, they were to order the Mitylenians to deliver up their ships and to pull down their walls, and if they did not obey, to declare war. The ships accordingly set out; the ten galleys, forming the contingent of the Mitylenians present with the fleet according to the terms of the alliance, being detained by the Athenians, and their crews placed in custody. However, the Mitylenians were informed of the expedition by a man who crossed from Athens to Eubœa, and going overland to Geræstus, sailed from thence by a merchantman which he found on the point of putting to sea, and so arrived at Mitylene the third day after leaving Athens.‡ The Mitylenians accordingly refrained from going out to the temple at Malea, and moreover barricaded and kept guard round the half-finished parts of their walls and harbours.

4. When the Athenians sailed in not long after and saw how things stood, the generals delivered their orders, and upon the Mitylenians refusing to obey, commenced hostilities. The Mitylenians, thus compelled to go to war without notice and unprepared, at first sailed out with their fleet and made some show of fighting, a little in front of the harbour; but being driven back by the Athenian ships, immediately offered to treat with the commanders, wishing, if possible, to get the ships away for the present upon any tolerable terms. The Athenian commanders accepted their offers, being themselves fearful that they might not be able to cope with the whole of Lesbos; and an armistice having been concluded, the Mitylenians sent to Athens one of the informers, already repentant of his conduct, and others with him, to try to persuade the Athenians of the innocence of their intentions and to get the fleet recalled. In the meantime, having no great hope of a favourable answer from Athens, they also sent off a galley with en-

---

*Thucydides comments sardonically on wishes overriding evidence.

†Malean Apollo (not Panhellenic Apollo or Panionian Apollo) was the focus of a local Lesbian cult shared by the population of its leading city, Mitylene.

‡This is a precious indication of how quickly on land by foot and on sea by ship an active traveler could cover the approximately 190 miles between Athens and Mitylene. The time required for this journey will later determine the Lesbians' life or death.

voys to Lacedæmon, unobserved by the Athenian fleet which was anchored at Malea to the north of the town.

While these envoys, reaching Lacedæmon after a difficult journey across the open sea, were negotiating for succours being sent them,

5. the ambassadors from Athens returned without having effected anything; and hostilities were at once begun by the Mitylenians and the rest of Lesbos, with the exception of the Methymnians, who came to the aid of the Athenians with the Imbrians and Lemnians and some few of the other allies. The Mitylenians made a sortie with all their forces against the Athenian camp; and a battle ensued, in which they gained some slight advantage, but retired notwithstanding, not feeling sufficient confidence in themselves to spend the night upon the field. After this they kept quiet, wishing to wait for the chance of reinforcements arriving from Peloponnese before making a second venture, being encouraged by the arrival of Meleas, a Laconian, and Hermæondas, a Theban, who had been sent off before the insurrection but had been unable to reach Lesbos before the Athenian expedition, and who now stole in in a galley after the battle, and advised them to send another galley and envoys back with them, which the Mitylenians accordingly did.*

6. Meanwhile the Athenians, greatly encouraged by the inaction of the Mitylenians, summoned allies to their aid, who came in all the quicker from seeing so little vigour displayed by the Lesbians, and bringing round their ships to a new station to the south of the town, fortified two camps, one on each side of the city, and instituted a blockade of both the harbours. The sea was thus closed against the Mitylenians, who however commanded the whole country, with the rest of the Lesbians who had now joined them; the Athenians only holding a limited area round their camps, and using Malea more as the station for their ships and their market.

While the war went on in this way at Mitylene,

7. the Athenians, about the same time in this summer, also sent thirty ships to Peloponnese under Asopius, son of Phormio; the Acarnanians insisting that the commander sent should be some son or relative of Phormio.† As the ships coasted along shore they ravaged the seaboard of Laconia; after which Asopius sent most of the fleet home, and himself went on with twelve vessels to Naupactus, and afterwards raising the whole Acarnanian population made an expedition against

---

*The Spartan hegemons and their immediate allies encouraged cities connected to them by blood, myth, or interest to join the revolt against Athens' empire.

†Thucydides shifts—the first of two times in the first fifty chapters of this massive book 3 (concerning Lesbos, Plataea, Corcyra, and northwestern Greece)—to one of the other theaters. The Acarnanians of the northwest knew the talents of the successful general Phormio and demanded a relative as their commander.

Œniadæ, the fleet sailing along the Achelous, while the army laid waste the country. The inhabitants, however, showing no signs of submitting, he dismissed the land forces and himself sailed to Leucas, and making a descent upon Nericus was cut off during his retreat, and most of his troops with him, by the people in those parts aided by some coast-guards; after which the Athenians sailed away, recovering their dead from the Leucadians under truce.*

8. Meanwhile the envoys of the Mitylenians sent out in the first ship were told by the Lacedæmonians to come to Olympia, in order that the rest of the allies might hear them and decide upon their matter, and so they journeyed thither. It was the Olympiad in which the Rhodian Dorieus gained his second victory,† and the envoys having been introduced to make their speech after the festival, spoke as follows:—

9. 'Lacedæmonians and allies, the rule established among the Hellenes is not unknown to us. Those who revolt in war and forsake their former confederacy are favourably regarded by those who receive them, in so far as they are of use to them, but otherwise are thought less well of, through being considered traitors to their former friends. Nor is this an unfair way of judging, where the rebels and the power from whom they secede are at one in policy and sympathy, and a match for each other in resources and power, and where no reasonable ground exists for the rebellion. But with us and the Athenians this was not the case; and no one need think the worse of us‡ for revolting from them in danger, after having been honoured by them in time of peace.

10. 'Justice and honesty will be the first topics of our speech, especially as we are asking for alliance; because we know that there can never be any solid friendship between individuals, or union between communities that is worth the name, unless the parties be persuaded of each other's honesty, and be generally congenial the one to the other; since from difference in feeling springs also difference in conduct. Between ourselves and the Athenians alliance began, when you withdrew from the Median war and they remained to finish the business.§ But we did not become allies of the Athenians for the subjugation of the Hellenes, but allies of the Hellenes for their liberation from the Mede; and as long as the Athenians led us fairly we followed them loyally; but when we saw them relax their hostility to the Mede, to try to compass

---

*The northwestern narrative will be continued in chapters 97–114.

†Thucydides reports little of athletic prowess and kudos, so significant in his day and ours. Dorieus won the vicious *pankration*, an all-out fighting event.

‡The Mitylenians of Lesbos (map 10) begin by justifying their long loyalty to the inveterate enemies of the Spartans.

§After 479, the Hellenes dwelling along the Ionian coast gladly accepted whatever aid they could find from the stronger, more secure mainland Greek powers.

the subjection of the allies, then our apprehensions began.* Unable, however, to unite and defend themselves on account of the number of confederates that had votes, all the allies were enslaved, except ourselves and the Chians, who continued to send our contingents as independent and nominally free.† Trust in Athens as a leader, however, we could no longer feel, judging by the examples already given; it being unlikely that she would reduce our fellow-confederates, and not do the same by us who were left, if ever she had the power.

11. 'Had we all been still independent, we could have had more faith in their not attempting any change; but the greater number being their subjects, while they were treating us as equals, they would naturally chafe under this solitary instance of independence as contrasted with the submission of the majority; particularly as they daily grew more powerful, and we more destitute. Now the only sure basis of an alliance is for each party to be equally afraid of the other:‡ he who would like to encroach is then deterred by the reflexion that he will not have odds in his favour. Again, if we were left independent, it was only because they thought they saw their way to empire more clearly by specious language and by the paths of policy than by those of force. Not only were we useful as evidence that powers who had votes, like themselves, would not, surely, join them in their expeditions, against their will, without the party attacked being in the wrong; but the same system also enabled them to lead the stronger states, against the weaker first, and so to leave the former to the last, stripped of their natural allies, and less capable of resistance. But if they had begun with us, while all the states still had their resources under their own control, and there was a centre to rally round, the work of subjugation would have been found less easy. Besides this, our navy gave them some apprehension: it was always possible that it might unite with you or with some other power, and become dangerous to Athens. The court which we paid to their commons and its leaders for the time being, also helped us to maintain our independence.§ However, we did not expect to be able to do so much longer, if this war had not broken out, from the examples that we had had of their conduct to the rest.

---

*The Lesbians cannot deny supporting Athens' empire, so they must explain when and why they experienced a change of heart.

†The Chians, the Lesbians, and the Samians until 440 (when the Athenians crushed their revolt) maintained a contribution in men and ships and thus an apparent, but in fact limited, autonomy.

‡Desertion of one alliance must be justified to the *hegemon* (leader) of the rival alliance. The Lesbians' speech provides reasons for many of the other rebellions from the Delian League.

§Thucydides' speaker acknowledges the need experienced by allies to flatter the Athenian common people, a point made less graciously by Aristophanes in *Wasps* and by the "Old Oligarch" in his pamphlet *Athenian Go ernment* (Fornara #107).

12. 'How then could we put our trust in such friendship or freedom as we had here? We accepted each other against our inclination; fear made them court us in war, and us them in peace; sympathy, the ordinary basis of confidence, had its place supplied by terror, fear having more share than friendship in detaining us in the alliance; and the first party that should be encouraged by the hope of impunity was certain to break faith with the other. So that to condemn us for being the first to break off, because they delay the blow that we dread, instead of ourselves delaying to know for certain whether it will be dealt or not, is to take a false view of the case. For if we were equally able with them to meet their plots and imitate their delay, we should be their equals and should be under no necessity of being their subjects; but the liberty of offence being always theirs, that of defence ought clearly to be ours.

13. 'Such, Lacedæmonians and allies, are the grounds and the reasons of our revolt; clear enough to convince our hearers of the fairness of our conduct, and sufficient to alarm ourselves, and to make us turn to some means of safety. This we wished to do long ago, when we sent to you on the subject while the peace yet lasted, but were baulked by your refusing to receive us; and now, upon the Bœotians inviting us, we at once responded to the call, and decided upon a twofold revolt, from the Hellenes and from the Athenians, not to aid the latter in harming the former, but to join in their liberation, and not to allow the Athenians in the end to destroy us, but to act in time against them. Our revolt, however, has taken place prematurely and without preparation—a fact which makes it all the more incumbent on you to receive us into alliance and to send us speedy relief, in order to show that you support your friends, and at the same time do harm to your enemies.* You have an opportunity such as you never had before.† Disease and expenditure have wasted the Athenians: their ships are either cruising round your coasts, or engaged in blockading us; and it is not probable that they will have any to spare, if you invade them a second time this summer by sea and land; but they will either offer no resistance to your vessels, or withdraw from both our shores. Nor must it be thought that this is a case of putting yourselves into danger for a country which is not yours. Lesbos may appear far off, but when help is wanted she will be found near enough.‡ It is not in

---

*The Lesbians try to convince the Lacedaemonians that they have no choice but to support the revolt once it has begun. Harming enemies and helping friends is a commonplace of Greek morality.

†Not only is aid ethical; it is also expedient at this time when Athenian forces are in trouble.

‡This promise turned out to be as unreal as that the Corcyreans made to the Athenians before the war. That is not to imply it was initially insincere.

Attica that the war will be decided, as some imagine,* but in the countries by which Attica is supported; and the Athenian revenue is drawn from the allies, and will become still larger if they reduce us; as not only will no other state revolt, but our resources will be added to theirs, and we shall be treated worse than those that were enslaved before. But if you will frankly support us, you will add to your side a state that has a large navy, which is your great want; you will smooth the way to the overthrow of the Athenians by depriving them of their allies, who will be greatly encouraged to come over;† and you will free yourselves from the imputation made against you, of not supporting insurrection. In short, only show yourselves as liberators, and you may count upon having the advantage in the war.

14. 'Respect, therefore, the hopes placed in you by the Hellenes, and that Olympian Zeus, in whose temple we stand as very suppliants;‡ become the allies and defenders of the Mitylenians, and do not sacrifice us, who put our lives upon the hazard, in a cause in which general good will result to all from our success, and still more general harm if we fail through your refusing to help us; but be the men that the Hellenes think you, and our fears desire.'

15. Such were the words of the Mitylenians. After hearing them out, the Lacedæmonians and confederates granted what they urged, and took the Lesbians into alliance, and deciding in favour of the invasion of Attica, told the allies present to march as quickly as possible to the Isthmus with two-thirds of their forces; and arriving there first themselves, got ready hauling machines to carry their ships across from Corinth to the sea on the side of Athens, in order to make their attack by sea and land at once. However, the zeal which they displayed was not imitated by the rest of the confederates, who came in but slowly, being engaged in harvesting their grain and sick of making expeditions.§

16. Meanwhile the Athenians, aware that the preparations of the enemy were due to his conviction of their weakness, and wishing to show him that he was mistaken, and that they were able, without moving the Lesbian fleet, to repel with ease that with which they were

---

*The Lesbians realize that the Spartan strategy would not work and could not work. They speak this unpleasant truth politely, however.

†This argument about the paradigmatic value of desertion reappears in Cleon's subsequent argument about why the Lesbians deserve especially severe punishment.

‡Suppliants in Thucydides' day were sometimes ignored or, worse, butchered. Although the Mitylenians carry the oratorical day, they lose the killing battle. But they are employing the atmosphere of the Panhellenic sanctuary to persuade their audience.

§Peloponnesian morale was low, as Pericles predicted, after three years of inconclusive disruption, invasion, and insecurity. Twenty-five years of combat with interruptions remained.

menaced from Peloponnese, manned a hundred ships by embarking the citizens of Athens, except the knights and Pentecosiomedimni, and the resident aliens;* and putting out to the Isthmus, displayed their power, and made descents upon Peloponnese wherever they pleased. A disappointment so signal made the Lacedæmonians think that the Lesbians had not spoken the truth; and embarrassed by the non-appearance of the confederates, coupled with the news that the thirty ships round Peloponnese were ravaging the lands near Sparta, they went back home. Afterwards, however, they got ready a fleet to send to Lesbos, and ordering a total of forty ships from the different cities in the league, appointed Alcidas to command the expedition in his capacity of high admiral. Meanwhile the Athenians in the hundred ships, upon seeing the Lacedæmonians go home, went home likewise.

17. If at the time that this fleet was at sea, Athens had almost the largest number of first-rate ships in commission that she ever possessed at any one moment, she had as many or even more when the war began.† At that time one hundred guarded Attica, Eubœa, and Salamis; a hundred more were cruising round Peloponnese, besides those employed at Potidæa and in other places;‡ making a grand total of two hundred and fifty vessels employed on active service in a single summer. It was this, with Potidæa, that most exhausted her revenues—Potidæa being blockaded by a force of heavy infantry (each drawing two drachmæ a day, one for himself and another for his servant),§ which amounted to three thousand at first, and was kept at this number down to the end of the siege; besides sixteen hundred with Phormio who went away before it was over; and the ships being all paid at the same rate. In this way her money was wasted at first; and this was the largest number of ships ever manned by her.

18. About the same time that the Lacedæmonians were at the Isthmus, the Mitylenians marched by land with their mercenaries against Methymna, which they thought to gain by treachery. After assaulting the town, and not meeting with the success that they anticipated, they withdrew to Antissa, Pyrrha, and Eresus; and taking measures for the

---

*The knights (*hippeis*) were Athenian citizens who could afford to feed a horse in their fields and on campaign. They were not as rich as the top class, the men who produced 500 bushels each year of grain or its equivalent, thus called "500-bushels-a-year" citizens (*pentakosiomedimnoi*), but they owned greater assets than the yeoman farmers who maintained a yoke of oxen (the *zeugites*), or citizens below that threshold (the *thetes*), landholders or not. The resident aliens (*metics*) could not own real property or exercise political rights but were nevertheless subject to taxes and military service.

†A digression examines Athenian war resources. Some scholars think the paragraph has been displaced from a more suitable, earlier location.

‡Potidaea had capitulated earlier (2.70; map 7), so this note seems awkward here.

§Two drachmae per day was double the usual hoplite pay, but the duty was onerous.

better security of these towns and strengthening their walls, hastily returned home. After their departure the Methymnians marched against Antissa, but were defeated in a sortie by the Antissians and their mercenaries, and retreated in haste after losing many of their number. Word of this reaching Athens, and the Athenians learning that the Mitylenians were masters of the country and their own soldiers unable to hold them in check, they sent out about the beginning of autumn Paches, son of Epicurus, to take the command, and a thousand Athenian heavy infantry; who worked their own passage, and arriving at Mitylene, built a single wall all round it, forts being erected at some of the strongest points. Mitylene was thus blockaded strictly on both sides, by land and by sea; and winter now drew near.

19. The Athenians needing money for the siege, although they had for the first time raised a contribution of two hundred talents from their own citizens,* now sent out twelve ships to levy subsidies from their allies, with Lysicles and four others in command. After cruising to different places and laying them under contribution, Lysicles went up the country from Myus, in Caria, across the plain of the Maender, as far as the hill of Sandius; and being attacked by the Carians and the people of Anaia, was slain with many of his soldiers.

20. The same winter the Platæans, who were still being besieged by the Peloponnesians and Bœotians,† distressed by the failure of their provisions, and seeing no hope of relief from Athens, nor any other means of safety, formed a scheme with the Athenians besieged with them for escaping, if possible, by forcing their way over the enemy's walls; the attempt having been suggested by Theænetus, son of Tolmides, a soothsayer, and Eupompides, son of Daïmachus, one of their generals. At first all were to join: afterwards, half hung back, thinking the risk great; about two hundred and twenty, however, voluntarily persevered in the attempt, which was carried out in the following way. Ladders were made to match the height of the enemy's wall, which they measured by the layers of bricks, the side turned towards them not being thoroughly whitewashed. These were counted by many persons at once; and though some might miss the right calculation, most would hit upon it, particularly as they counted over and over again, and were no great way from the wall, but could see it easily enough for their purpose.‡ The length required for the ladders was thus obtained, being calculated from the breadth of the brick.

---

*The profits of empire had enabled the Athenians to remove taxes on persons and property within the citizen body.

†The narrative of Plataea resumes from 2.78 with an exciting escape.

‡Thucydides can be abstract, but he also has vivid patches such as this one, where we are invited to place ourselves in the action. The double circumvallation is unique in fifth-century warfare.

21. Now the wall of the Peloponnesians was constructed as follows. It consisted of two lines drawn round the place, one against the Platæans, the other against any attack on the outside from Athens, about sixteen feet apart. The intermediate space of sixteen feet was occupied by huts portioned out among the soldiers on guard, and built in one block, so as to give the appearance of a single thick wall with battlements on either side. At intervals of every ten battlements were towers of considerable size, and the same breadth as the wall, reaching right across from its inner to its outer face, with no means of passing except through the middle. Accordingly on stormy and wet nights the battlements were deserted, and guard kept from the towers, which were not far apart and roofed in above.

22. Such being the structure of the wall by which the Platæans were blockaded, when their preparations were completed, they waited for a stormy night of wind and rain and without any moon,* and then set out, guided by the authors of the enterprise. Crossing first the ditch that ran round the town, they next gained the wall of the enemy unperceived by the sentinels, who did not see them in the darkness, or hear them, as the wind drowned with its roar the noise of their approach; besides which they kept a good way off from each other, that they might not be betrayed by the clash of their weapons. They were also lightly equipped, and had only the left foot shod to preserve them from slipping in the mire.† They came up to the battlements at one of the intermediate spaces where they knew them to be unguarded: those who carried the ladders went first and planted them; next twelve light-armed soldiers with only a dagger and a breastplate mounted, led by Ammias, son of Corœbus, who was the first on the wall; his followers getting up after him and going six to each of the towers. After these came another party of light troops armed with spears, whose shields, that they might advance the easier, were carried by men behind, who were to hand them to them when they found themselves in presence of the enemy. After a good many had mounted they were discovered by the sentinels in the towers, by the noise made by a tile which was knocked down by one of the Platæans as he was laying hold of the battlements.‡ The alarm was instantly

---

*The dark, cold, and stormy night aided the heavily outnumbered break-out band of plucky Plataeans.

†Why only one shoe off? Thucydides argues in order to increase traction (illogically, but to rationalize). He eschews religious explanations, as he does personal explanations, especially those involving females, that he and other later historians have associated with the less power-obsessed historiography of Herodotus.

‡"For want of a nail"—or as here, for the smash of a tile—a battle or war may be won or lost. Thucydides emphasizes chance occurrences, those that no one could foretell, not even Themistocles.

given, and the troops rushed to the wall, not knowing the nature of the danger, owing to the dark night and stormy weather; the Platæans in the town having also chosen that moment to make a sortie against the wall of the Peloponnesians upon the side opposite to that on which their men were getting over, in order to divert the attention of the besiegers. Accordingly they remained distracted at their several posts, without any venturing to stir to give help from his own station, and at a loss to guess what was going on. Meanwhile the three hundred set aside for service on emergencies went outside the wall in the direction of the alarm. Fire-signals of an attack were also raised towards Thebes; but the Platæans in the town at once displayed a number of others, prepared beforehand for this very purpose,* in order to render the enemy's signals unintelligible, and to prevent his friends getting a true idea of what was passing and coming to his aid, before their comrades who had gone out should have made good their escape and be in safety.

23. Meanwhile the first of the scaling-party that had got up, after carrying both the towers and putting the sentinels to the sword, posted themselves inside to prevent any one coming through against them; and rearing ladders from the wall, sent several men up on the towers, and from their summit and base kept in check all of the enemy that came up, with their missiles, while their main body planted a number of ladders against the wall, and knocking down the battlements, passed over between the towers; each as soon as he had got over taking up his station at the edge of the ditch, and plying from thence with arrows and darts any who came along the wall to stop the passage of his comrades. When all were over, the party on the towers came down, the last of them not without difficulty, and proceeded to the ditch, just as the three hundred came up carrying torches. The Platæans, standing on the edge of the ditch in the dark, had a good view of their opponents, and discharged their arrows and darts upon the unarmed parts of their bodies, while they themselves could not be so well seen in the obscurity for the torches; and thus even the last of them got over the ditch, though not without effort and difficulty; as ice had formed in it, not strong enough to walk upon, but of that watery kind which generally comes with a wind more east than north, and the snow which this wind had caused to fall during the night had made the water in the ditch rise, so that they could scarcely breast it as they crossed.† However, it was mainly the violence of the storm that enabled them to effect their escape at all.

---

*On the other hand, Thucydides admires successful advance planning, of which these telegraphic torches are one example.

†The summer tourist may mistakenly disbelieve reports of the snow and ice of a bitter Greek winter. Even helping factors can hinder a good plan.

24. Starting from the ditch, the Platæans went all together along the road leading to Thebes, keeping the chapel of the hero Androcrates upon their right; considering that the last road which the Peloponnesians would suspect them of having taken would be that towards their enemies' country. Indeed they could see them pursuing with torches upon the Athens road towards Cithæron and Druos-kephalai or Oakheads. After going for rather more than half a mile upon the road to Thebes, the Platæans turned off and took that leading to the mountain, to Erythræ and Hysiæ, and reaching the hills, made good their escape to Athens, two hundred and twelve men in all; some of their number having turned back into the town before getting over the wall, and one archer having been taken prisoner at the outer ditch. Meanwhile the Peloponnesians gave up the pursuit and returned to their posts; and the Platæans in the town, knowing nothing of what had passed, and informed by those who had turned back that not a man had escaped,* sent out a herald as soon as it was day to make a truce for the recovery of the dead bodies, and then learning the truth, desisted. In this way the Platæan party got over and were saved.

25. Towards the close of the same winter, Salæthus, a Lacedæmonian, was sent out in a galley from Lacedæmon to Mitylene. Going by sea to Pyrrha, and from thence overland, he passed along the bed of a torrent, where the line of circumvallation was passable, and thus entering unperceived into Mitylene, told the magistrates that Attica would certainly be invaded, and the forty ships destined to relieve them arrive, and that he had been sent on to announce this and to superintend matters generally. The Mitylenians upon this took courage, and laid aside the idea of treating with the Athenians; and now this winter ended, and with it ended the fourth year of the war of which Thucydides was the historian.†

26. The next summer the Peloponnesians sent off the forty-two ships for Mitylene, under Alcidas, their high admiral, and themselves and their allies invaded Attica, their object being to distract the Athenians by a double movement, and thus to make it less easy for them to act against the fleet sailing to Mitylene. The commander in this invasion was Cleomenes, in the place of King Pausanias, son of Pleistoanax, his nephew, who was still a minor.‡ Not content with laying

---

*Thucydides' recordings of the exchange and recovery of corpses include surprised reactions at misguided expectations of both smaller or disastrous losses (compare the dramatic dialogue of 3.113).

†The formulaic pause marks the end of another year of the conflict and the "trademark" or "signature ending" of the author. On occasion, as in the case of book 3, such pauses appear at book's end.

‡Spring 427 includes preparations for another year, the fifth, and for an important campaign, this time under the Spartan regent for a minor. His father had been banished for accepting a bribe. As one recollects from the earlier Pausanias, Spartans had trouble with unlimited temptations.

waste whatever had shot up in the parts which they had before devastated, the invaders now extended their ravages to lands passed over
in their previous incursions; so that this invasion was more severely
felt by the Athenians than any except the second;* the enemy staying
on and on until they had overrun most of the country, in the expectation of hearing from Lesbos of something having been achieved by
their fleet, which they thought must now have got over. However, as
they did not obtain any of the results expected, and their provisions
began to run short, they retreated and dispersed to their different
cities.

27. In the meantime the Mitylenians, finding their provisions failing, while the fleet from Peloponnese was loitering on the way instead
of appearing at Mitylene, were compelled to come to terms with the
Athenians in the following manner. Salæthus having himself ceased
to expect the fleet to arrive, now armed the commons with heavy armour, which they had not before possessed, with the intention of
making a sortie against the Athenians.† The commons, however, no
sooner found themselves possessed of arms than they refused any
longer to obey their officers;‡ and forming in knots together, told the
authorities to bring out in public the provisions and divide them
amongst them all, or they would themselves come to terms with the
Athenians and deliver up the city.

28. The government, aware of their inability to prevent this, and of
the danger they would be in, if left out of the capitulation, publicly
agreed with Paches and the army to surrender Mitylene at discretion
and to admit the troops into the town; upon the understanding that
the Mitylenians should be allowed to send an embassy to Athens to
plead their cause, and that Paches should not imprison, make slaves
of, or put to death any of the citizens until its return. Such were the
terms of the capitulation; in spite of which the chief authors of the negotiation with Lacedæmon were so completely overcome by terror
when the army entered, that they went and seated themselves by the
altars, from which they were raised up by Paches under promise that
he would do them no wrong, and lodged by him in Tenedos, until he

---

*The length of the incursion and its thorough destruction of capital goods (timber,
olive trees, grapevines) afflicted the Athenian victims, but the Peloponnesians were
also disappointed in the results.

†The Spartan Salaethus misestimates the loyalty of the Mitylenean population toward
the revolt, which the wealthy seem to have begun. This miscalculation costs him his life.

‡It is unclear from Thucydides' account whether the *demos* had been originally enthusiastic about the revolt but changed its attitude or whether merely their lack of
weaponry made them compliant at first.

should learn the pleasure of the Athenians concerning them. Paches also sent some galleys and seized Antissa, and took such other military measures as he thought advisable.

29. Meanwhile the Peloponnesians in the forty ships, who ought to have made all haste to relieve Mitylene, lost time in coming round Peloponnese itself, and proceeding leisurely on the remainder of the voyage, made Delos without having been seen by the Athenians at Athens, and from thence arriving at Icarus and Myconus, there first heard of the fall of Mitylene. Wishing to know the truth, they put into Embatum, in the Erythræid, about seven days after the capture of the town. Here they learned the truth, and began to consider what they were to do; and Teutiaplus, an Elean, addressed them as follows:—*

30. 'Alcidas and Peloponnesians who share with me the command of this armament, my advice is to sail just as we are to Mitylene, before we have been heard of. We may expect to find the Athenians as much off their guard† as men generally are who have just taken a city: this will certainly be so by sea, where they have no idea of any enemy attacking them, and where our strength, as it happens, mainly lies; while even their land forces are probably scattered about the houses in the carelessness of victory. If therefore we were to fall upon them suddenly and in the night, I have hopes, with the help of the well-wishers that we may have left inside the town, that we shall become masters of the place. Let us not shrink from the risk, but let us remember that this is just the occasion for one of the baseless panics common in war; and that to be able to guard against these in one's own case, and to detect the moment when an attack will find an enemy at this disadvantage, is what makes a successful general.'

31. These words of Teutiaplus failing to move Alcidas, some of the Ionian exiles and the Lesbians with the expedition began to urge him, since this seemed too dangerous, to seize one of the Ionian cities or the Æolic town of Cyme, to use as a base for effecting the revolt of Ionia. This was by no means a hopeless enterprise, as their coming was welcome everywhere;‡ their object would be by this move to deprive Athens of her chief source of revenue,§ and at the same time to saddle her with expense, if she chose to blockade them; and they

---

*Like Diodotus of Athens in the Mitylenian debate soon after, Teutiaplus of Elis is otherwise unknown. His good advice has no effect except to show us what might have happened with a commander more resolute than the despicable Spartiate Alcidas.

†As in the parallel account of Spartan reluctance to strike at 2.29, the element of surprise can be worth a battalion. The Spartan Brasidas appreciated alacrity, when an attack has been properly prepared.

‡Thucydides plainly indicates the unpopularity of the Athenian empire in Ionia.

§Thucydides plainly indicates the centrality of Ionia to Athenian imperial income.

would probably induce Pissuthnes to join them in the war.* However, Alcidas gave this proposal as bad a reception as the other, being eager, since he had come too late for Mitylene, to find himself back in Peloponnese as soon as possible.†

32. Accordingly he put out from Embatum and proceeded along shore; and touching at the Teian town, Myonnesus, there butchered most of the prisoners that he had taken on his passage.‡ Upon his coming to anchor at Ephesus, envoys came to him from the Samians at Anaia, and told him that he was not going the right way to free Hellas in massacring men who had never raised a hand against him, and who were not enemies of his, but allies of Athens against their will, and that if he did not stop he would turn many more friends into enemies than enemies into friends.§ Alcidas agreed to this, and let go all the Chians still in his hands and some of the others that he had taken; the inhabitants, instead of flying at the sight of his vessels, rather coming up to them, taking them for Athenian, having no sort of expectation that while the Athenians commanded the sea Peloponnesian ships would venture over to Ionia.

33. From Ephesus Alcidas set sail in haste and fled. He had been seen by the Salaminian and Paralian galleys,‖ which happened to be sailing from Athens, while still at anchor off Clarus; and fearing pursuit he now made across the open sea, fully determined to touch nowhere, if he could help it, until he got to Peloponnese. Meanwhile news of him had come in to Paches from the Erythræid, and indeed from all quarters. As Ionia was unfortified, great fears were felt that the Peloponnesians coasting along shore, even if they did not intend to stay, might make descents in passing and plunder the towns; and now the Paralian and Salaminian, having seen him at Clarus, themselves brought intelligence of the fact. Paches accordingly gave hot chase, and continued the pursuit as far as the isle of Patmos, and then finding that Alcidas had got on too far to be overtaken, came back again. Meanwhile he thought it fortunate that, as he had not fallen in with them out at sea, he had not overtaken them anywhere where

---

*The Persian connection, long sought by both sides, would play, in the last stages of the war, a decisive role in dashing Athenian hopes of victory.

†Early Peloponnesian attempts to detach the allies of Athens do more harm than good, at least to the alleged beneficiaries of Spartan support.

‡Alcidas serves as a paradigm for the Spartans' inability to gain the goodwill that the Hellenes were eager to throw at them. This stupidity is criminal.

§Some Samians were as eager as any Greeks to drive out the Athenians. In their friendly mouths, Thucydides puts the case against Spartans killing potential friends.

‖These two high-speed, elite triremes were the Athenian state's official diplomatic and messenger ships. The *demos* paid their crews more and trained them better than the *thetes* (the ordinary, lower-class oarsmen) of the battle-triremes.

they would have been forced to encamp, and so give him the trouble of blockading them.

34. On his return along shore he touched, among other places, at Notium, the port of Colophon, where the Colophonians had settled after the capture of the upper town by Itamenes and the barbarians, who had been called in by certain individuals in a party quarrel. The capture of the town took place about the time of the second Peloponnesian invasion of Attica. However, the refugees, after settling at Notium, again split up into factions, one of which called in Arcadian and barbarian mercenaries from Pissuthnes, and entrenching these in a quarter apart, formed a new community with the Median party* of the Colophonians who joined them from the upper town. Their opponents had retired into exile, and now called in Paches, who invited Hippias, the commander of the Arcadians in the fortified quarter, to a parley, upon condition that, if they could not agree, he was to be put back safe and sound in the fortification. However, upon his coming out to him, he put him into custody, though not in chains, and attacked suddenly and took by surprise the fortification, and putting the Arcadians and the barbarians found in it to the sword, afterwards took Hippias into it as he had promised, and, as soon as he was inside, seized him and shot him down.† Paches then gave up Notium to the Colophonians not of the Median party; and settlers were afterwards sent out from Athens, and the place colonised according to Athenian laws, after collecting all the Colophonians found in any of the cities.‡

35. Arrived at Mitylene, Paches reduced Pyrrha and Eresus; and finding the Lacedæmonian, Salæthus, in hiding in the town, sent him off to Athens, together with the Mitylenians that he had placed in Tenedos, and any other persons that he thought concerned in the revolt. He also sent back the greater part of his forces, remaining with the rest to settle Mitylene and the rest of Lesbos as he thought best.

36. Upon the arrival of the prisoners with Salæthus, the Athenians at once put the latter to death, although he offered, among other things, to procure the withdrawal of the Peloponnesians from Platæa,

---

*"The Median party" refers to Greeks, native Anatolians, and mixed-bloods who were ready again to exchange Greek masters for Persian—for one thing, taxes might be lower. Many fifth-century Greeks use the word "Median" interchangeably with the more accurate (at this time) word for their successor, "Persian." The Persians, on their side, tended to call all Greeks "Ionians."

†This fairytale-like anecdote of the promise fulfilled, if in an unpleasant way for Hippias, characterizes the relatively lawless state of Greek warfare and the careful observation of religious letter rather than spirit.

‡The Athenians reward the Colophonians who remain loyal to them and confiscate territory (map 10) for their own citizens' profit.

which was still under siege;* and after deliberating as to what they should do with the former, in the fury of the moment determined to put to death not only the prisoners at Athens, but the whole adult male population of Mitylene, and to make slaves of the women and children.† It was remarked that Mitylene had revolted without being, like the rest, subjected to the empire; and what above all swelled the wrath of the Athenians was the fact of the Peloponnesian fleet having ventured over to Ionia to her support, a fact which was held to argue a long meditated rebellion. They accordingly sent a galley to communicate the decree to Paches, commanding him to lose no time in despatching the Mitylenians. The morrow brought repentance with it and reflexion on the horrid cruelty of a decree,‡ which condemned a whole city to the fate merited only by the guilty. This was no sooner perceived by the Mitylenian ambassadors at Athens and their Athenian supporters, than they moved the authorities to put the question again to the vote; which they the more easily consented to do, as they themselves plainly saw that most of the citizens wished some one to give them an opportunity for reconsidering the matter. An assembly was therefore at once called, and after much expression of opinion upon both sides, Cleon, son of Cleænetus, the same who had carried the former motion of putting the Mitylenians to death, the most violent man at Athens, and at that time by far the most powerful with the commons, came forward again and spoke as follows:—§

37. 'I have often before now been convinced that a democracy is incapable of empire, and never more so than by your present change of mind in the matter of Mitylene. Fears or plots being unknown to

---

*Salaethus seems not to have had a trial, nor did the Athenians see fit to trade him for other prisoners of their own. His promise looks unlikely, a desperate way to buy time.

†This severe and indiscriminate sentence of death and enslavement was within the parameters for unconditional surrender of a city. It seems clearly inappropriate and impolitic in the Mitylenian situation. Perhaps a majority of the citizens surrendered to the Athenians as soon as they could do so.

‡Revenge gave way to calculation; the unusual phrase "horrid cruelty" may be the Athenians' thought, Thucydides', or (probably) that of both.

§Thucydides' inexplicit habits when introducing speakers are noteworthy. In the first place, we only hear two of the many opinions expressed in the assembly, those delivered by two leaders of Athenian factions and those most opposed to each other. Second, Cleon receives a superlative adjective here and other unflattering descriptors elsewhere (see the concluding "epitaph" at 5.10 and 16). He will be the dominant voice in Athenian politics until his death in 422, fighting Brasidas at Amphipolis. His death allowed the peace treaty (sometimes called the Peace of Nicias) of that year. Some scholars surmise that Cleon had been responsible for Thucydides' banishment from Athens when he failed to save Amphipolis (4.106–107; 5.26). Thucydides does not say. This speech is notable for twisted echoes of Pericles' imperial logic and for its aggressive, indeed bullying tone—an attitude that enemies of Athenian democracy associated with the so-called demagogues, leaders of the people.

you in your daily relations with each other, you feel just the same with regard to your allies, and never reflect that the mistakes into which you may be led by listening to their appeals, or by giving way to your own compassion,* are full of danger to yourselves, and bring you no thanks for your weakness from your allies; entirely forgetting that your empire is a despotism and your subjects disaffected conspirators,† whose obedience is insured not by your suicidal concessions, but by the superiority given you by your own strength and not their loyalty.‡ The most alarming feature in the case is the constant change of measures with which we appear to be threatened, and our seeming ignorance of the fact that bad laws which are never changed are better for a city than good ones that have no authority; that unlearned loyalty is more serviceable than quick-witted insubordination; and that ordinary men usually manage public affairs better than their more gifted fellows.§ The latter are always wanting to appear wiser than the laws, and to overrule every proposition brought forward, thinking that they cannot show their wit in more important matters, and by such behaviour too often ruin their country; while those who mistrust their own cleverness are content to be less learned than the laws, and less able to pick holes in the speech of a good speaker; and being fair judges rather than rival athletes, generally conduct affairs successfully. These we ought to imitate, instead of being led on by cleverness and intellectual rivalry to advise your people against our real opinions.

38. 'For myself, I adhere to my former opinion,‖ and wonder at those who have proposed to reopen the case of the Mitylenians, and who are thus causing a delay which is all in favour of the guilty, by making the sufferer proceed against the offender with the edge of his anger blunted; although where vengeance follows most closely upon the wrong, it best equals it and most amply requites it. I wonder also who will be the man who will maintain the contrary, and will pretend to show that the crimes of the Mitylenians are of service to us, and our misfortunes injurious to the allies. Such a man must plainly either have such confidence in his rhetoric# as to adventure to prove that what has been once for all decided is still undetermined, or be bribed

---

*Cleon despises intrusions of sentiment into realpolitik such as pity.

†The bald statement that the empire is a tyranny echoes Pericles (2.63).

‡Cleon argues that overwhelming military superiority will alone bring obedience.

§The Sicilian rhetorician and sophist Gorgias may lie behind this series of antitheses. Many Thucydidean speakers employ them. Thucydides' balanced clauses are usually slightly and intentionally unbalanced in thought or syntactical structure.

‖Another echo of Pericles' claim of sticking to a fixed policy (2.61).

#Cleon disguised his attack on discussion as an attack on slick speakers, a commonplace *ad hominem* remark in the second half of the fifth century.

to try to delude us by elaborate sophisms.* In such contests the state
gives the rewards to others, and takes the dangers for herself. The
persons to blame are you who are so foolish as to institute these contests; who go to see an oration as you would to see a sight, take your
facts on hearsay, judge of the practicability of a project by the wit of
its advocates, and trust for the truth as to past events not to the fact
which you saw more than to the clever strictures which you heard;
the easy victims of new-fangled arguments, unwilling to follow received conclusions; slaves to every new paradox, despisers of the
commonplace;† the first wish of every man being that he could speak
himself, the next to rival those who can speak by seeming to be quite
up with their ideas by applauding every hit almost before it is made,
and by being as quick in catching an argument as you are slow in
foreseeing its consequences; asking, if I may so say, for something
different from the conditions under which we live, and yet compre-
hending inadequately those very conditions; very slaves‡ to the pleasure of the ear, and more like the audience of a rhetorician than the
council of a city.

39. 'In order to keep you from this, I proceed to show that no one
state has ever injured you as much as Mitylene. I can make allowance
for those who revolt because they cannot bear our empire, or who
have been forced to do so by the enemy. But for those who possessed
an island with fortifications; who could fear our enemies only by sea,
and there had their own force of galleys to protect them; who were independent and held in the highest honour by you—to act as these
have done, this is not revolt—revolt implies oppression; it is deliberate and wanton aggression; an attempt to ruin us by siding with our
bitterest enemies; a worse offence than a war undertaken on their
own account in the acquisition of power. The fate of those of their
neighbours who had already rebelled and had been subdued was no
lesson to them; their own prosperity could not dissuade them from af-
fronting danger; but blindly confident in the future, and full of hopes
beyond their power though not beyond their ambition, they declared
war and made their decision to prefer might to right, their attack
being determined not by provocation but by the moment which
seemed propitious. The truth is that great good fortune coming sud-

---

*Another such attack questions the motives of one's opponent, suggests that someone
bribed him. Aristophanes, in his comedies paid for from public revenues, often hurls
this very charge against Cleon himself. (See Fornara #131 for Cleon's political allies.)

†This jeremiad against the Athenian *demos* is remarkably blunt—even offensive. Thucydides is representing the violence of Cleon's expression and his policy.

‡To call the citizens amusement- and pleasure-seekers and slaves of every novel idea
is more insulting than most legislative or quasi-judicial bodies—then or now—would
tolerate.

denly and unexpectedly tends to make a people insolent;* in most cases it is safer for mankind to have success in reason than out of reason; and it is easier for them, one may say, to stave off adversity than to preserve prosperity.† Our mistake has been to distinguish the Mitylenians as we have done: had they been long ago treated like the rest, they never would have so far forgotten themselves, human nature being as surely made arrogant by consideration, as it is awed by firmness. Let them now therefore be punished as their crime requires, and do not, while you condemn the aristocracy, absolve the people. This is certain, that all attacked you without distinction, although they might have come over to us, and been now again in possession of their city. But no, they thought it safer to throw in their lot with the aristocracy and so joined their rebellion! Consider therefore: if you subject to the same punishment the ally who is forced to rebel by the enemy, and him who does so by his own free choice, which of them, think you, is there that will not rebel upon the slightest pretext; when the reward of success is freedom, and the penalty of failure nothing so very terrible? We meanwhile shall have to risk our money and our lives against one state after another; and if successful, shall receive a ruined town from which we can no longer draw the revenue upon which our strength depends; while if unsuccessful, we shall have an enemy the more upon our hands, and shall spend the time that might be employed in combating our existing foes in warring with our own allies.

40. 'No hope, therefore, that rhetoric may instil or money purchase, of the mercy due to human infirmity must be held out to the Mitylenians.‡ Their offence was not involuntary, but of malice and deliberate; and mercy is only for unwilling offenders. I therefore now as before persist against your reversing your first decision, or giving way to the three failings most fatal to empire—pity, sentiment, and indulgence. Compassion is due to those who can reciprocate the feeling, not to those who will never pity us in return, but are our natural and necessary foes: the orators who charm us with sentiment may find other less important arenas for their talents, in the place of one where the city pays a heavy penalty for a momentary pleasure, themselves receiving fine acknowledgments for their fine phrases; while indulgence should be shown towards those who will be our friends in fu-

---

*Cleon comments on hubris, insolent self-confidence, a favorite topic of contemporary tragedy and an idea frequently found in Herodotus as well.

†Crawley's clever jingles (might/right, in reason/out of reason, adversity/prosperity) attempt to catch the flavor of the sophist Gorgias' contributions to Thucydides' Athenian oratory—antithesis, rhythm, and rhyming prose.

‡Cleon summarizes his rational objections to his opponents' motives (rhetoric, money) and to sparing the conquered Mityleneans (mercy, infirmity).

ture, instead of towards men who will remain just what they were, and as much our enemies as before. To sum up shortly, I say that if you follow my advice you will do what is just towards the Mitylenians, and at the same time expedient; while by a different decision you will not oblige them so much as pass sentence upon yourselves. For if they were right in rebelling, you must be wrong in ruling. However, if, right or wrong, you determine to rule, you must carry out your principle and punish the Mitylenians as your interest requires; or else you must give up your empire and cultivate honesty without danger.* Make up your minds, therefore, to give them like for like; and do not let the victims who escaped the plot be more insensible than the conspirators who hatched it; but reflect what they would have done if victorious over you, especially as they were the aggressors. It is they who wrong their neighbour without a cause, that pursue their victim to the death, on account of the danger which they foresee in letting their enemy survive; since the object of a wanton wrong is more dangerous, if he escape, than an enemy who has not this to complain of. Do not, therefore, be traitors to yourselves, but recall as nearly as possible the moment of suffering and the supreme importance which you then attached to their reduction; and now pay them back in their turn, without yielding to present weakness or forgetting the peril that once hung over you. Punish them as they deserve, and teach your other allies by a striking example that the penalty of rebellion is death.† Let them once understand this and you will not have so often to neglect your enemies while you are fighting with your own confederates.'

41. Such were the words of Cleon. After him Diodotus,‡ son of Eucrates, who had also in the previous assembly spoken most strongly against putting the Mitylenians to death, came forward and spoke as follows:—

42. 'I do not blame the persons who have reopened the case of the Mitylenians, nor do I approve the protests which we have heard against important questions being frequently debated. I think the two things most opposed to good counsel are haste and passion; haste usually goes hand in hand with folly, passion with coarseness and narrowness of mind. As for the argument that speech ought not to be the exponent of action, the man who uses it must be either senseless or biassed by personal interest: senseless if he believes it possible to treat of the uncertain future through any other medium;

---

*Cleon boldly states that empire and justice are incompatible. He vaguely echoes Pericles' view that national success requires a different view of interstate morality.

†Cleon believes that a fierce policy of murderous repression will prevent further rebellions. Diodotus, we shall hear, espouses a different view.

‡Nothing other than this speech is known about Diodotus. His points against Cleon carry the day in the assembly and gain the historian's sympathy.

biassed if wishing to carry a disgraceful measure and doubting his ability to speak well in a bad cause, he thinks to frighten opponents and hearers by well-aimed calumny. What is still more intolerable is to accuse a speaker of making a display in order to be paid for it. If ignorance only were imputed, an unsuccessful speaker might retire with a reputation for honesty, if not for wisdom; while the charge of dishonesty makes him suspected, if successful, and thought, if defeated, not only a fool but a rogue. The city is no gainer by such a system, since fear deprives it of its advisers; although in truth, if our speakers are to make such assertions, it would be better for the country if they could not speak at all, as we should then make fewer blunders. The good citizen ought to triumph not by frightening his opponents but by beating them fairly in argument; and a wise city without over-distinguishing its best advisers, will nevertheless not deprive them of their due, and far from punishing an unlucky counsellor will not even regard him as disgraced. In this way successful orators would be least tempted to sacrifice their convictions to popularity, in the hope of still higher honours, and unsuccessful speakers to resort to the same popular arts in order to win over the multitude.

43. 'This is not our way; and, besides, the moment that a man is suspected of giving advice, however good, from corrupt motives, we feel such a grudge against him for the gain which after all we are not certain he will receive, that we deprive the city of its certain benefit. Plain good advice has thus come to be no less suspected than bad; and the advocate of the most monstrous measures is not more obliged to use deceit to gain the people, than the best counsellor is to lie in order to be believed. The city and the city only, owing to these refinements, can never be served openly and without disguise; he who does serve it openly being always suspected of serving himself in some secret way in return. Still, considering the magnitude of the interests involved, and the position of affairs, we orators must make it our business to look a little further than you who judge offhand; especially as we, your advisers, are responsible, while you, our audience, are not so. For if those who gave the advice, and those who took it, suffered equally, you would judge more calmly; as it is, you visit the disasters into which the whim of the moment may have led you, upon the single person of your adviser, not upon yourselves, his numerous companions in error.*

44. 'However, I have not come forward either to oppose or to accuse in the matter of Mitylene; indeed, the question before us as sen-

---

*Diodotus and Cleon share the theme of the disconnect between speakers and the listeners who vote. Both chastise the *demos* for neglecting its own role in bad decisions.

sible men is not their guilt, but our interests.* Though I prove them ever so guilty, I shall not, therefore, advise their death, unless it be expedient; nor though they should have claims to indulgence, shall I recommend it, unless it be clearly for the good of the country. I consider that we are deliberating for the future more than for the present; and where Cleon is so positive as to the useful deterrent effects that will follow from making rebellion capital, I who consider the interests of the future quite as much as he, as positively maintain the contrary. And I require you not to reject my useful considerations for his specious ones: his speech may have the attraction of seeming the more just in your present temper against Mitylene; but we are not in a court of justice, but in a political assembly; and the question is not justice, but how to make the Mitylenians useful to Athens.†

45. 'Now of course communities have enacted the penalty of death for many offences far lighter than this: still hope leads men to venture, and no one ever yet put himself in peril without the inward conviction that he would succeed in his design. Again, was there ever city rebelling that did not believe that it possessed either in itself or in its alliances resources adequate to the enterprise? All, states and individuals, are alike prone to err, and there is no law that will prevent them; or why should men have exhausted the list of punishments in search of enactments to protect them from evil-doers? It is probable that in early times the penalties for the greatest offences were less severe, and that, as these were disregarded, the penalty of death has been by degrees in most cases arrived at, which is itself disregarded in like manner. Either then some means of terror more terrible than this must be discovered, or it must be owned that this restraint is useless; and that as long as poverty gives men the courage of necessity, or plenty fills them with the ambition which belongs to insolence and pride, and the other conditions of life remain each under the thraldom of some fatal and master passion, so long will the impulse never be wanting to drive men into danger. Hope also and cupidity, the one leading and the other following, the one conceiving the attempt, the other suggesting the facility of succeeding, cause the widest ruin, and, although invisible agents, are far stronger than the dangers that are seen. Fortune,‡ too, powerfully helps the delusion, and by the unex-

---

*Diodotus outflanks the alleged realism of angry Cleon by claiming that self-interest and not compassion should lead to sparing the Lesbian *demos*. He turns the argument for the deterrence value of genocide against its brutal author.

†Diodotus sets aside justice (*dike*) in international affairs, a subject of constant debate in Greek and subsequent thought, at least from Hesiod and Homer onward, for cool utilitarian considerations about international relations.

‡Fortune (*tyche*), an excuse for the weak and a difficult issue for historiographical analysis, leads many men to irrational decisions and acts.

pected aid that she sometimes lends, tempts men to venture with inferior means; and this is especially the case with communities, because the stakes played for are the highest, freedom or empire, and, when all are acting together, each man irrationally magnifies his own capacity. In fine, it is impossible to prevent, and only great simplicity can hope to prevent, human nature doing what it has once set its mind upon, by force of law or by any other deterrent force whatsoever.

46. 'We must not, therefore, commit ourselves to a false policy through a belief in the efficacy of the punishment of death, or exclude rebels from the hope of repentance and an early atonement of their error. Consider a moment! At present, if a city that has already revolted perceive that it cannot succeed, it will come to terms while it is still able to refund expenses, and pay tribute afterwards. In the other case, what city think you would not prepare better than is now done, and hold out to the last against its besiegers, if it is all one whether it surrender late or soon? And how can it be otherwise than hurtful to us to be put to the expense of a siege, because surrender is out of the question; and if we take the city, to receive a ruined town from which we can no longer draw the revenue which forms our real strength against the enemy? We must not, therefore, sit as strict judges of the offenders to our own prejudice, but rather see how by moderate chastisements we may be enabled to benefit in future by the revenue-producing powers of our dependencies; and we must make up our minds to look for our protection not to legal terrors but to careful administration. At present we do exactly the opposite. When a free community, held in subjection by force, rises, as is only natural,* and asserts its independence, it is no sooner reduced than we fancy ourselves obliged to punish it severely; although the right course with freemen is not to chastise them rigorously when they do rise, but rigorously to watch them before they rise, and to prevent their ever entertaining the idea, and, the insurrection suppressed, to make as few responsible for it as possible.†

47. 'Only consider what a blunder you would commit in doing as Cleon recommends. As things are at present, in all the cities the people is your friend,‡ and either does not revolt with the oligarchy, or, if

---

*Thucydides recognizes the common Hellenic impulse to conserve local sovereignty in the autonomous *polis* unit.

†Diodotus voices the humane and politic view that limiting those prosecuted will be best for Athenian imperial interests. (Fornara #68 translates an agreement about litigation between Phaselites and Athenians.)

‡Thucydides' speaker here states that the cities' democratic masses were inclined to find the Athenian imperial rule more attuned to their interests than that of the oligarchic/aristocratic regimes that were endemic at all periods of Greek history (Ste. Croix). Recall that the Athenian democracy was a recognized anomaly even during its dominant period. Alcibiades, for a Spartan audience, at 6.89 calls it "an acknowledged folly."

forced to do so, becomes at once the enemy of the insurgents; so that in the war with the hostile city you have the masses on your side. But if you butcher the people of Mitylene, who had nothing to do with the revolt, and who, as soon as they got arms, of their own will surrendered the town, first you will commit the crime of killing your benefactors; and next you will play directly into the hands of the higher classes, who when they induce their cities to rise, will immediately have the people on their side, through your having announced in advance the same punishment for those who are guilty and for those who are not. On the contrary, even if they were guilty, you ought to seem not to notice it, in order to avoid alienating the only class still friendly to us. In short, I consider it far more useful for the preservation of our empire voluntarily to put up with injustice, than to put to death, however justly, those whom it is our interest to keep alive. As for Cleon's idea that in punishment the claims of justice and expediency can both be satisfied, facts do not confirm the possibility of such a combination.

48. 'Confess, therefore, that this is the wisest course, and without conceding too much either to pity or to indulgence, by neither of which motives do I any more than Cleon* wish you to be influenced, upon the plain merits of the case before you, be persuaded by me to try calmly those of the Mitylenians whom Paches sent off as guilty, and to leave the rest undisturbed. This is at once best for the future, and most terrible to your enemies at the present moment; inasmuch as good policy against an adversary is superior to the blind attacks of brute force.'

49. Such were the words of Diodotus. The two opinions thus expressed were the ones that most directly contradicted each other;† and the Athenians, notwithstanding their change of feeling, now proceeded to a division, in which the show of hands was almost equal, although the motion of Diodotus carried the day. Another galley was at once sent off in haste, for fear that the first might reach Lesbos in the interval, and the city be found destroyed; the first ship having about a day and a night's start. Wine and barley-cakes were provided for the vessel by the Mitylenian ambassadors, and great promises made if they arrived in time; which caused the men to use such diligence upon the voyage that they took their meals of barley-cakes kneaded with oil and wine as they rowed, and only slept by turns while the others were at the oar. Luckily they met with no contrary wind, and the first ship

---

*Diodotus emphasizes that he does not intend his argument to be merciful, although it may be, but merely the smartest policy for Athens to follow.

†Thucydides never wrote that his method was to select the two speeches most sharply opposed, although it may be the case. This debate, as many in Thucydides, states an issue that recurred many times, but in other cases, he will report only the assembly's ultimate decision.

making no haste upon so horrid an errand,* while the second pressed on in the manner described, the first arrived so little before them, that Paches had only just had time to read the decree, and to prepare to execute the sentence, when the second put into port and prevented the massacre. The danger of Mitylene had indeed been great.†

50. The other party whom Paches had sent off as the prime movers in the rebellion, were upon Cleon's motion put to death by the Athenians, the number being rather more than a thousand.‡ The Athenians also demolished the walls of the Mitylenians, and took possession of their ships. Afterwards tribute was not imposed upon the Lesbians; but all their land, except that of the Methymnians, was divided into three thousand allotments, three hundred of which were reserved as sacred for the gods,§ and the rest assigned by lot to Athenian shareholders, who were sent out to the island.‖ With these the Lesbians agreed to pay a rent of two minæ a year for each allotment, and cultivated the land themselves.# The Athenians also took possession of the towns on the continent belonging to the Mitylenians, which thus became for the future subject to Athens. Such were the events that took place at Lesbos.

Fifth Year of the War — Trial and Execution of the Platæans — Corcyræan Revolution

51. During the same summer, after the reduction of Lesbos, the Athenians under Nicias,** son of Niceratus, made an expedition against

---

*This phrase suggests editorial judgment, or it could be the soldiers' or sailors'. This word appears nowhere else in Thucydides. ("Monstrous" might now better translate the Greek than "horrid.")

†Thucydides repeats this summary dramatic judgment about the nick of time for the danger of Syracuse (7.2).

‡Cleon pops up, something like a Punch and Judy figure, whenever the Athenians vote to do something monstrous. A thousand principal plotters is a high number for the small ancient Greek city-states.

§Selecting and dedicating a tenth of campaign proceeds for the gods is a standard Hellenic religious practice.

‖The use of sortition is basic to Athenian democratic procedures. 2,700 allotments or shares each producing two minae amounts to 90 talents of rent or tribute a year, a huge sum, and the Lesbians had lost their essential wealth, their property. There were 100 drachmae in a mina, and 60 minae in a talent, or 6,000 drachmae in a talent (this last term denotes a unit of accounting, not an available coin or currency).

#The Lesbians are not killed, but they have lost their capital in land and are now sharecroppers. This solution would not promote appreciation or loyalty.

**Thucydides shifts back to the mainland briefly, to Nicias' siege of Megarian Minoa (map 2). Nicias, a rich and popular politician and general, would unwillingly serve in his final command on the expedition against Syracuse and Selinus.

the island of Minoa, which lies off Megara and was used as a fortified post by the Megarians, who had built a tower upon it. Nicias wished to enable the Athenians to maintain their blockade from this nearer station instead of from Budorum and Salamis; to stop the Peloponnesian galleys and privateers sailing out unobserved from the island, as they had been in the habit of doing; and at the same time prevent anything from coming into Megara. Accordingly, after taking two towers projecting on the side of Nisæa, by engines from the sea, and clearing the entrance into the channel between the island and the shore, he next proceeded to cut off all communication by building a wall on the mainland at the point where a bridge across a morass enabled succours to be thrown into the island, which was not far off from the continent. A few days sufficing to accomplish this, he afterwards raised some works in the island also, and leaving a garrison there, departed with his forces.

52. About the same time in this summer, the Platæans being now without provisions, and unable to support the siege, surrendered to the Peloponnesians in the following manner. An assault had been made upon the wall, which the Platæans were unable to repel. The Lacedæmonian commander, perceiving their weakness, wished to avoid taking the place by storm; his instructions from Lacedæmon having been so conceived, in order that if at any future time peace should be made with Athens, and they should agree each to restore the places that they had taken in the war, Platæa might be held to have come over voluntarily, and not be included in the list.* He accordingly sent a herald to them to ask if they were willing voluntarily to surrender the town to the Lacedæmonians, and accept them as their judges, upon the understanding that the guilty should be punished, but no one without form of law. The Platæans were now in the last state of weakness, and the herald had no sooner delivered his message than they surrendered the town. The Peloponnesians fed them for some days until the judges from Lacedæmon, who were five in number, arrived. Upon their arrival no charge was preferred; they simply called up the Platæans, and asked them whether they had done the Lacedæmonians and allies any service in the war then raging. The Platæans asked leave to speak at greater length, and deputed two of their number to represent them; Astymachus, son of Asopolaus, and Lacon, son of Aeimnestus, *Proxenus* of the Lacedæmonians,† who came forward and spoke as follows:—

---

*Thucydides notes examples of literalism by which states can manipulate treaties for their long-term advantage. The siege of Plataea reduced the native defenders to the last stage of starvation.

†The Plataeans choose as their spokesman someone with a Laconian name and a known relationship as informal Plataean host for visiting Lacedæmonians.

53. 'Lacedæmonians, when we surrendered our city we trusted in you, and looked forward to a trial more agreeable to the forms of law than the present, to which we had no idea of being subjected; the judges also in whose hands we consented to place ourselves were you, and you only (from whom we thought we were most likely to obtain justice), and not other persons, as is now the case. As matters stand, we are afraid that we have been doubly deceived. We have good reason to suspect, not only that the issue to be tried is the most terrible of all, but that you will not prove impartial; if we may argue from the fact that no accusation was first brought forward for us to answer, but we had ourselves to ask leave to speak, and from the question being put so shortly,* that a true answer to it tells against us, while a false one can be contradicted. In this dilemma, our safest, and indeed our only course, seems to be to say something at all risks: placed as we are, we could scarcely be silent without being tormented by the damning thought that speaking might have saved us. Another difficulty that we have to encounter is the difficulty of convincing you. Were we unknown to each other we might profit by bringing forward new matter with which you were unacquainted: as it is, we can tell you nothing that you do not know already, and we fear, not that you have condemned us in your own minds of having failed in our duty towards you, and make this our crime, but that to please a third party we have to submit to a trial the result of which is already decided.

54. 'Nevertheless, we will place before you what we can justly urge, not only on the question of the quarrel which the Thebans have against us, but also as addressing you and the rest of the Hellenes; and we will remind you of our good services, and endeavour to prevail with you.

'To your short question, whether we have done the Lacedæmonians and allies any service in this war, we say, if you ask us as enemies, that to refrain from serving you was not to do you injury; if as friends, that you are more in fault for having marched against us. During the peace, and against the Mede, we acted well: we have not now been the first to break the peace, and we were the only Bœotians who then joined in defending against the Mede the liberty of Hellas.† Although an inland people, we were present at the action at Artemisium; in the battle that took place in our territory we fought by the side of your-

---

*The Spartans and their Theban allies had designed an inquest that insured that the Plataeans would die.

†The Plataeans hope that past service, especially in the national heroic conflict against the Persians, would buy them a lighter penalty. Since the Spartans began the war in the name of Hellenic liberty, the Plataeans argue that killing the inhabitants of the city where the Greeks once had won the final battle for that freedom would hurt their cause. (Fornara translates documents of that great victory at #57–#59.)

selves and Pausanias; and in all the other Hellenic exploits of the time we took a part quite out of proportion to our strength. Besides, you, as Lacedæmonians, ought not to forget that at the time of the great panic at Sparta, after the earthquake, caused by the secession of the Helots to Ithome, we sent the third part of our citizens to assist you.*

55. 'On these great and historical occasions such was the part that we chose, although afterwards we became your enemies. For this you were to blame. When we asked for your alliance against our Theban oppressors, you rejected our petition, and told us to go to the Athenians who were our neighbours, as you lived too far off.† In the war we never have done to you, and never should have done to you, anything unreasonable. If we refused to desert the Athenians when you asked us, we did no wrong; they had helped us against the Thebans when you drew back, and we could no longer give them up with honour; especially as we had obtained their alliance and had been admitted to their citizenship at our own request, and after receiving benefits at their hands; but it was plainly our duty loyally to obey their orders. Besides, the faults that either of you may commit in your supremacy must be laid, not upon the followers, but on the chiefs that lead them astray.

56. 'With regard to the Thebans, they have wronged us repeatedly, and their last aggression, which has been the means of bringing us into our present position, is within your own knowledge. In seizing our city in time of peace, and what is more at a holy time in the month, they justly encountered our vengeance, in accordance with the universal law which sanctions resistance to an invader;‡ and it cannot now be right that we should suffer on their account. By taking your own immediate interest and their animosity as the test of justice, you will prove yourselves to be rather waiters on expediency than judges of right; although if they seem useful to you now, we and the rest of the Hellenes gave you much more valuable help at a time of greater need. Now you are the assailants, and others fear you; but at the crisis to which we allude, when the barbarian threatened all with slavery, the Thebans were on his side. It is just, therefore, to put our

---

*The Plataeans helped the Spartans when the helots revolted and captured a hilltop redoubt at Ithome (compare 1.101–103; map 4). Does this not deserve gratitude?

†Spartan recommendation prompted the Plataeans' alliance with the Athenians. Can one criticize them for following Spartan advice? Probably the Spartans had been trying, then as later, to keep their powerful ally Thebes from becoming too strong a power.

‡The Plataeans engaged in self-defense against their neighbors, the Thebans. All nations recognize this necessary right of self-protection. Plataean fellow citizens, one recalls, led in the invaders, another example of civil strife (*stasis*). Such conflict was prominent in Lesbos and, later in this book (starting at 3.70), will be central in Thucydides' account of the events in Corcyra.

patriotism then against our error now, if error there has been; and you will find the merit outweighing the fault, and displayed at a juncture when there were few Hellenes who would set their valour against the strength of Xerxes, and when greater praise was theirs who preferred the dangerous path of honour to the safe course of consulting their own interest with respect to the invasion. To these few we belonged, and highly were we honoured for it; and yet we now fear to perish by having again acted on the same principles, and chosen to act well with Athens sooner than wisely with Sparta. Yet in justice the same cases should be decided in the same way, and policy should not mean anything else than lasting gratitude for the service of a good ally combined with a proper attention to one's own immediate interest.

57. 'Consider also that at present the Hellenes generally regard you as a pattern of worth and honour; and if you pass an unjust sentence upon us in this which is no obscure cause, but one in which you, the judges, are as illustrious as we, the prisoners, are blameless, take care that displeasure be not felt at an unworthy decision* in the matter of honourable men made by men yet more honourable than they, and at the consecration in the national temples of spoils taken from the Platæans, the benefactors of Hellas. Shocking indeed will it seem for Lacedæmonians to destroy Platæa, and for the city whose name your fathers inscribed upon the tripod at Delphi for its good service,† to be by you blotted out from the map of Hellas, to please the Thebans. To such a depth of misfortune have we fallen, that while the Medes' success had been our ruin, Thebans now supplant us in your once fond regards; and we have been subjected to two dangers, the greatest of any—that of dying of starvation then, if we had not surrendered our town, and now of being tried for our lives. So that we Platæans, after exertions beyond our power in the cause of the Hellenes, are rejected by all, forsaken and unassisted; helped by none of our allies, and reduced to doubt the stability of our only hope, yourselves.

58. 'Still, in the name of the gods who once presided over our confederacy, and of our own good service in the Hellenic cause, we adjure you to relent; to recall the decision which we fear that the Thebans may have obtained from you; to ask back the gift that you have given them, that they disgrace not you by slaying us; to gain a

---

*In addition to arguments from history and justice, the Plataeans argue from political consequences. The Spartans, like the Athenians, must keep the allies they have and not chase potential others away. They repeat the point in their last sentence.

†The tripod, a three-legged stand, was a standard dedication in Panhellenic sanctuaries. The Roman emperor Constantine seized and took this one to Istanbul. He refounded the city of Byzantium (and renamed it Constantinople); there the tripod with its inscription still survives (Fornara #59).

pure instead of a guilty gratitude, and not to gratify others to be yourselves rewarded with shame. Our lives may be quickly taken, but it will be a heavy task to wipe away the infamy of the deed; as we are no enemies whom you might justly punish, but friends forced into taking arms against you. To grant us our lives would be, therefore, a righteous judgment; if you consider also that we are prisoners who surrendered of their own accord, stretching out our hands for quarter, whose slaughter Hellenic law forbids, and who besides were always your benefactors.* Look at the sepulchres of your fathers, slain by the Medes and buried in our country, whom year by year we honoured with garments and all other dues, and the first fruits of all that our land produced in their season, as friends from a friendly country and allies to our old companions in arms! Should you not decide aright, your conduct would be the very opposite to ours. Consider only: Pausanias buried them thinking that he was laying them in friendly ground and among men as friendly; but you, if you kill us and make the Platæan territory Theban, will leave your fathers and kinsmen in a hostile soil and among their murderers, deprived of the honours which they now enjoy. What is more, you will enslave the land in which the freedom of the Hellenes was won, make desolate the temples of the gods to whom they prayed before they overcame the Medes, and take away your ancestral sacrifices from those who founded and instituted them.†

59. 'It were not to your glory, Lacedæmonians, either to offend in this way against the common law of the Hellenes and against your own ancestors, or to kill us your benefactors to gratify another's hatred without having been wronged yourselves: it were more so to spare us and to yield to the impressions of a reasonable compassion; reflecting not merely on the awful fate in store for us, but also on the character of the sufferers, and on the impossibility of predicting how soon misfortune may fall even upon those who deserve it not. We, as we have a right to do and as our need impels us, entreat you, calling aloud upon the gods at whose common altar all the Hellenes worship, to hear our request, to be not unmindful of the oaths which your fathers swore, and which we now plead—we supplicate you by the

---

*In Thucydides appeals for mercy are conspicuous for their failure. The historian comments in the last chapter of the introduction on how traditional practices were abandoned during this war. Here is one outstanding example.

†The Plataeans have strong moral and emotional arguments but weak political ones. The moral significance of Plataea in the Greek imagination will not save it from conveying immediate political benefits to the Peloponnesians through depopulation and executions. The arguments about Plataean sacrifices in honor of Spartan fathers receive only tortuous response from the Boeotians (who had expediently joined the Persian invaders in 480).

tombs of your fathers, and appeal to those that are gone to save us
from falling into the hands of the Thebans, and their dearest friends
from being given up to their most detested foes.* We also remind you
of that day on which we did the most glorious deeds, by your fathers'
sides, we who now on this are like to suffer the most dreadful fate. Finally, to do what is necessary and yet most difficult for men in our situation—that is, to make an end of speaking, since with that ending
the peril of our lives draws near—in conclusion we say that we did
not surrender our city to the Thebans (to that we would have preferred inglorious starvation), but trusted in and capitulated to you;
and it would be just, if we fail to persuade you, to put us back in the
same position and let us take the chance that falls to us. And at the
same time we adjure you not to give us up,—your suppliants, Lacedæmonians, out of your hands and faith, Platæans foremost of the Hellenic patriots, to Thebans, our most hated enemies,—but to be our
saviours, and not, while you free the rest of the Hellenes, to bring us
to destruction.'†

60. Such were the words of the Platæans. The Thebans, afraid that
the Lacedæmonians might be moved by what they had heard, came
forward and said that they too desired to address them, since the
Platæans had, against their wish, been allowed to speak at length instead of being confined to a simple answer to the question. Leave
being granted, the Thebans spoke as follows:—

61. 'We should never have asked to make this speech if the Platæans
on their side had contented themselves with shortly answering the
question, and had not turned round and made charges against us, coupled with a long defence of themselves upon matters outside the present inquiry and not even the subject of accusation, and with praise of
what no one finds fault with. However, since they have done so, we
must answer their charges and refute their self-praise, in order that neither our bad name nor their good may help them, but that you may
hear the real truth on both points, and so decide.

'The origin of our quarrel was this. We settled Platæa some time
after the rest of Bœotia, together with other places out of which we
had driven the mixed population. The Platæans not choosing to
recognise our supremacy, as had been first arranged, but separating
themselves from the rest of the Bœotians, and proving traitors to
their nationality, we used compulsion; upon which they went over to

---

*Appeals—to gods, oaths, and tombs—fall on deaf ears. These are significant argu-
ments, but they do not sway the Spartan judges—and probably nothing else could have.
†The Plataean speech gains the sympathy of readers, both distant in time and merciful
because their interests are not at risk. The following Theban speech repels the reader,
but the Plataeans can only focus on past service to the Peloponnesians and not present
assistance or even goodwill.

the Athenians, and with them did much harm, for which we naturally retaliated.

62. 'Next, when the barbarian invaded Hellas, they say that they were the only Bœotians who did not Medise; and this is where they most glorify themselves and abuse us. We say that if they did not Medise, it was because the Athenians did not do so either; just as afterwards when the Athenians attacked the Hellenes they, the Platæans, were again the only Bœotians who Atticised. And yet consider the forms of our respective governments when we so acted. Our city at that juncture had neither an oligarchical constitution in which all the nobles enjoyed equal rights nor a democracy, but that which is most opposed to law and good government and nearest a tyranny—the rule of a close cabal. These, hoping to strengthen their individual power by the success of the Mede, kept down by force the people, and brought him into the town. The city as a whole was not its own mistress when it so acted, and ought not to be reproached for the errors that it committed while deprived of its constitution. Examine only how we acted after the departure of the Mede and the recovery of the constitution; when the Athenians attacked the rest of Hellas and endeavoured to subjugate our country, the greater part of which faction had already made them masters. Did not we fight and conquer at Coronea and liberate Bœotia,* and do we not now actively contribute to the liberation of the rest, providing horses to the cause and a force unequalled by that of any other state in the confederacy?

63. 'Let this suffice to excuse us for our Medism. We will now endeavour to show that you have injured the Hellenes more than we, and are more deserving of condign punishment. It was in defence against us, say you, that you became allies and citizens of Athens. If so, you ought only to have called in the Athenians against us, instead of joining them in attacking others: it was open to you to do this if you ever felt that they were leading you where you did not wish to follow, as Lacedæmon was already your ally against the Mede, as you so much insist; and this was surely sufficient to keep us off, and above all to allow you to deliberate in security. Nevertheless, of your own choice and without compulsion you chose to throw your lot in with Athens. And you say that it had been base for you to betray your benefactors; but it was surely far baser and more iniquitous to sacrifice the whole body of the Hellenes, your fellow-confederates, who were liberating Hellas, than the Athenians only, who were enslaving it. The return that you made them was therefore neither equal nor

---

*The Thebans' case, based on self-interest but cloaked in patriotic rhetoric, comes down to a veiled threat to remove their vital military (especially cavalry) support from the Peloponnesian alliance.

honourable, since you called them in, as you say, because you were being oppressed yourselves, and then became their accomplices in oppressing others; although baseness rather consists in not returning like for like than in not returning what is justly due but must be unjustly paid.

64. 'Meanwhile, after thus plainly showing that it was not for the sake of the Hellenes that you alone then did not Medise, but because the Athenians did not do so either, and you wished to side with them and to be against the rest; you now claim the benefit of good deeds done to please your neighbours. This cannot be admitted: you chose the Athenians, and with them you must stand or fall. Nor can you plead the league then made and claim that it should now protect you. You abandoned that league, and offended against it by helping instead of hindering the subjugation of the Æginetans* and others of its members, and that not under compulsion, but while in enjoyment of the same institutions that you enjoy to the present hour, and no one forcing you as in our case. Lastly, an invitation was addressed to you before you were blockaded to be neutral and join neither party: this you did not accept. Who then merit the detestation of the Hellenes more justly than you, you who sought their ruin under the mask of honour? The former virtues that you allege you now show not to be proper to your character; the real bent of your nature has been at length damningly proved: when the Athenians took the path of injustice you followed them.

'Of our unwilling Medism and your wilful Atticising this then is our explanation.

65. 'The last wrong of which you complain consists in our having, as you say, lawlessly invaded your town in time of peace and festival. Here again we cannot think that we were more in fault than yourselves. If solely from our own interest we made an armed attack upon your city and ravaged your territory, we are guilty; but if the first men among you in estate and family,† wishing to put an end to the foreign connexion and to restore you to the common Bœotian country, of their own free will invited us, wherein is our crime? Where wrong is done, those who lead, as you say, are more to blame than those who follow. Not that, in our judgment, wrong was done either by them or by us. Citizens like yourselves, and with more at stake than you, they opened their own walls and introduced us into their own city, not as foes but as friends, to prevent the bad among you from becoming worse; to give honest men their due; to reform principles without at-

---

*The Plataeans were loyal allies of the Athenians for more than ninety years. The Aeginetans were unwilling allies. They were first defeated in battle, then subjugated, and finally expelled from their ancestral lands around 457 (1.108).

†The Thebans point out that oligarchs of Plataea led the attempt to overthrow the current government. They were just helping these good friends.

tacking persons, since you were not to be banished from your city, but brought home to your kindred, nor to be made enemies to any, but friends alike to all.

66. 'That our intention was not hostile is proved by our behaviour. We did no harm to any one, but publicly invited those who wished to live under a national, Bœotian government to come over to us; which at first you gladly did, and made an agreement with us and remained tranquil, until you became aware of the smallness of our numbers. Now it is possible that there may have been something not quite fair in our entering without the consent of your commons.* At any rate you did not repay us in kind. Instead of refraining, as we had done, from violence, and inducing us to retire by negotiation, you fell upon us in violation of your agreement, and slew some of us in fight, of which we do not so much complain, for in that there was a certain justice; but others who held out their hands and received quarter, and whose lives you subsequently promised us, you lawlessly butchered. If this was not abominable, what is? And after these three crimes committed one after the other—the violation of your agreement, the murder of the men afterwards, and the lying breach of your promise not to kill them, if we refrained from injuring your property in the country—you still affirm that we are the criminals and yourselves pretend to escape justice. Not so, if these your judges decide aright, but you will be punished for all together.

67. 'Such, Lacedæmonians, are the facts. We have gone into them at some length both on your account and on our own, that you may feel that you will justly condemn the prisoners, and we, that we have given an additional sanction to our vengeance. We would also prevent you from being melted by hearing of their past virtues, if any such they had: these may be fairly appealed to by the victims of injustice, but only aggravate the guilt of criminals, since they offend against their better nature. Nor let them gain anything by crying and wailing, by calling upon your fathers' tombs and their own desolate condition.† Against this we point to the far more dreadful fate of our youth, butchered at their hands; the fathers of whom either fell at Coronea, bringing Bœotia over to you, or seated, forlorn old men by desolate hearths, with far more reason implore your justice upon the prisoners. The pity which they appeal to is rather due to men who suffer unworthily; those who suffer justly as they do, are on the contrary subjects for triumph.‡ For their present desolate condition they have

---

*Theban concessions in arguing their case are disingenuous and not significant.

†The Thebans coldly mock the Plataeans' desperate pleas for mercy.

‡The Thebans employ the rational argument that those who pursue wrong policies intentionally do not deserve mercy but rather those who have been forced to do what they did. The Boeotian Thebans, in good Greek style, justify even their gloating.

themselves to blame, since they wilfully rejected the better alliance. Their lawless act was not provoked by any action of ours: hate, not justice, inspired their decision; and even now the satisfaction which they afford us is not adequate; they will suffer by a legal sentence, not as they pretend as suppliants asking for quarter in battle, but as prisoners who have surrendered upon agreement to take their trial. Vindicate, therefore, Lacedæmonians, the Hellenic law which they have broken; and to us, the victims of its violation, grant the reward merited by our zeal. Nor let us be supplanted in your favour by their harangues, but offer an example to the Hellenes, that the contests to which you invite them are of deeds, not words: good deeds can be shortly stated, but where wrong is done a wealth of language is needed to veil its deformity. However, if leading powers were to do what you are now doing, and putting one short question to all alike were to decide accordingly, men would be less tempted to seek fine phrases to cover bad actions.'

68. Such were the words of the Thebans. The Lacedæmonian judges decided that the question whether they had received any service from the Platæans in the war, was a fair one for them to put; as they had always invited them to be neutral, agreeably to the original covenant of Pausanias after the defeat of the Mede, and had again definitely offered them the same conditions before the blockade. This offer having been refused, they were now, they conceived, by the loyalty of their intention released from their covenant; and having, as they considered, suffered evil at the hands of the Platæans, they brought them in again one by one and asked each of them the same question, that is to say, whether they had done the Lacedæmonians and allies any service in the war; and upon their saying that they had not, took them out and slew them, all without exception. The number of Platæans thus massacred was not less than two hundred, with twenty-five Athenians who had shared in the siege.* The women were taken as slaves. The city the Thebans gave for about a year to some political emigrants from Megara, and to the surviving Platæans of their own party to inhabit, and afterwards razed it to the ground from the very foundations,† and built on to the precinct of Hera an

---

*Most of the Plataeans had left before the blockade was total. The Spartans and their allies killed all the defenders that they took. Thucydides' deadpan reports evoke sympathy by never appealing to it.

†The destruction of the physical plant of an ancient city, primitive as the engineering was, amounted to a terrible and unconditional rejection of everything it had stood for. The eradication of Plataea must have been meant to serve as a cautionary example, but both Diodotus and Samians sympathetic to the "liberationist rhetoric" of Sparta have argued against extreme measures earlier in this book. They may disincline the uncertain hesitators to join a cause or initiate resistance. As the historian says, the Spartans were out to please their allies, the Thebans, and did not think about further consequences.

inn two hundred feet square, with rooms all round above and below, making use for this purpose of the roofs and doors of the Platæans: of the rest of the materials in the wall, the brass and the iron, they made couches which they dedicated to Hera, for whom they also built a stone temple of a hundred feet square.* The land they confiscated and let out on a ten-years' lease to Theban occupiers. The adverse attitude of the Lacedæmonians in the whole Platæan affair was mainly adopted to please the Thebans, who were thought to be useful in the war at that moment raging. Such was the end of Platæa, in the ninety-third year after she became the ally of Athens.

69. Meanwhile, the forty ships of the Peloponnesians that had gone to the relief of the Lesbians, and which we left flying across the open sea, pursued by the Athenians, were caught in a storm off Crete, and scattering from thence made their way to Peloponnese, where they found at Cyllene thirteen Leucadian and Ambraciot triremes, with Brasidas,† son of Tellis, lately arrived as counsellor to Alcidas; the Lacedæmonians, upon the failure of the Lesbian expedition, having resolved to strengthen their fleet and sail to Corcyra, where a revolution had broken out, so as to arrive there before the twelve Athenian ships at Naupactus could be reinforced from Athens. Brasidas and Alcidas began to prepare accordingly.

70. The Corcyræan revolution‡ began with the return of the prisoners taken in the sea-fights off Epidamnus. These the Corinthians had released, nominally upon the security of eight hundred talents given by their *Proxeni*, but in reality upon their engagement to bring over Corcyra to Corinth. These men proceeded to canvass each of the citizens, and to intrigue with the view of detaching the city from Athens. Upon the arrival of an Athenian and a Corinthian vessel, with envoys on board, a conference was held in which the Corcyræans voted to remain allies of the Athenians according to their agreement, but to be friends of the Peloponnesians as they had been formerly. Meanwhile, the returned prisoners brought Peithias, a volunteer *Proxenus* of the Athenians and leader of the commons, to trial, upon

---

Hekatompedon temples, measuring 100 feet in Hellenic measuring systems, were built to a standard model. The choice of Hera as recipient of the honor is obvious: She was a Peloponnesian and Boeotian favorite and the nearby goddess to whom the earlier Pausanias had once prayed for victory (Herodotus 9.61).

†Brasidas, a central and commanding Spartan figure from this point until his death at the battle of Amphipolis at the beginning of book 5, must have been known for his willingness to take risks, if victory were a reasonable expectation.

‡The third great panel of book 3 concerns the large and prosperous community of Corcyra, the northerly island of Corfu (map 1) off the Albanian coast. It serves as a paradigm of murderous civil war within peripheral communities that were dragged into the Aegean-wide conflict between Athens and Sparta.

the charge of enslaving Corcyra to Athens.* He, being acquitted, retorted by accusing five of the richest of their number of cutting stakes in the ground sacred to Zeus and Alcinous; the legal penalty being a stater for each stake. Upon their conviction, the amount of the penalty being very large, they seated themselves as suppliants in the temples, to be allowed to pay it by instalments; but Peithias, who was one of the senate, prevailed upon that body to enforce the law; upon which the accused, rendered desperate by the law, and also learning that Peithias had the intention, while still a member of the senate, to persuade the people to conclude a defensive and offensive alliance with Athens, banded together armed with daggers, and suddenly bursting into the senate killed Peithias and sixty others, senators and private persons;† some few only of the party of Peithias taking refuge in the Athenian galley, which had not yet departed.

71. After this outrage, the conspirators summoned the Corcyræans to an assembly, and said that this would turn out for the best, and would save them from being enslaved by Athens: for the future, they moved to receive neither party unless they came peacefully in a single ship, treating any larger number as enemies. This motion made, they compelled it to be adopted, and instantly sent off envoys to Athens to justify what had been done and to dissuade the refugees there from any hostile proceedings which might lead to a reaction.

72. Upon the arrival of the embassy the Athenians arrested the envoys and all who listened to them, as revolutionists, and lodged them in Ægina. Meanwhile a Corinthian galley arriving in the island with Lacedæmonian envoys, the dominant Corcyræan party attacked the commons and defeated them in battle. Night coming on, the commons took refuge in the Acropolis and the higher parts of the city, and concentrated themselves there, having also possession of the Hyllaic harbour; their adversaries occupying the market-place, where most of them lived, and the harbour adjoining, looking towards the mainland.

73. The next day passed in skirmishes of little importance, each party sending into the country to offer freedom to the slaves and to invite them to join them.‡ The mass of the slaves answered the appeal of the commons; their antagonists being reinforced by eight hundred mercenaries§ from the continent.

---

*Thucydides rapidly sketches the local politics, played out in accusations and lawsuits.

†The oligarchs, failing at law, resort to violence, in fear of what the other side might do, and kill members of their own political state-council (*boule*) and personal enemies.

‡An invitation to slaves to join one party or the other would be another sign of the failure of traditional civility and the usual rules of political dispute and engagement.

§Mercenaries, the bane of fourth-century politics although a boon for hungry younger sons of farmers who inherited no property, became an important factor in this war.

74. After a day's interval hostilities recommenced, victory remaining with the commons, who had the advantage in numbers and position, the women also valiantly assisting them, pelting with tiles from the houses, and supporting the mêlée with a fortitude beyond their sex.* Towards dusk, the oligarchs in full rout, fearing that the victorious commons might assault and carry the arsenal and put them to the sword, fired the houses round the market-place and the lodging-houses, in order to bar their advance; sparing neither their own, nor those of their neighbours; by which much stuff of the merchants was consumed and the city risked total destruction, if a wind had come to help the flame by blowing on it. Hostilities now ceasing, both sides kept quiet, passing the night on guard, while the Corinthian ship stole out to sea upon the victory of the commons, and most of the mercenaries passed over secretly to the continent.

75. The next day the Athenian general, Nicostratus, son of Diitrephes, came up from Naupactus with twelve ships and five hundred Messenian heavy infantry. He at once endeavoured to bring about a settlement, and persuaded the two parties to agree together to bring to trial ten of the ringleaders, who presently fled, while the rest were to live in peace, making terms with each other, and entering into a defensive and offensive alliance with the Athenians. This arranged, he was about to sail away, when the leaders of the commons induced him to leave them five of his ships to make their adversaries less disposed to move, while they manned and sent with him an equal number of their own. He had no sooner consented, than they began to enroll their enemies for the ships;† and these fearing that they might be sent off to Athens, seated themselves as suppliants in the temple of the Dioscuri. An attempt on the part of Nicostratus to reassure them and to persuade them to rise proving unsuccessful, the commons armed upon this pretext, alleging the refusal of their adversaries to sail with them as a proof of the hollowness of their intentions, and took their arms out of their houses, and would have dispatched some whom they fell in with, if Nicostratus had not prevented it. The rest of the party seeing what was going on, seated themselves as suppliants in the temple of Hera, being not less than four hundred in number;‡ until the

---

*Thucydides, unlike Herodotus, rarely mentions women, sometimes perhaps suppressing their importance. Here he notes their violent participation in civil conflict as another sign of the degradation of norms.

†The Corcyreans manipulate the Athenian admiral Nicostratus. The democratic faction tries to send the oligarchic supporters away with the Athenian navy, a smart move to get them off island.

‡The four hundred oligarchs, rightly fearful of their enemies' intentions, act in a way that brings out the worst in them. Their remaining option is to seek sanctuary as suppliants, always one step closer to disaster in the *History*.

commons, fearing that they might adopt some desperate resolution, induced them to rise, and conveyed them over to the island in front of the temple, where provisions were sent across to them.

76. At this stage in the revolution, on the fourth or fifth day after the removal of the men to the island, the Peloponnesian ships arrived from Cyllene where they had been stationed since their return from Ionia, fifty-three in number, still under the command of Alcidas, but with Brasidas also on board as his adviser; and dropping anchor at Sybota, a harbour on the mainland, at daybreak made sail for Corcyra.

77. The Corcyræans in great confusion and alarm at the state of things in the city and at the approach of the invader, at once proceeded to equip sixty vessels, which they sent out, as fast as they were manned, against the enemy, in spite of the Athenians recommending them to let them sail out first, and to follow themselves afterwards with all their ships together. Upon their vessels coming up to the enemy in this straggling fashion, two immediately deserted: in others the crews were fighting among themselves, and there was no order in anything that was done; so that the Peloponnesians seeing their confusion, placed twenty ships to oppose the Corcyræans, and ranged the rest* against the twelve Athenian ships, amongst which were the two vessels *Salaminia* and *Paralus*.

78. While the Corcyræans, attacking without judgment and in small detachments, were already crippled by their own misconduct, the Athenians, afraid of the numbers of the enemy and of being surrounded, did not venture to attack the main body or even the centre of the division opposed to them, but fell upon its wing and sank one vessel; after which the Peloponnesians formed in a circle, and the Athenians rowed round them and tried to throw them into disorder. Perceiving this, the division opposed to the Corcyræans, fearing a repetition of the disaster of Naupactus,† came to support their friends, and the whole fleet now bore down, united, upon the Athenians, who retired before it, backing water, retiring as leisurely as possible in order to give the Corcyræans time to escape, while the enemy was thus kept occupied. Such was the character of this sea-fight, which lasted until sunset.

79. The Corcyræans now feared that the enemy would follow up their victory and sail against the town and rescue the men in the is-

---

*The Peloponnesians were so well aware of Athenian naval superiority in tactics and training that they allocated thirty-three ships against the measly Athenian twelve, among which were two usually non-combatant vessels, the ambassadorial triremes.

†The reason for hesitation was the Peloponnesian recollection of the battle at Naupactus, so they pit their thirty-three ships against the Athenian twelve and still advance with caution, allowing the Athenians to escape. The other twenty faced the Corcyrean fleet of sixty.

land, or strike some other blow equally decisive, and accordingly carried the men over again to the temple of Hera, and kept guard over the city. The Peloponnesians, however, although victorious in the sea-fight, did not venture to attack the town, but took the thirteen Corcyræan vessels which they had captured, and with them sailed back to the continent from whence they had put out. The next day equally they refrained from attacking the city, although the disorder and panic were at their height, and though Brasidas, it is said, urged Alcidas, his superior officer, to do so,* but they landed upon the promontory of Leukimme and laid waste the country.

80. Meanwhile the commons in Corcyra, being still in great fear of the fleet attacking them, came to a parley with the suppliants and their friends, in order to save the town; and prevailed upon some of them to go on board the ships, of which they still manned thirty, against the expected attack. But the Peloponnesians after ravaging the country until midday sailed away, and towards nightfall were informed by beacon signals of the approach of sixty Athenian vessels from Leucas, under the command of Eurymedon, son of Thucles; which had been sent off by the Athenians upon the news of the revolution and of the fleet with Alcidas being about to sail for Corcyra.

81. The Peloponnesians accordingly at once set off in haste by night for home, coasting along shore; and hauling their ships across the Isthmus of Leucas, in order not to be seen doubling it, so departed. The Corcyræans, made aware of the approach of the Athenian fleet and of the departure of the enemy, brought the Messenians from outside the walls into the town, and ordered the fleet which they had manned to sail round into the Hyllaic harbour; and while it was so doing, slew such of their enemies as they laid hands on, dispatching afterwards as they landed them, those whom they had persuaded to go on board the ships.† Next they went to the sanctuary of Hera and persuaded about fifty men to take their trial, and condemned them all to death. The mass of the suppliants who had refused to do so, on seeing what was taking place, slew each other there in the consecrated ground; while some hanged themselves upon the trees, and others destroyed themselves as they were severally able. During seven days that Eurymedon stayed with his sixty ships, the Corcyræans were engaged in butchering those of their fellow-citizens whom they regarded as their enemies: and although the crime imputed was that of attempting to put down the democracy, some were slain also for private hatred, others by their debtors because of the monies owed to

---

*Brasidas, as earlier at 2.93–94, urges an aggressive and unexpected attack. Again his bold strategy is rejected.

†The Corcyrean democratic faction with bad faith butchers its political foes.

them.* Death thus raged in every shape; and, as usually happens at such times, there was no length to which violence did not go; sons were killed by their fathers, and suppliants dragged from the altar or slain upon it; while some were even walled up in the temple of Dionysus and died there.

82. So bloody was the march of the revolution, and the impression which it made was the greater as it was one of the first to occur.† Later on, one may say, the whole Hellenic world was convulsed; struggles being everywhere made by the popular chiefs to bring in the Athenians, and by the oligarchs to introduce the Lacedæmonians.‡ In peace there would have been neither the pretext nor the wish to make such an invitation; but in war, with an alliance always at the command of either faction for the hurt of their adversaries and their own corresponding advantage, opportunities for bringing in the foreigner were never wanting to the revolutionary parties. The sufferings which revolution entailed upon the cities were many and terrible, such as have occurred and always will occur, as long as the nature of mankind remains the same; though in a severer or milder form, and varying in their symptoms, according to the variety of the particular cases.§ In peace and prosperity states and individuals have better sentiments, because they do not find themselves suddenly confronted with imperious necessities; but war takes away the easy supply of daily wants, and so proves a rough master, that brings most men's characters to a level with their fortunes.‖ Revolution thus ran its course from city to city, and the places which it arrived at last, from having heard what had been done before, carried to a still greater excess the refinement of their inventions, as manifested in the cunning of their enterprises and the atrocity of their reprisals. Words had to change their ordinary meaning and to take that which was now given them.# Reckless audacity came to be considered the courage of a loyal ally; prudent hesitation, specious cowardice; moderation was held to be a cloak for

---

*The political conflict becomes an opportunity for some to settle private hostilities and to rid themselves of debts.

†Corcyra serves Thucydides as the paradigm of *stasis* (civil conflict). He emphasizes the psychological impact on the Hellenic world as well as the immediate local consequences.

‡Local rivalries intensified opportunities to bring in the major powers. The democrats turned to the Athenians, the oligarchs to the Spartans.

§Thucydides emphasizes his belief that one can discern stable, repeating patterns in human nature and history.

‖Thucydides establishes war as the paradigmatic subject of history. The reason is that it brings out extreme behaviors in human beings.

#The perversion of words by individuals, factions, and states forms a noteworthy part of the *kinesis* (disruptive motion) that Thucydides spoke of in his opening paragraph.

unmanliness; ability to see all sides of a question inaptness to act on any.* Frantic violence became the attribute of manliness; cautious plotting, a justifiable means of self-defence. The advocate of extreme measures was always trustworthy; his opponent a man to be suspected. To succeed in a plot was to have a shrewd head, to divine a plot a still shrewder; but to try to provide against having to do either was to break up your party and to be afraid of your adversaries. In fine, to forestall an intending criminal, or to suggest the idea of a crime where it was wanting, was equally commended, until even blood became a weaker tie than party, from the superior readiness of those united by the latter to dare everything without reserve; for such associations had not in view the blessings derivable from established institutions but were formed by ambition for their overthrow; and the confidence of their members in each other rested less on any religious sanction than upon complicity in crime. The fair proposals of an adversary were met with jealous precautions by the stronger of the two, and not with a generous confidence. Revenge also was held of more account than self-preservation. Oaths of reconciliation, being only proffered on either side to meet an immediate difficulty, only held good so long as no other weapon was at hand; but when opportunity offered, he who first ventured to seize it and to take his enemy off his guard, thought this perfidious vengeance sweeter than an open one, since, considerations of safety apart, success by treachery won him the palm of superior intelligence. Indeed it is generally the case that men are readier to call rogues clever than simpletons honest, and are as ashamed of being the second as they are proud of being the first.

The cause of all these evils was the lust for power arising from greed and ambition;† and from these passions proceeded the violence of parties once engaged in contention. The leaders in the cities, each provided with the fairest professions, on the one side with the cry of political equality of the people, on the other of a moderate aristocracy, sought prizes for themselves in those public interests which they pretended to cherish,‡ and, recoiling from no means in their struggles

---

*Thucydides emphasizes that words not merely changed meanings but took on opposite signification under the stress of bloody conflict. These antitheses struck the author as disastrous for Hellenic values and self-respect. The compact analyses of Thucydides are as acute here as anywhere.

†Desire for power, greed, and ambition are the primary human motivators, an unflattering but probably accurate view of human nature.

‡Ideology, here the deformation of truth in service of an idea, successfully cloaks personal animosities and desires. Thucydides does not assert that political ideals are unreal but questions their significance for the motives of factional chiefs and followers. (The Greeks did not have enduring political parties of the modern sort that campaign on a platform.)

for ascendancy, engaged in the direst excesses; in their acts of vengeance they went to even greater lengths, not stopping at what justice or the good of the state demanded, but making the party caprice of the moment their only standard, and invoking with equal readiness the condemnation of an unjust verdict or the authority of the strong arm to glut the animosities of the hour. Thus religion was in honour with neither party; but the use of fair phrases to arrive at guilty ends was in high reputation. Meanwhile the moderate part of the citizens perished between the two, either for not joining in the quarrel, or because envy would not suffer them to escape.*

83. Thus every form of iniquity took root in the Hellenic countries by reason of the troubles. The ancient simplicity into which honour so largely entered was laughed down and disappeared;† and society became divided into camps in which no man trusted his fellow. To put an end to this, there was neither promise to be depended upon, nor oath that could command respect; but all parties dwelling rather in their calculation upon the hopelessness of a permanent state of things, were more intent upon self-defence than capable of confidence. In this contest the blunter wits were most successful. Apprehensive of their own deficiencies and of the cleverness of their antagonists, they feared to be worsted in debate and to be surprised by the combinations of their more versatile opponents, and so at once boldly had recourse to action: while their adversaries, arrogantly thinking that they should know in time, and that it was unnecessary to secure by action what policy afforded, often fell victims to their want of precaution.

84. Meanwhile Corcyra gave the first example of most of the crimes alluded to; of the reprisals exacted by the governed who had never experienced equitable treatment or indeed aught but insolence from their rulers‡—when their hour came; of the iniquitous resolves of those who desired to get rid of their accustomed poverty, and ardently coveted their neighbours' goods; and lastly, of the savage and pitiless excesses into which men who had begun the struggle not in a class but in a party spirit, were hurried by their ungovernable passions. In the confusion into which life was now thrown in the cities,

---

*Thucydides notes how ineffective in revolutionary situations are men of moderation on both sides. Further, they were prime targets for quick liquidation.

†Thucydides contrasts traditional values to his war-torn world, in which trust disappeared. He blames this change not on intellectual developments such as the sophists and pre-Socratics but on the pressures of war.

‡Most editors think this chapter is a later addition and not by Thucydides, although not for reasons of content. Thucydides observes that oligarchic regimes tend not to be fair or just to the inferior classes.

human nature, always rebelling against the law and now its master, gladly showed itself ungoverned in passion, above respect for justice, and the enemy of all superiority; since revenge would not have been set above religion, and gain above justice, had it not been for the fatal power of envy. Indeed men too often take upon themselves in the prosecution of their revenge to set the example of doing away with those general laws to which all alike can look for salvation in adversity, instead of allowing them to subsist against the day of danger when their aid may be required.*

85. While the revolutionary passions thus for the first time displayed themselves in the factions of Corcyra, Eurymedon and the Athenian fleet sailed away; after which some five hundred Corcyræan exiles who had succeeded in escaping, took some forts on the mainland, and becoming masters of the Corcyræan territory over the water, made this their base to plunder their countrymen in the island, and did so much damage as to cause a severe famine in the town. They also sent envoys to Lacedæmon and Corinth to negotiate their restoration; but meeting with no success, afterwards got together boats and mercenaries and crossed over to the island, being about six hundred in all; and burning their boats so as to have no hope except in becoming masters of the country, went up to Mount Istone, and fortifying themselves there, began to annoy those in the city and obtained command of the country.

86. At the close of the same summer the Athenians sent twenty ships under the command of Laches, son of Melanopus, and Charœades, son of Euphiletus, to Sicily, where the Syracusans and Leontines were at war.† The Syracusans had for allies all the Dorian cities except Camarina—these had been included in the Lacedæmonian confederacy from the commencement of the war, though they had not taken any active part in it—the Leontines had Camarina and the Chalcidian cities. In Italy the Locrians were for the Syracusans, the Rhegians for their Leontine kinsmen. The allies of the Leontines now sent to Athens and appealed to their ancient alliance and to their Ionian origin, to persuade the Athenians to send them a fleet, as the Syracusans were blockading them by land and sea. The Athenians sent it upon the plea of their common descent, but in reality to prevent the exportation of Sicilian grain to Peloponnese and to test the possibility of bringing Sicily into subjection. Accordingly they estab-

---

*Impulses for momentary gain lead to the abrogation of rules that exist for the benefit of all. Leaders today in need of a moment's advantage still disregard this obvious principle.

†Thucydides shifts back to the Sicilian front. This will be the focus for events in books 6 and 7. The Athenians sent Laches' twenty ships to test the waters. Inscriptions record these distant alliances (Fornara #124 and #125).

lished themselves at Rhegium in Italy, and from thence carried on the war in concert with their allies.

Sixth Year of the War—Campaigns of Demosthenes in Western Greece—Ruin of Ambracia

Summer was now over.

87. The winter following, the plague a second time attacked the Athenians; for although it had never entirely left them, still there had been a notable abatement in its ravages. The second visit lasted no less than a year, the first having lasted two; and nothing distressed the Athenians and reduced their power more than this. No less than four thousand four hundred heavy infantry in the ranks died of it and three hundred cavalry, besides a number of the multitude that was never ascertained. At the same time took place the numerous earthquakes in Athens, Eubœa, and Bœotia, particularly at Orchomenus in the last-named country.*

88. The same winter the Athenians in Sicily and the Rhegians, with thirty ships, made an expedition against the islands of Æolus; it being impossible to invade them in summer, owing to the want of water. These islands are occupied by the Liparæans, a Cnidian colony, who live in one of them of no great size called Lipara; and from this as their headquarters cultivate the rest, Didyme, Strongyle, and Hiera. In Hiera the people in those parts believe that Hephæstus has his forge,† from the quantity of flame which they see it send out by night, and of smoke by day. These islands lie off the coast of the Sicels and Messinese, and were allies of the Syracusans. The Athenians laid waste their land, and as the inhabitants did not submit, sailed back to Rhegium. Thus the winter ended, and with it ended the fifth year of this war, of which Thucydides was the historian.

89. The next summer‡ the Peloponnesians and their allies set out to invade Attica under the command of Agis, son of Archidamus, and went as far as the Isthmus, but numerous earthquakes occurring, turned back again without the invasion taking place. About the same

---

*The return of the plague in late 427 and the occurrence of earthquakes are part of the unforeseeable, non-human disruption that Thucydides, in his opening chapters, notes as remarkable. He never connects the two catastrophes to any divine plan. The year 426 begins.

†Mythological references occur primarily in geographically exotic contexts. Thucydides' references to local belief or tradition do not suggest that he gives them credibility.

‡The annual Peloponnesian invasion of Attica in 426 stops before its goal and accomplishes nothing, but the notice, just as the preceding signature to year five of the war helps provide a rhythm by its formulaic regularity.

time that these earthquakes were so common, the sea at Orobiæ, in Eubœa, retiring from the then line of coast, returned in a huge wave and invaded a great part of the town, and retreated leaving some of it still under water; so that what was once land is now sea; such of the inhabitants perishing as could not run up to the higher ground in time. A similar inundation also occurred at Atalanta, the island off the Opuntian-Locrian coast, carrying away part of the Athenian fort and wrecking one of two ships which were drawn up on the beach. At Peparethus also the sea retreated a little, without however any inundation following; and an earthquake threw down part of the wall, the town-hall, and a few other buildings. The cause, in my opinion, of this phenomenon must be sought in the earthquake.* At the point where its shock has been the most violent the sea is driven back, and suddenly recoiling with redoubled force, causes the inundation. Without an earthquake I do not see how such an accident could happen.

90. During the same summer different operations were carried on by the different belligerents in Sicily; by the Siceliots themselves against each other, and by the Athenians and their allies: I shall however confine myself to the actions in which the Athenians took part, choosing the most important. The death of the Athenian general Charœades, killed by the Syracusans in battle, left Laches in the sole command of the fleet, which he now directed in concert with the allies against Mylæ, a place belonging to the Messinese. Two Messinese battalions in garrison at Mylæ laid an ambush for the party landing from the ships, but were routed with great slaughter by the Athenians and their allies, who thereupon assaulted the fortification and compelled them to surrender the Acropolis and to march with them upon Messina. This town afterwards also submitted upon the approach of the Athenians and their allies, and gave hostages and all other securities required.

91. The same summer the Athenians sent thirty ships round Peloponnese under Demosthenes, son of Alcisthenes, and Procles, son of Theodorus, and sixty others, with two thousand heavy infantry, against Melos, under Nicias, son of Niceratus; wishing to reduce the Melians, who, although islanders, refused to be subjects of Athens or even to join her confederacy.† The devastation of their land not procuring

---

*Thucydides had scientific interests, as his account of the plague at Athens has shown. Resolutely empirical in his causality, he never in his own voice attributes (compare Nicias, 7.69) human fortune or misfortune to divine beings.

†The Athenians have sent twenty ships to Sicily, thirty around the Peloponnese, and sixty now to Melos. Melos became the Thucydidean poster-child of apparent victims of unlimited Athenian aggression. Their tale resumes in book 5. (Fornara #132 translates an inscription recording a Melian contribution to the Peloponnesian war fund; depending on its date, the inscription may throw into question the impartiality of Thucydides' account.)

their submission, the fleet, weighing from Melos, sailed to Oropus in the territory of Græa, and landing at nightfall, the heavy infantry started at once from the ships by land for Tanagra in Bœotia, where they were met by the whole levy from Athens, agreeably to a concerted signal, under the command of Hipponicus, son of Callias, and Eurymedon, son of Thucles. They encamped, and passing that day in ravaging the Tanagræan territory, remained there for the night; and next day, after defeating those of the Tanagræans who sallied out against them and some Thebans who had come up to help the Tanagræans, took some arms, set up a trophy, and retired, the troops to the city and the others to the ships. Nicias with his sixty ships coasted along shore and ravaged the Locrian seaboard, and so returned home.

92. About this time the Lacedæmonians founded their colony of Heraclea in Trachis, their object being the following. The Malians form in all three tribes, the Paralians, the Hiereans, and the Trachinians. The last of these having suffered severely in a war with their neighbours the Œtæans, at first intended to give themselves up to Athens; but afterwards fearing not to find in her the security that they sought, sent to Lacedæmon, having chosen Tisamenus for their ambassador. In this embassy joined also the Dorians from the mother country of the Lacedæmonians, with the same request, as they themselves also suffered from the same enemy. After hearing them, the Lacedæmonians determined to send out the colony, wishing to assist the Trachinians and Dorians, and also because they thought that the proposed town would lie conveniently for the purposes of the war against the Athenians.* A fleet might be got ready there against Eubœa, with the advantage of a short passage to the island; and the town would also be useful as a station on the road to Thrace. In short, everything made the Lacedæmonians eager to found the place. After first consulting the god at Delphi and receiving a favourable answer, they sent off the colonists, Spartans and Periœci, inviting also any of the rest of the Hellenes who might wish to accompany them, except Ionians, Achæans, and certain other nationalities; three Lacedæmonians leading as founders of the colony, Leon, Alcidas, and Damagon.† The settlement effected, they fortified anew the city, now called Heraclea, distant about four miles and a half from Thermopylæ and two miles and a quarter from the sea, and commenced building docks,

---

*Central Greece is a major battleground of the early war. Various towns invite in the principal combatants for security against local enemies. The results do not always accord with their expectations.

†One notes that the names of the colony-founders include Damagon (Leader of the People) and Alcidas, whose name is a (grandfather's) patronymic of Heracles. Probably, as Hornblower notes, this was an intended ominous "coincidence" for a colony called Heraclea (map 4).

closing the side towards Thermopylæ just by the pass itself, in order that they might be easily defended.

93. The foundation of this town, evidently meant to annoy Eubœa (the passage across to Cenæum in that island being a short one), at first caused some alarm at Athens, which the event however did nothing to justify, the town never giving them any trouble. The reason of this was as follows. The Thessalians, who were sovereign in those parts, and whose territory was menaced by its foundation, were afraid that it might prove a very powerful neighbour, and accordingly continually harassed and made war upon the new settlers, until they at last wore them out in spite of their originally considerable numbers, people flocking from all quarters to a place founded by the Lacedæmonians, and thus thought secure of prosperity. On the other hand the Lacedæmonians themselves, in the persons of their governors, did their full share towards ruining its prosperity and reducing its population, as they frightened away the greater part of the inhabitants by governing harshly and in some cases not fairly,* and thus made it easier for their neighbours to prevail against them.

94. The same summer, about the same time that the Athenians were detained at Melos, their fellow-citizens in the thirty ships cruising round Peloponnese, after cutting off some guards in an ambush at Ellomenus in Leucadia, subsequently went against Leucas itself with a large armament, having been reinforced by the whole levy of the Acarnanians except Œniadæ, and by the Zacynthians and Cephallenitans and fifteen ships from Corcyra.† While the Leucadians witnessed the devastation of their land, without and within the isthmus upon which the town of Leucas and the temple of Apollo stand, without making any movement on account of the overwhelming numbers of the enemy, the Acarnanians urged Demosthenes, the Athenian general, to build a wall so as to cut off the town from the continent, a measure which they were convinced would secure its capture and rid them once and for all of a most troublesome enemy.

95. Demosthenes however had in the meanwhile been persuaded by the Messenians that it was a fine opportunity for him, having so large an army assembled, to attack the Ætolians, who were not only the enemies of Naupactus, but whose reduction would further make it easy to gain the rest of that part of the continent for the Athenians. The Ætolian nation, although numerous and warlike, yet dwelt in un-

---

*The strategic concept was sound, but the execution was flawed. The commanders on both sides were often deficient in political skills.

†The Corcyreans supply some assistance in the northwest to the Athenians. The Leucadians were Peloponnesian allies, and the Athenians are trying to encircle the enemy's base (map 4).

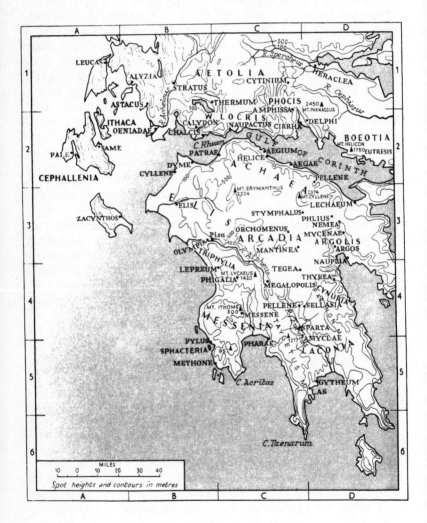

MAP 4. SOUTHWESTERN GREECE

MAP 5. SOUTHEASTERN GREECE

walled villages scattered far apart,* and had nothing but light armour, and might, according to the Messenians, be subdued without much difficulty before succours could arrive. The plan which they recommended was to attack first the Apodotians, next the Ophionians, and after these the Eurytanians, who are the largest tribe in Ætolia, and speak, as is said, a language exceedingly difficult to understand, and eat their flesh raw. These once subdued, the rest would easily come in.

To this plan Demosthenes consented, not only to please the Messenians, but also in the belief that by adding the Ætolians to his other continental allies he would be able, without aid from home, to march against the Bœotians by way of Ozolian Locris to Kytinium in Doris, keeping Parnassus on his right until he descended to the Phocians, whom he could force to join him if their ancient friendship for Athens did not, as he anticipated, at once decide them to do so. Arrived in Phocis he was already upon the frontier of Bœotia. He accordingly weighed from Leucas, against the wish of the Acarnanians, and with his whole armament sailed along the coast to Sollium, where he communicated to them his intention; and upon their refusing to agree to it on account of the non-investment of Leucas, himself with the rest of the forces, the Cephallenians, the Messenians, and Zacynthians, and three hundred Athenian marines from his own ships (the fifteen Corcyræan vessels having departed), started on his expedition against the Ætolians. His base he established at Œneon in Locris, as the Ozolian Locrians were allies of Athens and were to meet him with all their forces in the interior. Being neighbours of the Ætolians and armed in the same way, it was thought that they would be of great service upon the expedition, from their acquaintance with the localities and the warfare of the inhabitants.

96. After bivouacking with the army in the precinct of Nemean Zeus, in which the poet Hesiod is said to have been killed by the people of the country, according to an oracle which had foretold that he should die in Nemea, Demosthenes set out at daybreak to invade Ætolia. The first day he took Potidania, the next Krokyle, and the third Tichium, where he halted and sent back the booty to Eupalium in Locris, having determined to pursue his conquests as far as the Ophionians, and in the event of their refusing to submit, to return to Naupactus and make them the objects of a second expedition. Meanwhile the Ætolians had been aware of his design from the moment of its formation, and as soon as the army invaded their country came up in great force with all their tribes; even the most remote Ophionians,

---

*Northwestern Greece was primitive, as Thucydides mentions at 1.5–6, and its varied inhabitants still were not familiar with the full panoply of political procedures, those practices found in mature *poleis*.

the Bomiensians, and Calliensians, who extend towards the Malian Gulf, being among the number.

97. The Messenians, however, adhered to their original advice. Assuring Demosthenes that the Ætolians were an easy conquest, they urged him to push on as rapidly as possible, and to try to take the villages as fast as he came up to them, without waiting until the whole nation should be in arms against him. Led on by his advisers and trusting in his fortune, as he had met with no opposition, without waiting for his Locrian reinforcements, who were to have supplied him with the light-armed darters in which he was most deficient, he advanced and stormed Ægitium, the inhabitants flying before him and posting themselves upon the hills above the town, which stood on high ground about nine miles from the sea. Meanwhile the Ætolians had gathered to the rescue, and now attacked the Athenians and their allies, running down from the hills on every side and darting their javelins, falling back when the Athenian army advanced, and coming on as it retired;* and for a long while the battle was of this character, alternate advance and retreat, in both which operations the Athenians had the worst.

98. Still as long as their archers had arrows left and were able to use them, they held out, the light-armed Ætolians retiring before the arrows; but after the captain of the archers had been killed and his men scattered, the soldiers, wearied out with the constant repetition of the same exertions and hard pressed by the Ætolians with their javelins, at last turned and fled, and falling into pathless gullies and places that they were unacquainted with, thus perished, the Messenian Chromon, their guide, having also unfortunately been killed. A great many were overtaken in the pursuit by the swift-footed and light-armed Ætolians, and fell beneath their javelins; the greater number however missed their road and rushed into the wood, which had no ways out, and which was soon fired and burnt round them by the enemy. Indeed the Athenian army fell victims to death in every form, and suffered all the vicissitudes of flight; the survivors escaped with difficulty to the sea and Œneon in Locris, whence they had set out. Many of the allies were killed, and about one hundred and twenty Athenian heavy infantry, not a man less, and all in the prime of life. These were by far the best men in the city of Athens that fell during this war.† Among the slain, was also Procles, the colleague of Demosthenes. Meanwhile the Athenians took up their dead under

---

*Guerrilla tactics and light-armed warfare became more important as the war progressed. The hoplite phalanx, heavily armed and dependent on a tight formation, could cope well only against a similar formation in open battle.

†Thucydides remarkably singles out these 120 hoplites as Athens' finest. One of the generals, Procles, also fell.

truce from the Ætolians, and retired to Naupactus, and from thence went in their ships to Athens; Demosthenes staying behind in Naupactus and in the neighbourhood, being afraid to face the Athenians after the disaster.

99. About the same time the Athenians on the coast of Sicily sailed to Locris, and in a descent which they made from the ships defeated the Locrians who came against them, and took a fort upon the river Halex.

100. The same summer the Ætolians, who before the Athenian expedition had sent an embassy to Corinth and Lacedæmon, composed of Tolophus, an Ophionian, Boriades, an Eurytanian, and Tisander, an Apodotian, obtained that an army should be sent them against Naupactus, which had invited the Athenian invasion. The Lacedæmonians accordingly sent off towards autumn three thousand heavy infantry of the allies, five hundred of whom were from Heraclea, the newly-founded city in Trachis, under the command of Eurylochus, a Spartan, accompanied by Macarius and Menedaïus, also Spartans.

101. The army having assembled at Delphi, Eurylochus sent a herald to the Ozolian Locrians; the road to Naupactus lying through their territory, and he having besides conceived the idea of detaching them from Athens. His chief abettors in Locris were the Amphissians, who were alarmed at the hostility of the Phocians. These first gave hostages themselves, and induced the rest to do the same for fear of the invading army; first, their neighbours the Myonians, who held the most difficult of the passes, and after them the Ipnians, Messapians, Tritæans, Chalæans, Tolophonians, Hessians, and Œanthians, all of whom joined in the expedition; the Olpæans contenting themselves with giving hostages, without accompanying the invasion; and the Hyæans refusing to do either, until the capture of Polis, one of their villages.

102. His preparations completed, Eurylochus lodged the hostages in Kytinium, in Doris, and advanced upon Naupactus through the country of the Locrians, taking upon his way Œneon and Eupalium, two of their towns that refused to join him. Arrived in the Naupactian territory, and having been now joined by the Ætolians, the army laid waste the land and took the suburb of the town, which was unfortified; and after this Molycrium also, a Corinthian colony subject to Athens. Meanwhile the Athenian Demosthenes, who since the affair in Ætolia had remained near Naupactus, having had notice of the army and fearing for the town, went and persuaded the Acarnanians, although not without difficulty because of his departure from Leucas, to go to the relief of Naupactus. They accordingly sent with him on board his ships a thousand heavy infantry, who threw themselves into the place and saved it; the extent of its wall and the small number of its defenders otherwise placing it in the greatest danger. Meanwhile Eurylochus and his companions, finding that this force had entered and that it was impossible to storm the town, withdrew, not to Peloponnese, but to the country once called Æolis, and now Calydon and Pleuron, and to the places in that neighbourhood, and Proschium in Ætolia; the Ambraciots having come and urged them to combine with them in attacking Amphilochian Argos and the rest of Amphilochia and Acarnania; affirming that the conquest of these countries would bring all the continent into alliance with Lacedæmon. To this Eurylochus consented, and dismissing the Ætolians, now remained quiet with his army in those parts, until the time should come for the Ambraciots to take the field, and for him to join them before Argos.

Summer was now over.

103. The winter ensuing, the Athenians in Sicily with their Hellenic allies, and such of the Sicel subjects or allies of Syracuse as had revolted from her and joined their army, marched against the Sicel town Inessa, the Acropolis of which was held by the Syracusans, and after attacking it without being able to take it, retired. In the retreat, the allies retreating after the Athenians were attacked by the Syracusans from the fort, and a large part of their army routed with great slaughter. After this, Laches and the Athenians from the ships made some descents in Locris, and defeating the Locrians, who came against them with Proxenus, son of Capaton, upon the river Caïcinus, took some arms and departed.

104. The same winter the Athenians purified Delos, in compliance, it appears, with a certain oracle.* It had been purified before by Pisistratus the tyrant; not indeed the whole island, but as much of it as could be seen from the temple. All of it was, however, now purified in the following way. All the sepulchres of those that had died in Delos were taken up, and for the future it was commanded that no one should be allowed either to die or to give birth to a child in the island;† but that they should be carried over to Rhenea, which is so near to Delos that Polycrates, tyrant of Samos, having added Rhenea to his other island conquests during his period of naval ascendancy, dedicated it to the Delian Apollo by binding it to Delos with a chain.

The Athenians, after the purification, celebrated, for the first time,

---

*The purification was historical; the oracular cause produces a Thucydidean disclaimer ("it appears"). Delos was a Panhellenic sanctuary (like Olympia, Nemea, Delphi, and the Isthmus) but especially sacred to the ethnic Ionians. Here the Athenians had first established their defensive league, and here until 455/454 they stored the Delian (or Hellenic) League's income and treasure. The removal of the treasury to Athens along with the regular synods of the alliance reduced Delos' importance except as a religious shrine (and festival locale).

†Hellenic ritual purity excluded various acts thought to confer pollution. Many societies include birth and death among these. The Athenians repeat an action performed almost a century earlier by their tyrant Pisistratus.

the quinquennial festival of the Delian games. Once upon a time, indeed, there was a great assemblage of the Ionians and the neighbouring islanders at Delos, who used to come to the festival, as the Ionians now do to that of Ephesus, and athletic and poetical contests took place there, and the cities brought choirs of dancers. Nothing can be clearer on this point than the following verses of Homer,* taken from a hymn to Apollo:—

> Phœbus, where'er thou strayest, far or near,
> Delos was still of all thy haunts most dear.
> Thither the robed Ionians take their way
> With wife and child to keep thy holiday,
> Invoke thy favour on each manly game,
> And dance and sing in honour of thy name.

That there was also a poetical contest in which the Ionians went to contend, again is shown by the following, taken from the same hymn. After celebrating the Delian dance of the women, he ends his song of praise with these verses, in which he also alludes to himself:—

> Well, may Apollo with Artemis keep you all! and so,
> Fare ye well, good-bye—yet tell me not I go
> Out from your hearts; and if in after hours
> Some other wanderer in this world of ours
> Touch at your shores, and ask your maidens here
> Who sings the songs the sweetest to your ear,
> Think of me then, and answer with a smile,
> "A blind old man of Chios' rocky isle."

Homer thus attests that there was anciently a great assembly and festival at Delos. In later times, although the islanders and the Athenians continued to send the choirs of dancers with sacrifices, the contests and most of the ceremonies were abolished, probably through adversity, until the Athenians celebrated the games upon this occasion with the novelty of horse-races.

105. The same winter the Ambraciots, as they had promised Eurylochus when they retained his army, marched out against Amphilochian Argos with three thousand heavy infantry, and invading the Argive territory occupied Olpæ, a stronghold on a hill near the sea, which had

---

*Thucydides has criticized Homer as a source (for example, at 1.9 and 2.41) but has used him before (1.3, 10) when nothing better was available. Classicists no longer believe that Homer wrote the *Homeric Hymns*, a collection of narratives and preludic verses, but some of them were written within a generation of the composition of the two great Homeric epics.

been formerly fortified by the Acarnanians and used as the place of judicial trials for their nation, and which is about two miles and three-quarters from the city of Argos upon the sea-coast. Meanwhile the Acarnanians went with a part of their forces to the relief of Argos, and with the rest encamped in Amphilochia at the place called Crenæ, or the Wells, to watch for Eurylochus and his Peloponnesians, and to prevent their passing through and effecting their junction with the Ambraciots; while they also sent for Demosthenes, the commander of the Ætolian expedition, to be their leader, and for the twenty Athenian ships that were cruising off Peloponnese under the command of Aristotle, son of Timocrates, and Hierophon, son of Antimnestus. On their part, the Ambraciots at Olpæ sent a messenger to their own city, to beg them to come with their whole levy to their assistance, fearing that the army of Eurylochus might not be able to pass through the Acarnanians, and that they might themselves be obliged to fight single-handed, or be unable to retreat, if they wished it, without danger.

106. Meanwhile Eurylochus and his Peloponnesians, learning that the Ambraciots at Olpæ had arrived, set out from Proschium with all haste to join them, and crossing the Achelous advanced through Acarnania, which they found deserted by its population, who had gone to the relief of Argos; keeping on their right the city of the Stratians and its garrison, and on their left the rest of Acarnania. Traversing the territory of the Stratians, they advanced through Phytia, next, skirting Medeon, through Limnæa; after which they left Acarnania behind them and entered a friendly country, that of the Agræans. From thence they reached and crossed Mount Thyamus, which belongs to the Agræans, and descended into the Argive territory after nightfall, and passing between the city of Argos and the Acarnanian posts at Crenæ, joined the Ambraciots at Olpæ.

107. Uniting here at daybreak, they sat down at the place called Metropolis, and encamped. Not long afterwards the Athenians in the twenty ships came into the Ambracian Gulf to support the Argives, with Demosthenes and two hundred Messenian heavy infantry, and sixty Athenian archers. While the fleet off Olpæ blockaded the hill from the sea, the Acarnanians and a few of the Amphilochians, most of whom were kept back in force by the Ambraciots, had already arrived at Argos, and were preparing to give battle to the enemy, having chosen Demosthenes to command the whole of the allied army in concert with their own generals. Demosthenes led them near to Olpæ and encamped, a great ravine separating the two armies. During five days they remained inactive; on the sixth both sides formed in order of battle. The army of the Peloponnesians was the largest and outflanked their opponents; and Demosthenes fearing that his right might be surrounded, placed in ambush in a hollow way overgrown with bushes some four hundred heavy infantry and light troops, who were to rise up at the moment of the onset behind the projecting left wing of the enemy, and to take them in the rear.* When both sides were ready they joined battle; Demosthenes being on the right wing with the Messenians and a few Athenians, while the rest of the line was made up of the different divisions of the Acarnanians, and of the Amphilochian darters. The Peloponnesians and Ambraciots were drawn up pell-mell together, with the exception of the Mantineans, who were massed on the left, without however reaching to the extremity of the wing, where Eurylochus and his men confronted the Messenians and Demosthenes.

108. The Peloponnesians were now well engaged and with their outflanking wing were upon the point of turning their enemy's right; when the Acarnanians from the ambuscade set upon them from behind, and broke them at the first attack, without their staying to resist; while the panic into which they fell caused the flight of most of their army, terrified beyond measure at seeing the division of Eurylochus and their best troops cut to pieces. Most of the work was done by Demosthenes and his Messenians, who were posted in this part of the field. Meanwhile the Ambraciots (who are the best soldiers in those countries) and the troops upon the right wing, defeated the division opposed to them and pursued it to Argos. Returning from the pursuit, they found their main body defeated; and hard pressed by the Acarnanians, with difficulty made good their passage to Olpæ, suffering heavy loss on the way, as they dashed on without discipline or order, the Mantineans excepted, who kept their ranks best of any in the army during the retreat.

The battle did not end until the evening.

109. The next day Menedaïus, who on the death of Eurylochus and Macarius had succeeded to the sole command, being at a loss after so signal a defeat how to stay and sustain a siege, cut off as he was by land and by the Athenian fleet by sea, and equally so how to retreat in safety, opened a parley with Demosthenes and the Acarnanian generals for a truce and permission to retreat, and at the same time for the recovery of the dead. The dead they gave back to him, and setting up a trophy took up their own also to the number of about three hundred. The retreat demanded they refused publicly to the army; but permission to depart without delay was secretly granted to the Mantineans and to Menedaïus and the other commanders and principal men of the Peloponnesians by Demosthenes and his Acarna-

---

*Demosthenes, unlike most generals, learned from his mistakes and his enemies. He employs a guerrilla ambush with his own local Acarnanian and Amphilochian allies to defeat the combined Peloponnesian and local Ambraciot force. Many locations that Thucydides mentions in this narrative are unknown (maps 4 and 5).

nian colleagues; who desired to strip the Ambraciots and the mercenary host of foreigners of their supporters; and, above all, to discredit
the Lacedæmonians and Peloponnesians with the Hellenes in those
parts, as traitors and self-seekers.*

While the enemy was taking up his dead and hastily burying them
as he could, and those who obtained permission were secretly planning their retreat,

110. word was brought to Demosthenes and the Acarnanians that
the Ambraciots from the city, in compliance with the first message
from Olpæ, were on the march with their whole levy through Amphilochia to join their countrymen at Olpæ, knowing nothing of what
had occurred. Demosthenes prepared to march with his army against
them, and meanwhile sent on at once a strong division to beset the
roads and occupy the strong positions.

111. In the meantime the Mantineans and others included in the
agreement went out under the pretence of gathering herbs and firewood,† and stole off by twos and threes, picking on the way the things
which they professed to have come out for, until they had gone some
distance from Olpæ, when they quickened their pace. The Ambraciots
and such of the rest as had accompanied them in larger parties, seeing them going on, pushed on in their turn, and began running in
order to catch them up. The Acarnanians at first thought that all alike
were departing without permission, and began to pursue the Peloponnesians; and believing that they were being betrayed, even threw
a dart or two at some of their generals who tried to stop them and
told them that leave had been given. Eventually, however, they let
pass the Mantineans and Peloponnesians, and slew only the Ambraciots, there being much dispute and difficulty in distinguishing
whether a man was an Ambraciot or a Peloponnesian.‡ The number
thus slain was about two hundred; the rest escaped into the bordering
territory of Agræa, and found refuge with Salynthius, the friendly
king of the Agræans.

112. Meanwhile the Ambraciots from the city arrived at Idomene.
Idomene consists of two lofty hills, the highest of which the troops

---

*Demosthenes employs psychological warfare, allowing some Peloponnesian enemy
troops to depart without the knowledge of their local Aetolian comrades in order to
discredit their home governments' commitment to this theater of war. The skulking
behavior of the Spartan Menedaius does not conform to Spartan traditions.

†It is difficult to see how this Peloponnesian plan could have been successful. Thucydides is interested in the desperation of the disloyal. Note that Hellenic troops had to
forage for themselves in most situations—no supply divisions helped them.

‡The complicity of the Mantineans and other Peloponnesians in this desertion of their
Ambraciot allies, and the Athenians' partial permission for some enemy combatants to
depart, led to understandable confusion on both sides—and the death of 200 soldiers.

sent on by Demosthenes succeeded in occupying after nightfall, un-observed by the Ambraciots, who had meanwhile ascended the smaller and bivouacked upon it. After supper Demosthenes set out with the rest of the army, as soon as it was evening; himself with half his force making for the pass, and the remainder going by the Amphilochian hills. At dawn he fell upon the Ambraciots while they were still abed,* ignorant of what had passed, and fully thinking that it was their own countrymen,—Demosthenes having purposely put the Messenians in front with orders to address them in the Doric dialect, and thus to inspire confidence in the sentinels, who would not be able to see them as it was still night. In this way he routed their army as soon as he attacked it, slaying most of them where they were, the rest breaking away in flight over the hills. The roads, however, were already occupied, and while the Amphilochians knew their own country, the Ambraciots were ignorant of it and could not tell which way to turn, and had also heavy armour as against a light-armed enemy, and so fell into ravines and into the ambushes which had been set for them, and perished there. In their manifold efforts to escape some even turned to the sea, which was not far off, and seeing the Athenian ships coasting along shore just while the action was going on, swam off to them, thinking it better in the panic they were in, to perish, if perish they must, by the hands of the Athenians, than by those of the barbarous and detested Amphilochians. Of the large Ambraciot force destroyed in this manner, a few only reached the city in safety; while the Acarnanians, after stripping the dead and setting up a trophy, returned to Argos.

113. The next day arrived a herald from the Ambraciots who had fled from Olpæ to the Agræans, to ask leave to take up the dead that had fallen after the first engagement, when they left the camp with the Mantineans and their companions, without, like them, having had permission to do so. At the sight of the arms of the Ambraciots from the city, the herald was astonished at their number,† knowing nothing of the disaster and fancying that they were those of their own party. Some one asked him what he was so astonished at, and how many of

---

*The first Ambraciot force having been defeated, and forced to retreat to a local ally, Demosthenes brilliantly turns to face the main contingent and falls upon them in the night (a tactic he again attempted at Syracuse, but with less success, 7.43–44). His advance guards speak Doric, the better to deceive the Dorian enemy.

†Book 3 closes with a uniquely pathetic dialogic exchange between the official representative of the defeated and an unnamed victorious soldier. The point is the ignorance of the combatants and the breakdown of diplomacy and even communication in the face of sheer catastrophe. The error is double; here the Ambraciot herald comes for permission to recover the dead from their first defeat but meets the equipment from the unimagined second defeat.

them had been killed, fancying in his turn that this was the herald from the troops at Idomene.* He replied, 'About two hundred'; upon which his interrogator took him up, saying, 'Why, the arms you see here are of more than a thousand.' The herald replied, 'Then they are not the arms of those who fought with us?' The other answered, 'Yes, they are, if at least you fought at Idomene yesterday.' 'But we fought with no one yesterday; but the day before in the retreat.' 'However that may be, we fought yesterday with those who came to reinforce you from the city of the Ambraciots.' When the herald heard this and knew that the reinforcement from the city had been destroyed, he broke into wailing,† and stunned at the magnitude of the present evils, went away at once without having performed his errand, or again asking for the dead bodies. Indeed, this was by far the greatest disaster that befell any one Hellenic city in an equal number of days during this war; and I have not set down the number of the dead, because the amount stated seems so out of proportion to the size of the city as to be incredible.‡ In any case I know that if the Acarnanians and Amphilochians had wished to take Ambracia as the Athenians and Demosthenes advised, they would have done so without striking a blow; as it was, they feared that if the Athenians had it they would be worse neighbours to them than the present ones.

114. After this the Acarnanians allotted a third of the spoils to the Athenians, and divided the rest among their own different towns. The share of the Athenians was captured on the voyage home; the arms now deposited in the Attic temples are three hundred panoplies, which the Acarnanians set apart for Demosthenes, and which he brought to Athens in person, his return to his country after the Ætolian disaster being rendered less hazardous by this exploit. The Athenians in the twenty ships also went off to Naupactus. The Acarnanians and Amphilochians, after the departure of Demosthenes and the Athenians, granted the Ambraciots and Peloponnesians who had taken refuge with Salynthius and the Agræans a free retreat from

---

*The interlocutor, in his turn, wrongly assumes that the herald is from the remnants of the army in the second defeat at Idomene.

†The herald, once aware that two armies of his comrades have been destroyed, cannot continue with his official task and falls into inarticulate grief. Did Thucydides observe this interchange? Was he the unnamed interlocutor?

‡Thucydides likes to report superlatives, some of them extended and convoluted (compare 7.30 on little Mycalessus), here the greatest Hellenic loss in the shortest time "during this war." This last phrase, seemingly innocuous, is important for the compositional question of the *Histories*. Does Thucydides mean the Ten Years' War, ending in 421, or the twenty-seven year war, ending in 404? Probably he has in mind the former, given the Athenian losses at the end of the campaign in Sicily. Nowhere else does Thucydides refuse to report something that he claims to know. The figure is probably in excess of 1,000 casualties.

Œniadæ, to which place they had removed from the country of Salynthius, and for the future concluded with the Ambraciots a treaty and alliance for one hundred years, upon the terms following. It was to be a defensive, not an offensive alliance; the Ambraciots could not be required to march with the Acarnanians against the Peloponnesians, nor the Acarnanians with the Ambraciots against the Athenians; for the rest the Ambraciots were to give up the places and hostages that they held of the Amphilochians, and not to give help to Anactorium, which was at enmity with the Acarnanians. With this arrangement they put an end to the war. After this the Corinthians sent a garrison of their own citizens to Ambracia, composed of three hundred heavy infantry, under the command of Xenocleides, son of Euthycles, who reached their destination after a difficult journey across the continent. Such was the history of the affair of Ambracia.

115. The same winter the Athenians in Sicily made a descent from their ships upon the territory of Himera, in concert with the Sicels, who had invaded its borders from the interior, and also sailed to the islands of Æolus. Upon their return to Rhegium they found the Athenian general, Pythodorus, son of Isolochus, come to supersede Laches in the command of the fleet. The allies in Sicily had sailed to Athens and induced the Athenians to send out more vessels to their assistance, pointing out that the Syracusans who already commanded their land were making efforts to get together a navy, to avoid being any longer excluded from the sea by a few vessels.* The Athenians proceeded to man forty ships to send to them, thinking that the war in Sicily would thus be the sooner ended, and also wishing to exercise their navy. One of the generals, Pythodorus, was accordingly sent out with a few ships; Sophocles, son of Sostratides, and Eurymedon, son of Thucles, being destined to follow with the main body. Meanwhile Pythodorus had taken the command of Laches' ships, and towards the end of winter sailed against the Locrian fort, which Laches had formerly taken, and returned after being defeated in battle by the Locrians.

116. In the first days of this spring, the stream of fire issued from Etna, as on former occasions, and destroyed some land of the Catanians, who live upon Mount Etna, which is the largest mountain in Sicily. Fifty years, it is said, had elapsed since the last eruption, there having been three in all since the Hellenes have inhabited Sicily.† Such were the events of this winter; and with it ended the sixth year of this war, of which Thucydides was the historian.

---

*Thucydides briefly returns to events in Sicily as the Athenians continue to be sucked in by invitations—here a chance to exercise a fleet of forty ships in western waters (see map 10 for the places mentioned).

†Volcanic eruption, another natural cataclysm, rounds off 426, the war's sixth year.

BOOK 4

Seventh Year of the War — Occupation of Pylos — Surrender of the Spartan Army in Sphacteria

1. Next summer, about the time of the grain's coming into ear, ten Syracusan and as many Locrian vessels sailed to Messina, in Sicily, and occupied the town upon the invitation of the inhabitants; and Messina revolted from the Athenians.* The Syracusans contrived this chiefly because they saw that the place afforded an approach to Sicily, and feared that the Athenians might hereafter use it as a base for attacking them with a larger force; the Locrians because they wished to carry on hostilities from both sides of the Strait† and to reduce their enemies, the people of Rhegium. Meanwhile, the Locrians had invaded the Rhegian territory with all their forces, to prevent their succouring Messina, and also at the instance of some exiles from Rhegium who were with them; the long factions by which that town had been torn rendering it for the moment incapable of resistance, and thus furnishing an additional temptation to the invaders.‡ After devastating the country the Locrian land forces retired, their ships remaining to guard Messina, while others were being manned for the same destination to carry on the war from thence.

2. About the same time in the spring, before the grain was ripe, the Peloponnesians and their allies invaded Attica under Agis, the son of Archidamus, king of the Lacedæmonians, and sat down and laid waste the country. Meanwhile the Athenians sent off the forty ships which they had been preparing to Sicily, with the remaining generals Eurymedon and Sophocles; their colleague Pythodorus having already preceded them thither.§ These had also instructions as they sailed by to look to the Corcyræans in the town, who were being plun-

---

*Messina, on the strategic northeast tip of Sicily (map 10), provides a western paradigm of political *stasis* leading to intervention by major powers, here Athens and Syracuse. Syracusans and Locrians (natives of Locri, on the east side of the "toe" of the Italian "boot") aided the disaffected Messinese in internal revolution at the beginning of 425.

†The Locrians were inveterately hostile to the Rhegians; Rhegium is at the western tip of the toe, opposite Sicily's Messina.

‡The war promoted factionalism and class warfare in cities large and small.

§Forty ships is a significant force. This commander is not the tragic poet Sophocles, although he too had earlier been elected to the office of *strategos*.

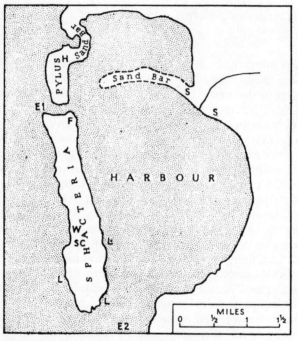

H = *Headland fortified by Athenians (Th.4.4.3)*
E1 & **E2**: *Two entries to the Harbour (4.8.6)*
F: *Old Fort used by Spartans (4.31.2; 35.1)*
W: *Water in "Meritt's cleft" (4.26.4; 31.2)*
SC: *Spartan Camp (4.31.2)*
L: *Landing places (4.31; 32.2)*
S: *Station of Spartan fleet (4.14.1)*

MAP 6. PYLOS (PYLUS) AND SPHACTERIA

dered by the exiles in the mountain. To support these exiles sixty Peloponnesian vessels had lately sailed, it being thought that the famine raging in the city would make it easy for them to reduce it. Demosthenes also, who had remained without employment since his return from Acarnania,* applied and obtained permission to use the fleet, if he wished it, upon the coast of Peloponnese.

3. Off Laconia they heard that the Peloponnesian ships were already at Corcyra, upon which Eurymedon and Sophocles wished to hasten to the island, but Demosthenes required them first to touch at Pylos and do what was wanted there, before continuing their voyage.† While they were making objections, a squall chanced‡ to come on and carried the fleet into Pylos. Demosthenes at once urged them to fortify the place, it being for this that he had come on the voyage, and made them observe there was plenty of stone and timber on the spot, and that the place was strong by nature, and together with much of the country round unoccupied; Pylos, or Coryphasium, as the Lacedæmonians call it, being about forty-five miles distant from Sparta, and situated in the old country of the Messenians.§ The commanders told him that there was no lack of desert headlands in Peloponnese if he wished to put the city to expense by occupying them.‖ He, however, thought that this place was distinguished from others of the kind by having a harbour close by; while the Messenians, the old natives of the country, speaking the same dialect as the Lacedæmonians, could do them the greatest mischief by their incursions from it, and would at the same time be a trusty garrison.#

4. After speaking to the captains of companies on the subject, and failing to persuade either the generals or the soldiers, he remained in-

---

*Demosthenes was often innovative but not always as successful as he had been recently. He was general-elect at this time but had not yet taken office.

†Thucydides presents Demosthenes' plan and place as if he had just conceived it, but the strategic implications of "permission to use the fleet . . . upon the coast of Peloponnese" and the obvious guerrilla-warfare possibilities with a native force of liberated, Doric-speaking Messenians suggest a carefully developed strategy.

‡The squall was not predictable, of course, but the delay helped the irregular commander achieve his unanticipated goal.

§The location at the corner of the Peloponnese was home to Homer's legendary Nestor, an important Achaean commander. It ceased to serve as a town after the Spartan conquest of Messenia (c.715) and the enserfment of its population (thenceforth, the helots). An intervening mountain range (including the refuge of Mount Ithome) renders the journey of 75 miles from Sparta in Laconia more difficult.

‖The reported strategic objection is a joke of which there are precious few in Thucydides (although there are many in Herodotus). Another jibe appears at 4.40.

#The military base in this spot (map 6) is easily reinforced by sea, is manned by a force that knows the territory well, and is a dependable, unrelenting force for damaging enemies.

active with the rest from stress of weather; until the soldiers themselves wanting occupation were seized with a sudden impulse to go
round and fortify the place. Accordingly they set to work in earnest,
and having no iron tools, picked up stones, and put them together as
they happened to fit, and where mortar was needed, carried it on
their backs for want of hods, stooping down to make it stay on, and
clasping their hands together behind to prevent it falling off; sparing
no effort to be able to complete the most vulnerable points before the
arrival of the Lacedæmonians, most of the place being sufficiently
strong by nature without further fortification.

5. Meanwhile the Lacedæmonians were celebrating a festival, and
also at first made light of the news, in the idea that whenever they
chose to take the field the place would be immediately evacuated by
the enemy or easily taken by force;* the absence of their army before
Athens having also something to do with their delay. The Athenians
fortified the place on the land side, and where it most required it, in six
days, and leaving Demosthenes with five ships to garrison it, with the
main body of the fleet hastened on their voyage to Corcyra and Sicily.

6. As soon as the Peloponnesians in Attica heard of the occupation
of Pylos, they hurried back home; the Lacedæmonians and their king
Agis thinking that the matter touched them nearly. Besides having
made their invasion early in the season, and while the grain was still
green, most of their troops were short of provisions: the weather also
was unusually bad for the time of year, and greatly distressed their
army. Many reasons thus combined to hasten their departure and to
make this invasion a very short one; indeed they only stayed fifteen
days in Attica.†

7. About the same time the Athenian general Simonides getting
together a few Athenians from the garrisons, and a number of the allies in those parts, took Eion in Thrace, a Mendæan colony and hostile to Athens, by treachery,‡ but had no sooner done so than the
Chalcidians and Bottiæans came up and beat him out of it, with the
loss of many of his soldiers.

8. On the return of the Peloponnesians from Attica the Spartans
themselves and the nearest of the Periœci§ at once set out for Pylos,

---

*The Spartans miscalculate repeatedly the potential damage of the base in their terri-
tory. Their religious calendar on several occasions is blamed for preventing rapid responses. They regard the attack as a momentary finger in the eye rather than a cancer
of permanent fortification.

†An unexpected dividend of Demosthenes' plan for the Athenians is the curtailed annual invasion of the Peloponnesians into Attica.

‡This is not the famous Thraceward Eion but another undetermined location nearby
of the same name.

§These second-class citizens remain loyal to the Spartiate ruling class.

the other Lacedæmonians following more slowly as they had just come in from another campaign. Word was also sent round Peloponnese to come up as quickly as possible to Pylos; while the sixty Peloponnesian ships were sent for from Corcyra, and being dragged by their crews across the isthmus of Leucas, passed unperceived by the Athenian squadron at Zacynthus, and reached Pylos, where the land forces had arrived before them. Before the Peloponnesian fleet sailed in, Demosthenes found time to send out unobserved two ships to inform Eurymedon and the Athenians on board the fleet at Zacynthus of the danger of Pylos and to summon them to his assistance. While the ships hastened on their voyage in obedience to the orders of Demosthenes, the Lacedæmonians prepared to assault the fort by land and sea, hoping to capture with ease a work constructed in haste, and held by a feeble garrison. Meanwhile, as they expected the Athenian ships to arrive from Zacynthus, they intended, if they failed to take the place before, to block up the entrances of the harbour to prevent their being able to anchor inside it.

For the island of Sphacteria, stretching along in a line close in front of the harbour, at once makes it safe and narrows its entrances, leaving a passage for two ships on the side nearest Pylos and the Athenian fortifications, and for eight or nine on that next the rest of the mainland:* for the rest, the island was entirely covered with wood, and without paths through not being inhabited, and about one mile and five furlongs in length.† The inlets the Lacedæmonians meant to close with a line of ships placed close together, with their prows turned towards the sea, and, meanwhile, fearing that the enemy might make use of the island to operate against them, carried over some heavy infantry thither, stationing others along the coast.‡ By this means the island and the continent would be alike hostile to the Athenians, as they would be unable to land on either; and the shore of Pylos itself outside the inlet towards the open sea having no harbour, and, therefore, presenting no point which they could use as a base to relieve their countrymen, they, the Lacedæmonians, without sea-fight or risk would in all probability become masters of the place, occupied, as it had been on the spur of the moment, and unfurnished

---

*The geography of this campaign poses problems, when it can be checked. Either Thucydides miscalculated the distances or the manuscripts misreport his once-accurate figures.

†The forested nature of this isolated location will play a part in Demosthenes' delayed attack, until by chance an Athenian soldier burns off the cover.

‡The built-up part of Pylos was located north of the deserted island Sphacteria. The Spartans intelligently anticipate the need to seize the island (why did Demosthenes not occupy it in the first place?) but not the successful Athenian blockade. Pylos has no other real harbor.

with provisions. This being determined, they carried over to the island the heavy infantry, drafted by lot from all the companies. Some others had crossed over before in relief parties, but these last who were left there were four hundred and twenty in number, with their Helot attendants, commanded by Epitadas, son of Molobrus.*

9. Meanwhile Demosthenes, seeing the Lacedæmonians about to attack him by sea and land at once, himself was not idle. He drew up under the fortification and enclosed in a stockade the triremes remaining to him of those which had been left him, arming the sailors taken out of them with poor shields made most of them of osier, it being impossible to procure arms in such a desert place, and even these having been obtained from a thirty-oared Messenian privateer and a boat belonging to some Messenians who happened to have come to them. Among these Messenians were forty heavy infantry, whom he made use of with the rest. Posting most of his men, unarmed and armed, upon the best fortified and strong points of the place towards the interior, with orders to repel any attack of the land forces, he picked sixty heavy infantry and a few archers from his whole force, and with these went outside the wall down to the sea, where he thought that the enemy would most likely attempt to land. Although the ground was difficult and rocky, looking towards the open sea, the fact that this was the weakest part of the wall would, he thought, encourage their ardour, as the Athenians, confident in their naval superiority, had here paid little attention to their defences, and the enemy if he could force a landing might feel secure of taking the place. At this point, accordingly, going down to the water's edge, he posted his heavy infantry to prevent, if possible, a landing, and encouraged them in the following terms:—†

10. 'Soldiers and comrades in this adventure, I hope that none of you in our present strait will think to show his wit by exactly calculating all the perils that encompass us, but that you will rather hasten to close with the enemy, without staying to count the odds, seeing in this your best chance of safety. In emergencies like ours calculation is out of place; the sooner the danger is faced the better. To my mind also most of the chances are for us, if we will only stand fast and not throw away our advantages, overawed by the numbers of the enemy. One of the points in our favour is the awkwardness of the landing. This, however, only helps us if we stand our ground. If we give way it will be practicable enough, in spite of its natural difficulty, without a

---

*Four hundred and twenty Spartiates and their multiple attendants constitute a significant commitment, but this was Spartan home territory, and a helot rebellion was always greatly feared (compare 4.80).

†Demosthenes' speech of encouragement sticks to the tactical situation. This form of soldierly exhortation does not appear in Herodotus.

defender; and the enemy will instantly become more formidable from the difficulty he will have in retreating, supposing that we succeed in repulsing him, which we shall find it easier to do, while he is on board his ships, than after he has landed and meets us on equal terms. As to his numbers, these need not too much alarm you. Large as they may be he can only engage in small detachments, from the impossibility of anchoring. Besides, the numerical superiority that we have to meet is not that of an army on land with everything else equal, but of troops on board ship, upon an element where many favourable accidents are required to act with effect. I therefore consider that his difficulties may be fairly set against our numerical deficiencies, and at the same time I charge you, as Athenians who know by experience what landing from ships on a hostile territory means, and how impossible it is to drive back an enemy determined enough to stand his ground and not to be frightened away by the surf and the terrors of the ships sailing in, to stand fast in the present emergency, beat back the enemy at the water's edge, and save yourselves and the place.'

11. Thus encouraged by Demosthenes, the Athenians felt more confident, and went down to meet the enemy, posting themselves along the edge of the sea. The Lacedæmonians now put themselves in movement and simultaneously assaulted the fortification with their land forces and with their ships, forty-three in number, under their admiral, Thrasymelidas, son of Cratesicles, a Spartan, who made his attack just where Demosthenes expected.* The Athenians had thus to defend themselves on both sides, from the land and from the sea; the enemy rowing up in small detachments, the one relieving the other— it being impossible for many to bring to at once—and showing great ardour and cheering each other on, in the endeavour to force a passage and to take the fortification. He who most distinguished himself was Brasidas. Captain of a trireme, and seeing that the captains and steersmen, impressed by the difficulty of the position, hung back even where a landing might have seemed possible, for fear of wrecking their vessels, he shouted out to them, that they must never allow the enemy to fortify himself in their country for the sake of saving timber, but must shiver their vessels and force a landing; and bade the allies, instead of hesitating in such a moment to sacrifice their ships for Lacedæmon in return for her many benefits, to run them boldly aground, land in one way or another, and make themselves masters of the place and its garrison.

12. Not content with this exhortation, he forced his own steersman

---

*Demosthenes correctly anticipates the Lacedaemonian attack from the sea. Brasidas distinguishes himself in battle, as always. Thucydides reports his hortatory words only indirectly. Map 6 posits the specific locations that Thucydides mentions.

to run his ship ashore, and stepping on to the gangway, was endeavouring to land, when he was cut down by the Athenians, and after receiving many wounds fainted away.* Falling into the bows, his shield
slipped off his arm into the sea, and being thrown ashore was picked
up by the Athenians, and afterwards used for the trophy which they
set up for this attack. The rest also did their best, but were not able to
land, owing to the difficulty of the ground and the unflinching tenacity of the Athenians. It was a strange reversal of the order of things†
for Athenians to be fighting from the land, and from Laconian land
too, against Lacedæmonians coming from the sea; while Lacedæmonians were trying to land from shipboard in their own country, now
become hostile, to attack Athenians, although the former were chiefly
famous at the time as an inland people and superior by land, the latter as a maritime people with a navy that had no equal.

13. After continuing their attacks during that day and most of the
next, the Peloponnesians desisted, and the day after sent some of their
ships to Asine for timber to make engines, hoping to take by their aid,
in spite of its height, the wall opposite the harbour, where the landing
was easiest. At this moment the Athenian fleet from Zacynthus arrived, now numbering fifty sail, having been reinforced by some of the
ships on guard at Naupactus and by four Chian vessels. Seeing the
coast and the island both crowded with heavy infantry, and the hostile
ships in harbour showing no signs of sailing out, at a loss where to anchor, they sailed for the moment to the desert island of Prote,‡ not far
off, where they passed the night. The next day they got under way in
readiness to engage in the open sea if the enemy chose to sail out to
meet them, being determined in the event of his not doing so to sail in
and attack him. The Lacedæmonians did not sail out to sea, and having omitted to close the inlets as they had intended, remained quiet on
shore, engaged in manning their ships and getting ready, in the case of
any one sailing in, to fight in the harbour, which is a fairly large one.

14. Perceiving this, the Athenians advanced against them by each
inlet, and falling on the enemy's fleet, most of which was by this time
afloat and in line, at once put it to flight, and giving chase as far as the
short distance allowed, disabled a good many vessels, and took five,
one with its crew on board; dashing in at the rest that had taken
refuge on shore, and battering some that were still being manned, be-

---

*Ancient commanders fought in the front lines, and Brasidas will die later leading
there at Amphipolis.

†Thucydides marks superlatives of many sorts but also, as here, reversals of the natural or usual order. The Spartans, a land power, attack from the sea the Athenians, a sea
power, dug in on land—the Spartans' own at that. Thucydides here again marks the
role of *tyche* (chance), as he often does in this campaign.

‡This uninhabitable island is found about 8 miles north of the theater of fighting.

fore they could put out, and lashing on to their own ships and towing off empty others whose crews had fled. At this sight the Lacedæmonians, maddened by a disaster which cut off their men on the island, rushed to the rescue, and going into the sea with their heavy armour, laid hold of the ships and tried to drag them back, each man thinking that success depended on his individual exertions. Great was the mêlée, and quite in contradiction to the naval tactics usual to the two combatants; the Lacedæmonians in their excitement and dismay being actually engaged in a sea-fight on land, while the victorious Athenians, in their eagerness to push their success as far as possible, were carrying on a land-fight from their ships.* After great exertions and numerous wounds on both sides they separated, the Lacedæmonians saving their empty ships, except those first taken; and both parties returning to their camp, the Athenians set up a trophy, gave back the dead, secured the wrecks, and at once began to cruise round and jealously watch the island, with its intercepted garrison, while the Peloponnesians on the mainland, whose contingents had now all come up, stayed where they were before Pylos.

15. When the news of what had happened at Pylos reached Sparta, the disaster was thought so serious that the Lacedæmonians resolved that the authorities should go down to the camp, and decide on the spot what was best to be done. There seeing that it was impossible to help their men, and not wishing to risk their being reduced by hunger or overpowered by numbers, they determined, with the consent of the Athenian generals, to conclude an armistice at Pylos and send envoys to Athens to obtain a convention, and to endeavour to get back their men as quickly as possible.

16. The generals accepting their offers, an armistice was concluded upon the terms following:—

That the Lacedæmonians should bring to Pylos and deliver up to the Athenians the ships that had fought in the late engagement, and all in Laconia that were vessels of war, and should make no attack on the fortification either by land or by sea.

That the Athenians should allow the Lacedæmonians on the mainland to send to the men in the island a certain fixed quantity of grain ready kneaded, that is to say, two quarts of barley meal, one pint of wine, and a piece of meat for each man, and half the same quantity for a servant.

That this allowance should be sent in under the eyes of the Athenians, and that no boat should sail to the island except openly.

---

*Thucydides marks another reversal of the usual military situation, here referring to tactics. The antitheses are also congenial to his way of thinking and his organization of sentences.

That the Athenians should continue to guard the island the same as before, without however landing upon it, and should refrain from attacking the Peloponnesian troops either by land or by sea.

That if either party should infringe any of these terms in the slightest particular, the armistice should be at once void.

That the armistice should hold good until the return of the Lacedæmonian envoys from Athens—the Athenians sending them thither in a trireme and bringing them back again—and upon the arrival of the envoys should be at an end, and the ships be restored by the Athenians in the same state as they received them.

Such were the terms of the armistice, and the ships were delivered over to the number of sixty,* and the envoys sent off accordingly. Arrived at Athens they spoke as follows:—

17. 'Athenians, the Lacedæmonians sent us to try to find some way of settling the affair of our men on the island, that shall be at once satisfactory to your interests, and as consistent with our dignity in our misfortune as circumstances permit. We can venture to speak at some length without any departure from the habit of our country. Men of few words where many are not wanted,† we can be less brief when there is a matter of importance to be illustrated and an end to be served by its illustration. Meanwhile we beg you to take what we may say, not in a hostile spirit, nor as if we thought you ignorant and wished to lecture you, but rather as a suggestion on the best course to be taken, addressed to intelligent judges. You can now, if you choose, employ your present success to advantage, so as to keep what you have got and gain honour and reputation besides, and you can avoid the mistake of those who meet with an extraordinary piece of good fortune, and are led on by hope to grasp continually at something further, through having already succeeded without expecting it.‡ While those who have known most vicissitudes of good and bad, have also justly least faith in their prosperity; and to teach your city and ours this lesson experience has not been wanting.

---

*The extremity of Spartan anxiety for their men is patent in this delivery of all their sixty ships as part of the armistice.

†Spartans were proud of their disdain for words. They explain that rather than arising from national character, here their relative wordiness results from an impossible situation.

‡Unexpected success and the consequent impulse to expect further good fortune provide vocabulary and motifs that Thucydides endorses in his own narrative (for example, at 4.21 and 41). This correspondence of speech and authorial judgment leads some critics to doubt the veracity in phrase and substance of Thucydidean speeches. Cornford (*Thucydides Mythistoricus*) and Hunter (*Thucydides: The Artful Reporter*) regard the correspondence of this section of the *Histories* to the tragic pattern of "prosperity–excessive good fortune–arrogance–delusion" as the imposition of an archaic and tragic pattern and outlook on the irregular events of history (accidents, as Aristotle calls them).

18. 'To be convinced of this you have only to look at our present misfortune. What power in Hellas stood higher than we did? and yet we are come to you, although we formerly thought ourselves more able to grant what we are now here to ask. Nevertheless, we have not been brought to this by any decay in our power, or through having our heads turned by aggrandisement; no, our resources are what they have always been, and our error has been an error of judgment, to which all are equally liable. Accordingly, the prosperity which your city now enjoys, and the accession that it has lately received, must not make you fancy that fortune will be always with you. Indeed sensible men are prudent enough to treat their gains as precarious, just as they would also keep a clear head in adversity, and think that war, so far from staying within the limit to which a combatant may wish to confine it, will run the course that its chances prescribe; and thus, not being puffed up by confidence in military success, they are less likely to come to grief, and most ready to make peace, if they can, while their fortune lasts. This, Athenians, you have a good opportunity to do now with us, and thus to escape the possible disasters which may follow upon your refusal, and the consequent imputation of having owed to accident even your present advantages, when you might have left behind you a reputation for power and wisdom which nothing could endanger.

19. 'The Lacedæmonians accordingly invite you to make a treaty and to end the war, and offer peace and alliance and the most friendly and intimate relations in every way and on every occasion between us;* and in return ask for the men on the island, thinking it better for both parties not to stand out to the end, on the chance of some favourable accident enabling the men to force their way out, or of their being compelled to succumb under the pressure of blockade. Indeed if great enmities are ever to be really settled, we think it will be, not by the system of revenge and military success, and by forcing an opponent to swear to a treaty to his disadvantage, but when the more fortunate combatant waives these his privileges, to be guided by gentler feelings, conquers his rival in generosity, and accords peace on more moderate conditions than he expected. From that moment, instead of the debt of revenge which violence must entail, his adversary owes a debt of generosity to be paid in kind, and is inclined by honour to stand to his agreement. And men oftener act in this manner towards their greatest enemies than where the quarrel is of less importance; they are also by nature as glad to give way to those who

---

*The Lacedaemonians are offering a sweet deal and one that would have led to the dissolution of their alliances, if they kept to the terms. The four hundred and more hostages were apparently too great a loss for them to imagine sustaining.

first yield to them, as they are apt to be provoked by arrogance to risks condemned by their own judgment.

20. 'To apply this to ourselves: if peace was ever desirable for both parties, it is surely so at the present moment, before anything irremediable befall us and force us to hate you eternally, personally as well as politically, and you to miss the advantages that we now offer you. While the issue is still in doubt, and you have reputation and our friendship in prospect, and we the compromise of our misfortune before anything fatal occur, let us be reconciled, and for ourselves choose peace instead of war, and grant to the rest of the Hellenes a remission from their sufferings, for which be sure they will think they have chiefly you to thank. The war that they labour under they know not which began, but the peace that concludes it, as it depends on your decision, will by their gratitude be laid to your door. By such a decision you can become firm friends with the Lacedæmonians at their own invitation, which you do not force from them, but oblige them by accepting. And from this friendship consider the advantages that are likely to follow: when Attica and Sparta are at one, the rest of Hellas, be sure, will remain in respectful inferiority before its heads.'

21. Such were the words of the Lacedæmonians, their idea being that the Athenians, already desirous of a truce and only kept back by their opposition, would joyfully accept a peace freely offered, and give back the men. The Athenians, however, having the men on the island, thought that the treaty would be ready for them whenever they chose to make it, and grasped at something further.* Foremost to encourage them in this policy was Cleon, son of Cleænetus, a popular leader of the time and very powerful with the multitude,† who persuaded them to answer as follows: First, the men in the island must surrender themselves and their arms and be brought to Athens. Next, the Lacedæmonians must restore Nisæa, Pegæ, Trœzen, and Achaia, all places acquired not by arms, but by the previous convention, under which they had been ceded by Athens herself at a moment of disaster, when a truce was more necessary to her than at present. This done they might take back their men, and make a truce for as long as both parties might agree.

22. To this answer the envoys made no reply, but asked that com-

---

*The Spartan speech has no corresponding Athenian reply. It is impossible to predict when Thucydides will report both positions (or more), but the Athenian mood is summarized.

†Cleon receives another formal introduction, perhaps a sign of his significance, perhaps a sign that Thucydides composed this narrative and the Mitylenian separately. The so-called analyst critics discover many signs of separate periods for the composition of sections of the *History*, narratives that Thucydides has not yet satisfactorily united.

missioners might be chosen with whom they might confer on each point, and quietly talk the matter over and try to come to some agreement.* Hereupon Cleon violently assailed them, saying that he knew from the first that they had no right intentions, and that it was clear enough now by their refusing to speak before the people, and wanting to confer in secret with a committee of two or three. No! if they meant anything honest let them say it out before all. The Lacedæmonians, however, seeing that whatever concessions they might be prepared to make in their misfortune, it was impossible for them to speak before the multitude and lose credit with their allies for a negotiation which might after all miscarry, and on the other hand, that the Athenians would never grant what they asked upon moderate terms, returned from Athens without having effected anything.†

23. Their arrival at once put an end to the armistice at Pylos, and the Lacedæmonians asked back their ships according to the convention. The Athenians, however, alleged an attack on the fort in contravention of the truce, and other grievances seemingly not worth mentioning, and refused to give them back,‡ insisting upon the clause by which the slightest infringement made the armistice void. The Lacedæmonians, after denying the contravention and protesting against their bad faith in the matter of the ships, went away and earnestly addressed themselves to the war. Hostilities were now carried on at Pylos upon both sides with vigour. The Athenians cruised round the island all day with two ships going different ways; and by night, except on the seaward side in windy weather, anchored round it with their whole fleet, which having been reinforced by twenty ships from Athens come to aid in the blockade, now numbered seventy sail; while the Peloponnesians remained encamped on the continent, making attacks on the fort, and on the look-out for any opportunity which might offer itself for the deliverance of their men.

24. Meanwhile the Syracusans and their allies in Sicily had brought up to the squadron guarding Messina the reinforcement which they

---

*The Spartans here, as do the Melian oligarchs in the next book (5.84–85), prefer discrete diplomatic negotiations to public disputation. Cleon, who does not want a peace treaty, pointedly humiliates the Spartan ambassadors.

†The Spartans fear public revelation to their allies of how far they are willing to abandon their alliance, at least before they see whether these negotiations with the enemy will succeed. Here and elsewhere, one cannot be sure whether Thucydides heard from Spartan sources what they were thinking at the time or speculated on why they gave up. In addition, he seems to commend or endorse their reasoning in his own judgment, but does not state that approval clearly.

‡Thucydides more clearly suggests here that the Athenian excuses for not returning the Spartan ships were bogus.

were preparing,* and carried on the war from thence, incited chiefly by the Locrians from hatred of the Rhegians, whose territory they had invaded with all their forces. The Syracusans also wished to try their fortune at sea, seeing that the Athenians had only a few ships actually at Rhegium, and hearing that the main fleet destined to join them was engaged in blockading the island. A naval victory, they thought, would enable them to blockade Rhegium by sea and land, and easily to reduce it; a success which would at once place their affairs upon a solid basis, the promontory of Rhegium in Italy and Messina in Sicily being so near each other that it would be impossible for the Athenians to cruise against them and command the strait. The strait in question consists of the sea between Rhegium and Messina, at the point where Sicily approaches nearest to the continent, and is the Charybdis through which the story makes Ulysses sail; and the narrowness of the passage and the strength of the current that pours in from the vast Tyrrhenian and Sicilian mains, have rightly given it a bad reputation.†

25. In this strait the Syracusans and their allies were compelled to engage, late in the day, about the passage of a boat, putting out with rather more than thirty ships against sixteen Athenian and eight Rhegian vessels. Defeated by the Athenians they hastily set off, each for himself, to their own stations at Messina and Rhegium, with the loss of one ship; night coming on before the battle was finished. After this the Locrians retired from the Rhegian territory, and the ships of the Syracusans and their allies united and came to anchor at Cape Pelorus, in the territory of Messina, where their land forces joined them. Here the Athenians and Rhegians sailed up, and seeing the ships unmanned, made an attack, in which they in their turn lost one vessel, which was caught by a grappling iron, the crew saving themselves by swimming.‡ After this the Syracusans got on board their ships, and while they were being towed along shore to Messina, were again attacked by the Athenians, but suddenly got out to sea and became the assailants, and caused them to lose another vessel. After thus holding their own in the voyage along shore and in the engagement as above described, the Syracusans sailed on into the harbour of Messina.

Meanwhile the Athenians, having received warning that Camarina

---

*Thucydides, with his desire to keep contemporary events together, awkwardly interrupts the long Pylos narrative (through chapter 40) for a return to 4.1, the Sicilian narrative.

†Thucydides pauses on geographical details (map 10) to describe the geostrategic importance of the straits of Messina, but tosses in a mythological reference.

‡Not all sailors in antiquity or more recent centuries learned to swim. Here other allied ships farther out to sea must have picked them up.

was about to be betrayed to the Syracusans by Archias and his party, sailed thither; and the Messinese took this opportunity to attack by sea and land with all their forces their Chalcidian neighbour, Naxos. The first day they forced the Naxians to keep their walls, and laid waste their country; the next they sailed round with their ships, and laid waste their land on the river Akesines, while their land forces menaced the city. Meanwhile the Sicels came down from the high country in great numbers, to aid against the Messinese; and the Naxians, elated at the sight, and animated by a belief that the Leontines and their other Hellenic allies were coming to their support, suddenly sallied out from the town, and attacked and routed the Messinese, killing more than a thousand of them; while the remainder suffered severely in their retreat home, being attacked by the barbarians on the road, and most of them cut off. The ships put in to Messina, and afterwards dispersed for their different homes. The Leontines and their allies, with the Athenians, upon this at once turned their arms against the now weakened Messina, and attacked, the Athenians with their ships on the side of the harbour, and the land forces on that of the town. The Messinese, however, sallying out with Demoteles and some Locrians who had been left to garrison the city after the disaster, suddenly attacked and routed most of the Leontine army, killing a great number; upon seeing which the Athenians landed from their ships, and falling on the Messinese in disorder chased them back into the town, and setting up a trophy retired to Rhegium. After this the Hellenes in Sicily continued to make war on each other by land, without the Athenians.*

26. Meanwhile the Athenians at Pylos were still besieging the Lacedæmonians in the island, the Peloponnesian forces on the continent remaining where they were. The blockade was very laborious for the Athenians from want of food and water; there was no spring except one in the citadel of Pylos itself, and that not a large one, and most of them were obliged to grub up the shingle on the sea beach and drink such water as they could find. They also suffered from want of room, being encamped in a narrow space; and as there was no anchorage for the ships, some took their meals on shore in their turn, while the others were anchored out at sea. But their greatest discouragement arose from the unexpectedly long time which it took to reduce a body of men shut up in a desert island, with only brackish water to drink, a matter which they had imagined would take them only a few days. The fact was that the Lacedæmonians had made advertisement for volunteers to carry into the island ground grain, wine, cheese, and any other food useful in a siege; high prices being offered, and freedom promised to

*The petty rivalries of the Sicilian and southern Italian cities are not yet decided by Athenian intervention in lands more than 1,200 miles distant. The Athenians will return.

any of the Helots who should succeed in doing so.* The Helots accordingly were most forward to engage in this risky traffic, putting off from this or that part of Peloponnese, and running in by night on the seaward side of the island. They were best pleased, however, when they could catch a wind to carry them in. It was more easy to elude the look-out of the galleys, when it blew from the seaward, as it became impossible for them to anchor round the island; while the Helots had their boats rated at their value in money, and ran them ashore, without caring how they landed, being sure to find the soldiers waiting for them at the landing-places. But all who risked it in fair weather were taken. Divers[†] also swam in under water from the harbour, dragging by a cord in skins poppy-seed mixed with honey, and bruised linseed; these at first escaped notice, but afterwards a look-out was kept for them. In short, both sides tried every possible contrivance, the one to throw in provisions, and the other to prevent their introduction.

27. At Athens, meanwhile, the news that the army was in great distress, and that grain found its way in to the men in the island caused no small perplexity; and the Athenians began to fear that winter might come on and find them still engaged in the blockade. They saw that the convoying of provisions round Peloponnese would be then impossible. The country offered no resources in itself, and even in summer they could not send round enough. The blockade of a place without harbours could no longer be kept up; and the men would either escape by the siege being abandoned, or would watch for bad weather and sail out in the boats that brought in their grain. What caused still more alarm was the attitude of the Lacedæmonians, who must, it was thought by the Athenians, feel themselves on strong ground not to send them any more envoys; and they began to repent having rejected the treaty. Cleon, perceiving the disfavour with which he was regarded for having stood in the way of the convention, now said that their informants did not speak the truth; and upon the messengers recommending them, if they did not believe them, to send some commissioners to see, Cleon himself and Theagenes were chosen by the Athenians as commissioners. Aware that he would now be obliged either to say what had been already said by the men whom he was slandering, or be proved a liar if he said the contrary,[‡] he told

---

*This extreme measure on the part of the Spartans—offering freedom to the helots—marks their dire view of the situation. Thucydides indirectly comments on morale.

†The close Athenian watch rendered the attempts at provisioning extremely dangerous and unlikely to succeed.

‡Without flattering the change of heart of the Athenian *demos*, Thucydides skewers the alleged motives and proposals of Cleon, the detested, unelected leader of the people (in Greek, "demogogue," a word that appears only here in Thucydides, where it can be seen developing a pejorative connotation that it did not originally have).

the Athenians, whom he saw to be not altogether disinclined for a fresh expedition, that instead of sending commissioners and wasting their time and opportunities, if they believed what was told them, they ought to sail against the men. And pointing at Nicias, son of Niceratus, then general, whom he hated,* he tauntingly said that it would be easy, if they had men for generals, to sail with a force and take those in the island, and that if he had himself been in command, he would have done it.

28. Nicias, seeing the Athenians murmuring against Cleon for not sailing now if it seemed to him so easy, and further seeing himself the object of attack, told him that for all that the generals cared, he might take what force he chose and make the attempt. At first Cleon fancied that this resignation was merely a figure of speech,† and was ready to go, but finding that it was seriously meant, he drew back, and said that Nicias, not he, was general, being now frightened, and having never supposed that Nicias would go so far as to retire in his favour. Nicias, however, repeated his offer, and resigned the command against Pylos, and called the Athenians to witness that he did so. And as the multitude is wont to do,‡ the more Cleon shrank from the expedition and tried to back out of what he had said, the more they encouraged Nicias to hand over his command, and clamoured at Cleon to go. At last, not knowing how to get out of his words, he undertook the expedition, and came forward and said that he was not afraid of the Lacedæmonians, but would sail without taking any one from the city with him, except the Lemnians and Imbrians that were at Athens, with some targeteers that had come up from Ænus, and four hundred archers from other quarters. With these and the soldiers at Pylos, he would within twenty days either bring the Lacedæmonians alive, or kill them on the spot.§ The Athenians could not help

---

*In trying to force his personal and political enemy, the general Nicias, to bring an additional force against the Spartans on Sphacteria, Cleon insults Nicias' manliness. Thucydides rarely reports conflicts between individuals.

†Nicias, not known for political agility, offers to resign his military office in favor of Cleon, if he thinks conquest of the Spartan-held island to be so easy. Cleon mistakenly walks into the offer and then cannot escape.

‡Nicias' brusque offer, perhaps a bluff, risks the lives of Athenian soldier-citizens, but they are themselves in the assembly implicated in promoting this risky solution. The negative reflection on crowd psychology, here and elsewhere, supports the view that Thucydides, who might have attended this debate, did not highly respect the ratiocinative and strategic decisions of the Athenian assembly (which, however, elected him general within a year!).

§Cleon's trapped promise seemed brash. Its success astounded the *strategos* Thucydides, who faithfully records it, but Cleon probably had information from his colleague-to-be, Demosthenes, that they could succeed in their plan with sufficient reinforcement.

laughing at his fatuity, while sensible men comforted themselves with the reflexion that they must gain in either circumstance; either they would be rid of Cleon, which they rather hoped, or if disappointed in this expectation, would reduce the Lacedæmonians.*

29. After he had settled everything in the assembly, and the Athenians had voted him the command of the expedition, he chose as his colleague Demosthenes, one of the generals at Pylos, and pushed forward the preparations for his voyage. His choice fell upon Demosthenes because he heard that he was contemplating a descent on the island; the soldiers distressed by the difficulties of the position, and rather besieged than besiegers, being eager to fight it out, while the firing of the island had increased the confidence of the general. He had been at first afraid, because the island having never been inhabited was almost entirely covered with wood and without paths, thinking this to be in the enemy's favour, as he might land with a large force, and yet might suffer loss by an attack from an unseen position. The mistakes and forces of the enemy the wood would in a great measure conceal from him, while every blunder of his own troops would be at once detected, and they would be thus able to fall upon him unexpectedly just where they pleased, the attack being always in their power. If, on the other hand, he should force them to engage in the thicket, the smaller number who knew the country would, he thought, have the advantage over the larger who were ignorant of it, while his own army might be cut off imperceptibly, in spite of its numbers, as the men would not be able to see where to succour each other.†

30. The Ætolian disaster, which had been mainly caused by the wood, had not a little to do with these reflexions. Meanwhile, one of the soldiers who were compelled by want of room to land on the extremities of the island and take their dinners, with outposts fixed to prevent a surprise, set fire to a little of the wood without meaning to do so;‡ and as it came on to blow soon afterwards, almost the whole was consumed before they were aware of it. Demosthenes was now able for the first time to see how numerous the Lacedæmonians really were, having up to this moment been under the impression that they took in provisions for a smaller number; he also saw that the Athenians thought success important and were anxious about it, and that it was now easier to land on the island, and accordingly got ready for the attempt, sent for troops from the allies in the neighbourhood, and pushed forward his other preparations. At this moment Cleon arrived

---

*Athenian laughter and sensible men's comfort seem heedless of the potential loss of other citizens' lives.

†Demosthenes' reasoning is sound, and based on learning from prior experience (a rare Thucydidean virtue), but would he himself not think of burning down the trees?

‡Again, unintended consequences feed the Athenians' fortune.

at Pylos with the troops which he had asked for, having sent on word to say that he was coming. The first step taken by the two generals after their meeting was to send a herald to the camp on the mainland, to ask if they were disposed to avoid all risk and to order the men on the island to surrender themselves and their arms, to be kept in gentle custody until some general convention should be concluded.

31. On the rejection of this proposition the generals let one day pass, and the next embarking all their heavy infantry on board a few ships, put out by night, and a little before dawn, landed on both sides of the island from the open sea and from the harbour, being about eight hundred strong, and advanced with a run against the first post in the island.* The enemy had distributed his force as follows:—In this first post there were about thirty heavy infantry; the centre and most level part, where the water was, was held by the main body, and by Epitadas their commander; while a small party guarded the very end of the island, towards Pylos, which was precipitous on the seaside and very difficult to attack from the land, and where there was also a sort of old fort of stones rudely put together, which they thought might be useful to them, in case they should be forced to retreat. Such was their disposition.

32. The advanced post thus attacked by the Athenians was at once put to the sword, the men being scarcely out of bed and still arming, the landing having taken them by surprise, as they fancied the ships were only sailing as usual to their stations for the night. As soon as day broke, the rest of the army landed, that is to say, all the crews of rather more than seventy ships, except the lowest rank of oars, with the arms they carried, eight hundred archers, and as many targeteers, the Messenian reinforcements, and all the other troops on duty round Pylos, except the garrison on the fort. The tactics of Demosthenes had divided them into companies of two hundred, more or less, and made them occupy the highest points in order to paralyse the enemy by surrounding him on every side and thus leaving him without any tangible adversary, exposed to the cross-fire of their host; plied by those in his rear if he attacked in front, and by those on one flank if he moved against those on the other. In short, wherever he went he would have the assailants behind him, and these light-armed assailants, the most awkward of all; arrows, darts,† stones, and slings making them formidable at a distance, and there being no means of getting at them at

---

*Demosthenes plans an encirclement. Thucydides grants Cleon no credit for the military maneuvers. The Athenians have a nearly two-to-one advantage in manpower.

†Thucydides refers here and elsewhere to short (5 to 6 feet), light javelins with a throwing loop, which are different from the hoplites' long (up to 8 feet), heavy thrusting spears. (See Hanson, *Hoplites: The Classical Greek Battle Experience*, and van Wees, *War and Violence in Ancient Greece*.)

close quarters, as they could conquer flying, and the moment their pursuer turned they were upon him.* Such was the idea that inspired Demosthenes in his conception of the descent, and presided over its execution.

33. Meanwhile the main body of the troops in the island (that under Epitadas), seeing their outpost cut off and an army advancing against them, serried their ranks and pressed forward to close with the Athenian heavy infantry in front of them, the light troops being upon their flanks and rear. However, they were not able to engage or to profit by their superior skill, the light troops keeping them in check on either side with their missiles, and the heavy infantry remaining stationary instead of advancing to meet them; and although they routed the light troops wherever they ran up and approached too closely, yet they retreated fighting, being lightly equipped, and easily getting the start in their flight, from the difficult and rugged nature of the ground,† in an island hitherto desert, over which the Lacedæmonians could not pursue them with their heavy armour.

34. After this skirmishing had lasted some little while, the Lacedæmonians became unable to dash out with the same rapidity as before upon the points attacked, and the light troops, finding that they now fought with less vigour, became more confident. They could see with their own eyes that they were many times more numerous than the enemy; they were now more familiar with his aspect and found him less terrible, the result not having justified the apprehensions which they had suffered, when they first landed in slavish dismay at the idea of attacking Lacedæmonians;‡ and accordingly their fear changing to disdain, they now rushed all together with loud shouts upon them, and pelted them with stones, darts, and arrows, whichever came first to hand. The shouting accompanying their onset confounded§ the Lacedæmonians, unaccustomed to this mode of fighting; dust rose from the newly-burnt wood, and it was impossible to see in front of one with the arrows and stones flying through clouds of dust from the hands of numerous assailants. The Lacedæmonians had now to sustain a rude conflict; their caps would not keep out the arrows, darts had broken off in the armour of the wounded, while they themselves

---

*The heavily armored Spartan hoplites cannot effectively respond to the swift, light-armed attack and retreat tactics.

†The uncleared and uneven ground further impedes the Spartans, who had no functioning equivalent to the Athenians' auxiliary troops.

‡Spartan valor had maintained its unspotted reputation, one reinforced by all the Greeks after their heroic stand to the death at Thermopylae (mentioned at 4.36).

§Spartans did not efficiently improvise in unforeseen circumstances. They suffer paralyzing confusion. Here the noise, the dust, the attack from several directions, the lack of reserves or retreat, and the variety of missiles reasonably disheartened them.

were helpless for offence, being prevented from using their eyes to see what was before them, and unable to hear the words of command for the hubbub raised by the enemy; danger encompassed them on every side, and there was no hope of any means of defence or safety.

35. At last, after many had been already wounded in the confined space in which they were fighting, they formed in close order and re-tired on the fort at the end of the island, which was not far off, and to their friends who held it. The moment they gave way, the light troops became bolder and pressed upon them, shouting louder than ever, and killed as many as they came up with in their retreat, but most of the Lacedæmonians made good their escape to the fort, and with the garrison in it ranged themselves all along its whole extent to repulse the enemy wherever it was assailable. The Athenians pursuing, unable to surround and hem them in, owing to the strength of the ground, at-tacked them in front and tried to storm the position. For a long time, indeed for most of the day, both sides held out against all the tor-ments of the battle, thirst, and sun, the one endeavouring to drive the enemy from the high ground, the other to maintain himself upon it, it being now more easy for the Lacedæmonians to defend themselves than before, as they could not be surrounded upon the flanks.

36. The struggle began to seem endless, when the commander of the Messenians came to Cleon and Demosthenes, and told them that they were losing their labour: but that if they would give him some archers and light troops to go round on the enemy's rear by a way he would undertake to find, he thought he could force the approach. Upon receiving what he asked for, he started from a point out of sight in order not to be seen by the enemy, and creeping on wherever the precipices of the island permitted, and where the Lacedæmonians, trusting to the strength of the ground, kept no guard, succeeded after the greatest difficulty in getting round without their seeing him, and suddenly appeared on the high ground in their rear, to the dismay of the surprised enemy and the still greater joy of his expectant friends. The Lacedæmonians thus placed between two fires, and in the same dilemma, to compare small things with great,* as at Thermopylæ, where the defenders were cut off through the Persians getting round by the path, being now attacked in front and behind, began to give way, and overcome by the odds against them and exhausted from want of food, retreated.

37. The Athenians were already masters of the approaches when Cleon and Demosthenes perceiving that, if the enemy gave way a sin-gle step further, they would be destroyed by their soldiery, put a stop

---

*One puzzles over why Thucydides qualifies his statement with "to compare small things with great," since more men were lost (although not killed) here than at the battle of Thermopylae in 480. At 1.23, Thucydides tendentiously minimized Herodotus' great war.

to the battle and held their men back; wishing to take the Lacedæ-monians alive to Athens, and hoping that their stubbornness might relax on hearing the offer of terms, and that they might surrender and yield to the present overwhelming danger. Proclamation was accordingly made, to know if they would surrender themselves and their arms to the Athenians to be dealt with at their discretion.

38. The Lacedæmonians hearing this offer, most of them lowered their shields and waved their hands to show that they accepted it.* Hostilities now ceased, and a parley was held between Cleon and Demosthenes and Styphon, son of Pharax, on the other side; since Epitadas, the first of the previous commanders, had been killed, and Hippagretas, the next in command, left for dead among the slain, though still alive, and thus the command had devolved upon Styphon according to the law, in case of anything happening to his superiors. Styphon and his companions said they wished to send a herald to the Lacedæmonians on the mainland, to know what they were to do. The Athenians would not let any of them go, but themselves called for heralds from the mainland, and after questions had been carried backwards and forwards two or three times, the last man that passed over from the Lacedæmonians on the continent brought this message: 'The Lacedæmonians bid you to decide for yourselves so long as you do nothing dishonourable;'† upon which after consulting together they surrendered themselves and their arms. The Athenians, after guarding them that day and night, the next morning set up a trophy in the island, and got ready to sail, giving their prisoners in batches to be guarded by the captains of the galleys; and the Lacedæmonians sent a herald and took up their dead. The number of the killed and prisoners taken in the island was as follows: four hundred and twenty heavy infantry had passed over; three hundred all but eight were taken alive to Athens; the rest were killed. About a hundred and twenty of the prisoners were Spartans.‡ The Athenian loss was small, the battle not having been fought at close quarters.

39. The blockade in all, counting from the fight at sea to the battle in the island, had lasted seventy-two days. For twenty of these, during the absence of the envoys sent to treat for peace, the men had provisions given them, for the rest they were fed by the smugglers. Grain and other victual was found in the island; the commander Epitadas

---

*The Spartans non-verbally assent to an armistice, if not a surrender.

†The Spartans have lost two commanders; the third asks for direction from his superiors and receives an ambiguous response, perhaps to free the authorities from consent to surrender.

‡The Athenians took 292 prisoners, of which 120 were full Spartan citizen-warriors. Camp illustrates one of their shields (illustration 65). The psychological effect (see 4.40) perhaps eclipsed the significant military victory (not forgetting those 60 ships).

having kept the men upon half rations. The Athenians and Peloponnesians now each withdrew their forces from Pylos, and went home, and crazy as Cleon's promise was, he fulfilled it, by bringing the men to Athens within the twenty days as he had pledged himself to do.*

40. Nothing that happened in the war surprised the Hellenes so much as this. It was the opinion that no force or famine could make the Lacedæmonians give up their arms, but that they would fight on as they could, and die with them in their hands: indeed people could scarcely believe that those who had surrendered were of the same stuff as the fallen; and an Athenian ally, who some time after insultingly asked one of the prisoners from the island if those that had fallen were men of honour, received for answer that the *atraktos*— that is, the arrow—would be worth a great deal if it could tell men of honour from the rest; in allusion to the fact that the killed were those whom the stones and the arrows happened to hit.†

41. Upon the arrival of the men the Athenians determined to keep them in prison until the peace,‡ and if the Peloponnesians invaded their country in the interval, to bring them out and put them to death. Meanwhile the defence of Pylos was not forgotten; the Messenians from Naupactus sent to their old country, to which Pylos formerly belonged, some of the likeliest of their number, and began a series of incursions into Laconia, which their common dialect rendered most destructive.§ The Lacedæmonians, hitherto without experience of incursions or a warfare of the kind, finding the Helots deserting, and fearing the march of revolution in their country, began to be seriously uneasy, and in spite of their unwillingness to betray this to the Athenians began to send envoys to Athens, and tried to recover Pylos and the prisoners. The Athenians, however, kept grasping at more, and dismissed envoy after envoy without their having effected anything.‖ Such was the history of the affair of Pylos.

---

*Thucydides declines to acknowledge rational calculations behind Cleon's promise, but he cannot deny the achievement.

†Hellenic astonishment at this Spartan surrender reveals the recognized myth of Spartan "do or die" heroics. Thucydides dallies to report soldierly badinage—insult from the Athenian side (not from an Athenian, though) and Spartan laconic retort.

‡The Agora excavations have yielded a shield inscribed by a punch as booty from the Pylos victory (see Camp, illustration 65).

§Demosthenes' original plan, to harass Laconia (and their conquered territory of Messenia) from the new Peloponnesian base, now went into effect. Apart from the enemy's windfall victory, this setback was very costly to Spartan and Peloponnesian morale.

‖The narrative ends with the refrain of both endless Athenian desires for more and the formulaic phrase indicating closure of an incident and change of venue.

Seventh and Eighth Years of the War—End of Corcyrœan
Revolution—Peace of Gela—Capture of Nisœa

42. The same summer, directly after these events, the Athenians made an expedition against the territory of Corinth with eighty ships and two thousand Athenian heavy infantry, and two hundred cavalry on board horse transports, accompanied by the Milesians, Andrians, and Carystians from the allies, under the command of Nicias, son of Niceratus, with two colleagues. Putting out to sea they made land at daybreak between Chersonese and Rheitus, at the beach of the country underneath the Solygian hill, upon which the Dorians in old times established themselves and carried on war against the Æolian inhabitants of Corinth, and where a village now stands called Solygia. The beach where the fleet came to is about a mile and a half from the village, seven miles from Corinth, and two and a quarter from the Isthmus. The Corinthians had heard from Argos of the coming of the Athenian armament, and had all come up to the Isthmus long before, with the exception of those who lived beyond it, and also of five hundred who were away in garrison in Ambracia and Leucadia; and they were there in full force watching for the Athenians to land. These last, however, gave them the slip by coming in the dark; and being informed by signals of the fact, the Corinthians left half their number at Cenchreæ, in case the Athenians should go against Crommyon, and marched in all haste to the rescue.*

43. Battus, one of the two generals present at the action, went with a company to defend the village of Solygia, which was unfortified; Lycophron remaining to give battle with the rest. The Corinthians first attacked the right wing of the Athenians, which had just landed in front of Chersonese, and afterwards the rest of the army. The battle was an obstinate one, and fought throughout hand to hand. The right wing of the Athenians and Carystians, who had been placed at the end of the line, received and with some difficulty repulsed the Corinthians, who thereupon retreated to a wall upon the rising ground behind, and throwing down the stones upon them, came on again singing the pæan,† and being received by the Athenians, were again engaged at close quarters. At this moment a Corinthian company having come to the relief of the left wing, routed and pursued the Athenian right to the sea, whence they were in their turn driven

---

*All these towns in the territory of Corinth are found in the northwestern corner of the Saronic Gulf (map 5).

†A paean is a song of praise, typically to Apollo, but such hymns, like the American "Battle Hymn of the Republic," often had a military and patriotic element. They served well as rhythmic marching songs for the advancing phalanx, the hoplite battle line.

back by the Athenians and Carystians from the ships. Meanwhile the rest of the army on either side fought on tenaciously, especially the right wing of the Corinthians, where Lycophron sustained the attack of the Athenian left, which it was feared might attempt the village of Solygia.

44. After holding on for a long while without either giving way, the Athenians aided by their horse, of which the enemy had none, at length routed the Corinthians, who retired to the hill and halting remained quiet there, without coming down again. It was in this rout of the right wing that they had the most killed, Lycophron their general being among the number. The rest of the army, broken and put to flight in this way without being seriously pursued or hurried, retired to the high ground and there took up its position. The Athenians, finding that the enemy no longer offered to engage them, stripped his dead and took up their own and immediately set up a trophy. Meanwhile, the half of the Corinthians left at Cenchreæ to guard against the Athenians sailing on Crommyon, although unable to see the battle for Mount Oneion, found out what was going on by the dust, and hurried up to the rescue.; as did also the older Corinthians from the town, upon discovering what had occurred. The Athenians seeing them all coming against them, and thinking that they were reinforcements arriving from the neighbouring Peloponnesians, withdrew in haste to their ships with their spoils and their own dead, except two that they left behind,* not being able to find them, and going on board crossed over to the islands opposite, and from thence sent a herald, and took up under truce the bodies which they had left behind. Two hundred and twelve Corinthians fell in the battle, and rather less than fifty Athenians.

45. Weighing from the islands, the Athenians sailed the same day to Crommyon in the Corinthian territory, about thirteen miles from the city, and coming to anchor laid waste the country, and passed the night there. The next day, after first coasting along to the territory of Epidaurus and making a descent there, they came to Methana between Epidaurus and Trœzen, and drew a wall across and fortified the isthmus of the peninsula, and left a post there from which incursions were henceforth made upon the country of Trœzen, Haliæ, and Epidaurus.† After walling off this spot the fleet sailed off home.

46. While these events were going on, Eurymedon and Sophocles had put to sea with the Athenian fleet from Pylos on their way to Sicily, and arriving at Corcyra, joined the townsmen in an expedition against

---

*Thucydides regularly reports request and receipt of the dead. The recognition of failure to account for two bodies indicates a respectably comprehensive "buddy" system.

†South of the Corinthian territory is the Argolid; some of its cities (map 5) allied with Athens' enemies.

the party established on Mount Istone, who had crossed over after the revolution,* and become masters of the country, to the great hurt of the inhabitants. Their stronghold having been taken by an attack, the garrison took refuge in a body upon some high ground and there capitulated, agreeing to give up their mercenary auxiliaries, lay down their arms, and commit themselves to the discretion of the Athenian people. The generals carried them across under truce to the island of Ptychia, to be kept in custody until they could be sent to Athens, upon the understanding that if any were caught running away, all would lose the benefit of the treaty. Meanwhile the leaders of the Corcyræan commons, afraid that the Athenians might spare the lives of the prisoners, had recourse to the following stratagem.† They gained over some few men on the island by secretly sending friends with instructions to provide them with a boat, and to tell them, as if for their own sakes, that they had best escape as quickly as possible, as the Athenian generals were going to give them up to the Corcyræan people.

47. These representations succeeding, it was so arranged that the men were caught sailing out in the boat that was provided, and the treaty became void accordingly, and the whole body were given up to the Corcyræans. For this result the Athenian generals were in a great measure responsible; their evident disinclination to sail for Sicily, and thus to leave to others the honour of conducting the men to Athens, encouraged the intriguers in their design and seemed to affirm the truth of their representations. The prisoners thus handed over were shut up by the Corcyræans in a large building, and afterwards taken out by twenties and led past two lines of heavy infantry, one on each side, being bound together, and beaten and stabbed by the men in the lines whenever any saw pass a personal enemy; while men carrying whips went by their side and hastened on the road those that walked too slowly.‡

48. As many as sixty men were taken out and killed in this way without the knowledge of their friends in the building, who fancied they were merely being moved from one prison to another. At last, however, some one opened their eyes to the truth, upon which they called upon the Athenians to kill them themselves, if such was their pleasure, and refused any longer to go out of the building, and said they would do all they could to prevent any one coming in. The Corcyræans, not liking themselves to force a passage by the doors, got up on the top of the

---

*Thucydides returns to 4.2, the continuing *stasis* that destroyed Corcyra, later called Corfu by the Italians.

†Allies double-cross their friends; just as the major powers use their satellites, so do those lesser states appeal to and abuse the expectations of their "protectors."

‡The sadistic slaughter of the surrendered is one of many signs of the degeneration of civilization in wartime. Similar forms of horrifying cruelty are reported from the Spanish Civil War and elsewhere.

building, and breaking through the roof, threw down the tiles and let fly arrows at them, from which the prisoners sheltered themselves as well as they could. Most of their number, meanwhile, were engaged in dispatching themselves by thrusting into their throats the arrows shot by the enemy, and hanging themselves with the cords taken from some beds that happened to be there, and with strips made from their clothing; adopting, in short, every possible means of self-destruction, and also falling victims to the missiles of their enemies on the roof. Night came on while these horrors were enacting, and most of it had passed before they were concluded. When it was day the Corcyræans threw them in layers upon waggons and carried them out of the city. All the women taken in the stronghold were sold as slaves. In this way the Corcyræans of the mountain were destroyed by the commons; and so after terrible excesses the party strife came to an end, at least as far as the period of this war is concerned, for of one party there was practically nothing left.* Meanwhile the Athenians sailed off to Sicily, their primary destination, and carried on the war with their allies there.

49. At the close of the summer, the Athenians at Naupactus and the Acarnanians made an expedition against Anactorium, the Corinthian town lying at the mouth of the Ambracian gulf, and took it by treachery; and the Acarnanians themselves sending settlers from all parts of Acarnania occupied the place.

Summer was now over.

50. During the winter ensuing Aristides, son of Archippus, one of the commanders of the Athenian ships sent to collect money from the allies,† arrested at Eion on the Strymon Artaphernes, a Persian, on his way from the king to Lacedæmon. He was conducted to Athens, where the Athenians got his despatches translated from the Assyrian character and read them.‡ With numerous references to other subjects, they in substance told the Lacedæmonians that the king did not

---

*The *stasis* ends only because one side was completely victorious and eradicated its oligarchic opponents. Every time Thucydides mentions "this war," one wonders whether he means the Ten Years' or Archidamian War reported in books 1–5.24, or the entire Peloponnesian War from 431 to 404, for which Thucydides did not finish his account (the last book breaks off in 411). Here he seems to refer to the longer conflict.

†The Athenians reassessed and increased most tributes in the winter of 425/424 (compare Fornara #136). Thucydides shows less interest in material resources and finance than we think necessary. The Athenians collected tribute from their "allies" annually. They gave one-sixtieth to the goddess Athena. We have reconstructed the records of these "tithes" from hundreds of broken stone fragments found on and below the Acropolis, an original and invaluable inscriptional supplement to the information the historian gives (for example, Fornara #142).

‡"Assyrian" is a common, erroneous Hellenic designation for the typically Aramaic language and script of Persian imperial communications. Ancient sources rarely refer to translators or to the problems of translation.

know what they wanted, as of the many ambassadors they had sent him no two ever told the same story; if however they were prepared to speak plainly they might send him some envoys with this Persian. The Athenians afterwards sent back Artaphernes in a galley to Ephesus, and ambassadors with him, who heard there of the death of King Artaxerxes, son of Xerxes, which took place about that time, and so returned home.*

51. The same winter the Chians pulled down their new wall at the command of the Athenians, who suspected them of meditating an insurrection,[†] after first however obtaining pledges from the Athenians, and security as far as this was possible for their continuing to treat them as before. Thus the winter ended, and with it ended the seventh year of this war of which Thucydides is the historian.

52. In the first days of the next summer there was an eclipse of the sun at the time of new moon, and in the early part of the same month an earthquake. Meanwhile, the Mitylenian and other Lesbian exiles set out, for the most part from the continent, with mercenaries hired in Peloponnese, and others levied on the spot, and took Rhœteum, but restored it without injury on the receipt of two thousand Phocæan staters. After this they marched against Antandrus and took the town by treachery, their plan being to free Antandrus and the rest of the Actæan towns, formerly owned by Mitylene but now held by the Athenians. Once fortified there, they would have every facility for shipbuilding from the vicinity of Ida and the consequent abundance of timber, and plenty of other supplies, and might from this base easily ravage Lesbos, which was not far off, and make themselves masters of the Æolian towns on the continent.

53. While these were the schemes of the exiles, the Athenians in the same summer made an expedition with sixty ships, two thousand heavy infantry, a few cavalry, and some allied troops from Miletus and other parts, against Cythera, under the command of Nicias, son of Niceratus, Nicostratus, son of Diotrephes, and Autocles, son of Tolmæus. Cythera is an island lying off Laconia, opposite Malea; the inhabitants are Lacedæmonians of the class of the Periœci; and an officer called the Judge of Cythera went over to the place annually from Sparta. A garrison of heavy infantry was also regularly sent there, and great attention paid to the island, as it was the landing-place for the merchantmen from Egypt and Libya, and at the same time secured

---

*The Athenians may have signed a treaty with the Persian king about this time (see Fornara #138) and even earlier (Peace of Callias, 449; see Fornara #95; map 12).

†Chios was the last independent ally standing after the Samian revolt of 440 and the Mitylenean revolt of 428/427. At 8.5, the Chians themselves rise, believing that now the Athenians can no longer prevent their quest to recover their autonomy. The year 424 begins.

Laconia from the attacks of privateers from the sea, at the only point where it is assailable, as the whole coast rises abruptly towards the Sicilian and Cretan seas.

54. Coming to land here with their armament, the Athenians with ten ships and two thousand Milesian heavy infantry took the town of Scandea, on the sea;* and with the rest of their forces landing on the side of the island looking towards Malea, went against the lower town of Cythera, where they found all the inhabitants encamped. A battle ensuing, the Cytherians held their ground for some little while, and then turned and fled into the upper town, where they soon afterwards capitulated to Nicias and his colleagues, agreeing to leave their fate to the decision of the Athenians, their lives only being safe. A correspondence had previously been going on between Nicias and certain of the inhabitants, which caused the surrender to be effected more speedily, and upon terms more advantageous, present and future, for the Cytherians; who would otherwise have been expelled by the Athenians on account of their being Lacedæmonians and their island being so near to Laconia. After the capitulation, the Athenians occupied the town of Scandea near the harbour, and appointing a garrison for Cythera, sailed to Asine, Helus, and most of the places on the sea, and making descents and passing the night on shore at such spots as were convenient, continued ravaging the country for about seven days.

55. The Lacedæmonians seeing the Athenians masters of Cythera, and expecting descents of the kind upon their coasts, nowhere opposed them in force, but sent garrisons here and there through the country, consisting of as many heavy infantry as the points menaced seemed to require, and generally stood very much upon the defensive. After the severe and unexpected blow that had befallen them in the island, the occupation of Pylos and Cythera, and the apparition on every side of a war whose rapidity defied precaution, they lived in constant fear of internal revolution,† and now took the unusual step of raising four hundred horse and a force of archers, and became more timid than ever in military matters, finding themselves involved

---

*Demaratus (Herodotus 7.235) had recommended to King Xerxes that he could capture the Peloponnese from a base on the island of Cythera (map 5). Two thousand allies from one city is an unusually large number. Miletus on the Ionian coast had been the leading city of Ionia in the previous century and still possessed a major army.

†Spartan morale has reached a low point. This is but one of six such notices that Thucydides planted in book 4 and the opening of book 5 (Hornblower, *Commentary*). Thucydides mentions the occupations of Peloponnesian territory, the speed of Athenian offensives by sea, and the constant fear of a helot uprising. However brutal the Spartans, one admits that they had prevented such servile insurrections from occurring, with one exception (described at 1.101–103).

in a maritime struggle, which their organisation had never contemplated, and that against Athenians, with whom an enterprise unattempted was always looked upon as a success sacrificed. Besides this, their late numerous reverses of fortune, coming close one upon another without any reason, had thoroughly unnerved them, and they were always afraid of a second disaster like that on the island, and thus scarcely dared to take the field, but fancied that they could not stir without a blunder, for being new to the experience of adversity they had lost all confidence in themselves.

56. Accordingly they now allowed the Athenians to ravage their seaboard, without making any movement, the garrisons in whose neighbourhood the descents were made always thinking their numbers insufficient, and sharing the general feeling. A single garrison which ventured to resist, near Cotyrta and Aphrodisia, struck terror by its charge into the scattered mob of light troops, but retreated, upon being received by the heavy infantry, with the loss of a few men and some arms, for which the Athenians set up a trophy, and then sailed off to Cythera. From thence they sailed round to the Limeran Epidaurus, ravaged part of the country, and so came to Thyrea in the Cynurian territory, upon the Argive and Laconian border. This district had been given by its Lacedæmonian owners to the expelled Æginetans to inhabit, in return for their good offices at the time of the earthquake and the rising of the Helots; and also because, although subjects of Athens, they had always sided with Lacedæmon.

57. While the Athenians were still at sea, the Æginetans evacuated a fort which they were building upon the coast, and retreated into the upper town where they lived, rather more than a mile from the sea. One of the Lacedæmonian district garrisons which was helping them in the work, refused to enter here with them at their entreaty, thinking it dangerous to shut themselves up within the wall, and retiring to the high ground remained quiet, not considering themselves a match for the enemy. Meanwhile the Athenians landed, and instantly advanced with all their forces and took Thyrea. The town they burnt, pillaging what was in it; the Æginetans who were not slain in action they took with them to Athens, with Tantalus, son of Patrocles, their Lacedæmonian commander, who had been wounded and taken prisoner. They also took with them a few men from Cythera whom they thought it safest to remove. These the Athenians determined to lodge in the islands: the rest of the Cytherians were to retain their lands and pay four talents tribute; the Æginetans captured to be all put to death, on account of the old inveterate feud; and Tantalus to share the imprisonment of the Lacedæmonians taken on the island.

58. The same summer, the inhabitants of Camarina and Gela in Sicily first made an armistice with each other, after which embassies from all the other Sicilian cities assembled at Gela to try to bring about a pacification. After many expressions of opinion on one side and the other, according to the griefs and pretensions of the different parties complaining, Hermocrates,* son of Hermon, a Syracusan, the most influential man among them, addressed the following words to the assembly:—

59. 'If I now address you, Sicilians, it is not because my city is the least in Sicily or the greatest sufferer by the war, but in order to state publicly what appears to me to be the best policy for the whole island. That war is an evil is a proposition so familiar to every one that it would be tedious to develop it. No one is forced to engage in it by ignorance, or kept out of it by fear, if he fancies there is anything to be gained by it. To the former the gain appears greater than the danger, while the latter would rather stand the risk than put up with any immediate sacrifice. But if both should happen to have chosen the wrong moment for acting in this way, advice to make peace would not be unserviceable; and this, if we did but see it, is just what we stand most in need of at the present juncture.

'I suppose that no one will dispute that we went to war at first, in order to serve our own several interests, that we are now, in view of the same interests, debating how we can make peace; and that if we separate without having as we think our rights, we shall go to war again.

60. 'And yet, as men of sense, we ought to see that our separate interests are not alone at stake in the present congress: there is also the question whether we have still time to save Sicily, the whole of which in my opinion is menaced by Athenian ambition;† and we ought to find in the name of that people more imperious arguments for peace than any which I can advance, when we see the first power in Hellas watching our mistakes with the few ships that she has at present in our waters, and under the fair name of alliance speciously seeking to turn to account the natural hostility that exists between us. If we go to war, and call in to help us a people that are ready enough to carry their arms even where they are not invited; and if we injure ourselves at our own expense, and at the same time serve as the pioneers of their dominion, we may expect when they see us worn out, that they will one day come with a larger armament, and seek to bring all of us into subjection.

---

*Thucydides, although recognizing that other views were expressed, reports but one speech from this Sicilian conference at Gela (map 10). Hermocrates will be lauded (6.72) for his Themistoclean foresight and intelligence, as he directs the Syracusan defense against the Athenian invasion.

†Hermocrates emphasizes, both here and in the next chapter, the Athenian desire to have more than their rightful share, but the Syracusan recognizes the inherent desire to exercise power wherever possible.

61. 'And yet as sensible men, if we call in allies and court danger, it should be in order to enrich our different countries with new acquisitions, and not to ruin what they possess already; and we should understand that the internal discords which are so fatal to communities generally, will be equally so to Sicily, if we, its inhabitants, absorbed in our local quarrels, neglect the common enemy.* These considerations should reconcile individual with individual, and city with city, and unite us in a common effort to save the whole of Sicily.† Nor should any one imagine that the Dorians only are enemies of Athens, while the Chalcidian race is secured by its Ionian blood; the attack in question is not inspired by hatred of one of two ethnicities,‡ but by a desire for the good things in Sicily, the common property of us all. This is proved by the Athenian reception of the Chalcidian invitation: an ally who has never given them any assistance whatever, at once receives from them almost more than the treaty entitles him to. That the Athenians should cherish this ambition and practise this policy is very excusable; and I do not blame those who wish to rule, but those who are over-ready to serve. It is just as much in men's nature to rule those who submit to them, as it is to resist those who molest them; one is not less invariable than the other. Meanwhile all who see these dangers and refuse to provide for them properly, or who have come here without having made up their minds that our first duty is to unite to get rid of the common peril, are mistaken. The quickest way to be rid of it is to make peace with each other; since the Athenians menace us not from their own country, but from that of those who invited them here. In this way instead of war issuing in war, peace quietly ends our quarrels; and the guests who come hither under fair pretences for bad ends, will have good reason for going away without having attained them.

62. 'So far as regards the Athenians, such are the great advantages proved inherent in a wise policy. Independently of this, in the face of the universal consent that peace is the first of blessings, how can we refuse to make it amongst ourselves; or do you not think that the good which you have, and the ills that you complain of, would be better preserved and cured by quiet than by war; that peace has its hon-

---

*Hermocrates correctly observes that the Athenians threaten the autonomy of all the cities of Sicily. He neglects to point out that his city of Syracuse always threatened to dominate and control all the lesser cities of the island.

†The rhetoric of this passage suggests the influence of Gorgias, known for his rhythmic and rhyming effects on oratory and on Thucydides' prose.

‡Thucydides and his speakers in various locations refer to the ethnic rivalries of Dorians (Peloponnesians and their colonists) and Ionians (Athenians and their Anatolian colonists). It remains unclear how important a factor this prejudice was in contemporary rhetoric and in politics.

ours and splendours of a less perilous kind, not to mention the numerous other blessings that one might dilate on, with the not less numerous miseries of war? These considerations should teach you not to disregard my words, but rather to look in them every one for his own safety.

'If there be any here who feels certain either by right or might to effect his object, let not this surprise be to him too severe a disappointment. Let him remember that many before now have tried to chastise a wrongdoer, and failing to punish their enemy have not even saved themselves; while many who have trusted in force to gain an advantage, instead of gaining anything more, have been doomed to lose what they had. Vengeance is not necessarily successful because wrong has been done, or strength sure because it is confident; but the incalculable element in the future* exercises the widest influence, and is the most treacherous, and yet in fact the most useful of all things, as it frightens us all equally, and thus makes us consider before attacking each other.

63. 'Let us therefore now allow the undefined fear of this unknown future, and the immediate terror of the Athenians' presence to produce their natural impression, and let us consider any failure to carry out the programmes that we may each have sketched out for ourselves as sufficiently accounted for by these obstacles, and send away the intruder from the country; and if everlasting peace be impossible between us, let us at all events make a treaty for as long a term as possible, and put off our private differences to another day. In fine, let us recognise that the adoption of my advice will leave us each citizens of a free state,† and as such arbiters of our own destiny, able to return good or bad offices with equal effect; while its rejection will make us dependent on others, and thus not only impotent to repel an insult, but on the most favourable supposition, friends to our direst enemies, and at feud with our natural friends.

64. 'For myself, though, as I said at first, the representative of a great city, and able to think less of defending myself than of attacking others, I am prepared to concede something in prevision of these dangers. I am not inclined to ruin myself for the sake of hurting my enemies, or so blinded by animosity as to think myself equally master of my own plans and of fortune which I cannot command; but I am ready to give up anything in reason. I call upon the rest of you to imitate my conduct of your own free will, without being forced to do so

---

*Hermocrates disconnects right and wrong from success and failure. Further, he emphasizes the element of chance in history and employs it to discourage others' imperialist ventures.

†Hermocrates appeals to the universal inclination of a *polis* to autonomy, and to a strategy that recognizes common interests among the Hellenic Sicilians. He makes a good case for the Sicilian rejection of outside intervention in their internecine quarrels.

by the enemy. There is no disgrace in connexions giving way to one another, a Dorian to a Dorian, or a Chalcidian to his brethren; above and beyond this we are neighbours, live in the same country, are girt by the same sea, and go by the same name of Sicilians. We shall go to war again, I suppose, when the time comes, and again make peace among ourselves by means of future congresses; but the foreign invader, if we are wise, will always find us united against him, since the hurt of one is the danger of all; and we shall never, in future, invite into the island either allies or mediators. By so acting we shall at the present moment do for Sicily a double service, ridding her at once of the Athenians, and of civil war, and in future shall live in freedom at home, and be less menaced from abroad.'

65. Such were the words of Hermocrates. The Sicilians took his advice, and came to an understanding among themselves to end the war, each keeping what they had—the Camarinæans taking Morgantina at a price fixed to be paid to the Syracusans—and the allies of the Athenians called the officers in command, and told them that they were going to make peace and that they would be included in the treaty. The generals assenting, the peace was concluded, and the Athenian fleet afterwards sailed away from Sicily. Upon their arrival at Athens, the Athenians banished Pythodorus and Sophocles, and fined Eurymedon for having taken bribes to depart when they might have subdued Sicily.* So thoroughly had the present prosperity persuaded the citizens that nothing could withstand them, and that they could achieve what was possible and impracticable alike, with means ample or inadequate it mattered not. The secret of this was their general extraordinary success, which made them confuse their strength with their hopes.†

66. The same summer the Megarians in the city, pressed by the hostilities of the Athenians, who invaded their country twice every year with all their forces, and harassed by the incursions of their own exiles at Pegæ, who had been expelled in a revolution by the popular party, began to ask each other whether it would not be better to receive back their exiles, and free the town from one of its two scourges. The friends of the emigrants perceiving the agitation, now more openly than before demanded the adoption of this proposition; and the leaders of the

---

*Thucydides indicates without comment the inability of the Athenian assembly to recognize that not every defeat was the fault of one or more of their generals. Thucydides (at 2.65) had commented on democratic displeasure with, and competition among, commanders, a problem Thucydides knew at first hand. This passage also plainly states the confidence of the *demos* in the possibility of success in Sicily.

†Recent Athenian success was undeniable, but Thucydides clearly thought that the Athenians squandered their opportunities and failed to keep their desires in line with their capacities. The ominous note about buoyant hope anticipates their disasters in books 7 and 8 and their eventual defeat.

commons, seeing that the sufferings of the times had tired out the constancy of their supporters, entered in their alarm into correspondence with the Athenian generals, Hippocrates, son of Ariphron, and Demosthenes, son of Alcisthenes, and resolved to betray the town, thinking this less dangerous to themselves than the return of the party which they had banished. It was accordingly arranged that the Athenians should first take the long walls extending for nearly a mile from the city to the port of Nisæa, to prevent the Peloponnesians coming to the rescue from that place, where they formed the sole garrison to secure the fidelity of Megara; and that after this the attempt should be made to put into their hands the upper town, which it was thought would then come over with less difficulty.

67. The Athenians, after plans had been arranged between themselves and their correspondents both as to words and actions, sailed by night to Minoa, the island off Megara, with six hundred heavy infantry under the command of Hippocrates, and took post in a quarry not far off, out of which bricks used to be taken for the walls; while Demosthenes, the other commander, with a detachment of Platæan light troops and another of Peripoli,* placed himself in ambush in the precinct of Enyalius, which was still nearer. No one knew of it, except those whose business it was to know that night. A little before daybreak, the traitors in Megara began to act. Every night for a long time back, under pretence of marauding, in order to have a means of opening the gates, they had been used, with the consent of the officer in command, to carry by night a sculling boat upon a cart along the ditch to the sea, and so to sail out, bringing it back again before day upon the cart, and taking it within the wall through the gates, in order, as they pretended, to baffle the Athenian blockade at Minoa, there being no boat to be seen in the harbour. On the present occasion the cart was already at the gates, which had been opened in the usual way for the boat, when the Athenians, with whom this had been concerted, saw it, and ran at the top of their speed from the ambush in order to reach the gates before they were shut again, and while the cart was still there to prevent their being closed; their Megarian accomplices at the same moment killing the guard at the gates. The first to run in was Demosthenes with his Platæans and Peripoli, just where the trophy now stands;† and he was no sooner within the gates than

---

*The *peripoli* were young citizen-soldiers engaged in military training from age eighteen to twenty, a kind of coast and frontier guard. Since Megara bordered Attica, Demosthenes had not drawn them far from home.

†The topographical indication offers an example of autopsy (Thucydides' firsthand experience) but would not mean much to most of his readership, ancient or modern. It stands awkwardly with notices telling us what might seem obvious, such as 2.93, noting that Piraeus is the port of Athens.

the Platæans engaged and defeated the nearest party of Peloponnesians who had taken the alarm and come to the rescue, and secured
the gates for the approaching Athenian heavy infantry.

68. After this, each of the Athenians as fast as they entered went
against the wall. A few of the Peloponnesian garrison stood their
ground at first, and tried to repel the assault, and some of them were
killed; but the main body took fright and fled; the night attack and the
sight of the Megarian traitors in arms against them making them think
that all Megara had gone over to the enemy. It so happened also that
the Athenian herald of his own idea called out and invited any of the
Megarians that wished, to join the Athenian ranks; and this was no
sooner heard by the garrison than they gave way, and, convinced that
they were the victims of a concerted attack, took refuge in Nisæa. By
daybreak, the walls being now taken and the Megarians in the city in
great agitation, the persons who had negotiated with the Athenians,
supported by the rest of the popular party which was privy to the plot,
said that they ought to open the gates and march out to battle. It had
been concerted between them that the Athenians should rush in, the
moment that the gates were opened, while the conspirators were to be
distinguished from the rest by being anointed with oil,* and so to avoid
being hurt. They could open the gates with more security, as four thousand Athenian heavy infantry from Eleusis, and six hundred horse, had
marched all night, according to agreement, and were now close at hand.
The conspirators were all ready anointed and at their posts by the
gates, when one of their accomplices denounced the plot to the opposite party, who gathered together and came in a body, and roundly said
that they must not march out—a thing they had never yet ventured on
even when in greater force than at present—or wantonly compromise
the safety of the town, and that if what they said was not attended to,
the battle would have to be fought in Megara. For the rest, they gave
no signs of their knowledge of the intrigue, but stoutly maintained that
their advice was the best, and meanwhile kept close by and watched the
gates, making it impossible for the conspirators to effect their purpose.

69. The Athenian generals seeing that some obstacle had arisen,
and that the capture of the town by force was no longer practicable,
at once proceeded to invest Nisæa, thinking that if they could take it
before relief arrived, the surrender of Megara would soon follow.†

---

*Modern commentators puzzle over this stratagem, wondering how olive oil on the
body can immediately mark out a man wearing a full suit of armor as an ally.

†Like Athens—with its port, Piraeus—the inland *polis* of Megara has a port, Nisaea
(map 2). Similar long walls connected the main town to its harbor facilities. The Athenians attempt to cut off the one from the other. Thucydides is interested in siege-
operations and their machines; compare 4.115. Brasidas and the Peloponnesians come
to the aid of their exposed ally.

Iron, stone-masons, and everything else required quickly coming up from Athens, the Athenians started from the wall which they occupied, and from this point built a cross wall looking towards Megara down to the sea on either side of Nisæa; the ditch and the walls being divided among the army, stones and bricks taken from the suburb, and the fruit-trees and timber cut down to make a palisade wherever this seemed necessary; the houses also in the suburb with the addition of battlements sometimes entering into the fortification. The whole of this day the work continued, and by the afternoon of the next the wall was all but completed, when the garrison in Nisæa, alarmed by the absolute want of provisions, which they used to take in for the day from the upper town, not anticipating any speedy relief from the Peloponnesians, and supposing Megara to be hostile, capitulated to the Athenians on condition that they should give up their arms, and should each be ransomed for a stipulated sum; their Lacedæmonian commander, and any others of his countrymen in the place, being left to the discretion of the Athenians. On these conditions they surrendered and came out, and the Athenians broke down the long walls at their point of junction with Megara, took possession of Nisæa, and went on with their other preparations.

70. Just at this time the Lacedæmonian Brasidas, son of Tellis, happened to be in the neighbourhood of Sicyon and Corinth, getting ready an army for Thrace. As soon as he heard of the capture of the walls, fearing for the Peloponnesians in Nisæa and the safety of Megara, he sent to the Bœotians to meet him as quickly as possible at Tripodiscus, a village so called of the Megarid, under Mount Geraneia, and went himself, with two thousand seven hundred Corinthian heavy infantry, four hundred Phliasians, six hundred Sicyonians, and such troops of his own as he had already levied, expecting to find Nisæa not yet taken. Hearing of its fall (he had marched out by night to Tripodiscus), he took three hundred picked men from the army, without waiting till his coming should be known, and came up to Megara unobserved by the Athenians, who were down by the sea, ostensibly, and really if possible, to attempt Nisæa, but above all to get into Megara and secure the town. He accordingly invited the townspeople to admit his party, saying that he had hopes of recovering Nisæa.

71. However, one of the Megarian factions feared that he might expel them and restore the exiles; the other that the commons, apprehensive of this very danger, might set upon them, and the city be thus destroyed by a battle within its gates under the eyes of the ambushed Athenians. He was accordingly refused admittance, both parties electing to remain quiet and await the event; each expecting a battle between the Athenians and the relieving army, and thinking it safer to see their friends victorious before declaring in their favour.

Unable to carry his point, Brasidas went back to the rest of the army.

72. At daybreak the Bœotians joined him. Having determined to relieve Megara, whose danger they considered their own, even before hearing from Brasidas, they were already in full force at Platæa, when his messenger arrived to add spurs to their resolution; and they at once sent on to him two thousand two hundred heavy infantry, and six hundred horse, returning home with the main body. The whole army thus assembled numbered six thousand heavy infantry. The Athenian heavy infantry were drawn up by Nisæa and the sea; but the light troops being scattered over the plain were attacked by the Bœotian horse and driven to the sea, being taken entirely by surprise, as on previous occasions no relief had ever come to the Megarians from any quarter. Here the Bœotians were in their turn charged and engaged by the Athenian horse, and a cavalry action ensued which lasted a long time, and in which both parties claimed the victory. The Athenians killed and stripped the leader of the Bœotian horse and some few of his comrades who had charged right up to Nisæa, and remaining masters of the bodies gave them back under truce, and set up a trophy; but regarding the action as a whole the forces separated without either side having gained a decisive advantage, the Bœotians returning to their army and the Athenians to Nisæa.

73. After this Brasidas and the army came nearer to the sea and to Megara, and taking up a convenient position, remained quiet in order of battle, expecting to be attacked by the Athenians and knowing that the Megarians were waiting to see which would be the victor. This attitude seemed to present two advantages. Without taking the offensive or willingly provoking the hazards of a battle, they openly showed their readiness to fight, and thus without bearing the burden of the day would fairly reap its honours; while at the same time they effectually served their interests at Megara. For if they had failed to show themselves, they would not have had a chance, but would have certainly been considered vanquished, and have lost the town. As it was, the Athenians might possibly not be inclined to accept their challenge, and their object would be attained without fighting. And so it turned out. The Athenians formed outside the long walls, and the enemy not attacking, there remained motionless; their generals having decided that the risk was too unequal. In fact most of their objects had been already attained; and they would have to begin a battle against superior numbers, and if victorious could only gain Megara, while a defeat would destroy the flower of their heavy soldiery. For the enemy it was different; as even the states actually represented in his army risked each only a part of its entire force, he might well be more audacious. Accordingly after waiting for some time without either side attacking, the Athenians withdrew to Nisæa, and the Pelo-

ponnesians after them to the point from which they had set out.* The
friends of the Megarian exiles now threw aside their hesitation, and
opened the gates to Brasidas and the commanders from the different
states—looking upon him as the victor and upon the Athenians as
having declined the battle—and receiving them into the town proceeded to discuss matters with them; the party in correspondence
with the Athenians being paralysed by the turn things had taken.

74. Afterwards Brasidas let the allies go home, and himself went
back to Corinth, to prepare for his expedition to Thrace, his original
destination. The Athenians also returning home, the Megarians in the
city most implicated in the Athenian negotiation, knowing that they
had been detected, presently disappeared; while the rest conferred with
the friends of the exiles, and restored the party at Pegæ, after binding
them under solemn oaths to take no vengeance for the past, and only
to consult the real interests of the town. However, as soon as they were
in office, they held a review of the heavy infantry, and separating the
battalions, picked out about a hundred of their enemies, and of those
who were thought to be most involved in the correspondence with the
Athenians, brought them before the people, and compelling the vote to
be given openly, had them condemned and executed, and established a
close oligarchy in the town—a revolution which lasted a very long
while, although effected by the fewest partisans.†

*Eighth and Ninth Years of the War — Invasion of Bœotia —
Fall of Amphipolis — Successes of Brasidas*

75. The same summer the Mitylenians were about to fortify Antandrus, as they had intended, when Demodocus and Aristides, the commanders of the Athenian squadron engaged in levying tribute, heard on
the Hellespont of what was being done to the place (Lamachus their
colleague having sailed with ten ships into the Pontus) and conceived
fears of its becoming a second Anaia,—the place in which the Samian
exiles had established themselves to annoy Samos, helping the Peloponnesians by sending pilots to their navy, and keeping the city in agitation and receiving all its outlaws. They accordingly got together a force
from the allies and set sail, defeated in battle the troops that met them

---

*Brasidas later misrepresents this draw as an Athenian unwillingness to do battle
against his forces (4.85, 108). The Athenian attack on Megara (4.66–74) was not successful, and the oligarchy became more firmly established.

†Thucydides generously distributes superlatives, the greatest war, the most fatal disease, the most eclipses, the most lamentable disaster, the greatest military loss, the most
unexpected occurrence, or, as here, the longest revolution by the fewest men. He is not
prone to exaggerate, however.

from Antandrus, and retook the place. Not long after, Lamachus, who had sailed into the Pontus, lost his ships at anchor in the river Calex,* in the territory of Heraclea, rain having fallen in the interior and the flood coming suddenly down upon them; and himself and his troops passed by land through the Bithynian Thracians on the Asiatic side, and arrived at Chalcedon, the Megarian colony at the mouth of the Pontus.

76. The same summer the Athenian general, Demosthenes, arrived at Naupactus with forty ships immediately after the return from the Megarid. Hippocrates and Demosthenes had had overtures made to them by certain men in the cities in Bœotia, who wished to change the constitution and introduce a democracy as at Athens; Ptœodorus, a Theban exile, being the chief mover in this intrigue. The seaport town of Siphæ, in the bay of Crisæ, in the Thespian territory, was to be betrayed to them by one party; Chæronea (a dependency of what was formerly called the Minyan, now the Bœotian, Orchomenus), to be put into their hands by another from that town, whose exiles were very active in the business, hiring men in Peloponnese. Some Phocians also were in the plot, Chæronea being the frontier town of Bœotia and close to Phanotis in Phocis. Meanwhile the Athenians were to seize Delium, the sanctuary of Apollo, in the territory of Tanagra looking towards Eubœa; and all these events† were to take place simultaneously upon a day appointed, in order that the Bœotians might be unable to unite to oppose them at Delium, being everywhere detained by disturbances at home. Should the enterprise succeed, and Delium be fortified, its authors confidently expected that even if no revolution should immediately follow in Bœotia, yet with these places in their hands, and the country being harassed by incursions, and a refuge in each instance near for the partisans engaged in them, things would not remain as they were, but that the rebels being supported by the Athenians and the forces of the oligarchs divided, it would be possible after a while to settle matters according to their wishes.

---

*The Pontus is one Greek name for the Black Sea (map 1). Lamachus will be among the first group of generals chosen for the Sicilian expedition. Aristophanes satirizes him in *Acharnians*, a play about war fever and frustrations. This loss of ships at anchor, not due to hostile action, is unique. The reference to tribute-collection explains the presence of the three Athenian generals but fails to provide any statement of the degree of the Athenians' dependence on this region, one of the five administrative regions created for collecting imperial revenues. This paragraph gathers various incidents.

†The Athenians develop an aggressive strategy on their northern border after their western border strategy fails. Delium, in the southeastern corner of Boeotia, was the site of a shrine to Apollo. Tanagra is the local *polis*, site of the major Athenian defeat of 457 (compare 1.108; map 2). Both sides will try to profit from the off-limits nature of the sanctuary. Demosthenes' bold and complicated plan depended on careful synchronization, a factor that soon ruined this particular idea.

77. Such was the plot in contemplation. Hippocrates with a force raised at home awaited the proper moment to take the field against the Bœotians; while he sent on Demosthenes with the forty ships above mentioned to Naupactus, to raise in those parts an army of Acarnanians and of the other allies, and sail and receive Siphæ from the conspirators; a day having been agreed on for the simultaneous execution of both these operations. Demosthenes on his arrival found Œniadæ already compelled by the united Acarnanians to join the Athenian confederacy, and himself raising all the allies in those countries marched against and subdued Salynthius and the Agræans; after which he devoted himself to the preparations necessary to enable him to be at Siphæ by the time appointed.

78. About the same time in the summer, Brasidas set out on his march for the Thracian places* with seventeen hundred heavy infantry, and arriving at Heraclea in Trachis, from thence sent on a messenger to his friends at Pharsalus, to ask them to conduct himself and his army through the country. Accordingly there came to Melitia in Achaia Panærus, Dorus, Hippolochidas, Torylaus, and Strophacus, the Chalcidian *Proxenus*, under whose escort he resumed his march, being accompanied also by other Thessalians, among whom was Niconidas from Larissa, a friend of Perdiccas. It was never very easy to traverse Thessaly without an escort; and throughout all Hellas for an armed force to pass without leave through a neighbour's country was a delicate step to take. Besides this the Thessalian people had always sympathised with the Athenians. Indeed if instead of the customary close oligarchy there had been a constitutional government in Thessaly, he would never have been able to proceed; since even as it was, he was met on his march at the river Enipeus by certain of the opposite party who forbade his further progress, and complained of his making the attempt without the consent of the nation. To this his escort answered that they had no intention of taking him through against their will; they were only friends in attendance on an unexpected visitor. Brasidas himself added that he came as a friend to Thessaly and its inhabitants; his arms not being directed against them but against the Athenians, with whom he was at war, and that although he knew of no quarrel between the Thessalians and Lacedæmonians to prevent the two nations having access to each other's territory, he neither would nor could proceed against their wishes; he could only beg them not to stop him. With this answer they went away, and he took the advice of his escort, and pushed on without halting, before a greater force might

---

*Brasidas is notably successful in Thrace (4.78–88). Perdiccas, king of Macedon, was an undependable ally for all parties, but a powerful force because of his soldiers and cavalry, and his control of both timber and gold and silver mines. A century after this, his descendant Alexander III ("the Great") would rule most of the known world.

gather to prevent him. Thus in the day that he set out from Melitia he performed the whole distance to Pharsalus, and encamped on the river Apidanus; and so to Phacium, and from thence to Perrhæbia. Here his Thessalian escort went back, and the Perrhæbians, who are subjects of Thessaly, set him down at Dium in the dominions of Perdiccas, a Macedonian town under Mount Olympus, looking towards Thessaly.

79. In this way Brasidas hurried through Thessaly before any one could be got ready to stop him, and reached Perdiccas and Chalcidice. The departure of the army from Peloponnese had been procured by the Thracian towns in revolt against Athens and by Perdiccas, alarmed at the successes of the Athenians.* The Chalcidians thought that they would be the first objects of an Athenian expedition, not that the neighbouring towns which had not yet revolted did not also secretly join in the invitation; and Perdiccas also had his apprehensions on account of his old quarrels with the Athenians, although not openly at war with them, and above all wished to reduce Arrhabæus, king of the Lyncestians.† It had been less difficult for them to get an army to leave Peloponnese, because of the ill fortune of the Lacedæmonians at the present moment.

80. The attacks of the Athenians upon Peloponnese, and in particular upon Laconia, might, it was hoped, be diverted most effectually by annoying them in return, and by sending an army to their allies, especially as they were willing to maintain it and asked for it to aid them in revolting. The Lacedæmonians were also glad to have an excuse for sending some of the Helots out of the country, for fear that the present aspect of affairs and the occupation of Pylos might encourage them to move. Indeed fear of their numbers and shiftiness even persuaded the Lacedæmonians to the following action, their policy at all times having been governed by the necessity of taking precautions against them.‡ The

---

*Perdiccas intended to use the major war to settle minor scores with his neighbor king to the west. He further reasonably believed the static Spartans would threaten his dominions considerably less than the aggressive Athenians, who managed a maritime empire and nearby Thraceward colonies such as Amphipolis.

†The relations of the northern tribes were fluid and personal. At 2.80, the two groups were friendly.

‡The helots outnumbered the Spartans at all times. Spartan politics and economics depended on the docility of their servile population and/or on terrorizing their underlings. It might surprise us that the Spartans could trust them to remain loyal to the army when abroad, and on their serving as front-line hoplites, as the 700 presumably did on this military expedition. One can only imagine the threats made about the safety of their families left at home, should they misbehave. (Crawley offered "obstinacy" for the Greek word translated here as "shiftiness" and by others as "stupidity.") The Spartans, whose viewpoint and shaky morale this sentence reflects, needed to despise the humans whom they brutally exploited. Where this translation now gives "shiftiness," most manuscripts read "youthfulness," another word that makes little sense given the fact that helotage was a life-long and inherited status.

Helots were invited by a proclamation to pick out those of their number who claimed to have most distinguished themselves against the enemy, in order that they might receive their freedom; the object being to test them, as it was thought that the first to claim their freedom would be the most high-spirited and the most apt to rebel. As many as two thousand were selected accordingly, who crowned themselves and went round the temples, rejoicing in their new freedom. The Spartans, however, soon afterwards did away with them, and no one ever knew how each of them perished.* The Spartans now therefore gladly sent seven hundred as heavy infantry with Brasidas, who recruited the rest of his force by means of money in Peloponnese.

81. Brasidas himself was sent out by the Lacedæmonians mainly at his own desire, although the Chalcidians also were eager to have a man so thorough as he had shown himself whenever there was anything to be done at Sparta, and whose after-service abroad proved of the utmost use to his country.† At the present moment his just and moderate conduct towards the towns generally succeeded in procuring their revolt, besides the places which he managed to take by treachery; and thus when the Lacedæmonians desired to treat, as they ultimately did, they had places to offer in exchange, and the burden of war meanwhile shifted from Peloponnese. Later on in the war, after the events in Sicily, the present valour and conduct of Brasidas, known by experience to some, by hearsay to others, was what mainly created in the allies of Athens a feeling for the Lacedæmonians.‡ He was the first who went out and showed himself so good a man at all points as to leave behind him the conviction that the rest were like him.

82. Meanwhile his arrival in the Thracian country no sooner became known to the Athenians than they declared war against Perdic-

---

*This anecdote, acknowledging insufficient information, reflects Spartan mercilessness and paranoia as well as the pathos of the helots' pleasure in freedom. Thucydides says nothing about the Spartan selection process or its criminal injustice against those 2,000 men in bondage who had loyally served Sparta.

†Thucydides acknowledges Brasidas' popularity abroad and his discomfort at home (compare 4.108, jealousy at home). His policies were good for the Spartan war aims but not always appreciated as such.

‡Thucydides usually keeps within his chronology, sticking to events in the order that they happened. The exceptions, such as 2.65, convey his attempts at comprehensive evaluations. Here he looks forward to the period after the death of Brasidas in 421 and even to after 413, the year of the Athenian defeat in Sicily, to book 8 and beyond. He wants to explain one basis for the Hellenes' warm welcomes of the Spartans, who elsewhere are described as inefficient and impolitic, in speech and deed, toward the allies—for example, Pausanias in the previous war (1.108), Alcidas and Polydamidas in this one (3.32; 4.130), and others later in the final, Ionian phase of the war (411–404). Brasidas was a singularly impressive Lacedaemonian in his ability to profit from circumstances (see 4.121 for his popularity).

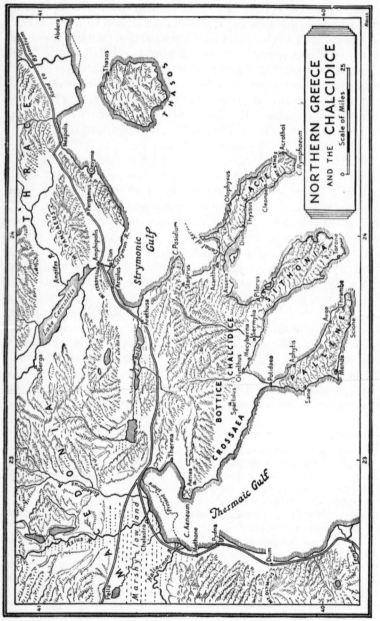

MAP 7. NORTHERN GREECE AND THE CHALCIDICE

cas, whom they regarded as the author of the expedition, and kept a closer watch on their allies in that quarter.

83. Upon the arrival of Brasidas and his army, Perdiccas immediately started with them and with his own forces against Arrhabæus, son of Bromerus, king of the Lyncestian Macedonians, his neighbour, with whom he had a quarrel and whom he wished to subdue. However, when he arrived with his army and Brasidas at the pass leading into Lyncus, Brasidas told him that before commencing hostilities he wished to go and try to persuade Arrhabæus to become the ally of Lacedæmon, this latter having already made overtures intimating his willingness to make Brasidas arbitrator between them, and the Chalcidian envoys accompanying him having warned him not to remove the apprehensions of Perdiccas, in order to insure his greater zeal in their cause. Besides, the envoys of Perdiccas had talked at Lacedæmon about his bringing many of the places round him into alliance with them; and thus Brasidas thought he might take a larger view of the question of Arrhabæus. Perdiccas however retorted that he had not brought him with him to arbitrate in their quarrel, but to put down the enemies whom he might point out to him;* and that while he, Perdiccas, maintained half his army it was a breach of faith for Brasidas to parley with Arrhabæus. Nevertheless Brasidas disregarded the wishes of Perdiccas and held the parley in spite of him, and suffered himself to be persuaded to lead off the army without invading the country of Arrhabæus; after which Perdiccas, holding that faith had not been kept with him, contributed only a third instead of half of the support of the army.

84. The same summer, without loss of time, Brasidas marched with the Chalcidians against Acanthus, a colony of the Andrians, a little before vintage. The inhabitants were divided into two parties on the question of receiving him; those who had joined the Chalcidians in inviting him, and the popular party. However, fear for their fruit, which was still out, enabled Brasidas to persuade the multitude to admit him alone, and to hear what he had to say before making a decision; and he was admitted accordingly and appeared before the people, and not being a bad speaker for a Lacedæmonian, addressed them as follows:—†

85. 'Acanthians, the Lacedæmonians have sent out me and my

---

*Perdiccas shows his cards. Brasidas stands firm and thus loses some of the already questionable dependability of this barbarian ally.

†The speech to the rationally dithering Acanthians (map 7) in winter 424/423 serves as the paradigm of Brasidas' exhortations to many towns thinking about revolt from Athens. His other attempts at persuasion (4.114 and 120) summarize or allude to it. Thucydides acknowledges that Spartans were generally inferior speakers. Acanthus was on the northeastern coast of the easternmost of the three peninsulas of the Chalcidice (map 7).

army to make good the reason that we gave for the war when we began it, viz. that we were going to war with the Athenians in order to free Hellas.* Our delay in coming has been caused by mistaken expectations as to the war at home, which led us to hope, by our own unassisted efforts and without your risking anything, to effect the speedy downfall of the Athenians; and you must not blame us for this, as we are now come the moment that we were able, prepared with your aid to do our best to subdue them. Meanwhile I am astonished at finding your gates shut against me, and at not meeting with a better welcome. We Lacedæmonians thought of you as allies eager to have us, to whom we should come in spirit even before we were with you in body; and in this expectation undertook all the risks of a march of many days through a strange country, so far did our zeal carry us. It will be a terrible thing if after this you have other intentions, and mean to stand in the way of your own and Hellenic freedom. It is not merely that you oppose me yourselves; but wherever I may go people will be less inclined to join me, on the score that you, to whom I first came—an important town like Acanthus, and prudent men like the Acanthians†—refused to admit me. I shall have nothing to prove that the reason which I advance is the true one; it will be said either that there is something unfair in the freedom which I offer, or that I am here in insufficient force and unable to protect you against an attack from Athens. Yet when I went with the army which I now have to the relief of Nisæa, the Athenians did not venture to engage me although in greater force than I;‡ and it is not likely they will ever send across sea against you an army as numerous as they had at Nisæa.

86. 'And for myself, I have come here not to hurt but to free the Hellenes, witness the solemn oaths by which I have bound my government that the allies that I may bring over shall be independent; and besides my object in coming is not by force or fraud to obtain your alliance, but to offer you mine to help you against your Athenian masters. I protest, therefore, against any suspicions of my intentions after the guarantees which I offer, and equally so against doubts of my ability to protect you, and I invite you to join me without hesitation.

---

*Brasidas' repeated keynote or catchword is the "freedom of the Greeks." But, hints of menace and threat are also present, should the locals choose not to revolt. He must explain Peloponnesian delays and respond to northern Greek suspicions that the forces sent cannot protect local towns from imperial Athenian reprisals. He developed a successful line of patter.

†The flattery is relevant to the importance of this first attempt to gain local adhesion to the Peloponnesian cause.

‡Brasidas' words are inaccurate in at least three ways: The army of Brasidas is different from what it was; it outnumbered the Athenians at Nisaea; and there *both* sides refused battle. Thucydides himself notes fraudulent statements and promises at 4.108.

'Some of you may hang back because they have private enemies, and fear that I may put the city into the hands of a party: none need be more tranquil than they. I am not come here to help this party or that; and I do not consider that I should be bringing you freedom in any real sense, if I should disregard your constitution, and enslave the many to the few or the few to the many. This would be heavier than a foreign yoke; and we Lacedæmonians instead of being thanked for our pains, should get neither honour nor glory, but contrariwise reproaches. The charges which strengthen our hands in the war against the Athenians would on our own showing be merited by ourselves, and more hateful in us than in those who make no pretensions to honesty; as it is more disgraceful for persons of character to take what they covet by fair-seeming fraud than by open force; the one aggression having for its justification the might which fortune gives, the other being simply a piece of clever roguery.

87. 'A matter which concerns us thus nearly we naturally look to most jealously; and over and above the oaths that I have mentioned, what stronger assurance can you have, when you see that our words, compared with the actual facts, produce the necessary conviction that it is our interest to act as we say?

'If to these considerations of mine you put in the plea of inability, and claim that your friendly feeling should save you from being hurt by your refusal; if you say that freedom, in your opinion, is not without its dangers, and that it is right to offer it to those who can accept it, but not to force it on any against their will, then I shall take the gods and heroes of your country to witness that I came for your good and was rejected, and shall do my best to compel you by laying waste your land. I shall do so without scruple, being justified by the necessity which constrains me, first, to prevent the Lacedæmonians from being damaged by you, their friends, in the event of your non-adhesion, through the monies that you pay to the Athenians; and secondly, to prevent the Hellenes from being hindered by you in shaking off their servitude. Otherwise indeed we should have no right to act as we propose; except in the name of some public interest, what call should we Lacedæmonians have to free those who do not wish it? Empire we do not aspire to: it is what we are labouring to put down; and we should wrong the greater number if we allowed you to stand in the way of the independence that we offer to all.* Endeavour, therefore, to decide wisely, and strive to begin the work of liberation for the Hellenes,

---

*What is good policy for the Acanthians is unclear (4.84), but they are in immediate danger of losing their crops to Brasidas before the vintage. It is paradoxical to destroy a community, if it does not choose independence and adherence to another alliance. Their vote was clearly uneasy as well as secret.

and lay up for yourselves endless renown, while you escape private loss, and cover your commonwealth with glory.'

88. Such were the words of Brasidas. The Acanthians, thus after much had been said on both sides of the question, gave their votes in secret, and the majority, influenced by the seductive arguments of Brasidas and by fear for their fruit, decided to revolt from Athens; not however admitting the army until they had taken his personal security for the oaths sworn by his government before they sent him out, assuring the independence of the allies whom he might bring over. Not long after, Stagirus, a colony of the Andrians, followed their example and revolted.

89. Such were the events of this summer. It was in the first days of the winter following that the places in Bœotia were to be put into the hands of the Athenian generals, Hippocrates and Demosthenes, the latter of whom was to go with his ships to Siphæ, the former to Delium. A mistake, however, was made in the days on which they were each to start;* and Demosthenes sailing first to Siphæ, with the Acarnanians and many of the allies from those parts on board, failed to effect anything, through the plot having been betrayed by Nicomachus, a Phocian from Phanotis, who told the Lacedæmonians, and they the Bœotians. Succours accordingly flocked in from all parts of Bœotia, Hippocrates not being yet there to make his diversion, and Siphæ and Chæronea were promptly secured, and the conspirators, informed of the mistake, did not venture on any movement in the towns.

90. Meanwhile Hippocrates made a levy in mass of the citizens, resident aliens, and foreigners in Athens, and arrived at his destination after the Bœotians had already come back from Siphæ, and encamping his army began to fortify Delium, the sanctuary of Apollo, in the following manner. A trench was dug all round the temple and the consecrated ground, and the earth thrown up from the excavation was made to do duty as a wall, in which stakes were also planted, the vines round the sanctuary being cut down and thrown in, together with stones and bricks pulled down from the houses near; every means, in short, being used to run up the rampart. Wooden towers were also erected where they were wanted, and where there was no part of the temple buildings left standing, as on the side where the gallery once existing had fallen in. The work was begun on the third day after leaving home, and continued during the fourth, and till dinner-time on the fifth, when most of it being now finished the army removed from

---

*The invasion of Boeotia at Delium had been fatally flawed from the start. Demosthenes failed to take Siphae on the north, and Hippocrates had to meet the Boeotian army in battle before he had finished fortifying the sanctuary.

Delium about a mile and a quarter on its way home. From this point most of the light troops went straight on, while the heavy infantry halted and remained where they were; Hippocrates having stayed behind at Delium to arrange the posts, and to give directions for the completion of such part of the outworks as had been left unfinished.

91. During the days thus employed the Bœotians were mustering at Tanagra, and by the time that they had come in from all the towns, found the Athenians already on their way home. The rest of the eleven Bœotarchs* were against giving battle, as the enemy was no longer in Bœotia, the Athenians being just over the Oropian border, when they halted; but Pagondas, son of Æolidas, one of the Bœotarchs of Thebes (Arianthides, son of Lysimachidas, being the other), and then commander-in-chief, thought it best to hazard a battle. He accordingly called the men to him, company after company, to prevent their all leaving their arms at once, and urged them to attack the Athenians, and stand the issue of a battle, speaking as follows:—

92. 'Bœotians, the idea that we ought not to give battle to the Athenians unless we came up with them in Bœotia, is one which should never have entered into the head of any of us, your generals. It was to annoy Bœotia that they crossed the frontier and built a fort in our country; and they are therefore, I imagine, our enemies wherever we may come up with them, and from wheresoever they may have come to act as enemies do. And if any one has taken up with the idea in question for reasons of safety, it is high time for him to change his mind. The party attacked, whose own country is in danger, can scarcely discuss what is prudent with the calmness of men who are in full enjoyment of what they have got, and are thinking of attacking a neighbour in order to get more. It is your national habit, in your country or out of it, to oppose the same resistance to a foreign invader; and when that invader is Athenian, and lives upon your frontier besides, it is doubly imperative to do so. As between neighbours generally, freedom means simply a determination to hold one's own; and with neighbours like these, who are trying to enslave near and far alike, there is nothing for it but to fight it out to the last.

'Look at the condition of the Eubœans and of most of the rest of Hellas, and be convinced that others have to fight with their neighbours for this frontier or that, but that for us conquest means one frontier for the whole country, about which no dispute can be made, for they will simply come and take by force what we have. So much

---

*Eleven Boeotarchs composed an executive council and commanded the troops of the confederacy, headed by Thebes, which contributed two of them. Thebes dominated the independent cities as much as she could. Plataea had been recalcitrant and suffered extinction for it. Pagondas' speech provides a window into the thinking of allied but non-Peloponnesian communities that faced Athenian aggression.

more have we to fear from this neighbour than from another. Besides, people who, like the Athenians in the present instance, are tempted by pride of strength to attack their neighbours, usually march most confidently against those who keep still, and only defend themselves in their own country, but think twice before they grapple with those who meet them outside their frontier and strike the first blow if opportunity offers. The Athenians have shown us this themselves; the defeat which we inflicted upon them at Coronea, at the time when our quarrels had allowed them to occupy the country,* has given great security to Bœotia until the present day. Remembering this, the old must equal their ancient exploits, and the young, the sons of the heroes of that time, must endeavour not to disgrace their native valour; and trusting in the help of the god whose temple has been sacrilegiously fortified,† and in the victims which in our sacrifices have proved propitious, we must march against the enemy, and teach him that he must go and get what he wants by attacking some one who will not resist him, but that men whose glory it is to be always ready to give battle for the liberty of their own country, and never unjustly to enslave that of others, will not let him go without a struggle.'

93. By these arguments Pagondas persuaded the Bœotians to attack the Athenians, and quickly breaking up his camp led his army forward, it being now late in the day. On nearing the enemy, he halted in a position where a hill intervening prevented the two armies from seeing each other, and then formed and prepared for action. Meanwhile Hippocrates at Delium, informed of the approach of the Bœotians, sent orders to his troops to throw themselves into line, and himself joined them not long afterwards, leaving about three hundred horse behind him at Delium, at once to guard the place in case of attack, and to watch their opportunity and fall upon the Bœotians during the battle. The Bœotians placed a detachment to deal with these, and when everything was arranged to their satisfaction appeared over the hill, and halted in the order which they had determined on, to the number of seven thousand heavy infantry, more than ten thousand light troops, one thousand horse, and five hundred targeteers. On their right were the Thebans and those of their province, in the centre the Haliartians, Coronæans, Copæans, and the other people around the lake, and on the left the Thespians, Tanagræans, and Or-

---

*The Boeotian general naturally refers to earlier victory over the Athenians, here at Coronea, fought in 447 (see 1.108 and 113). This battle had ended Athenian control over much of Boeotia. He also refers to Boeotian internal disputes and factions.

†Most claims of divine support in Thucydides meet with disaster, but this observation furnishes a counter-example to the wretched Plataeans or to Nicias pleading in desperation in Sicily. The back-and-forth about sacrilege is hard to justify and seems included to show the devolution of religion to the status of political pawn.

chomenians, the cavalry and the light troops being at the extremity of each wing. The Thebans formed twenty-five shields deep,* the rest as they pleased. Such was the strength and disposition of the Bœotian army.

94. On the side of the Athenians, the heavy infantry throughout the whole army formed eight deep, being in numbers equal to the enemy, with the cavalry upon the two wings. Light troops regularly armed there were none in the army, nor had there ever been any at Athens. Those who had joined in the invasion, though many times more numerous than those of the enemy, had mostly followed unarmed, as part of the levy in mass of the citizens and foreigners at Athens, and having started first on their way home were not present in any number.† The armies being now in line and upon the point of engaging, Hippocrates, the general, passed along the Athenian ranks, and encouraged them as follows:—

95. 'Athenians, I shall only say a few words to you, but brave men require no more, and they are addressed more to your understanding than to your courage. None of you must fancy that we are going out of our way to run this risk in the country of another. Fought in their territory the battle will be for ours: if we conquer, the Peloponnesians will never invade your country without the Bœotian horse, and in one battle you will win Bœotia and in a manner free Attica. Advance to meet them then like citizens of a country in which you all glory as the first in Hellas, and like sons of the fathers who beat them at Œnophyta with Myronides and thus gained possession of Bœotia.'

96. Hippocrates had got half through the army with his exhortation,‡ when the Bœotians, after a few more hasty words from Pagondas, struck up the pæan, and came against them from the hill; the Athenians advancing to meet them, and closing at a run. The extreme wing of neither army came into action, one like the other being stopped by the water-courses in the way; the rest engaged with the utmost obstinacy, shield against shield. The Bœotian left, as far as the centre, was worsted by the Athenians. The Thespians in that part of

---

*The Thebans file their phalanx to a great depth (eight was standard; compare Pritchett, *The Greek State at War*, part 1, chapter 11), a tactic that Epaminondas (Philip of Macedon's teacher) in the early part of the next century was to develop to perfection, leading to the short-lived Theban hegemony (372–361; see Plutarch's *Life of Epaminondas*).

†There was a full levy on both sides, but many Athenians (why unarmed?) had returned home. The Athenians did not have specialized light-armed forces, and Thucydides states they never had maintained such a force composed of Athenians—perhaps contradicting views he had encountered while in exile from Athens.

‡Hippocrates' brief encouragement, however delivered (repeated in substance to fire up the separate units along the front line?) would vary for different units. The Boeotian attack cut him short.

the field suffered most severely. The troops alongside them having given way, they were surrounded in a narrow space and cut down fighting hand to hand; some of the Athenians also fell into confusion in surrounding the enemy and mistook and so killed each other. In this part of the field the Bœotians were beaten, and retreated upon the troops still fighting; but the right, where the Thebans were, got the better of the Athenians and shoved them further and further back, though gradually at first. It so happened also that Pagondas, seeing the distress of his left, had sent two squadrons of horse, where they could not be seen, round the hill, and their sudden appearance struck a panic into the victorious wing of the Athenians, who thought that it was another army coming against them. At length in both parts of the field, disturbed by this panic, and with their line broken by the advancing Thebans, the whole Athenian army took to flight. Some made for Delium and the sea, some for Oropus, others for Mount Parnes, or wherever they had hopes of safety, pursued and cut down by the Bœotians, and in particular by the cavalry, composed partly of Bœotians and partly of Locrians, who had come up just as the rout began. Night however coming on to interrupt the pursuit, the mass of the fugitives escaped more easily than they would otherwise have done. The next day the troops at Oropus and Delium returned home by sea, after leaving a garrison in the latter place, which they continued to hold notwithstanding the defeat.

97. The Bœotians set up a trophy, took up their own dead, and stripped those of the enemy, and leaving a guard over them retired to Tanagra, there to take measures for attacking Delium. Meanwhile a herald came from the Athenians to ask for the dead, but was met and turned back by a Bœotian herald, who told him that he would effect nothing until the return of himself the Bœotian herald, and who then went on to the Athenians, and told them on the part of the Bœotians that they had done wrong in transgressing the law of the Hellenes. Of what use was the universal custom protecting the temples in an invaded country, if the Athenians were to fortify Delium and live there, acting exactly as if they were on unconsecrated ground, and drawing and using for their purposes the water which they, the Bœotians, never touched except for sacred uses? Accordingly for the god as well as for themselves, in the name of the deities concerned, and of Apollo, the Bœotians invited them first to evacuate the temple, if they wished to take up the dead that belonged to them.*

98. After these words from the herald, the Athenians sent their

---

*Both sides try to exploit hallowed conventions regarding sacred ground through their diplomatic agents, the heralds. The Athenians lost twice as many men as the Boeotians (4.101).

own herald to the Bœotians to say that they had not done any wrong to the temple, and for the future would do it no more harm than they could help; not having occupied it originally in any such design, but to defend themselves from it against those who were really wronging them. The law of the Hellenes was that conquest of a country, whether more or less extensive, carried with it possession of the temples in that country, with the obligation to keep up the usual ceremonies, at least as far as possible. The Bœotians and most other people who had turned out the owners of a country, and put themselves in their places by force, now held as of right the temples which they originally entered as usurpers. If the Athenians could have conquered more of Bœotia this would have been the case with them: as things stood, the piece of it which they had got they should treat as their own, and not quit unless obliged. The water they had disturbed under the impulsion of a necessity which they had not wantonly incurred, having been forced to use it in defending themselves against the Bœotians who had first invaded Attica.

Besides, anything done under the pressure of war and danger might reasonably claim indulgence even in the eye of the god; or why, pray, were the altars the asylum for involuntary offences? Transgression also was a term applied to presumptuous offenders, not to the victims of adverse circumstances. In short, which were most impious—the Bœotians who wished to barter dead bodies for holy places, or the Athenians who refused to give up holy places to obtain what was theirs by right? The condition of evacuating Bœotia must therefore be withdrawn. They were no longer in Bœotia. They stood where they stood by the right of the sword. All that the Bœotians had to do was to tell them to take up their dead under a truce according to the national custom.*

99. The Bœotians replied that if they were in Bœotia, they must evacuate that country before taking up their dead; if they were in their own territory, they could do as they pleased: for they knew that, although the Oropid where the bodies as it chanced were lying (the battle having been fought on the borders) was subject to Athens, yet the Athenians could not get them without their leave. Besides, why should they grant a truce for Athenian ground? And what could be fairer than to tell them to evacuate Bœotia if they wished to get what they asked? The Athenian herald accordingly returned with this answer, without having accomplished his object.

100. Meanwhile the Bœotians at once sent for darters and slingers from the Malian gulf, and with two thousand Corinthian heavy in-

---

*The Athenians unpersuasively claim that they have conquered Delium and therefore are no longer on enemy territory, only surrounded by enemy territory, so their corpses should be returned. They also claim divine indulgence for doing only what they had to do, perhaps a weaker claim.

fantry who had joined them after the battle, the Peloponnesian garrison which had evacuated Nisæa, and some Megarians with them, marched against Delium, and attacked the fort, and after divers efforts finally succeeded in taking it by an engine of the following description. They sawed in two and scooped out a great beam from end to end, and fitting it nicely together again like a pipe, hung by chains a cauldron at one extremity, with which communicated an iron tube projecting from the beam, which was itself in great part plated with iron. This they brought up from a distance upon carts to the part of the wall principally composed of vines and timber, and when it was near, inserted huge bellows into their end of the beam and blew with them. The blast passing closely confined into the cauldron, which was filled with lighted coals, sulphur and pitch, made a great blaze, and set fire to the wall, which soon became untenable for its defenders, who left it and fled; and in this way the fort was taken. Of the garrison some were killed and two hundred made prisoners; most of the rest got on board their ships and returned home.

101. Soon after the fall of Delium, which took place seventeen days after the battle, the Athenian herald, without knowing what had happened, came again for the dead, which were now restored by the Bœotians, who no longer answered as at first.* Not quite five hundred Bœotians fell in the battle, and nearly one thousand Athenians, including Hippocrates the general, besides a great number of light troops and camp followers.

Soon after this battle Demosthenes, after the failure of his voyage to Siphæ and of the plot on the town, availed himself of the Acarnanian and Agræan troops and of the four hundred Athenian heavy infantry which he had on board, to make a descent on the Sicyonian coast. Before however all his ships had come to shore, the Sicyonians came up and routed and chased to their ships those that had landed, killing some and taking others prisoners; after which they set up a trophy, and gave back the dead under truce.

About the same time with the affair of Delium took place the death of Sitalces, king of the Odrysians, who was defeated in battle, in a campaign against the Triballi; Seuthes, son of Sparadocus, his nephew, succeeding to the kingdom of the Odrysians, and of the rest of Thrace ruled by Sitalces.

102. The same winter Brasidas, with his allies in the Thracian places, marched against Amphipolis, the Athenian colony on the river Strymon. A settlement upon the spot on which the city now stands was before attempted by Aristagoras, the Milesian (when he fled

---

*The Boeotian engineers capture and chase out the Athenian garrison at Delium. The Athenians again request their dead and receive them now, because they have abandoned the sacred precinct.

from king Darius), who was however dislodged by the Edonians;*
and thirty-two years later by the Athenians, who sent thither ten
thousand settlers of their own citizens, and whoever else chose to go.
These were cut off at Drabescus by the Thracians. Twenty-nine years
after, the Athenians returned (Hagnon, son of Nicias, being sent out
as leader of the colony) and drove out the Edonians, and founded a
town on the spot, formerly called Ennea-hodoi or Nine Ways.† The
base from which they started was Eion, their commercial seaport at
the mouth of the river, not more than three miles from the present
town, which Hagnon named Amphipolis, because the Strymon flows
round it on two sides, and he built it so as to be conspicuous from the
sea and land alike, running a long wall across from river to river, to
complete the circumference.

103. Brasidas now marched against this town, starting from Arne in
Chalcidice. Arriving about dusk at Aulon and Bromiscus, where the
lake of Bolbe runs into the sea, he supped there, and went on during
the night. The weather was stormy and it was snowing a little, which encouraged him to hurry on, in order, if possible, to take every one at Amphipolis by surprise, except the party who were to betray it. The plot
was carried on by some natives of Argilus, an Andrian colony, residing
in Amphipolis, where they had also other accomplices gained over by
Perdiccas or the Chalcidians. But the most active in the matter were the
inhabitants of Argilus itself, which is close by, who had always been suspected by the Athenians, and had had designs on the place. These men
now saw their opportunity arrive with Brasidas, and having for some
time been in correspondence with their countrymen in Amphipolis for
the betrayal of the town, at once received him into Argilus, and revolted from the Athenians, and that same night took him on to the
bridge over the river; where he found only a small guard to oppose him,
the town being at some distance from the passage, and the walls not
reaching down to it as at present. This guard he easily drove in, partly
through there being treason in their ranks, partly from the stormy state
of the weather and the suddenness of his attack, and so got across the
bridge, and immediately became master of all the property outside; the
Amphipolitans having houses all over the quarter.

---

*Thucydides often connects his narrative to that of his great, if unnamed, predecessor,
Herodotus. Aristagoras, a tyrant and adventurer, had tried to escape Persian control by
settling in European Thrace (in 499; Herodotus 5.11 and 124–126). Amphipolis was a
strategic location, combining north–south and east–west access to the riches of Thrace
and the interior. The Strymon River (map 7) provided some protection against Macedonian attacks on Athenian dependencies from the west.

†In 465, the Athenians settled a colony in the same place, but it soon came to disaster,
and for the third time in 437/436, Hagnon settled it with Athenians and other Greeks.
He was the official founder and fortifier.

104. The passage of Brasidas was a complete surprise to the people in the town; and the capture of many of those outside, and the flight of the rest within the wall, combined to produce great confusion among the citizens; especially as they did not trust one another. It is even said that if Brasidas, instead of stopping to pillage, had advanced straight against the town, he would probably have taken it. In fact, however, he established himself where he was and overran the country outside, and for the present remained inactive, vainly awaiting a demonstration on the part of his friends within.* Meanwhile the party opposed to the traitors proved numerous enough to prevent the gates being immediately thrown open, and in concert with Eucles, the general, who had come from Athens to defend the place, sent to the other commander in Thrace, Thucydides, son of Olorus,† the author of this history, who was at the isle of Thasos, a Parian colony, half a day's sail from Amphipolis, to tell him to come to their relief. On receipt of this message he at once set sail with seven ships which he had with him, in order, if possible, to reach Amphipolis in time to prevent its capitulation, or in any case to save Eion.

105. Meanwhile Brasidas, afraid of succours arriving by sea from Thasos, and learning that Thucydides possessed the right of working the gold mines in that part of Thrace, and had thus great influence with the inhabitants of the continent,‡ hastened to gain the town, if possible, before the people of Amphipolis should be encouraged by his arrival to hope that he could save them by getting together a force of allies from the sea and from Thrace, and so refuse to surrender. He accordingly offered moderate terms, proclaiming that any of the Amphipolitans and Athenians who chose, might continue to enjoy their property with full rights of citizenship; while those who did not wish to stay had five days to depart, taking their property with them.

---

*Brasidas' usual celerity confounded the Athenian defenders of Amphipolis. There is no reason to doubt this fact, although it also helps to clear Thucydides, commander of a very small fleet of seven ships nearby, from the charge of failure to relieve the town in a timely fashion. He does not explain why he was anchored at Thasos, about 50 miles away, but Brasidas, here as before and after, surprised everyone with his sudden arrivals.

†Thucydides speaks of himself in the third person and does not directly exculpate himself. But his giving Eucles responsibility for Amphipolis' defense and his ascribing fear of himself to Brasidas certainly color him favorably—as does his subsequent success in saving Eion on the coast. Did Thucydides in exile get to interview the Spartan responsible for his twenty-year exile?

‡Thucydides reports very little about himself, but here he divulges that he was a mine-owner in this region, and that his local connections were responsible for his assignment to a military command here. Only later does he describe the penalty of exile that he suffered for his failure to save Amphipolis (5.26).

106. The bulk of the inhabitants, upon hearing this, began to change their minds, especially as only a small number of the citizens were Athenians, the majority having come from different quarters, and many of the prisoners outside had relations within the walls. They found the proclamation a fair one in comparison of what their fear had suggested; the Athenians being glad to go out, as they thought they ran more risk than the rest, and further, did not expect any speedy relief, and the multitude generally being content at being left in possession of their civic rights, and at such an unexpected reprieve from danger. The partisans of Brasidas now openly advocated this course, seeing that the feeling of the people had changed, and that they no longer gave ear to the Athenian general present; and thus the surrender was made and Brasidas was admitted by them on the terms of his proclamation. In this way they gave up the city, and late in the same day Thucydides and his ships entered the harbour of Eion, Brasidas having just got hold of Amphipolis, and having been within a night of taking Eion: had the ships been less prompt in relieving it, in the morning it would have been his.*

107. After this Thucydides put all in order at Eion to secure it against any present or future attack of Brasidas, and received such as had elected to come there from the interior according to the terms agreed on. Meanwhile Brasidas suddenly sailed with a number of boats down the river to Eion to see if he could not seize the point running out from the wall, and so command the entrance; at the same time he attempted it by land, but was beaten off on both sides and had to content himself with arranging matters at Amphipolis and in the neighbourhood. Myrcinus, an Edonian town, also came over to him; the Edonian king Pittacus having been killed by the sons of Goaxis and his own wife Brauro; and Galepsus and Œsime, which are Thasian colonies, not long after followed its example. Perdiccas too came up immediately after the capture and joined in these arrangements.

108. The news that Amphipolis was in the hands of the enemy caused great alarm at Athens. Not only was the town valuable for the timber it afforded for shipbuilding, and the money that it brought in;† but also, although the escort of the Thessalians gave the Lacedæmo-

---

*Brasidas succeeded in capturing Amphipolis by remarkable military and diplomatic skills, but Thucydides claims that he himself saved Eion by his own alacrity and subsequent arrangements, arriving on the same day that he heard the news about Brasidas' success, fortifying the port, and protecting the exiles who had come from Amphipolis.

†Amphipolis was the source or shipping point for the long timbers needed to build the large Athenian fleets. In addition, it provided revenues, probably drawn largely from the nearby mines. It does not appear in the meticulously recorded tribute lists because it is an Athenian colony, not a subject-ally.

nians a means of reaching the allies of Athens as far as the Strymon, yet as long as they were not masters of the bridge but were watched on the side of Eion by the Athenian triremes, and on the land side impeded by a large and extensive lake formed by the waters of the river, it was impossible for them to go any further. Now, on the contrary, the path seemed open. There was also the fear of the allies revolting, owing to the moderation displayed by Brasidas in all his conduct, and to the declarations which he was everywhere making that he was sent out to free Hellas. The towns subject to the Athenians, hearing of the capture of Amphipolis and of the terms accorded to it, and of the gentleness of Brasidas,* felt most strongly encouraged to change their condition, and sent secret messages to him, begging him to come on to them; each wishing to be the first to revolt.

Indeed there seemed to be no danger in so doing; their mistake in their estimate of the Athenian power was as great as that power afterwards turned out to be, and their judgment was based more upon blind wishing than upon any sound prevision; for it is a habit of mankind to entrust to careless hope what they long for, and to use sovereign reason to thrust aside what they do not fancy.† Besides the late severe blow which the Athenians had met with in Bœotia, joined to the seductive, though untrue, statements of Brasidas, about the Athenians not having ventured to engage his single army at Nisæa, made the allies confident, and caused them to believe that no Athenian force would be sent against them.‡ Above all the wish to do what was agreeable at the moment, and the likelihood that they should find the Lacedæmonians full of zeal at starting, made them eager to venture. Observing this, the Athenians sent garrisons to the different towns, as far as was possible at such short notice and in winter; while Brasidas sent despatches to Lacedæmon asking for reinforcements, and himself made preparations for building triremes in the Strymon. The Lacedæmonians however did not send him any, partly through envy on the part of their chief men, partly because they were more bent on recovering the prisoners of the island and ending the war.§

---

*As the Spartans feared revolt by the helots, so Athenians feared revolts by the subject-cities. Brasidas' claims and his proven record for mild and moderate behavior promoted rebellion and fears of further ones by Athenian dependencies.

†While the Athenians bear the brunt of Thucydides' scorn for letting dreams trump reason in national decision-making, here their present and former allies are the parties guilty of such self-delusion.

‡Athenian defeat in Boeotia and Thrace encouraged allied states' hopes of liberation; Brasidas misrepresented his former achievements as well.

§The Spartans did not universally admire what he had achieved, perhaps from envy, but also not all of them agreed with his strategy of bringing the Athenians to the peace-table by attacking their sources of income. We hear once again of the prisoners in Athens.

109. The same winter the Megarians took and razed to the foundations the long walls which had been occupied by the Athenians; and Brasidas after the capture of Amphipolis marched with his allies against Acte, a promontory running out from the king's dike with an inward curve, and ending in Athos, a lofty mountain looking towards the Ægean sea. In it are various towns, Sane, an Andrian colony, close to the canal, and facing the sea in the direction of Eubœa; the others being Thyssus, Cleone, Acrothoi, Olophyxus, and Dium, inhabited by mixed barbarian races speaking the two languages. There is also a small Chalcidian element; but the greater number are Tyrrheno-Pelasgians once settled in Lemnos and Athens, and Bisaltians, Crestonians, and Edonians; the towns being all small ones. Most of these came over to Brasidas; but Sane and Dium held out and saw their land ravaged by him and his army.

110. Upon their not submitting, he at once marched against Torone in Chalcidice, which was held by an Athenian garrison, having been invited by a few persons who were prepared to hand over the town. Arriving in the dark a little before daybreak, he sat down with his army near the temple of the Dioscuri, rather more than a quarter of a mile from the city. The rest of the town of Torone and the Athenians in garrison did not perceive his approach; but his partisans knowing that he was coming (a few of them had secretly gone out to meet him), were on the watch for his arrival, and were no sooner aware of it than they took in to them seven light-armed men with daggers, who alone of twenty men ordered on this service dared to enter, commanded by Lysistratus an Olynthian. These passed through the sea wall, and without being seen went up and put to the sword the garrison of the highest post in the town, which stands on a hill, and broke open the postern on the side of Canastræum.

111. Brasidas meanwhile came a little nearer and then halted with his main body, sending on one hundred targeteers to be ready to rush in first, the moment that a gate should be thrown open and the beacon lighted as agreed. After some time passed in waiting and wondering at the delay, the targeteers by degrees got up close to the town. The Toronæans inside at work with the party that had entered, had by this time broken down the postern and opened the gates leading to the market-place by cutting through the bar, and first brought some men round and let them in by the postern, in order to strike a panic into the surprised townsmen by suddenly attacking them from behind and on both sides at once; after which they raised the fire-signal as had been agreed, and took in by the market gates the rest of the targeteers.

112. Brasidas seeing the signal told the troops to rise, and dashed forward amid the loud hurrahs of his men, which carried dismay among the astonished townspeople. Some burst in straight by the

gate, others over some square pieces of timber placed against the wall
(which had fallen down and was being rebuilt) to draw up stones;
Brasidas and the greater number making straight uphill for the higher
part of the town, in order to take it from top to bottom, and once for
all, while the rest of the multitude spread in all directions.

113. The capture of the town was effected before the great body of
the Toronæans had recovered from their surprise and confusion; but
the conspirators and the citizens of their party at once joined the invaders. About fifty of the Athenian heavy infantry happened to be
sleeping in the market-place when the alarm reached them. A few of
these were killed fighting; the rest escaped, some by land, others to
the two ships on the station, and took refuge in Lecythus, a fort garrisoned by their own men in the corner of the town running out into
the sea and cut off by a narrow isthmus; where they were joined by
the Toronæans of their party.

114. Day now arrived, and the town being secured, Brasidas made
a proclamation to the Toronæans who had taken refuge with the
Athenians, to come out, as many as chose, to their homes without
fearing for their rights or persons, and sent a herald to invite the
Athenians to accept a truce, and to evacuate Lecythus with their
property, as being Chalcidian ground. The Athenians refused this
offer, but asked for a truce for a day to take up their dead. Brasidas
granted it for two days, which he employed in fortifying the houses
near, and the Athenians in doing the same to their positions. Meanwhile he called a meeting of the Toronæans, and said very much what
he had said at Acanthus,* namely, that they must not look upon those
who had negotiated with him for the capture of the town as bad men
or as traitors, as they had not acted as they had done from corrupt
motives or in order to enslave the city, but for the good and freedom
of Torone; nor again must those who had not shared in the enterprise
fancy that they would not equally reap its fruits, as he had not come
to destroy either city or individual. This was the reason of his proclamation to those that had fled for refuge to the Athenians: he thought
none the worse of them for their friendship for the Athenians; he believed that they had only to make trial of the Lacedæmonians to like
them as well, or even much better, as acting much more justly: it was
for want of such a trial that they were now afraid of them. Meanwhile
he exhorted all of them to prepare to be staunch allies, and for being
held responsible for all faults in future: for the past, they had not
wronged the Lacedæmonians but had been wronged by others who

---

*Thucydides presents Brasidas' "stump speech," why the Toronaeans (at the end of the
middle finger of the Chalcidic peninsula; map 7) should do what the Acanthians already had done. His last remarks, reported indirectly, contain velvet-gloved warnings
and threats.

were too strong for them, and any opposition that they might have offered him could be excused.

115. Having encouraged them with this address, as soon as the truce expired he made his attack upon Lecythus; the Athenians defending themselves from a poor wall and from some houses with parapets. One day they beat him off; the next the enemy were preparing to bring up an engine against them from which they meant to throw fire upon the wooden defences, and the troops were already coming up to the point where they fancied they could best bring up the engine, and where the place was most assailable; meanwhile the Athenians put a wooden tower upon a house opposite, and carried up a quantity of jars and casks of water and big stones, and a large number of men also climbed up. The house thus laden too heavily suddenly broke down with a loud crash; at which the men who were near and saw it were more vexed than frightened; but those not so near, and still more those furthest off thought that the place was already taken at that point, and fled in haste to the sea and the ships.*

116. Brasidas, perceiving that they were deserting the parapet, and seeing what was going on, dashed forward with his troops, and immediately took the fort, and put to the sword all whom he found in it. In this way the place was evacuated by the Athenians, who went across in their boats and ships to Pallene. Now there is a temple of Athene in Lecythus, and Brasidas had proclaimed in the moment of making the assault, that he would give thirty silver minæ to the man first on the wall.† Being now of opinion that the capture was scarcely due to human means, he gave the thirty minæ to the goddess for her temple, and razed and cleared Lecythus, and made the whole of it consecrated ground. The rest of the winter he spent in settling the places in his hands, and in making designs upon the rest; and with the expiration of the winter the eighth year of this war ended.‡

117. In the spring of the summer following, the Lacedæmonians and Athenians made an armistice for a year; the Athenians thinking that they would thus have full leisure to take their precautions before Brasidas could procure the revolt of any more of their towns, and might also, if it suited them, conclude a general peace; the Lacedæ-

---

*Lecythus is a peninsular extension of Torone, more easily defensible. The collapsing house does very little damage to those on it but determines defeat for the Athenians, when Brasidas descries their misperception that the enemy had breached the town's wall.

†Thirty minae would salary a man for ten years; the huge amount promised may justify for the historian his rare mention of such *aristeai* (prizes) for military valor.

‡Brasidas, like the Athenians, is always plotting his next advance. The years of the war naturally receive different lengths of treatment depending on how much had happened. He treats this eighth year in but seventeen chapters. The year 423 now begins.

monians divining the actual fears of the Athenians, and thinking that after once tasting a respite from trouble and misery they would be more disposed to consent to a reconciliation, and to give back the prisoners, and make a treaty for the longer period. The great idea of the Lacedæmonians was to get back their men while Brasidas' good fortune lasted: further successes might make the struggle a less unequal one in Chalcidice, but would leave them still deprived of their men, and even in Chalcidice not more than a match for the Athenians and by no means certain of victory. An armistice was accordingly concluded by Lacedæmon and her allies upon the terms following:—*

118. 1. *As to the temple and oracle of the Pythian Apollo, we are agreed that whosoever will shall have access to it, without fraud or fear, according to the usages of his forefathers. The Lacedæmonians and the allies present agree to this, and promise to send heralds to the Bœotians and Phocians, and to do their best to persuade them to agree likewise.*

2. *As to the treasure of the god, we agree to exert ourselves to detect all wrongdoers, truly and honestly following the customs of our forefathers, we and you and all others willing to do so, all following the customs of our forefathers. As to these points the Lacedæmonians and the other allies are agreed as has been said.*

3. *As to what follows, the Lacedæmonians and the other allies agree, if the Athenians conclude a treaty, to remain, each of us in our own territory, retaining our respective acquisitions;† the garrison in Coryphasium keeping within Buphras and Tomeus; that in Cythera attempting no communication with the Peloponnesian confederacy, neither we with them, nor they with us; that in Nisæa and Minoa not crossing the road leading from the gates of the temple of Nisus to that of Poseidon and from thence straight to the bridge at Minoa; the Megarians and the allies being equally bound not to cross this road, and the Athenians retaining the island they have taken, without any communication on either side; as to Trœzen, each side retaining what it has, and as was arranged with the Athenians.*

4. *As to the use of the sea, so far as refers to their own coast and to that of their confederacy, that the Lacedæmonians and their allies may voyage upon it in any vessel rowed by oars and of not more than five hundred talents tonnage, not a vessel of war.*

5. *That all heralds and embassies, with as many attendants as they please, for concluding the war and adjusting claims, shall have free*

---

*Four documents describe the armistice of 423/422, three from the Peloponnesian side. The first concerns a Spartan-Peloponnesian agreement about Delphic matters (compare Fornara #38, a Spartan dedication at Olympia). Ancient historians very rarely included verbatim treaties, laws, or other documents in their texts.

†The principle of *uti possidetis* ("you keep what you possess" at the time of the agreement) is to be observed, according to the second document.

passage, going and coming, to Peloponnese or Athens by land and by sea.

6. *That during the truce, deserters, whether bond or free shall be received neither by you, nor by us.*

7. *Further, that satisfaction shall be given by you to us and by us to you according to the public law of our several countries, all disputes being settled by law without recourse to hostilities.*

The Lacedæmonians and allies agree to these articles: but if you have anything fairer or juster to suggest, come to Lacedæmon and let us know; whatever shall be just will meet with no objection either from the Lacedæmonians or from the allies. Only let those who come come with full powers, as you desire us. The truce shall be for one year.

Approved by the people.

The tribe of Acamantis had the prytany, Phœnippus was secretary, Niciades chairman. Laches moved, in the name of the good luck of the Athenians, that they should conclude the armistice upon the terms agreed upon by the Lacedæmonians and the allies. It was agreed accordingly in the popular assembly, that the armistice should be for one year, beginning that very day, the fourteenth of the month of Elaphebolion;* during which time ambassadors and heralds should go and come between the two countries to discuss the bases of a pacification. That the generals and prytanes should call an assembly of the people, in which the Athenians should first consult on the peace, and on the mode in which the embassy for putting an end to the war should be admitted. That the embassy now present should at once take the engagement before the people to keep well and truly this truce for one year.

119. On these terms the Lacedæmonians concluded with the Athenians and their allies on the twelfth day of the Spartan month Gerastius;† the allies also taking the oaths. Those who concluded and poured the libation were Taurus, son of Echetimides, Athenæus, son of Pericleidas, and Philocharidas, son of Eryxidaidas, Lacedæmonians; Æneas, son of Ocytus, and Euphamidas, son of Aristonymus, Corinthians; Damotimus, son of Naucrates, and Onasimus, son of Megacles, Sicyonians; Nicasus, son of Cecalus, and Menecrates, son of Amphidorus, Megarians; and Amphias, son of Eupaidas, an Epidaurian; and the Athenian generals Nicostratus, son of Diitrephes, Nicias, son of Niceratus, and Autocles, son of Tolmæus. Such was the

---

*The third document records an Athenian decree of March 423 accepting the terms proposed and adding some others.

†The fourth document, indirectly reported, records the Spartan and Peloponnesian ratification of the revised terms. They envisioned the drafting of a more general peace treaty in the immediate future.

armistice, and during the whole of it conferences went on on the subject of a pacification.

120. In the days in which they were going backwards and forwards to these conferences, Scione, a town in Pallene, revolted from Athens, and went over to Brasidas.* The Scionæans say that they are Pallenians from Peloponnese, and that their first founders on their voyage from Troy were carried in to this spot by the storm which the Achæans were caught in, and there settled. The Scionæans had no sooner revolted than Brasidas crossed over by night to Scione, with a friendly trireme ahead and himself in a small boat some way behind; his idea being that if he fell in with a vessel larger than the boat he would have the trireme to defend him, while a ship that was a match for the trireme, would probably neglect the small vessel to attack the large one, and thus leave him time to escape. His passage effected, he called a meeting of the Scionæans and spoke to the same effect as at Acanthus and Torone,† adding that they merited the utmost commendation, in that, in spite of Pallene within the isthmus being cut off by the Athenian occupation of Potidæa and of their own practically insular position, they had of their own free will gone forward to meet their liberty instead of timorously waiting until they had been by force compelled to their own manifest good. This was a sign that they would valiantly undergo any trial, however great; and if he should order affairs as he intended, he should count them among the truest and sincerest friends of the Lacedæmonians, and would in every other way honour them.‡

121. The Scionæans were elated by his language, and even those who had at first disapproved of what was being done catching the general confidence, they determined on a vigorous conduct of the war, and welcomed Brasidas with all possible honours, publicly crowning him with a crown of gold as the liberator of Hellas; while private persons crowded round him and decked him with garlands as though he had been an athlete.§ Meanwhile Brasidas left them a small garrison for the present and crossed back again, and not long after-

---

*Scione's revolt violated the *uti possidetis* diplomatic principle (see note on p. 280). Brasidas certainly did not discourage this action of a city on the southwestern corner of the westernmost peninsula of the Chalcidice (map 7). The rebellion clearly violated the treaty.

†Thucydides refers to former speeches but provides a few new twists. Potidaea's allegiance was one of the original causes of the war.

‡The original audience would understand the flattery and appreciate the irony. In 5.32, we hear summarily of the Athenian capture of Scione, the killing of all the adult males in retaliation for the revolt, the enslavement of the rest, and the gift of the land to the homeless Plataean allies. The Spartans eventually had abandoned the town in accordance with the treaty.

§Brasidas has his moments of joy; the comparison to a sportsman is notable. Later there will be religious honors for "the liberator of Hellas."

wards sent over a larger force, intending with the help of the Scionæans to attempt Mende and Potidæa before the Athenians should arrive; Scione, he felt, being too like an island for them not to relieve it. He had besides intelligence in the above towns about their betrayal.

122. In the midst of his designs upon the towns in question, a trireme arrived with the commissioners carrying round the news of the armistice, Aristonymus for the Athenians and Athenæus for the Lacedæmonians. The troops now crossed back to Torone, and the commissioners gave Brasidas notice of the convention. All the Lacedæmonian allies in Thrace accepted what had been done; and Aristonymus made no difficulty about the rest, but finding, on counting the days, that the Scionæans had revolted after the date of the convention, refused to include them in it.* To this Brasidas earnestly objected, asserting that the revolt took place before, and would not give up the town. Upon Aristonymus reporting the case to Athens, the people at once prepared to send an expedition to Scione. Upon this, envoys arrived from Lacedæmon, alleging that this would be a breach of the truce, and laying claim to the town upon the faith of the assertion of Brasidas, and meanwhile offering to submit the question to arbitration. Arbitration, however, was what the Athenians did not choose to risk; being determined to send troops at once to the place, and furious at the idea of even the islanders now daring to revolt, in a vain reliance upon the power of the Lacedæmonians by land. Besides the facts of the revolt were rather as the Athenians contended, the Scionæans having revolted two days after the convention.† Cleon accordingly succeeded in carrying a decree to reduce and put to death the Scionæans; and the Athenians employed the leisure which they now enjoyed in preparing for the expedition.

123. Meanwhile Mende revolted, a town in Pallene and a colony of the Eretrians, and was received without scruple by Brasidas, in spite of its having patently come over during the armistice, on account of certain infringements of the truce alleged by him against the Athenians. This audacity of Mende was partly caused by seeing Brasidas forward in the matter and by the conclusions drawn from his refusal to betray Scione; and besides, the conspirators in Mende were few, and had carried on their practices too long not to fear detection for themselves, and not to wish to force the inclination of the multitude.‡ This news

---

*Scione unfortunately, in a time of slow communications, had revolted in ignorance that the parties already had signed an armistice.

†Thucydides rarely offers alternative versions of events, but here the difference was itself a cause of continuing disagreement (see 2.5 and 8.87 for two others). Brasidas was simply wrong on his dates or comfortably misrepresenting them for Spartan advantage.

‡The Mendaeans were patently in the wrong in expecting support for their revolt. Brasidas' quibbling did them no good, although he did make a good-faith effort to preserve the women and children and defend the cities.

made the Athenians more furious than ever, and they at once prepared against both towns. Brasidas expecting their arrival conveyed
away to Olynthus in Chalcidice the women and children of the
Scionæans and Mendæans, and sent over to them five hundred Peloponnesian heavy infantry and three hundred Chalcidian targeteers,
all under the command of Polydamidas.

124. Leaving these two towns to prepare together against the
speedy arrival of the Athenians, Brasidas and Perdiccas started on a
second joint expedition into Lyncus against Arrhabæus; the latter
with the forces of his Macedonian subjects, and a corps of heavy infantry composed of Hellenes domiciled in the country; the former
with the Peloponnesians whom he still had with him and the Chalcidians, Acanthians, and the rest in such force as they were able. In all
there were about three thousand Hellenic heavy infantry, accompanied by all the Macedonian cavalry with the Chalcidians, near one
thousand strong, besides an immense crowd of barbarians. On entering the country of Arrhabæus, they found the Lyncestians encamped
awaiting them, and themselves took up a position opposite. The infantry on either side were upon a hill, with a plain between them, into
which the horse of both armies first galloped down, and engaged a
cavalry action.

After this the Lyncestian heavy infantry advanced from their hill
to join their cavalry and offered battle; upon which Brasidas and
Perdiccas also came down to meet them, and engaged and routed
them with heavy loss; the survivors taking refuge upon the heights
and there remaining inactive. The victors now set up a trophy and
waited two or three days for the Illyrian mercenaries who were to
join Perdiccas. Perdiccas then wished to go on and attack the villages
of Arrhabæus, and to sit still no longer; but Brasidas, afraid that the
Athenians might sail up during his absence, and of something happening to Mende, and seeing besides that the Illyrians did not appear,
far from seconding this wish was anxious to return.

125. While they were thus disputing, the news arrived that the Illyrians had actually betrayed Perdiccas and had joined Arrhabæus;
and the fear inspired by their warlike character made both parties
now think it best to retreat.* However, owing to the dispute, nothing
had been settled as to when they should start; and night coming on,
the Macedonians and the barbarian crowd took fright in a moment in
one of those mysterious panics to which great armies are liable; and
persuaded that an army many times more numerous than that which
had really arrived was advancing and all but upon them, suddenly

---

*Perdiccas proved more trouble than he was worth as anyone's ally. The Macedonian
kingdom eventually absorbed the Illyrians, to their west.

broke and fled in the direction of home, and thus compelled Perdiccas, who at first did not perceive what had occurred, to depart without seeing Brasidas, the two armies being encamped at a considerable distance from each other.

At daybreak Brasidas, perceiving that the Macedonians had gone on, and that the Illyrians and Arrhabæus were on the point of attacking him, formed his heavy infantry into a square, with the light troops in the centre, and himself also prepared to retreat. Posting his youngest soldiers to dash out wherever the enemy should attack them, he himself with three hundred picked men in the rear intended to face about during the retreat and beat off the most forward of their assailants. Meanwhile, before the enemy approached, he sought to sustain the courage of his soldiers with the following hasty exhortation:—

126. 'Peloponnesians, if I did not suspect you of being dismayed at being left alone to sustain the attack of a numerous and barbarian enemy, I should just have said a few words to you as usual without further explanation. As it is, in the face of the desertion of our friends and the numbers of the enemy, I have some advice and information to offer, which, brief as they must be, will, I hope, suffice for the more important points. The bravery that you habitually display in war does not depend on your having allies at your side in this or that encounter, but on your native courage; nor have numbers any terrors for citizens of states like yours, in which the many do not rule the few, but rather the few the many, owing their position to nothing else than to superiority in the field. Inexperience now makes you afraid of barbarians; and yet the trial of strength which you had with the Macedonians among them, and my own judgment, confirmed by what I hear from others, should be enough to satisfy you that they will not prove formidable. Where an enemy seems strong but is really weak, a true knowledge of the facts makes his adversary the bolder, just as a serious antagonist is encountered most confidently by those who do not know him. Thus the present enemy might terrify an inexperienced imagination, they are formidable in outward bulk, their loud yelling is unbearable, and the brandishing of their weapons in the air has a threatening appearance.

'But when it comes to real fighting with an opponent who stands his ground, they are not what they seemed; they have no regular order that they should be ashamed of deserting their positions when hard pressed; flight and attack are with them equally honourable, and afford no test of courage; their independent mode of fighting never leaving any one who wants to run away without a fair excuse for so doing. In short, they think frightening you at a secure distance a surer game than meeting you hand to hand; otherwise they would have done the one and not the other. You can thus plainly see that the terrors with which they were at first invested are in fact trifling enough, though to the eye and ear very prominent. Stand your ground therefore when they advance, and again wait your opportunity to retire in good order, and you will reach a place of safety all the sooner, and will know for ever afterwards that rabble such as these, to those who sustain their first attack, do but show off their courage by threats of the terrible things that they are going to do, at a distance, but with those who give way to them are quick enough to display their heroism in pursuit when they can do so without danger.'

127. With this brief address Brasidas began to lead off his army. Seeing this, the barbarians came on with much shouting and hubbub, thinking that he was flying and that they would overtake him and cut him off. But wherever they charged they found the young men ready to dash out against them, while Brasidas with his picked company* sustained their onset. Thus the Peloponnesians withstood the first attack, to the surprise of the enemy, and afterwards received and repulsed them as fast as they came on, retiring as soon as their opponents became quiet. The main body of the barbarians ceased therefore to molest the Hellenes with Brasidas in the open country, and leaving behind a certain number to harass their march, the rest went on after the flying Macedonians, slaying those with whom they came up, and so arrived in time to occupy the narrow pass between two hills that leads into the country of Arrhabæus. They knew that this was the only way by which Brasidas could retreat, and now proceeded to surround him just as he entered the most impracticable part of the road, in order to cut him off.

128. Brasidas, perceiving their intention, told his three hundred to run on without order, each as quickly as he could, to the hill which seemed easiest to take, and to try to dislodge the barbarians already there, before they should be joined by the main body closing round him.† These attacked and overpowered the party upon the hill, and the main army of the Hellenes now advanced with less difficulty towards it; the barbarians being terrified at seeing their men on that side driven from the height, and no longer following the main body, who, they considered, had gained the frontier and made good their escape. The heights once gained, Brasidas now proceeded more securely, and the same day arrived at Arnisa, the first town in the dominions of Perdiccas. The soldiers, enraged at the desertion of the

---

*Brasidas had apparently studied the sloppy barbarian tactics. His younger men were his lightning squadron, and his battle-hardened 300 older troops defended the rear of the retreating units against other attackers.

†Brasidas dispatches the best soldiers in haste but in no formation to seize a hill supplied with few barbarian defenders. After this tactic, his retreat to friendly territory is not difficult.

Macedonians, vented their rage on all their yokes of oxen which they found on the road, and on any baggage which had tumbled off (as might easily happen in the panic of a night retreat), by unyoking and cutting down the cattle and taking the baggage for themselves. From this moment Perdiccas began to regard Brasidas as an enemy and to feel against the Peloponnesians a hatred which could not be congenial to the adversary of the Athenians. However, he departed from his natural interests and made it his endeavour to come to terms with the latter and to get rid of the former.

129. On his return from Macedonia to Torone, Brasidas found the Athenians already masters of Mende, and remained quiet where he was, thinking it now out of his power to cross over into Pallene and assist the Mendæans, but he kept good watch over Torone. For about the same time as the campaign in Lyncus, the Athenians sailed upon the expedition which they were preparing against Mende and Scione, with fifty ships, ten of which were Chians, one thousand Athenian heavy infantry and six hundred archers, one hundred Thracian mercenaries and some targeteers drawn from their allies in the neighbourhood, under the command of Nicias, son of Niceratus, and Nicostratus, son of Diitrephes. Weighing from Potidæa, the fleet came to land opposite the temple of Poseidon, and proceeded against Mende; the men of which town, reinforced by three hundred Scionæans, with their Peloponnesian auxiliaries, seven hundred heavy infantry in all, under Polydamidas, they found encamped upon a strong hill outside the city.* These Nicias, with one hundred and twenty light-armed Methonæans, sixty picked men from the Athenian heavy infantry, and all the archers, tried to reach by a path running up the hill, but received a wound and found himself unable to force the position; while Nicostratus, with all the rest of the army, advancing upon the hill, which was naturally difficult, by a different approach further off, was thrown into utter disorder; and the whole Athenian army narrowly escaped being defeated. For that day, as the Mendæans and their allies showed no signs of yielding, the Athenians retreated and encamped, and the Mendæans at nightfall returned into the town.

130. The next day the Athenians sailed round to the Scione side and took the suburb, and all day plundered the country, without any one coming out against them, partly because of internal disturbances in the town; and the following night the three hundred Scionæans returned home. On the morrow Nicias advanced with half the army to

---

*During the truce, the Athenians can focus their energies on the recovery of Mende and Scione. They sail from Potidaea on the same Pallene peninsula. Small Mende received Scione's military support as well as 700 Peloponnesian troops with a Spartan commander.

the frontier of Scione and laid waste the country; while Nicostratus with the remainder sat down before the town near the upper gate on the road to Potidæa. The arms of the Mendæans and of their Peloponnesian auxiliaries within the wall happened to be piled in that quarter, where Polydamidas accordingly began to draw them up for battle, encouraging the Mendæans to make a sortie.

At this moment one of the popular party answered him in a partisan manner that they would not go out and did not want a war, and for thus answering was dragged by the arm and knocked about by Polydamidas. Hereupon the infuriated commons at once seized their arms and rushed at the Peloponnesians and at their allies of the opposite faction.* The troops thus assaulted were at once routed, partly from the suddenness of the conflict and partly through fear of the gates being opened to the Athenians, with whom they imagined that the attack had been concerted. As many as were not killed on the spot took refuge in the citadel, which they had held from the first; and the whole Athenian army, Nicias having by this time returned and being close to the city, now burst into Mende, which had opened its gates without any convention, and sacked it just as if they had taken it by storm, the generals even finding some difficulty in restraining them from also massacring the inhabitants.†

After this the Athenians told the Mendæans that they might retain their civil rights, and themselves judge the supposed authors of the revolt; and cut off the party in the citadel by a wall built down to the sea on either side, appointing troops to maintain the blockade. Having thus secured Mende, they proceeded against Scione.

131. The Scionæans and Peloponnesians marched out against them, occupying a strong hill in front of the town, which had to be captured by the enemy before they could invest the place. The Athenians stormed the hill, defeated and dislodged its occupants, and having encamped and set up a trophy, prepared for the work of circumvallation. Not long after they had begun their operations, the auxiliaries besieged in the citadel of Mende forced the guard by the seaside and arrived by night at Scione, into which most of them succeeded in entering, passing through the besieging army.

132. While the investment of Scione was in progress, Perdiccas sent a herald to the Athenian generals and made peace with the Atheni-

---

*The Spartan lieutenant had not the delicate political touch of Brasidas. The anti-war activists spoke up; Polydamidas lost the city with his rude and imperious behavior—Spartans trained their young to deliver barbed insults.

†The victorious army, composed largely of Athenians, was angry with the rebels of Mende (compare 4.122 and 123)—even though it was by the aid of the commons that they retook the city without a siege or even a serious battle. Compare the final situations of Mitylene in Lesbos (3.27 and 47) or tendencies at Chios (8.9 and 24).

ans, through spite against Brasidas for the retreat from Lyncus, from which moment indeed he had begun to negotiate.* The Lacedæmonian Ischagoras was just then upon the point of starting with an army overland to join Brasidas; and Perdiccas, being now required by Nicias to give some proof of the sincerity of his reconciliation to the Athenians, and being himself no longer disposed to let the Peloponnesians into his country, put in motion his friends in Thessaly, with whose chief men he always took care to have relations, and so effectually stopped the army and its preparation that they did not even try the Thessalians. Ischagoras himself, however, with Ameinias and Aristeus, succeeded in reaching Brasidas; they had been commissioned by the Lacedæmonians to inspect the state of affairs, and brought out from Sparta (in violation of all precedent) some of their young men to put in command of the towns, to guard against their being entrusted to the persons upon the spot.† Brasidas accordingly placed Clearidas, son of Cleonymus, in Amphipolis, and Pasitelidas, son of Hegesander, in Torone.

133. The same summer the Thebans dismantled the wall of the Thespians on the charge of Atticism, having always wished to do so, and now finding it an easy matter, as the flower of the Thespian youth had perished in the battle with the Athenians.‡ The same summer also the temple of Hera at Argos was burnt down, through Chrysis, the priestess, placing a lighted torch near the garlands and then falling asleep, so that they all caught fire and were in a blaze before she observed it. Chrysis that very night fled to Phlius for fear of the Argives, who, agreeably to the law in such a case, appointed another priestess named Phæinis. Chrysis at the time of her flight had been priestess for eight years of the present war and half the ninth.§ At the close of the summer the investment of Scione was completed, and the Athenians, leaving a detachment to maintain the blockade, returned with the rest of their army.

134. During the winter following the Athenians and Lacedæmonians were kept quiet by the armistice; but the Mantineans and

---

*Peloponnesian remnants from Mende's citadel reach Scione, nearby to the southeast, but Perdiccas abandons his Peloponnesian and Thracian allies.

†The Spartans, contrary to their usual practice of appointing senior administrators, send young men out as governors. Whether this is intended to provide specially trained administrators (unlike Polydamidas) or shows distrust of Brasidas' own arrangements and choices, it does not look like autonomy (compare 4.86) for these cities.

‡The Thebans reward their allies by dismantling their walls, a sign of deep distrust, indeed a slap in the face.

§The Argive priestess, first mentioned in establishing the date at which the war began (2.2), flees for her life. This shrine of Hera, along with the Samian Heraion, was one of her two main sanctuaries in Greece. The substructure survives.

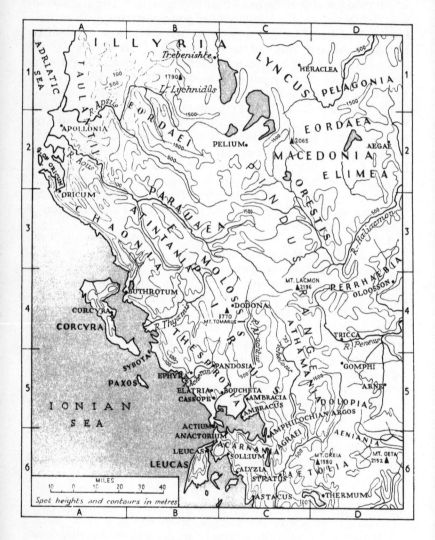

MILES
10   0   10   20   30   40

Spot heights and contours in metres

MAP 8. NORTHWESTERN GREECE

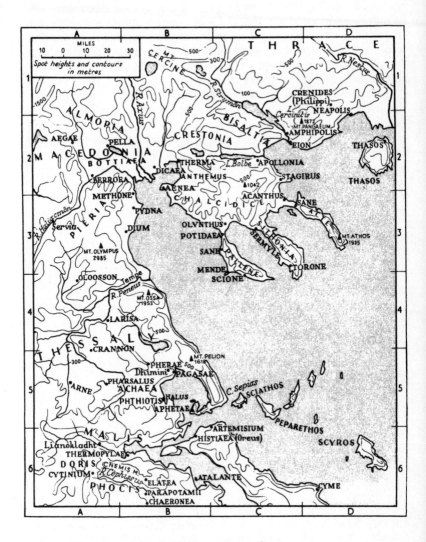

MAP 9. NORTHEASTERN GREECE

Tegeans, and their respective allies, fought a battle at Laodicium, in the Oresthid. The victory remained doubtful, as each side routed one of the wings opposed to them, and both set up trophies and sent spoils to Delphi. After heavy loss on both sides the battle was undecided, and night interrupted the action; yet the Tegeans passed the night on the field and set up a trophy at once, while the Mantineans withdrew to Bucolion and set up theirs afterwards.

135. At the close of the same winter, in fact almost in spring, Brasidas made an attempt upon Potidæa.* He arrived by night, and succeeded in planting a ladder against the wall without being discovered, the ladder being planted just in the interval between the passing round of the bell and the return of the man who brought it back.† Upon the garrison, however, taking the alarm immediately afterwards, before his men came up, he quickly led off his troops, without waiting until it was day. So ended the winter and the ninth year of this war of which Thucydides is the historian.‡

---

*Brasidas continues to ignore the armistice, either because he hopes to improve Sparta's position in negotiation or because he does not want the war to end. He formally claims that the Athenians are already in breach of the agreements (4.123). Potidaea is the most important city on the three Chalcidic promontories.

†The system of the watch intended to keep all the sentries awake and the blood flowing in the cold Thracian night. It left a section of each sentry's wall briefly unguarded.

‡This long book has taken us from the seventh summer to the tenth winter. The next book begins with the end of the first war in 421, a second preface, and the start of the second major phase, the unstable peace that preceded the battle of Mantinea (map 4) and that patchily endured until the Athenians' ill-starred attack on all Sicily (415).

BOOK 5

Tenth Year of the War — Death of Cleon and
Brasidas — Peace of Nicias

1. The next summer the truce for a year ended, after lasting until the Pythian games. During the armistice the Athenians expelled the Delians from Delos, concluding that they must have been polluted by some old offence at the time of their consecration, and that this had been the omission in the previous purification of the island, which, as I have related, had been thought to have been duly accomplished by the removal of the graves of the dead. The Delians had Atramyttium in Asia given them by Pharnaces, and settled there as they removed from Delos.*

2. Meanwhile Cleon prevailed on the Athenians to let him set sail at the expiration of the armistice for the towns in the direction of Thrace† with twelve hundred heavy infantry and three hundred horse from Athens, a larger force of the allies, and thirty ships. First touching at the still besieged Scione, and taking some heavy infantry from the army there, he next sailed into Cophos, a harbour in the territory of Torone, which is not far from the town. From thence, having learnt from deserters that Brasidas was not in Torone, and that its garrison was not strong enough to give him battle, he advanced with his army against the town, sending ten ships to sail round into the harbour. He first came to the fortification lately thrown up in front of the town by Brasidas in order to take in the suburb, to do which he had pulled down part of the original wall and made it all one city.

3. To this point Pasitelidas, the Lacedæmonian commander, with such garrison as there was in the place, hurried to repel the Athenian assault; but finding himself hard pressed, and seeing the ships that

---

*Thucydides begins a new summer for 422. Our manuscripts indicate a new book. There is a summary of important Panhellenic events: games and armistice; reference to the pollution, purification, and (re-)consecration of Panhellenic Delos—with a cross-reference to 3.104 (compare also 1.8). Thucydides notes again the expulsion of a small subject population by the Athenians. Cross-referencing persons or events, common practice in Herodotus, occurs elsewhere in Thucydides' more focused narrative only at 6.94.

†"Towns [the Greek actually reads "territories"] in the direction of Thrace" is an administrative phrase found in official Athenian documents like the Athenian Tribute Lists. These massive inscriptions record the sixtieth of the imperial tax paid to the goddess Athena.

had been sent round sailing into the harbour, Pasitelidas began to be afraid that they might get up to the city before its defenders were there, and the fortification being also carried, he might be taken prisoner, and so abandoned the outwork and ran into the town. But the Athenians from the ships had already taken Torone, and their land forces following at his heels burst in with him with a rush over the part of the old wall that had been pulled down, killing some of the Peloponnesians and Toronæans in the mêlée, and making prisoners of the rest, and Pasitelidas their commander amongst them. Brasidas meanwhile had advanced to relieve Torone, and had only about four miles more to go when he heard of its fall on the road, and turned back again. Cleon and the Athenians set up two trophies, one by the harbour, the other by the fortification, and making slaves of the wives and children of the Toronæans, sent the men with the Peloponnesians and any Chalcidians that were there, to the number of seven hundred, to Athens; whence, however, they all came home afterwards, the Peloponnesians on the conclusion of peace, and the rest of being exchanged against other prisoners with the Olynthians.* About the same time Panactum, a fortress on the Athenian border, was taken by treachery by the Bœotians. Meanwhile Cleon, after placing a garrison in Torone, weighed anchor and sailed round Athos on his way to Amphipolis.

4. About the same time Phæax, son of Erasistratus, set sail with two colleagues as ambassador from Athens to Italy and Sicily. The Leontines, upon the departure of the Athenians from Sicily after the pacification, had placed a number of new citizens upon the roll, and the commons had a design for redividing the land; but the upper classes, aware of their intention, called in the Syracusans and expelled the commons. These last were scattered in various directions; but the upper classes came to an agreement with the Syracusans, abandoned and laid waste their city, and went and lived at Syracuse, where they were made citizens. Afterwards some of them were dissatisfied, and leaving Syracuse occupied Phocææ, a quarter of the town of Leontini, and Bricinniæ, a strong place in the Leontine country, and being there joined by most of the exiled commons carried on war from the fortifications. The Athenians hearing this, sent Phæax to see if they could not by some means so convince their allies there and the rest of the Sicilians of the ambitious designs of Syracuse, as to induce them to form a general coalition against her, and thus save the commons of Leontini. Arrived in Sicily, Phæax succeeded at Camarina and Agri-

---

*Cleon is the major Athenian expansionist imperialist from the death of Pericles (429) through the end of the "first" war (421; 5.20). His slight victory here is undercut by the forward reference to the exchange of troops at the peace.

gentum, but meeting with a repulse at Gela did not go on to the rest, as he saw that he should not succeed with them, but returned through the country of the Sicels to Catana, and after visiting Bricinniæ as he passed, and encouraging its inhabitants, sailed back to Athens.

5. During his voyage along the coast to and from Sicily, he treated with some cities in Italy on the subject of friendship with Athens, and also fell in with some Locrian settlers exiled from Messina, who had been sent thither when the Locrians were called in by one of the factions that divided Messina after the pacification of Sicily, and Messina came for a time into the hands of the Locrians. These being met by Phæax on their return home received no injury at his hands, as the Locrians had agreed with him for a treaty with Athens. They were the only people of the allies who, when the reconciliation between the Sicilians took place, had not made peace with her; nor indeed would they have done so now, if they had not been pressed by a war with the Hipponians and Medmæans who lived on their border, and were colonists of theirs. Phæax meanwhile proceeded on his voyage, and at length arrived at Athens.

6. Cleon, on his voyage from Torone to Amphipolis, made Eion his base, and after an unsuccessful assault upon the Andrian colony of Stagirus, took Galepsus, a colony of Thasos, by storm. He now sent envoys to Perdiccas to command his attendance with an army, as provided by the alliance; and others to Thrace, to Polles, king of the Odomantians, who was to bring as many Thracian mercenaries as possible; and himself remained inactive in Eion, awaiting their arrival. Informed of this, Brasidas on his part took up a position of observation upon Cerdylium, a place situated in the Argilian country on high ground across the river, not far from Amphipolis, and commanding a view on all sides, and thus made it impossible for Cleon's army to move without his seeing it; for he fully expected that Cleon, despising the scanty numbers of his opponent, would march against Amphipolis with the force that he had got with him. At the same time Brasidas made his preparations, calling to his standard fifteen hundred Thracian mercenaries, and all the Edonians, horse and targeteers; he also had a thousand Myrcinian and Chalcidian light-armed troops,* besides those in Amphipolis, and a force of heavy infantry numbering altogether about two thousand, and three hundred Hellenic horse. Fifteen hundred of these he had with him upon Cerdylium; the rest were stationed with Clearidas in Amphipolis.

---

*The Greek word *peltastes* was translated as "targeteers" by Crawley, but I have altered that to "light-armed troops" or "light infantry." It refers to men carrying less offensive and defensive equipment than the hoplites. They served as mobile protectors and advance troops for the highly compact, heavily burdened, hoplite phalanx. The hoplites carried two long spears, a shield, a sword, and metal body armor.

7. After remaining quiet for some time, Cleon was at length obliged to do as Brasidas expected. His soldiers, tired of their inactivity, began also seriously to reflect on the weakness and incompetence of their commander and the skill and valour that would be opposed to him, and on their own original unwillingness to accompany him. These murmurs coming to the ears of Cleon, he resolved not to disgust the army by keeping it in the same place, and broke up his camp and advanced. The temper of the general was what it had been at Pylos, his success on that occasion having given him confidence in his capacity. He never dreamed of any one coming out to fight him, but said that he was rather going up to view the place; and if he waited for his reinforcements it was not in order to make victory secure in case he should be compelled to engage, but to be enabled to surround and storm the city. He accordingly came and posted his army upon a strong hill in front of Amphipolis, and proceeded to examine the lake formed by the Strymon, and how the town lay on the side of Thrace. He thought to retire at pleasure without fighting, as there was no one to be seen upon the wall or coming out of the gates, all of which were shut. Indeed, it seemed a mistake not to have brought down engines with him; he could then have taken the town, there being no one to defend it.

8. As soon as Brasidas saw the Athenians in motion he descended himself from Cerdylium and entered Amphipolis. He did not venture to go out in regular order against the Athenians: he mistrusted his strength, and thought it inadequate to the attempt; not in numbers—these were not so unequal—but in quality, the flower of the Athenian army being in the field, with the best of the Lemnians and Imbrians. He therefore prepared to assail them by stratagem.* By showing the enemy the number of his troops, and the shifts which he had been put to to arm them, he thought that he should have less chance of beating him than by not letting him have a sight of them, and thus learn how good a right he had to despise them. He accordingly picked out a hundred and fifty heavy infantry, and putting the rest under Clearidas determined to attack suddenly before the Athenians retired; thinking that he should not have again such a chance of catching them alone, if their reinforcements were once allowed to come up; and so calling all his soldiers together in order to encourage them and explain his intention, spoke as follows:—

9. 'Peloponnesians, the character of the country from which we have come, one which has always owed its freedom to valour, and the fact that you are Dorians and the enemy you are about to fight Ioni-

---

*Brasidas envisions cautious stratagems (Greek: *techne*, whence our word "technique") while Cleon is over-confident. These two men furnish the principal Spartan hero and Athenian villain of the "first" Ten Years' War.

ans, whom you are accustomed to beat, are things that do not need further comment. But the plan of attack that I propose to pursue, this it is as well to explain, in order that the fact of our adventuring with a part instead of with the whole of our forces may not damp your courage by the apparent disadvantage at which it places you. I imagine it is the poor opinion that he has of us, and the fact that he has no idea of any one coming out to engage him, that has made the enemy march up to the place and carelessly look about him as he is doing, without noticing us. But the most successful soldier will always be the man who most happily detects a blunder like this,* and who carefully consulting his own means makes his attack not so much by open and regular approaches, as by seizing the opportunity of the moment; and these stratagems, which do the greatest service to our friends by most completely deceiving our enemies, have the most brilliant name in war. Therefore, while their careless confidence continues, and they are still thinking, as in my judgment they are now doing, more of retreat than of maintaining their position, while their spirit is slack and not high-strung with expectation, I with the men under my command will, if possible, take them by surprise and fall with a run upon their centre; and do you, Clearidas, afterwards, when you see me already upon them, and, as is likely, dealing terror among them, take with you the Amphipolitans, and the rest of the allies, and suddenly open the gates and dash at them, and hasten to engage as quickly as you can. That is our best chance of establishing a panic among them, as a fresh assailant has always more terrors for an enemy than the one he is immediately engaged with. Show yourself a brave man, as a Spartan should; and do you, allies, follow him like men, and remember that zeal, honour, and obedience mark the good soldier, and that this day will make you either free men and allies of Lacedæmon, or slaves of Athens;† even if you escape without personal loss of liberty or life, your bondage will be on harsher terms than before, and you will also hinder the liberation of the rest of the Hellenes. No cowardice then on your part, seeing the greatness of the issues at stake, and I will show that what I preach to others I can practise myself.'

10. After this brief speech Brasidas himself prepared for the sally, and placed the rest with Clearidas at the Thracian gates to support him as had been agreed. Meanwhile he had been seen coming down from Cerdylium and then in the city, which is overlooked from the outside, sacrificing near the temple of Athene; in short, all his move-

---

*Brasidas' speech provides the analysis in advance for the important battle of Amphipolis (map 9).
†Brasidas' propaganda again exploits the antithesis of free allies of Lacedaemon or slaves of Athens. Just below, he speaks of the liberation of the Hellenes, a goal that he may have endorsed but that the Spartans did not practice when successful.

ments had been observed, and word was brought to Cleon, who had at the moment gone on to look about him, that the whole of the enemy's force could be seen in the town, and that the feet of horses and men in great numbers were visible under the gates, as if a sally were intended. Upon hearing this he went up to look, and having done so, being unwilling to venture upon the decisive step of a battle before his reinforcements came up, and fancying that he would have time to retire, bid the retreat be sounded and sent orders to the men to effect it by moving on the left wing in the direction of Eion, which was indeed the only way practicable. This however not being quick enough for him, he joined the retreat in person and made the right wing wheel round, thus turning its unarmed side to the enemy. It was then that Brasidas seeing the Athenian force in motion and his opportunity come,* said to the men with him and the rest, 'Those fellows will never stand before us, one can see that by the way their spears and heads are going. Troops which do as they do seldom stand a charge. Quick, some one, and open the gates I spoke of, and let us be out and at them with no fears for the result.'

Accordingly issuing out by the palisade gate and by the first in the long wall then existing, he ran at the top of his speed along the straight road, where the trophy now stands as you go by the steepest part of the hill, and fell upon and routed the centre of the Athenians, panic-stricken by their own disorder and astounded at his audacity.†
At the same moment Clearidas in execution of his orders issued out from the Thracian gates to support him, and also attacked the enemy. The result was that the Athenians, suddenly and unexpectedly attacked on both sides, fell into confusion; and their left towards Eion, which had already got on some distance, at once broke and fled. Just as it was in full retreat and Brasidas was passing on to attack the right, he received a wound; but his fall was not perceived by the Athenians, as he was taken up by those near him and carried off the field. The Athenian right made a better stand, and though Cleon, who from the first had no thought of fighting, at once fled and was overtaken and slain by a Myrcinian advance-soldier, his infantry forming in close order upon the hill twice or thrice repulsed the attacks of Clearidas, and did not finally give way until they were surrounded and routed by the missiles of the Myrcinian and Chalcidian horse and the light-armed troops. Thus the Athenian army was all now in flight; and such as escaped being killed in the battle or by the Chalcidian horse and the light-armed troops, dispersed among the hills, and with difficulty

---

*Patient self-restraint, awaiting the opportunity (Greek: *kairos*) is a defining Thucydidean excellence.

†Brasidas' audacious plan has been well thought out; it eschews the foolhardy recklessness that certain commanders show in this text.

made their way to Eion. The men who had taken up and rescued Brasidas, brought him into the town with the breath still in him: he lived to hear of the victory of his troops, and not long after expired. The rest of the army returning with Clearidas from the pursuit stripped the dead and set up a trophy.

11. After this all the allies attended in arms and buried Brasidas at the public expense in the city, in front of what is now the market-place, and the Amphipolitans having enclosed his tomb, ever afterwards sacrifice to him as a hero and have given to him the honour of games and annual offerings.* They constituted him the founder of their colony, and pulled down the Hagnonic buildings and obliterated everything that could be interpreted as a memorial of his having founded the place; for they considered that Brasidas had been their preserver, and courting as they did the alliance of Lacedæmon for fear of Athens, in their present hostile relations with the latter they could no longer with the same advantage or satisfaction pay Hagnon his honours.† They also gave the Athenians back their dead. About six hundred of the latter had fallen and only seven of the enemy, owing to there having been no regular engagement, but the affair of accident and panic that I have described.‡ After taking up their dead the Athenians sailed off home, while Clearidas and his troops remained to arrange matters at Amphipolis.

12. About the same time three Lacedæmonians—Ramphias, Autocharidas, and Epicydidas—led a reinforcement of nine hundred heavy infantry to the towns in the direction of Thrace, and arriving at Heraclea in Trachis reformed matters there as seemed good to them. While they delayed there, this battle took place and so the summer ended.

13. With the beginning of the winter following Ramphias and his companions penetrated as far as Pierium in Thessaly; but as the Thessalians opposed their further advance, and Brasidas whom they came to reinforce was dead, they turned back home, thinking that the moment had gone by, the Athenians being defeated and gone, and themselves not equal to the execution of Brasidas' designs. The main cause however of their return was because they knew that when they set out, Lacedæmonian opinion was really in favour of peace.

14. Indeed it so happened that directly after the battle of Am-

---

*The heroization of a Spartan soldier is unexpected. Thucydides would include it for that reason alone, but he is also interested in religious innovations. The language implies that a long time has passed between the inauguration of 421 and the time of Thucydides' writing.

†Hagnon, the Athenian true founder of the commercial and strategic colonial chokepoint, suffers a Hellenic *damnatio memoriae* (official disappearance from records). The political factors far outweigh any religious significance invested in the heroic honors.

‡600 to 7, the proportion of casualties, quietly endorses Brasidas' plan.

phipolis and the retreat of Ramphias from Thessaly, both sides ceased to prosecute the war and turned their attention to peace. Athens had suffered severely at Delium, and again shortly afterwards at Amphipolis, and had no longer that confidence* in her strength which had made her before refuse to treat, in the belief of ultimate victory which her success at the moment had inspired; besides, she was afraid of her allies being tempted by her reverses to rebel more generally, and repented having let go the splendid opportunity for peace which the affair of Pylos had offered. Lacedæmon, on the other hand, found the event of the war falsify her notion that a few years would suffice for the overthrow of the power of the Athenians by the devastation of their land. She had suffered on the island a disaster hitherto unknown at Sparta; she saw her country plundered from Pylos and Cythera; the Helots were deserting, and she was in constant apprehension that those who remained in Peloponnese would rely upon those outside and take advantage of the situation to renew their old attempts at revolution. Besides this, as chance would have it, her thirty years' truce with the Argives was upon the point of expiring;† and they refused to renew it unless Cynuria were restored to them; so that it seemed impossible to fight Argos and Athens at once. She also suspected some of the cities in Peloponnese of intending to go over to the enemy, as was indeed the case.

15. These considerations made both sides disposed for an accommodation; the Lacedæmonians being probably the most eager, as they ardently desired to recover the men taken upon the island, the Spartans among whom belonged to the first families and were accordingly related to the governing body in Lacedæmon. Negotiations had been begun directly after their capture, but the Athenians in their hour of triumph would not consent to any reasonable terms; though after their defeat at Delium Lacedæmon, knowing that they would be now more inclined to listen, at once concluded the armistice for a year, during which they were to confer together and see if a longer period could not be agreed upon.

16. Now, however, after the Athenian defeat at Amphipolis, and the death of Cleon and Brasidas, who had been the two principal opponents of peace on either side—the latter from the success and honour which war gave him, the former because he thought that, if

---

*Thucydides often comments on civic morale, high or low. Pericles' preparations, then Cleon and Demosthenes' success at capturing Spartans at Pylos, had over-inflated Athenian egos.

†Argos is ever the looming source of subversion and threat for the Spartans, who must control their "inferiors," including the helots of Laconia. Argos is also the decisive ally that the ever-hopeful Athenians expect will enable them to win the war. This book is much concerned with eliminating the Argives as spoilers.

tranquillity were restored, his crimes would be more open to detection and his slanders less credited*—the foremost candidates for power in either city, Pleistoanax, son of Pausanias, king of Lacedæmon, and Nicias, son of Niceratus, the most fortunate general of his time, each desired peace more ardently than ever.[†] Nicias, while still happy and honoured, wished to secure his good fortune, to obtain a present release from trouble for himself and his countrymen, and hand down to posterity a name as an ever-successful statesman, and thought the way to do this was to keep out of danger and commit himself as little as possible to fortune, and that peace alone made this keeping out of danger possible. Pleistoanax, again, was assailed by his enemies for his restoration, and regularly held up by them to the prejudice of his countrymen, upon every reverse that befell them, as though his unjust restoration were the cause; the accusation being that he and his brother Aristocles had bribed the prophetess of Delphi[‡] to tell the Lacedæmonian deputations which successively arrived at the temple to bring home the seed of the demigod son of Zeus from abroad, else they would have to plough with a silver share. In this way, it was insisted, in time he had induced the Lacedæmonians in the nineteenth year of his exile to Lycæum (whither he had gone when banished on suspicion of having been bribed to retreat from Attica, and had built half his house within the consecrated precinct of Zeus for fear of the Lacedæmonians), to restore him with the same dances and sacrifices[§] with which they had instituted their kings upon the first settlement of Lacedæmon. The smart of this accusation, and the reflexion that in peace no disaster could occur, and that when Lacedæmon had recovered her men there would be nothing for his enemies to take hold of (whereas, while war lasted the highest station must always bear the scandal of everything that went wrong), made him ardently desire a settlement.

17. Accordingly this winter was employed in conferences; and as

---

*Cleon and Brasidas contrast in their motives, but neither comes out looking very creditable, even if Cleon seems worse. Thucydides' animus against this leader has been explained as personal animosity, political rivalry, or disgust with post-Periclean politicians' ambition and selfish purposes.

†Pleistoanax of Sparta and Nicias of Athens emerge as proponents of a peace after ten years of war. Their motives likewise are less patriotic than personal. Many think that Thucydides was friendly with and to Nicias. However, most positive passages about his talents and his decisions are ambiguous, in books 6 and 7 especially.

‡Spartans bribed the leading Hellenic shrine a number of times—perhaps many more than our sources knew.

§This unusual reference to dance in a historian with limited anthropological patience conforms to his attention to Spartan ceremonies and religious elements relevant to politics.

spring rapidly approached, the Lacedæmonians sent round orders to the cities to prepare for a fortified occupation of Attica, to induce the Athenians to listen to their overtures; and at last, after many claims had been urged on either side at the conferences, a peace was agreed on upon the following basis. Each party was to restore its conquests,* but Athens was to keep Nisæa; her demand for Platæa being met by the Thebans asserting that they had acquired the place not by force or treachery, but by the voluntary adhesion upon agreement of its citizens; and the same, according to the Athenian account, being the history of her acquisition of Nisæa. This arranged, the Lacedæmonians summoned their allies, and all voting for peace except the Bœotians, Corinthians, Eleans, and Megarians, who did not approve of these proceedings, they concluded the treaty and made peace, each of the contracting parties swearing to the following articles:—†

18. *The Athenians and Lacedæmonians and their allies made a treaty, and swore to it, city by city, as follows:—*

1. *Touching the national temples, there shall be a free passage by land and by sea to all who wish it, to sacrifice, travel, consult, and attend the oracle or games, according to the customs of their countries.*

2. *The temple and shrine of Apollo at Delphi and the Delphians shall be governed by their own laws, taxed by their own state, and judged by their own judges, the land and the people, according to the custom of their country.*

3. *The treaty shall be binding for fifty years upon the Athenians and the allies of the Athenians, and upon the Lacedæmonians and the allies of the Lacedæmonians, without fraud or hurt by land or by sea.*

4. *It shall not be lawful to take up arms, with intent to do hurt, either for the Lacedæmonians and their allies against the Athenians and their allies, or for the Athenians and their allies against the Lacedæmonians and their allies, in any way or means whatsoever. But should any difference arise between them they are to have recourse to law and oaths, according as may be agreed between the parties.*

5. *The Lacedæmonians and their allies shall give back Amphipolis to the Athenians. Nevertheless, in the case of cities given up by the Lacedæmonians to the Athenians, the inhabitants shall be allowed to*

---

*The restoration of conquered territories offered no one a clear claim of victory. If they had agreed to keep their conquests (the Latin term in international law is *uti possidetis*—"as you hold them," maintaining the status quo), Athens would have been holding part of Messenia, a result unacceptable to the Peloponnesian League and especially to Lacedaemon. (See a disputed application at 5.31.)

†Herodotus and subsequent historians rarely quote treaties precisely. The presence of the quotation here suggests Thucydides' respect for reporting original words—when that option was possible—or his inadequate or incomplete revision of books 5 and 8, the only sections in which such verbatim documents appear.

go where they please and to take their property with them; and the cities shall be independent, paying only the tribute of Aristides.* And it shall not be lawful for the Athenians or their allies to carry on war against them after the treaty has been concluded, so long as the tribute is paid. The cities referred to are Argilus, Stagirus, Acanthus, Scolus, Olynthus, and Spartolus. These cities shall be neutral, allies neither of the Lacedæmonians nor of the Athenians; but if the cities consent, it shall be lawful for the Athenians to make them their allies, provided always that the cities wish it. The Mecybernæans, Sanæans, and Singæans shall inhabit their own cities, as also the Olynthians and Acanthians; but the Lacedæmonians and their allies shall give back Panactum to the Athenians.

6. The Athenians shall give back Coryphasium, Cythera, Methana, Pteleum, and Atalanta to the Lacedæmonians, and also all Lacedæmonians that are in the prison at Athens or elsewhere in the Athenian dominions, and shall let go the Peloponnesians besieged in Scione, and all others in Scione that are allies of the Lacedæmonians, and all whom Brasidas sent in there, and any others of the allies of the Lacedæmonians that may be in the prison at Athens or elsewhere in the Athenian dominions.

7. The Lacedæmonians and their allies shall in like manner give back any of the Athenians or their allies that they may have in their hands.

8. In the case of Scione, Torone, and Sermylium, and any other cities that the Athenians may have, the Athenians may adopt such measures as they please.

9. The Athenians shall take an oath to the Lacedæmonians and their allies, city by city. Every man shall swear by the most binding oath of his country, seventeen from each city. The oath shall be as follows:—'I will abide by this agreement and treaty honestly and without deceit.' In the same way an oath shall be taken by the Lacedæmonians and their allies to the Athenians; and the oath shall be renewed annually by both parties. Pillars shall be erected at Olympia, Pythia, the Isthmus, at Athens in the Acropolis, and at Lacedæmon in the temple at Amyclæ.†

10. If anything be forgotten, whatever it be, and on whatever point, it shall be consistent with their oath for both parties the Athenians and Lacedæmonians to alter it, according to their discretion.

---

*The tribute (tax) of 460 talents (see 1.96), established in 479 by Aristides at the creation of the Delian (or Hellenic) League, was a benchmark of fairness and less than the allies were now able to pay. The independence or autonomy of the cities was a standard harder to define.

†Annual renewal of the oath is noteworthy. Pillars at the Panhellenic shrines of Olympia, Delphi, and the Isthmus, and at the two chief shrines of the two chief combatant cities constitute the "official" publication of the treaty.

19. *The treaty begins from the Ephoralty of Pleistolas in Lacedæ-mon, on the 27th day of the month of Artemisium, and from the Archonship of Alcæus at Athens, on the 25th day of the month of Elaphebolion. Those who took the oath and poured the libations for the Lacedæmonians were Pleistoanax, Agis, Pleistolas, Damagetus, Chionis, Metagenes, Acanthus, Daithus, Ischagoras, Philocharidas, Zeuxidas, Antippus, Tellis, Alcinadas, Empedias, Menas, and Laphilus; for the Athenians, Lampon, Isthmionicus, Nicias, Laches, Euthydemus, Procles, Pythodorus, Hagnon, Myrtilus, Thrasycles, Theagenes, Aristocrates, Iolcius, Timocrates, Leon, Lamachus, and Demosthenes.*

20. This treaty was made in the spring, just at the end of winter, directly after the city festival of Dionysus, just ten years, with the difference of a few days, from the first invasion of Attica and the commencement of this war.* This must be calculated by the seasons rather than by trusting to the enumeration of the names of the several magistrates or offices of honour that are used to mark past events. Accuracy is impossible where an event may have occurred in the beginning, or middle, or at any period in their tenure of office. But by computing by summers and winters, the method adopted in this history,† it will be found that, each of these amounting to half a year, there were ten summers and as many winters contained in this first war.

21. Meanwhile the Lacedæmonians, to whose lot it fell to begin the work of restitution, immediately set free all the prisoners of war in their possession, and sent Ischagoras, Menas, and Philocharidas as envoys to the towns in the direction of Thrace, to order Clearidas to hand over Amphipolis to the Athenians, and the rest of their allies each to accept the treaty as it affected them. They, however, did not like its terms, and refused to accept it; Clearidas also, willing to oblige the Chalcidians, would not hand over the town, averring his inability to do so against their will. Meanwhile he hastened in person to Lacedæmon with envoys from the place, to defend his disobedience against the possible accusations of Ischagoras and his companions, and also to see whether it was too late for the agreement to be altered; and on finding the Lacedæmonians were bound, quickly set out back again with instructions from them to hand over the place, if possible, or at all events to bring out the Peloponnesians that were in it.

22. The allies happened to be present in person at Lacedæmon, and those who had not accepted the treaty were now asked by the

---

*The Athenian city festival of Dionysus occurred in late January or early February. Thucydides is precise in calling this a war of "ten years."

†Thucydides defends his innovative historical chronology, explaining why other methods, used by local historians, magistrates, and others, could not convey precisely how much time had passed.

Lacedæmonians to adopt it. This, however, they refused to do, for the same reasons as before, unless a fairer one than the present were agreed upon; and remaining firm in their determination were dismissed by the Lacedæmonians, who now decided on forming an alliance with the Athenians, thinking that Argos, who had refused the application of Ampelidas and Lichas for a renewal of the treaty, would without Athens be no longer formidable, and that the rest of the Peloponnese would be most likely to keep quiet, if the coveted alliance of Athens were shut against them. Accordingly, after conference with the Athenian ambassadors, an alliance was agreed upon and oaths were exchanged, upon the terms following:—

23. 1. *The Lacedæmonians shall be allies of the Athenians for fifty years.*

2. *Should any enemy invade the territory of Lacedæmon and injure the Lacedæmonians, the Athenians shall help them in such way as they most effectively can, according to their power. But if the invader be gone after plundering the country, that city shall be the enemy of Lacedæmon and Athens, and shall be chastised by both, and one shall not make peace without the other. This to be honestly, loyally, and without fraud.*

3. *Should any enemy invade the territory of Athens and injure the Athenians, the Lacedæmonians shall help them in such way as they most effectively can, according to their power. But if the invader be gone after plundering the country, that city shall be the enemy of Lacedæmon and Athens, and shall be chastised by both, and one shall not make peace without the other. This to be honestly, loyally, and without fraud.*

4. *Should the slave population rise, the Athenians shall help the Lacedæmonians with all their might, according to their power.*

5. *This treaty shall be sworn to by the same persons on either side that swore to the other. It shall be renewed annually by the Lacedæmonians going to Athens for the Dionysia, and the Athenians to Lacedæmon for the Hyacinthia, and a pillar shall be set up by either party; at Lacedæmon near the statue of Apollo at Amyclæ, and at Athens on the Acropolis near the statue of Athens. Should the Lacedæmonians and Athenians see fit to add to or take away from the alliance in any particular, it shall be consistent with their oaths for both parties to do so, according to their discretion.*

24. *Those who took the oath for the Lacedæmonians were Pleistoanax, Agis, Pleistolas, Damagetus, Chionis, Metagenes, Acanthus, Daithus, Ischagoras, Philocharidas, Zeuxidas, Antippus, Alcinadas, Tellis, Empedias, Menas, and Laphilus; for the Athenians, Lampon, Isthmionicus, Laches, Nicias, Euthydemus, Procles, Pythodorus, Hagnon, Myrtilus, Thrasycles, Theagenes, Aristocrates, Iolcius, Timocrates, Leon, Lamachus, and Demosthenes.*

This alliance was made not long after the treaty; and the Athenians gave back the men from the island to the Lacedæmonians, and the summer of the eleventh year began. This completes the history of the first war, which occupied the whole of the ten years previously.*

Feeling against Sparta in Peloponnese—League of the Mantineans, Eleans, Argives, and Athenians—Battle of Mantinea and Break Up of the League

25. After the treaty and the alliance between the Lacedæmonians and Athenians, concluded after the ten years' war, in the Ephorate of Pleistolas at Lacedæmon, and the Archonship of Alcæus at Athens, the states which had accepted them were at peace;† but the Corinthians and some of the cities in Peloponnese trying to disturb the settlement, a fresh agitation was instantly commenced by the allies against Lacedæmon. Further, the Lacedæmonians, as time went on, became suspected by the Athenians through their not performing some of the provisions in the treaty; and though for six years and ten months‡ they abstained from invasion of each other's territory, yet abroad an unstable armistice did not prevent either party doing the other the most effectual injury, until they were finally obliged to break the treaty made after the ten years' war and to have recourse to open hostilities.

26. The history of this period has been also written by the same Thucydides, an Athenian, in the chronological order of events by summers and winters, to the time when the Lacedæmonians and their allies put an end to the Athenian empire, and took the Long Walls and Piræus.§ The war had then lasted for twenty-seven years in all. Only a mistaken judgment can object to including the interval of

---

*Again, Thucydides did not create the current divisions into paragraph sections (first provided in John Hudson's edition, published in 1696 at Oxford), book-like chapters (Crawley), and eight books (ancient, perhaps Alexandrian, although the ancients knew other divisions into nine and thirteen books, perhaps conforming better to the contents of papyrus rolls). The language of this first part of book 5 suggests it was completed long before the remainder of the book (which covers an unusually high number of years because of the armistice to follow), but phrases such as the "first war" show revision after the later war had started or perhaps even ended. In 421, the Archidamian war ended, but the book brings events down to 416.

†The identification of the Spartan ephor and the Athenian archon solemnly opens the period of uneasy peace (421) and provides a cross-reference for historians, chroniclers, and official archival dates that used this clumsy and parochial means to date events.

‡Six years and ten months separated the first (Archidamian) war from the second (Sicilian and Ionian) war (415–404).

§This chapter proves that Thucydides survived to and beyond the end of the twenty-seven-year Peloponnesian War. It ended with the unconditional surrender of Athens and the destruction of her strategic shield at home, the long walls that encircled the city and extended to the port of Piraeus (map 3).

treaty in the war.* Looked at by the light of facts it cannot, it will be found, be rationally considered a state of peace, where neither party either gave or got back all that they had agreed, apart from the violations of it which occurred on both sides in the Mantinean and Epidaurian wars and other instances,† and the fact that the allies in the direction of Thrace were in as open hostility as ever, while the Bœotians had only a truce renewed every ten days. So that the first ten years' war, the treacherous armistice that followed it, and the subsequent war will, calculating by the seasons, be found to make up the number of years which I have mentioned, with the difference of a few days, and to afford an instance of faith in oracles being for once justified by the event.‡ I certainly all along remember from the beginning to the end of the war its being commonly declared that it would last thrice nine years.§ I lived through the whole of it, being of an age to comprehend events, and giving my attention to them in order to know the exact truth about them.‖ It was also my fate to be an exile from my country for twenty years after my command at Amphipolis; and being present with both parties, and more especially with the Peloponnesians by reason of my exile, I had leisure to observe affairs somewhat particularly.# I will accordingly now relate the differences that arose after the ten years' war, the breach of the treaty, and the hostilities that followed.

27. After the conclusion of the fifty years' truce and of the subsequent alliance,** the embassies from Peloponnese which had been

---

*Thucydides argues here against unnamed (as always) opponents in discussion or writing who saw the two wars as separate. No historian since Thucydides has maintained that position. His argument is powerful.

†We call these "campaigns" rather than separate "wars."

‡This tepid endorsement of an oracle makes clear how little Thucydides shared the religiosity of some of his fellow Hellenes.

§ The oracle is mentioned only because it lends feeble support to Thucydides' thesis of a twenty-seven-year war.

‖This precious sentence of self-revelation and innovation suggests that Thucydides was over twenty years of age when the war began. Since the Athenians elected him one of the ten Athenian generals (*strategoi*) in 424, he was probably well over thirty when the war began, putting his birth in the 460s and his death some years after 404.

#The exile lasted from 424 to 404, dating from his failure to preserve the vital forward outpost in Thrace to the restoration of the exiles and the end of the Athenian democracy. Thucydides casually mentions association with the Peloponnesians. He seems proud of his knowledge of the secretive and xenophobic Spartans.

**The Spartans and the Athenians not only stopped their warfare against each other but also entered into a *symmachia* (defensive alliance). This sign of good faith was taken amiss in particular by Corinth, whose interests the peace did not serve, and by Argos, whose profitable, previous neutrality now put it at risk of further and immediate Spartan aggression.

summoned for this business returned from Lacedæmon. The rest went straight home, but the Corinthians first turned aside to Argos and opened negotiations with some of the men in office there, pointing out that Lacedæmon could have no good end in view, but only the subjugation of Peloponnese, or she would never have entered into treaty and alliance with the once detested Athenians, and that the duty of consulting for the safety of Peloponnese had now fallen upon Argos, who should immediately pass a decree inviting any Hellenic state that chose, such state being independent and accustomed to meet fellow-powers upon the fair and equal ground of law and justice, to make a defensive alliance with the Argives; appointing a few individuals with plenipotentiary powers, instead of making the people the medium of negotiation, in order that, in the case of an applicant being rejected, the fact of his overtures might not be made public.* They said that many would come over from hatred of the Lacedæmonians. After this explanation of their views the Corinthians returned home.

28. The persons with whom they had communicated reported the proposal to their government and people, and the Argives passed the decree and chose twelve men to negotiate an alliance for any Hellenic state that wished it, except Athens and Lacedæmon, neither of which should be able to join without reference to the Argive people. Argos came in to the plan the more readily because she saw that they were going to be at war with Lacedæmon, the truce being on the point of expiring; and also because she hoped to gain the supremacy of Peloponnese. For at this time Lacedæmon had sunk very low in public estimation because of her disasters, while the Argives were in a most flourishing condition, having taken no part in the Attic war, but having on the contrary profited largely by their neutrality.† The Argives accordingly prepared to receive into alliance any of the Hellenes that desired it.

29. The Mantineans and their allies were the first to come over through fear of the Lacedæmonians. Having taken advantage of the war against Athens to reduce a large part of Arcadia into subjection,‡ they thought that Lacedæmon would not leave them undisturbed in

---

*Thucydides notes the anti-democratic Corinthians' secret negotiations with neutral Argives and their desire to maintain deniability, should the new "third force" alliance fall through.

†The Argives hoped to profit from having sat out the war. They now need allies in order to face the Spartan war machine. They could become, perhaps, the leaders of the "third world," at least along with the Corinthians, who were more powerful at sea. The name "Attic war," unparalleled (except at 5.31), reflects the Peloponnesian point of view.

‡Arcadia refers to the region of the central Peloponnese, north of Laconia. This mountainous area (map 4) is large, landlocked, and infertile. Mantinea, the chief city of the region, usually faced threats from its more powerful neighbors, Sparta and Argos.

their conquests, now that she had leisure to interfere, and consequently gladly turned to a powerful city like Argos, the historical enemy of the Lacedæmonians, and a sister democracy. Upon the defection of Mantinea the rest of Peloponnese at once began to agitate the propriety of following her example, conceiving that the Mantineans would not have changed sides without good reason; besides which they were angry with Lacedæmon among other reasons for having inserted in the treaty with Athens that it should be consistent with their oaths for both parties, Lacedæmonians and Athenians, to add to or take away from it according to their discretion. It was this clause that was the real origin of the panic in Peloponnese, by exciting suspicions of a Lacedæmonian and Athenian combination against their liberties:* any alteration should properly have been made conditional upon the consent of the whole body of the allies. With these apprehensions there was a very general desire in each state to place itself in alliance with Argos.

30. In the meantime the Lacedæmonians perceiving the agitation going on in Peloponnese, and that Corinth was the author of it and was herself about to enter into alliance with the Argives, sent ambassadors thither in the hope of preventing what was in contemplation. They accused her of having brought it all about, and told her that she could not desert Lacedæmon and become the ally of Argos, without adding violation of her oaths to the crime which she had already committed in not accepting the treaty with Athens, when it had been expressly agreed that the decision of the majority of the allies should be binding, unless the gods or heroes stood in the way. Corinth in her answer, delivered before those of her allies who had like her refused to accept the treaty, and whom she had previously invited to attend, refrained from openly stating the injuries she complained of, such as the non-recovery of Sollium or Anactorium from the Athenians, or any other point in which she thought she had been prejudiced, but took shelter under the pretext† that she could not give up her Thracian allies, to whom her separate individual security had been given, when they first rebelled with Potidæa, as well as upon subsequent occasions. She denied, therefore, that she committed any violation of her oaths to the allies in not entering into the treaty with Athens; hav-

---

*The small city-states (*poleis*) of ancient Greece were perpetually suspicious of their neighbors. Their larger enemies—Persia, Macedon, and eventually Rome—were able to manipulate justified local paranoia into diplomatic and military strategies for subjecting large numbers of their unallied, loosely allied, or squabbling opponents.

†The contrast between openly stated policies (often attractive or locally popular pretexts) and actual motives is one to which Thucydides repeatedly returns. He first drew this major distinction in his carefully phrased account of the "truest cause" of the war (1.23). Thucydides thought that he had discovered the decisive propelling forces;

ing sworn upon the faith of the gods to her Thracian friends, she could not honestly give them up. Besides, the expression was, 'unless the gods or heroes stand in the way.' Now here, as it appeared to her, the gods stood in the way. This was what she said on the subject of her former oaths. As to the Argive alliance she would confer with her friends, and do whatever was right. The Lacedæmonian envoys returning home, some Argive ambassadors who happened to be in Corinth pressed her to conclude the alliance without further delay, but were told to attend at the next congress to be held at Corinth.

31. Immediately afterwards an Elean embassy arrived, and first making an alliance with Corinth went on from thence to Argos, according to their instructions, and became allies of the Argives, their country being just then at enmity with Lacedæmon and Lepreum. Some time back* there had been a war between the Lepreans and some of the Arcadians; and the Eleans being called in by the former with the offer of half their lands, had put an end to the war, and leaving the land in the hands of its Leprean occupiers had imposed upon them the tribute of a talent to the Olympian Zeus. Till the Attic war this tribute was paid by the Lepreans, who then took the war as an excuse for no longer doing so, and upon the Eleans using force appealed to Lacedæmon. The case was thus submitted to her arbitrament; but the Eleans, suspecting the fairness of the tribunal, renounced the reference and laid waste the Leprean territory. The Lacedæmonians nevertheless decided that the Lepreans were independent and the Eleans aggressors, and as the latter did not abide by the arbitration, sent a garrison of heavy infantry into Lepreum. Upon this the Eleans, holding that Lacedæmon had received one of their rebel subjects, put forward the convention providing that each confederate should come out of the Attic war in possession of what he had when he went into it, and considering that justice had not been done them went over to the Argives, and now made the alliance through their ambassadors, who had been instructed for that purpose. Immediately after them the Corinthians and the Thracian Chalcidians became allies of Argos. Meanwhile the Bœotians and Megarians, who acted together, remained quiet, being left to do as they pleased by Lacedæmon, and thinking that the Argive democracy would not suit so well with their aristocratic government as the Lacedæmonian constitution.†

32. About the same time in this summer Athens succeeded in reducing Scione, put the adult males to death, and making slaves of the

---

*Thucydides does not try to provide exact dates when he cannot. Lepreum, a minor locale, sits on the border of Messene and Elis (map 4).

†The ideological conflict between democrats and aristocrats is a theme of the *History* developed most fully in the Corcyrean civil war (3.70–84) and in book 8.

women and children, gave the land for the Platæans to live in.* She also brought back the Delians to Delos, moved by her misfortunes in the field and by the commands of the god at Delphi. Meanwhile the Phocians and Locrians commenced hostilities. The Corinthians and Argives being now in alliance, went to Tegea to bring about its defection from Lacedæmon, seeing that if so considerable a state could be persuaded to join, all Peloponnese would be with them. But when the Tegeans said that they would do nothing against Lacedæmon, the hitherto zealous Corinthians relaxed their activity, and began to fear that none of the rest would now come over. Still they went to the Bœotians and tried to persuade them to alliance and a common action generally with Argos and themselves, and also begged them to go with them to Athens and obtain for them a ten days' truce similar to that made between the Athenians and Bœotians not long after the fifty years' treaty, and in the event of the Athenians refusing, to throw up the armistice, and not make any truce in future without Corinth. These were the requests of the Corinthians. The Bœotians stopped them on the subject of the Argive alliance, but went with them to Athens, where however they failed to obtain the ten days' truce; the Athenian answer being that the Corinthians had truce already, as being allies of Lacedæmon. Nevertheless the Bœotians did not throw up their ten days' truce, in spite of the prayers and reproaches of the Corinthians for their breach of faith; and these last had to content themselves with a *de facto* armistice with Athens.

33. The same summer the Lacedæmonians marched into Arcadia with their whole levy under Pleistoanax, son of Pausanias, king of Lacedæmon, against the Parrhasians, who were subjects of Mantinea, and a faction of whom had invited their aid. They also meant to demolish, if possible, the fort of Cypsela which the Mantineans had built and garrisoned in the Parrhasian territory, to annoy the district of Sciritis in Laconia. The Lacedæmonians accordingly laid waste the Parrhasian country, and the Mantineans, placing their town in the hands of an Argive garrison, addressed themselves to the defence of their confederacy, but being unable to save Cypsela or the Parrhasian towns went back to Mantinea. Meanwhile the Lacedæmonians made the Parrhasians independent, razed the fortress and returned home.

34. The same summer the soldiers from Thrace who had gone out with Brasidas came back, having been brought from thence after the treaty by Clearidas; and the Lacedæmonians decreed that the Helots who had fought with Brasidas should be free and allowed to live

---

*Thucydides is heartless, realistic, or understated. Here he reports the conclusion of the dominant Athenian empire's campaign against Scione, a city fighting for its autonomy (compare 4.120–123). The irony is that one city's desolation becomes a gift to the surviving Plataeans, who had suffered a similar fate at Spartan hands.

where they liked, and not long afterwards settled them with the Neodamodes* at Lepreum, which is situated on the Laconian and Elean
border; Lacedæmon being at this time at enmity with Elis. Those however of the Spartans who had been taken prisoners on the island and
had surrendered their arms might, it was feared, suppose that they
were to be subjected to some degradation in consequence of their
misfortune, and so make some attempt at revolution, if left in possession of their franchise.† These were therefore at once disfranchised,
although some of them were in office at the time, and thus placed
under a disability to take office, or buy and sell anything.‡ After some
time, however, the franchise was restored to them.

35. The same summer the Dians took Thyssus, a town on Acte by
Athos in alliance with Athens. During the whole of this summer intercourse between the Athenians and Peloponnesians continued, although each party began to suspect the other directly after the treaty,
because of the places specified in it not being restored. Lacedæmon,
to whose lot it had fallen to begin by restoring Amphipolis and the
other towns, had not done so.§ She had equally failed to get the treaty
accepted by her Thracian allies, or by the Bœotians or the Corinthians; although she was continually promising to unite with Athens in
compelling their compliance, if it were longer refused. She also kept
fixing a time at which those who still refused to come in were to be
declared enemies to both parties, but took care not to bind herself by
any written agreement. Meanwhile the Athenians, seeing none of
these professions performed in fact, began to suspect the honesty of
her intentions, and consequently not only refused to comply with her
demands for Pylos, but also repented having given up the prisoners
from the island, and kept tight hold of the other places, until Lacedæmon's part of the treaty should be fulfilled. Lacedæmon, on the other
hand, said she had done what she could, having given up the Athenian
prisoners of war in her possession, evacuated Thrace, and performed

---

Neodamodes (literally "new citizens") were helots liberated in return for major services to the *homoioi* (the Spartan "equals"). Thucydides does not define the term, although elsewhere (1.101) he does define helots (for their services, compare 4.26).

†Ancient and modern ideologues, hostile and friendly, commonly exaggerate the stability of the Spartan regime, as this mean fear of its own citizens suggests. If stability is
bought only by protective punishments carried out in anxious anticipation of possible
dissatisfaction, it produces many unhappy outcasts.

‡Disenfranchisement included loss of political participation and economic membership in the messes (communal meals) and the allotments (the distribution of land and
helots for family income and tax payments). The Spartans could and did do worse to
the lower classes (see 4.80).

§The new peace and alliance were doomed from the start, since the Spartans themselves were divided on its wisdom. The allies were disinclined to participate in a peace
that did almost nothing for them.

everything else in her power. Amphipolis it was out of her ability to restore; but she would endeavour to bring the Bœotians and Corinthians in to the treaty, to recover Panactum, and send home all the Athenian prisoners of war in Bœotia. Meanwhile she required that Pylos should be restored, or at all events that the Messenians and Helots should be withdrawn, as her troops had been from Thrace, and the place garrisoned, if necessary, by the Athenians themselves. After a number of different conferences held during the summer she succeeded in persuading Athens to withdraw from Pylos the Messenians and the rest of the Helots and deserters from Laconia, who were accordingly settled by her at Cranii in Cephallenia. Thus during this summer there was peace and intercourse between the two peoples.

36. Next winter, however, the Ephors under whom the treaty had been made were no longer in office, and some of their successors were directly opposed to it.* Embassies now arrived from the Lacedæmonian confederacy, and the Athenians, Bœotians, and Corinthians also presented themselves at Lacedæmon, and after much discussion and no agreement between them, separated for their several homes; when Cleobulus and Xenares, the two Ephors who were the most anxious to break off the treaty, took advantage of this opportunity to communicate privately with the Bœotians and Corinthians, and advising them to act as much as possible together, instructed the former first to enter into alliance with Argos, and then try and bring themselves and the Argives into alliance with Lacedæmon. The Bœotians would so be least likely to be compelled to come in to the Attic treaty; and the Lacedæmonians would prefer gaining the friendship and alliance of Argos even at the price of the hostility of Athens and the rupture of the treaty.† The Bœotians knew that an honourable friendship with Argos had been long the desire of Lacedæmon; for the Lacedæmonians believed that this would considerably facilitate the conduct of the war outside Peloponnese. Meanwhile they begged the Bœotians to place Panactum in her hands in order that she might, if possible, obtain Pylos in exchange for it, and so be more in a position to resume hostilities with Athens.

37. After receiving these instructions for their governments from Xenares and Cleobulus and their other friends at Lacedæmon, the Bœotians and Corinthians departed. On their way home they were joined by two persons high in office at Argos who had waited for them on the road, and who now sounded them upon the possibility of the Bœotians joining the Corinthians, Eleans, and Mantineans in be-

---

*The fragile peace became more fragile with the entry at Sparta of new ephors, a yearly office.

†The Spartans worried about the neighboring Argives stirring up revolt with the always restive helots. Still, this speedy willingness to dump the recent treaty is surprising.

coming the allies of Argos, in the idea that if this could be effected they would be able, thus united, to make peace or war as they pleased either against Lacedæmon or any other power. The Bœotian envoys were pleased at thus hearing themselves accidentally asked to do what their friends at Lacedæmon had told them; and the two Argives perceiving that their proposal was agreeable, departed with a promise to send ambassadors to the Bœotians. On their arrival the Bœotians reported to the Bœotarchs* what had been said to them at Lacedæmon and also by the Argives who had met them, and the Bœotarchs, pleased with the idea, embraced it with the more eagerness from the lucky coincidence of Argos soliciting the very thing wanted by their friends at Lacedæmon. Shortly afterwards ambassadors appeared from Argos with the proposals indicated; and the Bœotarchs approved of the terms and dismissed the ambassadors with a promise to send envoys to Argos to negotiate the alliance.

38. In the meantime it was decided by the Bœotarchs, the Corinthians, the Megarians, and the envoys from Thrace first to interchange oaths together to give help to each other whenever it was required and not to make war or peace except in common; after which the Bœotians and Megarians, who acted together, should make the alliance with Argos. But before the oaths were taken the Bœotarchs communicated these proposals to the four councils of the Bœotians,† in whom the supreme power resides, and advised them to interchange oaths with all such cities as should be willing to enter into a defensive league with the Bœotians. But the members of the Bœotian councils refused their assent to the proposal, being afraid of offending Lacedæmon by entering into a league with the deserter Corinth; the Bœotarchs not having acquainted them with what had passed at Lacedæmon and with the advice given by Cleobulus and Xenares and the Bœotian partisans there, namely, that they should become allies of Corinth and Argos as a preliminary to a junction with Lacedæmon; fancying that, even if they should say nothing about this, the councils would not vote against what had been decided and advised by the Bœotarchs. This difficulty arising, the Corinthians and the envoys from Thrace departed without anything having been concluded; and the Bœotarchs, who had previously intended after carrying this to try

---

*The Bœotarchs were the elected leaders of the Bœotian League (compare 2.2 and 4.91), a loose confederation of nine to eleven *poleis* dominated by the leading city of Bœotia, Thebes (map 2).

†The four councils are not well documented or understood, not least because Thucydides mentions them nowhere else. A "footnote" (that is, parenthetical explanation) would be useful here, as we reach the end of 421. Thucydides takes knowledge of some institutions for granted, but sometimes explains what is obvious even for us. His intended audience is only loosely defined (1.22).

and effect the alliance with Argos, now omitted to bring the Argive question before the councils, or to send to Argos the envoys whom they had promised; and a general coldness and delay ensued in the matter.

39. In this same winter Mecyberna was assaulted and taken by the Olynthians, having an Athenian garrison inside it.

All this while negotiations had been going on between the Athenians and Lacedæmonians about the conquests still retained by each, and Lacedæmon, hoping that if Athens were to get back Panactum from the Bœotians she might herself recover Pylos, now sent an embassy to the Bœotians, and begged them to place Panactum and their Athenian prisoners in her hands, in order that she might exchange them for Pylos. This the Bœotians refused to do, unless Lacedæmon made a separate alliance with them as she had done with Athens. Lacedæmon knew that this would be a breach of faith to Athens, as it had been agreed that neither of them should make peace or war without the other; yet wishing to obtain Panactum which she hoped to exchange for Pylos, and the party who pressed for the dissolution of the treaty strongly affecting the Bœotian connexion, she at length concluded the alliance just as winter gave way to spring; and Panactum was instantly razed. And so the eleventh year of the war ended.

40. In the first days of the summer following, the Argives, seeing that the promised ambassadors from Bœotia did not arrive, and that Panactum was being demolished, and that a separate alliance had been concluded between the Bœotians and Lacedæmonians, began to be afraid that Argos might be left alone, and all the confederacy go over to Lacedæmon. They fancied that the Bœotians had been persuaded by the Lacedæmonians to raze Panactum and to enter into the treaty with the Athenians, and that Athens was privy to this arrangement, and even her alliance, therefore, no longer open to them—a resource which they had always counted upon, by reason of the dissensions existing, in the event of the non-continuance of their treaty with Lacedæmon. In this strait the Argives, afraid that, as the result of refusing to renew the treaty with Lacedæmon and of aspiring to the supremacy in Peloponnese, they would have the Lacedæmonians, Tegeans, Bœotians, and Athenians on their hands all at once, now hastily sent off Eustrophus and Æson, who seemed the persons most likely to be acceptable, as envoys to Lacedæmon, with the view of making as good a treaty as they could with the Lacedæmonians, upon such terms as could be got, and being left in peace.

41. Having reached Lacedæmon, their ambassadors proceeded to negotiate the terms of the proposed treaty. What the Argives first demanded was that they might be allowed to refer to the arbitration of some state or private person the question of the Cynurian land, a piece of frontier-territory about which they have always been disputing, and which contains the towns of Thyrea and Anthene, and is occupied by the Lacedæmonians. The Lacedæmonians at first said that they could not allow this point to be discussed, but were ready to conclude upon the old terms. Eventually, however, the Argive ambassadors succeeded in obtaining from them this concession:—For the present there was to be a truce for fifty years, but it should be competent for either party, there being neither plague nor war in Lacedæmon or Argos, to give a formal challenge and decide the question of this territory by battle, as on a former occasion, when both sides claimed the victory; pursuit not being allowed beyond the frontier of Argos or Lacedæmon. The Lacedæmonians at first thought this mere folly;* but at last, anxious in any case to have the friendship of Argos, they agreed to the terms demanded, and reduced them to writing. However, before any of this should become binding, the ambassadors were to return to Argos and communicate with their people, and in the event of their approval, to come at the Feast of the Hyacinthia and take the oaths.

42. The envoys returned accordingly. In the meantime, while the Argives were engaged in these negotiations, the Lacedæmonian ambassadors, Andromedes, Phædimus, and Antimenidas, who were to receive the prisoners from the Bœotians and restore them and Panactum to the Athenians, found that the Bœotians had themselves razed Panactum, upon the plea that oaths had been anciently exchanged between their people and the Athenians, after a dispute on the subject, to the effect that neither should inhabit the place, but that they should graze it in common. As for the Athenian prisoners of war in the hands of the Bœotians, these were delivered over to Andromedes and his colleagues, and by them conveyed to Athens and given back. The envoys at the same time announced the razing of Panactum, which to them seemed as good as its restitution, as it would no longer lodge an enemy of Athens. This announcement was received with great indignation by the Athenians,† who thought that the Lacedæmonians had played them false, both in the matter of the demolition of Panactum, which ought to have been restored to them standing, and in having, as they now heard, made a separate alliance with the Bœotians, in spite of their previous promise to join Athens in compelling the adhesion of those who refused to accede to the treaty. The Athenians also considered the other points in which

---

*Presumably, such heroic resolution of conflicts seemed archaic to the persons directing foreign policy for Sparta. The Argives needed to come to the assembly with some possible form of restitution of the disputed territory (Cynuria, map 5).

†The destruction of the strategic Athenian fort on the marches of Boeotia (map 2) was contrary to custom and expectation, but clearly many Athenians wanted to see the treaty and peace fail.

Lacedæmon had failed in her compact, and thinking that they had been overreached, gave an angry answer to the ambassadors and sent them away.

43. The breach between the Lacedæmonians and Athenians having gone thus far, the party at Athens, also, who wished to cancel the treaty, immediately put themselves in motion. Foremost amongst these was Alcibiades, son of Clinias, a man yet young in years for any other Hellenic city, but distinguished by the splendour of his ancestry.* Alcibiades thought the Argive alliance really preferable, not that personal pique had not also a great deal to do with his opposition;† he being offended with the Lacedæmonians for having negotiated the treaty through Nicias and Laches, and having overlooked him on account of his youth, and also for not having shown him the respect due to the ancient connexion of his family with them as their *Proxeni*,‡ which, renounced by his grandfather, he had lately himself thought to renew by his attentions to their prisoners taken in the island. Being thus, as he thought, slighted on all hands, he had in the first instance spoken against the treaty, saying that the Lacedæmonians were not to be trusted, but that they only treated, in order to be enabled by this means to crush Argos, and afterwards to attack Athens alone; and now, immediately upon the above breach occurring, he sent privately to the Argives, telling them to come as quickly as possible to Athens, accompanied by the Mantineans and Eleans, with proposals of alliance; as the moment was propitious and he himself would do all he could to help them.

44. Upon receiving this message and discovering that the Athenians, far from being privy to the Bœotian alliance, were involved in a serious quarrel with the Lacedæmonians, the Argives paid no further attention to the embassy which they had just sent to Lacedæemon on the subject of the treaty, and began to incline rather towards the Athenians, reflecting that, in the event of war, they would thus have on their side a city that was not only an ancient ally of Argos, but a sister democracy and very powerful at sea. They accordingly at once sent ambassadors to Athens to treat for an alliance, accompanied by others from Elis and and Mantinea.

---

*Here Alcibiades, who will dominate much of the remaining history and the text, appears with the formulaic information of his ancestry and the particular fact of his youth. He was related to Pericles (see Plutarch's biographies of both men, written half a millennium later).

†We cannot say that Thucydides had special access to Alcibiades' motives, but he often describes both a public and a private reason given for his behavior. This unscrupulous selfishness had been generalized for Pericles' successors at 2.65.

‡A *proxenos* was a semi-official representative of a foreign state. He would protect and promote that foreign city's national interests and the interests of its nationals in his home state. Here Alcibiades is identified as *proxenos* of Sparta at Athens.

At the same time arrived in haste from Lacedæmon an embassy consisting of persons reputed well disposed towards the Athenians—Philocharidas, Leon, and Endius, for fear that the Athenians in their irritation might conclude alliance with the Argives, and also to ask back Pylos in exchange for Panactum, and in defence of the alliance with the Bœotians to plead that it had not been made to hurt the Athenians.

45. Upon the envoys speaking in the senate upon these points, and stating that they had come with full powers to settle all others at issue between them, Alcibiades became afraid that if they were to repeat these statements to the popular assembly, they might gain the multitude, and the Argive alliance might be rejected, and accordingly had recourse to the following stratagem.* He persuaded the Lacedæmonians by a solemn assurance that if they would say nothing of their full powers in the assembly, he would give back Pylos to them (himself, the present opponent of its restitution, engaging to obtain this from the Athenians), and would settle the other points at issue. His plan was to detach them from Nicias and to disgrace them before the people, as being without sincerity in their intentions, or even common consistency in their language, and so to get the Argives, Eleans, and Mantineans taken into alliance. This plan proved successful. When the envoys appeared before the people, and upon the question being put to them, did not say as they had said in the senate, that they had come with full powers, the Athenians lost all patience, and carried away by Alcibiades, who thundered more loudly than ever against the Lacedæmonians, were ready instantly to introduce the Argives and their companions and to take them into alliance. An earthquake, however, occurring, before anything definite had been done, this assembly was adjourned.†

46. In the assembly held the next day, Nicias, in spite of the Lacedæmonians having been deceived themselves, and having allowed him to be deceived also in not admitting that they had come with full powers, still maintained that it was best to be friends with the Lacedæmonians, and, letting the Argive proposals stand over, to send once more to Lacedæmon and learn her intentions. The adjournment of the war could only increase their own prestige and injure that of their rivals; the excellent state of their affairs making it their interest

---

*The senate (*boule*) of 500 received representatives of foreign governments and set the agenda for the Athenian assembly. Alcibiades maneuvers his way by means of personal contacts and public procedures. It is not clear why the Spartan ambassadors would have much reason to trust him.

†Some Greeks and Romans (for instance, Nicias and the sailors frightened at 7.50) regarded exceptional natural phenomena (earthquakes and eclipses, but also famines, droughts, and other longer-lasting events) as an indication of divine displeasure. Nothing indicates that this earthquake was severe, but the interruption may have served the interests of various factions.

to preserve this prosperity as long as possible, while those of Lacedæmon were so desperate that the sooner she could try her fortune again the better. He succeeded accordingly in persuading them to send ambassadors, himself being among the number, to invite the Lacedæmonians, if they were really sincere, to restore Panactum intact with Amphipolis, and to abandon their alliance with the Bœotian (unless they consented to accede to the treaty), agreeably to the stipulation which forbade either party to treat without the other. The ambassadors were also directed to say that the Athenians, had they wished to play false, might already have made alliance with the Argives, who were indeed come to Athens for that very purpose, and went off furnished with instructions as to any other complaints that the Athenians had to make. Having reached Lacedæmon they communicated their instructions, and concluded by telling the Lacedæmonians that unless they gave up their alliance with the Bœotians, in the event of their not acceding to the treaty, the Athenians for their part would ally themselves with the Argives and their friends. The Lacedæmonians, however, refused to give up the Bœotian alliance— the party of Xenares the Ephor, and such as shared their view, carrying the day upon this point—but renewed the oaths at the request of Nicias, who feared to return without having accomplished anything and to be disgraced; as was indeed his fate, he being held the author of the treaty with Lacedæmon.* When he returned, and the Athenians heard that nothing had been done at Lacedæmon, they flew into a passion, and deciding that faith had not been kept with them, took advantage of the presence of the Argives and their allies, who had been introduced by Alcibiades, and made a treaty and alliance with them upon the terms following:—

47. *The Athenians, Argives, Mantineans, and Eleans, acting for themselves and the allies in their respective empires, made a treaty for a hundred years, to be without fraud or hurt by land and by sea.*

1. *It shall not be lawful to carry on war, either for the Argives, Eleans, Mantineans, and their allies, against the Athenians, or the allies in the Athenian empire; or for the Athenians and their allies against the Argives, Eleans, Mantineans, or their allies, in any way or means whatsoever.*

The Athenians, Argives, Eleans, and Mantineans shall be allies for a hundred years upon the terms following:—

2. *If an enemy invade the country of the Athenians, the Argives, Eleans, and Mantineans shall go to the relief of Athens, according as the Athenians may require by message, in such way as they most effectually can, to the best of their power. But if the invader be gone after*

---

*Nicias, older and more conservative than Alcibiades but his antagonist and opponent until his death, especially in the matter of deciding to attack Sicily (books 6 and 7), is often outfoxed by the younger man.

plundering the territory, the offending state shall be the enemy of the Argives, Mantineans, Eleans, and Athenians, and war shall be made against it by all these cities; and no one of the cities shall be able to make peace with that state, except all the above cities agree to do so.

3. *Likewise the Athenians shall go to the relief of Argos, Mantinea, and Elis, if an enemy invade the country of Elis, Mantinea, or Argos, according as the above cities may require by message, in such way as they most effectually can, to the best of their power. But if the invader be gone after plundering the territory, the state offending shall be the enemy of the Athenians, Argives, Mantineans, and Eleans, and war shall be made against it by all these cities, and peace may not be made with that state except all the above cities agree to it.*

4. *No armed force shall be allowed to pass for hostile purposes through the country of the powers contracting, or of the allies in their respective empires, or to go by sea, except all the cities—that is to say, Athens, Argos, Mantinea, and Elis—vote for such passage.*

5. *The relieving troops shall be maintained by the city sending them for thirty days from their arrival in the city that has required them, and upon their return in the same way; if their services be desired for a longer period the city that sent for them shall maintain them, at the rate of three Æginetan obols per day for a heavy-armed soldier, archer, or light soldier, and an Æginetan drachma for a trooper.* *

6. *The city sending for the troops shall have the command when the war is in its own country; but in case of the cities resolving upon a joint expedition the command shall be equally divided among all the cities.*

7. *The treaty shall be sworn to by the Athenians for themselves and their allies, by the Argives, Mantineans, Eleans, and their allies, by each state individually. Each shall swear the oath most binding in his country over full-grown victims; the oath being as follows:*

'I WILL STAND BY THE ALLIANCE AND ITS ARTICLES, JUSTLY, INNO-CENTLY, AND SINCERELY, AND I WILL NOT TRANSGRESS THE SAME IN ANY WAY OR MEANS WHATSOEVER.'

The oath shall be taken at Athens by the Senate and the magistrates, the Prytanes, administering it;† at Argos by the Senate, the Eighty, and the

---

*Six obols make a drachma; Aeginetan obols were heavier than Athenian, so this is an adequate provision for a trooper's ration allowance. See 3.17 for the high pay of two drachmas a day; the usual rate was one drachma (6.8, 31; 8.29). The Athenian Acropolis construction accounts also record pay of one drachma a day for a skilled workman in the middle and late fifth century.

†The actual words of the treaty provide us with precious evidence for the names of officials and governmental bodies in various leading cities. In Athens, the *prytanes* were the 50 members of the council or senate of 500 who in a given month, chosen by lot, day and night manned the *prytaneion* (the *tholos*, or round building), in the Agora (see Camp, pp. 69–70 and illustration 66). At least one-third of them had to remain inside at all times, according to the Aristotelian *Constitution of Athens*.

Artynæ, the Eighty administering it; at Mantinea by the Demiurgi, the Senate, and the other magistrates, the Theori and Polemarchs administering it; at Elis by the Demiurgi, the magistrates, and the Six Hundred, the Demiurgi and the Thesmophylaces administering it. The oaths shall be renewed by the Athenians going to Elis, Mantinea, and Argos thirty days before the Olympic games; by the Argives, Mantineans, and Eleans going to Athens ten days before the great feast of the Panathenæa. The articles of the treaty, the oaths, and the alliance shall be inscribed on a stone pillar by the Athenians in the citadel, by the Argives in the market-place, in the temple of Apollo; by the Mantineans in the temple of Zeus, in the market-place; and a brazen pillar shall be erected jointly by them at the Olympic games now at hand. Should the above cities see good to make any addition to these article, whatever all the above cities shall agree upon, after consulting together, shall be binding.*

48. Although the treaty and alliances were thus concluded, still the treaty between the Lacedæmonians and Athenians was not renounced by either party. Meanwhile Corinth, although the ally of the Argives, did not accede to the new treaty, any more than she had done to the alliance, defensive and offensive, formed before this between the Eleans, Argives, and Mantineans, when she declared herself content with the first alliance, which was defensive only, and which bound them to help each other, but not to join in attacking any.† The Corinthians thus stood aloof from their allies, and again turned their thoughts towards Lacedæmon.

49. At the Olympic games which were held this summer, and in which the Arcadian Androsthenes was victor the first time in the wrestling and boxing, the Lacedæmonians were excluded from the temple by the Eleans, and thus prevented from sacrificing or contending, for having refused to pay the fine specified in the Olympic law imposed upon them by the Eleans, who alleged that they had attacked Fort Phyrcus, and sent heavy infantry of theirs into Lepreum during the Olympic truce. The amount of the fine was two thousand minæ, two for each heavy-armed soldier, as the law prescribes.‡ The Lacedæmonians sent envoys, and pleaded that the imposition was unjust; saying that the truce had not yet been proclaimed at Lacedæmon

---

Demiurgi as a term for a magistracy means "those who work the community's concerns"; *thesmophylaces* means "guardians of the established laws." Thucydides does not explain these and the other parochial institutions mentioned here.

†The Hellenes distinguished solely defensive from defensive and offensive alliances, the latter obviously arising only when states saw a real community of interests.

‡The mina was worth 100 drachmas, the common coin (equal to 6 obols), and amounted to 1/60 of a talent. Mina and talent were units of weight and large-sum accounting too large to coin. Two minae is commonly the ransom of a hoplite. Thirty-three talents is a very large sum.

when the heavy infantry were sent off. But the Eleans affirmed that the armistice with them had already begun (they proclaim it first among themselves), and that the aggression of the Lacedæmonians had taken them by surprise while they were living quietly as in time of peace, and not expecting anything. Upon this the Lacedæmonians submitted, that if the Eleans really believed that they had committed an aggression, it was useless after that to proclaim the truce at Lacedæmon; but they had proclaimed it notwithstanding, as believing nothing of the kind, and from that moment the Lacedæmonians had made no attack upon their country. Nevertheless the Eleans adhered to what they had said, that nothing would persuade them that an aggression had not been committed; if, however, the Lacedæmonians would restore Lepreum, they would give up their own share of the money and pay that of the god for them.*

50. As this proposal was not accepted, the Eleans tried a second. Instead of restoring Lepreum, if this was objected to, the Lacedæmonians should ascend the altar of the Olympian Zeus, as they were so anxious to have access to the temple, and swear before the Hellenes that they would surely pay the fine at a later day. This being also refused, the Lacedæmonians were excluded from the temple, the sacrifice, and the games, and sacrificed at home; the Lepreans being the only other Hellenes who did not attend. Still the Eleans were afraid of the Lacedæmonians sacrificing by force, and kept guard with a heavy-armed company of their young men; being also joined by a thousand Argives, the same number of Mantineans, and by some Athenian cavalry who stayed at Harpina during the feast. Great fears were felt in the assembly of the Lacedæmonians coming in arms, especially after Lichas, son of Arcesilaus, a Lacedæmonian, had been scourged on the course by the umpires; because, upon his horses being the winners, and the Bœotian people being proclaimed the victor on account of his having no right to enter, he came forward on the course and crowned the charioteer, in order to show that the chariot was his.† After this incident all were more afraid than ever, and firmly looked for a disturbance: the Lacedæmonians, however, kept quiet, and let the feast pass by, as we have seen. After the Olympic games, the Argives and the allies repaired to Corinth to invite her to come

---

*The Olympics became involved in political and military struggles. The political entity of Elis was a weak sister in the northwestern Peloponnese (map 4) and therefore even more inclined to use its one good card: It was home to the Olympic games. The endless diplomatic wrangling and hair-splitting of book 5 seemed to Thucydides an important aspect of the changes in the Hellenic world brought about by the Peloponnesian War.
†Lichas was a prominent Spartiate (compare 5.22, 8.39, and 8.97, and see Index). If he had been whipped for his illegal activity, the Elean fear was reasonable enough. Thucydides' notice of a sporting event, even one with military implications, is unusual.

over to them. There they found some Lacedæmonian envoys; and a long discussion ensued, which after all ended in nothing, as an earthquake occurred, and they dispersed to their different homes.

Summer was now over.

51. The winter following a battle took place between the Heracleots in Trachinia and the Ænianians, Dolopians, Malians, and certain of the Thessalians, all tribes bordering on and hostile to the town, which directly menaced their country. Accordingly, after having opposed and harassed it from its very foundation by every means in their power, they now in this battle defeated the Heracleots, Xenares, son of Cnidis, their Lacedæmonian commander, being among the slain.* Thus the winter ended and the twelfth year of this war ended also.

52. After the battle Heraclea was so terribly reduced that in the first days of the summer following the Bœotians occupied the place and sent away the Lacedæmonian Agesippidas for misgovernment, fearing that the town might be taken by the Athenians while the Lacedæmonians were distracted with the affairs of Peloponnese. The Lacedæmonians, nevertheless, were offended with them for what they had done.†

The same summer Alcibiades, son of Clinias, now one of the generals at Athens, in concert with the Argives and the allies, went into Peloponnese with a few Athenian heavy infantry and archers, and some of the allies in those parts whom he took up as he passed, and with this army marched here and there through Peloponnese, and settled various matters connected with the alliance, and among other things induced the Patrians to carry their walls down to the sea, intending himself also to build a fort near the Achæan Rhium. However, the Corinthians and Sicyonians, and all others who would have suffered by its being built, came up and hindered him.

53. The same summer war broke out between the Epidaurians and Argives. The pretext‡ was that the Epidaurians did not send an offer-

---

*The winter ends and the new year of 419 begins with the intrusive Spartan colony at Heracleia in Trachis (map 5) suffering a serious defeat, including the death of the resident Spartan general.

†Boeotian interests were not identical with Spartan, and the Spartans generally take umbrage at any other state's making decisions for them. The Boeotians were much closer on the ground in this case, and more worried about an Athenian outpost nearby.

‡Greek *poleis* frequently operate on the principle that one's immediate neighbor is a competitor for territory, so the neighbor on the other side of one's neighbor is a potential ally, or at least a useful threat to the immediate neighbor. Argos stood between Sparta and Epidaurus. Again, the pretext of religious ritual failure serves to promote a hostile policy for strategic Athenian advantage.

ing for their pasture-land to Apollo Pythæus, as they were bound to do, the Argives having the chief management of the temple; but, apart from this pretext, Alcibiades and the Argives were determined, if possible, to gain possession of Epidaurus, and thus to insure the neutrality of Corinth and give the Athenians a shorter passage for their reinforcements from Ægina than if they had to sail round Scyllæum. The Argives accordingly prepared to invade Epidaurus by themselves, to exact the offering.

54. About the same time the Lacedæmonians marched out with all their people to Leuctra upon their frontier, opposite to Mount Lycæum, under the command of Agis, son of Archidamus, without any one knowing their destination, not even the cities that sent the contingents. The sacrifices, however, for crossing the frontier not proving propitious,* the Lacedæmonians returned home themselves, and sent word to the allies to be ready to march after the month ensuing, which happened to be the month of Carneus, a holy time for the Dorians. Upon the retreat of the Lacedæmonians the Argives marched out on the last day but three of the month before Carneus, and keeping this as the day during the whole time that they were out, invaded and plundered Epidaurus. The Epidaurians summoned their allies to their aid, some of whom pleaded the month as an excuse; others came as far as the frontier of Epidaurus and there remained inactive.

55. While the Argives were in Epidaurus embassies from the cities assembled at Mantinea, upon the invitation of the Athenians. The conference having begun, the Corinthian Euphamidas said that their actions did not agree with their words; while they were sitting deliberating about peace, the Epidaurians and their allies and the Argives were arrayed against each other in arms; deputies from each party should first go and separate the armies, and then the talk about peace might be resumed. In compliance with this suggestion they went and brought back the Argives from Epidaurus, and afterwards reassembled, but without succeeding any better in coming to a conclusion; and the Argives a second time invaded Epidaurus and plundered the country. The Lacedæmonians also marched out to Caryæ; but the frontier sacrifices again proving unfavourable, they went back again, and the Argives, after ravaging about a third of the Epidaurian territory, returned home. Meanwhile a thousand Athenian heavy infantry had come to their aid under the command of Alcibiades, but finding that the Lacedæmonian expedition was at an end, and that they were no longer wanted, went back again.

---

*The extent to which religious phenomena were and are cynically manipulated for political aggrandizement is not known. The Spartans were famous (as were the Romans) for observing omens with religious zeal, and, like the Romans, they would persist in taking omens until they received the one they wanted.

So passed the summer.

56. The next winter the Lacedæmonians managed to elude the vigilance of the Athenians, and sent in a garrison of three hundred men to Epidaurus, under the command of Agesippidas. Upon this the Argives went to the Athenians and complained of their having allowed an enemy to pass by sea, in spite of the clause in the treaty by which the allies were not to allow an enemy to pass through their country. Unless, therefore, they now put the Messenians and Helots in Pylos to annoy the Lacedæmonians, they, the Argives, should consider that faith had not been kept with them. The Athenians were persuaded by Alcibiades to inscribe at the bottom of the Laconian pillar that the Lacedæmonians had not kept their oaths, and to convey the Helots at Cranii to Pylos to plunder the country; but for the rest they remained quiet as before. During this winter hostilities went on between the Argives and Epidaurians, without any pitched battle taking place, but only forays and ambuscades, in which the losses were small and fell now on one side and now on the other. At the close of the winter, towards the beginning of spring, the Argives went with scaling-ladders to Epidaurus, expecting to find it left unguarded on account of the war and to be able to take it by assault, but returned unsuccessful. And the winter ended, and with it the thirteenth year of the war ended also.*

57. In the middle of the next summer the Lacedæmonians, seeing the Epidaurians, their allies, in distress, and the rest of Peloponnese either in revolt or disaffected, concluded that it was high time for them to interfere if they wished to stop the progress of the evil, and accordingly with their full force, the Helots included, took the field against Argos, under the command of Agis, son of Archidamus, king of the Lacedæmonians.† The Tegeans and the other Arcadian allies of Lacedæmon joined in the expedition. The allies from the rest of Peloponnese and from outside mustered at Phlius; the Bœotians with five thousand heavy infantry and as many light troops, and five hundred horse and the same number of dismounted troopers; the Corinthians with two thousand heavy infantry; the rest more or less as might happen; and the Phliasians with all their forces, the army being in their country.

58. The preparations of the Lacedæmonians from the first had been known to the Argives, who did not, however, take the field until

---

*The thirteenth year has occupied but three pages in the text. This book covers the end of the first war (422–421) and the interval until open hostilities recommence (421–416).

†In 418 Agis (reigned c.427–400) leads the Spartans into the Argolid, the territory of Argos. His father, Archidamus, who led the Peloponnesians into Attica in the first three years of the war, presumably died around 427; we hear nothing of him after that. Agis will be victorious at Mantinea and ferociously destructive of Attica in 413 and following years, when he establishes the permanent raiding-base at Deceleia.

the enemy was on his road to join the rest at Phlius. Reinforced by the Mantineans with their allies, and by three thousand Elean heavy infantry, they advanced and fell in with the Lacedæmonians at Methydrium in Arcadia. Each party took up its position upon a hill, and the Argives prepared to engage the Lacedæmonians while they were alone; but Agis eluded them by breaking up his camp in the night, and proceeded to join the rest of the allies at Phlius. The Argives discovering this at daybreak, marched first to Argos and then to the Nemean road, by which they expected the Lacedæmonians and their allies would come down. However, Agis, instead of taking this road as they expected, gave the Lacedæmonians, Arcadians, and Epidaurians their orders, and went along another difficult road, and descended into the plain of Argos. The Corinthians, Pellenians, and Phliasians marched by another steep road; while the Bœotians, Megarians, and Sicyonians had instructions to come down by the Nemean road where the Argives were posted, in order that if the enemy advanced into the plain against the troops of Agis, they might fall upon his rear with the cavalry. These dispositions concluded, Agis invaded the plain and began to ravage Saminthus and other places.

59. Discovering this, the Argives came up from Nemea, day having now dawned. On their way they fell in with the troops of the Phliasians and Corinthians, and killed a few of the Phliasians, and had perhaps a few more of their own men killed by the Corinthians. Meanwhile the Bœotians, Megarians, and Sicyonians, advancing upon Nemea according to their instructions, found the Argives no longer there, as they had gone down on seeing their property ravaged, and were now forming for battle, the Lacedæmonians imitating their example. The Argives were now completely surrounded; from the plain the Lacedæmonians and their allies shut them off from their city; above them were the Corinthians, Phliasians, and Pellenians; and on the side of Nemea the Bœotians, Sicyonians, and Megarians. Meanwhile their army was without cavalry, the Athenians alone among the allies not having yet arrived. Now the bulk of the Argives and their allies did not see the danger of their position, but thought that they could not have a fairer field, having intercepted the Lacedæmonians in their own country and close to the city.* Two men, however, in the Argive army, Thrasylus, one of the five generals, and Alciphron, the Lacedæmonian *Proxenus*, just as the armies were upon the point of engaging, went and held a parley with Agis and urged him not to bring on a battle, as the Argives were ready to refer to fair and equal

---

*Thucydides presents both sides as thinking they have a solid advantage in the battle to come.

arbitration whatever complaints the Lacedæmonians might have against them, and to make a treaty and live in peace in future.

60. The Argives who made these statements did so upon their own authority, not by order of the people, and Agis on his accepted their proposals, and without himself either consulting the majority, simply communicated the matter to a single individual, one of the high officers accompanying the expedition, and granted the Argives a truce for four months, in which to fulfil their promises;* after which he immediately led off the army without giving any explanation to any of the other allies. The Lacedæmonians and allies followed their general out of respect for the law, but amongst themselves loudly blamed Agis for going away from so fair a field (the enemy being hemmed in on every side by infantry and cavalry) without having done anything worthy of their strength.† Indeed this was by far the finest Hellenic army ever yet brought together;‡ and it should have been seen while it was still united at Nemea, with the Lacedæmonians in full force, the Arcadians, Bœotians, Corinthians, Sicyonians, Pellenians, Phliasians, and Megarians, and all these the flower of their respective populations, thinking themselves a match not merely for the Argive confederacy, but for another such added to it. The army thus retired blaming Agis, and returned every man to his home. The Argives, however, blamed still more loudly the persons who had concluded the truce without consulting the people, themselves thinking that they had let escape with the Lacedæmonians an opportunity such as they should never see again; as the struggle would have been under the walls of their city, and by the side of many and brave allies. On their return accordingly they began to stone Thrasylus in the bed of the Charadrus, where they try all military causes before entering the city. Thrasylus fled to the altar, and so saved his life; his property however they confiscated.§

61. After this arrived a thousand Athenian heavy infantry and three hundred horse, under the command of Laches and Nicostratus; whom the Argives, being nevertheless loath to break the truce with the Lacedæmonians, begged to depart, and refused to bring before the people, to whom they had a communication to make, until compelled to do

---

*Agis had the legal authority, as king in the field, to treat with the enemy as plenipotentiary, but many Spartans and their Peloponnesian and Boeotian allies disapproved of his allowing the Argive forces to escape to fight another day. Both sides were angry that no battle had taken place.

†The contrast between behavior and evaluation is notable. It does seem to Thucydides that Agis had lost a great opportunity.

‡Thucydides points out two things: the superlative nature of this Hellenic land force and the fact that later armies surpassed even this one.

§The Argive commander Thrasylus was disgraced and almost murdered by stoning. Altars still served as asylum at Argos (compare Corcyra, 3.75, 81).

so by the entreaties of the Mantineans and Eleans, who were still at Argos. The Athenians, by the mouth of Alcibiades their ambassador there present, told the Argives and the allies that they had no right to make a truce at all without the consent of their fellow-confederates, and now that the Athenians had arrived so opportunely the war ought to be resumed. These arguments proving successful with the allies, they immediately marched upon Orchomenos, all except the Argives, who, although they had consented like the rest, stayed behind at first, but eventually joined the others. They now all sat down and besieged Orchomenos, and made assaults upon it; one of their reasons for desiring to gain this place being that hostages from Arcadia had been lodged there by the Lacedæmonians. The Orchomenians, alarmed at the weakness of their wall and the numbers of the enemy, and at the risk they ran of perishing before relief arrived, capitulated upon condition of joining the league, of giving hostages of their own to the Mantineans, and giving up those lodged with them by the Lacedæmonians.

62. Orchomenos thus secured, the allies now consulted as to which of the remaining places they should attack next. The Eleans were urgent for Lepreum; the Mantineans for Tegea; and the Argives and Athenians giving their support to the Mantineans, the Eleans went home in a rage at their not having voted for Lepreum; while the rest of the allies made ready at Mantinea for going against Tegea, which a party inside had arranged to put into their hands.

63. Meanwhile the Lacedæmonians, upon their return from Argos after concluding the four months' truce, vehemently blamed Agis for not having subdued Argos, after an opportunity such as they thought they had never had before; for it was no easy matter to bring so many and so good allies together. But when the news arrived of the capture of Orchomenos, they became more angry than ever, and, departing from all precedent,* in the heat of the moment had almost decided to raze his house, and to fine him ten thousand drachmæ. Agis however entreated them to do none of these things, promising to atone for his fault by good service in the field, failing which they might then do to him whatever they pleased; and they accordingly abstained from razing his house or fining him as they had threatened to do, and now made a law, hitherto unknown at Lacedæmon, attaching to him ten Spartans as counsellors, without whose consent he should have no power to lead an army out of the city.†

---

*The Spartans moved at a legendarily slow pace, with exceptions. Here their fury recalls the vocabulary of Athenian democratic passions, as in the Mytilenean debate. Ten thousand drachmae constitutes a crushing fine for any individual.

†The more significant departure from tradition is the assignment of ten Spartiates as military counselors. This provision does not seem to have been long lasting (compare Agis' situation later, at 8.5 or 8.9).

64. At this juncture arrived word from their friends in Tegea that unless they speedily appeared, Tegea would go over from them to the Argives and their allies, if it had not gone over already. Upon this news a force marched out from Lacedæmon, of the Spartans and Helots and all their people, and that instantly and upon a scale never before witnessed. Advancing to Orestheum in Mænalia, they directed the Arcadians in their league to follow close after them to Tegea, and going on themselves as far as Orestheum, from thence sent back the sixth part of the Spartans, consisting of the oldest and youngest men, to guard their homes, and with the rest of their army arrived at Tegea; where their Arcadian allies soon after joined them. Meanwhile they sent to Corinth, to the Bœotians, the Phocians, and Locrians, with orders to come up as quickly as possible to Mantinea. These had but short notice; and it was not easy except all together, and after waiting for each other, to pass through the enemy's country, which lay right across and blocked up the line of communication. Nevertheless they made what haste they could. Meanwhile the Lacedæmonians with the Arcadian allies that had joined them, entered the territory of Mantinea, and encamping near the temple of Heracles began to plunder the country.

65. Here they were seen by the Argives and their allies, who immediately took up a strong and difficult position, and formed in order of battle. The Lacedæmonians at once advanced against them, and came on within a stone's throw or javelin's cast, when one of the older men, seeing the enemy's position to be a strong one, hallooed to Agis that he was minded to cure one evil with another; meaning that he wished to make amends for his retreat, which had been so much blamed, from Argos, by his present untimely precipitation. Meanwhile Agis, whether in consequence of this halloo or of some sudden new idea of his own, quickly led back his army without engaging, and entering the Tegean territory, began to turn off into that of Mantinea the water about which the Mantineans and Tegeans are always fighting,* on account of the extensive damage it does to whichever of the two countries it falls into. His object in this was to make the Argives and their allies come down from the hill, to resist the diversion of the water, as they would be sure to do when they knew of it, and thus to fight the battle in the plain. He accordingly stayed that day where he was, engaged in turning off the water. The Argives and their allies were at first amazed at the sudden retreat of the enemy after advancing so near, and did not know what to make of it; but when he

---

*The Tegeans and Mantineans (map 4), like many other contiguous Hellenic communities, fought over water rights, water being a precious resource in the dry geology of Greece. Here, unusually, the problem is too much water. Agis employs the perennial conflict to draw the enemy from their strong defensive position.

had gone away and disappeared, without their having stirred to pursue him, they began anew to find fault with their generals, who had not only let the Lacedæmonians get off before, when they were so happily intercepted before Argos, but who now again allowed them to run away, without any one pursuing them, and to escape at their leisure while the Argive army was leisurely betrayed. The generals, half-stunned for the moment, afterwards led them down from the hill, and went forward and encamped in the plain, with the intention of attacking the enemy.

66. The next day the Argives and their allies formed in the order in which they meant to fight, if they chanced to encounter the enemy; and the Lacedæmonians returning from the water to their old encampment by the temple of Heracles, suddenly saw their adversaries close in front of them, all in complete order, and advanced from the hill. A shock like that of the present moment the Lacedæmonians do not ever remember to have experienced:* there was scant time for preparation, as they instantly and hastily fell into their ranks, Agis, their king, directing everything, agreeably to the law. For when a king is in the field all commands proceed from him: he gives the word to the Polemarchs; they to the Lochages; these to the Pentecostyes; these again to the Enomotarchs, and these last to the Enomoties.† In short all orders required pass in the same way and quickly reach the troops; as almost the whole Lacedæmonian army, save for a small part, consists of officers under officers, and the care of what is to be done falls upon many.

67. In this battle the left wing was composed of the Sciritæ, who in a Lacedæmonian army have always that post to themselves alone; next to these were the soldiers of Brasidas from Thrace, and the Neodamodes with them; then came the Lacedæmonians themselves, company after company, with the Arcadians of Heræa at their side. After these were the Mænalians, and on the right wing the Tegeans with a few of the Lacedæmonians at the extremity; their cavalry being posted upon the two wings. Such was the Lacedæmonian formation. That of their opponents was as follows:—On the right were the Mantineans, the action taking place in their country;‡ next to them the allies from Arcadia; after whom came the thousand picked men of the

---

*The Argives are at first clueless; then the Lacedaemonians are equally surprised, but they recover, prompted by Spartan discipline.

†Thucydides supplies the apparently little-known chain of command among the Spartan units. He may have observed the battle as an Athenian exile.

‡The right wing was the place of honor in a hoplite battle, because it was the place of greatest danger; each man, as the line tends to move toward his right, tried to protect his unprotected right arm using the shield in the left hand of the man to his right (see 5.71). The Mantineans, fighting for their own land, were expected to hold the line from shifting rightward.

Argives, to whom the state had given a long course of military training at the public expense; next to them the rest of the Argives, and
after them their allies, the Cleonæans and Orneans, and lastly the
Athenians on the extreme left, and their own cavalry with them.

68. Such were the order and the forces of the two combatants. The
Lacedæmonian army looked the largest;* though as to putting down the
numbers of either host, or of the contingents composing it, I could not
do so with any accuracy.† Owing to the secrecy of their government the
number of the Lacedæmonians was not known, and men are so apt to
brag about the forces of their country that the estimate of their opponents was not trusted.‡ The following calculation, however, makes it possible to estimate the numbers of the Lacedæmonians present upon this
occasion. There were seven companies in the field without counting the
Sciritæ, who numbered six hundred men: in each company there were
four Pentecostyes, and in the Pentecosty four Enomoties. The first rank
of the Enomoty was composed of four soldiers: as to the depth, although
they had not been all drawn up alike, but as each captain chose, they
were generally ranged eight deep; the first rank along the whole line, ex-
clusive of the Sciritæ, consisted of four hundred and forty-eight men.

69. The armies being now on the eve of engaging, each contingent
received some words of encouragement from its own commander.
The Mantineans were reminded that they were going to fight for
their country and to avoid returning to the experience of servitude
after having tasted that of empire; the Argives, that they would contend for their ancient supremacy, to regain their once equal share of
Peloponnese of which they had been so long deprived, and to punish an enemy and a neighbour for a thousand wrongs; the Athenians, of the glory of gaining the honours of the day with so many and
brave allies in arms, and that a victory over the Lacedæmonians in
Peloponnese would cement and extend their empire, and would besides preserve Attica from all invasions in future. These were the in-
citements addressed to the Argives and their allies. The
Lacedæmonians meanwhile, man to man, and with their war-songs
in the ranks,§ exhorted each brave comrade to remember what he

---

*This eyewitness phrase suggests that Thucydides observed the battle.

†Thucydides' figures allow for some guessing estimates in the range of 10,000 Peloponnesians (the larger army; see 5.71) facing 9,000 Argives and allies. His unwillingness
to give an exact number should mean that when elsewhere he does report one, he had
warrant for what he writes. These numbers seem low (as Gomme and Andrewes point
out in *A Historical Commentary on Thucydides*).

‡The historian's irritation in the face of official secrets and patriotic exaggeration
(compare 1.20–21, 5.74) is patent.

§Spartan military technique was one of a kind, and we here learn something of their
cheerleading and other group self-motivation.

had learnt before; well aware that the long training of action was of more saving virtue than any brief verbal exhortation, though never so well delivered.*

70. After this they joined battle, the Argives and their allies advancing with haste and fury, the Lacedæmonians slowly and to the music of many flute-players—a standing institution in their army, that has nothing to do with religion, but is meant to make them advance evenly, stepping in time, without breaking their order, as large armies are apt to do in the moment of engaging.

71. Just before the battle joined, King Agis resolved upon the following manœuvre. All armies are alike in this: on going into action they get forced out rather on their right wing, and one and the other overlap with this their adversary's left; because fear makes each man do his best to shelter his unarmed side with the shield of the man next him in the right, thinking that the closer the shields are locked together the better will he be protected. The man primarily responsible for this is the first upon the right wing, who is always striving to withdraw from the enemy his unarmed side; and the same apprehension makes the rest follow him.† On the present occasion the Mantineans reached with their wing far beyond the Sciritæ, and the Lacedæmonians and Tegeans still farther beyond the Athenians, as their army was the largest. Agis, afraid of his left being surrounded, and thinking that the Mantineans outflanked it too far, ordered the Sciritæ and Brasideans to move out from their place in the ranks and make the line even with the Mantineans, and told the Polemarchs Hipponoidas and Aristocles to fill up the gap thus formed, by throwing themselves into it with two companies taken from the right wing; thinking that his right would still be strong enough and to spare, and that the line fronting the Mantineans would gain in solidity.

72. However, as he gave these orders in the moment of the onset, and at short notice, it so happened that Aristocles and Hipponoidas would not move over, for which offence they were afterwards banished from Sparta, as having been guilty of cowardice;‡ and the enemy meanwhile closed before the Sciritæ (whom Agis on seeing that the two companies did not move over ordered to return to their place) had time to fill up the breach in question. Now it was, however, that the Lacedæmonians, utterly worsted in respect of skill, showed

---

*It is unclear whether this last comment is part of the mutual exhortations of the Spartans, Thucydides' own observation, or both.

†Agis correctly calculated that the Argive right might extend beyond the Peloponnesian left, not by planned tactic but by normal inclinations toward self-preservation.

‡Polemarchs, second in command, should not have hesitated to follow a Spartan king's orders, but disengaging part of a hoplite line was no easy task.

themselves as superior in point of courage.* As soon as they came to close quarters with the enemy, the Mantinean right broke their Sciritæ and Brasideans, and bursting in with their allies and the thousand picked Argives into the unclosed breach in their line cut up and surrounded the Lacedæmonians, and drove them in full rout to the waggons, slaying some of the older men on guard there. But the Lacedæmonians, worsted in this part of the field, with the rest of their army, and especially the centre, where the three hundred knights, as they are called, fought round King Agis, fell on the older men of the Argives and the five companies so named, and on the Cleonæans, the Orneans, and the Athenians next them, and instantly routed them; the greater number not even waiting to strike a blow, but giving way the moment that they came on, some even being trodden under foot, in their fear of being overtaken by their assailants.

73. The army of the Argives and their allies having given way in this quarter was now completely cut in two, and the Lacedæmonian and Tegean right simultaneously closing round the Athenians with the troops that outflanked them, these last found themselves placed between two fires, being surrounded on one side and already defeated on the other.† Indeed they would have suffered more severely than any other part of the army, but for the services of the cavalry which they had with them. Agis also on perceiving the distress of his left opposed to the Mantineans and the thousand Argives, ordered all the army to advance to the support of the defeated wing; and while this took place, as the enemy moved past and slanted away from them, the Athenians escaped at their leisure, and with them the beaten Argive division. Meanwhile the Mantineans and their allies and the picked body of the Argives ceased to press the enemy, and seeing their friends defeated and the Lacedæmonians in full advance upon them, took to flight. Many of the Mantineans perished; but the bulk of the picked body of the Argives made good their escape. The flight and retreat, however, were neither hurried nor long; the Lacedæmonians fighting long and stubbornly until the rout of their enemy, but that once effected, pursuing for a short time and not far.

74. Such was the battle, as nearly as possible as I have described it; the greatest that had occurred for a very long while among the Hel-

---

*The Lacedaemonians are skilled and experienced battlers, but here they are bested by the break-through "skills" of the determined locals. Thucydides says that they saved the day, however, by their "courage." His narrative does not support this odd judgment. Rather their steadiness illustrates both discipline and bravery. Sometimes love of contrast seems to cloud Thucydides' judgment.

†The Spartan victory over the center turns Argive victory into defeat and endangers their Athenian allies with encirclement.

lenes, and joined by the most considerable states.* The Lacedæmonians took up a position in front of the enemy's dead, and immediately set up a trophy and stripped the slain; they took up their own dead and carried them back to Tegea, where they buried them, and restored those of the enemy under truce. The Argives, Orneans, and Cleonæans had seven hundred killed; the Mantineans two hundred, and the Athenians and Æginetans also two hundred, with both their generals. On the side of the Lacedæmonians, the allies did not suffer any loss worth speaking of: as to the Lacedæmonians themselves it was difficult to learn the truth; it is said, however, that there were slain about three hundred of them.

75. While the battle was impending, Pleistoanax,† the other king, set out with a reinforcement composed of the oldest and youngest men, and got as far as Tegea, where he heard of the victory and went back again. The Lacedæmonians also sent and turned back the allies from Corinth and from beyond the Isthmus, and returning themselves dismissed their allies, and kept the Carnean holidays, which happened to be at that time. The imputations cast upon them by the Hellenes at the time, whether of cowardice on account of the disaster in the island, or of mismanagement and slowness generally, were all wiped out by this single action:‡ fortune, it was thought, might have humbled them, but the men themselves were the same as ever.

The day before this battle, the Epidaurians with all their forces invaded the deserted Argive territory, and cut off many of the guards left there in the absence of the Argive army. After the battle three thousand Elean heavy infantry arriving to aid the Mantineans, and a reinforcement of one thousand Athenians, all these allies marched at once against Epidaurus, while the Lacedæmonians were keeping the Carnea, and dividing the work among them began to build a wall round the city. The rest left off; but the Athenians finished at once the part assigned to them round Cape Heræum; and having all joined in leaving a garrison in the fortification in question, they returned to their respective cities.

---

*Thucydides marks more superlatives, although, given the numbers provided, it is hard to believe this was the greatest battle, however long "a very long time" might mean (forty years at most?).

†The Spartan dual kingship meant that the state usually had another commander in reserve, but this danger to Lacedaemonian hegemony was so serious that Pleistoanax, the senior king (reigned c.458–408), was dispatched with the reserve infantry of young and older troops.

‡The moral force of Agis' victory at Mantinea restored severely damaged Spartan prestige. That glorious image (or mirage) had been severely reduced by the Spartans' defeat and their surrender to the Athenians at Pylos in 425 (4.2 ff.). The Spartans' decisive victory here irrationally modified and diminished their deserved reputation for mismanagement and slowness.

Summer now came to an end.

76. In the first days of the next winter, when the Carnean holidays were over, the Lacedæmonians took the field, and arriving at Tegea sent on to Argos proposals of accommodation. They had before had a party in the town desirous of overthrowing the democracy; and after the battle that had been fought, these were now far more in a position to persuade the people to listen to terms. Their plan was first to make a treaty with the Lacedæmonians, to be followed by an alliance, and after this to fall upon the commons. Lichas, son of Arcesilaus, the Argive *Proxenus*, accordingly arrived at Argos with two proposals from Lacedæmon, to regulate the conditions of war or peace, according as they preferred the one or the other. After much discussion, Alcibiades happening to be in the town, the Lacedæmonian party who now ventured to act openly, persuaded the Agives to accept the proposal for an accommodation; which ran as follows:—

77. *The assembly of the Lacedæmonians agrees to treat with the Argives upon the terms following—*

1. *The Argives shall restore to the Orchomenians their children, and to the Mænalians their men, and shall restore the men they have in Mantinea to the Lacedæmonians.*

2. *They shall evacuate Epidaurus, and raze the fortification there. If the Athenians refuse to withdraw from Epidaurus, they shall be declared enemies of the Argives and of the Lacedæmonians, and of the allies of the Lacedæmonians and the allies of the Argives.*

3. *If the Lacedæmonians have any children in their custody, they shall restore them every one to his city.*

4. *As to the offering to the god, the Argives, if they wish, shall impose an oath upon the Epidaurians, but, if not, they shall swear it themselves.*

5. *All the cities in Peloponnese, both small and great, shall be independent according to the customs of their country.*

6. *If any of the powers outside Peloponnese invade Peloponnesian territory, the parties contracting shall unite to repel them, on such terms as they may agree upon, as being most fair for the Peloponnesians.*

7. *All allies of the Lacedæmonians outside Peloponnese shall be on the same footing as the Lacedæmonians, and the allies of the Argives shall be on the same footing as the Argives, being left in enjoyment of their own possessions.*

8. *This treaty shall be shown to the allies, and shall be concluded, if they approve: if the allies think fit, they may send the treaty to be considered at home.*

78. The Argives began by accepting this proposal, and the Lacedæmonian army returned home from Tegea. After this intercourse was renewed between them, and not long afterwards the same party contrived that the Argives should give up the league with the Mantineans, Eleans, and Athenians, and should make a treaty and alliance with the Lacedæmonians; which was consequently done upon the terms following:—

79. *The Lacedæmonians and Argives agree to a treaty and alliance for fifty years upon the terms following:—*

1. *All disputes shall be decided by fair and impartial arbitration, agreeably to the customs of the two countries.*

2. *The rest of the cities in Peloponnese may be included in this treaty and alliance, as independent and sovereign, in full enjoyment of what they possess; all disputes being decided by fair and impartial arbitration, agreeably to the customs of the said cities.*

3. *All allies of the Lacedæmonians outside Peloponnese shall be upon the same footing as the Lacedæmonians themselves, and the allies of the Argives shall be upon the same footing as the Argives themselves, continuing to enjoy what they possess.*

4. *If it shall be anywhere necessary to make an expedition in common, the Lacedæmonians and Argives shall consult upon it and decide, as may be most fair for the allies.*

5. *If any of the cities, whether inside or outside Peloponnese, have a question whether of frontiers or otherwise, it must be settled; but if one allied city should have a quarrel with another allied city, it must be referred to some third city thought impartial by both parties. Private citizens shall have their disputes decided according to the laws of their several countries.*

80. The treaty and above alliance concluded, each party at once released everything whether acquired by war or otherwise, and thenceforth acting in common voted to receive neither herald nor embassy from the Athenians unless they evacuated their forts and withdrew from Peloponnese, and also to make neither peace nor war with any, except jointly. Zeal was not wanting: both parties sent envoys to the Thracian places and to Perdiccas, and persuaded the latter to join their league. Still he did not at once break off from Athens, although minded to do so upon seeing the way shown him by Argos, the original home of his family. They also renewed their old oaths with the Chalcidians and took new ones: the Argives, besides, sent ambassadors to the Athenians, bidding them evacuate the fort at Epidaurus. The Athenians, seeing their own men outnumbered by the rest of the garrison, sent Demosthenes to bring them out. This general, under colour of a gymnastic contest which he arranged on his arrival, got the rest of the garrison out of the place, and shut the gates behind them. Afterwards the Athenians renewed their treaty with the Epidaurians, and by themselves gave up the fortress.

81. After the defection of Argos from the league, the Mantineans, though they held out at first, in the end finding themselves powerless without the Argives, themselves too came to terms with Lacedæmon, and gave up their sovereignty over the towns.* The Lacedæmonians and Argives, each a thousand strong, now took the field together, and the former first went by themselves to Sicyon and made the government there more oligarchical than before, and then both, uniting, put down the democracy at Argos and set up an oligarchy favourable to Lacedæmon. These events occurred at the close of the winter, just before spring; and the fourteenth year of the war ended.†

82. The next summer the people of Dium, in Athos, revolted from the Athenians to the Chalcidians, and the Lacedæmonians settled affairs in Achæa in a way more agreeable to the interests of their country. Meanwhile the popular party at Argos little by little gathered new consistency and courage, and waited for the moment of the Gymnopædic festival at Lacedæmon, and then fell upon the oligarchs.‡ After a fight in the city victory declared for the commons, who slew some of their opponents and banished others. The Lacedæmonians for a long while let the messages of their friends at Argos remain without effect. At last they put off the Gymnopædiæ and marched to their succour, but learning at Tegea the defeat of the oligarchs, refused to go any further in spite of the entreaties of those who had escaped, and returned home and kept the festival. Later on, envoys arrived with messages from the Argives in the town and from the exiles, when the allies were also at Sparta; and after much had been said on both sides, the Lacedæmonians decided that the party in the town had done wrong, and resolved to march against Argos, but kept delaying and putting off the matter. Meanwhile the commons at Argos, in fear of the Lacedæmonians, began again to court the Athenian alliance, which they were convinced would be of the greatest service to them; and accordingly proceeded to build long walls to the sea, in order that in case of a blockade by land, with the help of the Athenians they might have the advantage of importing what they wanted by sea. Some of the cities in Peloponnese were

---

*The entire Athenian initiative in the Peloponnese came crashing down, once Argos made peace with Sparta. The Mantineans could not maintain an autonomous foreign policy without Argive support. Alcibiades' mischief had done no one any good. His persuasive powers, however, never failed him.

†The political consequences of Lacedaemonian victory is changes of governments in various cities, not least in Argos, where the supporters of oligarchy seize their chance to take over the government. Thus ends 418; the new year 417 begins with further internal revolutions (*stasis*).

‡While the Lacedaemonians otherwise occupy themselves with the "Naked Youths" mid-summer festival, the commons at Argos takes back its government.

also privy to the building of these walls; and the Argives with all their people, women and slaves not excepted, addressed themselves to the work, while carpenters and masons came to them from Athens.*

Summer was now over.

83. The winter following the Lacedæmonians, hearing of the walls that were building, marched against Argos with their allies, the Corinthians excepted, being also not without intelligence in the city itself; Agis, son of Archidamus, their king, was in command. The intelligence which they counted upon within the town came to nothing; they however took and razed the walls which were being built, and after capturing the Argive town Hysiæ and killing all the freemen that fell into their hands, went back and dispersed every man to his city. After this the Argives marched into Phlius and plundered it for harbouring their exiles, most of whom had settled there, and so returned home. The same winter the Athenians blockaded Macedonia, on the score of the league entered into by Perdiccas with the Argives and Lacedæmonians, and also of his breach of his engagements on the occasion of the expedition prepared by Athens against the Chalcidians in the direction of Thrace and against Amphipolis, under the command of Nicias, son of Niceratus, which had to be broken up mainly because of his desertion.† He was therefore proclaimed an enemy. And thus the winter ended, and the fifteenth year of the war ended with it.

Sixteenth Year of the War — The Melian Conference — Fate of Melos

84. The next summer Alcibiades sailed with twenty ships to Argos and seized the suspected persons still left of the Lacedæmonian faction to the number of three hundred, whom the Athenians forthwith lodged in the neighbouring islands of their empire. The Athenians also made an expedition against the isle of Melos with thirty ships of their own, six Chian, and two Lesbian vessels, twelve hundred heavy infantry, three hundred archers, and twenty mounted archers from Athens, and about fifteen hundred heavy infantry from the allies and

---

*Note the participation of women and slaves in the building of long walls connecting the inland town to the Athenian-dominated Argolic Gulf and Cretan Sea. This geopolitical strategy mimics the Athenian democracy's connection of Athens to the Saronic Gulf and the Aegean Sea.

†The Macedonian Perdiccas, pursuing his own local interests on the northern front (map 7), was never anyone's dependable ally. Nicias engages here in another unsuccessful campaign.

the islanders. The Melians are a colony of Lacedæmon that would not submit to the Athenians like the other islanders,* and at first remained neutral and took no part in the struggle,† but afterwards upon the Athenians using violence and plundering their territory, assumed an attitude of open hostility. Cleomedes, son of Lycomedes, and Tisias, son of Tisimachus, the generals, encamping in their territory with the above armament, before doing any harm to their land, sent envoys to negotiate.‡ These the Melians did not bring before the people, but bade them state the object of their mission to the magistrates and the few; upon which the Athenian envoys spoke as follows:—

85. *Athenians.*—'Since the negotiations are not to go on before the people, in order that we may not be able to speak straight on without interruption, and deceive the ears of the multitude by seductive arguments which would pass without refutation§ (for we know that this is the meaning of our being brought before the few), what if you who sit there were to pursue a method more cautious still! Make no set speech yourselves, but take us up at whatever you do not like, and settle that before going any farther. And first tell us if this proposition of ours suits you.'

86. The Melian commissioners answered:—

---

*In 416, the sixteenth year of Thucydides' war, the peace and treaties will be abrogated in fact, if not in declaration. Melos, an island about 75 miles east of the Laconian coast (map 1), and colonized by the Spartans, claimed to be an ally of neither confederacy. Therefore, as a neutral, it had the option to join the Athenian alliance, since the treaty of 421 (5.18, section 5) ignores relations with unnamed unaligned powers. Thus, attack within the terms of the peace treaty does not seem ruled out, although the Athenians have no reasonable justification and deny or mock the very concept of neutrality.

†There is evidence that Melos had been assessed to contribute to both the Athenians' Delian (or Hellenic) League (Fornara #136) and to the Peloponnesian war fund (Fornara #132), but no proof that she did so. Thucydides here, in one of his most difficult passages, provides an unprecedentedly dialogical examination of the psychology and morality of power, both for the oppressors and the oppressed. He juxtaposes this manifestation of the Athenian doctrine of "rule where you can" to the following Athenian expedition against Sicily, where the doctrine comes crashing down. The Melians oppose might to right, a distinction that the Machiavellian and amoral Athenians reject for the realm of international politics. Thucydides' experimental disquisition explores unequal power and its tendency to blind and/or corrupt.

‡The Athenian generals are not well-known individuals, but that suits their personality-free representation of Athenian state policy. It is only rational to request surrender before destroying the capital (fruit trees, vines, hydraulic infrastructure, etc.) of the "enemy," here a middling state that prudently (he implies) tried to avoid involvement in the war.

§The Athenians unexpectedly reject discussion with the commons, usually a group that would welcome their intervention and seductive arguments. The attractions of Athenian-style democracy often leveraged Athenian interests in neutral states typically ruled, as most Hellenic cities were, by oligarchies.

Melians.—'To the fairness of quietly instructing each other as you propose there is nothing to object; but your military preparations are too far advanced to agree with what you say, as we see you are come to be judges in your own cause, and that all we can reasonably expect from this negotiation is war, if we prove to have right on our side and refuse to submit, and in the contrary case, slavery.'

87. *Athenians.*—'If you have met to reason about presentiments of the future, or for anything else than to consult for the safety of your state* upon the facts that you see before you, we will give over; otherwise we will go on.'

88. *Melians.*—'It is natural and excusable for men in our position to turn more ways than one both in thought and utterance. However, the question in this conference is, as you say, the safety of our country; and the discussion, if you please, can proceed in the way which you propose.'

89. *Athenians.*—'For ourselves, we shall not trouble you with specious pretences†—either of how we have a right to our empire because we overthrew the Mede, or are now attacking you because of wrong that you have done us—and make a long speech which would not be believed; and in return we hope that you, instead of thinking to influence us by saying that you did not join the Lacedæmonians, although their colonists, or that you have done us no wrong, will aim at what is feasible, holding in view the real sentiments of us both: since you know as well as we do that right, as the world goes, is only in question between equals in power,‡ while the strong do what they can and the weak suffer what they must.'

90. *Melians.*—'As we think, at any rate, it is expedient—we speak as we are obliged, since you enjoin us to let right alone and talk only of interest§—that you should not destroy what is our common protection, the privilege of being allowed in danger to invoke what is fair and right, and even to profit by arguments not strictly valid if they can be got to pass current. And you are as much interested in this as any, as your fall would be a signal for the heaviest vengeance and an example for the world to meditate upon.'‖

---

*The Athenians try to shut off immediately discussion of what is right. Self-interest, not morality, is at stake in a military confrontation.

†The Athenians do not wish to make use of arguments from the past and from justice.

‡Only military equals can invoke "right," and presumably there too it is only expedient talk.

§The Melians attempt to turn the argument from expediency back on the Athenians by describing morality as itself a practical shield for all.

‖The Melians, like Herodotus, can foresee the likely downfall and end of every city and empire—sooner or later, often sooner. In 404, when the war ended with Athens' total defeat, the Thebans did wish to eradicate Athens and enslave the population, but the Spartans objected, presciently calculating that Athens could serve as a useful counterweight or puppet for moderating future Boeotian claims and exercises of power.

91. *Athenians.*—'The end of our empire, if end it should, does not frighten us: a rival empire like Lacedæmon, even if Lacedæmon was our real antagonist, is not so terrible to the vanquished as subjects who by themselves attack and overpower their rulers. This, however, is a risk that we are content to take. We will now proceed to show you that we are come here in the interest of our empire, and that we shall say what we are now going to say, for the preservation of your country; as we would fain exercise that empire over you without trouble, and see you preserved for the good of us both.'

92. *Melians.*—'And how, pray, could it turn out as good for us to serve as for you to rule?'

93. *Athenians.*—'Because you would have the advantage of submitting before suffering the worst, and we should gain by not destroying you.'

94. *Melians.*—'So that you would not consent to our being neutral, friends instead of enemies, but allies of neither side.'

95. *Athenians.*—'No; for your hostility cannot so much hurt us as your friendship will be an argument to our subjects of our weakness, and your enmity of our power.'*

96. *Melians.*—'Is that your subjects' idea of equity, to put those who have nothing to do with you in the same category with peoples that are most of them your own colonists, and some conquered rebels?'

97. *Athenians.*—'As far as right goes they think one has as much of it as the other,† and that if any maintain their independence it is because they are strong, and that if we do not molest them it is because we are afraid; so that besides extending our empire we should gain in security by your subjection; the fact that you are islanders and weaker than others rendering it all the more important that you should not succeed in baffling the masters of the sea.'

98. *Melians.*—'But do you consider that there is no security in the policy which we indicate? For here again if you debar us from talking about justice and invite us to obey your interest, we also must explain ours, and try to persuade you, if the two happen to coincide. How can you avoid making enemies of all existing neutrals who shall look at our case and conclude from it that one day or another you will attack them?‡ And what is this but to make greater the enemies that you

---

*This statement encapsulates an ugly and inexpedient distortion of human values: Now Melian friendship would suggest Athenian weakness, while their hostility indicates Athenian power.

†The Athenians argue that "right" does not depend on tradition or on former relations. There is a reflection here of contemporary sophistic debates on the superior power of nurture or nature, custom or nature, *nomos* (human law) or *physis* (natural law).

‡The Melians reasonably argue that if neutrals are attacked, all remaining neutral countries will perforce join forces with Athens' enemies.

have already, and to force others to become so who would otherwise have never thought of it?'

99. *Athenians.*—'Why, the fact is that continentals generally give us but little alarm; the liberty which they enjoy will long prevent their taking precautions against us; it is rather islanders like yourselves, outside our empire, and subjects smarting under the yoke, who would be the most likely to take a rash step and lead themselves and us into obvious danger.'

100. *Melians.*—'Well then, if you risk so much to retain your empire, and your subjects to get rid of it, it were surely great baseness and cowardice in us who are still free not to try everything that can be tried, before submitting to your yoke.'

101. *Athenians.*—'Not if you are well advised, the contest not being an equal one, with honour as the prize and shame as the penalty, but a question of self-preservation and of not resisting those who are far stronger than you are.'

102. *Melians.*—'But we know that the fortune of war is sometimes more impartial than the disproportion of numbers might lead one to suppose; to submit is to give ourselves over to despair, while action still preserves for us a hope that we may stand erect.'

103. *Athenians.*—'Hope, danger's comforter,* may be indulged in by those who have abundant resources, if not without loss at all events without ruin; but its nature is to be extravagant, and those who go so far as to put their all upon the venture see it in its true colours only when they are ruined; but so long as the discovery would enable them to guard against it, it is never found wanting. Let not this be the case with you, who are weak and hang on a single turn of the scale; nor be like the vulgar, who, abandoning such security as human means may still afford, when visible hopes fail them in extremity, turn to invisible, to prophecies and oracles, and other such inventions that delude men with hopes to their destruction.'†

104. *Melians.*—'You may be sure that we are as well aware as you of the difficulty of contending against your power and fortune, unless the terms be equal. But we trust that the gods may grant us fortune as good as yours, since we are just men fighting against unjust,‡ and that what we want in power will be made up by the alliance of the Lacedæmonians, who are bound, if only for very shame, to come to

---

*Hope, a positive value in Jewish and Christian and many other traditions, is often negative in early Greek thought. Hesiod described two kinds, the constructive and competitive, but also the destructive and debilitating. Thucydides thinks that hope leads governing bodies into dangerous calculations that are contrary to reason.

†The weak states especially should avoid pinning their fortunes on unlikely outcomes.

‡The Melians, hammered down to their last arguments, call on the gods and justice, as the Plataeans had done—to no better result.

the aid of their kindred.* Our confidence, therefore, after all is not so utterly irrational.'

105. *Athenians.*—'When you speak of the favour of the gods, we may as fairly hope for that as yourselves; neither our pretensions nor our conduct being in any way contrary to what men believe of the gods, or practise among themselves. Of the gods we believe, and of men we know, that by a necessary law of their nature they rule wherever they can. And it is not as if we were the first to make this law, or to act upon it when made: we found it existing before us, and shall leave it to exist for ever after us; all we do is to make use of it, knowing that you and everybody else, having the same power as we have, would do the same as we do. Thus, as far as the gods are concerned, we have no fear and no reason to fear that we shall be at a disadvantage. But when we come to your notion about the Lacedæmonians, which leads you to believe that shame will make them help you, here we bless your simplicity but do not envy your folly. The Lacedæmonians, when their own interests or their country's laws are in question, are the worthiest men alive; of their conduct towards others much might be said, but no clearer idea of it could be given than by shortly saying that of all the men we know they are most conspicuous in considering what is agreeable honourable, and what is expedient just.† Such a way of thinking does not promise much for the safety which you now unreasonably count upon.'

106. *Melians.*—'But it is for this very reason that we now trust to their respect for expediency to prevent them from betraying the Melians, their colonists, and thereby losing the confidence of their friends in Hellas and helping their enemies.'

107. *Athenians.*—'Then you do not adopt the view that expediency goes with security, while justice and honour cannot be followed without danger; and danger the Lacedæmonians generally court as little as possible.'‡

108. *Melians.*—'But we believe that they would be more likely to face even danger for our sake, and with more confidence than for others, as our nearness to Peloponnese makes it easier for them to act, and our common blood insures our fidelity.'

109. *Athenians.*—'Yes, but what an intending ally trusts to, is not the goodwill of those who ask his aid, but a decided superiority of

---

*The Lacedaemonians will surely acknowledge ethnic bonds, since both the Melians and the Spartans are Dorians, and the Melians are bonded closer than many, because they were colonists sent from Lacedaemon. Shame constitutes another unreliable reed for them (and others) to lean upon.

†The Athenians have a cynical and justified view of the Spartans' realpolitik.

‡The Athenians rightly judge the Spartans as both averse to risks and aware that their security requires them to stick close to home and avoid the sea, the Athenians' realm.

power for action; and the Lacedæmonians look to this even more than others. At least, such is their distrust of their home resources that it is only with numerous allies that they attack a neighbour; now is it likely that while we are masters of the sea they will cross over to an island?'*

110. *Melians.*—'But they would have others to send. The Cretan sea is a wide one, and it is more difficult for those who command it to intercept others, than for those who wish to elude them to do so safely. And should the Lacedæmonians miscarry in this, they would fall upon your land, and upon those left of your allies whom Brasidas did not reach; and instead of places which are not yours, you will have to fight for your own country and your own confederacy.'

111. *Athenians.*—'Some diversion of the kind you speak of you may one day experience, only to learn, as others have done, that the Athenians never once yet withdrew from a siege for fear of any. But we are struck by the fact, that after saying you would consult for the safety of your country, in all this discussion you have mentioned nothing which men might trust in and think to be saved by. Your strongest arguments depend upon hope and the future, and your actual resources are too scanty, as compared with those arrayed against you, for you to come out victorious. You will therefore show great blindness of judgment, unless, after allowing us to retire, you can find some counsel more prudent than this. You will surely not be caught by that idea of disgrace, which in dangers that are disgraceful, and at the same time too plain to be mistaken, proves so fatal to mankind; since in too many cases the very men that have their eyes perfectly open to what they are rushing into, let the thing called disgrace, by the mere influence of a seductive name, lead them on to a point at which they become so enslaved by the phrase as in fact to fall wilfully into hopeless disaster, and incur disgrace more disgraceful as the companion of error, than when it comes as the result of misfortune.† This, if you are well advised, you will guard against; and you will not think it dishonourable to submit to the greatest city in Hellas, when it makes you the moderate offer of becoming its tributary ally, without ceasing to enjoy the country that belongs to you; nor when you have the choice given you between war and security, will you be so blinded as to choose

---

*The Athenian Empire developed among the islanders of the Aegean and along its coasts. The Athenians could blockade the Peloponnese and in general forced the Spartans and their allies to do without seaborne provisioning and materiel. Islanders were at the naval empire's mercy.

†The Athenians, having derided arguments based on hope and the future, turn to honor, and tell the Melians that rushing into predictable disaster is more disgraceful than surrender and regular tribute payments.

the worse.* And it is certain that those who do not yield to their equals, who keep terms with their superiors, and are moderate towards their inferiors, on the whole succeed best. Think over the matter, therefore, after our withdrawal, and reflect once and again that it is for your country that you are consulting, that you have not more than one, and that upon this one deliberation depends its prosperity or ruin.'

112. The Athenians now withdrew from the conference; and the Melians, left to themselves, came to a decision corresponding with what they had maintained in the discussion, and answered, 'Our resolution, Athenians, is the same as it was at first. We will not in a moment deprive of freedom a city that has been inhabited these seven hundred years; but we put our trust in the fortune by which the gods have preserved it until now, and in the help of men, that is, of the Lacedæmonians; and so we will try and save ourselves. Meanwhile we invite you to allow us to be friends to you and foes to neither party, and to retire from our country after making such a treaty as shall seem fit to us both.'

113. Such was the answer of the Melians. The Athenians now departing from the conference said, 'Well, you alone, as it seems to us, judging from these resolutions, regard what is future as more certain than what is before your eyes, and what is out of sight, in your eagerness, as already coming to pass; and as you have staked most on, and trusted most in, the Lacedæmonians, your fortune, and your hopes, so will you be most completely deceived.'

114. The Athenian envoys now returned to the army; and the Melians showing no signs of yielding, the generals at once betook themselves to hostilities, and drew a line of circumvallation round the Melians, dividing the work among the different states. Subsequently the Athenians returned with most of their army, leaving behind them a certain number of their own citizens and of the allies to keep guard by land and sea. The force thus left stayed on and besieged the place.

115. About the same time the Argives invaded the territory of Phlius and lost eighty men cut off in an ambush by the Phliasians and Argive exiles. Meanwhile the Athenians at Pylos took so much plunder from the Lacedæmonians that the latter, although they still refrained from breaking off the treaty and going to war with Athens, yet proclaimed that any of their people that chose might plunder the

---

*The loss of autonomy in the face of the greatest power in Hellas is nothing dishonorable compared to war and community destruction. The debate ends without anyone persuading anyone. The situation returns to the *status quo ante*, and the Athenians' superior force will decide it. (Fornara #142 records various cities' tributary quotas for 418, an ordinary year for the Athenian treasury.)

Athenians.* The Corinthians also commenced hostilities with the Athenians for private quarrels of their own; but the rest of the Peloponnesians stayed quiet. Meanwhile the Melians attacked by night and took the part of the Athenian lines over against the market, and killed some of the men, and brought in grain and all else that they could find useful to them, and so returned and kept quiet, while the Athenians took measures to keep better guard in future.

Summer was now over.

116. The next winter the Lacedæmonians intended to invade the Argive territory, but arriving at the frontier found the sacrifices for crossing unfavourable, and went back again.† This intention of theirs gave the Argives suspicions of certain of their fellow-citizens, some of whom they arrested; others, however, escaped them. About the same time the Melians again took another part of the Athenian lines which were but feebly garrisoned. Reinforcements afterwards arriving from Athens in consequence, under the command of Philocrates, son of Demeas, the siege was now pressed vigorously; and some treachery taking place inside, the Melians surrendered at discretion to the Athenians, who put to death all the grown men whom they took, and sold the women and children for slaves, and subsequently sent out five hundred colonists and inhabited the place themselves.‡

---

*War is resumed without any public abrogations of the treaty.

†Those wondering about Lacedaemonian intentions toward their Melian colonists find a silent answer here. Their initiatives ignore their fellow Dorians and their colonists, the Melians.

‡The Melians, battered by internal conflict, surrender at last. All the men are executed, the women and children sold into slavery, as at Scione. Thucydides, as is his wont, understates the callous brutality while endorsing the Athenians' predictions (but not their policy or morality). Melos became the paradigm for what was wrong with imperialism for the ancient world and for later critics—for example, Senator J. William Fulbright's criticisms of American attacks on Vietnam in the late 1960s.

BOOK 6

Seventeenth Year of the War — The Sicilian Campaign —
Affair of the Herms — Departure of the Expedition

1. The same winter the Athenians resolved to sail again to Sicily, with a greater armament than that under Laches and Eurymedon, and, if possible, to conquer the island; most of them being ignorant of its size and of the number of its inhabitants, Hellenic and barbarian, and of the fact that they were undertaking a war not much inferior to that against the Peloponnesians.* For the voyage round Sicily in a merchantman is not far short of eight days; and yet, large as the island is, there are only two miles of sea to prevent its being mainland.

2. It was settled originally as follows, and the peoples that occupied it are these. The earliest inhabitants spoken of in any part of the country are the Cyclopes and Læstrygones; but I cannot tell of what race they were, or whence they came or whither they went, and that must suffice which the poets have said of them and what may be generally known concerning them.† The Sicanians appear to have been the next settlers, although they pretend to have been the first of all and aborigines; but the facts show that they were Iberians, driven by the Ligurians from the river Sicanus in Iberia. It was from them that the island, before called Trinacria, took its name of Sicania, and to the present day they inhabit the west of Sicily. On the fall of Ilium,‡ some of the Trojans escaped from the Achæans, came in ships to Sicily, and settled next to the Sicanians under the general name of Elymi; their towns being called Eryx and Egesta. With them settled some of the Phocians carried on their way from Troy by a storm, first to Libya, and afterwards from thence to Sicily. The Sicels crossed over to Sicily from their first home Italy, flying from the Opicans, as tradition says

---

*Thucydides stresses the magnitude of the task (Sicily's circumference is approximately 500 miles) and the ignorance of those Athenians voting in early 415 to invade and conquer a distant territory.

†The geographic-ethnographic discussion may owe much to Antiochus of Syracuse, a contemporary of Thucydides who wrote an account of his native island (map 10). Thucydides mentions no earlier author except Hellanicus (1.97), a native of Lesbos who also wrote a history of Attica. The reference to poets, and mythological creatures as well, conveys Thucydides' low regard for these ahistorical sources and subjects.

‡Thucydides regarded the Trojan War as historical, as one sees in his prefatory "archaeology" (1.8–12), but not Homer's elaboration of the details.

MAP 10. SOUTHERN ITALY AND SICILY

and as seems not unlikely, upon rafts, having watched till the wind set down the strait to effect the passage; although perhaps they may have sailed over in some other way. Even at the present day there are still Sicels in Italy; and the country got its name of Italy from Italus, a king of the Sicels, so called. These went with a great host to Sicily, defeated the Sicanians in battle and forced them to remove to the south and west of the island, which thus came to be called Sicily instead of Sicania, and after they crossed over continued to enjoy the richest parts of the country for near three hundred years before any Hellenes came to Sicily; indeed they still hold the centre and north of the island. There were also Phœnicians living all round Sicily, who had occupied promontories upon the sea coasts and the islets adjacent for the purpose of trading with the Sicels. But when the Hellenes began to arrive in considerable numbers by sea, the Phœnicians abandoned most of their stations, and drawing together took up their abode in Motye, Soloeis, and Panormus, near the Elymi, partly because they confided in their alliance, and also because these are the nearest points, for the voyage between Carthage and Sicily.*

These were the barbarians in Sicily, settled as I have said.

3. Of the Hellenes, the first to arrive were Chalcidians from Eubœa with Thucles, their founder. They founded Naxos and built the altar to Apollo Archegetes, which now stands outside the town, and upon which the deputies for the Olympic and other games sacrifice before sailing from Sicily.† Syracuse was founded the year afterwards by Archias, one of the Heraclids from Corinth, who began by driving out the Sicels from the island upon which the inner city now stands, though it is no longer surrounded by water: in process of time the outer town also was taken within the walls and became populous. Meanwhile Thucles and the Chalcidians set out from Naxos in the fifth year after the foundation of Syracuse, and drove out the Sicels by arms and founded Leontini and afterwards Catana; the Catanians themselves choosing Evarchus as their founder.

4. About the same time Lamis arrived in Sicily with a colony from Megara, and after founding a place called Trotilus beyond the river

---

*The Phoenicians (here Carthaginians who had settled near modern Tunis) were strong in the western and southern parts of Sicily, as well as in western north Africa and Iberia. The strait across the Mediterranean from Sicily to North Africa measures less than 90 miles.

†Apollo enjoyed the epithet of the colonizing "chief leader." Distribution of information about markets and settlements abroad was one important function of Apollo at Delphi in central Hellas. Like the other Hellenic cities abroad, Naxos, the first Sicilian colony, founded on the east coast around 733, sent contestants and officials to the Panhellenic games in the homeland. Pindar's victory odes often celebrate Sicilian victors. (See Fornara #5 and map 10 for Sicilian colonization.)

Pantacyas, and afterwards leaving it and for a short while joining the Chalcidians at Leontini, was driven out by them and founded Thapsus. After his death his companions were driven out of Thapsus, and founded a place called the Hyblæan Megara; Hyblon, a Sicel king, having given up the place and inviting them thither. Here they lived two hundred and forty-five years; after which they were expelled from the city and the country by the Syracusan tyrant Gelo. Before their expulsion, however, a hundred years after they had settled there, they sent out Pamillus and founded Selinus; he having come from their mother country Megara to join them in its foundation. Gela was founded by Antiphemus from Rhodes and Entimus from Crete, who joined in leading a colony thither, in the forty-fifth year after the foundation of Syracuse. The town took its name from the river Gelas, the place where the citadel now stands, and which was first fortified, being called Lindii. The institutions which they adopted were Dorian.

Near one hundred and eight years after the foundation of Gela, the Geloans founded Acragas (Agrigentum), so called from the river of that name, and made Aristonous and Pystilus their founders; giving their own institutions to the colony. Zancle was originally founded by pirates from Cuma, the Chalcidian town in the country of the Opicans: afterwards, however, large numbers came from Chalcis and the rest of Eubœa, and helped to people the place; the founders being Perieres and Cratæmenes from Cuma and Chalcis respectively. It first had the name of Zancle given it by the Sicels, because the place is shaped like a sickle, which the Sicels call *Zanclon*; but upon the original settlers being afterwards expelled by some Samians and other Ionians who landed in Sicily flying from the Medes, and the Samians in their turn not long afterwards by Anaxilas, tyrant of Rhegium, the town was by him colonised with a mixed population, and its name changed to Messina, after his old country.*

5. Himera was founded from Zancle by Euclides, Simus, and Sacon, most of those who went to the colony being Chalcidians; though they were joined by some exiles from Syracuse, defeated in a civil war, called the Myletidæ. The language was a mixture of Chalcidian and Doric, but the institutions which prevailed were the Chalcidian. Acræ and Casmenæ were founded by the Syracusans; Acræ seventy years after Syracuse, Casmenæ nearly twenty after Acræ. Camarina was first founded by the Syracusans, close upon a hundred and thirty-five years

---

*The catalogue of cities, like the Homeric catalogue of contingents at Troy, emphasizes the numbers and introduces a major campaign. Strategically placed on the northeastern corner, Zancle, later Messina, experienced many changes of government, engineered from within and without. Herodotus (6.22–24) recounts the flight from Ionia. (For the tyrant Gelon, see Fornara #52 and #54.)

after the building of Syracuse; its founders being Daxon and Meneco-lus. But the Camarinæans being expelled by arms by the Syracusans for having revolted, Hippocrates, tyrant of Gela, some time later receiving their land in ransom for some Syracusan prisoners, resettled Camarina, himself acting as its founder. Lastly, it was again depopulated by Gelo, and settled once more for the third time by the Geloans.*

6. Such is the list of the peoples, Hellenic and barbarian, inhabiting Sicily, and such the magnitude of the island which the Athenians were now bent upon invading; being ambitious in real truth of conquering the whole, although they had also the plausible design of succouring their kindred and other allies in the island.† But they were especially incited by envoys from Egesta, who had come to Athens and invoked their aid more urgently than ever. The Egestæans had gone to war with their neighbours the Selinuntines upon questions of marriage and disputed territory, and the Selinuntines had procured the alliance of the Syracusans, and pressed Egesta hard by land and sea. The Egestæans now reminded the Athenians of the alliance made in the time of Laches, during the former Leontine war, and begged them to send a fleet to their aid, and among a number of other considerations urged as a capital argument, that if the Syracusans were allowed to go unpunished for their depopulation of Leontini, to ruin the allies still left to Athens in Sicily, and to get the whole power of the island into their hands, there would be a danger of their one day coming with a large force, as Dorians, to the aid of their Dorian brethren, and as colonists, to the aid of the Peloponnesians who had sent them out, and joining these in pulling down the Athenian empire.‡ The Athenians would, therefore, do well to unite with the allies still left to them, and to make a stand against the Syracusans; especially as they, the Egestæans, were prepared to furnish money sufficient for the war. The Athenians, hearing these arguments constantly repeated in their assemblies by the Egestæans and their supporters, voted first to send

---

*The Greeks settled from east to west, in general, in the century following Syracuse's foundation c. 733. The survey ends abruptly, and Thucydides returns to the proper theme of Athenian imperialism.

†Thucydides expresses a deeper reality in the phrase "in real truth." The same peculiar phrase appears to explain the cause (Spartan fear) of the entire war (1.23). He contrasts that reality with the fair-sounding phrases of helping both their diplomatic allies (Egesta, modern Segesta, a partly Greek city inland near the western corner; see the inscription of alliance [Fornara #81]) and their nominal kin (such as Ionian Leontini, northwest of Syracuse, a few miles inland from the eastern shore; map 10).

‡The Leontines work on Athenian fear of their enemies cooperating, just as the Corinthians had worked on Spartan fear, but their goal is more congenial to the Athenian expansionists. After the Athenian debacle, the Syracusans and other Sicilians did join in the Ionian War, the last phase of the Peloponnesian War.

envoys to Egesta, to see if there was really the money that they talked of in the treasury and temples, and at the same time to ascertain in what posture was the war with the Selinuntines.

7. The envoys of the Athenians were accordingly despatched to Sicily. The same winter the Lacedæmonians and their allies, the Corinthians excepted, marched into the Argive territory, and ravaged a small part of the land, and took some yokes of oxen and carried off some grain. They also settled the Argive exiles at Orneæ, and left them a few soldiers taken from the rest of the army; and after making a truce for a certain while, according to which neither Orneatæ nor Argives were to injure each other's territory, returned home with the army. Not long afterwards the Athenians came with thirty ships and six hundred heavy infantry, and the Argives joining them with all their forces, marched out and besieged the men in Orneæ for one day; but the garrison escaped by night, the besiegers having bivouacked some way off. The next day the Argives, discovering it, razed Orneæ to the ground, and went back again; after which the Athenians went home in their ships. Meanwhile the Athenians took by sea to Methone on the Macedonian border some cavalry of their own and the Macedonian exiles that were at Athens, and plundered the country of Perdiccas. Upon this the Lacedæmonians sent to the Thracian Chalcidians, who had a truce with Athens from one period of ten days to another, urging them to join Perdiccas in the war, which they refused to do. And the winter ended, and with it ended the sixteenth year of this war of which Thucydides is the historian.

8. Early in the spring of the following summer the Athenian envoys arrived from Sicily, and the Egestæans with them, bringing sixty talents of uncoined silver, as a month's pay for sixty ships, which they were to ask to have sent them.* The Athenians held an assembly, and after hearing from the Egestæans and their own envoys a report, as attractive as it was untrue,† upon the state of affairs generally, and in particular as to the money, of which, it was said, there was abundance in the temples and the treasury, voted to send sixty ships to Sicily,

---

*Sixty talents is a considerable sum. It would support sixty ships for a month (at 200 oarsmen per trireme receiving one drachma a day). That amount will not go far in the campaign to bring a huge island into subjection. The debate over the decision (6.8–26) includes rare discussions of internal politics as well as external aggression. (Fornara #146 translates several decrees relating to this expedition.)

†Thucydides plainly states that fraud and misperception drove the Athenian decision. One recalls that Thucydides (2.65) thought more optimistically of Athenian opportunity for success. There he says the Athenian error arose more from failure to support the expedition than from miscalculation of the opposition's strength. He probably wrote that analysis later, since it explicitly mentions the end of the war. We have now reached 415; Thucydides retards the pace for his most extensively developed narrative, the expedition to Sicily.

under the command of Alcibiades, son of Clinias, Nicias, son of Niceratus, and Lamachus, son of Xenophanes, who were appointed with full powers; they were to help the Egestæans against the Selinuntines, to restore Leontini upon gaining any advantage in the war, and to order all other matters in Sicily as they should deem best for the interests of Athens. Five days after this a second assembly was held, to consider the speediest means of equipping the ships, and to vote whatever else might be required by the generals for the expedition; and Nicias, who had been chosen to the command against his will, and who thought that the state was not well advised, but upon a slight and specious pretext was aspiring to the conquest of the whole of Sicily, a great matter to achieve, came forward in the hope of diverting the Athenians from the enterprise,* and gave them the following counsel:—

9. 'Although this assembly was convened to consider the preparations to be made for sailing to Sicily, I think, notwithstanding, that we have still this question to examine, whether it be better to send out the ships at all, and that we ought not to give so little consideration to a matter of such moment, or let ourselves be persuaded by foreigners into undertaking a war with which we have nothing to do. And yet, individually, I gain in honour by such a course, and fear as little as other men for my person—not that I think a man need be any the worse citizen for taking some thought for his person and estate; on the contrary, such a man would for his own sake desire the prosperity of his country more than others—nevertheless, as I have never spoken against my convictions to gain honour, I shall not begin to do so now, but shall say what I think best. Against your character any words of mine would be weak enough; if I were to advise your keeping what you have got and not risking what is actually yours for advantages which are dubious in themselves, and which you may or may not attain. I will, therefore, content myself with showing that your ardour is out of season, and your ambition not easy of accomplishment.

10. 'I affirm, then, that you leave many enemies behind you here to

---

*Nicias is a senior statesman and general. We have seen him active in several theaters, at the first attack on Melos, in the Pylos debate, etc. As in the discussion of Pylos, Nicias hopes to divert the Athenians from new strategic schemes (as Pericles had advised), but his methods again lead to the opposite result. Thucydides respected the man (see his "epitaph," 7.86) but could hardly have admired his political savvy (as compared to Pericles' or Themistocles'). His desire to maintain the peace of 421 also grew out of his role and credit for chaperoning that treaty. Plutarch has composed a biography of him, and he also draws from sources other than Thucydides. Alcibiades, a younger politician from the prominent Alcmaeonid family (which included Pericles), was capable but selfish. He would switch sides several times before the end of the war. Plutarch has written his biography also. Lamachus, found in Aristophanes' comedy *Acharnians* (early 425), is relatively colorless, in comparison to his fellow generals; he would meet death fighting bravely early in the campaign.

go yonder and bring more back with you. You imagine, perhaps, that the treaty which you have made can be trusted; a treaty that will continue to exist nominally, as long as you keep quiet—for nominal it has become, owing to the practices of certain men here and at Sparta—but which in the event of a serious reverse in any quarter would not delay our enemies a moment in attacking us; first, because the convention was forced upon them by disaster and was less honourable to them than to us; and secondly, because in this very convention there are many points that are still disputed. Again, some of the most powerful states have never yet accepted the arrangement at all. Some of these are at open war with us; others (as the Lacedæmonians do not yet move) are restrained by truces renewed every ten days, and it is only too probable that if they found our power divided, as we are hurrying to divide it, they would attack us vigorously with the Siceliots, whose alliance they would have in the past valued as they would that of few others. A man ought, therefore, to consider these points, and not to think of running risks with a country placed so critically, or of grasping at another empire before we have secured the one we have already; for in fact the Thracian Chalcidians have been all these years in revolt from us without being yet subdued, and others on the continents yield us but a doubtful obedience. Meanwhile the Egestæans, our allies, have been wronged, and we run to help them, while the rebels who have so long wronged us still wait for punishment.

11. 'And yet the latter, if brought under, might be kept under; while the Sicilians, even if conquered, are too far off and too numerous to be ruled without difficulty.* Now it is folly to go against men who could not be kept under even if conquered, while failure would leave us in a very different position from that which we occupied before the enterprise. The Siceliots, again, to take them as they are at present, in the event of a Syracusan conquest (the favourite bugbear of the Egestæans), would to my thinking be even less dangerous to us than before. At present they might possibly come here as separate states for love of Lacedæmon; in the other case one empire would scarcely attack another; for after joining the Peloponnesians to overthrow ours, they could only expect to see the same hands overthrow their own in the same way. The Hellenes in Sicily would fear us most if we never went there at all, and next to this, if after displaying our power we went away again as soon as possible. We all know that that which is farthest off and the reputation of which can least be tested, is the object of admiration; at the least reverse they would at once

---

*Nicias rightly points out that the Athenians have many enemies closer to home that will benefit from the division of Athenian military resources. Even if they can conquer Sicily, he doubts they can successfully rule it.

begin to look down upon us, and would join our enemies here against us. You have yourselves experienced this with regard to the Lacedæmonians and their allies, whom your unexpected success, as compared with what you feared at first, has made you suddenly despise, tempting you further to aspire to the conquest of Sicily. Instead, however, of being puffed up by the misfortunes of your adversaries, you ought to think of breaking their spirit before giving yourselves up to confidence, and to understand that the one thought awakened in the Lacedæmonians by their disgrace is how they may even now, if possible, overthrow us and repair their dishonour; inasmuch as military reputation is their oldest and chiefest study. Our struggle, therefore, if we are wise, will not be for the barbarian Egestæans in Sicily,* but how to defend ourselves most effectually against the oligarchical machinations of Lacedæmon.

12. 'We should also remember that we are but now enjoying some respite from a great pestilence and from war, to the no small benefit of our estates and persons, and that it is right to employ these at home on our own behalf, instead of using them on behalf of these exiles whose interest it is to lie as fairly as they can, who do nothing but talk themselves and leave the danger to others, and who if they succeed will show no proper gratitude, and if they fail will drag down their friends with them. And if there be any man here,† overjoyed at being chosen to command, who urges you to make the expedition, merely for ends of his own—especially if he be still too young to command—who seeks to be admired for his stud of horses, but on account of its heavy expenses hopes for some profit from his appointment, do not allow such an one to maintain his private splendour at his country's risk, but remember that such persons injure the public fortune while they squander their own, and that this is a matter of importance, and not for a young man to decide or hastily to take in hand.

13. 'When I see such persons now sitting here at the side of that same individual and summoned by him, alarm seizes me; and I, in my turn, summon any of the older men that may have such a person sitting next him, not to let himself be shamed down, for fear of being thought a coward if he do not vote for war, but, remembering how rarely success is got by wishing and how often by forecast, to leave to

---

*The Egestaeans belonged to the non-Hellenic Elymian race. Their temple (divinity unknown) today stands unfinished in the middle of a vast and empty landscape. Nicias hints at further oligarchical plots between the Spartans and certain Athenians—a theme picked up in the hysteria over oligarchy and tyranny that just precedes the sailing of the Athenian fleet.

†Nicias identifies Alcibiades by habits and policies, not by name, but he clearly regarded this rival as the chief proponent for the over-reaching expedition.

them the mad dream of conquest,* and as a true lover of his country, now threatened by the greatest danger in its history, to hold up his hand on the other side; to vote that the Siceliots be left in the limits now existing between us, limits of which no one can complain (the Ionian sea for the coasting voyage, and the Sicilian across the open main), to enjoy their own possessions and to settle their own quarrels; that the Egestæans, for their part, be told to end by themselves with the Selinuntines the war which they began without consulting the Athenians; and that for the future we do not enter into alliance, as we have been used to do, with people whom we must help in their need, and who can never help us in ours.

14. 'And you, Prytanis,† if you think it your duty to care for the commonwealth, and if you wish to show yourself a good citizen, put the question to the vote, and take a second time the opinions of the Athenians. If you are afraid to move the question again, consider that a violation of the law cannot carry any prejudice with so many abettors, that you will be the physician of your misguided city, and that the virtue of men in office is briefly this, to do their country as much good as they can, or in any case no harm that they can avoid.'

15. Such were the words of Nicias. Most of the Athenians that came forward spoke in favour of the expedition, and of not annulling what had been voted, although some spoke on the other side. By far the warmest advocate of the expedition was, however, Alcibiades, son of Clinias,‡ who wished to thwart Nicias both as his political opponent and also because of the attack he had made upon him in his speech, and who was, besides, exceedingly ambitious of a command by which

---

*Alcibiades' charm, brains, looks, and daring were extraordinary. His wild lifestyle attracted admirers but frightened traditionalists like Nicias. Nicias' incisive analysis is outflanked and overwhelmed by the "mad dream of conquest."

†The *prytanis* is one man of fifty members of his civic tribe (there were ten Attic tribes in all) in a group called a *prytany*. For one month (of the ten-month civil year) in a rotation determined by lot, the *prytaneis* presided over civil and military business. One member each day, an unelected official called the *epistates*, was chosen by lot from the presiding *prytany* of the *boule* (the senate or Council of Five Hundred) to run meetings (if any) of the *ecclesia* (assembly). Thucydides normally takes knowledge of Athenian civil affairs for granted. Reconsideration of an enacted decree was not illegal.

‡Thucydides reports Alcibiades' motives as if they are clearly known, although this historian does not indicate whether he is speculating, had personal information from Alcibiades, or gained such information from others. According to Thucydides the policies developed from Alcibiades' desire for further wealth (of which he had considerable) and political repute; rivalry with Nicias, who was opposed to any further campaigns; and ambition for glory. Alcibiades had come to prominence partly through athletic victories; his stable and racing chariots had been successful at Olympia (with others driving them, as was the custom of the aristocrats and tyrants).

he hoped to reduce Sicily and Carthage,* and personally to gain in wealth and reputation by means of his successes. For the position he held among the citizens led him to indulge his tastes beyond what his real means would bear, both in keeping horses and in the rest of his expenditure; and this later on had not a little to do with the ruin of the Athenian state.† Alarmed at the greatness of his license in his own life and habits, and of the ambition which he showed in all things soever that he undertook, the mass of the people set him down as a pretender to the tyranny, and became his enemies;‡ and although publicly his conduct of the war was as good as could be desired, individually, his habits gave offence to every one, and caused them to commit affairs to other hands, and thus before long to ruin the city. Meanwhile he now came forward and gave the following advice to the Athenians:—

16. 'Athenians, I have a better right to command than others—I must begin with this as Nicias has attacked me—and at the same time I believe myself to be worthy of it. The things for which I am abused, bring fame to my ancestors and to myself, and to the country profit besides. The Hellenes, after expecting to see our city ruined by the war, concluded it to be even greater than it really is, by reason of the magnificence with which I represented it at the Olympic games, when I sent into the competition seven chariots, a number never before entered by any private person, and won the first prize, and was second and fourth, and took care to have everything else in a style worthy of my victory.§

'Custom regards such displays as honourable, and they cannot be made without leaving behind them an impression of power. Again,

---

*Talk of nearby Carthage comes as a surprise, but it must have seemed a logical next step to unredeemed imperialists, once and if the Athenians could reduce Sicily to subject status.

†A forward-looking statement puts serious responsibility for Athenian disaster on the shoulders of this one extravagant individual. Thucydides distinguishes Alcibiades' damaging ambition from his significant military skills.

‡Thucydides, famous for his focus on national forces and system disequilibria, here blames an individual's caprices for the ruin of Athens' unique achievement. The two factors here are compatible. Alcibiades violated Athenian customs and tolerance to the point that he gained popular disapproval. The accusation of aiming at tyranny was very real and one previously mocked in Aristophanes' comic portrait of Cleon in *Wasps* (winter 422).

§Alcibiades does not deny the accusations of ambition and pride, but he turns them back on both Nicias and his fellow-citizens as appropriate exhibitions of patriotic magnificence in athletics and munificence in choral competitions in the theater of Dionysus (map 3, inset). Wealthy men were expected to fund voluntarily competitive equipages and charitable gifts to demesmen and the city (Cimon was famous for this generosity two generations before). In addition, the rich were legally required to fund choral performances and the outfitting of triremes (tax obligations called "liturgies").

any splendour that I may have exhibited at home in providing choruses or otherwise, is naturally envied by my fellow-citizens, but in the eyes of foreigners has an air of strength as in the other instance. And this is no useless folly, when a man at his own private cost benefits not himself only, but his city: nor is it unfair that he who prides himself on his position should refuse to be upon an equality with the rest. He who is badly off has his misfortunes all to himself, and as we do not see men courted in adversity, on the like principle a man ought to accept the insolence of prosperity; or else, let him first mete out equal measure to all, and then demand to have it meted out to him.

'What I know is that persons of this kind and all others that have attained to any distinction, although they may be unpopular in their lifetime in their relations with their fellow-men and especially with their equals, leave to posterity the desire of claiming connexion with them even without any ground, and are vaunted by the country to which they belonged, not as strangers or ill-doers, but as fellow-countrymen and heroes. Such are my aspirations, and however I am abused for them in private, the question is whether any one manages public affairs better than I do. Having united the most powerful states of Peloponnese, without great danger or expense to you, I compelled the Lacedæmonians to stake their all upon the issue of a single day at Mantinea; and although victorious in the battle, they have never since fully recovered confidence.

17. 'Thus did my youth and so-called monstrous folly find fitting arguments to deal with the power of the Peloponnesians, and by its ardour win their confidence and prevail. And do not be afraid of my youth now, but while I am still in its flower, and Nicias appears fortunate, avail yourselves to the utmost of the services of us both. Do not rescind your resolution to sail to Sicily, on the ground that you would be going to attack a great power. The cities in Sicily are peopled by motley rabbles, and easily change their institutions and adopt new ones in their stead; and consequently the inhabitants, being without any feeling of patriotism, are not provided with arms for their persons, and have not regularly established themselves on the land; every man thinks that either by fair words or by party strife he can obtain something at the public expense, and then in the event of a catastrophe settle in some other country, and makes his preparations accordingly. From a mob like this you need not look for either unanimity in counsel or concert in action; but they will probably one by one come in as they get a fair offer, especially if they are torn by civil strife as we are told. Moreover, the Siceliots have not so many heavy infantry as they boast; just as the Hellenes generally did not prove so numerous as each state reckoned itself, but Hellas greatly over-estimated their numbers, and has hardly had an adequate force of heavy infantry throughout this war.

'The states in Sicily, therefore, from all that I can hear, will be found as I say, and I have not pointed out all our advantages, for we shall have the help of many barbarians, who from their hatred of the Syracusans will join us in attacking them; nor will the powers at home prove any hindrance, if you judge rightly. Our fathers with these very adversaries, which it is said we shall now leave behind us when we sail, and the Mede as their enemy as well, were able to win the empire, depending solely on their superiority at sea. The Peloponnesians had never so little hope against us as at present; and let them be ever so sanguine, although strong enough to invade our country even if we stay at home, they can never hurt us with their navy, as we leave one of our own behind us that is a match for them.

18. 'In this state of things what reason can we give to ourselves for holding back, or what excuse can we offer to our allies in Sicily for not helping them? They are our confederates, and we are bound to assist them, without objecting that they have not assisted us. We did not take them into alliance to have them to help us in Hellas, but that they might so annoy our enemies in Sicily as to prevent them from coming over here and attacking us. It is thus that empire has been won, both by us and by all others that have held it, by a constant readiness to support all, whether barbarians or Hellenes, that invite assistance; since if all were to keep quiet or to pick and choose whom they ought to assist, we should make but few new conquests, and should imperil those we have already won. Men do not rest content with parrying the attacks of a superior, but often strike the first blow to prevent the attack being made. And we cannot fix the exact point at which our empire shall stop;* we have reached a position in which we must not be content with retaining but must scheme to extend it, for, if we cease to rule others, we are in danger of being ruled ourselves. Nor can you look at inaction from the same point of view as others, unless you are prepared to change your habits and make them like theirs.

'Be convinced then that we shall augment our power at home by this adventure abroad, and let us make the expedition, and so humble the pride of the Peloponnesians by sailing off to Sicily, and letting them see how little we care for the peace that we are now enjoying; and at the same time we shall either become masters, as we very easily may, of the whole of Hellas through the accession of the Sicilian Hellenes, or in any case ruin the Syracusans, to the no small advantage of ourselves and our allies. The faculty of staying if successful, or of returning, will be secured to us by our navy, as we shall be superior at sea to all the Siceliots put together.

---

*Alcibiades echoes Pericles' metaphor from physics about momentum carrying empires along in perpetual aggression.

'Do not let the do-nothing policy which Nicias advocates, or his setting of the young against the old, turn you from your purpose, but in the good old fashion by which our fathers, old and young together, by their united counsels brought our affairs to their present height, do you endeavour still to advance them; understanding that neither youth nor old age can do anything the one without the other, but that levity, sobriety, and deliberate judgment are strongest when united, and that, by sinking into inaction, the city, like everything else, will wear itself out, and its skill in everything decay; while each fresh struggle will give it fresh experience, and make it more used to defend itself not in word but in deed. In short, my conviction is that a city not inactive by nature could not choose a quicker way to ruin itself than by suddenly adopting such a policy, and that the safest rule of life is to take one's character and institutions for better and for worse, and to live up to them as closely as one can.'

19. Such were the words of Alcibiades. After hearing him and the Egestæans and some Leontine exiles, who came forward reminding them of their oaths and imploring their assistance, the Athenians became more eager for the expedition than before. Nicias, perceiving that it would be now useless to try to deter them by the old line of argument, but thinking that he might perhaps alter their resolution by the extravagance of his estimates, came forward a second time and spoke as follows:—*

20. 'I see, Athenians, that you are thoroughly bent upon the expedition, and therefore hope that all will turn out as we wish, and proceed to give you my opinion at the present juncture. From all that I hear we are going against cities that are great and not subject to one another, or in need of change, so as to be glad to pass from enforced servitude to an easier condition, or in the least likely to accept our rule in exchange for freedom; and, to take only the Hellenic towns, they are very numerous for one island. Besides Naxos and Catana, which I expect to join us from their connexion with Leontini, there are seven others armed at all points just like our own power, particularly Selinus and Syracuse, the chief objects of our expedition. These are full of heavy infantry, archers, and javelin-men, have triremes in abundance and crowds to man them; they have also money, partly in the hands of private persons, partly in the temples at Selinus, and at Syracuse first-fruits from some of the barbarians as well. But their chief advantage over us lies in the number

---

*Nicias almost mechanically and somewhat comically expects that the cost of the expedition in men and supplies might discourage the enthusiastic assembly. He reviews the size and number of their potential enemies.

of their horses, and in the fact that they grow their grain at home instead of importing it.*

21. 'Against a power of this kind it will not do to have merely a weak naval armament, but we shall want also a large land army to sail with us, if we are to do anything worthy of our ambition, and are not to be shut out from the country by a numerous cavalry; especially if the cities should take alarm and combine, and we should be left without friends (except the Egestæans) to furnish us with horse to defend ourselves with. It would be disgraceful to have to retire under compulsion, or to send back for reinforcements, owing to want of reflexion at first:† we must therefore start from home with a competent force, seeing that we are going to sail far from our country, and upon an expedition not like any which you may have undertaken in the quality of allies, among your subject states here in Hellas, where any additional supplies needed were easily drawn from the friendly territory; but we are cutting ourselves off, and going to a land entirely strange, from which during four months in winter it is not even easy for a messenger to get to Athens.

22. 'I think, therefore, that we ought to take great numbers of heavy infantry, both from Athens and from our allies, and not merely from our subjects, but also any we may be able to get for love or for money in Peloponnese, and great numbers also of archers and slingers, to make head against the Sicilian horse. Meanwhile we must have an overwhelming superiority at sea, to enable us the more easily to carry in what we want; and we must take our own grain in merchant vessels, that is to say, wheat and parched barley, and bakers from the mills compelled to serve for pay in the proper proportion; in order that in case of our being weather-bound the armament may not want provisions, as it is not every city that will be able to entertain numbers like ours. We must also provide ourselves with everything else as far as we can, so as not to be dependent upon others; and above all we must take with us from home as much money as possible, as the sums talked of as ready at Egesta are readier, you may be sure, in talk than in any other way.

23. 'Indeed, even if we leave Athens with a force not only equal to that of the enemy except in the number of heavy infantry in the field, but even at all points superior to him, we shall still find it difficult to conquer Sicily or save ourselves. We must not disguise from ourselves

---

*Their assets include untouched gold and silver, their superiority in cavalry, and their food supply. In Herodotus (7.49), Xerxes' uncle Artabanus had emphasized some of these same inherent barriers in invading the territory of an enemy far distant, however superior the aggressor may be in manpower.

†Shame and disgrace are prominent always in Nicias' thinking. His prediction of few allies for the Athenians holds true, and the need for reinforcements appears quickly.

that we go to found a city among strangers and enemies, and that he who undertakes such an enterprise should be prepared to become master of the country the first day he lands, or failing in this to find everything hostile to him. Fearing this, and knowing that we shall have need of much good counsel and more good fortune—a hard matter for mortal men to aspire to—I wish as far as may be to make myself independent of fortune before sailing, and when I do sail, to be as safe as a strong force can make me.* This I believe to be surest for the country at large, and safest for us who are to go on the expedition. If any one thinks differently I resign to him my command.'†

24. With this Nicias concluded, thinking that he should either disgust the Athenians by the magnitude of the undertaking, or, if obliged to sail on the expedition, would thus do so in the safest way possible. The Athenians, however, far from having their taste for the voyage taken away by the burdensomeness of the preparations, became more eager for it than ever; and just the contrary took place of what Nicias had thought, as it was held that he had given good advice, and that the expedition would be the safest in the world. All alike fell in love with the enterprise.‡ The older men thought that they would either subdue the places against which they were to sail, or at all events, with so large a force, meet with no disaster; those in the prime of life felt a longing for foreign sights and spectacles, and had no doubt that they should come safe home again; while the idea of the common people and the soldiery was to earn wages at the moment, and make conquests that would supply a never-ending fund of pay for the future. With this enthusiasm of the majority, the few that liked it not, feared to appear unpatriotic by holding up their hands against it, and so kept quiet.

25. At last one of the Athenians came forward and called upon Nicias and told him that he ought not to make excuses or put them off, but say at once before them all what forces the Athenians should vote him. Upon this he said, not without reluctance, that he would advise upon that matter more at leisure with his colleagues; as far however as he could see at present, they must sail with at least one hundred triremes—the Athenians providing as many transports

---

*Nicias wisely fears their dependence on fortune, but in the end he himself will be forced to appeal to precisely that. His desire to anticipate all difficulties is rational, but his bluffing strategy for talking the Athenians out of the expedition fails.

†Nicias again offers to resign his command (see 4.28). Cleon, forced to assume it on the Pylos campaign, is now dead. Nicias, who had no desire to go to Sicily, will endure its every horror.

‡Nicias miscalculates the mood of the people. His ploy backfires, and he gains his every extravagant request. Thucydides' vocabulary equates the expedition with a passionate folly, a doomed lust. Again, his opponents call Nicias' bluff.

as they might determine, and sending for others from the allies—not less than five thousand heavy infantry in all, Athenian and allied, and if possible more; and the rest of the armament in proportion; archers from home and from Crete, and slingers, and whatever else might seem desirable, being got ready by the generals and taken with them.

26. Upon hearing this the Athenians at once voted that the generals should have full powers in the matter of the numbers of the army and of the expedition generally, to do as they judged best for the interests of Athens. After this the preparations began; messages being sent to the allies and the rolls drawn up at home. And as the city had just recovered from the plague and the long war, and a number of young men had grown up and capital had accumulated by reason of the truce, everything was the more easily provided.*

27. In the midst of these preparations all the stone Herms in the city of Athens, that is to say the customary square figures, so common in the doorways of private houses and temples, had in one night most of them their faces mutilated.† No one knew who had done it, but large public rewards were offered to find the authors; and it was further voted that any one who knew of any other act of impiety having been committed should come and give information without fear of consequences, whether he were citizen, alien, or slave. The matter was taken up the more seriously, as it was thought to be ominous for the expedition, and part of a conspiracy to bring about a revolution and to upset the democracy.‡

28. Information was given accordingly by some resident aliens and body servants, not about the Herms but about some previous mutilations of other images perpetrated by young men in a drunken frolic,

---

*Thucydides admits Athenian readiness for an ambitious imperial enterprise. It has been six years since combatants signed the Peace of Nicias; new financial reserves were stored (compare 6.31 and 8.1 for other notices of financial resources); and a new generation, unaware of war's indiscriminate destruction, was ready to fight. The plague seems to be a distant memory.

†The doorways of many Athenian houses featured a pillar (intended to protect the household from evil) topped by an image of the head of Hermes, god of travelers and good fortune; an erect phallus was carved into the pillar's middle (see Camp, illustration 62; Osborne, illustration 82). The desecration of the pillars, which could have begun as a prank of drunken revelers stumbling home from a symposium in the dark, may in fact have been otherwise (the numbers support the idea of a pre-concerted plan), a signal in an oligarchical plot such as occurred afterwards within five years. The desecration of many images in a single night required coordination.

‡The religious element in Athens interpreted the event as portending bad fortune, and the politically minded thought it might portend a conspiracy that Alcibiades had concocted. He was not involved in this foolishness or plot, but the reference to other acts of impiety widened the investigation into a kind of witch-hunt.

and of mock celebrations of the Mysteries,* averred to take place in private houses. Alcibiades being implicated in this charge, it was taken hold of by those who could least endure him, because he stood in the way of their obtaining the undisturbed direction of the people, and who thought that if he were once removed the first place would be theirs.† These accordingly magnified the matter and loudly proclaimed that the affair of the mysteries and the mutilation of the Herms were part of a scheme to overthrow the democracy, and that nothing of all this had been done without Alcibiades; the proofs alleged being the general and undemocratic license of his life and habits.

29. Alcibiades repelled on the spot the charges in question, and also before going on the expedition, the preparations for which were now complete, offered to stand his trial, that it might be seen whether he was guilty of the acts imputed to him; desiring to be punished if found guilty, but, if acquitted, to take the command. Meanwhile he protested against their receiving slanders against him in his absence, and begged them rather to put him to death at once if he were guilty, and pointed out the imprudence of sending him out at the head of so large an army, with so serious a charge still undecided. But his enemies feared that he would have the army for him if he were tried immediately, and that the people might relent in favour of the man whom they already caressed as the cause of the Argives and some of the Mantineans joining in the expedition, and did their utmost to get this proposition rejected, putting forward other orators who said that he ought at present to sail and not delay the departure of the army, and be tried on his return within a fixed number of days; their plan being to have him sent for and brought home for trial upon some graver charge, which they would the more easily get up in his absence. Accordingly it was decreed that he should sail.

30. After this the departure for Sicily took place, it being now about midsummer. Most of the allies, with the grain transports and the smaller craft and the rest of the expedition, had already received orders to muster at Corcyra, to cross the Ionian sea from thence in a body to the Iapygian promontory. But the Athenians themselves, and such of their allies as happened to be with them, went down to Piræus upon a day appointed at daybreak, and began to man the ships for

---

*The Mysteries were a religious ritual reserved for the appreciation and edification of initiates of Demeter at nearby Attic Eleusis (14 miles west; see map 2). To reveal to the uninitiated what transpired in the closed building was punishable by death. To mock the rituals was even more offensive.

†Someone implicated Alcibiades in this second ill-omened and perhaps politically related charge. Thucydides implies his enemies were selfishly motivated but does not exculpate the rash Alcibiades.

putting out to sea. With them also went down the whole population, one may say, of the city, both citizens and foreigners; the inhabitants of the country each escorting those that belonged to them, their friends, their relatives, or their sons, with hope and lamentation upon their way, as they thought of the conquests which they hoped to make, or of the friends whom they might never see again, considering the long voyage which they were going to make from their country.

31. Indeed, at this moment, when they were now upon the point of parting from one another, the danger came more home to them than when they voted for the expedition; although the strength of the armament, and the profuse provision which they remarked in every department, was a sight that could not but comfort them. As for the foreigners and the rest of the crowd, they simply went to see a sight worth looking at and passing all belief.*

This armament that first sailed out was by far the most costly and splendid Hellenic force that had ever been sent out by a single city up to that time.† In mere number of ships and heavy infantry that against Epidaurus under Pericles, and the same when going against Potidæa under Hagnon, was not inferior; containing as it did four thousand Athenian heavy infantry, three hundred horse, and one hundred galleys accompanied by fifty Lesbian and Chian vessels and many allies besides. But these were sent upon a short voyage and with a scanty equipment. The present expedition was formed in contemplation of a long term of service by land and sea alike, and was furnished with ships and troops so as to be ready for either as required. The fleet had been elaborately equipped at great cost to the captains and the state;‡ the treasury giving a drachma a day to each seaman, and providing empty ships, sixty men of war and forty transports, and manning these with the best crews obtainable; while the captains gave a bounty in addition to the pay from the treasury to the *thranitæ* and crews generally, besides spending lavishly upon figure-heads and equipments, and one and all making the utmost exertions to enable their own ships to excel in beauty and fast sailing.

Meanwhile the land forces had been picked from the best musterrolls, and vied with each other in paying great attention to their arms and personal accoutrements. From this resulted not only a rivalry

---

*The embarkation and departure of the fleet resembles a religious procession and celebration. Thucydides implies that the entertainment values of the experience overwhelmed the rational fears of danger far off.

†Although there is no explicit comparison to the Trojan expedition, the thought is inescapable (compare 1.9–11). Not only the numbers but the supplies and preparations were on a hitherto unmatched scale.

‡Athenian *eros* (enthusiasm) led individual captains to outfit their ships beyond what was required of them. The Athenians sent the flower of the military—soldiers, sailors, and marines—that now was not otherwise engaging an enemy.

among themselves in their different departments, but an idea among the rest of the Hellenes that it was more a display of power and resources than an armament against an enemy. For if any one had counted up the public expenditure of the state, and the private outlay of individuals—that is to say, the sums which the state had already spent upon the expedition and was sending out in the hands of the generals, and those which individuals had expended upon their personal outfit, or as captains of triremes had laid out and were still to lay out upon their vessels; and if he had added to this the journey money which each was likely to have provided himself with, independently of the pay from the treasury, for a voyage of such length, and what the soldiers or traders took with them for the purpose of exchange—it would have been found that many talents in all were being taken out of the city.

Indeed the expedition became not less famous for its wonderful boldness and for the splendour of its appearance, than for its overwhelming strength as compared with the peoples against whom it was directed, and for the fact that this was the longest passage from home hitherto attempted, and the most ambitious in its objects considering the resources of those who undertook it.

32. The ships being now manned, and everything put on board with which they meant to sail, the trumpet commanded silence, and the prayers customary before putting out to sea were offered, not in each ship by itself, but by all together to the voice of a herald; and bowls of wine were mixed through all the armament, and libations made by the soldiers and their officers in gold and silver goblets. In their prayers joined also the crowds on shore, the citizens and all others that wished them well. The hymn sung and the libations finished, they put out to sea, and first sailing out in column then raced each other as far as Ægina, and so hastened to reach Corcyra, where the rest of the allied forces were also assembling.*

Seventeenth Year of the War—Parties at Syracuse—Story of Harmodius and Aristogiton—Disgrace of Alcibiades

Meanwhile at Syracuse news came in from many quarters of the expedition, but for a long while met with no credence whatever. Indeed, an assembly was held in which speeches, as will be seen, were

---

*The solemn moment (prayers, libations, fancy goblets, hymns) befits a two-book construction in which an action begun solemnly and with high hopes of success comes completely a cropper. Corcyra was the common way-station on the coastal route to Sicily (compare 1.44) for small ancient ships that preferred to hug the shore and trust to the open sea as little as possible. Corcyra lies only 65 miles from the heel of Italy (map 8).

delivered by different orators, believing or contradicting the report of
the Athenian expedition; among whom Hermocrates, son of Hermon,
came forward, being persuaded that he knew the truth of the matter,
and gave the following counsel:—

33. 'Although I shall perhaps be no better believed than others
have been when I speak upon the reality of the expedition, and although I know that those who either make or repeat statements
thought not worthy of belief not only gain no converts, but are
thought fools for their pains, I shall certainly not be frightened into
holding my tongue when the state is in danger, and when I am persuaded that I can speak with more authority on the matter than other
persons. Much as you wonder at it, the Athenians nevertheless have
set out against us with a large force, naval and military, professedly to
help the Egestæans and to restore Leontini, but really to conquer
Sicily, and above all our city, which once gained, the rest, they think,
will easily follow.* Make up your minds, therefore, to see them speedily here, and see how you can best repel them with the means under
your hand, and do not be taken off your guard through despising the
news, or neglect the common weal through disbelieving it.

'Meanwhile those who believe me need not be dismayed at the
force or daring of the enemy. They will not be able to do us more hurt
than we shall do them; nor is the greatness of their armament altogether without advantage to us. Indeed, the greater it is the better,
with regard to the rest of the Siceliots, whom dismay will make more
ready to join us; and if we defeat or drive them away, disappointed of
the objects of their ambition (for I do not fear for a moment that they
will get what they want), it will be a most glorious exploit for us, and
in my judgment by no means an unlikely one.

'Few indeed have been the large armaments, either Hellenic or
barbarian, that have gone far from home and been successful. They
cannot be more numerous than the people of the country and their
neighbours, all of whom fear leagues together; and if they miscarry
for want of supplies in a foreign land, to those against whom their
plans were laid none the less they leave renown, although they may
themselves have been the main cause of their own discomfort. Thus
these very Athenians rose by the defeat of the Mede,† in a great mea-

---

*Hermocrates is a great Syracusan patriot, and serves the best interests of Sicily, what-
ever his own imperialistic ambitions for his hegemonic *polis*. Like Themistocles, he
clearly perceives what Athens is capable of and engaged in.

†Like Herodotus, Hermocrates (or Thucydides, who wrote this version of this speech)
understands the logistical issues of overseas campaigns. The Persian *casus belli* had been
Athenian support for the Ionian revolt (see Herodotus books 5–6). He downplays the
vigor and foresight of Athenians in defeating the Persian Empire and in creating their
own equivalent.

sure due to accidental causes, from the mere fact that Athens had been the object of his attack; and this may very well be the case with us also.

34. 'Let us, therefore, confidently begin preparations here; let us send and confirm some of the Sicels, and obtain the friendship and alliance of others, and despatch envoys to the rest of Sicily to show that the danger is common to all, and to Italy to get them to become our allies, or at all events to refuse to receive the Athenians. I also think that it would be best to send to Carthage as well; they are by no means there without apprehension, but it is their constant fear that the Athenians may one day attack their city, and they may perhaps think that they might themselves suffer by letting Sicily be sacrificed, and be willing to help us secretly if not openly, in one way if not in another.* They are the best able to do so, if they will, of any of the present day, as they possess most gold and silver, by which war, like everything else, flourishes.

'Let us also send to Lacedæmon and Corinth, and ask them to come here and help us as soon as possible, and to keep alive the war in Hellas. But the true thing of all others, in my opinion, to do at the present moment, is what you, with your constitutional love of quiet, will be slow to see, and what I must nevertheless mention. If we Siceliots, all together, or at least as many as possible besides ourselves, would only launch the whole of our actual navy with two months' provisions, and meet the Athenians at Tarentum and the Iapygian promontory, and show them that before fighting for Sicily they must first fight for their passage across the Ionian sea, we should strike dismay into their army, and set them on thinking that we have a base for our defensive—for Tarentum is ready to receive us†—while they have a wide sea to cross with all their armament, which could with difficulty keep its order through so long a voyage, and would be easy for us to attack as it came on slowly and in small detachments. On the other hand, if they were to lighten their vessels, and draw together their fast sailers and with these attack us, we could either fall upon them when they were wearied with rowing, or if we did not choose to do so, we could retire to Tarentum; while they, having crossed with few provisions just to give battle, would be hard put to it in desolate places, and would either have to remain and be blockaded, or to try

---

*Hermocrates thinks Carthage might be a target of Athenian aggression and therefore a possible ally of the Sicilians. Nothing seems to have come of this potential alliance at this time.

†Hermocrates advocated a forward strategy of repelling the Athenians at the southern edge of Italy, even before they reach Sicily. Public opinion did not support this strategy. It may well have failed in open waters, where the superior training of the still-fresh Athenian fleet might have destroyed the relatively untrained Sicilian alliance.

to sail along the coast, abandoning the rest of their armament, and being further discouraged by not knowing for certain whether the cities would receive them.

'In my opinion this consideration alone would be sufficient to deter them from putting out from Corcyra; and what with deliberating and reconnoitring our numbers and whereabouts, they would let the season go on until winter was upon them, or, confounded by so unexpected a circumstance, would break up the expedition, especially as their most experienced general has, as I hear, taken the command against his will, and would grasp at the first excuse offered by any serious demonstration of ours.

'We should also be reported, I am certain, as more numerous than we really are, and men's minds are affected by what they hear, and, besides the first to attack, or to show that they mean to defend themselves against an attack, inspire greater fear because men see that they are ready for the emergency. This would just be the case with the Athenians at present. They are now attacking us in the belief that we shall not resist, having a right to judge us severely because we did not help the Lacedæmonians in crushing them;* but if they were to see us showing a courage for which they are not prepared, they would be more dismayed by the surprise than they could ever be by our actual power.

'I could wish to persuade you to show this courage; but if this cannot be, at all events lose not a moment in preparing generally for the war; and remember all of you that contempt for an assailant is best shown by bravery in action, but that for the present the best course is to accept the preparations which fear inspires as giving the surest promise of safety, and to act as if the danger was real. That the Athenians are coming to attack us, and are already upon the voyage, and all but here—this is what I am sure of.'

35. Thus spoke Hermocrates. Meanwhile the people of Syracuse were at great strife among themselves; some contending that the Athenians had no idea of coming and that there was no truth in what he said; some asking if they did come what harm they could do that would not be repaid them tenfold in return; while others made light of the whole affair and turned it into ridicule. In short, there were few that believed Hermocrates and feared for the future. Meanwhile Athenagoras, the leader of the people and very powerful at that time with the masses, came forward and spoke as follows:—

36. 'For the Athenians, he who does not wish that they may be as

---

*In the Persian War, the Sicilians did not come to the aid of their motherland in large numbers, but they did have their own campaign to fight against the opportunistic Carthaginians. The Lacedaemonians had asked for Sicilian support in the Ten Years' War (2.7) and failed to receive it.

misguided as they are supposed to be, and that they may come here to become our subjects, is either a coward or a traitor to his country; while as for those who carry such tidings and fill you with so much alarm, I wonder less at their audacity than at their folly if they flatter themselves that we do not see through them. The fact is that they have their private reasons to be afraid, and wish to throw the city into consternation to have their own terrors cast into the shade by the public alarm.

'In short, this is what these reports are worth; they do not arise of themselves, but are concocted by men who are always causing agitation here in Sicily. However, if you are well advised, you will not be guided in your calculation of probabilities by what these persons tell you, but by what shrewd men and of large experience, as I esteem the Athenians to be, would be likely to do.* Now it is not likely that they would leave the Peloponnesians behind them, and before they have well ended the war in Hellas wantonly come in quest of a new war quite as arduous, in Sicily; indeed, in my judgment, they are only too glad that we do not go and attack them, being so many and so great cities as we are.

37. 'However, if they should come as is reported, I consider Sicily better able to go through with the war than Peloponnese, as being at all points better prepared, and our city by itself far more than a match for this pretended army of invasion, even were it twice as large again. I know that they will not have horses with them, or get any here, except a few perhaps from the Egestæans; or be able to bring a force of heavy infantry equal in number to our own, in ships which will already have enough to do to come all this distance, however lightly laden, not to speak of the transport of the other stores required against a city of this magnitude, which will be no slight quantity. In fact, so strong is my opinion upon the subject, that I do not well see how they could avoid annihilation if they brought with them another city as large as Syracuse, and settled down and carried on war from our frontier; much less can they hope to succeed with all Sicily hostile to them, as all Sicily will be, and with only a camp pitched from the ships, and composed of tents and bare necessaries, from which they would not be able to stir far for fear of our cavalry.

38. 'But the Athenians see this as I tell you, and as I have reason to know are looking after their possessions at home, while persons here

---

*The Syracusan Athenagoras exemplifies the ignorant and dangerous demagogue. Thucydides introduces him with language reminiscent of Cleon. Any reader of Thucydides knows Athenagoras is wrong in rejecting reports of the launching of the Athenian expeditionary force. In arguing the unlikelihood of the shrewd Athenians attacking, he reinforces Thucydides' theme of the significance of chance and miscalculation. Mere logic can be fatal.

invent stories that neither are true nor ever will be. Nor is this the first time that I see these persons, when they cannot resort to deeds, trying by such stories and by others even more abominable to frighten your people and get into their hands the government: it is what I see always. And I cannot help fearing that trying so often they may one day succeed, and that we, as long as we do not feel the smart, may prove too weak for the task of prevention, or, when the offenders are known, of pursuit. The result is that our city is rarely at rest, but is subject to constant troubles and to contests as frequent against herself as against the enemy, not to speak of occasional tyrannies and infamous cabals.

'However, I will try, if you will support me, to let nothing of this happen in our time, by gaining you, the many, and by chastising the authors of such machinations, not merely when they are caught in the act—a difficult feat to accomplish—but, also for what they have the wish though not the power to do; as it is necessary to punish an enemy not only for what he does, but also beforehand for what he intends to do, if the first to relax precaution would not be also the first to suffer.

'I shall also reprove, watch, and on occasion warn the few—the most effectual way, in my opinion, of turning them from their evil courses. And after all, as I have often asked—What would you have, young men? Would you hold office at once? The law forbids it, a law enacted rather because you are not competent than to disgrace you when competent. Meanwhile you would not be on a legal equality with the many! But how can it be right that citizens of the same state should be held unworthy of the same privileges?

39. 'It will be said, perhaps, that democracy is neither wise nor equitable, but that the holders of property are also the best fitted to rule. I say, on the contrary, first, that the word *demos*, or people, includes the whole state, oligarchy only a part; next, that if the best guardians of property are the rich, and the best counsellors the wise, none can hear and decide so well as the many; and that all these talents, severally and collectively, have their just place in a democracy. But an oligarchy gives the many their share of the danger, and not content with the largest part takes and keeps the whole of the profit; and this is what the powerful and young among you aspire to, but in a great city cannot possibly obtain.

40. 'But even now, foolish men, most senseless of all the Hellenes that I know, if you have no sense of the wickedness of your designs, or most criminal if you have that sense and still dare to pursue them,—even now, if it is not a case for repentance, you may still learn wisdom, and thus advance the interest of the country, the common interest of us all.

'Reflect that in the country's prosperity the men of merit in your ranks will have a share and a larger share than the great mass of your

fellow-countrymen, but that if you have other designs you run a risk
of being deprived of all; and desist from reports like these, as the people know your object and will not put up with it. If the Athenians arrive, this city will repulse them in a manner worthy of itself; we have,
moreover, generals who will see to this matter.

'And if nothing of this be true, as I incline to believe, the city will
not be thrown into a panic by your intelligence, or impose upon itself
a self-chosen servitude by choosing you for its rulers; the city itself
will look into the matter, and will judge your words as if they were
acts, and instead of allowing itself to be deprived of its liberty by listening to you, will strive to preserve that liberty by taking care to
have always at hand the means of making itself respected.'

41. Such were the words of Athenagoras. One of the generals now
stood up and stopped any other speakers coming forward, adding
these words of his own with reference to the matter in hand:—'It is
not well for speakers to utter calumnies against one another, or for
their hearers to entertain them; we ought rather to look to the intelligence that we have received, and see how each man by himself and
the city as a whole may best prepare to repel the invaders. Even if
there be no need, there is no harm in the state being furnished with
horses and arms and all other equipment of war; and we will undertake to see to and order this, and to send round to the cities to reconnoitre and do all else that may appear desirable. Part of this we
have seen to already, and whatever we discover shall be laid before
you.' After these words from the general, the Syracusans departed
from the assembly.

42. In the meantime the Athenians with all their allies had now arrived at Corcyra. Here the generals began by again reviewing the armament, and made arrangements as to the order in which they were
to anchor and encamp, and dividing the whole fleet into three divisions, allotted one to each of their number, to avoid sailing all together and being thus embarrassed for water, harbourage, or
provisions at the stations which they might touch at, and at the same
time to be generally better ordered and easier to handle, by each
squadron having its own commander. Next they sent on three ships to
Italy and Sicily to find out which of the cities would receive them,
with instructions to meet them on the way and let them know before
they put in to land.

43. After this the Athenians weighed from Corcyra, and proceeded to cross to Sicily with an armament now consisting of one
hundred and thirty-four triremes in all (besides two Rhodian fifty-
oared ships), of which one hundred were Athenian vessels—sixty
men-of-war, and forty troopships—and the remainder from Chios
and the other allies; five thousand and one hundred heavy infantry in
all, that is to say, fifteen hundred Athenian citizens from the rolls at

Athens and seven hundred *Thetes* shipped as marines, and the rest allied troops, some of them Athenian subjects, and besides these five hundred Argives, and two hundred and fifty Mantineans serving for hire; four hundred and eighty archers in all, eighty of whom were Cretans, seven hundred slingers from Rhodes, one hundred and twenty light-armed exiles from Megara, and one horse-transport carrying thirty horses.*

44. Such was the strength of the first armament that sailed over for the war. The supplies for this force were carried by thirty ships of burden laden with grain, which conveyed the bakers, stone-masons and carpenters, and the tools for raising fortifications, accompanied by one hundred boats, like the former pressed into the service, besides many other boats and ships of burden which followed the armament voluntarily for purposes of trade; all of which now left Corcyra and struck across the Ionian sea together. The whole force making land at the Iapygian promontory and Tarentum, with more or less good fortune, coasted along the shores of Italy, the cities shutting their markets and gates against them, and according them nothing but water and liberty to anchor, and Tarentum and Locri not even that, until they arrived at Rhegium, the extreme point of Italy. Here at length they reunited, and not gaining admission, within the walls pitched a camp outside the city in the precinct of Artemis, where a market was also provided for them, and drew their ships on shore and kept quiet.

Meanwhile they opened negotiations with the Rhegians, and called upon them as Chalcidians to assist their Leontine kinsmen; to which the Rhegians replied that they would not side with either party, but should await the decision of the rest of the Italiots, and do as they did. Upon this the Athenians now began to consider what would be the best action to take in the affairs of Sicily, and meanwhile waited for the ships sent on to come back from Egesta, in order to know whether there was really there the money mentioned by the messengers at Athens.

45. In the meantime came in from all quarters to the Syracusans, as well as from their own officers sent to reconnoitre, the positive tidings that the fleet was at Rhegium; upon which they laid aside their incredulity and threw themselves heart and soul into the work of preparation. Guards or envoys, as the case might be, were sent round to the Sicels, garrisons put into the posts of the Peripoli in the country, horses and arms reviewed in the city to see that nothing was wanting, and all other steps taken to prepare for a war which might be upon them at any moment.

---

*The Athenians have a very large fleet but insufficient cavalry. They plan to reinforce this number from their allies and victims in Sicily.

46. Meanwhile the three ships that had been sent on came from Egesta to the Athenians at Rhegium, with the news that so far from there being the sums promised, all that could be produced was thirty talents. The generals were not a little disheartened at being thus disappointed at the outset, and by the refusal to join in the expedition of the Rhegians, the people they had first tried to gain and had had most reason to count upon, from their relationship to the Leontines and constant friendship for Athens. If Nicias was prepared for the news from Egesta, his two colleagues were taken completely by surprise.

The Egestæans had had recourse to the following stratagem, when the first envoys from Athens came to inspect their resources. They took the envoys in question to the temple of Aphrodite at Eryx and showed them the treasures deposited there; bowls, wine-ladles, censers, and a large number of other pieces of plate, which from being in silver gave an impression of wealth quite out of proportion to their really small value.

They also privately entertained the ships' crews, and collected all the cups of gold and silver that they could find in Egesta itself or could borrow in the neighbouring Phœnician and Hellenic towns, and each brought them to the banquets as their own; and as all used pretty nearly the same, and everywhere a great quantity of plate was shown, the effect was most dazzling upon the Athenian sailors, and made them talk loudly of the riches they had seen when they got back to Athens. The dupes in question—who had in their turn persuaded the rest—when the news got abroad that there was not the money supposed at Egesta, were much blamed by the soldiers.*

Meanwhile the generals consulted upon what was to be done.†

47. The opinion of Nicias was to sail with all the armament to Selinus, the main object of the expedition, and if the Egestæans could provide money for the whole force, to advise accordingly; but if they could not, to require them to supply provisions for the sixty ships that they had asked for, to stay and settle matters between

---

*Thucydides reports the diplomatic deception and the delusion much in the manner of Herodotus. Nicias had somehow anticipated the inflation of Egestæan resources, but he remained in the minority.

†Someone provided Thucydides (in exile, hypothetically in Sicily, but if so, not with the Athenians) with a summary of the three commanders' opinions. Nicias wanted to strike surgically on one matter that provided the public-relations cover for the expedition— aid to Egesta by attacking Selinus—and then go home. Alcibiades wanted to conquer Sicily starting with potential allies and eventually attacking Selinus and Syracuse. Lamachus, the swing vote, wanted to attack Syracuse directly and conquer their most powerful opponent. Thucydides endorses this Brasidas-like strategy, insofar as he thought the Athenians had a good chance at success (compare Demosthenes' reasoning at 7.42).

them and the Selinuntines either by force or by agreement, and then to coast past the other cities, and after displaying the power of Athens and proving their zeal for their friends and allies, to sail home again (unless they should have some sudden and unexpected opportunity of serving the Leontines, or of bringing over some of the other cities), and not to endanger the state by wasting its home resources.

48. Alcibiades said that a great expedition like the present must not disgrace itself by going away without having done anything; heralds must be sent to all the cities except Selinus and Syracuse, and efforts be made to make some of the Sicels revolt from the Syracusans, and to obtain the friendship of others, in order to have grain and troops; and first of all to gain the Messinese, who lay right in the passage and entrance to Sicily, and would afford an excellent harbour and base for the army. Thus, after bringing over the towns and knowing who would be their allies in the war, they might at length attack Syracuse and Selinus; unless the latter came to terms with Egesta and the former ceased to oppose the restoration of Leontini.

49. Lamachus, on the other hand, said that they ought to sail straight to Syracuse, and fight their battle at once under the walls of the town while the people were still unprepared, and the panic at its height. Every armament was most terrible at first; if it allowed time to run on without showing itself, men's courage revived, and they saw it appear at last almost with indifference. By attacking suddenly, while Syracuse still trembled at their coming, they would have the best chance of gaining a victory for themselves and of striking a complete panic into the enemy by the aspect of their numbers—which would never appear so considerable as at present—by the anticipation of coming disaster, and above all by the immediate danger of the engagement. They might also count upon surprising many in the fields outside, incredulous of their coming; and at the moment that the enemy was carrying in his property the army would not want for booty if it sat down in force before the city. The rest of the Siceliots would thus be immediately less disposed to enter into alliance with the Syracusans, and would join the Athenians, without waiting to see which were the strongest. They must make Megara their naval station as a place to retreat to and a base from which to attack: it was an uninhabited place at no great distance from Syracuse either by land or by sea.*

50. After speaking to this effect, Lamachus nevertheless gave his sup-

---

*Megara (Hyblaea) in Sicily had been left deserted by the Syracusan tyrant Gelon (6.4). It was an early colony of the Megarians in the homeland bordering Attica on the west (map 2).

port to the opinion of Alcibiades.* After this Alcibiades sailed in his own vessel across to Messina with proposals of alliance, but met with no success, the inhabitants answering that they could not receive him within their walls, though they would provide him with a market outside. Upon this he sailed back to Rhegium. Immediately upon his return the generals manned and victualled sixty ships cut of the whole fleet and coasted along to Naxos, leaving the rest of the armament behind them at Rhegium with one of their number. Received by the Naxians, they then coasted on to Catana, and being refused admittance by the inhabitants, there being a Syracusan party in the town, went on to the river Terias. Here they bivouacked, and the next day sailed in single file to Syracuse with all their ships except ten which they sent on in front to sail into the great harbour and see if there was any fleet launched, and to proclaim by herald from shipboard that the Athenians were come to restore the Leontines to their country, as being their allies and kinsmen, and that such of them, therefore, as were in Syracuse should leave it without fear and join their friends and benefactors the Athenians. After making this proclamation and reconnoitring the city and the harbours, and the features of the country which they would have to make their base of operations in the war, they sailed back to Catana.

51. An assembly being held here, the inhabitants refused to receive the armament, but invited the generals to come in and say what they desired; and while Alcibiades was speaking and the citizens were intent on the assembly, the soldiers broke down an ill-walled-up postern-gate without being observed, and getting inside the town, flocked into the market-place. The Syracusan party in the town no sooner saw the army inside than they became frightened and withdrew, not being at all numerous; while the rest voted for an alliance with the Athenians and invited them to fetch the rest of their forces from Rhegium. After this the Athenians sailed to Rhegium, and put off, this time with all the armament, for Catana, and fell to work at their camp immediately upon their arrival.

52. Meanwhile word was brought them from Camarina that if they went there the town would go over to them, and also that the Syracusans were manning a fleet. The Athenians accordingly sailed along shore with all their armament, first to Syracuse, where they found no fleet manning, and so always along the coast to Camarina, where they brought to at the beach, and sent a herald to the people, who, however, refused to receive them, saying that their oaths bound them to receive the Athenians only with a single vessel, unless they them-

---

*Thucydides does not explain Lamachus' support for Alcibiades. He was inferior in prestige to the other two *strategoi*, and the Athenian *demos* had sided with the aggressive policy. If he had to choose between the two others who had dug their heels in deep, it might well be safer to side with the more popular, as well as more charismatic, leader.

selves sent for more. Disappointed here, the Athenians now sailed back again, and after landing and plundering on Syracusan territory and losing some stragglers from their light infantry through the coming up of the Syracusan horse, so got back to Catana.

53. There they found the Salaminia come from Athens for Alcibiades, with orders for him to sail home to answer the charges which the state brought against him, and for certain others of the soldiers who with him were accused of sacrilege in the matter of the mysteries and of the Herms. For the Athenians, after the departure of the expedition, had continued as active as ever in investigating the facts of the mysteries and of the Herms, and, instead of testing the informers, in their suspicious temper welcomed all indifferently, arresting and imprisoning the best citizens upon the evidence of rascals,* and preferring to sift the matter to the bottom sooner than to let an accused person of good character pass unquestioned, owing to the rascality of the informer. The commons had heard how oppressive the tyranny of Pisistratus and his sons had become before it ended, and further that that tyranny had been put down at last, not by themselves and Harmodius, but by the Lacedæmonians, and so were always in fear and took everything suspiciously.

54. Indeed, the daring action of Aristogiton and Harmodius was undertaken in consequence of a love affair, which I shall relate at some length, to show that the Athenians are not more accurate than the rest of the world in their accounts of their own tyrants and of the facts of their own history.† Pisistratus dying at an advanced age in possession of the tyranny, was succeeded by his eldest son, Hippias, and not Hipparchus, as is vulgarly believed. Harmodius was then in the flower of youthful beauty, and Aristogiton, a citizen in the middle rank of life, was his lover and possessed him. Solicited without success by Hipparchus, son of Pisistratus, Harmodius told Aristogiton, and the enraged lover, afraid that the powerful Hipparchus might take Harmodius by force, immediately formed a design, such as his condition in life permitted, for overthrowing the tyranny. In the meantime Hipparchus, after a second solicitation of Harmodius, attended with no better success, unwilling to use violence, arranged to insult‡ him in

---

*The investigation, however sincere, became embroiled in the politics of Alcibiades. Reputation meant little, and arrests were widespread. Proud Athenian democrats kept alive their passionate memories of the tyranny, some of them incorrect.

†This digression (6.54–59) serves Thucydides' argument that history is not a careful concern of ordinary folk, the Athenians included (compare 1.20–22). Harmodius and Aristogiton became national heroes for defending their honor in a homosexual affair.

‡Insult to honor, direct or through proxies (such as Harmodius' sister) was common in relatively tolerant ancient Athens (compare Pericles' idealized remarks, not true for daily life, at 2.37). Although son and brother of the tyrants, Hipparchus had to discover a way to infuriate Harmodius that did not depend on his raw power.

some covert way. Indeed, generally their government was not grievous to the multitude, or in any way odious in practice; and these
tyrants cultivated wisdom and virtue as much as any, and without exacting from the Athenians more than a twentieth of their income,
splendidly adorned their city, and carried on their wars, and provided
sacrifices for the temples.* For the rest, the city was left in full enjoyment of its existing laws, except that care was always taken to have
the offices in the hands of some one of the family.† Among those of
them that held the yearly archonship at Athens was Pisistratus, son of
the tyrant Hippias, and named after his grandfather, who dedicated
during his term of office the altar to the twelve gods in the market-
place, and that of Apollo in the Pythian precinct. The Athenian people afterwards built on to and lengthened the altar in the
market-place, and obliterated the inscription; but that in the Pythian
precinct can still be seen, though in faded letters,‡ and is to the following effect:—

> Pisistratus, the son of Hippias,
> Set up this record of his archonship
> In precinct of Apollo Pythias.

55. That Hippias was the eldest son and succeeded to the government, is what I positively assert as a fact upon which I have had more
exact accounts than others, and may be also ascertained by the following circumstance.§ He is the only one of the legitimate brothers
that appears to have had children; as the altar shows, and the pillar
placed in the Athenian Acropolis, commemorating the crime of the
tyrants, which mentions no child of Thessalus or of Hipparchus, but
five of Hippias, which he had by Myrrhine, daughter of Callias, son of
Hyperechides; and naturally the eldest would have married first.

---

*Pisistratus' 5 percent tax was reasonable, and his policies beautified Athens and its
shrines. They further provided work to the commoners.

†Hellenic tyrannies, unlike modern ones, depended on control of the political process
without removal of the existing regime. In fact, the tyrants' administration in Athens
co-opted many of the aristocracy, a fact that they subsequently suppressed whenever
possible but that an epigraphical fragment confirms (Fornara #23c).

‡This inscription, without its paint (thus "faded"?) but with the letters deeply carved,
survives well (Fornara #37).

§Thucydides emphatically asserts Hippias' priority both by oral tradition and by sound
arguments: Only he had fathered children; his name is mentioned first on more than
one inscription (compare Fornara #30); and it was easier for an established tyrant in office to hold on to power than to establish a new tyrant. More to the detriment of
Athenian pride, unless events were successfully misremembered, it was not this nearly
fruitless and entirely fatal, botched assassination that ended the tyranny but foreign interference by a Spartan army (6.59).

Again, his name comes first on the pillar after that of his father; and this too is quite natural, as he was the eldest after him, and the reigning tyrant. Nor can I ever believe that Hippias would have obtained the tyranny so easily,* if Hipparchus had been in power when he was killed, and he, Hippias, had had to establish himself upon the same day; but he had no doubt been long accustomed to over-awe the citizens, and to be obeyed by his mercenaries, and thus not only conquered, but conquered with ease, without experiencing any of the embarrassment of a younger brother unused to the exercise of authority. It was the sad fate which made Hipparchus famous that got him also the credit with posterity of having been tyrant.

56. To return to Harmodius; Hipparchus having been repulsed in his solicitations insulted him as he had resolved, by first inviting a sister of his, a young girl, to come and bear a basket in a certain procession, and then rejecting her, on the plea that she had never been invited at all owing to her unworthiness.† If Harmodius was indignant at this, Aristogiton for his sake now became more exasperated than ever; and having arranged everything with those who were to join them in the enterprise, they only waited for the great feast of the Panathenæa, the sole day upon which the citizens forming part of the procession could meet together in arms without suspicion.‡ Aristogiton and Harmodius were to begin, but were to be supported immediately by their accomplices against the bodyguard. The conspirators were not many, for better security, besides which they hoped that those not in the plot would be carried away by the example of a few daring spirits, and use the arms in their hands to recover their liberty.

57. At last the festival arrived; and Hippias with his bodyguard was outside the city in the Ceramicus, arranging how the different parts of the procession were to proceed.§ Harmodius and Aristogiton had already their daggers and were getting ready to act, when seeing one of their accomplices talking familiarly with Hippias, who was easy of ac-

---

*Various memorials in song (Fornara #39) and stone commemorated the injustice of the tyrants and the virtues of the so-called tyrannicides. Popular tradition focused on the younger brother killed for his insult, even though this happenstance meant that the reigning tyrant survived and his power grew more oppressive for three more years.

†The apparent pettiness of this insult may be explained by the implication that her unworthiness for the parade (the Panathenaic Procession, according to the Aristotelian *Constitution of the Athenians*) resulted from her no longer being a virgin—a lethal insult to her noble brother and family.

‡The Pisistratids promoted national unity by festivals that brought together the citizens of Attica, but they discouraged political assemblies of the citizens and their coming together for any purpose with weapons.

§The city wall cut through the Ceramicus, the center of the Athenian pottery industry and the site (beyond the walls) of important tombs.

cess to every one, they took fright, and concluded that they were discovered and on the point of being taken; and eager if possible to be re-
venged first upon the man who had wronged them and for whom they
had undertaken all this risk, they rushed, as they were, within the gates,
and meeting with Hipparchus by the Leocorium recklessly fell upon
him at once, infuriated, Aristogiton by love, and Harmodius by insult,
and smote him and slew him.* Aristogiton escaped the guards at the
moment, through the crowd running up, but was afterwards taken and
dispatched in no merciful way: Harmodius was killed on the spot.

58. When the news was brought to Hippias in the Ceramicus, he at
once proceeded not to the scene of action, but to the armed men in
the procession, before they, being some distance away, knew anything
of the matter, and composing his features for the occasion, so as not
to betray himself, pointed to a certain spot, and bade them repair
thither without their arms. They withdrew accordingly, fancying he
had something to say; upon which he told the mercenaries to remove
the arms, and there and then picked out the men he thought guilty
and all found with daggers, the shield and spear being the usual
weapons for a procession.†

59. In this way offended love first led Harmodius and Aristogiton
to conspire, and the alarm of the moment to commit the rash action
recounted. After this the tyranny pressed harder on the Athenians,
and Hippias, now grown more fearful, put to death many of the citizens, and at the same time began to turn his eyes abroad for a refuge
in case of revolution. Thus, although an Athenian, he gave his daughter, Archedice, to a Lampsacene, Æantides, son of the tyrant of Lampsacus, seeing that they had great influence with Darius.‡ And there is
her tomb in Lampsacus with this inscription:—

> Archedice lies buried in this earth,
> Hippias her sire, and Athens gave her birth;
> Unto her bosom pride was never known,
> Though daughter, wife, and sister to the throne.

---

*Even the two assassins differed in their motives. They killed the insulter, but their cel-
ebrated sacrifice left the government intact, since Hippias' quick-witted parade tactics
disarmed their supporters. The Leocorium building honored a legendary Attic hero
who sacrificed his daughters. It sat near the Ceramicus and the Dipylon gate (map 3),
northwest of the Acropolis. Parades mustered their marching men and women here.

†The daggers identified the conspirators, who had no legitimate reason for hidden
weapons in the planned, pacific civic procession.

‡The tyrant's reign became more severe than his father's had been, a common pattern
in Hellenic tyrannies. He allied through his daughter's marriage with another tyrant established in the Asian Propontis (map 10) and thereby secured a refuge and possible
support from the Persian king, Darius. Once again, Thucydides the archaeologist
quotes an inscription, here an epitaph.

Hippias, after reigning three years longer over the Athenians, was deposed in the fourth by the Lacedæmonians and the banished Alcmæonidæ, and went with a safe conduct to Sigeum, and to Æantides at Lampsacus, and from thence to King Darius; from whose court he set out twenty years after, in his old age, and came with the Medes to Marathon.*

60. With these events in their minds, and recalling everything they knew by hearsay on the subject, the Athenian people grew difficult of humour and suspicious of the persons charged in the affair of the mysteries, and persuaded that all that had taken place was part of an oligarchical and tyrannical conspiracy. In the state of irritation thus produced, many persons of consideration had been already thrown into prison, and far from showing any signs of abating, public feeling grew daily more savage, and more arrests were made; until at last one of those in custody, thought to be the most guilty of all, was induced by a fellow-prisoner to make a revelation, whether true or not is a matter on which there are two opinions, no one having been able, either then or since, to say for certain who did the deed.† However this may be, the other found arguments to persuade him, that even if he had not done it, he ought to save himself by gaining a promise of impunity, and free the state of its present suspicions; as he would be surer of safety if he confessed after promise of impunity than if he denied and were brought to trial. He accordingly made a revelation, affecting himself and others in the affair of the Herms; and the Athenian people, glad at last, as they supposed, to get at the truth, and furious until then at not being able to discover those who had conspired against the commons, at once let go the informer and all the rest whom he had not denounced, and bringing the accused to trial executed as many as were apprehended, and condemned to death such as had fled and set a price upon their heads. In this it was, after all, not clear whether the sufferers had been punished unjustly, while in any case the rest of the city received immediate and manifest relief.‡

---

*The Alcmaeonidae claimed hostility to tyranny but had worked with the Pisistratids (Fornara #23 and #40). Hippias returned to Attica and the family stomping-grounds at Marathon in 490 as a Persian collaborator and puppet for Darius (Herodotus 6.94–120).

†Oligarchy and tyranny were equally unacceptable to the *demos*; Alcibiades could be involved in either. The witch-hunt grew fiercer, and a man named Andocides eventually turned witness on a grant of immunity (see Fornara #105) for his family. Those men and women implicated by him were not necessarily guilty, and certainly they were not all of them guilty.

‡The capital sentence was further exacerbated by confiscation of the property of the convicted (see Fornara #147).

61. To return to Alcibiades: public feeling was very hostile to him, being worked on by the same enemies who had attacked him before he went out; and now that the Athenians fancied that they had got at the truth of the matter of the Herms, they believed more firmly than ever that the affair of the mysteries also, in which he was implicated, had been contrived by him in the same intention and was connected with the plot against the democracy. Meanwhile it so happened that, just at the time of this agitation, a small force of Lacedæmonians had advanced as far as the Isthmus, in pursuance of some scheme with the Bœotians. It was now thought that this had come by appointment, at his instigation, and not on account of the Bœotians, and that if the citizens had not acted on the information received, and forestalled them by arresting the prisoners, the city would have been betrayed. The citizens went so far as to sleep one night armed in the temple of Theseus within the walls. The friends also of Alcibiades at Argos were just at this time suspected of a design to attack the commons; and the Argive hostages deposited in the islands were given up by the Athenians to the Argive people to be put to death upon that account: in short, everywhere something was found to create suspicion against Alcibiades.

It was therefore decided to bring him to trial and execute him, and the Salaminia was sent to Sicily for him and the others named in the information, with instructions to order him to come and answer the charges against him, but not to arrest him, because they wished to avoid causing any agitation in the army or among the enemy in Sicily, and above all to retain the services of the Mantineans and Argives, who, it was thought, had been induced to join by his influence.* Alcibiades, with his own ship and his fellow-accused, accordingly sailed off with the Salaminia from Sicily, as though to return to Athens, and went with her as far as Thurii, and there they left the ship and disappeared, being afraid to go home for trial with such a prejudice existing against them. The crew of the Salaminia stayed some time looking for Alcibiades and his companions, and at length, as they were nowhere to be found, set sail and departed. Alcibiades, now an outlaw, crossed in a boat not long after from Thurii to Peloponnese; and the Athenians passed sentence of death by default upon him and those in his company.†

---

*Alcibiades' unique prestige with allies led the recalled general to an opportunity for escape that he seized immediately.

†Thurii had been a Panhellenic colony, founded with Athens' overseas energy already (444/443) in the heyday of Periclean imperialism (Fornara #108 and map 10). *In absentia*, Alcibiades was condemned, but he escaped and survived to wreak havoc on his compatriots. When he was recalled (8.97), he did Athens good service (8.108). When he did eventually return to Athens in 407, he received the welcome of a military hero and served as a religious procession leader (Xenophon, *Hellenica* 1.4.11–20)!

Seventeenth and Eighteenth Years of the War—Inaction of the Athenian Army—Alcibiades at Sparta—Investment (Siege) of Syracuse

62. The Athenian generals left in Sicily now divided the armament into two parts, and each taking one by lot, sailed with the whole for Selinus and Egesta, wishing to know whether the Egestæans would give the money, and to look into the question of Selinus and ascertain the state of the quarrel between her and Egesta. Coasting along Sicily, with the shore on their left, on the side towards the Tyrrhene Gulf, they touched at Himera, the only Hellenic city in that part of the island, and being refused admission resumed their voyage. On their way they took Hyccara, a petty Sicanian seaport, nevertheless at war with Egesta, and making slaves of the inhabitants gave up the town to the Egestæans, some of whose horse had joined them; after which the army proceeded through the territory of the Sicels until it reached Catana, while the fleet sailed along the coast with the slaves on board. Meanwhile Nicias sailed straight from Hyccara along the coast and went to Egesta, and after transacting his other business and receiving thirty talents, rejoined the forces. They now sold their slaves for the sum of one hundred and twenty talents, and sailed round to their Sicel allies to urge them to send troops; and meanwhile went with half their own force to the hostile town of Hybla in the territory of Gela, but did not succeed in taking it. Summer was now over.

63. The winter following, the Athenians at once began to prepare for moving on Syracuse, and the Syracusans on their side for marching against them. From the moment when the Athenians failed to attack them instantly as they at first feared and expected, every day that passed did something to revive their courage; and when they saw them sailing far away from them on the other side of Sicily, and going to Hybla only to fail in their attempts to storm it, they thought less of them than ever, and called upon their generals, as the multitude is apt to do in its moments of confidence, to lead them to Catana, since the enemy would not come to them. Parties also of the Syracusan horse employed in reconnoitring constantly rode up to the Athenian armament, and among other insults asked them whether they had not really come to settle with the Syracusans in a foreign country rather than to resettle the Leontines in their own.*

64. Aware of this, the Athenian generals determined to draw them out in mass as far as possible from the city, and themselves in the

---

*Thucydides' report of Syracusan psychology affirms Lamachus' strategy. The report of insults traded between the two camps confirms Thucydides' interest in psychological warfare.

meantime to sail by night along shore, and take up at their leisure a convenient position. This they knew they could not so well do, if they had to disembark from their ships in front of a force prepared for them, or to go by land openly. The numerous cavalry of the Syracusans (a force which they were themselves without), would then be able to do the greatest mischief to their light troops and the crowd that followed them; but this plan would enable them to take up a position in which the horse could do them no hurt worth speaking of, some Syracusan exiles with the army having told them of the spot near the Olympieum, which they afterwards occupied.

In pursuance of their idea, the generals imagined the following stratagem. They sent to Syracuse a man devoted to them, and by the Syracusan generals thought to be no less in their interest; he was a native of Catana, and said he came from persons in that place, whose names the Syracusan generals were acquainted with, and whom they knew to be among the members of their party still left in the city. He told them that the Athenians passed the night in the town, at some distance from their arms, and that if the Syracusans would name a day and come with all their people at daybreak to attack the armament, they, their friends, would close the gates upon the troops in the city, and set fire to the vessels, while the Syracusans would easily take the camp by an attack upon the stockade. In this they would be aided by many of the Catanians, who were already prepared to act, and from whom he himself came.

65. The generals of the Syracusans, who did not want confidence, and who had intended even without this to march on Catana, believed the man without any sufficient inquiry,* fixed at once a day upon which they would be there, and dismissed him, and the Selinuntines and others of their allies having now arrived, gave orders for all the Syracusans to march out in mass. Their preparations completed, and the time fixed for their arrival being at hand, they set out for Catana, and passed the night upon the river Symæthus, in the Leontine territory. Meanwhile, the Athenians no sooner knew of their approach than they took all their forces and such of the Sicels or others as had joined them, put them on board their ships and boats, and sailed by night to Syracuse. Thus, when morning broke the Athenians were landing opposite the Olympieum ready to seize their camping ground,† and the Syracusan

---

*Double-agents became even more frequent in internecine fourth-century warfare. Thucydides reproves the excessive alacrity of the Syracusan commanders to abandon the city and march north to Catana.

†The Athenians move quickly when their ruse succeeds. To follow the detailed description of the feints, retreats, and advances of the two sides, one must often refer to map 11. The location of many fortifications and other features has not been definitely determined. The city and Epipolae (Heights [in plateau form] above the Town) are north of the Great Harbor; the Olympieum and the Anapus River are west of it.

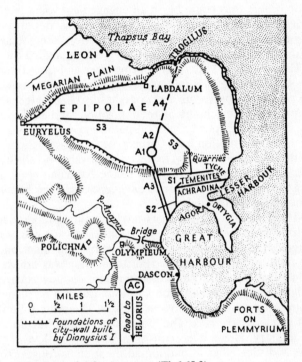

AC: *Original Athenian camp (Th.6.65.3)*
A1: *Athenian round fort (6.98.2)*
A2: *Athenian north wall (6.99.1)*
A3: *Athenian south wall (6.101.1; 103.1)*
A4: *Athenian incomplete wall (7.2.4)*
S1: *First Syracusan counterwall (6.99.2–3; 100.2)*
S2: *Second Syracusan counterwork, palisade & trench (6.101.2)*
S3: *Third Syracusan counterwall (7.4.1; 5.1; 6.4; 7.1; 42.4)*

MAP 11. THE SYRACUSE CAMPAIGN

horse having ridden up first to Catana and found that all the armament had put to sea, turned back and told the infantry, and then all turned back together, and went to the relief of the city.

66. In the meantime, as the march before the Syracusans was a long one, the Athenians quietly sat down their army in a convenient position, where they could begin an engagement when they pleased, and where the Syracusan cavalry would have least opportunity of annoying them, either before or during the action, being fenced off on one side by walls, houses, trees, and by a marsh, and on the other by cliffs. They also felled the neighbouring trees and carried them down to the sea, and formed a palisade alongside of their ships, and with stones which they picked up and wood hastily raised a fort at Daskon, the most vulnerable point of their position, and broke down the bridge over the Anapus.* These preparations were allowed to go on without any interruption from the city, the first hostile force to appear being the Syracusan cavalry, followed afterwards by all the foot together. At first they came close up to the Athenian army, and then, finding that they did not offer to engage, crossed the Helorine road and encamped for the night.

67. The next day the Athenians and their allies prepared for battle, their dispositions being as follows:—Their right wing was occupied by the Argives and Mantineans, the centre by the Athenians, and the rest of the field by the other allies. Half their army was drawn up eight deep in advance, half close to their tents in a hollow square, formed also eight deep, which had orders to look out and be ready to go to the support of the troops hardest pressed. The camp followers were placed inside this reserve. The Syracusans, meanwhile, formed their heavy infantry sixteen deep, consisting of the mass-levy of their own people, and such allies as had joined them, the strongest contingent being that of the Selinuntines; next to them the cavalry of the Geloans, numbering two hundred in all, with about twenty horse and fifty archers from Camarina. The cavalry was posted on their right, full twelve hundred strong, and next to it the darters. As the Athenians were about to begin the attack, Nicias went along the lines, and addressed these words of encouragement to the army and the nations composing it:—

68. 'Soldiers, a long exhortation is little needed by men like ourselves, who are here to fight in the same battle, the force itself being, to my thinking, more fit to inspire confidence than a fine speech with a weak army. Where we have Argives, Mantineans, Athenians, and the

---

*Daskon was near the harbor's edge, but either Thucydides did not know the details of the topography, because he had not been to Syracuse, or he expects an unwarranted familiarity with features such as this location and the bridge.

first of the islanders in the ranks together, it were strange indeed, with so many and so brave companions in arms, if we did not feel confident of victory; especially when we have mass-levies opposed to our picked troops, and what is more, Siceliots, who may disdain us but will not stand against us, their skill not being at all commensurate to their rashness. You may also remember that we are far from home and have no friendly land near,* except what your own swords shall win you; and here I put before you a motive just the reverse of that which the enemy are appealing to; their cry being that they shall fight for their country, mine that we shall fight for a country that is not ours, where we must conquer or hardly get away, as we shall have their horse upon us in great numbers. Remember, therefore, your renown, and go boldly against the enemy, thinking the present strait and necessity more terrible than they.'

69. After this address Nicias at once led on the army. The Syracusans were not at that moment expecting an immediate engagement, and some had even gone away to the town, which was close by; these now ran up as hard as they could, and though behind time, took their places here or there in the main body as fast as they joined it. Want of zeal or daring was certainly not the fault of the Syracusans, either in this or the other battles, but although not inferior in courage, so far as their military science might carry them, when this failed them they were compelled to give up their resolution also.

On the present occasion, although they had not supposed that the Athenians would begin the attack, and although constrained to stand upon their defence at short notice, they at once took up their arms and advanced to meet them. First, the stone-throwers, slingers, and archers of either army began skirmishing, and routed or were routed by one another, as might be expected between light troops; next, soothsayers brought forward the usual victims, and trumpeters urged on the heavy infantry to the charge; and thus they advanced, the Syracusans to fight for their country, and each individual for his safety that day and liberty hereafter; in the enemy's army, the Athenians to make another's country theirs and to save their own from suffering by their defeat; the Argives and independent allies to help them in getting what they came for, and to earn by victory another sight of the country they had left behind; while the subject allies owed most of their ardour to the desire of self-preservation, which they could only hope for if victorious; next to which, as a secondary motive, came the

---

*Nicias' pessimistic exhortation betrays the not unreasonable lack of confidence he had always felt. The lack of friendly territory to which he could retreat differentiates this campaign from most fought in Greece proper. He attacks promptly and unexpectedly, however.

chance of serving on easier terms, after helping the Athenians to a fresh conquest.

70. The armies now came to close quarters, and for a long while fought without either giving ground. Meanwhile there occurred some claps of thunder with lightning and heavy rain, which did not fail to add to the fears of the party fighting for the first time, and very little acquainted with war; while to their more experienced adversaries these phenomena appeared to be produced by the time of year, and much more alarm was felt at the continued resistance of the enemy.

At last the Argives drove in the Syracusan left, and after them the Athenians routed the troops opposed to them, and the Syracusan army was thus cut in two and betook itself to flight. The Athenians did not pursue far, being held in check by the numerous and undefeated Syracusan horse, who attacked and drove back any of their heavy infantry whom they saw pursuing in advance of the rest; in spite of which the victors followed so far as was safe in a body, and then went back and set up a trophy. Meanwhile the Syracusans rallied at the Helorine road, where they reformed as well as they could under the circumstances, and even sent a garrison of their own citizens to the Olympieum, fearing that the Athenians might lay hands on some of the treasures there. The rest returned to the town.

71. The Athenians, however did not go to the temple, but collected their dead and laid them upon a pyre, and passed the night upon the field. The next day they gave the enemy back their dead under truce, to the number of about two hundred and sixty, Syracusans and allies, and gathered together the bones of their own, some fifty, Athenians and allies, and taking the spoils of the enemy, sailed back to Catana. It was now winter; and it did not seem possible for the moment to carry on the war before Syracuse, until horse should have been sent for from Athens and levied among the allies in Sicily—to do away with their utter inferiority in cavalry—and money should have been collected in the country and received from Athens, and until some of the cities, which they hoped would be now more disposed to listen to them after the battle, should have been brought over, and grain and all other necessaries provided, for a campaign in the spring against Syracuse.

72. With this intention they sailed off to Naxos and Catana for the winter. Meanwhile the Syracusans burned their dead, and then held an assembly, in which Hermocrates, son of Hermon, a man who with a general ability of the first order had given proofs of military capacity and brilliant courage in the war, came forward and encouraged them, and told them not to let what had occurred make them give way, since their spirit had not been conquered, but their want of discipline had done the mischief.

Still they had not been beaten by so much as might have been expected, especially as they were, one might say, novices in the art of war, an army of artisans opposed to the most practised soldiers in Hellas. What had also done great mischief was the number of the generals (there were fifteen of them) and the quantity of orders given, combined with the disorder and insubordination of the troops. But if they were to have a few skilful generals, and used this winter in preparing their heavy infantry, finding arms for such as had not got any, so as to make them as numerous as possible, and forcing them to attend to their training generally, they would have every chance of beating their adversaries, courage being already theirs and discipline in the field having thus been added to it.

Indeed, both these qualities would improve, since danger would exercise them in discipline, while their courage would be led to surpass itself by the confidence which skill inspires. The generals should be few and elected with full powers, and an oath should be taken to leave them entire discretion in their command: if they adopted this plan, their secrets would be better kept, all preparations would be properly made, and there would be no room for excuses.

73. The Syracusans heard him, and voted everything as he advised, and elected three generals, Hermocrates himself, Heraclides, son of Lysimachus, and Sicanus, son of Execestes. They also sent envoys to Corinth and Lacedæmon to procure a force of allies to join them, and to induce the Lacedæmonians for their sakes openly to address themselves in real earnest to the war against the Athenians, that they might either have to leave Sicily or be less able to send reinforcements to their army there.*

74. The Athenian forces at Catana now at once sailed against Messina, in the expectation of its being betrayed to them. The intrigue, however, after all came to nothing: Alcibiades, who was in the secret, when he left his command upon the summons from home, foreseeing that he would be outlawed, gave information of the plot to the friends of the Syracusans in Messina, who had at once put to death its authors, and now rose in arms against the opposite faction with those of their way of thinking, and succeeded in preventing the admission of the Athenians. The latter waited for thirteen days, and then, as they were exposed to the weather and without provisions, and met with no success, went back to Naxos, where they made places for their ships to lie in, erected a palisade round their camp, and re-

---

*Hermocrates rallies the Syracusans after the initial Athenian victory. He presents the problems but has realistic solutions as well. Thucydides emphasizes the importance of the presence of a Spartan commander as well as Peloponnesian reinforcements, even if the Peloponnesians do not open a new front in the homeland to draw the Athenians away while the treaty is still ostensibly in force. Hermocrates had advised this before the Athenians arrived (6.34).

tired into winter quarters; meanwhile they sent a trireme to Athens for money and cavalry to join them in the spring.

75. During the winter the Syracusans built a wall on to the city, so as to take in the statue of Apollo Temenites, all along the side looking towards Epipolæ, to make the task of circumvallation longer and more difficult, in case of their being defeated, and also erected a fort at Megara and another in the Olympieum, and stuck palisades along the sea wherever there was a landing place.* Meanwhile, as they knew that the Athenians were wintering at Naxos, they marched with all their people to Catana, and ravaged the land and set fire to the tents and encampment of the Athenians, and so returned home. Learning also that the Athenians were sending an embassy to Camarina, on the strength of the alliance concluded in the time of Laches, to gain, if possible, that city, they sent another from Syracuse to oppose them. They had a shrewd suspicion that the Camarinæans had not sent what they did send for the first battle very willingly; and they now feared that they would refuse to assist them at all in future, after seeing the success of the Athenians in the action, and would join the latter on the strength of their old friendship. Hermocrates, with some others, accordingly arrived at Camarina from Syracuse, and Euphemus and others from the Athenians; and an assembly of the Camarinæans having been convened, Hermocrates spoke as follows, in the hope of prejudicing them against the Athenians:—

76. 'Camarinæans, we did not come on this embassy because we were afraid of your being frightened by the actual forces of the Athenians, but rather of your being gained by what they would say to you before you heard anything from us. They are come to Sicily with the pretext that you know, and the intention which we all suspect,† in my opinion less to restore the Leontines to their homes than to oust us from ours; as it is out of all reason that they should restore in Sicily the cities that they lay waste in Hellas, or should cherish the Leontine Chalcidians because of their Ionian blood, and keep in servitude the Eubœan Chalcidians, of whom the Leontines are a colony.

'No; but the same policy which has proved so successful in Hellas is now being tried in Sicily. After being chosen as the leaders of the Ionians and of the other allies of Athenian origin, to punish the Mede,

---

*The sanctuary of Apollo lay between the Heights and the city. This wall (built in winter 415) and the palisades in the harbor reveal sensible Syracusan fears that they will be on the defensive with the forces currently available to them.

†Hermocrates served as an envoy to the congress at Camarina, southwest of Syracuse on the southern coast. Thucydides has Hermocrates employ his (and many other Greeks') frequent antithesis between pretext and real intention. He ridicules arguments from ethnic ties, as is his interest. His exhortation for Sicilian unity betrays other Gorgianic features of rhetoric, such as the wordplay at the end of 6.76.

the Athenians accused some of failure in military service, some of fighting against each other, and others, as the case might be, upon any colourable pretext that could be found, until they thus subdued them all. In fine, in the struggle against the Medes, the Athenians did not fight for the liberty of the Hellenes, or the Hellenes for their own liberty, but the former to make their countrymen serve them instead of him, the latter to change one master for another, wiser indeed than the first, but wiser for evil.

77. 'But we are not now come to declare to an audience familiar with them the misdeeds of a state so open to accusation as is the Athenian, but much rather to blame ourselves, who, with the warnings we possess in the Hellenes in those parts that have been enslaved through not supporting each other, and seeing the same sophisms being now tried upon ourselves—such as restorations of Leontine kinsfolk and support of Egestæan allies—do not stand together and resolutely show them that here are no Ionians, or Hellespontines, or islanders, who change continually, but always serve a master, sometimes the Mede and sometimes some other, but free Dorians from independent Peloponnese, dwelling in Sicily.

'Or, are we waiting until we be taken in detail, one city after another; knowing as we do that in no other way can we be conquered, and seeing that they turn to this plan, so as to divide some of us by words, to draw some by the bait of an alliance into open war with each other, and to ruin others by such flattery as different circumstances may render acceptable? And do we fancy when destruction first overtakes a distant fellow-countryman that the danger will not come to each of us also, or that he who suffers before us will suffer in himself alone?

78. 'As for the Camarinæan, who says that it is the Syracusan, not he, that is the enemy of the Athenian, and who thinks it hard to have to encounter risk in behalf of my country, I would have him bear in mind that he will fight in my country, not more for mine than for his own, and by so much the more safety in that he will enter on the struggle not alone, after the way has been cleared by my ruin, but with me as his ally; and that the object of the Athenian is not so much to punish the enmity of the Syracusan as to use me as a blind to secure the friendship of the Camarinæan. As for him who envies or even fears us (and envied and feared great powers must always be), and who on this account wishes Syracuse to be humbled to teach us a lesson, but would still have her survive in the interest of his own security, the wish that he indulges is not humanly possible.

'A man can control his own desires, but he cannot likewise control circumstances; and in the event of his calculations proving mistaken, he may live to bewail his own misfortune, and wish to be again envying my prosperity. An idle wish, if he now sacrifice us and refuse to take his share of perils which are the same, in reality though not in name, for him as for us; what is nominally the preservation of our power being really his own salvation.

'It was to be expected that you, of all people in the world, Camarinæans, being our immediate neighbours and the next in danger, would have foreseen this, and instead of supporting us in the lukewarm way that you are now doing, would rather come to us of your own accord, and be now offering at Syracuse the aid which you would have asked for at Camarina, if to Camarina the Athenians had first come, to encourage us to resist the invader. Neither you, however, nor the rest have as yet bestirred yourselves in this direction.

79. 'Fear perhaps will make you study to do right both by us and by the invaders, and plead that you have an alliance with the Athenians. But you made that alliance, not against your friends, but against the enemies that might attack you, and to help the Athenians when they were wronged by others, not when as now they are wronging their neighbours. Even the Rhegians, Chalcidians though they be, refuse to help to restore the Chalcidian Leontines; and it would be strange if, while they suspect the gist of this fine pretence and are wise without reason, you, with every reason on your side, should yet choose to assist your natural enemies, and should join with their direst foes in undoing those whom nature has made your own kinsfolk. This is not to do right; but you should help us without fear of their armament, which has no terrors if we hold together, but only if we let them succeed in their endeavours to separate us; since even after attacking us by ourselves and being victorious in battle, they had to go off without effecting their purpose.

80. 'United, therefore, we have no cause to despair, but rather new encouragement to league together; especially as succours will come to us from the Peloponnesians, in military matters the undoubted superiors of the Athenians. And you need not think that your prudent policy of taking sides with neither, because allies of both, is either safe for you or fair to us. Practically it is not as fair as it pretends to be. If the vanquished be defeated, and the victor conquer, through your refusing to join, what is the effect of your abstention but to leave the former to perish unaided, and to allow the latter to offend unhindered? And yet it were more honourable to join those who are not only the injured party, but your own kindred, and by so doing to defend the common interests of Sicily and save your friends the Athenians from doing wrong.

'In conclusion, we Syracusans say that it is useless for us to demonstrate either to you or to the rest what you know already as well as we do; but we entreat, and if our entreaty fail, we protest that we are menaced by our eternal enemies the Ionians, and are betrayed by you our fellow Dorians. If the Athenians reduce us, they will owe their victory to your decision, but in their own name will reap the honour, and will receive as the prize of their triumph the very men who enabled them to gain it. On the other hand, if we are the conquerors, you will have to pay for having been the cause of our danger.* Consider, therefore; and now make your choice between the security which present servitude offers and the prospect of conquering with us and so escaping disgraceful submission to an Athenian master and avoiding the lasting enmity of Syracuse.'

81. Such were the words of Hermocrates; after whom Euphemus,[†] the Athenian ambassador, spoke as follows:—

82. 'Although we came here only to renew the former alliance, the attack of the Syracusans compels us to speak of our empire and of the good right we have to it. The best proof of this the speaker himself furnished, when he called the Ionians eternal enemies of the Dorians. It is the fact; and the Peloponnesian Dorians being our superiors in numbers and next neighbours, we Ionians looked out for the best means of escaping their domination. After the Median war we had a fleet, and so got rid of the empire and supremacy of the Lacedæmonians, who had no right to give orders to us more than we to them, except that of being the strongest at that moment; and being appointed leaders of the king's former subjects, we continue to be so, thinking that we are least likely to fall under the dominion of the Peloponnesians, if we have a force to defend ourselves with, and in strict truth having done nothing unfair in reducing to subjection the Ionians and islanders, the kinsfolk whom the Syracusans say we have enslaved. They, our kinsfolk, came against their mother country, that is to say against us, together with the Mede, and instead of having the courage to revolt and sacrifice their property as we did when we abandoned our city, chose to be slaves themselves, and to try to make us so.[‡]

83. 'We, therefore, deserve to rule because we placed the largest fleet and an unflinching patriotism at the service of the Hellenes, and because these, our subjects, did us mischief by their ready subservience to the Medes; and, just deserts apart, we seek to strengthen ourselves against the Peloponnesians. We make no fine professions of having a right to rule because we overthrew the barbarian single-

---

*Hermocrates, like Brasidas and many other speakers, combines threats with his encouragement and sweet-talk. "Liberation" and "slavery" were catchwords of the Peloponnesian cause and popular in anti-Athenian communities (compare 6.83; a weak response).

†Euphemus (whose name means "Good-Talker," similar to an Aristophanic tell-tale name and otherwise unknown) echoes some of the arguments of the anonymous Athenian speaker at Sparta before the Ten Years' War began. He rehearses how the Athenians went from victim of the Persians to rulers of the Aegean.

‡He draws a bleak picture of the Asiatic Ionians in this and the next chapter.

handed, or because we risked what we did risk for the freedom of the subjects in question any more than for that of all, and for our own: no one can be quarrelled with for providing for his proper safety.* If we are now here in Sicily, it is equally in the interest of our security, with which we perceive that your interest also coincides. We prove this from the conduct which the Syracusans cast against us and which you somewhat too timorously suspect; knowing that those whom fear has made suspicious, may be carried away by the charm of eloquence for the moment; but when they come to act follow their interests.

'Now, as we have said, fear makes us hold our empire in Hellas, and fear makes us now come, with the help of our friends, to order safely matters in Sicily, and not to enslave any but rather to prevent any from being enslaved.

84. 'Meanwhile, let no one imagine that we are interesting ourselves in you without your having anything to do with us, seeing that if you are preserved and able to make head against the Syracusans, they will be less likely to harm us by sending troops to the Peloponnesians. In this way you have everything to do with us, and on this account it is perfectly reasonable for us to restore the Leontines, and to make them, not subjects like their kinsmen in Eubœa, but as powerful as possible, to help us by annoying the Syracusans from their frontier. In Hellas we are alone a match for our enemies; and as for the assertion that it is out of all reason that we should free the Sicilian, while we enslave the Chalcidian, the fact is that the latter is useful to us by being without arms and contributing money only; while the former, the Leontines and our other friends, cannot be too independent.

85. 'Besides,† for tyrant and imperial city nothing is unreasonable if expedient, no one a kinsman unless sure; but friendship or enmity is everywhere an affair of time and circumstance. Here, in Sicily, our interest is not to weaken our friends, but by means of their strength to cripple our enemies.

'Why doubt this? In Hellas we treat our allies as we find them useful. The Chians and Methymnians govern themselves and furnish ships; most of the rest have harder terms and pay tribute in money; while others, although islanders and easy for us to take, are free altogether, because they occupy convenient positions round Peloponnese. In our settlement of the states here in Sicily, we should, therefore, naturally be guided by our interest, and by fear, as we say, of the Syracusans. Their ambition is to rule you, their object to use the suspicions that we excite to unite you, and then, when we have gone

---

*Fear and security are keynotes of his speech and of those who find a textbook justifying power struggle and aggression in this historian.

†Euphemus acknowledges the rule of expediency, at least for tyrants and empires, and here he too belittles the significance of ethnic ties.

away without effecting anything, by force or through your isolation, to become the masters of Sicily. And masters they must become, if you unite with them; as a force of that magnitude would be no longer easy for us to deal with united, and they would be more than a match for you as soon as we were away.

86. 'Any other view of the case is condemned by the facts. When you first asked us over, the fear which you held out was that of danger to Athens if we let you come under the dominion of Syracuse; and it is not right now to mistrust the very same argument by which you claimed to convince us, or to give way to suspicion because we are come with a larger force against the power of that city. Those whom you should really distrust are the Syracusans. We are not able to stay here without you, and if we proved perfidious enough to bring you into subjection, we should be unable to keep you in bondage, owing to the length of the voyage and the difficulty of guarding large, and in a military sense continental, towns: they, the Syracusans, live close to you, not in a camp, but in a city greater than the force we have with us, plot always against you, never let slip an opportunity once offered, as they have shown in the case of the Leontines and others, and now have the face, just as if you were fools, to invite you to aid them against the power that hinders this, and that has thus far maintained Sicily independent. We, as against them, invite you to a much more real safety, when we beg you not to betray that common safety which we each have in the other, and to reflect that they, even without allies, will, by their numbers, have always the way open to you, while you will not often have the opportunity of defending yourselves with such numerous auxiliaries; if, through your suspicions, you once let these go away unsuccessful or defeated, you will wish to see if only a handful of them back again, when the day is past in which their presence could do anything for you.

87. 'But we hope, Camarinæans, that the calumnies of the Syracusans will not be allowed to succeed either with you or with the rest: we have told you the whole truth upon the things we are suspected of, and will now briefly recapitulate, in the hope of convincing you. We assert that we are rulers in Hellas in order not to be subjects; liberators in Sicily that we may not be harmed by the Sicilians; that we are compelled to interfere in many things, because we have many things to guard against; and that now, as before, we are come as allies to those of you who suffer wrong in this island, not without invitation but upon invitation.

'Accordingly, instead of making yourselves judges or censors of our conduct, and trying to turn us away, which it were now difficult to do, so far as there is anything in our interfering policy or in our character, that chimes in with your interest, take this and make use of it; and be sure that far from being injurious to all alike, to most of the Hellenes that policy is even beneficial. Thanks to it, all men in all places, even where we are not, who either apprehend or meditate aggression, from the near prospect before them, in the one case, of obtaining our intervention in their favour, in the other, of our arrival making the venture dangerous, find themselves constrained, respectively, to be moderate against their will, and to be preserved without trouble of their own. Do not you reject this security that is open to all who desire it, and is now offered to you; but do like others, and instead of being always on the defensive against the Syracusans, unite with us, and in your turn at last threaten them.'

88. Such were the words of Euphemus. What the Camarinæans felt was this. Sympathising with the Athenians, except in so far as they might be afraid of their subjugating Sicily, they had always been at enmity with their neighbour Syracuse. From the very fact, however, that they were their neighbours, they feared the Syracusans most of the two, and being apprehensive of their conquering the Athenians even without them, both sent them in the first instance the few horsemen mentioned, and for the future determined to support them most in fact, although as sparingly as possible; but for the moment in order not to seem to slight the Athenians, especially as they had been successful in the engagement, to answer both alike. Agreeably to this resolution they answered that as both the contending parties happened to be allies of theirs, they thought it most consistent with their oaths, at present, to side with neither; with which answer the ambassadors of either party departed.

In the meantime, while Syracuse pursued her preparations for war, the Athenians were encamped at Naxos, and tried by negotiation to gain as many of the Sicels as possible. Those more in the low lands, and subjects of Syracuse, mostly held aloof; but the peoples of the interior who had never been otherwise than independent, with few exceptions, at once joined the Athenians, and brought down grain to the army, and in some cases even money. The Athenians marched against those who refused to join, and forced some of them to do so; in the case of others they were stopped by the Syracusans sending garrisons and reinforcements. Meanwhile the Athenians moved their winter quarters from Naxos to Catana, and reconstructed the camp burnt by the Syracusans, and stayed there the rest of the winter. They also sent a galley to Carthage, with proffers of friendship,* on the chance of obtaining assistance, and another to the cities of Etruria; some of the cities there having spontaneously offered to join them in the war. They also sent round to the Sicels and to Egesta, desiring them to

---

*Such a treaty of friendship seems to have become a reality within a decade (see the inscription translated in Fornara #165).

send them as many horses as possible, and meanwhile prepared bricks, iron, and all other things necessary for the work of circumvallation, intending by the spring to begin hostilities.

In the meantime the Syracusan envoys despatched to Corinth and Lacedæmon tried as they passed along the coast to persuade the Italiots to interfere with the proceedings of the Athenians, which threatened Italy quite as much as Syracuse, and having arrived at Corinth made a speech calling on the Corinthians to assist them on the ground of their common origin. The Corinthians voted at once to aid them with all enthusiasm themselves, and then sent on envoys with them to Lacedæmon, to help them to persuade her also to prosecute the war with the Athenians more openly at home and to send succour to Sicily. The envoys from Corinth having reached Lacedæmon found there Alcibiades with his fellow-refugees, who had at once crossed over in a trading vessel from Thurii, first to Cyllene in Elis, and afterwards from thence to Lacedæmon; upon the Lacedæmonians' own invitation, after first obtaining a safe conduct, as he feared them for the part he had taken in the affair of Mantinea. The result was that the Corinthians, Syracusans, and Alcibiades, pressing all the same request in the assembly of the Lacedæmonians, succeeded in persuading them; but as the Ephors and the authorities, although resolved to send envoys to Syracuse to prevent their surrendering to the Athenians, showed no disposition to send them any assistance, Alcibiades now came forward and inflamed and stirred the Lacedæmonian by speaking as follows:—

89. 'I am forced first to speak to you of the prejudice with which I am regarded, in order that suspicion may not make you disinclined to listen to me upon public matters. The connexion with you as your *Proxeni*, which the ancestors of our family by reason of some discontent renounced, I personally tried to renew by my good offices towards you, in particular upon the occasion of the disaster at Pylos.* But although I maintained this friendly attitude, you yet chose to negotiate the peace with the Athenians through my enemies, and thus to strengthen them and to discredit me. You had therefore no right to complain if I turned to the Mantineans and Argives, and seized other occasions of thwarting and injuring you; and the time has now come when those among you, who in the bitterness of the moment may have been then unfairly angry with me, should look at the matter in its true light, and take a different view.

---

*Alcibiades, the leading Athenian politician in opposition to Sparta after the death of Cleon, here (6.88–93) addresses the Spartan assembly to whip up their enthusiasm for renewing war against Athens. His family had served as *proxenoi* (unofficial consuls for foreign nationals) for the Spartans in the past. His speech absurdly inclines to equate his individual interests to those of another state.

'Those again who judged me unfavourably, because I leaned rather to the side of the commons, must not think that their dislike is any better founded. We have always been hostile to tyrants, and all who oppose arbitrary power are called commons; hence we continued to act as leaders of the multitude; besides which, as democracy was the government of the city, it was necessary in most things to conform to established conditions. However, we endeavoured to be more moderate than the licentious temper of the times; and while there were others, formerly as now, who tried to lead the multitude astray, the same who banished me, our party was that of the whole people, our creed being to do our part in preserving the form of government under which the city enjoyed the utmost greatness and freedom, and which we had found existing.

'As for democracy, the men of sense among us knew what it was, and I perhaps as well as any, as I have the more cause to complain of it; but there is nothing new to be said of a patent absurdity*—meanwhile we did not think it safe to alter it under the pressure of your hostility.

90. 'So much then for the prejudices with which I am regarded: I now can call your attention to the questions you must consider, and upon which superior knowledge perhaps permits me to speak. We sailed to Sicily first to conquer, if possible, the Siceliots, and after them the Italiots also, and finally to assail the empire and city of Carthage. In the event of all or most of these schemes succeeding, we were then to attack Peloponnese, bringing with us the entire force of the Hellenes lately acquired in those parts, and taking a number of barbarians into our pay, such as the Iberians and others in those countries, confessedly the most warlike known, and building numerous triremes in addition to those which we had already, timber being plentiful in Italy; and with this fleet blockading Peloponnese from the sea and assailing it with our armies by land, taking some of the cities by storm, drawing works of circumvallation round others, we hoped without difficulty to effect its reduction, and after this to rule the whole of the Hellenic name. Money and grain meanwhile for the better execution of these plans were to be supplied in sufficient quantities by the newly acquired places in those countries, independently of our revenues here at home.

91. 'You have thus heard the history of the present expedition from the man who most exactly knows what our objects were; and the remaining generals will, if they can, carry these out just the same. But that

---

*Alcibiades' defense of his democratic postures is bold and self-serving. He seems to argue that the democracy changed while he was trying to lead it. There is truth in this view, but the speech conveys the effrontery of his scheming. To call the Athenian democracy a "patent absurdity" will fly in Sparta, but such words only ratify the criticisms made of him before and after this occasion in Athens.

the states in Sicily must succumb if you do not help them, I will now show. Although the Siceliots, with all their inexperience, might even now be saved if their forces were united, the Syracusans alone, beaten already in one battle with all their people and blockaded from the sea, will be unable to withstand the Athenian armament that is now there.

'But if Syracuse falls, all Sicily falls also, and Italy immediately afterwards; and the danger which I just now spoke of from that quarter will before long be upon you. None need therefore fancy that Sicily only is in question; Peloponnese will be so also, unless you speedily do as I tell you, and send on board ship to Syracuse troops that shall be able to row their ships themselves, and serve as heavy infantry the moment that they land; and what I consider even more important than the troops, a Spartan as commanding officer to discipline the forces already on foot and to compel recusants to serve. The friends that you have already will thus become more confident, and the waverers will be encouraged to join you.

'Meanwhile you must carry on the war here more openly, that the Syracusans seeing that you do not forget them, may put heart into their resistance, and that the Athenians may be less able to reinforce their armament.

'You must fortify Decelea in Attica, the blow of which the Athenians are always most afraid and the only one that they think they have not experienced in the present war;* the surest method of harming an enemy being to find out what he most fears, and to choose this means of attacking him, since every one naturally knows best his own weak points and fears accordingly. The fortification in question, while it benefits you, will create difficulties for your adversaries, of which I shall pass over many, and shall only mention the chief.

'Whatever property there is in the country will most of it become yours, either by capture or surrender; and the Athenians will at once be deprived of their revenues from the silver mines at Laurium, of their present gains from their land and from the law courts, and above all of the revenue from their allies, which will be paid less regularly, as they lose their awe of Athens, and see you addressing yourselves with vigour to the war.

92. 'The zeal and speed with which all this shall be done depends,

---

*The general of the Athenians certainly knows what the Spartans can do to harm the Athenians most. He tells them to support the Siceliots with men, matériel, and a commander, to open a second front, to permanently occupy a base in Attica (something they should have thought of long since). Deceleia lay in north-central Attica (map 2), in easy communication with the Peloponnese. Thereby the Spartans could cut the Athenians off from their silver mines at Laurium (southeastern Attica) and from their fields. These actions will disrupt further incoming allied revenues and encourage Aegean allies to revolt.

Lacedæmonians, upon yourselves; as to its possibility, I am quite confident, and I have little fear of being mistaken.

'Meanwhile I hope that none of you will think any the worse of me if after having hitherto passed as a lover of my country, I now actively join its worst enemies in attacking it, or will suspect what I say as the fruit of an outlaw's enthusiasm. I am an outlaw from the iniquity of those who drove me forth, not, if you will be guided by me, from your service: my worst enemies are not you who only harmed your foes, but they who forced their friends to become enemies; and love of country is what I do not feel when I am wronged, but what I felt when secure in my rights as a citizen. Indeed I do not consider that I am now attacking a country that is still mine; I am rather trying to recover one that is mine no longer;* and the true lover of his country is not he who consents to lose it unjustly rather than attack it, but he who longs for it so much that he will go all lengths to recover it.

'For myself, therefore, Lacedæmonians, I beg you to use me without scruple for danger and trouble of every kind, and to remember the argument in every one's mouth, that if I did you great harm as an enemy, I could likewise do you good service as a friend, inasmuch as I know the plans of the Athenians, while I only guessed yours. For yourselves I entreat you to believe that your most capital interests are now under deliberation; and I urge you to send without hesitation the expeditions to Sicily and Attica; by the presence of a small part of your forces you will save important cities in that island, and you will destroy the power of Athens both present and prospective; after this you will dwell in security and enjoy the supremacy over all Hellas, resting not on force but upon consent and affection.'

93. Such were the words of Alcibiades. The Lacedæmonians, who had themselves before intended to march against Athens, but were still waiting and looking about them, at once became much more in earnest when they received this particular information from Alcibiades, and considered that they had heard it from the man who best knew the truth of the matter. Accordingly they now turned their attention to the fortifying of Decelea and sending immediate aid to the Sicilians; and naming Gylippus, son of Cleandridas, to the command of the Syracusans,† bade him consult with that people and with the

---

*Alcibiades' sophistic defense of treason is tortuous and unpersuasive. Exiles and turncoats must somehow justify their behavior. Whether he truly desired revenge or just reinstallation, the Spartans adopted his intelligent stratagems.

†The *epiteichismos* (fortification in enemy territory) was to prove to be one of the most effective tactics in Sparta's many campaigns against the Athenians who were most vulnerable on land. Gylippus receives less description than Brasidas had been granted, perhaps because Thucydides had become acquainted only with the latter. Gylippus' influence on the outcome of the war is as great as Brasidas'.

Corinthians and arrange for succour reaching the island, in the best and speediest way possible under the circumstances. Gylippus desired the Corinthians to send him at once two ships to Asine, and to prepare the rest that they intended to send, and to have them ready to sail at the proper time. Having settled this, the envoys departed from Lacedæmon.

In the meantime arrived the Athenian galley from Sicily sent by the generals for money and cavalry; and the Athenians, after hearing what they wanted, voted to send the supplies for the armament and the cavalry. And the winter ended, and with it ended the seventeenth year of the present war of which Thucydides is the historian.*

94. The next summer, at the very beginning of the season, the Athenians in Sicily put out from Catana, and sailed along shore to Megara in Sicily, from which, as I have mentioned above, the Syracusans expelled the inhabitants in the time of their tyrant Gelo, themselves occupying the territory. Here the Athenians landed and laid waste the country, and after an unsuccessful attack upon a fort of the Syracusans, went on with the fleet and army to the river Terias, and advancing inland laid waste the plain and set fire to the grain; and after killing some of a small Syracusan party which they encountered, and setting up a trophy, went back again to their ships. They now sailed to Catana and took in provisions there, and going with their whole force against Centoripa, a town of the Sicels, acquired it by capitulation, and departed, after also burning the grain of the Inessæans and Hybleans. Upon their return to Catana they found the horsemen arrived from Athens, to the number of two hundred and fifty (with their equipment, but without their horses which were to be procured upon the spot), and thirty mounted archers and three hundred talents of silver.

95. The same spring the Lacedæmonians marched against Argos, and went as far as Cleonæ, when an earthquake occurred and caused them to return. After this the Argives invaded the Thyreatid, which is on their border, and took much booty from the Lacedæmonians, which was sold for no less than twenty-five talents. The same summer, not long after, the Thespian commons made an attack upon the party in office, which was not successful, but succour arrived from Thebes, and some were caught, while others took refuge at Athens.

96. The same summer the Syracusans learned that the Athenians

---

*The Athenians, not yet faced with the consequence of Alcibiades' advice, vote generous additional support to their expeditionary forces. Thucydides' formula of closure for winter 415 incorporates his belief that the series of events from 431 to 404 amounted to one war composed of various campaigns and occasional lulls. The next spring (of 414), the Athenians try a more aggressive policy and are initially successful. This account of this campaign extends from 6.94 to 7.18.

had been joined by their cavalry, and were on the point of marching against them; and seeing that without becoming masters of Epipolæ, a precipitous spot situated exactly over the town, the Athenians could not, even if victorious in battle, easily invest them,* they determined to guard its approaches, in order that the enemy might not ascend unobserved by this, the sole way by which ascent was possible, as the remainder is lofty ground, and falls right down to the city, and can all be seen from inside; and as it lies above the rest the place is called by the Syracusans Epipolæ or Overtown. They accordingly went out in mass at daybreak into the meadow along the river Anapus, their new generals, Hermocrates and his colleagues, having just come into office, and held a review of their heavy infantry, from whom they first selected a picked body of six hundred, under the command of Diomilus, an exile from Andros, to guard Epipolæ, and to be ready to muster at a moment's notice to help wherever help should be required.

97. Meanwhile the Athenians, the very same morning, were holding a review, having already made land unobserved with all the armament from Catana, opposite a place called Leon, not much more than half a mile from Epipolæ, where they disembarked their army, bringing the fleet to anchor at Thapsus, a peninsula running out into the sea, with a narrow isthmus, and not far from the city of Syracuse either by land or water. While the naval force of the Athenians threw a stockade across the isthmus and remained quiet at Thapsus, the land army immediately went on at a run to Epipolæ, and succeeded in getting up by Euryelus before the Syracusans perceived them, or could come up from the meadow and the review.† Diomilus with his six hundred and the rest advanced as quickly as they could, but they had nearly three miles to go from the meadow before reaching them. Attacking in this way in considerable disorder, the Syracusans were defeated in battle at Epipolæ and retired to the town, with a loss of about three hundred killed, and Diomilus among the number. After this the Athenians set up a trophy and restored to the Syracusans their dead under truce, and next day descended to Syracuse itself; and no one coming out to meet them, reascended and built a fort at Labdalum, upon the edge of the cliffs of Epipolæ, looking towards Megara, to serve as secure storage for their baggage and money, whenever they advanced to give battle or to work at the lines.

98. Not long afterwards three hundred cavalry came to them from

---

*The Syracusans calculate correctly but somewhat tardily that Epipolae is key to the Athenian plans of land and sea blockade.

†The Athenians land at Leon, north of Epipolae, where they cannot be seen. Then they advance up Leon's western side to a high region known as Euryelus (map 11). This advance and the subsequent battle were crucial Athenian victories, but they failed to make the necessarily prompt use of them that might have won them all of Syracuse.

Egesta, and about a hundred from the Sicels, Naxians, and others; and thus, with the two hundred and fifty from Athens, for whom they had got horses from the Egestæans and Catanians, besides others that they bought, they now mustered six hundred and fifty cavalry in all. After posting a garrison in Labdalum, they advanced to Syca, where they sat down and quickly built the Circle or centre of their wall of circumvallation. The Syracusans, appalled at the rapidity with which the work advanced, determined to go out against them and give battle and interrupt it; and the two armies were already in battle array, when the Syracusan generals observed that their troops found such difficulty in getting into line, and were in such disorder, that they led them back into the town, except part of the cavalry. These remained and hindered the Athenians from carrying stones or dispersing to any great distance, until a tribe of the Athenian heavy infantry,* with all the cavalry, charged and routed the Syracusan horse with some loss; after which they set up a trophy for the cavalry action.

99. The next day the Athenians began building the wall to the north of the Circle, at the same time collecting stone and timber, which they kept laying down towards Trogilus along the shortest line for their works from the great harbour to the sea; while the Syracusans, guided by their generals, and above all by Hermocrates, instead of risking any more general engagements, determined to build a counterwork in the direction in which the Athenians were going to carry their wall.† If this could be completed in time the enemy's lines would be cut; and meanwhile, if he were to attempt to interrupt them by an attack, they would send a part of their forces against him, and would secure the approaches beforehand with their stockade, while the Athenians would have to leave off working with their whole force in order to attend to them.

They accordingly sallied forth and began to build, starting from their city, running a cross wall below the Athenian Circle, cutting down the olives and erecting wooden towers. As the Athenian fleet had not yet sailed round into the great harbour, the Syracusans still commanded the sea-coast, and the Athenians brought their provisions by land from Thapsus.

Syca means "fig," and the fortifiable spot was one from which the Athenians could build circumvallations in two directions at once. The Syracusan command decides not to enter battle with troops in disarray. The cavalry, however, harassed the Athenian wall-builders. The Athenian military units—here the hoplites—were organized by their ten civic tribes constituted (artificially) by the original "democrat," Cleisthenes (c.560–490).

†Hermocrates decides that the Syracusans, at this moment, can protect themselves better by counter-walls than by open battle. It will be one of three counter-walls (map 11) designed to keep the Athenians from walling them off from the rest of Sicily.

100. The Syracusans now thought the stockades and stone-work of their counter-wall sufficiently far advanced; and as the Athenians, afraid of being divided and so fighting at a disadvantage, and intent upon their own wall, did not come out to interrupt them, they left one tribe to guard the new work and went back into the city. Meanwhile the Athenians destroyed their pipes of drinking-water carried underground into the city;* and watching until the rest of the Syracusans were in their tents at midday, and some even gone away into the city, and those in the stockade keeping but indifferent guard, appointed three hundred picked men of their own, and some men picked from the light troops and armed for the purpose, to run suddenly as fast as they could to the counterwork, while the rest of the army advanced in two divisions, the one with one of the generals to the city in case of a sortie, the other with the other general to the stockade by the postern gate. The three hundred attacked and took the stockade, abandoned by its garrison, who took refuge in the outworks round the statue of Apollo Temenites. Here the pursuers burst in with them, and after getting in were beaten out by the Syracusans, and some few of the Argives and Athenians slain; after which the whole army retired, and having demolished the counterwork and pulled up the stockade, carried away the stakes to their own lines, and set up a trophy.†

101. The next day the Athenians from the Circle proceeded to fortify the cliff above the marsh which on this side of Epipolæ looks towards the great harbour; this being also the shortest line for their work to go down across the plain and the marsh to the harbour. Meanwhile the Syracusans marched out and began a second stockade, starting from the city, across the middle of the marsh, digging a trench alongside to make it impossible for the Athenians to carry their wall down to the sea. As soon as the Athenians had finished their work at the cliff they again attacked the stockade and ditch of the Syracusans.

Ordering the fleet to sail round from Thapsus into the great harbour of Syracuse, they descended at about dawn from Epipolæ into the plain, and laying doors and planks over the marsh where it was muddy and firmest, crossed over on these, and by day-break took the ditch and the stockade, except a small portion which they captured afterwards. A battle now ensued, in which the Athenians were victorious, the right wing of the Syracusans flying to the town and the left to

---

*Athenian engineers hope to reduce the Syracusans by cutting off their water supply coming in from higher ground. The fountain of Arethusa near the sea would always supply some fresh water, however.

†Such an onslaught depends on speed; the Athenians were successful and the Syracusans retreated.

the river. The three hundred picked Athenians, wishing to cut off their passage, pressed on at a run to the bridge, when the alarmed Syracusans, who had with them most of their cavalry, closed and routed them, hurling them back upon the Athenian right wing, the first tribe of which was thrown into a panic by the shock. Seeing this, Lamachus came to their aid from the Athenian left with a few archers and with the Argives, and crossing a ditch, was left alone with a few that had crossed with him, and was killed with five or six of his men.* These the Syracusans managed immediately to snatch up in haste and get across the river into a place of security, themselves retreating as the rest of the Athenian army now came up.

Meanwhile those who had at first fled for refuge to the city, seeing the turn affairs were taking, now rallied from the town and formed against the Athenians in front of them, sending also a part of their number to the Circle on Epipolæ, which they hoped to take while denuded of its defenders.

102. These took and destroyed the Athenian out-work of a thousand feet, the Circle itself being saved by Nicias, who happened to have been left in it through illness,† and who now ordered the servants to set fire to the engines and timber thrown down before the wall; want of men, as he was aware, rendering all other means of escape impossible. This step was justified by the result, the Syracusans not coming any further on account of the fire, but retreating. Meanwhile succour was coming up from the Athenians below, who had put to flight the troops opposed to them; and the fleet also, according to orders, was sailing from Thapsus into the great harbour. Seeing this, the troops on the heights retired in haste, and the whole army of the Syracusans re-entered the city, thinking that with their present force they would no longer be able to hinder the wall reaching the sea.

103. After this the Athenians set up a trophy and restored to the Syracusans their dead under truce, receiving in return Lamachus and those who had fallen with him. The whole of their forces, naval and military, being now with them, they began from Epipolæ and the cliffs and enclosed the Syracusans with a double wall down to the sea.

Provisions were now brought in for the armament from all parts of Italy; and many of the Sicels, who had hitherto been looking to see how things went, came as allies to the Athenians: there also arrived

---

*The amphibious plan, audacious and successful for the most part, might well have been Lamachus'. His death in a minor skirmish, however, was a catastrophic loss for the Athenians, for now there was but one commander, and that was Nicias, who was constitutionally timid and currently ill with serious internal complaints (compare 7.15, kidney problems).

†Nicias, left behind by chance, saves by his bold action the central stronghold of the Athenian strategy.

three ships of fifty oars from the Etruscans. Meanwhile everything else progressed favourably for their hopes. The Syracusans began to despair of finding safety in arms, no relief having reached them from Peloponnese, and were now proposing terms of capitulation among themselves and to Nicias, who after the death of Lamachus was left sole commander. No decision was come to, but as was natural with men in difficulties and besieged more straitly than before, there was much discussion with Nicias and still more in the town. Their present misfortunes had also made them suspicious of one another; and the blame of their disasters was thrown upon the ill-fortune or treachery of the generals under whose command they had happened; and these were deposed and others, Heraclides, Eucles, and Tellias, elected in their stead.

104. Meanwhile the Lacedæmonian, Gylippus, and the ships from Corinth were now off Leucas, intent upon going with all haste to the relief of Sicily. The reports that reached them being of an alarming kind, and all of the reports agreeing in the falsehood that Syracuse was already completely blockaded,* Gylippus abandoned all hope of Sicily, and wishing to save Italy, rapidly crossed the Ionian Sea to Tarentum with the Corinthian, Pythen, two Laconian, and two Corinthian vessels, leaving the Corinthians to follow him after manning, in addition to their own ten, two Leucadian and two Ambraciot ships. From Tarentum Gylippus first went on an embassy to Thurii, and claimed anew the rights of citizenship which his father had enjoyed; failing to bring over the townspeople, he weighed anchor and coasted along Italy. Opposite the Terinæan gulf he was caught by the wind which blows violently and steadily from the north in that quarter, and was carried out to sea; and after experiencing very rough weather, remade Tarentum, where he hauled ashore and refitted such of his ships as had suffered most from the tempest. Nicias heard of his approach, but, like the Thurians, despised the scanty number of his ships, and set down piracy as the only probable object of the voyage, and so took no precautions for the present.†

105. About the same time in this summer, the Lacedæmonians invaded Argos with their allies, and laid waste most of the country. The

---

*Gylippus, misinformed about Syracuse's dire situation but eager to save southern Italy from the Athenians, hastens across the open Adriatic/Ionian Sea rather than making the usual and slower crossing to the north. He had connections in both Laconian (see Fornara #9) Tarentum and in Thurii, perhaps one reason for the Spartans' nomination of him for this crucial task.

†While Thucydides does not say so, Nicias' lack of interest in a few Spartans would prove decisive for the Athenian defeat. Gylippus proved to be an inspiring and effective Spartan commander of the united Syracusan and allied forces. We want to know more of him.

Athenians went with thirty ships to the relief of the Argives, thus breaking their treaty with the Lacedæmonians in the most overt manner.* Up to this time incursions from Pylos, descents on the coasts of the rest of Peloponnese, instead of on the Laconian, had been the extent of their co-operation with the Argives and Mantineans; and although the Argives had often begged them to land, if only for a moment, with their heavy infantry in Laconia, lay waste ever so little of it with them, and depart, they had always refused to do so. Now, however, under the command of Pythodorus, Læspodius, and Demaratus, they landed at Epidaurus, Limera, Prasiæ, and other places, and plundered the country; and thus furnished the Lacedæmonians with a better pretext for hostilities against Athens. After the Athenians had retired from Argos with their fleet, and the Lacedæmonians also, the Argives made an incursion into Phliasia, and returned home after ravaging their land and killing some of the inhabitants.

---

*The Lacedaemonians could invade Argos because she had no alliance to Athens at the time of the treaty of 421. It is odd, however, that Athenian assistance to their current allies, in fighting the Spartans, is regarded as the clear breach, while the ongoing guerrilla war from Pylos (Messenians!), the military incursions on the Peloponnese other than Laconia (such as on the Corinthia), the Mantinea campaign, etc. were not considered to be such clear breaches.

BOOK 7

*Eighteenth and Nineteenth Years of the War—Arrival of
Gylippus at Syracuse—Fortification of Decelea—
Successes of the Syracusans*

1. After refitting their ships, Gylippus and Pythen coasted along
from Tarentum to Epizephyrian Locris. They now received the more
correct information that Syracuse was not yet completely blockaded,
but that it was still possible for an army arriving by Epipolæ to effect
an entrance; and they consulted, accordingly, whether they should
keep Sicily on their right and risk sailing in by sea, or leaving it on
their left, should first sail to Himera, and taking with them the
Himeræans and any others that might agree to join them, go to Syracuse by land.*

Finally they determined to sail for Himera, especially as the four
Athenian ships which Nicias had at length sent off, on hearing that
they were at Locris, had not yet arrived at Rhegium. Accordingly, before these reached their post, the Peloponnesians crossed the strait,
and after touching at Rhegium and Messina, came to Himera. Arrived there, they persuaded the Himeræans to join in the war, and not
only to go with them themselves but to provide arms for the seamen
from their vessels which they had drawn ashore at Himera; and they
sent and appointed a place for the Selinuntines to meet them with all
their forces.† A few troops were also promised by the Geloans and
some of the Sicels, who were now ready to join them with much
greater alacrity, owing to the recent death of Archonidas, a powerful
Sicel king in that neighbourhood and friendly to Athens, and owing
also to the vigour shown by Gylippus in coming from Lacedæmon.

Gylippus now took with him about seven hundred of his sailors
and marines, that number only having arms, a thousand heavy infantry and light troops from Himera with a body of a hundred horse,
some light troops and cavalry from Selinus, a few Geloans, and Sicels
numbering a thousand in all, and set out on his march for Syracuse.

2. Meanwhile the Corinthian fleet from Leucas made all haste to
arrive; and one of their commanders, Gongylus, starting last with a

---

*Athenian control of the eastern Sicilian seas forces the Spartans to give their coastal
fleets a wide berth. Spartan caution pays off.

†Western Sicily, more than 100 miles distant from the armies of Syracuse, feared less
that city's dominance.

single ship, was the first to reach Syracuse, a little before Gylippus. Gongylus found the Syracusans on the point of holding an assembly to consider whether they should not put an end to the war. This he prevented, and reassured them by telling them that more vessels were still to arrive, and that Gylippus, son of Cleandridas, had been despatched by the Lacedæmonians to take the command.*

Upon this the Syracusans took courage, and immediately marched out with all their forces to meet Gylippus, who they found was now close at hand. Meanwhile Gylippus, after taking Ietæ, a fort of the Sicels, on his way, formed his army in order of battle, and so arrived at Epipolæ, and ascending by Euryelus, as the Athenians had done at first, now advanced with the Syracusans against the Athenian lines. His arrival chanced at the critical moment.[†] The Athenians had already finished a double wall of about 4,500 feet to the great harbour, with the exception of a small portion next the sea, which they were still engaged upon; and in the remainder of the circle towards Trogilus on the other sea, stones had been laid ready for building for the greater part of the distance, and some points had been left half finished, while others were entirely completed. The danger of Syracuse had indeed been great.[‡]

3. Meanwhile the Athenians, recovering from the confusion into which they had been at first thrown by the sudden approach of Gylippus and the Syracusans, formed in order of battle. Gylippus halted at a short distance off and sent on a herald to tell them that if they would evacuate Sicily with bag and baggage within five days' time, he was willing to make a truce accordingly. The Athenians treated this proposition with contempt, and dismissed the herald without an answer.[§] After this both sides began to prepare for action. Gylippus, observing that the Syracusans were in disorder and did not easily fall into line, drew off his troops more into the open ground, while Nicias did not lead on the Athenians but lay still by his own wall. When Gylippus saw that they did not come on, he led off his army to the citadel of the quarter of Apollo Temenites, and passed the night there. On the following day he led out the main body of his army, and draw-

---

*The desperate but determined Gongylus arrives in town at the low point of Syracusan morale and saves the city with news of help on the way.

†Gylippus arrived as the Athenians advanced their blockading walls north (toward Trogilus) and south (toward the Great Harbor).

‡This formulaic nick-of-time conclusion closely resembles that for Mitylenians about to be massacred (3.49). It exemplifies Thucydides' rhetoric of catastrophe and near catastrophe.

§Gylippus' offer does sound preposterous but may have been part of a (suppressed) religious ritual required for some concept of a just war. Byplay with heralds often attracts Thucydides' dramatic attention.

ing them up in order of battle before the walls of the Athenians to prevent their going to the relief of any other quarter, despatched a strong force against Fort Labdalum and took it, and put all whom he found in it to the sword, the place not being within sight of the Athenians. On the same day an Athenian galley that lay moored off the harbour was captured by the Syracusans.*

4. After this the Syracusans and their allies began to carry a single wall, starting from the city, in a slanting direction up Epipolæ, in order that the Athenians, unless they could hinder the work, might be no longer able to blockade them.† Meanwhile the Athenians, having now finished their wall down to the sea, had come up to the heights; and part of their wall being weak, Gylippus drew out his army by night and attacked it. However, the Athenians who happened to be bivouacking outside took the alarm and came out to meet him, upon seeing which he quickly led his men back again. The Athenians now built their wall higher, and in future kept guard at this point themselves, disposing their confederates along the remainder of the works, at the stations assigned to them. Nicias also determined to fortify Plemmyrium, a promontory over against the city, which juts out and narrows the mouth of the great harbour.‡ He thought that the fortification of this place would make it easier to bring in supplies, as they would be able to carry on their blockade from a less distance, near to the port occupied by the Syracusans; instead of being obliged, upon every movement of the enemy's navy, to put out against them from the bottom of the great harbour. Besides this, he now began to pay more attention to the war by sea, seeing that the coming of Gylippus had diminished their hopes by land. Accordingly, he conveyed over his ships and some troops, and built three forts in which he placed most of his baggage, and moored there for the future the larger craft and men-of-war. This was the first and chief occasion of the losses which the crews experienced. The water which they used was scarce and had to be fetched from far, and the sailors could not go out for firewood without being cut off by the Syracusan horse, who were masters of the country;§ a third of the enemy's cavalry being stationed at the little town of Olympieum, to prevent plundering incur-

---

*Gylippus tests the Athenian battle-readiness and executes some morale-building forays.
†The north–south Athenian wall and the east–west Syracusan counter-wall are difficult to follow. Map (9) offers one reconstruction. The southern part of the Athenian wall was designed to include the northern part of the great harbor south of the *polis* on the peninsula.
‡Fortification of Plemmyrium, the southern opening of the Great Harbor would have been a good idea, had the Athenians held control of the surrounding territory.
§The Syracusan cavalry controlled movement overland, and so the Athenians were wanting for water and firewood, not to mention other food supplies.

sions on the part of the Athenians at Plemmyrium. Meanwhile Nicias learned that the rest of the Corinthian fleet was approaching, and sent twenty ships to watch for them, with orders to be on the look-out for them about Locris and Rhegium and the approach to Sicily.

5. Gylippus, meanwhile, went on with the wall across Epipolæ, using the stones which the Athenians had laid down for their own wall, and at the same time constantly led out the Syracusans and their allies, and formed them in order of battle in front of the lines, the Athenians forming against him. At last he thought that the moment was come, and began the attack; and a hand-to-hand fight ensued between the lines, where the Syracusan cavalry could be of no use; and the Syracusans and their allies were defeated and took up their dead under truce, while the Athenians erected a trophy. After this Gylippus called the soldiers together, and said that the fault was not theirs but his; he had kept their lines too much within the works, and had thus deprived them of the services of their cavalry and darters. He would now, therefore, lead them on a second time. He begged them to remember that in material force they would be fully a match for their opponents, while, with respect to moral advantages, it were intolerable if Peloponnesians and Dorians should not feel confident of overcoming Ionians and islanders with the motley rabble that accompanied them, and of driving them out of the country.*

6. After this he embraced the first opportunity that offered of again leading them against the enemy. Now Nicias and the Athenians were of opinion that even if the Syracusans should not wish to offer battle, it was necessary for them to prevent the building of the cross wall, as it already almost overlapped the extreme point of their own, and if it went any further it would from that moment make no difference whether they fought ever so many successful actions, or never fought at all. They accordingly came out to meet the Syracusans. Gylippus led out his heavy infantry further from the fortifications than on the former occasion, and so joined battle; posting his horse and darters upon the flank of the Athenians in the open space, where the works of the two walls terminated. During the engagement the cavalry attacked and routed the left wing of the Athenians, which was opposed to them; and the rest of the Athenian army was in consequence defeated by the Syracusans and driven headlong within their lines. The night following the Syracusans carried their wall up to the Athenian works and passed them, thus putting it out of their power

---

*Gylippus appeals to ethnic and political prejudices. Just as important, he takes responsibility for the recent setback.

any longer to stop them, and depriving them, even if victorious in the field, of all chance of investing the city for the future.*

7. After this the remaining twelve vessels of the Corinthians, Ambraciots, and Leucadians sailed into the harbour under the command of Erasinides, a Corinthian, having eluded the Athenian ships on guard, and helped the Syracusans in completing the remainder of the cross wall. Meanwhile Gylippus went into the rest of Sicily to raise land and naval forces, and also to bring over any of the cities that either were lukewarm in the cause or had hitherto kept out of the war altogether. Syracusan and Corinthian envoys were also despatched to Lacedæmon and Corinth to get a fresh force sent over, in any way that might offer, either in merchant vessels or transports, or in any other manner likely to prove successful, as the Athenians too were sending for reinforcements; while the Syracusans proceeded to man a fleet and to exercise, meaning to try their fortune in this way also, and generally became exceedingly confident.†

8. Nicias perceiving this, and seeing the strength of the enemy and his own difficulties daily increasing, himself also sent to Athens. He had before sent frequent reports of events as they occurred, and felt it especially incumbent upon him to do so now, as he thought that they were in a critical position, and that unless speedily recalled or strongly reinforced from home, they had no hope of safety. He feared, however, that the messengers, either through inability to speak, or through failure of memory, or from a wish to please the multitude, might not report the truth, and so thought it best to write a letter, to insure that the Athenians should know his own opinion without its being lost in transmission,‡ and be able to decide upon the real facts of the case. His emissaries, accordingly, departed with the letter and the requisite verbal instructions; and he attended to the affairs of the army, making it his aim now to keep on the defensive and to avoid any unnecessary danger.

9. At the close of the same summer the Athenian general Euetion marched in concert with Perdiccas with a large body of Thracians against Amphipolis, and failing to take it brought some galleys round

---

*The Athenian besiegers' line has now been cut off, a vital victory for the besieged and presumably the cause of major shifts in morale.

†Gylippus recruits troops in western Sicily, envoys seek further support from the mainland, and the Syracusans begin to build and man a fleet.

‡Communication between the field and the Athenian home government is poorly documented. Nicias fears his own people as much as the enemy, and so has a letter prepared to be read verbatim. This letter reads much like a speech. Given Nicias' concerns about misrepresentation, one wonders whether Thucydides applied his usual principles for composition in its presentation here or some others. Would the Athenian archives have preserved a copy?

into the Strymon, and blockaded the town from the river, having his base at Himeræum.

Summer was now over.

10. The winter ensuing, the persons sent by Nicias, reaching Athens, gave the verbal messages which had been entrusted to them, and answered any questions that were asked them, and delivered the letter. The clerk of the city now came forward and read out to the Athenians the letter, which was as follows:—

11. 'Our past operations, Athenians, have been made known to you by many other letters;* it is now time for you to become equally familiar with our present condition, and to take your measures accordingly. We had defeated in most of our engagements with them the Syracusans, against whom we were sent, and we had built the works which we now occupy, when Gylippus arrived from Lacedæmon with an army obtained from Peloponnese and from some of the cities in Sicily. In our first battle with him we were victorious; in the battle on the following day we were overpowered by a multitude of cavalry and darters, and compelled to retire within our lines. We have now, therefore, been forced by the numbers of those opposed to us to discontinue the work of circumvallation, and to remain inactive; being unable to make use even of all the force we have, since a large portion of our heavy infantry is absorbed in the defence of our lines. Meanwhile the enemy have carried a single wall past our lines, thus making it impossible for us to invest them in future, until this cross wall be attacked by a strong force and captured. So that the besieger in name has become, at least from the land side, the besieged in reality; as we are prevented by their cavalry from even going for any distance into the country.†

12. 'Besides this, an embassy has been despatched to Peloponnese to procure reinforcements, and Gylippus has gone to the cities in Sicily, partly in the hope of inducing those that are at present neutral to join him in the war, partly of bringing from his allies additional contingents for the land forces and material for the navy. For I understand that they contemplate a combined attack, upon our lines with their land forces and with their fleet by sea. You must none of you be surprised that I say by sea also. They have discovered that the length of the time we have now been in commission has rotted our ships and wasted our crews, and that with the entireness of our crews

---

*Nicias assumes that the *demos* in its assembly will determine strategy for a theater more than 1,000 miles away. Nicias frankly admits that the invaders have been stymied in their offensive plans to conquer Syracuse.

†Active and passive roles have been reversed. Nicias anticipates the forthcoming naval strategy not only to defeat the Athenian invaders but to cut off their retreat by sea and land.

and the soundness of our ships the pristine efficiency of our navy has departed. For it is impossible for us to haul our ships ashore and careen them, because, the enemy's vessels being as many or more than our own, we are constantly anticipating an attack. Indeed, they may be seen exercising, and it lies with them to take the initiative; and not having to maintain a blockade, they have greater facilities for drying their ships.*

13. 'This we should scarcely be able to do, even if we had plenty of ships to spare, and were freed from our present necessity of exhausting all our strength upon the blockade. For it is already difficult to carry in supplies past Syracuse; and were we to relax our vigilance in the slightest degree it would become impossible. The losses which our crews have suffered and still continue to suffer arise from the following causes. Expeditions for fuel and for forage, and the distance from which water has to be fetched, cause our sailors to be cut off by the Syracusan cavalry; the loss of our previous superiority emboldens our slaves to desert; our foreign seamen are impressed by the unexpected appearance of a navy against us, and the strength of the enemy's resistance; such of them as were pressed into the service take the first opportunity of departing to their respective cities; such as were originally seduced by the temptation of high pay, and expected little fighting and large gains, leave us either by desertion to the enemy or by availing themselves of one or other of the various facilities of escape which the magnitude of Sicily affords them. Some even engage in trade themselves and prevail upon the captains to take Hyccaric slaves on board in their place; thus they have ruined the efficiency of our navy.

14. 'Now I need not remind you that the time during which a crew is in its prime is short, and that the number of sailors who can start a ship on her way and keep the rowing in time is small.† But by far my greatest trouble is, that holding the post which I do, I am prevented by the natural indocility of the Athenian seaman from putting a stop to these evils; and that meanwhile we have no source from which to recruit our crews, which the enemy can do from many quarters, but are compelled to depend both for supplying the crews in service and for making good our losses upon the men whom we brought with us. For our present confederates, Naxos and Catana, are incapable of supplying us. There is only one thing more wanting to our opponents, I mean the defection of our Italian markets. If they were to see you neglect to relieve us from our present condition, and were to go over

---

*The expeditionary force has insufficient food and other supplies. The Athenian ships have deteriorated through lack of dry-dock facilities and beaching opportunities.

†The desertion of their transported slaves, the lack of local money and allies, the inability to recruit locally, and the recent defeats have reduced Athenian and allied fighting trim. Thucydides does not say why trireme crews would quickly lose their edge.

to the enemy, famine would compel us to evacuate, and Syracuse would finish the war without a blow.*

'I might, it is true, have written to you something different and more agreeable than this, but nothing certainly more useful, if it is desirable for you to know the real state of things here before taking your measures. Besides I know that it is your nature to love to be told the best side of things, and then to blame the teller if the expectations which he has raised in your minds are not answered by the result; and I therefore thought it safest to declare to you the truth.†

15. 'Now you are not to think that either your generals or your soldiers have ceased to be a match for the forces originally opposed to them. But you are to reflect that a general Sicilian coalition is being formed against us; that a fresh army is expected from Peloponnese, while the force we have here is unable to cope even with our present antagonists; and you must promptly decide either to recall us or to send out to us another fleet and army as numerous again, with a large sum of money, and some one to succeed me, as a disease in the kidneys unfits me for retaining my post.‡ I have, I think, some claim on your indulgence, as while I was in my prime I did you much good service in my commands. But whatever you mean to do, do it at the commencement of spring and without delay, as the enemy will obtain his Sicilian reinforcements shortly, those from Peloponnese after a longer interval; and unless you attend to the matter the former will be here before you, while the latter will elude you as they have done before.'

16. Such were the contents of Nicias' letter. When the Athenians had heard it they refused to accept his resignation, but chose him two colleagues, naming Menander and Euthydemus, two of the officers at the seat of war, to fill their places until their arrival, that Nicias might not be left alone in his sickness to bear the whole weight of affairs. They also voted to send out another army and navy, drawn partly from the Athenians on the muster-roll, partly from the allies. The colleagues chosen for Nicias were Demosthenes, son of Alcisthenes, and Eurymedon, son of Thucles.§ Eurymedon was sent off at once, about

---

*Aggressive support from home is necessary not only for the soldiers present and for their adequate supplies but to keep the unaligned western Hellenic cities from joining the Syracusan cause.

†Nicias contrasts hopes with facts and chastises the assembly for preferring the former.

‡Nicias can no longer command. The Athenian choice is to recall the fleet and army or send out its equal. This clearly seems a covert plea for the former course of action. Nicias incorrectly anticipates reaction to another of his pessimistic analyses.

§Demosthenes, the daring and often successful general, probably sought the post. He had certainly proven himself a capable commander, if somewhat too optimistic (see books 3 and 4). Eurymedon had previously served in Sicily (4.2, 65) and might have wished to erase his former censure for leaving Sicily without conquering it.

the time of the winter solstice, with ten ships, a hundred and twenty talents of silver, and instructions to tell the army that reinforcements would arrive, and that care would be taken of them.

17. But Demosthenes stayed behind to organise the expedition, meaning to start as soon as it was spring, and sent for troops to the allies, and meanwhile got together money, ships, and heavy infantry at home.

The Athenians also sent twenty vessels round Peloponnese to prevent any one crossing over to Sicily from Corinth or Peloponnese. For the Corinthians, filled with confidence by the favourable alteration in Sicilian affairs which had been reported by the envoys upon their arrival, and convinced that the fleet which they had before sent out had not been without its use, were now preparing to despatch a force of heavy infantry in merchant vessels to Sicily, while the Lacedæmonians did the like for the rest of Peloponnese. The Corinthians also manned a fleet of twenty-five vessels, intending to try the result of a battle with the squadron on guard at Naupactus, and meanwhile to make it less easy for the Athenians there to hinder the departure of their merchantmen, by obliging them to keep an eye upon the galleys thus arrayed against them.

18. In the meantime the Lacedæmonians prepared for their invasion of Attica, in accordance with their own previous resolve, and at the instigation of the Syracusans and Corinthians, who wished for an invasion to arrest the reinforcements which they heard that Athens was about to send to Sicily. Alcibiades also urgently advised the fortification of Decelea, and a vigorous prosecution of the war. But the Lacedæmonians derived most encouragement from the belief that Athens, with two wars on her hands, against themselves and against the Siceliots, would be more easy to subdue, and from the conviction that she had been the first to infringe the truce.* In the former war, they considered, the offence had been more on their own side, both on account of the entrance of the Thebans into Platæa in time of peace, and also of their own refusal to listen to the Athenian offer of arbitration, in spite of the clause in the former treaty that where arbitration should be offered there should be no appeal to arms. For this reason they thought that they deserved their misfortunes, and took to heart seriously the disaster at Pylos and whatever else had befallen them.† But when, besides the ravages from Pylos, which went

---

*War on two fronts could only divide Athenian resources. The Syracusans and Corinthians promoted this Spartan observation, and Athenian aggression absolved them of any guilt (by association with the Thebans at Plataea) that they had assumed for starting the former Ten Tears' War.

†Thucydides credits the Lacedaemonians with a sentiment of divine interference that resembles principles of revenge or equalization found in Herodotus. He does not personally endorse the concept, however.

on without any intermission, the thirty Athenian ships came out from Argos and wasted part of Epidaurus, Prasiæ, and other places; when upon every dispute that arose as to the interpretation of any doubtful point in the treaty, their own offers of arbitration were always rejected by the Athenians,—the Lacedæmonians at length decided that Athens had now committed the very same offence as they had before done, and had become the guilty party; and they began to be full of ardour for the war. They spent this winter in sending round to their allies for iron, and in getting ready the other implements for building their fort; and meanwhile began raising at home, and also by forced requisitions in the rest of Peloponnese, a force to be sent out in the merchantmen to their allies in Sicily. Winter thus ended, and with it the eighteenth year of this war of which Thucydides is the historian.

19. In the first days of the spring following, at an earlier period than usual, the Lacedæmonians and their allies invaded Attica, under the command of Agis, son of Archidamus, king of the Lacedæmonians. They began by devastating the parts bordering upon the plain, and next proceeded to fortify Decelea, dividing the work among the different cities. Decelea is about thirteen or fourteen miles from the city of Athens, and the same distance or not much further from Bœotia; and the fort was meant to annoy the plain and the richest parts of the country, being in sight of Athens.* While the Peloponnesians and their allies in Attica were engaged in the work of fortification, their countrymen at home sent off, at about the same time, the heavy infantry in the merchant vessels to Sicily; the Lacedæmonians furnishing a picked force of Helots and Neodamodes (or freedmen), six hundred heavy infantry in all, under the command of Eccritus, a Spartan; and the Bœotians three hundred heavy infantry, commanded by two Thebans, Xenon and Nicon, and by Hegesander, a Thespian. These were among the first to put out into the open sea, starting from Tænarus in Laconia. Not long after their departure the Corinthians sent off a force of five hundred heavy infantry, consisting partly of men from Corinth itself, and partly of Arcadian mercenaries, placed under the command of Alexarchus, a Corinthian. The Sicyonians also sent off two hundred heavy infantry at the same time as the Corinthians, under the command of Sargeus, a Sicyonian. Meantime the five-and-twenty vessels manned by Corinth during the winter, lay confronting the twenty Athenian ships at Naupactus until the

---

*The Spartan fortification of Decelea (March 413) posed a continuing problem henceforth for the embattled Athenians. It constituted a permanent base in Attica (compare the less strategic, less central Pylos–Sphacteria base of the Athenians in the Peloponnese); it was an affront to Athenian power visible from the walls of Athens; and it lay on the final land leg of the route for seaborne supplies coming from and through Euboea (map 2).

heavy infantry in the merchantmen were fairly on their way from Peloponnese; thus fulfilling the object for which they had been manned originally, which was to divert the attention of the Athenians from the merchantmen to the galleys.

20. During this time the Athenians were not idle. Simultaneously with the fortification of Decelea, at the very beginning of spring, they sent thirty ships round Peloponnese, under Charicles, son of Apollodorus, with instructions to call at Argos and demand a force of their heavy infantry for the fleet, agreeably to the alliance. At the same time they despatched Demosthenes to Sicily, as they had intended, with sixty Athenian and five Chian vessels, twelve hundred Athenian heavy infantry from the muster-roll, and as many of the islanders as could be raised in the different quarters, drawing upon the other subject allies for whatever they could supply that would be of use for the war. Demosthenes was instructed first to sail round with Charicles and to operate with him upon the coasts of Laconia, and accordingly sailed to Ægina and there waited for the remainder of his armament, and for Charicles to fetch the Argive troops.

21. In Sicily about the same time in this spring, Gylippus came to Syracuse with as many troops as he could bring from the cities which he had persuaded to join. Calling the Syracusans together, he told them that they must man as many ships as possible, and try their hand at a sea-fight, by which he hoped to achieve an advantage in the war not unworthy of the risk. With him Hermocrates actively joined in trying to encourage his countrymen to attack the Athenians at sea, saying that the latter had not inherited their naval prowess nor would they retain it for ever; they had been landsmen even to a greater degree than the Syracusans, and had only become a maritime power when obliged by the Mede. Besides, to daring spirits like the Athenians, a daring adversary would seem the most formidable; and the Athenian plan of paralysing by the boldness of their attack a neighbour often not their inferior in strength, could now be used against them with as good effect by the Syracusans.* He was convinced also that the unlooked-for spectacle of Syracusans daring to face the Athenian navy would cause a terror to the enemy, the advantages of which would far outweigh any loss that Athenian science might inflict upon their inexperience. He accordingly urged them to throw aside their fears and to try their fortune at sea; and the Syracusans, under

---

*The Syracusans now resolve to fight at sea, the first naval battle. The Syracusans will fight fire with fire—that is, employ the daring and technological innovation that had served the Athenian fleets so well in the past. Both cities, it will be remembered, were democracies in an undemocratic world.

the influence of Gylippus and Hermocrates, and perhaps some others, made up their minds for the sea-fight and began to man their vessels.

22. When the fleet was ready, Gylippus led out the whole army by night; his plan being to assault in person the forts on Plemmyrium by land, while thirty-five Syracusan galleys sailed according to appointment against the enemy from the great harbour, and the forty-five remaining came round from the lesser harbour, where they had their arsenal, in order to effect a junction with those inside and simultaneously to attack Plemmyrium, and thus to distract the Athenians by assaulting them on two sides at once. The Athenians quickly manned sixty ships, and with twenty-five of these engaged the thirty-five of the Syracusans in the great harbour, sending the rest to meet those sailing round from the arsenal; and an action now ensued directly in front of the mouth of the great harbour, maintained with equal tenacity on both sides; the one wishing to force the passage, the other to prevent them.

23. In the meantime, while the Athenians in Plemmyrium were down at the sea, attending to the engagement, Gylippus made a sudden attack on the forts in the early morning and took the largest first, and afterwards the two smaller, whose garrisons did not wait for him, seeing the largest so easily taken. At the fall of the first fort, the men from it who succeeded in taking refuge in their boats and merchantmen, found great difficulty in reaching the camp, as the Syracusans were having the best of it in the engagement in the great harbour, and sent a fast-sailing galley to pursue them. But when the two others fell, the Syracusans were now being defeated; and the fugitives from these sailed along shore with more ease. The Syracusan ships fighting off the mouth of the harbour, forced their way through the Athenian vessels and sailing in without any order fell foul of one another, and transferred the victory to the Athenians; who not only routed the squadron in question, but also that by which they were at first being defeated in the harbour, sinking eleven of the Syracusan vessels and killing most of the men, except the crews of three ships whom they made prisoners. Their own loss was confined to three vessels; and after hauling ashore the Syracusan wrecks and setting up a trophy upon the islet in front of Plemmyrium, they retired to their own camp.

24. Unsuccessful at sea, the Syracusans had nevertheless the forts in Plemmyrium, for which they set up three trophies. One of the two last taken they razed, but put in order and garrisoned the two others. In the capture of the forts a great many men were killed and made prisoners, and a great quantity of property was taken in all. As the Athenians had used them as a magazine, there was a large stock of goods and grain of the merchants inside, and also a large stock belonging to the captains; the masts and other equipment of forty triremes being taken, besides three triremes which had been drawn up on shore. Indeed the first and chiefest cause of the ruin of the Athenian army was the capture of Plemmyrium; even the entrance of the harbour being now no longer safe for carrying in provisions, as the Syracusan vessels were stationed there to prevent it, and nothing could be brought in without fighting; besides the general impression of dismay and discouragement produced upon the army.*

25. After this the Syracusans sent out twelve ships under the command of Agatharchus, a Syracusan. One of these went to Peloponnese with ambassadors to describe the hopeful state of their affairs, and to incite the Peloponnesians to prosecute the war there even more actively than they were now doing, while the eleven others sailed to Italy, hearing that vessels laden with stores were on their way to the Athenians. After falling in with and destroying most of the vessels in question, and burning in the Caulonian territory a quantity of timber for ship-building, which had been got ready for the Athenians, the Syracusan squadron went to Locri, and one of the merchantmen from Peloponnese coming in, while they were at anchor there, carrying Thespian heavy infantry, took these on board and sailed along shore towards home. The Athenians were on the look-out for them with twenty ships at Megara, but were only able to take one vessel with its crew; the rest getting clear off to Syracuse. There was also some skirmishing in the harbour about the piles which the Syracusans had driven in the sea in front of the old docks, to allow their ships to lie at anchor inside, without being hurt by the Athenians sailing up and running them down. The Athenians brought up to them a ship of ten thousand talents burden furnished with wooden turrets and screens, and fastened ropes round the piles from their boats, wrenched them up and broke them, or dived down and sawed them in two.† Meanwhile the Syracusans plied them with missiles from the docks, to which they replied from their large vessel; until at last most of the piles were removed by the Athenians.

But the most awkward part of the stockade was the part out of sight: some of the piles which had been driven in did not appear above water, so that it was dangerous to sail up, for fear of running the ships upon them, just as upon a reef, through not seeing them. However divers went down and sawed off even these for reward; although the Syracusans drove in others. Indeed there was no end to

---

*Syracusan successes outweigh their setbacks. The Athenians could ill afford the loss in food and equipment of forty triremes. (When trireme crews prepared to fight at sea, they left behind their ships' masts, for example.)

†Thucydides meant us to understand that the ship was large, although a ship of nearly 400 tons seems too large. The ship was called a "ten-thousander" but we don't know what the understood unit was. In any case, Thucydides is interested in the inventive technology, determined sailors, and underwater demolition crews.

the contrivances to which they resorted against each other, as might be expected between two hostile armies confronting each other at such a short distance: and skirmishes and all kinds of other attempts were of constant occurrence.

Meanwhile the Syracusans sent embassies to the cities composed of Corinthians, Ambraciots, and Lacedæmonians, to tell them of the capture of Plemmyrium, and that their defeat in the sea-fight was due less to the strength of the enemy than to their own disorder; and generally, to let them know that they were full of hope, and to desire them to come to their help with ships and troops, as the Athenians were expected with a fresh army, and if the one already there could be destroyed before the other arrived, the war would be at an end.*

26. While the contending parties in Sicily were thus engaged, Demosthenes, having now got together the armament with which he was to go to the island, put out from Ægina, and making sail for Peloponnese, joined Charicles and the thirty ships of the Athenians. Taking on board the heavy infantry from Argos they sailed to Laconia, and after first plundering part of Epidaurus Limera, landed on the coast of Laconia, opposite Cythera, where the temple of Apollo stands, and laying waste part of the country, fortified a sort of isthmus, to which the Helots of the Lacedæmonians might desert, and from whence plundering incursions might be made as from Pylos.† Demosthenes helped to occupy this place, and then immediately sailed on to Corcyra to take up some of the allies in that island, and so to proceed without delay to Sicily; while Charicles waited until he had completed the fortification of the place, and leaving a garrison there, returned home subsequently with his thirty ships and the Argives also.

27. This same summer arrived at Athens thirteen hundred targeteers, Thracian swordsmen of the tribe of the Dii, who were to have sailed to Sicily with Demosthenes. Since they had come too late, the Athenians determined to send them back to Thrace, whence they had come; to keep them for the Decelean war appearing too expensive, as the pay of each man was a drachma a day. Indeed since Decelea had been first fortified by the whole Peloponnesian army during this summer, and then occupied for the annoyance of the country by the garrison from the cities relieving each other at stated intervals, it had

---

*The Syracusans repeatedly recognize that efficient early action can save many lives and battles fought on later, less attractive terms. Thucydides admires forethought more than anything.

†Demosthenes, on his way westward, again introduces his former winning strategy, but we hear nothing further about the success of this Peloponnesian base in receiving deserters and launching raids. Dover in his commentary (Gomme et al., vol. 4) points out that this spot was convenient, as it was both accessible to Athenian ships and remote from the town of Sparta.

been doing great mischief to the Athenians; in fact this occupation, by the destruction of property and loss of men which resulted from it, was one of the principal causes of their ruin.* Previously the invasions were short, and did not prevent their enjoying their land during the rest of the time: the enemy was now permanently fixed in Attica; at one time it was an attack in force, at another it was the regular garrison overrunning the country and making forays for its subsistence, and the Lacedæmonian king, Agis, was in the field and diligently prosecuting the war; great mischief was therefore done to the Athenians. They were deprived of their whole country: more than twenty thousand slaves had deserted, a great part of them artisans, and all their sheep and beasts of burden were lost; and as the cavalry rode out daily upon excursions to Decelea and to guard the country, their horses were either lamed by being constantly worked upon rocky ground, or wounded by the enemy.†

28. Besides, the transport of provisions from Eubœa, which had before been carried on so much more quickly over land by Decelea from Oropus, was now effected at great cost by sea round Sunium; everything the city required had to be imported from abroad, and instead of a city it became a fortress.‡ Summer and winter the Athenians were worn out by having to keep guard on the fortifications, during the day by turns, by night all together, the cavalry excepted, at the different military posts or upon the wall. But what most oppressed them was that they had two wars at once, and had thus reached a pitch of pertinacity which no one would have believed possible if he had heard of it before it had come to pass. For no one could have imagined§ that even when besieged by the Peloponnesians entrenched in Attica, they would still, instead of withdrawing from Sicily, stay on there besieging in like manner Syracuse, a city (taken

---

*The Spartan fortification of Decelea became a sheer disaster for the large and encircled Athenian population. The unrelenting (previous invasions had lasted no more than forty days) annoyance, material and psychological, arose from damage within sight of the walls and the desertion of thousands of slaves.

†Statistics were and are hard to find or evaluate in ancient texts. Twenty thousand slaves—specialists, workers in the lethal silver mines, general farmhands, and household slaves—is a large number in the Greek world. It represents a significant percentage of the Athenian workforce.

‡These general reflections look forward from this year to the end of the war nine years later. Euboea, a large island to the northeast of Athens, was important for its own produce and pasturage as well as for trans-shipment (compare 1.114; 2.14; 8.96). Trans-shipment through Oropus, a mainland port town northeast of Athens opposite Euboea, shortened a voyage that otherwise had to travel more than 40 miles south of Athens, around Cape Sunium, and then north into the Saronic Gulf to the port of Piraeus (map 2).

§Thucydides notes results contrary to calculation, a common event during war. Both sides suffer such surprises, incalculable reverses but also moments of good fortune.

as a city) in no way inferior to Athens, or would so thoroughly upset the Hellenic estimate of their strength and audacity, as to give the spectacle of a people which, at the beginning of the war, some thought might hold out one year, some two, none more than three, if the Peloponnesians invaded their country, now seventeen years after the first invasion, after having already suffered from all the evils of war, going to Sicily and undertaking a new war nothing inferior to that which they already had with the Peloponnesians.* These causes, the great losses from Decelea, and the other heavy charges that fell upon them, produced their financial embarrassment; and it was at this time that they imposed upon their subjects, instead of the tribute, the tax of a twentieth upon all imports and exports by sea, which they thought would bring them in more money; their expenditure being now not the same as at first, but having grown with the war while their revenues decayed.†

29. Accordingly, not wishing to incur expense in their present want of money, they sent back at once the Thracians who came too late for Demosthenes, under the conduct of Diitrephes, who was instructed, as they were to pass through the Euripus, to make use of them if possible in the voyage along shore to injure the enemy. Diitrephes first landed them at Tanagra and hastily snatched some booty; he then sailed across the Euripus in the evening from Chalcis in Eubœa and disembarking in Bœotia led them against Mycalessus. The night he passed unobserved near the temple of Hermes, not quite two miles from Mycalessus, and at daybreak assaulted and took the town, which is not a large one; the inhabitants being off their guard and not expecting that any one would ever come up so far from the sea to molest them, the wall too being weak, and in some places having tumbled down, while in others it had not been built to any height, and the gates also being left open through their feeling of security.‡ The Thracians bursting into Mycalessus sacked the houses and temples,

---

*Athenian pertinacity amazed the Hellenic world, but the financial and personal costs of the war kept mounting.

†This 5 percent export/import tax replaced the annually collected imperial tribute. That tribute had amounted to something like 900 talents. Thucydides does not explain the decline in the tribute—whether it had resulted from allies' economic hardships or from difficulties of collection.

‡The brief, interpolated Mycalessus narrative offers a vignette of the devastation of small communities consequent on the big-power quarrels. The barbarian mercenaries attacked a town that thought itself too unimportant to claim anyone's interest. The summary sentences in this paragraph and the next employ those superlatives of which Thucydides is fond. The indiscriminate slaughter illustrates the decline in civility and international norms mentioned in the preface (1.23). The Athenian commander Diitrephes either could not or did not control the Thracian troops that he was escorting home.

and butchered the inhabitants, sparing neither youth nor age, but killing all they fell in with, one after the other, children and women, and even beasts of burden, and whatever other living creatures they saw; the Thracian race, like the bloodiest of the barbarians, being ever most so when it has nothing to fear. Everywhere confusion reigned and death in all its shapes; and in particular they attacked a boys' school, the largest that there was in the place, into which the children had just gone, and massacred them all. In short, the disaster falling upon the whole town was unsurpassed in magnitude, and unapproached by any in suddenness and in horror.*

30. Meanwhile the Thebans heard of it and marched to the rescue, and overtaking the Thracians before they had gone far, recovered the plunder and drove them in panic to the Euripus and the sea, where the vessels which brought them were lying. The greatest slaughter took place while they were embarking, as they did not know how to swim, and those in the vessels on seeing what was going on on shore moored them out of bowshot: in the rest of the retreat the Thracians made a very respectable defence against the Theban horse, by which they were first attacked, dashing out and closing their ranks according to the tactics of their country, and lost only a few men in that part of the affair. A good number who were after plunder were actually caught in the town and put to death. Altogether the Thracians had two hundred and fifty killed out of thirteen hundred, the Thebans and the rest who came to the rescue about twenty, troopers and heavy infantry, with Scirphondas, one of the Bœotarchs. The Mycalessians lost a large proportion of their population. Mycalessus thus experienced a calamity, for its extent, as lamentable as any that happened in the war.

31. Demosthenes, then sailing to Corcyra, after the building of the fort in Laconia, found a merchantman lying at Phea in Elis, in which the Corinthian heavy infantry were to cross to Sicily. The ship he destroyed, but the men escaped, and subsequently got another in which they pursued their voyage. After this, arriving at Zacynthus and Cephallenia, he took a body of heavy infantry on board, and sending for some of the Messenians from Naupactus, crossed over to the opposite coast of Acarnania, to Alyzia, and to Anactorium which was held by the Athenians. While he was in these parts he was met by Eurymedon returning from Sicily, where he had been sent during the winter, with the money for the army, who told him the news, and also that he had heard, while at sea, that the Syracusans

---

*The pathos or suffering is highlighted by reference to the murder of children in school. It is notable that Thucydides not only includes but emphasizes the magnitude of the suffering in this small town northwest of Tanagra (map 2). Comparatively speaking, no disaster was greater.

had taken Plemmyrium.* Here, also, Conon came to them, the commander at Naupactus, with news that the twenty-five Corinthian ships stationed opposite to him, far from giving over the war, were meditating an engagement; and he therefore begged them to send him some ships, as his own eighteen were not a match for the enemy's twenty-five. Demosthenes and Eurymedon, accordingly, sent ten of their best sailers with Conon to reinforce the squadron at Naupactus, and meanwhile prepared for the muster of their forces; Eurymedon, who was now the colleague of Demosthenes, and had turned back in consequence of his appointment, sailing to Corcyra to tell them to man fifteen ships and to enlist heavy infantry; while Demosthenes raised slingers and darters from the parts about Acarnania.

32. Meanwhile the envoys who had gone from Syracuse to the cities after the capture of Plemmyrium, had succeeded in their mission, and were about to bring the army that they had collected, when Nicias got scent of it, and sent to the Centoripæ and Alicyæans and other of the friendly Sicels, who held the passes, not to let the enemy through, but to combine to prevent their passing, there being no other way by which they could even attempt it, as the Agrigentines would not give them a passage through their country.† Agreeably to this request the Sicels laid a triple ambuscade for the Siceliots upon their march, and attacking them suddenly, while off their guard, killed about eight hundred of them and all the envoys, the Corinthian only excepted, by whom fifteen hundred who escaped were conducted to Syracuse.

33. About the same time the Camarinæans also came to the assistance of Syracuse with five hundred heavy infantry, three hundred darters and as many archers, while the Geloans sent crews for five ships, four hundred darters, and two hundred horse. Indeed almost the whole of Sicily, except the Agrigentines, who were neutral, now ceased merely to watch events as it had hitherto done, and actively joined Syracuse against the Athenians.‡

---

*Eurymedon had already sailed toward Sicily (7.16) and now came back east. Conon was to become an important naval commander in the last years of the war, after Xenophon picks up his narrative in 411/410, when Thucydides' text breaks off. He is guarding against both Corinthians in the Corinthian Gulf and Peloponnesians sailing north toward the jump-off point for sailing across the open sea to Italy. The news of Plemmyrium's fall (with Nicias' camps) must have been discouraging.

†Nicias is trying to prevent the unification of the anti-Athenian forces. Agrigentum maintained its neutralities. The Sicels are pre-Greek inhabitants of Sicily, while the Siceliots are descendants of the Greek colonists (and their intermarriages).

‡Thucydides or his source exaggerates the extent of the Syracusan alliance. In addition to Egestans and many indigenous Sicels, the peoples of Naxos and Catana maintained their alliance with the Athenians.

While the Syracusans after the Sicel disaster put off any immediate attack upon the Athenians, Demosthenes and Eurymedon, whose forces from Corcyra and the continent were now ready, crossed the Ionian gulf with all their armament to the Iapygian promontory, and starting from thence touched at the Chœrades Isles lying off Iapygia, where they took on board a hundred and fifty Iapygian darters of the Messapian tribe, and after renewing an old friendship with Artas the chief, who had furnished them with the darters, arrived at Metapontium in Italy. Here they persuaded their allies the Metapontines, to send with them three hundred darters and two galleys, and with this reinforcement coasted on to Thurii, where they found the party hostile to Athens recently expelled by a revolution, and accordingly remained there to muster and review the whole army, to see if any had been left behind, and to prevail upon the Thurians resolutely to join them in their expedition, and in the circumstances in which they found themselves to conclude a defensive and offensive alliance with the Athenians.

34. About the same time the Peloponnesians in the twenty-five ships stationed opposite to the squadron at Naupactus to protect the passage of the transports to Sicily, had got ready for engaging, and manning some additional vessels, so as to be numerically little inferior to the Athenians, anchored off Erineus in Achaia in the Rhypic country. The place off which they lay being in the form of a crescent, the land forces furnished by the Corinthians and their allies on the spot, came up and ranged themselves upon the projecting headlands on either side, while the fleet, under the command of Polyanthes, a Corinthian, held the intervening space and blocked up the entrance. The Athenians under Diphilus* now sailed out against them with thirty-three ships from Naupactus, and the Corinthians, at first not moving, at length thought they saw their opportunity, raised the signal, and advanced and engaged the Athenians. After an obstinate struggle, the Corinthians lost three ships, and without sinking any altogether, disabled seven of the enemy, which were struck prow to prow and had their foreships stoven in by the Corinthian vessels, whose cheeks had been strengthened for this very purpose. After an action of this even character, in which either party could claim the victory (although the Athenians became masters of the wrecks through the wind driving them out to sea, the Corinthians not putting out again to meet them) the two combatants parted. No pursuit took place, and no prisoners were made on either side; the Corinthians and

---

*Diphilus has replaced Conon in command of the Athenian triremes at Naupactus, the choke point on the Gulf of Corinth.

Peloponnesians who were fighting near the shore escaping with ease, and none of the Athenian vessels having been sunk.

The Athenians now sailed back to Naupactus, and the Corinthians immediately set up a trophy as victors, because they had disabled a greater number of the enemy's ships. Moreover they held that they had not been worsted, for the very same reason that their opponent held that he had not been victorious; the Corinthians considering that they were conquerors, if not decidedly conquered, and the Athenians thinking themselves vanquished, because not decidedly victorious.* However, when the Peloponnesians sailed off and their land forces had dispersed, the Athenians also set up a trophy as victors in Achaia, about two miles and a quarter from Erineus, the Corinthian station.

This was the termination of the action at Naupactus.

35. Once the Thurians got ready to join in the expedition with seven hundred heavy infantry and three hundred darters, the two generals Demosthenes and Eurymedon ordered the ships to sail along the coast to the Crotonian territory, and meanwhile held a review of all the land forces upon the river Sybaris, and then led them through the Thurian country. Arrived at the river Hylias, they here received a message from the Crotonians, saying that they would not allow the army to pass through their country; upon which the Athenians descended towards the shore, and bivouacked near the sea and the mouth of the Hylias, where the fleet also met them, and the next day embarked and sailed along the coast touching at all the cities except Locri, until they came to Petra, in the Rhegian territory.

36. Meanwhile the Syracusans hearing of their approach resolved to make a second attempt with their fleet and their other forces on shore, which they had been collecting for this very purpose in order to do something before their arrival. In addition to other improvements suggested by the former sea-fight which they now adopted in the equipment of their navy, they cut down their prows to a smaller compass to make them more solid and made their cheeks stouter, and from these let stays into the vessel's sides for a length of 9 feet within and without, in the same way as the Corinthians had altered their prows before engaging the squadron at Naupactus.† The Syracusans

---

*The Corinthians kept the Athenians from open waters where their naval superiority would manifest itself. Further, they strengthened their triremes' foreships in order to ram the enemy head on. The trophy disputes reflect real uncertainty about what constituted a victory in such indecisive situations.

†The second naval battle at Syracuse occupies chapters 36–41. The Syracusans employ recent successful tactics of reinforced bows (reported at Naupactus) in hopes of foiling standard Athenian naval tactics. These depended on superior rowing skills, such as the *periplous* (rowing around) and the *diekplous* (breaking through enemy lines and coming about to ram enemies amidships).

thought that they would thus have an advantage over the Athenian vessels, which were not constructed with equal strength, but were slight in the bows, from their being more used to sail round and charge the enemy's side than to meet him prow to prow, and that the battle being in the great harbour, with a great many ships in not much room, was also a fact in their favour. Charging prow to prow, they would stave in the enemy's bows, by striking with solid and stout beaks against hollow and weak ones; and secondly, the Athenians for want of room would be unable to use their favourite manœuvre of breaking the line or of sailing round, as the Syracusans would do their best not to let them do the one, and want of room would prevent their doing the other. This charging prow to prow, which had hitherto been thought want of skill in a helmsman, would be the Syracusans' chief manœuvre, as being that which they should find most useful, since the Athenians, if repulsed, would not be able to back water in any direction except towards the shore, and that only for a little way, and in the little space in front of their own camp. The rest of the harbour would be commanded by the Syracusans; and the Athenians, if hard pressed, by crowding together in a small space and all to the same point, would run foul of one another and fall into disorder, which was, in fact, the thing that did the Athenians most harm in all the sea-fights, they not having, like the Syracusans, the whole harbour to retreat over. As to their sailing round into the open sea, this would be impossible, with the Syracusans in possession of the way out and in, especially as Plemmyrium would be hostile to them, and the mouth of the harbour was not large.

37. With these contrivances to suit their skill and ability, and now more confident after the previous sea-fight, the Syracusans attacked by land and sea at once. The town force Gylippus led out a little the first and brought them up to the wall of the Athenians, where it looked towards the city, while the force from the Olympieum, that is to say, the heavy infantry that were there with the horse and the light troops of the Syracusans, advanced against the wall from the opposite side; the ships of the Syracusans and allies sailing out immediately afterwards. The Athenians at first fancied that they were to be attacked by land only, and it was not without alarm that they saw the fleet suddenly approaching as well; and while some were forming upon the walls and in front of them against the advancing enemy, and some marching out in haste against the numbers of horse and darters coming from the Olympieum and from outside, others manned the ships or rushed down to the beach to oppose the enemy, and when the ships were manned put out with seventy-five sail against about eighty of the Syracusans.

38. After spending a great part of the day in advancing and retreating and skirmishing with each other, without either being able to gain any advantage worth speaking of, except that the Syracusans sank one or two of the Athenian vessels, they parted, the land force at the same time retiring from the lines. The next day the Syracusans remained quiet, and gave no signs of what they were going to do; but Nicias, seeing that the battle had been a drawn one, and expecting that they would attack again, compelled the captains to refit any of the ships that had suffered, and moored merchant vessels before the stockade which they had driven into the sea in front of their ships, to serve instead of an enclosed harbour, at about two hundred feet from each other, in order that any ship that was hard pressed might be able to retreat in safety and sail out again at leisure. These preparations occupied the Athenians all day until nightfall.

39. The next day the Syracusans began operations at an earlier hour, but with the same plan of attack by land and sea. A great part of the day the rivals spent as before, confronting and skirmishing with each other; until at last Ariston, son of Pyrrhicus, a Corinthian, the ablest helmsman in the Syracusan service, persuaded their naval commanders to send to the officials in the city, and tell them to move the sale market as quickly as they could down to the sea, and oblige every one to bring whatever eatables he had and sell them there, thus enabling the commanders to land the crews and dine at once close to the ships, and shortly afterwards, the selfsame day, to attack the Athenians again when they were not expecting it.

40. In compliance with this advice a messenger was sent and the market got ready, upon which the Syracusans suddenly backed water and withdrew to the town, and at once landed and took their dinner upon the spot; while the Athenians, supposing that they had returned to the town because they felt they were beaten, disembarked at their leisure and set about getting their dinners and about their other occupations, under the idea that they had done with fighting for that day. Suddenly the Syracusans manned their ships and again sailed against them; and the Athenians, in great confusion and most of them hungry, got on board, and with great difficulty put out to meet them.* For some time both parties remained on the defensive without engaging, until the Athenians at last resolved not to let themselves be worn out by waiting where they were, but to attack without delay, and giving a cheer, went into action. The Syracusans received them, and charging prow to prow as they had intended, stove in a great part of the Athenian foreships by the strength of their beaks; the darters on the decks also did great damage to the Athenians, but still greater damage was done by the Syracusans who went about in

---

*The Syracusan lunch-time ruse deceives the Athenians, who are caught off-guard. They thus suffer another setback in the Great Harbour.

small boats, ran in upon the oars of the Athenian galleys, and sailed against their sides, and discharged from thence their javelins upon the sailors.

41. At last, fighting hard in this fashion, the Syracusans gained the victory, and the Athenians turned and fled between the merchantmen to their own station. The Syracusan ships pursued them as far as the merchantmen, where they were stopped by the beams armed with dolphins suspended from those vessels over the passage.* Two of the Syracusan vessels went too near in the excitement of victory and were destroyed, one of them being taken with its crew. After sinking seven of the Athenian vessels and disabling many, and taking most of the men prisoners and killing others, the Syracusans retired and set up trophies for both the engagements, being now confident of having a decided superiority by sea, and by no means despairing of equal success by land.

Nineteenth Year of the War — Arrival of Demosthenes — Defeat of the Athenians at Epipolæ — Folly and Obstinacy of Nicias

42. In the meantime, while the Syracusans were preparing for a second attack upon both elements, Demosthenes and Eurymedon arrived with the succours from Athens, consisting of about seventy-three ships, including the foreigners; nearly five thousand heavy infantry, Athenian and allied; a large number of darters, Hellenic and barbarian, and slingers and archers and everything else upon a corresponding scale. The Syracusans and their allies were for the moment not a little dismayed at the idea that there was to be no term or ending to their dangers, seeing, in spite of the fortification of Decelea, a new army arrive nearly equal to the former, and the power of Athens proving so great in every quarter. On the other hand, the first Athenian armament regained a certain confidence in the midst of its misfortunes. Demosthenes, seeing how matters stood, felt that he could not drag on and fare as Nicias had done, who by wintering in Catana instead of at once attacking Syracuse had allowed the terror of his first arrival to evaporate in contempt, and had given time to Gylippus to arrive with a force from Peloponnese, which the Syracusans would never have sent for if he had attacked immediately; for they fancied that they were a match for him by themselves, and would not have discovered their inferiority until they were already invested, and even if they then sent for succours, they would no longer have been equally

---

*These "dolphins" are heavy iron weights swung on a pole and pulley that could be dropped into an enemy's ship to disable or sink it.

able to profit by their arrival.* Recollecting this, and well aware that it was now on the first day after his arrival that he like Nicias was most formidable to the enemy, Demosthenes determined to lose no time in drawing the utmost profit from the consternation at the moment inspired by his army; and seeing that the counterwall of the Syracusans, which hindered the Athenians from investing them, was a single one, and that he who should become master of the way up to Epipolæ, and afterwards of the camp there, would find no difficulty in taking it, as no one would even wait for his attack, made all haste to attempt the enterprise. This he took to be the shortest way of ending the war, as he would either succeed and take Syracuse, or would lead back the armament instead of frittering away the lives of the Athenians engaged in the expedition and the resources of the country at large.†

First therefore the Athenians went out and laid waste the lands of the Syracusans about the Anapus and carried all before them as at first by land and by sea, the Syracusans not offering to oppose them upon either element, unless it were with their cavalry and darters from the Olympieum.

43. Next Demosthenes resolved to attempt the counterwall first by means of engines. As however the engines that he brought up were burnt by the enemy fighting from the wall, and the rest of the forces repulsed after attacking at many different points, he determined to delay no longer, and having obtained the consent of Nicias and his fellow-commanders, proceeded to put in execution his plan of attacking Epipolæ. As by day it seemed impossible to approach and get up without being observed, he ordered provisions for five days, took all the masons and carpenters, and other things, such as arrows, and everything else that they could want for the work of fortification if successful; and after the first watch set out with Eurymedon and Menander and the whole army for Epipolæ, Nicias being left behind in the lines.

Having come up by the hill of Euryelus (where the former army had ascended at first), unobserved by the enemy's guards, they went up to the fort which the Syracusans had there, and took it, and put to the sword part of the garrison. The greater number, however, escaped

---

*Demosthenes' reasoning must have been laid out in the presence of an officer who survived his and Nicias' deaths. His criticism of Nicias' leadership encourages belief that Thucydides thought Lamachus' evaluation right initially (6.49; but compare 2.65, a passage written later). Demosthenes' battle-strategy everywhere had been to strike quickly, unexpectedly, and with all his forces.

†Demosthenes assessed the Athenian situation to be very desperate. Having come with a second fleet, he recognized the need to attempt an assault on Syracuse once more, but to leave Sicily if victory were not swift.

at once and gave the alarm to the camps, of which there were three upon Epipolæ, defended by outworks, one of the Syracusans, one of the other Siceliots, and one of the allies; and also to the six hundred Syracusans forming the original garrison for this part of Epipolæ. These at once advanced against the assailants, and falling in with Demosthenes and the Athenians, were routed by them after a sharp resistance, the victors immediately pushing on, eager to achieve the objects of the attack without giving time for their ardour to cool; meanwhile others from the very beginning were taking the counter-wall of the Syracusans, which was abandoned by its garrison, and pulling down the battlements.

The Syracusans and the allies, and Gylippus with the troops under his command, advanced to the rescue from the outworks, but engaged in some consternation (a night attack being a piece of audacity which they had never expected), and were at first compelled to retreat.* But while the Athenians, flushed with their victory, now advanced with less order, wishing to make their way as quickly as possible through the whole force of the enemy not yet engaged, without relaxing their attack or giving them time to rally, the Bœotians made the first stand against them, attacked them, routed them, and put them to flight.†

44. The Athenians now fell into great disorder and perplexity, so that it was not easy to get from one side or the other any detailed account of the affair.‡ By day certainly the combatants have a clearer notion, though even then by no means of all that takes place, no one knowing much of anything that does not go on in his own immediate neighbourhood; but in a night engagement (and this was the only one that occurred between great armies during the war) how could any one know anything for certain? Although there was a bright moon they saw each other only as men do by moonlight, that is to say, they could distinguish the form of the body, but could not tell for certain whether it was a friend or an enemy. Both had great numbers of heavy infantry moving about in a small space.

---

*Demosthenes' initial success arose from his unexpected audacity. His night attack was entirely unanticipated.

†The defenders, Boeotians in this case, formed up and resisted the Athenians advancing in sloppy order over unknown ground.

‡Thucydides occasionally comments on the difficulty of obtaining dependable information. At 1.22, he indicated the general problem; at 5.26, he mentions the advantage of exile allowing him to speak with participants in both camps. For Mantinea (5.68), he mentions the problem of overall numbers and Spartan secrecy. Here he discusses special problems connected with the limited visibility in a night battle (compare 2.3–4), where each man knows only what occurs near him. He offers rare, variant versions at 2.5 (Plataea) and 8.87 (the absence of the Phoenician fleet; Thucydides canvasses several explanations).

Some of the Athenians were already defeated, while others were coming up yet unconquered for their first attack. A large part also of the rest of their forces either had only just got up, or were still ascending, so that they did not know which way to march. Owing to the rout that had taken place all in front was now in confusion, and the noise made it difficult to distinguish anything. The victorious Syracusans and allies were cheering each other on with loud cries, by night the only possible means of communication, and meanwhile receiving all who came against them; while the Athenians were seeking for one another, taking all in front of them for enemies, even although they might be some of their now flying friends; and by constantly asking for the watchword,* which was their only means of recognition, not only caused great confusion among themselves by asking all at once, but also made it known to the enemy, whose own they did not so readily discover, as the Syracusans were victorious and not scattered, and thus less easily mistaken.

The result was that if the Athenians fell in with a party of the enemy that was weaker than they, it escaped them through knowing their watchword; while if they themselves failed to answer they were put to the sword. But what hurt them as much, or indeed more than anything else, was the singing of the Pæan, from the perplexity which it caused by being nearly the same on either side: the Argives and Corcyræans and any other Dorian peoples in the army, struck terror into the Athenians whenever they raised their Pæan, no less than did the enemy. Thus, after being once thrown into disorder, they ended by coming into collision with each other in many parts of the field, friends with friends, and citizens with citizens, and not only terrified one another, but even came to blows and could only be parted with difficulty. In the pursuit many perished by throwing themselves down the cliffs, the way down from Epipolæ being narrow; and of those who got down safely into the plain, although many, especially those who belonged to the first armament, escaped through their better acquaintance with the locality, some of the newcomers lost their way and wandered over the country, and were cut off in the morning by the Syracusan cavalry and killed.

45. The next day the Syracusans set up two trophies, one upon Epipolæ where the ascent had been made, and the other on the spot where the first check was given by the Bœotians; and the Athenians took back their dead under truce. A great many of the Athenians and allies were killed, although still more arms were taken than could be accounted for by the number of the dead, as some of those who were

---

*The "watchword" was the password by which friendly forces could identify each other. Here it leaked out, and the invaders were at a disadvantage in unfamiliar territory.

obliged to leap down from the cliffs without their shields escaped with their lives and did not perish like the rest.

46. After this the Syracusans, recovering their old confidence at such an unexpected stroke of good fortune, despatched Sicanus with fifteen ships to Agrigentum where there was a revolution, to induce if possible the city to join them; while Gylippus again went by land into the rest of Sicily to bring up reinforcements, being now in hope of taking the Athenian lines by storm, after the result of the affair on Epipolæ.

47. In the meantime the Athenian generals consulted upon the disaster which had happened, and upon the general weakness of the army. They saw themselves unsuccessful in their enterprises, and the soldiers disgusted with their stay; disease being rife among them owing to its being the sickly season of the year, and to the marshy and unhealthy nature of the spot in which they were encamped; and the state of their affairs generally being thought desperate.* Accordingly, Demosthenes was of opinion that they ought not to stay any longer; but agreeably to his original idea in risking the attempt upon Epipolæ, now that this had failed, he gave his vote for going away without further loss of time, while the sea might yet be crossed, and their late reinforcement might give them the superiority at all events on that element. He also said that it would be more profitable for the state to carry on the war against those who were building fortifications in Attica, than against the Syracusans whom it was no longer easy to subdue; besides which it was not right to squander large sums of money to no purpose by going on with the siege.

48. This was the opinion of Demosthenes. Nicias, without denying the bad state of their affairs, was unwilling to avow their weakness, or to have it reported to the enemy that the Athenians in full council were openly voting for retreat; for in that case they would be much less likely to effect it when they wanted without discovery. Moreover, his own particular information still gave him reason to hope that the affairs of the enemy would soon be in a worse state than their own, if the Athenians persevered in the siege;† as they would wear out the Syracusans by want of money, especially with the more extensive command of the sea now given them by their present navy. Besides this, there was a party in Syracuse who wished to betray the city to the

---

*Athenian problems included poor morale, failure to achieve easy victory, disease, poor encampment, few alternatives, and few "exit strategies." Demosthenes now, as before, recommended return to Athens.

†Nicias may have had inside information about Syracuse's factions. He could not rebut Demosthenes' case, but easily imagined charges of bribery, the rhetoric of insubordination to the popular will, and the fear of censure and worse back in Athens motivated opposition to the wiser military policy. His perverse determination carried the day.

Athenians, and kept sending him messages and telling him not to raise the siege. Accordingly, knowing this and really waiting because he hesitated between the two courses and wished to see his way more clearly, in his public speech on this occasion he refused to lead off the army, saying he was sure the Athenians would never approve of their returning without a vote of theirs.

Those who would vote upon their conduct, instead of judging the facts as eye-witnesses like themselves and not from what they might hear from hostile critics, would simply be guided by the calumnies of the first clever speaker; while many, indeed most, of the soldiers on the spot, who now so loudly proclaimed the danger of their position, when they reached Athens would proclaim just as loudly the opposite, and would say that their generals had been bribed to betray them and return.

For himself, therefore, who knew the Athenian temper, sooner than perish under a dishonourable charge and by an unjust sentence at the hands of the Athenians, he would rather take his chance and die, if die he must, a soldier's death at the hand of the enemy. Besides, after all, the Syracusans were in a worse case than themselves. What with paying mercenaries, spending upon fortified posts, and now for a full year maintaining a large navy, they were already at a loss and would soon be at a standstill: they had already spent two thousand talents and incurred heavy debts besides, and could not lose even ever so small a fraction of their present force through not paying it, without ruin to their cause; depending as they did more upon mercenaries than upon soldiers obliged to serve, like their own. He therefore said that they ought to stay and carry on the siege, and not depart defeated in point of money, in which they were much superior.

49. Nicias spoke positively because he had exact information of the financial distress at Syracuse, and also because of the strength of the Athenian party there which kept sending him messages not to raise the siege; besides which he had more confidence than before in his fleet, and felt sure at least of its success. Demosthenes, however, would not hear for a moment of continuing the siege, but said that if they could not lead off the army without a decree from Athens, and if they were obliged to stay on, they ought to remove to Thapsus or Catana; where their land forces would have a wide extent of country to over-run, and could live by plundering the enemy, and would thus do them damage; while the fleet would have the open sea to fight in, that is to say, instead of a narrow space which was all in the enemy's favour, a wide sea-room where their science would be of use, and where they could retreat or advance without being confined or circumscribed either when they put out or put in. In any case he was altogether opposed to their staying on where they were, and insisted on removing at once, as quickly and with as little delay as possible; and in this judgment Eurymedon agreed. Nicias however still objecting, a certain diffidence and hesitation came over them, with a suspicion that Nicias might have some further information to make him so positive.*

*Nineteenth Year of the War—Battles in the Great Harbour—
Retreat and Annihilation of the Athenian Army*

50. While the Athenians lingered on in this way without moving from where they were, Gylippus and Sicanus now arrived at Syracuse. Sicanus had failed to gain Agrigentum, the party friendly to the Syracusans having been driven out while he was still at Gela; but Gylippus was accompanied not only by a large number of troops raised in Sicily, but by the heavy infantry sent off in the spring from Peloponnese in the merchantmen, who had arrived at Selinus from Libya. They had been carried to Libya by a storm, and having obtained two galleys and pilots from the Cyrenians, on their voyage along shore had taken sides with the Euesperitæ and had defeated the Libyans who were besieging them, and from thence coasting on to Neapolis, a Carthaginian mart, and the nearest point on Sicily, from which it is only two days' and a night's voyage, there crossed over and came to Selinus. Immediately upon their arrival the Syracusans prepared to attack the Athenians again by land and sea at once.

The Athenian generals seeing a fresh army come to the aid of the enemy, and that their own circumstances, far from improving, were becoming daily worse, and above all distressed by the sickness of the soldiers, now began to repent of not having removed before; and Nicias no longer offering the same opposition, except by urging that there should be no open voting, they gave orders as secretly as possible for all to be prepared to sail out from the camp at a given signal. All was at last ready, and they were on the point of sailing away, when an eclipse of the moon, which was then at the full, took place. Most of the Athenians, deeply impressed by this occurrence, now urged the generals to wait; and Nicias, who was somewhat over-addicted to divination and practices of that kind, refused from that moment even to take the question of departure into consideration, until they had waited the thrice nine days prescribed by the soothsayers.†

---

*Demosthenes' "plan B" was to move the army from Syracuse to a Sicilian place friendlier to the Athenians where they could obtain provisions. Athenian lingering served Gylippus' hopes and plans for total victory.

†The Athenians' last best chance was to sail away back to Athens, but the eclipse of the moon (understood as purely an astronomical event by contemporary savants) swayed both the educated Nicias as well as the more understandably superstitious common sailors. Thucydides clearly does not approve of such devotion to divine signs or to its mouthpieces. "Thrice nine months" betrays the soothsayers' oracular phrasing.

51. The besiegers having already delayed stayed in the country; and the Syracusans getting wind of what had happened, became more eager than ever to press the Athenians, who had now themselves acknowledged that they were no longer their superiors either by sea or by land, as otherwise they would never have planned to sail away. Besides which the Syracusans did not wish them to settle in any other part of Sicily, where they would be more difficult to deal with, but desired to force them to fight at sea as quickly as possible, in a position favourable to themselves. Accordingly they manned their ships and practised for as many days as they thought sufficient. When the moment arrived they assaulted on the first day the Athenian lines, and upon a small force of heavy infantry and horse sallying out against them by certain gates, cut off some of the former and routed and pursued them to the lines, where, as the entrance was narrow, the Athenians lost seventy horses and some few of the heavy infantry.

52. Drawing off their troops for this day, on the next the Syracusans went out with a fleet of seventy-six sail, and at the same time advanced with their land forces against the lines. The Athenians put out to meet them with eighty-six ships, came to close quarters and engaged.* The Syracusans and their allies first defeated the Athenian centre, and then caught Eurymedon, the commander of the right wing, who was sailing out from the line more towards the land in order to surround the enemy, in the hollow and recess of the harbour, and killed him and destroyed the ships accompanying him; after which they now chased the whole Athenian fleet before them and drove them ashore.

53. Gylippus seeing the enemy's fleet defeated and carried ashore beyond their stockades and camp, ran down to the breakwater with some of his troops, in order to cut off the men as they landed and make it easier for the Syracusans to tow off the vessels by the shore being friendly ground. The Tyrrhenians who guarded this point for the Athenians seeing them come on in disorder, advanced out against them and attacked and routed their van, hurling it into the marsh of Lysimeleia. Afterwards the Syracusan and allied troops arrived in greater numbers, and the Athenians fearing for their ships came up also to the rescue, and engaged them, and defeated and pursued them to some distance and killed a few of their heavy infantry. They succeeded in rescuing most of their ships and brought them down by

---

*The third naval battle at Syracuse occupies chapters 52 through 54. Eurymedon tries to outflank the enemy, east of the Athenians on the northeastern end of the harbor, by sailing around his foes. He, along with a few other triremes, was cut off from his allies and killed. This setback led to a general rout of the Athenian ships.

their camp; eighteen however were taken by the Syracusans and their allies, and all the men killed. The rest the enemy tried to burn by means of an old merchantman which they filled with sticks and pine-wood, set on fire and let drift down the wind which blew full on the Athenians. The Athenians, however, alarmed for their ships, contrived means for stopping it and putting it out, and checking the flames and the nearer approach of the merchantman, thus escaped the danger.

54. After this the Syracusans set up a trophy for the sea-fight and for the heavy infantry whom they had cut off up at the lines, where they took the horses; and the Athenians for the rout of the foot driven by the Tyrrhenians into the marsh, and for their own victory with the rest of the army.*

55. The Syracusans had now gained a decisive victory at sea, where until now they had feared the reinforcement brought by Demosthenes, and deep, in consequence, was the despondency of the Athenians, and great their disappointment, and greater still their regret for having come on the expedition. These were the only cities that they had yet encountered, similar to their own in character, under democracies like themselves, which had ships and horses, and were of considerable magnitude. They had been unable to divide and bring them over by holding out the prospect of changes in their governments, or to crush them by their great superiority in force, but had failed in most of their attempts, and being already in perplexity, had now been defeated at sea, where defeat could never have been expected, and were thus plunged deeper in embarrassment than ever.†

56. Meanwhile the Syracusans immediately began to sail freely along the harbour, and determined to close up its mouth, so that the Athenians might not be able to steal out in future, even if they wished. Indeed, the Syracusans no longer thought only of saving themselves, but also how to hinder the escape of the enemy; thinking, and thinking rightly, that they were now much the strongest, and that to conquer the Athenians and their allies by land and sea would win them great glory in Hellas. The rest of the Hellenes would thus immediately be either freed or released from apprehension, as the remaining forces of Athens would be henceforth unable to sustain the war that would be waged against her; while they, the Syracusans, would be regarded as the authors of this deliverance, and would be held in high admiration, not only with all men now living but also with

---

*Both sides set up trophies, but the Syracusan victories mean more to their side than the Athenian successes to theirs.

†Thucydides observes the structural political similarities of the two antagonists. The Athenians regret their decision to attack Syracuse and now recognize that their usual advantages had done them little good.

posterity.* Nor were these the only considerations that gave dignity to the struggle. They would thus conquer not only the Athenians but also their numerous allies, and conquer not alone, but with their companions-in-arms, commanding side by side with the Corinthians and Lacedæmonians, having offered their city to stand in the van of danger, and having been in a great measure the pioneers of naval success.

57. Indeed, there were never so many peoples assembled before a single city, if we except the grand total gathered together in this war under Athens and Lacedæmon. The following were the states on either side who came to Syracuse to fight for or against Sicily, to help to conquer or defend the island.† Right or community of blood was not the bond of union between them, so much as interest or compulsion as the case might be. The Athenians themselves being Ionians went against the Dorians of Syracuse of their own free will; and the peoples still speaking Attic and using the Athenian laws, the Lemnians, Imbrians, and Æginetans, that is to say, the then occupants of Ægina, being their colonists, went with them. To these must be also added the Hestiæans dwelling at Hestiæa in Eubœa. Of the rest some joined in the expedition as subjects of the Athenians, others as independent allies, others as mercenaries. To the number of the subjects paying tribute belonged the Eretrians, Chalcidians, Styrians, and Carystians from Eubœa; the Ceans, Andrians, and Tenians from the islands; and the Milesians, Samians, and Chians from Ionia. The Chians, however, joined as independent allies, paying no tribute, but furnishing ships. Most of these were Ionians and descended from the Athenians, except the Carystians, who are Dryopes, and although subjects and obliged to serve, were still Ionians fighting against Dorians.

Besides these there were men of Æolic race, the Methymnians, subjects who provided ships, not tribute, and the Tenedians and Ænians who paid tribute. These Æolians fought against their Æolian founders, the Bœotians in the Syracusan army, because they were obliged, while the Platæans, the only native Bœotians opposed to Bœotians, did so upon a just quarrel.

Of the Rhodians and Cytherians, both Dorians, the latter, Lacedæmonian colonists, fought in the Athenian ranks against their Lacedæmonian countrymen with Gylippus; while the Rhodians, Argives by race, were compelled to bear arms against the Dorian Syracusans and their own colonists, the Geloans, serving with the Syracusans.

---

*Syracusan success led to great hopes of complete victory. The Aegean "allies" are mistaken in the reasonable expectation of the rapid defeat of Athens, which would hold out for nearly another decade and more than once come near to victory.

†Prior to the decisive battle, Thucydides offers a catalogue of combatants in the manner of Homer, the historians' prototype. The variety of the contingents and their geographical disconnectedness seems to have impressed this historian.

Of the islanders round Peloponnese, the Cephallenians and Zacynthians accompanied the Athenians as independent allies, although their insular position really left them little choice in the matter, owing to the maritime supremacy of Athens, while the Corcyræans, who were not only Dorians but Corinthians, were openly serving against Corinthians and Syracusans, although colonists of the former and of the same race as the latter, under colour of compulsion, but really out of free will through hatred of Corinth. The Messenians, as they are now called in Naupactus and from Pylos, then held by the Athenians, were taken with them to the war. There were also a few Megarian exiles, whose fate it was to be now fighting against the Megarian Selinuntines.

The engagement of the rest was more of a voluntary nature. It was less the league than hatred of the Lacedæmonians and the immediate private advantage of each individual that persuaded the Dorian Argives to join the Ionian Athenians in a war against Dorians; while the Mantineans and other Arcadian mercenaries, accustomed to go against the enemy pointed out to them at the moment, were led by interest to regard the Arcadians serving with the Corinthians as just as much their enemies as any others. The Cretans and Ætolians also served for hire, and the Cretans who had joined the Rhodians in founding Gela, thus came to consent to fight for pay against, instead of for, their colonists. There were also some Acarnanians paid to serve, although they came chiefly for love of Demosthenes and out of goodwill to the Athenians whose allies they were. These all lived on the Hellenic side of the Ionian gulf. Of the Italiots, there were the Thurians and Metapontines, dragged into the quarrel by the stern necessities of a time of revolution; of the Siceliots, the Naxians and the Catanians; and of the barbarians, the Egestæans, who called in the Athenians, most of the Sicels, and outside Sicily some Tyrrhenian enemies of Syracuse and Iapygian mercenaries.

Such were the peoples serving with the Athenians.

58. Against these the Syracusans had the Camarinæans their neighbours, the Geloans who live next them, and then passing over the neutral Agrigentines, the Selinuntines settled on the farther side of the island. These inhabit the part of Sicily looking towards Libya; the Himeræans came from the side towards the Tyrrhenian sea, being the only Hellenic inhabitants in that quarter, and the only people that came from thence to the aid of the Syracusans. Of the Hellenes in Sicily the above peoples joined in the war, all Dorians and independent, and of the barbarians the Sicels only, that is to say, such as did not go over to the Athenians.

Of the Hellenes outside Sicily there were the Lacedæmonians, who provided a Spartan to take the command, and a force of Neodamodes or Freedmen, and of Helots; the Corinthians, who alone joined with naval and land forces, with their Leucadian and Ambraciot kinsmen; some mercenaries sent by Corinth from Arcadia; some Sicyonians forced to serve, and from outside Peloponnese the Bœotians.

In comparison, however, with these foreign auxiliaries, the great Siceliot cities furnished more in every department—numbers of heavy infantry, ships and horses, and an immense multitude besides having been brought together; while in comparison, again, one may say, with all the rest put together, more was provided by the Syracusans themselves, both from the greatness of the city and from the fact that they were in the greatest danger.

59. Such were the auxiliaries brought together on either side, all of which had by this time joined, neither party experiencing any subsequent accession. It was no wonder, therefore, if the Syracusans and their allies thought that it would win them great glory if they could follow up their recent victory in the sea-fight by the capture of the whole Athenian armada, without letting it escape either by sea or by land. They began at once to close up the great harbour by means of boats, merchant vessels, and galleys moored broadside across its mouth, which is nearly a mile wide, and made all their other arrangements for the event of the Athenians again venturing to fight at sea. There was, in fact, nothing little either in their plans or their ideas.

60. The Athenians, seeing them closing up the harbour and informed of their further designs, called a council of war. The generals and colonels assembled and discussed the difficulties of the situation; the point which pressed most being that they no longer had provisions for immediate use (having sent on to Catana to tell them not to send any, in the belief that they were going away), and that they would not have any in future unless they could command the sea.

They therefore determined to evacuate their upper lines, to enclose with a cross-wall and garrison a small space close to the ships, only just sufficient to hold their stores and sick,* and manning all the ships, seaworthy or not, with every man that could be spared from the rest of their land forces, to fight it out at sea, and if victorious, to go to Catana, if not, to burn their vessels, form in close order, and retreat by land for the nearest friendly place they could reach, Hellenic or barbarian.

This was no sooner settled than carried into effect: they descended gradually from the upper lines and manned all their vessels, compelling all to go on board who were of age to be in any way of use. They thus succeeded in manning about one hundred and ten ships in

---

*The Athenians have abandoned their circumvallation efforts on Epipolae and other blockading walls. They pull in their lines to defend only what ground they need for their troops, stores, the wounded, and the sick.

all, on board of which they embarked a number of archers and darters taken from the Acarnanians and from the other foreigners, making all other provisions allowed by the nature of their plan and by the necessities which imposed it. All was now nearly ready, and Nicias, seeing the soldiery disheartened by their unprecedented and decided defeat at sea, and by reason of the scarcity of provisions eager to fight it out as soon as possible, called them all together, and first addressed them, speaking as follows:—

61. 'Soldiers of the Athenians and of the allies, we have all an equal interest in the coming struggle, in which life and country are at stake for us quite as much as they can be for the enemy; since if our fleet wins the day, each can see his native city again, wherever that city may be. You must not lose heart, or be like men without any experience, who fail in a first essay, and ever afterwards fearfully forebode a future as disastrous. But let the Athenians among you who have already had experience of many wars, and the allies who have joined us in so many expeditions, remember the surprises of war, and with the hope that fortune will not be always against us, prepare to fight again in a manner worthy of the number which you see yourselves to be.*

62. 'Now, whatever we thought would be of service against the crush of vessels in such a narrow harbour, and against the force upon the decks of the enemy, from which we suffered before, has all been considered with the helmsmen, and, as far as our means allowed, provided. A number of archers and darters will go on board, and a multitude that we should not have employed in an action in the open sea, where our science would be crippled by the weight of the vessels; but in the present land-fight that we are forced to make from shipboard all this will be useful. We have also discovered the changes in construction that we must make to meet theirs; and against the thickness of their cheeks, which did us the greatest mischief, we have provided grappling-irons, which will prevent an assailant backing water after charging, if the soldiers on deck here do their duty; since we are absolutely compelled to fight a land battle from the fleet, and it seems to be our interest neither to back water ourselves, nor to let the enemy do so, especially as the shore, except so much of it as may be held by our troops, is hostile ground.

63. 'You must remember this and fight on as long as you can, and must not let yourselves be driven ashore, but once alongside must make up your minds not to part company until you have swept the heavy infantry from the enemy's deck. I say this more for the heavy

---

*Nicias' encouragement before the final naval battle depends on surprise, hope, and fortune—three terms that shy away from vaunted Athenian superiority in courage and skill. Successful sieges reduced the Plataeans and the Melians to similar undependable confidence in miracles and unexpected luck.

infantry than for the seamen, as it is more the business of the men on deck; and our land forces are even now on the whole the strongest. The sailors I advise, and at the same time implore, not to be too much daunted by their misfortunes, now that we have our decks better armed and a greater number of vessels. Bear in mind how well worth preserving is the pleasure felt by those of you who through your knowledge of our language and imitation of our manners were always considered Athenians,* even though not so in reality, and as such were honoured throughout Hellas, and had your full share of the advantages of our empire, and more than your share in the respect of our subjects and in protection from ill treatment. You, therefore, with whom alone we freely share our empire, we now justly require not to betray that empire in its extremity, and in scorn of Corinthians, whom you have often conquered, and of Siceliots, none of whom so much as presumed to stand against us when our navy was in its prime, we ask you to repel them, and to show that even in sickness and disaster your skill is more than a match for the fortune and vigour of any other.

64. 'For the Athenians among you I add once more this reflexion:—you left behind you no more such ships in your docks as these, no more heavy infantry in their flower; if you do anything but conquer, our enemies here will immediately sail thither, and those that are left of us at Athens will become unable to repel their home assailants, reinforced by these new allies. Here you will fall at once into the hands of the Syracusans—I need not remind you of the intentions with which you attacked them—and your countrymen at home will fall into those of the Lacedæmonians. Since the fate of both thus hangs upon this single battle†—now, if ever, stand firm, and remember, each and all, that you who are now going on board are the army and navy of the Athenians, and all that is left of the state and the great name of Athens, in whose defence if any man has any advantage in skill or courage, now is the time for him to show it, and thus serve himself and save all.'

65. After this address Nicias at once gave orders to man the ships. Meanwhile Gylippus and the Syracusans could perceive by the preparations which they saw going on that the Athenians meant to fight at sea. They had also notice of the grappling-irons, against which they specially provided by stretching hides over the prows and much of the upper part of their vessels, in order that the irons when thrown

---

*Nicias specifically mentions Athenians, allies local and Aegean, resident aliens (*metics*), and mercenaries. He unpersuasively implies that all these groups benefit from Athenian domination.

†More persuasively, Nicias argues that immediate success or failure may mean the fall or survival of the Athenian empire. Those Athenians back home cannot survive the defeat of the Athenians here. Wrong again.

might slip off without taking hold. All being now ready, the generals
and Gylippus addressed them in the following terms:—

66. 'Syracusans and allies, the glorious character of our past
achievements and the no less glorious results at issue in the coming
battle are, we think, understood by most of you, or you would never
have thrown yourselves with such ardour into the struggle; and if
there be any one not as fully aware of the facts as he ought to be, we
will declare them to him. The Athenians came to this country first to
effect the conquest of Sicily, and after that, if successful, of Peloponnese and the rest of Hellas, possessing already the greatest empire yet
known, of present or former times, among the Hellenes.* Here for the
first time they found in you men who faced their navy which made
them masters everywhere; you have already defeated them in the
previous sea-fights, and will in all likelihood defeat them again now.
When men are once checked in what they consider their special excellence, their whole opinion of themselves suffers more than if they
had not at first believed in their superiority, the unexpected shock to
their pride causing them to give way more than their real strength
warrants; and this probably now the case with the Athenians.

67. 'With us it is different. The original estimate of ourselves which
gave us courage in the days of our unskilfulness has been strengthened, while the conviction super-added to it that we must be the best
seamen of the time, if we have conquered the best, has given a double measure of hope to every man among us; and, for the most part,
where there is the greatest hope, there is also the greatest ardour for
action. The means to combat us which they have tried to find in copying our armament are familiar to our warfare, and will be met by
proper provisions; while they will never be able to have a number of
heavy infantry on their decks, contrary to their custom, and a number
of darters (born landsmen, one may say; Acarnanians and others, embarked afloat, who will not know how to discharge their weapons
when they have to keep still), without hampering their vessels and
falling all into confusion among themselves through fighting not according to their own tactics.†

'For they will gain nothing by the number of their ships—I say this to
those of you who may be alarmed by having to fight against odds—as
a quantity of ships in a confined space will only be slower in executing

---

*This speech must stand for several delivered to the various anti-Athenian contingents.
Gylippus plainly states the Athenian goal of conquest and plainly admits the prior
achievements of their great empire.

†Gylippus again states that the progressive Athenians are now copying the even more
advanced Syracusan tactics and equipment (strengthened prows, increased numbers of
marines on decks), but these innovations are better suited to their situation than the
Athenian.

the movements required, and most exposed to injury from our means of offence. Indeed, if you would know the plain truth, as we are credibly informed, the excess of their sufferings, and the necessities of their present distress have made them desperate; they have no confidence in their force, but wish to try their fortune in the only way they can, and either to force their passage and sail out, or after this to retreat by land, it being impossible for them to be worse off than they are.

68. 'The fortune of our greatest enemies having thus betrayed itself, and their disorder being what I have described, let us engage in anger, convinced that, as between adversaries, nothing is more legitimate than to claim to sate the whole wrath of one's soul in punishing the aggressor, and nothing more sweet, as the proverb has it, than the vengeance upon an enemy, which it will now be ours to take. That enemies they are and mortal enemies you all know, since they came here to enslave our country,* and if successful had in reserve for our men all that is most dreadful, and for our children and wives all that is most dishonourable, and for the whole city the name which conveys the greatest reproach. None should therefore relent or think it gain if they go away without further danger to us. This they will do just the same, even if they get the victory; while if we succeed, as we may expect, in chastising them, and in handing down to all Sicily her ancient freedom strengthened and confirmed, we shall have achieved no mean triumph. And the rarest dangers are those in which failure brings little loss and success the greatest advantage.'

69. After the above address to the soldiers on their side, the Syracusan generals and Gylippus now perceived that the Athenians were manning their ships, and immediately proceeded to man their own also. Meanwhile Nicias, appalled by the position of affairs, realising the greatness and the nearness of the danger now that they were on the point of putting out from shore, and thinking, as men are apt to think in great crises, that when all has been done they have still something left to do, and when all has been said that they have not yet said enough, again called on the captains one by one, addressing each by his father's name and by his own, and by that of his tribe, and adjured them not to belie their own personal renown, or to obscure the hereditary virtues for which their ancestors were illustrious;† he reminded them of their country, the freest of the free, and of the unfettered discretion allowed in it to all to live as they pleased; and added other ar-

---

*Gylippus may have in mind the Athenian treatment of Torone, Scione, and Melos described in book 5, as well as other deracinations (for example, the Aeginetans).

†Nicias uniquely speaks again, in a speech notable for its appeal to "mom and apple pie"—that is, the clichés of the patriotic and the desperate. Nicias' referral to the values and pride of Pericles' celebratory funeral oration becomes more ironic by the speech's delivery on a foreign shore and in a despairing moment of battle-crisis.

guments such as men would use at such a crisis, and which, with little alteration, are made to serve on all occasions alike—appeals to wives, children, and national gods,—without caring whether they are thought common-place, but loudly invoking them in the belief that they will be of use in the consternation of the moment.* Having thus admonished them, not, he felt, as he would, but as he could, Nicias withdrew and led the troops to the sea, and ranged them in as long a line as he was able, in order to aid as far as possible in sustaining the courage of the men afloat; while Demosthenes, Menander, and Euthydemus, who took the command on board, put out from their own camp and sailed straight to the barrier across the mouth of the harbour and to the passage left open, to try to force their way out.†

70. The Syracusans and their allies had already put out with about the same number of ships as before, a part of which kept guard at the outlet, and the remainder all round the rest of the harbour, in order to attack the Athenians on all sides at once; while the land forces held themselves in readiness at the points at which the vessels might put into the shore. The Syracusan fleet was commanded by Sicanus and Agatharchus, who had each a wing of the whole force, with Pythen and the Corinthians in the centre. When the rest of the Athenians came up to the barrier, with the first shock of their charge they overpowered the ships stationed there, and tried to undo the fastenings; after this, as the Syracusans and allies bore down upon them from all quarters, the action spread from the barrier over the whole harbour, and was more obstinately disputed than any of the preceding ones.

On either side the rowers showed great zeal in bringing up their vessels at the boatswains' orders, and the helmsmen great skill in manœuvring, and great emulation one with another; while the ships once alongside, the soldiers on board did their best not to let the service on deck be outdone by the others; in short, every man strove to prove himself the first in his particular department. And as many ships were engaged in a small compass (for these were the largest fleets fighting in the narrowest space ever known, being together little short of two hundred),‡ the regular attacks with the beak were few, there being no opportunity of backing water or of breaking the line; while the collisions caused by one ship chancing to run foul of another, either in flying from or attacking a third, were more frequent.

---

*Thucydides uniquely comments on a speech's rhetoric. The speech is reported indirectly, perhaps a further comment on its relative lack of incisiveness or other merit.

†Nicias remains on shore while three other commanders board their ships.

‡In a battle reported with as much vividness as any other in Thucydides' text, 186 ships are engaged. We unexpectedly hear more about the onlookers' reactions than about the unusual technology and the course of the battle itself (compare the siege of Plataea: 2.1–5 and 2.75–78).

So long as a vessel was coming up to the charge the men on the decks rained darts and arrows and stones upon her; but once alongside, the heavy infantry tried to board each other's vessel, fighting hand to hand. In many quarters also it happened, by reason of the narrow room, that a vessel was charging an enemy on one side and being charged herself on another, and that two, or sometimes more ships had perforce got entangled round one, obliging the helmsmen to attend to defence here, offence there, not to one thing at once, but to many on all sides; while the huge din caused by the number of ships crashing together not only spread terror, but made the orders of the boatswains inaudible.

The boatswains on either side in the discharge of their duty and in the heat of the conflict shouted incessantly orders and appeals to their men; the Athenians they urged to force the passage out, and now if ever to show their mettle and lay hold of a safe return to their country; to the Syracusans and their allies they cried that it would be glorious to prevent the escape of the enemy, and conquering, to exalt the countries that were theirs. The generals, moreover, on either side, if they saw any in any part of the battle backing ashore without being forced to do so, called out to the captain by name and asked him— the Athenians, whether they were retreating because they thought the thrice hostile shore more their own than that sea which had cost them so much labour to win; the Syracusans, whether they were flying from the flying Athenians, whom they well knew to be eager to escape in whatever way they could.*

71. Meanwhile the two armies on shore, while victory hung in the balance, were a prey to the most agonising and conflicting emotions; the natives thirsting for more glory than they had already won, while the invaders feared to find themselves in even worse plight than before.† All hopes of the Athenians being set upon their fleet, their fear for the event was like nothing they had ever felt; while their view of the struggle was necessarily as chequered as the battle itself. Close to the scene of action and not all looking at the same point at once, some saw their friends victorious and took courage, and fell to calling upon heaven not to deprive them of salvation, while others who had their eyes turned upon the losers, wailed and cried aloud, and, although spectators, were more overcome than the actual combatants.

Others, again, were gazing at some spot where the battle was

---

*Thucydides breaks out the reactions of different groups—boatswains (helmsmen), Athenians, Syracusans, generals, captains, etc.

†This description of the men on shore clearly reflects Thucydides' sources. Thucydides pauses to expand when presenting spectacles, that of the Athenians once sailing out in glory and now perishing in misery. He expects readers to recall these bookend situations.

evenly disputed; as the strife was protracted without decision, their swaying bodies reflected the agitation of their minds, and they suffered the worst agony of all, ever just within reach of safety or just on the point of destruction. In short, in that one Athenian army as long as the sea-fight remained doubtful there was every sound to be heard at once, shrieks, cheers, 'We win,' 'We lose,' and all the other manifold exclamations that a great host would necessarily utter in great peril; and with the men in the fleet it was nearly the same; until at last the Syracusans and their allies, after the battle had lasted a long while, put the Athenians to flight, and with much shouting and cheering chased them in open rout to the shore.

The naval force, one one way, one another, as many as were not taken afloat, now ran ashore and rushed from on board their ships to their camp; while the army, no more divided, but carried away by one impulse, all with shrieks and groans deplored the event, and ran down, some to help the ships, others to guard what was left of their wall, while the remaining and most numerous part already began to consider how they should save themselves. Indeed, the panic of the present moment had never been surpassed.

They now suffered very nearly what they had inflicted at Pylos; as then the Lacedæmonians with the loss of their fleet lost also the men who had crossed over to the island, so now the Athenians had no hope of escaping by land, without the help of some extraordinary accident.

72. The sea-fight having been a severe one, and many ships and lives having been lost on both sides, the victorious Syracusans and their allies now picked up their wrecks and dead, and sailed off to the city and set up a trophy. The Athenians, overwhelmed by their misfortune, never even thought of asking leave to take up their dead or wrecks, but wished to retreat that very night.* Demosthenes, however, went to Nicias and gave it as his opinion that they should man the ships they had left and make another effort to force their passage out next morning; saying that they had still left more ships fit for service than the enemy, the Athenians having about sixty remaining as against less than fifty of their opponents. Nicias was quite of his mind; but when they wished to man the vessels, the sailors refused to go on board, being so utterly overcome by their defeat as no longer to believe in the possibility of success.†

---

*The battle account is brief, the aftermath protracted. The Athenians had lost twice as many ships (approximately 50) as the Syracusans (approximately 25). Not to ask for the return of their Athenian dead signals their extreme despair.

†The dilatory Nicias finally accedes to Demosthenes' bolder thinking, but at this point mutiny spreads through the ranks. The soldiers are irrationally, mutinously, and tragically unwilling to board ship again.

73. Accordingly they all now made up their minds to retreat by land. Meanwhile the Syracusan Hermocrates suspecting their intention, and impressed by the danger of allowing a force of that magnitude to retire by land, establish itself in some other part of Sicily, and from thence renew the war, went and stated his views to the authorities, and pointed out to them that they ought not to let the enemy get away by night, but that all the Syracusans and their allies should at once march out and block up the roads and seize and guard the passes. The authorities were entirely of his opinion, and thought that it ought to be done, but on the other hand felt sure that the people, who had given themselves over to rejoicing and were taking their ease after a great battle at sea, would not be easily brought to obey; besides, they were celebrating a festival, having on that day a sacrifice to Heracles, and most of them in their rapture at the victory had fallen to drinking at the festival, and would probably consent to anything sooner than to take up their arms and march out at that moment.* For these reasons the thing appeared impracticable to the magistrates; and Hermocrates, finding himself unable to do anything further with them, had now recourse to the following stratagem of his own. What he feared was that the Athenians might quietly get the start of them by passing the most difficult places during the night; and he therefore sent, as soon as it was dusk, some friends of his own to the camp with some horsemen who rode up within earshot and called out to some of the men, as though they were well-wishers of the Athenians, and told them to tell Nicias (who had in fact some correspondents who informed him of what went on inside the town), not to lead off the army by night as the Syracusans were guarding the roads, but to make his preparations at his leisure and to retreat by day. After saying this they departed; and their hearers informed the Athenian generals.

74. They put off going for that night on the strength of this message, not doubting its sincerity.†

Since after all they had not set out at once, they now determined to stay also the following day to give time to the soldiers to pack up as well as they could the most useful articles, and, leaving everything else behind, to start only with what was strictly necessary for their personal subsistence. Meanwhile the Syracusans and Gylippus marched out and blocked up the roads through the country by which

---

*Drunkenness in Syracuse (and in Tarentum) appears regularly in various disapproving Greek and Latin historical sources. The combination of naval victory and festival of Heracles (their Dorian patron hero) was volatile.

†Hermocrates' ruse works and the Athenians postpone their departure. There had been pro-Athenian Syracusans while an Athenian victory was conceivable (compare 7.48–49), but if any such partisans remained, they were not speaking up now.

the Athenians were likely to pass, and kept guard at the fords of the streams and rivers, posting themselves so as to receive them and stop the army where they thought best; while their fleet sailed up to the beach and towed off the ships of the Athenians. Some few were burned by the Athenians themselves as they had intended; the rest the Syracusans lashed on to their own at their leisure as they had been thrown up on shore, without any one trying to stop them, and conveyed to the town.

75. After this, Nicias and Demosthenes now thinking that enough had been done in the way of preparation, the removal of the army took place upon the second day after the sea-fight. It was a lamentable scene, not merely from the single circumstance that they were retreating after having lost all their ships, their great hopes gone, and themselves and the state in peril; but also in leaving the camp there were things most grievous for every eye and heart to contemplate. The dead lay unburied, and each man as he recognised a friend among them shuddered with grief and horror; while the living whom they were leaving behind, wounded or sick, were to the living far more shocking than the dead, and more to be pitied than those who had perished.* These fell to entreating and bewailing until their friends knew not what to do, begging them to take them and loudly calling to each individual comrade or relative whom they could see, hanging upon the necks of their tent-fellows in the act of departure, and following as far as they could, and when their bodily strength failed them, calling again and again upon heaven and shrieking aloud as they were left behind.†

So that the whole army being filled with tears and distracted after this fashion found it not easy to go, even from an enemy's land, where they had already suffered evils too great for tears and in the unknown future before them feared to suffer more. Dejection and self-condemnation were also rife among them. Indeed they could only be compared to a starved-out town, and that no small one, escaping; the whole multitude upon the march being not less than forty thousand men. All carried anything they could which might be of use, and the heavy infantry and troopers, contrary to their wont, while under arms carried their own victuals, in some cases for want of servants, in others through not trusting them; as they had long been deserting and now did so in greater numbers than ever. Yet even thus they did not carry enough, as there was no longer food in the camp.

---

*Thucydides describes the abandonment of camp and the Athenian retreat in highly colored, emotional terms. The descent from rulers of the Aegean to dead, disabled, and disheartened retreaters deserved detailed description.

†The unparalleled frequency of description of non-verbal behaviors (reaching, hanging on) and para-linguistic (vocal but non-verbal) indications (shrieking, moaning) marks Thucydides' engagement with *pathos*.

Moreover their disgrace generally, and the universality of their sufferings, however to a certain extent alleviated by being borne in company, were still felt at the moment a heavy burden, especially when they contrasted the splendour and glory of their setting out with the humiliation in which it had ended. For this was by far the greatest reverse that ever befell an Hellenic army.* They had come to enslave others, and were departing in fear of being enslaved themselves: they had sailed out with prayer, and pæans, and now started to go back with omens directly contrary; travelling by land instead of by sea, and trusting not in their fleet but in their heavy infantry. Nevertheless the greatness of the danger still impending made all this appear tolerable.

76. Nicias seeing the army dejected and greatly altered, passed along the ranks and encouraged and comforted them as far as was possible under the circumstances, raising his voice still higher and higher, as he went from one company to another in his earnestness, and in his anxiety that the benefit of his words might reach as many as possible:—

77. 'Athenians and allies, even in our present position we must still hope on, since men have ere now been saved from worse straits than this; and you must not condemn yourselves too severely either because of your disasters or because of your present unmerited sufferings. I myself who am not superior to any of you in strength—indeed you see how I am in my sickness—and who in the gifts of fortune am, I think, whether in private life or otherwise, the equal of any, am now exposed to the same danger as the meanest among you; and yet my life has been one of much devotion toward the gods, and of much justice and without offence toward men.† I have, therefore, still a strong hope for the future, and our misfortunes do not terrify me as much as they might. Indeed we may hope that they will be lightened: our enemies have had good fortune enough; and if any of the gods was offended at our expedition, we have been already amply punished.‡ Others before us have attacked their neighbours and have done what

---

*Thucydides now combines his interest in extremes of human experience with his interest in reversals in fortune and rhetorical antithesis.

†Nicias' earnest anxiety for his men does him credit, and his illness explains some of his stretched reasoning, but his arguments here appear deficient and self-serving. His acknowledged devotion to the gods can only call their existence into question. His comfort is cold, indeed.

‡Herodotus had developed in Hellenic historiography the ideas of both a cyclic flow of fortune good and bad, and of reciprocal balance, or cosmic revenge. The Hellenic idea that excess good fortune will eventually bring a swing of the pendulum was not accompanied by any idea that the gods would necessarily even out bad fortune also with something better. Thucydides rarely mentions *hubris* (in the psychological sense of contemptuous arrogance), but the related archaic (and Herodotean) concept of divine *phthonos* (envy or jealousy) is prominent in Nicias' reckoning. The Greeks were pessimistic in their theology and philosophy.

men will do without suffering more than they could bear; and we may now justly expect to find the gods more kind, for we have become fitter objects for their pity than their jealousy. And then look at yourselves, mark the numbers and efficiency of the heavy infantry marching in your ranks, and do not give way too much to despondency, but reflect that you are yourselves at once a city wherever you sit down, and that there is no other in Sicily that could easily resist your attack, or expel you when once established.

'The safety and order of the march is for yourselves to look to; the one thought of each man being that the spot on which he may be forced to fight must be conquered and held as his country and stronghold. Meanwhile we shall hasten on our way night and day alike, as our provisions are scanty; and if we can reach some friendly place of the Sicels, whom fear of the Syracusans still keeps true to us, you may forthwith consider yourselves safe. A message has been sent on to them with directions to meet us with supplies of food. To sum up, be convinced, soldiers, that you must be brave, as there is no place near for your cowardice to take refuge in, and that if you now escape from the enemy, you may all see again what your hearts desire, while those of you who are Athenians will raise up again the great power of the state, fallen though it be. Men make the city and not walls or ships without men in them.'*

78. As he made this address, Nicias went along the ranks, and brought back to their place any of the troops that he saw straggling out of the line; while Demosthenes did as much for his part of the army, addressing them in words very similar.

The army marched in a hollow square, the division under Nicias leading, and that of Demosthenes following, the heavy infantry being outside and the baggage-carriers and the bulk of the army in the middle. When they arrived at the ford of the river Anapus they there found drawn up a body of the Syracusans and allies, and routing these, made good their passage and pushed on, harassed by the charges of the Syracusan horse and by the missiles of their light troops. On that day they advanced about four miles and a half, halting for the night upon a certain hill. On the next they started early and got on about two miles further, and descended into a place in the plain and there encamped, in order to procure some eatables from the houses, as the place was inhabited, and to carry on with them water from thence, as for miles in front, in the direction in which they were going, it was not plentiful.

---

*The concluding observation is based on a verse surviving in the Lesbian lyric poet Alcaeus, but it had become a commonplace found in Aeschylus, Sophocles, and Euripides too. Some drafted Aegean cynics might have remarked that some decent walls and ships would be a comfort indeed in the present situation.

The Syracusans meanwhile went on and fortified the pass in front, where there was a steep hill with a rocky ravine on each side of it, called the Acræan cliff. The next day the Athenians advancing found themselves impeded by the missiles and charges of the horse and darters, both very numerous, of the Syracusans and allies; and after fighting for a long while, at length retired to the same camp, where they had no longer provisions as before, it being impossible to leave their position by reason of the cavalry.

79. Early next morning they started afresh and forced their way to the hill, which had been fortified, where they found before them the enemy's infantry drawn up many shields deep to defend the fortification, the pass being narrow. The Athenians assaulted the work, but were greeted by a storm of missiles from the hill, which told with the greater effect through its being a steep one, and unable to force the passage, retreated again and rested. Meanwhile occurred some claps of thunder and rain, as often happens towards autumn, which still further disheartened the Athenians, who thought all these things to be omens of their approaching ruin.*

While they were resting Gylippus and the Syracusans sent a part of their army to throw up works in their rear on the way by which they had advanced; however, the Athenians immediately sent some of their men and prevented them; after which they retreated more towards the plain and halted for the night. When they advanced the next day the Syracusans surrounded and attacked them on every side, and disabled many of them, falling back if the Athenians advanced and coming on if they retired, and in particular assaulting their rear, in the hope of routing them in detail, and thus striking a panic into the whole army. For a long while the Athenians persevered in this fashion, but after advancing about half a mile halted to rest in the plain, the Syracusans also withdrawing to their own camp.

80. During the night Nicias and Demosthenes, seeing the wretched condition of their troops, now in want of every kind of necessity, and numbers of them disabled in the numerous attacks of the enemy, determined to light as many fires as possible, and to lead off the army, no longer by the same route as they had intended, but towards the sea in the opposite direction to that guarded by the Syracusans. The

---

*The thunder and rain were not at all ominous, as the defeated thought, but were standard meteorological events of the Sicilian late summer. Thucydides disapproves of the reaction. He reports that the Athenian and allied forces, in the eight days following, travel with difficulty about 65 stades (7.4 miles, in six days, Demosthenes to the river Cacyparis) and 115 stades (13 miles, in eight days, Nicias to the river Assinaros). Their own weaknesses in morale, supplies, and health, and the constant attacks of their enemies made gaining every yard difficult. Marching in the defensive "hollow rectangle" formation, they were heading toward allied Catana, a coastal city about 30 miles north.

whole of this route was leading the army not to Catana but to the other side of Sicily, towards Camarina, Gela, and the other Hellenic and barbarian towns in that quarter. They accordingly lit a number of fires and set out by night. Now all armies, and the greatest most of all, are liable to fears and alarms, especially when they are marching by night through an enemy's country and with the enemy near; and the Athenians falling into one of these panics, the leading division, that of Nicias, kept together and got on a good way in front, while that of Demosthenes, comprising rather more than half the army, got separated and marched on in some disorder. By morning, however, they reached the sea, and getting into the Helorine Road,* pushed on in order to reach the river Cacyparis, and to follow the stream up through the interior, where they hoped to be met by the Sicels whom they had sent for. Arrived at the river, they found there also a Syracusan party engaged in barring the passage of the ford with a wall and a palisade, and forcing this guard, crossed the river and went on to another called the Erineus, according to the advice of their guides.

81. Meanwhile, when day came and the Syracusans and allies found that the Athenians were gone, most of them accused Gylippus of having let them escape on purpose, and hastily pursuing by the road which they had no difficulty in finding that they had taken, overtook them about dinner-time. They first came up with the troops under Demosthenes, who were behind and marching somewhat slowly and in disorder, owing to the night-panic above referred to, and at once attacked and engaged them, the Syracusan horse surrounding them with more ease now that they were separated from the rest, and hemming them in on one spot. The division of Nicias was five or six miles on in front, as he led them more rapidly, thinking that under the circumstances their safety lay not in staying and fighting, unless obliged, but in retreating as fast as possible, and only fighting when forced to do so. On the other hand, Demosthenes was, generally speaking, harassed more incessantly, as his post in the rear left him the first exposed to the attacks of the enemy; and now, finding that the Syracusans were in pursuit, he omitted to push on, in order to form his men for battle, and so lingered until he was surrounded by his pursuers and himself and the Athenians with him placed in the most distressing position, being huddled into an enclosure† with a wall

---

*The Helorine road headed in the opposite direction, southwest from Syracuse to Helorus, near the coast.

†The staunch Spartan ally Gylippus is himself accused of collusion with the Athenian invader. Demosthenes' army, guarding the rear, had the worst of the engagements with the pursuing enemies. Furthermore, these Athenian troops, originally more than 20,000 (see 7.80), became separated from Nicias' forces. Eventually, Demosthenes' force was surrounded.

all round it, a road on this side and on that, and olive-trees in great number, where missiles were showered in upon them from every quarter. This mode of attack the Syracusans had with good reason adopted in preference to fighting at close quarters, as to risk a struggle with desperate men was now more for the advantage of the Athenians than for their own; besides, their success had now become so certain that they began to spare themselves a little in order not to be cut off in the moment of victory, thinking too that, as it was, they would be able in this way to subdue and capture the enemy.

82. In fact, after plying the Athenians and allies all day long from every side with missiles, they at length saw that they were worn out with their wounds and other sufferings; and Gylippus and the Syracusans and their allies made a proclamation, offering their liberty to any of the islanders who chose to come over to them; and some few cities went over. Afterwards a capitulation was agreed upon for all the rest with Demosthenes, to lay down their arms on condition that no one was to be put to death either by violence or imprisonment or want of the necessaries of life. Upon this they surrendered to the number of six thousand in all,* laying down all the money in their possession, which filled the hollows of four shields, and were immediately conveyed by the Syracusans to the town.

83. Meanwhile Nicias with his division arrived that day at the river Erineus, crossed over and posted his army upon some high ground upon the other side. The next day the Syracusans overtook him and told him that the troops under Demosthenes had surrendered, and invited him to follow their example. Incredulous of the fact, Nicias asked for a truce to send a horseman to see, and upon the return of the messenger with the tidings that they had surrendered, sent a herald to Gylippus and the Syracusans, saying that he was ready to agree with them on behalf of the Athenians to repay whatever money the Syracusans had spent upon the war if they would let his army go; and offered until the money was paid to give Athenians as hostages, one for every talent.

The Syracusans and Gylippus rejected this proposition, and attacked this division as they had the other, standing all round and plying them with missiles until the evening. Food and necessities were as miserably wanting to the troops of Nicias as they had been to their comrades; nevertheless they watched for the quiet of the night to resume their march. But as they were taking up their arms the Syracusans perceived it and raised their pæan, upon which the Athenians,

---

*Only 6,000 were left to surrender after many perished in the skirmishes and from wounds and hunger. The capitulation was on terms, not favorable ones, but better than nothing—which was to be the fate of Nicias' contingent.

finding that they were discovered, laid them down again, except about three hundred men who forced their way through the guards and went on during the night as they were able.*

84. As soon as it was day Nicias put his army in motion, pressed, as before, by the Syracusans and their allies, pelted from every side by their missiles, and struck down by their javelins. The Athenians pushed on for the Assinarus, impelled by the attacks made upon them from every side by a numerous cavalry and the swarm of other arms, fancying that they should breathe more freely if once across the river, and driven on also by their exhaustion and craving for water. Once there they rushed in, and all order was at an end, each man wanting to cross first, and the attacks of the enemy making it difficult to cross at all; forced to huddle together, they fell against and trod down one another, some dying immediately upon the javelins, others getting entangled together and stumbling over the articles of baggage, without being able to rise again.†

Meanwhile the opposite bank, which was steep, was lined by the Syracusans, who showered missiles down upon the Athenians, most of them drinking greedily and heaped together in disorder in the hollow bed of the river. The Peloponnesians also came down and butchered them, especially those in the water, which was thus immediately spoiled, but which they went on drinking just the same, mud and all, bloody as it was, most even fighting to have it.‡

85. At last, when many dead now lay piled one upon another in the stream, and part of the army had been destroyed at the river, and the few that escaped from thence cut off by the cavalry, Nicias surrendered himself to Gylippus, whom he trusted more than he did the Syracusans, and told him and the Lacedæmonians to do what they liked with him, but to stop the slaughter of the soldiers. Gylippus, after this, immediately gave orders to take prisoners;§ upon which the rest were brought together alive, except a large

---

*Nicias was incredulous about the surrender of his fellow commander and all his troops. He offered to surrender on financial terms that the Syracusans rejected—money is more easily replaced than men. Their situation was more desperate now than even Demosthenes' had been.

†No one has definitively identified the Assinarus River. (Dover, in Gomme et al., opts for the Fiumara di Noto.) Thucydides underlines the hellish scene of thirst and butchery by the heedless confusion of the victims. The Sicilians take few more than 1,000 prisoners from a force that just eight days earlier consisted of nearly 20,000 men.

‡The Athenians have lost not only their military order but even any sense of self-preservation. They have become defenseless animals.

§Nicias, descended from the old aristocracy and a hereditary friend of Spartans, rightly thought it safer delivering himself to the Spartan commander. Until the losing commander arranged surrender, killing the enemy, however defenseless, constituted proper military etiquette. The local Sicilians seized many prisoners for private sale.

number secreted by the soldiery, and a party was sent in pursuit of the three hundred who had got through the guard during the night, and who were now taken with the rest. The number of the enemy collected as public property was not considerable; but that secreted was very large, and all Sicily was filled with them, no convention having been made in their case as for those taken with Demosthenes. Besides this, a large portion were killed outright, the carnage being very great, and not exceeded by any in this Sicilian war. In the numerous other encounters upon the march, not a few also had fallen. Nevertheless many escaped, some at the moment, others served as slaves, and then ran away subsequently. These found refuge at Catana.

86. The Syracusans and their allies now mustered and took up the spoils and as many prisoners as they could, and went back to the city. The rest of their Athenian and allied captives were deposited in the quarries, this seeming the safest way of keeping them;* but Nicias and Demosthenes were butchered, against the will of Gylippus, who thought that it would be the crown of his triumph if he could take the enemy's generals to Lacedæmon. One of them, as it happened, Demosthenes, was one of her greatest enemies, on account of the affair of the island and of Pylos; while the other, Nicias, was for the same reasons one of her greatest friends, owing to his exertions to procure the release of the prisoners by persuading the Athenians to make peace. For these reasons the Lacedæmonians felt kindly towards him; and it was in this that Nicias himself mainly confided when he surrendered to Gylippus. But some of the Syracusans who had been in correspondence with him were afraid, it was said, of his being put to the torture and troubling their success by his revelations; others, especially the Corinthians, of his escaping, as he was wealthy, by means of bribes, and living to do them further mischief; and these persuaded the allies and put him to death.† This or the like was the cause of the death of a man who, of all the Hellenes in my time, least deserved such a fate, seeing that the whole course

---

*The quarries were large and essentially an inescapable pit. One can still visit them today, east of the theater. Seven thousand is a dangerously large number of prisoners. Plutarch in his *Life of Nicias* (29) offers additional information about these prisoners, noting that some of them were bought out of the lethal prison as slaves—purchased because they had memorized the popular tragedies of Euripides.

†Gylippus wanted to bring home the enemy generals to crown his triumph. Demosthenes had engineered the Spartan humiliation at Pylos and now was in the opposite situation. Some Syracusans feared revelations of their own treasonous activities from Nicias. The Corinthians oddly fretted that the old and sick general might be ransomed by his family's riches so as to fight them again.

of his life had been regulated with strict attention to decency, morality, and courage.*

87. The prisoners in the quarries were at first hardly treated by the Syracusans. Crowded in a narrow hole, without any roof to cover them, the heat of the sun and the stifling closeness of the air tormented them during the day, and then the nights, which came on autumnal and chilly, made them ill by the violence of the change; besides, as they had to do everything in the same place for want of room, and the bodies of those who died of their wounds or from the variation in the temperature, or from similar causes, were left heaped together one upon another, intolerable stenches arose; while hunger and thirst never ceased to afflict them, each man during eight months having only half a pint of water and a pint of grain given him daily. In short, no single suffering to be apprehended by men thrust into such a place was spared them.† For some seventy days they thus lived all together, after which all, except the Athenians and any Siceliots or Italiots who had joined in the expedition, were sold. The total number of prisoners taken it would be difficult to state exactly, but it could not have been less than seven thousand.

This was the greatest Hellenic achievement of any in this war, or, in my opinion, in Hellenic history;‡ at once most glorious to the victors, and most calamitous to the conquered. They were beaten at all points and altogether; all that they suffered was great; they were destroyed, as the saying is, with a total destruction, their fleet, their army—everything was destroyed, and few out of many returned home.§ Such were the events in Sicily.

---

*Thucydides valued Nicias because he had been the opponent of Cleon and a decent person in his life (compare 5.16, an ambivalent estimate). He had long served his *polis*. His execution in cold blood after having surrendered was ugly, unscrupulous, and abnormal. However great his responsibility for the Athenian defeat and the deaths of thousands, he had not deserved this brutal treatment. Different scholars read differently this "epitaph," one of several planted in Thucydides' text. Some see it as frank praise, others read it ironically or even as a condemnation of Nicias' inveterate conformity to expectation.

†The Syracusans felt no inclination to mercy toward their invaders. The climate and the unsanitary conditions were tantamount to revenge and torture, while the medical assistance (if any) and the scant food provided were intentionally inadequate. The grain allowance is half what the Spartan *sla es* on Sphacteria had received. The Athenians who survived owed their survival and eventual purchase to their cash value—they were now salable property owned by the state.

‡Thucydides has in mind, at least, the two most likely competitors, the legendary Achaean expedition to Troy and Xerxes' expedition in 480 against Greece. He thereby trumps in magnitude anything in Homer and Herodotus, as he had claimed he would do, already in the preface. There are many parallels in the later two, overextended imperial ventures.

§Unique was both the magnitude and thoroughness of the Athenian collapse and loss of life. Thucydides expresses here either pity for his fellow citizens—Nicias, not least— or, more likely, sympathy for all human beings because of their murderous follies, their mistakes, and their suffering.

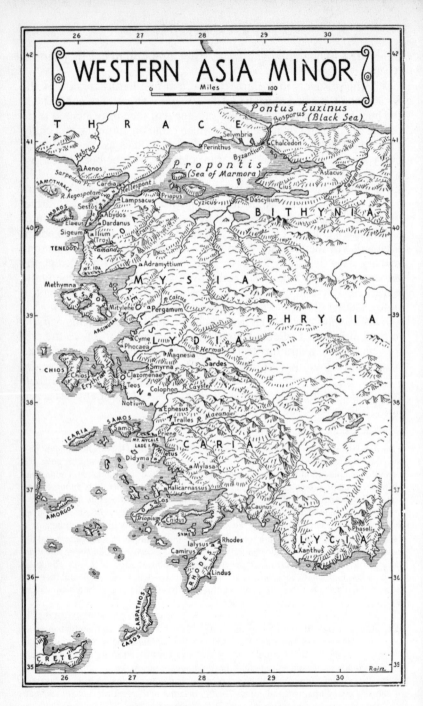

MAP 12. WESTERN ASIA MINOR

BOOK 8

*Nineteenth and Twentieth Years of the War — Revolt
of Ionia — Intervention of Persia — The War in Ionia*

1. When the news was brought to Athens, for a long while they
disbelieved even the most respectable of the soldiers who had
themselves escaped from the scene of action and clearly reported
the matter, a destruction so complete not being thought credible.
When the conviction was forced upon them, they were angry with
the orators who had joined in promoting the expedition, just as if
they had not themselves voted it, and were enraged also with the
reciters of oracles and soothsayers, and all other omen-mongers of
the time who had encouraged them to hope that they should conquer Sicily.*

Already distressed at all points and in all quarters, after what had
now happened, they were seized by the greatest fear and consternation. It was grievous enough for the state and for every man to lose
so many heavy infantry, cavalry, and able-bodied troops, and to see
none left to replace them; but when they saw, also, that they had not
sufficient ships in their docks, or money in the treasury, or crews for
the ships, they began to despair of salvation.†

They thought that their enemies in Sicily would immediately sail
with their fleet against Piræus, inflamed by so signal a victory; while
their adversaries at home, redoubling all their preparations, would
vigorously attack them by sea and land at once, aided by their own revolting confederates. Nevertheless, with such means as they had, it
was determined to resist to the last, and to provide timber and money,
and to equip a fleet as they best could, to take steps to secure their
confederates and above all Eubœa, to reform things in the city upon
a more economical footing, and to elect a board of elders to advise
upon the state of affairs as occasion should arise. In short, as is the

---

*Participants' or audiences' responses (credulity, incredulity, anger, amusement, etc.)
attract Thucydides' comment. Thucydides points to the *demos'* irrational irritation with
orators and oracle mongers, although he has little sympathy for either, insofar as they
encouraged the lust for attacking Sicily.

†Hoplites, triremes, the expensive timber to build them and crews to man them, and silver are the sinews of war. The *polis* seemed, to friend and foe, stripped of essential war
resources.

way of a democracy, in the panic of the moment they were ready to be as prudent as possible.*

These resolves were at once carried into effect. Summer was now over.

2. The winter ensuing saw all Hellas stirring under the impression of the great Athenian disaster in Sicily. Neutrals now felt that even if uninvited they ought no longer to stand aloof from the war, but should volunteer to march against the Athenians, who, as they severally reflected, would probably have come against them if the Sicilian campaign had succeeded. Besides, they considered that the war would now be short, and that it would be creditable for them to take part in it.[†] Meanwhile the allies of the Lacedæmonians felt all more anxious than ever to see a speedy end to their heavy labours. But above all, the subjects of the Athenians showed a readiness to revolt even beyond their ability, judging the circumstances with passion, and refusing even to hear of the Athenians being able to last out the coming summer.

Beyond all this, Lacedæmon was encouraged by the near prospect of being joined in great force in the spring by her allies in Sicily, lately forced by events to acquire their navy. With these reasons for confidence in every quarter, the Lacedæmonians now resolved to throw themselves without reserve into the war, considering that, once it was happily terminated, they would be finally delivered from such dangers as that which would have threatened them from Athens, if she had become mistress of Sicily, and that the overthrow of the Athenians would leave them in quiet enjoyment of the supremacy over all Hellas.

3. Their king, Agis, accordingly set out at once during this winter with some troops from Decelea, and levied from the allies contributions for the fleet, and turning towards the Malian gulf exacted a sum of money from the Œtæans by carrying off most of their cattle in reprisal for their old hostility, and, in spite of the protests and opposition of the Thessalians, forced the Achæans of Phthiotis and the other subjects of the Thessalians in those parts to give him money and hostages, and deposited the hostages at Corinth, and tried to bring their countrymen into the confederacy.[‡] The Lacedæmonians now is-

---

*Athenian resilience in 413 surprised Thucydides and her enemies, as he notes at 2.65 and 7.28. The board of [ten] senior advisers appears to be a constitutional attempt to prevent or retard overly hasty decisions of the *demos*.

†Rebellion seemed to the "allies" only prudent, since no one thought Athens could hold out long against the Peloponnesian, the Sicilian, and perhaps the Persian armed forces. Enemies, subjects, and neutrals contemplated joining the grand coalition developing against Athens.

‡During the winter of 413/412, King Agis was running the war in Attica independently of the government in Sparta or the advisers imposed on him after Mantinea (5.63; compare 8.5). Persuasion first, threat and force (including hostages for good behavior) afterward, were the prominent levers of the anti-Athenian alliance.

sued a requisition to the cities for building a hundred ships, fixing their own quota and that of the Bœotians at twenty-five each; that of the Phocians and Locrians together at fifteen; that of the Corinthians at fifteen; that of the Arcadians, Pellenians, and Sidyonians together at ten; and that of the Megarians, Trœzenians, Epidaurians, and Hermionians together at ten also; and meanwhile made every other preparation for commencing hostilities by the spring.

4. In the meantime the Athenians were not idle. During this same winter, as they had determined, they contributed timber and pushed on their ship-building, and fortified Sunium to enable their grain-ships to round it in safety, and evacuated the fort in Laconia which they had built on their way to Sicily;* while they also, for economy, cut down any other expenses that seemed unnecessary, and above all kept a careful look-out against the revolt of their confederates.

5. While both parties were thus engaged, and were as intent upon preparing for the war as they had been at the outset, the Eubœans first of all sent envoys during this winter to Agis to treat of their revolting from Athens. Agis accepted their proposals, and sent for Alcamenes, son of Sthenelaïdas, and Melanthus from Lacedæmon, to take the command in Eubœa. These accordingly arrived with some three hundred Neodamodes, and Agis began to arrange for their crossing over. But in the meanwhile arrived some Lesbians, who also wished to revolt; and these being supported by the Bœotians, Agis was persuaded to defer acting in the matter of Eubœa, and made arrangements for the revolt of the Lesbians, giving them Alcamenes, who was to have sailed to Eubœa, as governor, and himself promising them ten ships, and the Bœotians the same number.†

All this was done without instructions from home, as Agis while at Decelea with the army that he commanded had power to send troops to whatever quarter he pleased, and to levy men and money. During this period, one might say, the allies obeyed him much more than they did the Lacedæmonians in the city, as the force he had with him made him feared at once wherever he went. While Agis was engaged with the Lesbians, the Chians and Erythræans, who were also ready to revolt, applied, not to him but at Lacedæmon; where they arrived ac-

---

*As reported in 8.1, the Athenians retrenched on overseas bases and increased measures of security for their food supply and for keeping their restive subjects quiet. Lysander's grain blockade in 404 forced the Athenians finally to surrender, as Xenophon reports in the *Hellenica*, continuing the history of this war from the point in summer 411 when Thucydides stops.

†The rich island cities of the Euboeans were relatively secure subjects for the Athenians, but the Euboeans never appreciated their enforced membership in Athens' empire. Boeotia's proximity to Euboea at Chalcis made bringing Peloponnesian troops over relatively easy (map 5).

companied by an ambassador from Tissaphernes, the commander of
King Darius, son of Artaxerxes, in the maritime districts, who invited
the Peloponnesians to come over, and promised to maintain their
army.*

The king had lately called upon him for the tribute from his government, for which he was in arrears, being unable to raise it from the
Hellenic towns by reason of the Athenians; and he therefore calculated that by weakening the Athenians he should get the tribute better paid, and should also draw the Lacedæmonians into alliance with
the king; and by this means, as the king had commanded him, take
alive or dead Amorges, the bastard son of Pissuthnes, who was in rebellion on the coast of Caria.

6. While the Chians and Tissaphernes thus joined to effect the
same object, about the same time Calligeitus, son of Laophon, a
Megarian, and Timagoras, son of Athenagoras, a Cyzicene, both of
them exiles from their country and living at the court of Pharnabazus,
son of Pharnaces, arrived at Lacedæmon upon a mission from Pharnabazus, to procure a fleet for the Hellespont; by means of which, if
possible, he might himself effect the object of Tissaphernes' ambition,
and cause the cities in his government to revolt from the Athenians,
and so get the tribute, and by his own agency obtain for the king the
alliance of the Lacedæmonians.†

The emissaries of Pharnabazus and Tissaphernes treating apart, a
keen competition now ensued at Lacedæmon as to whether a fleet
and army should be sent first to Ionia and Chios, or to the Hellespont.
The Lacedæmonians, however, decidedly favoured the Chians and
Tissaphernes, who were seconded by Alcibiades, the family friend of
Endius, one of the Ephors for that year. Indeed, this is how their

---

*Agis decided to promote revolt first on the other side of the Aegean, in Lesbos. His
friction with the home authorities leads to Peloponnesian misfiring, when the Chians
and Erythraeans, neighbors south of Lesbos, come to Sparta with the envoy of Darius'
satrap (royal governor) Tissaphernes. Darius, king of Persia, naturally found the powerful and expansive Athenian empire a threat to his security and a hindrance to the
revenues from his once Persian, Ionian, and Hellespontine subjects (not to mention
those on the islands). The Athenians had earlier (c.450) imposed severe regulations on
several of the Anatolian subject communities, presumably after rebellions (for example, Erythrae; Fornara #71; map 12). Darius' rebellious underling Amorges had somehow set up an independent government in Caria, south of Ionia (map 1).

†Pharnabazus, satrap for the Hellespont and Propontis, was equal in authority to Tissaphernes. The two jockeyed for Darius' support and competed for alliance and action
with the Peloponnesian forces. Success might lead to restoration of the King's tribute,
currently collected by the Athenians for their empire. Hellenic portraits of both satraps
survive on contemporary coins, among the first Greek likenesses of living human beings ever produced. (See Levi, *The Greek World*, pp. 102–103, for basic facts about
Greek numismatics.)

house got its Laconic name, Alcibiades being the family name of Endius. Nevertheless the Lacedæmonians first sent to Chios Phrynis, one of the Periœci, to see whether they had as many ships as they said, and whether their city generally was as great as was reported;* and upon his bringing word that they had been told the truth, immediately entered into alliance with the Chians and Erythræans, and voted to send them forty ships, there being already, according to the statement of the Chians, not less than sixty in the island.

At first the Lacedæmonians meant to send ten of these forty themselves, with Melanchridas their admiral; but afterwards, an earthquake having occurred, they sent Chalcideus instead of Melanchridas, and instead of the ten ships equipped only five in Laconia. And the winter ended, and with it ended also the nineteenth year of this war of which Thucydides is the historian.

7. At the beginning of the next summer the Chians were urging that the fleet should be sent off, being afraid that the Athenians, from whom all these embassies were kept a secret, might find out what was going on, and the Lacedæmonians at once sent three Spartans to Corinth to haul the ships as quickly as possible across the Isthmus from the other sea to that on the side of Athens, and to order them all to sail to Chios, those which Agis was equipping for Lesbos not excepted. The number of ships from the allied states was thirty-nine in all.

8. Meanwhile Calligeitus and Timagoras did not join on behalf of Pharnabazus in the expedition to Chios or give the money—twenty-five talents—which they had brought with them to help in despatching a force, but determined to sail afterwards with another force by themselves. Agis, on the other hand, seeing the Lacedæmonians bent upon going to Chios first, himself came in to their views; and the allies assembled at Corinth and held a council, in which they decided to sail first to Chios under the command of Chalcideus, who was equipping the five vessels in Laconia, then to Lesbos, under the command of Alcamenes, the same whom Agis had fixed upon, and lastly to go to the Hellespont, where the command was given to Clearchus, son of Ramphias.

Meanwhile they would take only half the ships across the Isthmus first, and let those sail off at once, in order that the Athenians might attend less to the departing squadron than to those to be taken across afterwards, as no care had been taken to keep this voyage secret through contempt of the impotence of the Athenians, who had as yet

---

*Ionia and Chios were richer and closer to the Spartans than was Pharnabazus' northern domain. The political confidence placed in Phrynis, one of the Laconian *perioeci* ("dwellers round"; not the unfree helots but not full Spartiates either), is unexpected. The frequency of diplomatic fraud, or its expectation, is another surprise. So the year 413 ends.

no fleet of any account upon the sea.* Agreeably to this determination twenty-one vessels were at once conveyed across the Isthmus.

9. They were now impatient to set sail, but the Corinthians were not willing to accompany them until they had celebrated the Isthmian festival, which fell at that time. Upon this Agis proposed to them to save their scruples about breaking the Isthmian truce by taking the expedition upon himself. The Corinthians not consenting to this, a delay ensued, during which the Athenians conceived suspicions of what was preparing at Chios, and sent Aristocrates, one of their generals, and charged them with the fact, and upon the denial of the Chians, ordered them to send with them a contingent of ships, as faithful confederates. Seven were sent accordingly. The reason of the despatch of the ships lay in the fact that the mass of the Chians were not privy to the negotiations, while the few who were in the secret did not wish to break with the multitude until they had something positive to lean upon, and no longer expected the Peloponnesians to arrive by reason of their delay.†

10. In the meantime the Isthmian games took place, and the Athenians, who had been also invited, went to attend them, and now seeing more clearly into the designs of the Chians, as soon as they returned to Athens took measures to prevent the fleet putting out from Cenchreæ without their knowledge. After the festival the Peloponnesians set sail with twenty-one ships for Chios, under the command of Alcamenes. The Athenians first sailed against them with an equal number, drawing off towards the open sea.

The enemy, however, turning back before he had followed them far, the Athenians returned also, not trusting the seven Chian ships which formed part of their number, and afterwards manned thirty-seven vessels in all and chased him on his passage along shore into Spiræum, a desert Corinthian port on the edge of the Epidaurian frontier. After losing one ship out at sea, the Peloponnesians got the rest together and brought them to anchor. The Athenians now attacked not only from the sea with their fleet, but also disembarked upon the coast; and a mêlée ensued of the most confused and violent kind, in which the Athenians disabled most of the enemy's vessels and killed Alcamenes their commander, losing also a few of their own men.

---

*King Agis can act as a plenipotentiary. The Spartans regard the Athenians as impotent at sea, and although they built new triremes quickly, at this time they were not yet a serious threat.

†The current general Aristocrates is not well known, but he swore fealty to the earlier peace and alliance, and participated in the coup d'état and the dissolution of the Four Hundred (5.19, 24; 8.9, 89, 92). The Athenians understand the economic and strategic importance of the large, rich island of Chios. The Chian commons and conspirators are not frank with each other.

11. After this they separated, and the Athenians, detaching a sufficient number of ships to blockade those of the enemy, anchored with the rest at the islet adjacent, upon which they proceeded to encamp, and sent to Athens for reinforcements; the Peloponnesians having been joined on the day after the battle by the Corinthians, who came to help the ships, and by the other inhabitants in the vicinity, not long afterwards. These saw the difficulty of keeping guard in a desert place, and in their perplexity at first thought of burning the ships, but finally resolved to haul them up on shore and sit down and guard them with their land forces, until a convenient opportunity for escaping should present itself. Agis also, on being informed of the disaster, sent them a Spartan of the name of Thermon. The Lacedæmonians first received the news of the fleet having put out from the Isthmus, Alcamenes having been ordered by the Ephors to send off a horseman when this took place, and immediately resolved to despatch their own five vessels under Chalcideus, and Alcibiades with him. But while they were full of this resolution came the second news of the fleet having taken refuge in Spiræum; and disheartened at their first step in the Ionian war proving a failure, they laid aside the idea of sending the ships from their own country, and even wished to recall some that had already sailed.*

12. Perceiving this, Alcibiades again persuaded Endius and the other Ephors to persevere in the expedition, saying that the voyage would be made before the Chians heard of the fleet's misfortune, and that as soon as he set foot in Ionia, he should, by assuring them of the weakness of the Athenians and the zeal of Lacedæmon, have no difficulty in persuading the cities to revolt, as they would readily believe his testimony. He also represented to Endius himself in private that it would be glorious for him to be the means of making Ionia revolt and the king become the ally of Lacedæmon, instead of that honour being left to Agis (Agis was the enemy of Alcibiades); and Endius and his colleagues thus persuaded, he put to sea with the five ships and the Lacedæmonian Chalcideus, and made all haste upon the voyage.†

13. About this same time the sixteen Peloponnesian ships from Sicily, which had served through the war with Gylippus, were caught on their return off Leucadia and roughly handled by the twenty-seven Athenian vessels under Hippocles, son of Menippus, on the

---

*The Spartans don't react well to early defeat (compare 1.70; 8.96). Not only democracies in Thucydides falter when expectations crash.

†Alcibiades enjoys a hereditary guest-friendship with Endius and a significant enmity with Agis. Plutarch, in *Alcibiades* 23, claims it was based on the Athenian having seduced the Spartan king's wife. Thucydides does not report this significant scandal, rumor or not, or any other explanation for their consequential hostility.

look-out for the ships from Sicily. After losing one of their number the rest escaped from the Athenians and sailed into Corinth.

14. Meanwhile Chalcideus and Alcibiades seized all they met with on their voyage, to prevent news of their coming, and let them go at Corycus, the first point which they touched at in the continent. Here they were visited by some of their Chian correspondents, and being urged by them to sail up to the town without announcing their coming, arrived suddenly before Chios. The many were amazed and confounded, while the few had so arranged that the council should be sitting at the time; and after speeches from Chalcideus and Alcibiades stating that many more ships were sailing up, but saying nothing of the fleet being blockaded in Spiræum, the Chians revolted from the Athenians, and the Erythræans immediately afterwards.

After this three vessels sailed over to Clazomenæ, and made that city revolt also; and the Clazomenians immediately crossed over to the mainland and began to fortify Polichna, in order to retreat there, in case of necessity, from the island where they dwelt. Thus, the revolted places were all engaged in fortifying and preparing for the war.

15. News of Chios speedily reached Athens. The Athenians thought the danger by which they were now menaced great and unmistakable, and that the rest of their allies would not consent to keep quiet after the secession of the greatest of their number. In the consternation of the moment they at once took off the penalty attaching to whoever proposed or put to the vote a proposal for using the thousand talents which they had jealously avoided touching throughout the whole war,* and voted to employ them to man a large number of ships, and to send off at once under Strombichides, son of Diotimus, the eight vessels, forming part of the blockading fleet at Spiræum, which had left the blockade and had returned after pursuing and failing to overtake the vessels with Chalcideus. These were to be followed shortly afterwards by twelve more under Thrasycles, also taken from the blockade. They also recalled the seven Chian vessels, forming part of their squadron blockading the fleet in Spiræum, and giving the slaves on board their liberty, put the freemen in confinement, and speedily manned and sent out ten fresh ships to blockade the Peloponnesians in the place of all those that had departed, and decided to man thirty more. Zeal was not wanting, and no effort was spared to send relief to Chios.

16. In the meantime Strombichides with his eight ships arrived at

---

*The Chian revolt threatened the continued viability of the Athenian empire and perhaps the Athenian *polis* itself. No subject city was greater, none richer (8.45; compare 24 and 40).

Samos, and taking one Samian vessel, sailed to Teos and required them to remain quiet.* Chalcideus also set sail with twenty-three ships for Teos from Chios, the land forces of the Clazomenians and Erythræans moving along shore to support him. Informed of this in time, Strombichides put out from Teos before their arrival, and while out at sea, seeing the number of the ships from Chios, fled towards Samos, chased by the enemy. The Teians at first would not receive the land forces, but upon the flight of the Athenians took them into the town. There they waited for some time for Chalcideus to return from the pursuit, and as time went on without his appearing, began themselves to demolish the wall which the Athenians had built on the land side of the city of the Teians, being assisted by a few of the barbarians who had come up under the command of Stages, the lieutenant of Tissaphernes.

17. Meanwhile Chalcideus and Alcibiades, after chasing Strombichides into Samos, armed the crews of the ships from Peloponnese and left them at Chios, and filling their places with substitutes from Chios, and manning twenty others, sailed off to effect the revolt of Miletus. The wish of Alcibiades, who had friends among the leading men of the Milesians, was to bring over the town before the arrival of the ships from Peloponnese, and thus, by causing the revolt of as many cities as possible with the help of the Chian power and of Chalcideus, to secure the honour for the Chians and himself and Chalcideus, and, as he had promised, for Endius who had sent them out.† Not discovered until their voyage was nearly completed, they arrived a little before Strombichides and Thrasycles (who had just come with twelve ships from Athens, and had joined Strombichides in pursuing them), and occasioned the revolt of Miletus. The Athenians sailing up close on their heels with nineteen ships found Miletus closed against them, and took up their station at the adjacent island of Lade. The first alliance‡ between the king and the Lacedæmonians was now concluded immediately upon the revolt of the Milesians, by Tissaphernes and Chalcideus, and was as follows:—

18. *The Lacedæmonians and their allies made a treaty with the king and Tissaphernes upon the terms following:—*

---

*Strombichides plays a salient Athenian role in the Ionian War.

†Alcibiades procures the revolt of mainland Miletus, about 18 miles southeast across the Mycale strait from Samos (map 12), another crucial Athenian dependency and one more exposed, like mainland Teos, to attacks by the former ruler, the Persian king.

‡The revolt of Miletus, a good sign for general revolution within the empire, leads to the first of three documents of alliance (compare 8.37, 58), each one refining the previous contract, but none of them entirely satisfactory from the Peloponnesian point of view, as Lichas perceptively opines (8.43). The first draft betrays catchwords of Peloponnesian liberation, but it also returns most of the Athenian allies to the control of the Persian king.

1. *Whatever country or cities the king has, or the king's ancestors had, shall be the king's; and whatever came in to the Athenians from these cities, either money or any other thing, the king and the Lacedæmonians and their allies shalt jointly hinder the Athenians from receiving either money or any other thing.*

2. *The war with the Athenians shall be carried on jointly by the king and by the Lacedæmonians and their allies; and it shall not be lawful to make peace with the Athenians except both agree, the king on his side and the Lacedæmonians and their allies on theirs.*

3. *If any revolt from the king they shall be the enemies of the Lacedæmonians and their allies. And if any revolt from the Lacedæmonians and their allies they shall be the enemies of the king in like manner.*

19. This was the alliance. After this the Chians immediately manned ten more vessels and sailed for Anaia, in order to gain intelligence of those in Miletus, and also to make the cities revolt. A message, however, reaching them from Chalcideus to tell them to go back again, and that Amorges was at hand with an army by land, they sailed to the temple of Zeus, and there sighting ten more ships sailing up with which Diomedon had started from Athens after Thrasycles, fled, one ship to Ephesus, the rest to Teos. The Athenians took four of their ships empty, the men finding time to escape ashore; the rest took refuge in the city of the Teians; after which the Athenians sailed off to Samos, while the Chians put to sea with their remaining vessels, accompanied by the land forces, and caused Lebedos to revolt, and after it Eræ. After this they both returned home, the fleet and the army.

20. About the same time the twenty ships of the Peloponnesians in Spiræum, chased to land and blockaded by an equal number of Athenians, suddenly sallied out and defeated the blockading squadron, took four of their ships, and sailing back to Cenchreæ, prepared again for the voyage to Chios and Ionia. Here they were joined by Astyochus as high-admiral from Lacedæmon, henceforth invested with the supreme command at sea. The land forces now withdrawing from Teos, Tissaphernes repaired thither in person with an army and completed the demolition of anything that was left of the wall, and so departed. Not long after his departure Diomedon arrived with ten Athenian ships, and having made a convention by which the Teians admitted him as they had the enemy, coasted along to Eræ, and failing in an attempt upon the town, sailed back again.

21. About this time took place the rising of the commons at Samos against the upper classes, in concert with some Athenians, who were there in three vessels. The Samian commons put to death some two hundred in all of the upper classes, and banished four hundred more, and themselves took their land and houses; after which the Athenians decreed their independence, being now sure of their fidelity, and the commons henceforth governed the city, excluding the landholders from all share in affairs, and forbidding any of the commons to give his daughter in marriage to them or to take a wife from them in future.*

22. After this, during the same summer, the Chians, whose zeal continued as active as ever, and who even without the Peloponnesians found themselves in sufficient force to effect the revolt of the cities and also wished to have as many companions in peril as possible, made an expedition with thirteen ships of their own to Lesbos; the instructions from Lacedæmon being to go to that island next, and from thence to the Hellespont. Meanwhile the land forces of the Peloponnesians who were with the Chians and of the allies on the spot, moved along shore for Clazomenæ and Cuma, under the command of Eualas, a Spartan; while the fleet under Diniades, one of the Periœci,† first sailed up to Methymna and caused it to revolt, and, leaving four ships there, with the rest procured the revolt of Mitylene.

23. In the meantime Astyochus, the Lacedæmonian admiral, set sail from Cenchreæ with four ships, as he had intended, and arrived at Chios. On the third day after his arrival the Athenian ships, twenty-five in number, sailed to Lesbos under Diomedon and Leon, who had lately arrived with a reinforcement of ten ships from Athens. Late in the same day Astyochus put to sea, and taking one Chian vessel with him sailed to Lesbos to render what assistance he could.

Arrived at Pyrrha, and from thence the next day at Eresus, he there learned that Mitylene had been taken, almost without a blow, by the Athenians, who had sailed up and unexpectedly put into the harbour, had beaten the Chian ships, and landing and defeating the troops opposed to them, had become masters of the city. Informed of this by the Eresians and the Chian ships, which had been left with Eubulus at Methymna, and had fled upon the capture of Mitylene, and three of which he now fell in with, one having been taken by the Athenians, Astyochus did not go on to Mitylene, but raised and armed Eresus, and sending the heavy infantry from his own ships by land under Eteonicus to Antissa and Methymna, himself proceeded along shore thither with the ships which he had with him and with the three Chians, in the hope that the Methymnians upon seeing them would be encouraged to persevere in their revolt. As, however, everything went against him in Lesbos, he took up his own force and sailed

---

*The Samian *demos* declares for the Athenian government, a loyalty expressed in *stasis* that the Athenians do not soon forget (compare Fornara #166, a later decree honoring the Samians). Their granting of "independence" or autonomy is more a name than any political reality. The landholding upper classes, the "powerful," are excluded henceforth from intermarriage.

†Diniadas, a *perioec*, has military command of the fleet—either a reflection of extraordinary trust, or evidence of general Spartan inability on the seas.

back to Chios; the land forces on board, which were to have gone to the Hellespont, being also conveyed back to their different cities. After this six of the allied Peloponnesian ships at Cenchreæ joined the forces at Chios.

The Athenians, after restoring matters to their old state in Lesbos, set sail from thence and took Polichna, the place that the Clazomenians were fortifying on the continent, and carried the inhabitants back to their town upon the island, except the authors of the revolt, who withdrew to Daphnus; and thus Clazomenæ became once more Athenian.

24. The same summer the Athenians in the twenty ships at Lade blockading Miletus, made a descent at Panormus in the Milesian territory, and killed Chalcideus the Lacedæmonian commander, who had come with a few men against them, and the third day after sailed over and set up a trophy, which, as they were not masters of the country, was however pulled down by the Milesians.

Meanwhile, Leon and Diomedon with the Athenian fleet from Lesbos issuing from the Œnussæ, the isles off Chios, and from their forts of Sidussa and Pteleum in the Erythræid, and from Lesbos, carried on the war against the Chians from the ships, having on board heavy infantry from the rolls pressed to serve as marines. Landing in Cardamyle and in Bolissus they defeated with heavy loss the Chians that took the field against them, and laying desolate the places in that neighborhoos, defeated the Chians again in another battle at Phanæ, and in a third at Leuconium.

After this the Chians ceased to meet them in the field, while the Athenians devastated the country, which was beautifully stocked and had remained uninjured ever since the Median wars. Indeed, after the Lacedæmonians, the Chians are the only people that I have known who knew how to be wise in prosperity, and who ordered their city the more securely the greater it grew.* Nor was this revolt, in which they might seem to have erred on the side of rashness, ventured upon until they had numerous and gallant allies to share the danger with them, and until they perceived the Athenians after the Sicilian disaster themselves no longer denying the thoroughly desperate state of their affairs. And if they were thrown out by one of the surprises which upset human calculations, they found out their mistake in company with many others who believed, like them, in the speedy col-

---

*Astyochus is not an effective Spartan commander. The Athenians recover Lesbos and besiege Chios. Thucydides admires Chian self-control and institutional stability. (Fornara #19 describes the Chians' earlier oligarchy.) Since their reduction by Persia after the Ionian revolt (c.493; Herodotus 6.31), they had prospered under two empires and, for most of that time, had been as autonomous as Athenian allies could be, contributing men and ships, not mere tribute.

lapse of the Athenian power.* While they were thus blockaded from the sea and plundered by land, some of the citizens undertook to bring the city over to the Athenians. Apprised of this the authorities took no action themselves, but brought Astyochus, the admiral, from Erythræ, with four ships that he had with him, and considered how they could most quietly, either by taking hostages or by some other means, put an end to the conspiracy.

25. While the Chians were thus engaged, a thousand Athenian heavy infantry and fifteen hundred Argives (five hundred of whom were light troops furnished with armour by the Athenians), and one thousand of the allies, towards the close of the same summer sailed from Athens in forty-eight ships, some of which were transports, under the command of Phrynichus, Onomacles, and Scironides, and putting in to Samos crossed over and encamped at Miletus. Upon this the Milesians came out to the number of eight hundred heavy infantry, with the Peloponnesians who had come with Chalcideus, and some foreign mercenaries of Tissaphernes, Tissaphernes himself and his cavalry, and engaged the Athenians and their allies.

While the Argives rushed forward on their own wing with the careless disdain of men advancing against Ionians who would never stand their charge, and were defeated by the Milesians with a loss little short of three hundred men, the Athenians first defeated the Peloponnesians, and driving before them the barbarians and the ruck of the army, without engaging the Milesians, who after the rout of the Argives retreated into the town upon seeing their comrades worsted, crowned their victory by grounding their arms under the very walls of Miletus. Thus, in this battle, the Ionians on both sides overcame the Dorians, the Athenians defeating the Peloponnesians opposed to them, and the Milesians the Argives.† After setting up a trophy, the Athenians prepared to draw a wall round the place, which stood upon an isthmus; thinking that if they could gain Miletus, the other towns also would easily come over to them.

26. Meanwhile about dusk tidings reached them that the fifty-five ships from Peloponnese and Sicily might be instantly expected. Of these the Siceliots, urged principally by the Syracusan Hermocrates to join in giving the finishing blow to the power of Athens, furnished twenty-two—twenty from Syracuse, and two from Selinus; and the ships that were preparing in Peloponnese being now ready, both

---

*Stahl observes how often such mischances govern Thucydides' reports. Thucydides alleges that their reasoning was sound and logical, merely wrong. The *paralogos* (the incalculable) tripped up the carefully calculating Chians.

†The battle for Miletus shows that ethnic prejudice was not a factor that one could depend on.

squadrons had been entrusted to Therimenes, a Lacedæmonian, to take to Astyochus, the admiral.

They now put in first at Leros the island off Miletus, and from thence, discovering that the Athenians were before the town, sailed into the Iasic gulf, in order to learn how matters stood at Miletus. Meanwhile Alcibiades came on horseback to Teichiussa in the Milesian territory, the point of the gulf at which they had put in for the night, and told them of the battle, in which he had fought in person by the side of the Milesians and Tissaphernes, and advised them, if they did not wish to sacrifice Ionia and their cause, to fly to the relief of Miletus and hinder its siege.*

27. Accordingly they resolved to relieve it the next morning. Meanwhile Phrynichus, the Athenian commander, had received precise intelligence of the fleet from Leros, and when his colleagues expressed a wish to keep the sea and fight it out, flatly refused either to stay himself or to let them or any one else do so, if he could help it.† Where they could hereafter contend, after full and undisturbed preparation, with an exact knowledge of the number of the enemy's fleet and of the force which they could oppose to him, he would never allow the reproach of disgrace to drive him into a risk that was unreasonable. It was no disgrace for an Athenian fleet to retreat when it suited them: put it as they would, it would be more disgraceful to be beaten, and to expose the city not only to disgrace, but to the most serious danger. After its late misfortunes it could hardly be justified in voluntarily taking the offensive even with the strongest force, except in a case of absolute necessity: much less then without compulsion could it rush upon peril of its own seeking. He told them to take up their wounded as quickly as they could and the troops and stores which they had brought with them, and leaving behind what they had taken from the enemy's country, in order to lighten the ships, to sail off to Samos, and there concentrating all their ships to attack as opportunity served. As he spoke so he acted; and thus not now more than afterwards, nor in this alone but in all that he had to do with, did Phrynichus show himself a man of sense.‡ In this

---

*Leros lies 40 miles away, but it does command one of the approaches to the harbor of Miletus. The manuscripts are not unanimous about the island named. Alcibiades here gives advice from which his allies benefit.

†Phrynichus is one of several oligarchically inclined Athenians who earned Thucydides' admiration, here for his caution when Athens had few ships at sea. Although, like several others, he was originally elected by the democracy, he becomes determined to change Athens' form of government (see 8.48 ff.), although his motivation largely arose from personal differences with the dangerous Alcibiades (8.90; Phrynichus' assassination is reported at 8.92).

‡Thucydides' admiration for Phrynichus' intelligent caution here was not shared by all at the time (8.54) or by all later scholars. The word used for Phrynichus' good sense derives from the same stem as that employed for Themistocles'.

way that very evening the Athenians broke up from before Miletus, leaving their victory unfinished, and the Argives, mortified at their disaster, promptly sailed off home from Samos.

28. As soon as it was morning the Peloponnesians weighed from Teichiussa and put into Miletus after the departure of the Athenians; they stayed one day, and on the next took with them the Chian vessels originally chased into port with Chalcideus, and resolved to sail back for the tackle which they had put on shore at Teichiussa. Upon their arrival Tissaphernes came to them with his land forces and induced them to sail to Iasus, which was held by his enemy Amorges. Accordingly they suddenly attacked and took Iasus, whose inhabitants never imagined that the ships could be other than Athenian. The Syracusans distinguished themselves most in the action. Amorges, a bastard of Pissuthnes and a rebel from the king, was taken alive and handed over to Tissaphernes, to carry to the king, if he chose, according to his orders: Iasus was sacked by the army,* who found a very great booty there, the place being wealthy from ancient date. The mercenaries serving with Amorges the Peloponnesians received and enrolled in their army without doing them any harm, since most of them came from Peloponnese, and handed over the town to Tissaphernes with all the captives, bond or free, at the stipulated price of one Daric stater a head;† after which they returned to Miletus. Pedaritus, son of Leon, who had been sent by the Lacedæmonians to take the command at Chios, they despatched by land as far as Erythræ with the mercenaries taken from Amorges; appointing Philip to remain as governor of Miletus.

Summer was now over.

29. The winter following Tissaphernes put Iasus in a state of defence, and passing on to Miletus distributed a month's pay to all the ships as he had promised at Lacedæmon, at the rate of an Attic drachma a day for each man. In future, however, he was resolved not to give more than three obols, until he had consulted the king; when if the king should so order he would give, he said, the full drachma. However, upon the protest of the Syracusan general Hermocrates (for as Therimenes was not admiral, but only accompanied them in order to hand over the ships to Astyochus, he made little difficulty

---

*Tissaphernes persuades the Peloponnesians to do his dirty work. Iasus and the rebel Amorges are captured and the latter is not heard from again—but one can imagine his torture and execution from similar instances. The Athenians had not been able to support him sufficiently after Sicily, and the Peloponnesians did not care what became of him. Iasus on the mainland lies south of Miletus, toward Caria (map 12).

†A Daric stater was a gold coin worth 20 Athenian silver drachmas; it weighed approximately 8.4 grams. The ransom provided pay for the Peloponnesians and saved the lives of the Iasians.

about the pay), it was agreed that the amount of five ships' pay should be given over and above the three obols a day for each man; Tissaphernes paying thirty talents a month for fifty-five ships, and to the rest, for as many ships as they had beyond that number, at the same rate.*

30. The same winter the Athenians in Samos having been joined by thirty-five more vessels from home under Charminus, Strombichides, and Euctemon, called in their squadron at Chios and all the rest, intending to blockade Miletus with their navy, and to send a fleet and an army against Chios; drawing lots for the respective services. This intention they carried into effect; Strombichides, Onamacles, and Euctemon sailing against Chios, which fell to their lot, with thirty ships and a part of the thousand heavy infantry, who had been to Miletus, in transports; while the rest remained masters of the sea with seventy-four ships at Samos, and advanced upon Miletus.

31. Meanwhile Astyochus, at Chios collecting the hostages required in consequence of the conspiracy,† stopped upon learning that the fleet with Therimenes had arrived, and that the affairs of the league were in a more flourishing condition. Putting out to sea with ten Peloponnesian and as many Chian vessels, after a futile attack upon Pteleum, he coasted on to Clazomenæ, and ordered the Athenian party to remove inland to Daphnus, and to join the Peloponnesians, an order in which also joined Tamos the king's lieutenant in Ionia. This order being disregarded, Astyochus made an attack upon the town, which was unwalled, and having failed to take it was himself carried off by a strong gale to Phocæa and Cuma, while the rest of the ships put in at the islands adjacent to Clazomenæ, Marathussa, Pele, and Drymussa. Here they were detained eight days by the winds, and plundering and consuming all the property of the Clazomenians there deposited, put the rest on shipboard and sailed off to Phocæa and Cuma to join Astyochus.

32. While he was there, envoys arrived from the Lesbians who wished to revolt again. With Astyochus they were successful; but the Corinthians and the other allies being averse to it by reason of their former failure, he weighed anchor and set sail for Chios, where they

---

*Hermocrates took the agreement with Tissaphernes at face value, although no amount was specified at 8.5. Tissaphernes later suborned Astyochus and perhaps Therimenes. In winter 412/411, the rate was reduced from a drachma a day to half that, 3 obols plus change.

†Astyochus organized the securing of Chios town, and he maintained communication with the besieged Ionians and their Spartan commander Pedaritus at Miletus. He, however, had not the zest and resilience, much less the success, of Gylippus leading non-Spartan forces at Syracuse. Gylippus, to be sure, had the advantage of defending a city never subject to the Athenians.

eventually arrived from different quarters, the fleet having been scattered by a storm. After this, Pedaritus,* marching along the coast from Miletus, arrived at Erythræ, and thence crossed over with his army to Chios, where he found also about five hundred soldiers who had been left there by Chalcideus from the five ships with their arms. Meanwhile some Lesbians making offers to revolt, Astyochus urged upon Pedaritus and the Chians that they ought to go with their ships and effect the revolt of Lesbos, and so increase the number of their allies, or, if not successful, at all events harm the Athenians. The Chians, however, turned a deaf ear to this, and Pedaritus flatly refused to give up to him the Chian vessels.

33. Upon this Astyochus took five Corinthian and one Megarian vessel, with another from Hermione, and the ships which had come with him from Laconia, and set sail for Miletus to assume his command as admiral; after telling the Chians with many threats that he would certainly not come and help them if they should be in need.† At Corycus in the Erythræid he brought to for the night; the Athenian armament sailing from Samos against Chios being only separated from him by a hill, upon the other side of which it brought to; so that neither perceived the other. But a letter arriving in the night from Pedaritus to say that some liberated Erythræan prisoners had come from Samos to betray Erythræ, Astyochus at once put back to Erythræ, and so just escaped falling in with the Athenians. Here Pedaritus sailed over to join him; and after inquiry into the pretended treachery, finding that the whole story had been made up to procure the escape of the men from Samos, they acquitted them of the charge,‡ and sailed away, Pedaritus to Chios and Astyochus to Miletus, as he had intended.

34. Meanwhile the Athenian armament sailing round Corycus fell in with three Chian men of war off Arginus, and gave immediate chase. A great storm coming on, the Chians with difficulty took refuge in the harbour; the three Athenian vessels most forward in the pursuit being wrecked and thrown up near the city of Chios, and the crews slain or taken prisoners. The rest of the Athenian fleet took refuge in the harbour called Phœnicus, under Mount Mimas, and from thence afterwards put into Lesbos and prepared for the work of fortification.

---

*The Lesbians wanted to try revolt again, after their earlier defeat (8.22–23), but Chios seemed a surer hope of success to the Corinthians.

†Astyochus and Pedaritus were not in agreement, and the former, now commander of the Peloponnesian fleet stationed at Miletus, became angry with the besieged Chians.

‡The Erythraeans, from a coastal city on the peninsula opposite Chios, hatched an ostensibly pro-Athenian plan in order to obtain their liberty from their Samian captors. Once they were freed, the supposed treachery (against the Peloponnesian confederacy) was revealed as only a ruse to get away.

35. The same winter the Lacedæmonian Hippocrates sailed out from Peloponnese with ten Thurian ships under the command of Dorieus, son of Diagoras, and two colleagues, one Laconian and one Syracusan vessel, and arrived at Cnidus, which had already revolted at the instigation of Tissaphernes. When their arrival was known at Miletus, orders came to them to leave half their squadron to guard Cnidus, and with the rest to cruise round Triopium and seize all the merchantmen arriving from Egypt.* Triopium is a promontory of Cnidus and sacred to Apollo. This coming to the knowledge of the Athenians, they sailed from Samos and captured the six ships on the watch at Triopium, the crews escaping out of them. After this the Athenians sailed into Cnidus and made an assault upon the town, which was unfortified, and all but took it; and the next day assaulted it again, but with less effect, as the inhabitants had improved their defences during the night, and had been reinforced by the crews escaped from the ships at Triopium. The Athenians now withdrew, and after plundering the Cnidian territory sailed back to Samos.

36. About the same time Astyochus came to the fleet at Miletus. The Peloponnesian camp was still plentifully supplied, being in receipt of sufficient pay, and the soldiers having still in hand the large booty taken at Iasus. The Milesians also showed great ardour for the war. Nevertheless the Peloponnesians thought the first convention with Tissaphernes, made with Chalcideus, defective, and more advantageous to him than to them,[†] and consequently while Therimenes was still there concluded another, which was as follows:—

37. *The convention of the Lacedæmonians and the allies with King Darius and the sons of the king, and with Tissaphernes for a treaty and friendship, as follows:—*

1. Neither the Lacedæmonians nor the allies of the Lacedæmonians shall make war against or otherwise injure any country or cities that belong to King Darius or did belong to his father or to his ancestors: neither shall the Lacedæmonians nor the allies of the Lacedæmonians exact tribute from such cities. Neither shall King Darius nor any of the

---

*The Athenians fed themselves through overseas trade and tribute. Some of the grain came from Egypt, a dependency of the Persians that was sometimes in revolt. To cut off this basic provisioning would hasten the fall of Athens. Cnidus was situated on a promontory in southwestern Asia Minor, south of the island of Cos (map 12). Ships from Egypt could cross the open sea, or go up along the Levantine littoral, but when they reached southern Asia Minor, they would prefer the coastal route and cross through the islands, where harbors offer possible protection against storms.

†Therimenes' treaty gave away to the Persians less than Chalcideus' had allowed. Thucydides leaves it unclear whether the parties ratified either of the first two. He presents the third with fuller formalities.

subjects of the king make war against or otherwise injure the Lacedæmonians or their allies.

2. *If the Lacedæmonians or their allies should require any assistance from the king, or the king from the Lacedæmonians or their allies, whatever they both agree upon they shall be right in doing.*

3. *Both shall carry on jointly the war against the Athenians and their allies; and if they make peace, both shall do so jointly.*

4. *The expense of all troops in the king's country, sent for by the king, shall be borne by the king.* *

5. *If any of the states comprised in this convention with the king attack the king's country, the rest shall stop them and aid the king to the best of their power. And if any in the king's country or in the countries under the king's rule attack the country of the Lacedæmonians or their allies, the king shall stop it and help them to the best of his power.*

38. After this convention Therimenes handed over the fleet to Astyochus, sailed off in a small boat, and was lost. The Athenian armament had now crossed over from Lesbos to Chios, and being master by sea and land began to fortify Delphinium, a place naturally strong on the land side, provided with more than one harbour, and also not far from the city of Chios. Meanwhile the Chians remained inactive. Already defeated in so many battles, they were now also at discord among themselves; the execution of the party of Tydeus, son of Ion, by Pedaritus upon the charge of Atticism, followed by the forcible imposition of an oligarchy upon the rest of the city, having made them suspicious of one another; and they therefore thought neither themselves nor the mercenaries under Pedaritus a match for the enemy.† They sent, however, to Miletus to beg Astyochus to assist them, which he refused to do, and was accordingly denounced at Lacedæmon by Pedaritus as a traitor.‡ Such was the state of the Athenian affairs at Chios; while their fleet at Samos kept sailing out against the enemy in Miletus, until they found that he would not accept their challenge, and then retired again to Samos and remained quiet.

39. In the same winter the twenty-seven ships equipped by the Lacedæmonians for Pharnabazus through the agency of the Megarian

---

*The King will provide for his troops and the Peloponnesians while they are based in his nominal realm. This arrangement would be rather more attractive if his own troops ever had participated in significant numbers (such as the phantom of the long-awaited but never delivered 147 ships of the Phoenician fleet). See 8.87 for Thucydides' analysis of this continuing source of friction between the Persians and the Peloponnesians.

†Class warfare, or at least political division based on property, keeps the Chians from their most effective resistance.

‡Pedaritus needs the forces of Astyochus at Miletus, but true to his word, he does not assist them as they had not assisted him. This leads to a serious accusation at home.

Calligeitus, and the Cyzicene Timagoras, put out from Peloponnese and sailed for Ionia about the time of the solstice, under the command of Antisthenes, a Spartan. With them the Lacedæmonians also sent eleven Spartans as advisers to Astyochus; Lichas, son of Arcesilaus, being among the number.* Arrived at Miletus, their orders were to aid in generally superintending the good conduct of the war; to send off the above ships or a greater or less number to the Hellespont to Pharnabazus, if they thought proper, appointing Clearchus, son of Ramphias, who sailed with them, to the command; and further, if they thought proper, to make Antisthenes admiral, dismissing Astyochus, whom the letters of Pedaritus had caused to be regarded with suspicion. Sailing accordingly from Malea across the open sea, the squadron touched at Melos and there fell in with ten Athenian ships, three of which they took empty and burned. After this, being afraid that the Athenian vessels escaped from Melos might, as they in fact did, give information of their approach to the Athenians at Samos, they sailed to Crete, and having lengthened their voyage by way of precaution made land at Caunus in Asia, from whence considering themselves in safety they sent a message to the fleet at Miletus for a convoy along the coast.†

40. Meanwhile the Chians and Pedaritus, undeterred by the backwardness of Astyochus, went on sending messengers pressing him to come with all the fleet to assist them against their besiegers, and not to leave the greatest of the allied states in Ionia to be shut up by sea and overrun and pillaged by land.

There were more slaves at Chios than in any one other city except Lacedæmon, and being also by reason of their numbers punished more rigorously when they offended, most of them when they saw the Athenian armament firmly established in the island with a fortified position, immediately deserted to the enemy, and through their knowledge of the country did the greatest mischief.‡ The Chians therefore urged upon Astyochus that it was his duty to assist them, while there was still a hope and a possibility of stopping the enemy's progress, while Delphinium was still in process of fortification and unfinished, and before the completion of a higher rampart which was being added to protect the camp and fleet of their besiegers. Asty-

---

*A Spartan commander, after accusations and lack of victories, might be outfitted with overseers or advisers. Lichas is mentioned because he will be prominent in negotiations to follow.

†The Peloponnesians had lost their initial confidence after victory in Sicily and now advanced, keeping close to friendly shores.

‡Again, slaves can and will desert when a dependable opportunity presents itself, and Chios has been noted for its riches of all sorts. Athens as well as Sparta and Chios had huge numbers of slaves; recall that 20,000 deserted after the fortification of Decelea.

ochus now saw that the allies also wished it and prepared to go, in spite of his intention to the contrary owing to his prior threat.

41. In the meantime news came from Caunus of the arrival of the twenty-seven ships with the Lacedæmonian commissioners; and Astyochus postponing everything to the duty of convoying a fleet of that importance, in order to be more able to command the sea; and to the safe conduct of the Lacedæmonians sent as spies over his behaviour, at once gave up going to Chios and set sail for Caunus. As he coasted along he landed at the Meropid Cos and sacked the city, which was unfortified and had been lately laid in ruins by an earthquake, by far the greatest in living memory, and, as the inhabitants had fled to the mountains, overran the country and made booty of all it contained, letting go, however, the free men.

From Cos arriving in the night at Cnidus he was constrained by the representations of the Cnidians not to disembark the sailors, but to sail as he was straight against the twenty Athenian vessels, which with Charminus, one of the commanders at Samos, were on the watch for the very twenty-seven ships from Peloponnese which Astyochus was himself sailing to join; the Athenians in Samos having heard from Melos of their approach, and Charminus being on the look-out off Syme, Chalce, Rhodes, and Lycia, as he now heard that they were at Caunus.

42. Astyochus accordingly sailed as he was to Syme, before he was heard of, in the hope of catching the enemy somewhere out at sea. Rain, however, and foggy weather encountered him, and caused his ships to straggle and get into disorder in the dark. In the morning his fleet had parted company and was most of it still straggling round the island, and the left wing only in sight of Charminus and the Athenians. They took it for the squadron which they were watching for from Caunus, and hastily put out against it with part only of their twenty vessels, and attacking immediately sank three ships and disabled others, and had the advantage in the action until the main body of the fleet unexpectedly hove in sight, when they were surrounded on every side. Upon this they took to flight, and after losing six ships, with the rest escaped to Teutlussa or Beet Island, and from thence to Halicarnassus. After this the Peloponnesians put into Cnidus, and being joined by the twenty-seven ships from Caunus, sailed all together and set up a trophy in Syme, and then returned to anchor at Cnidus.

43. As soon as the Athenians knew of the sea-fight they sailed with all the ships at Samos to Syme, and without attacking or being attacked by the fleet at Cnidus, took the ships' tackle left at Syme, and touching at Lorymi on the main land sailed back to Samos. Meanwhile the Peloponnesian ships being now all at Cnidus, underwent such repairs as were needed; while the eleven Lacedæmonian commissioners conferred with Tissaphernes, who had come to meet them, upon the points which did not satisfy them in the past transactions, and upon the best and mutually most advantageous manner of conducting the war in future.*

The severest critic of the present proceedings was Lichas, who said that neither of the treaties could stand, neither that of Chalcideus, nor that of Therimenes; it being monstrous that the king should at this date pretend to the possession of all the country formerly ruled by himself or by his ancestors—a pretension which implicitly put back under the yoke all the islands, Thessaly, Locris, and everything as far as Bœotia, and made the Lacedæmonians give to the Hellenes instead of liberty a Median master.† He therefore invited Tissaphernes to conclude another and a better treaty, as they certainly would not recognise those existing and did not want any of his pay upon such conditions. This offended Tissaphernes so much that he went away in a rage without settling anything.

Twentieth and Twenty-first Years of the War—Intrigues of Alcibiades—Withdrawal of the Persian Subsidies—Oligarchical Coup d'État at Athens—Patriotism of the Army at Samos

44. The Peloponnesians now determined to sail to Rhodes, upon the invitation of some of the principal men there, hoping to gain an island powerful by the number of its seamen and by its land forces, and also thinking that they would be able to maintain their fleet from their own confederacy, without having to ask for money from Tissaphernes. They accordingly at once set sail that same winter from Cnidus, and first put in with ninety-four ships at Camirus in the Rhodian country, to the great alarm of the mass of the inhabitants, who were not privy to the intrigue, and who consequently fled, especially as the town was unfortified. They were afterwards, however, assembled by the Lacedæmonians together with the inhabitants of the two other towns of Lindus and Ialysus;‡ and the Rhodians were persuaded to revolt from the Athenians and the island went over to the

---

*Lichas recognizes that the appeal of the Lacedaemonians rests on the claim of "freedom of the Greeks." If they are to gain adherents from the Athenians' subjects, they need a different treaty with the Persians.

†Lichas correctly observes that the Persian's claim would restore the Greek world to the unfree *status quo ante* at the time of the Persian Wars.

‡Ancient Rhodes, largest island of the Dodecanese off the southwestern corner of Asia Minor, had three chief cities: Lindus, Ialysus, and Rhodes town itself. All were Dorian colonial foundations.

Peloponnesians. Meanwhile the Athenians had received the alarm and set sail with the fleet from Samos to forestall them, and came within sight of the island, but being a little too late sailed off for the moment to Chalce, and from thence to Samos, and subsequently waged war against Rhodes, issuing from Chalce, Cos, and Samos.

The Peloponnesians now levied a contribution thirty-two talents from the Rhodians, after which they hauled their ships ashore and for eighty days remained inactive.

45. During this time, and even earlier, before they removed to Rhodes, the following intrigues took place. After the death of Chalcideus and the battle at Miletus, Alcibiades began to be suspected by the Peloponnesians; and Astyochus received from Lacedæmon an order from them to put him to death, he being the personal enemy of Agis, and in other respects thought unworthy of confidence.

Alcibiades in his alarm first withdrew to Tissaphernes, and immediately began to do all he could with him to injure the Peloponnesian cause. Henceforth becoming his adviser in everything, he cut down the pay from an Attic drachma to three obols a day, and even this not paid too regularly; and told Tissaphernes to say to the Peloponnesians that the Athenians, whose maritime experience was of an older date than their own, only gave their men three obols, not so much from poverty as to prevent their seamen being corrupted by being too well off, and injuring their condition by spending money upon enervating indulgences, and also paid their crews irregularly in order to have a security against their deserting in the arrears which they would leave behind them. He also told Tissaphernes to bribe the captains and generals of the cities, and so to obtain their connivance—an expedient which succeeded with all except the Syracusans, Hermocrates alone opposing him on behalf of the whole confederacy.*

Meanwhile the cities asking for money Alcibiades sent off, by roundly telling them in the name of Tissaphernes, that it was great impudence in the Chians, the richest people in Hellas, not content with being defended by a foreign force, to expect others to risk not only their lives but their money as well in behalf of their freedom; while the other cities, he said, had had to pay largely to Athens before their rebellion, and could not justly refuse to contribute as much or even more now for their own selves. He also pointed out that Tissaphernes was at present carrying on the war at his own charges, and had good cause for economy, but that as soon as he received remit-

---

*Alcibiades plays all sides against each other for his own interest. Still appearing to be on Tissaphernes' good side, he had considerable leverage. Bribery further helped his self-promoting cause. Agis almost succeeded in having his enemy killed; Hermocrates protested against the reduction in Peloponnesian pay.

tances from the king he would give them their pay in full, and do what was reasonable for the cities.

46. Alcibiades further advised Tissaphernes not to be in too great a hurry to end the war, or to let himself be persuaded to bring up the Phœnician fleet which he was equipping, or to provide pay for more Hellenes, and thus put the power by land and sea into the same hands; but to leave each of the contending parties in possession of element, thus enabling the king when he found one troublesome to call in the other.* For if the command of the sea and land were united in one hand, he would not know where to turn for help to overthrow the dominant power; unless he at last chose to stand up himself, and go through with the struggle at great expense and hazard. The cheapest plan was to let the Hellenes wear each other out, at a small share of the expense and without risk to himself. Besides, he would find the Athenians the most convenient partners in empire as they did not aim at conquests on shore, and carried on the war upon principles and with a practice most advantageous to the king; being prepared to combine to conquer the sea for Athens, and for the king all the Hellenes inhabiting his country, whom the Peloponnesians, on the contrary, had come to liberate. Now it was not likely that the Lacedæmonians would free the Hellenes from the Hellenic Athenians, without freeing them also from the barbarian Mede, unless overthrown by him in the meanwhile.

Alcibiades therefore urged him to wear them both out at first, and after docking the Athenian power as much as he could, forthwith to rid the country of the Peloponnesians.† In the main Tissaphernes approved of this policy, so far at least as could be conjectured from his behaviour; since he now gave his confidence to Alcibiades in recognition of his good advice, and kept the Peloponnesians short of money, and would not let them fight at sea, but ruined their cause by pretending that the Phœnician fleet would arrive, and that they would thus be enabled to contend with the odds in their favour, and so made their navy lose its

---

*Alcibiades' advice to Tissaphernes was sound for Persian purposes. One wonders if the clever Persian needed it. Perhaps Alcibiades or an associate was Thucydides' informant at this time or later. Persia was not strong enough to expel either Hellenic power from Asia Minor, if one got the upper hand. Playing them against each other would give the Persians the most opportunities to recover their lost territories. This advice is both strategic and cheaper than trying to conclude the war with the help of one side or the other. The chosen ally would have to be paid for its services. Alcibiades' maneuvering in book 8 colors one's evaluation of his comments about his lack of patriotism when speaking at Sparta (6.89–92).

†Tissaphernes certainly followed this Machiavellian strategy of wearing down both sides. The Peloponnesians would be less of a nuisance but no more enthusiastic about Persian control of Greeks than the Athenians had been.

efficiency, which had been very remarkable, and generally betrayed a coolness in the war that was too plain to be mistaken.*

47. Alcibiades gave this advice to Tissaphernes and the king, with whom he then was, not merely because he thought it really the best, but because he was studying means to effect his restoration to his country, well knowing that if he did not destroy it he might one day hope to persuade the Athenians to recall him, and thinking that his best chance of persuading them lay in letting them see that he possessed the favour of Tissaphernes. The event proved him to be right.† When the Athenians at Samos found that he had influence with Tissaphernes, principally of their own motion (though partly also through Alcibiades himself sending word to their chief men to tell the best men in the army,‡ that if there were only an oligarchy in the place of the rascally democracy that had banished him, he would be glad to return to his country and to make Tissaphernes their friend), the captains and chief men in the armament at once embraced the idea of subverting the democracy.§

48. The design was first mooted in the camp; and afterwards from thence reached the city. Some persons crossed over from Samos and had an interview with Alcibiades, who immediately offered to make first Tissaphernes, and afterwards the king, their friend, if they would give up the democracy, and make it possible for the king to trust them. The higher class, who also suffered most severely from the war, now conceived great hopes of getting the government into their own hands, and of triumphing over the enemy.

Upon their return to Samos the emissaries formed their partisans into a club, and openly told the mass of the armament that the king would be their friend, and would provide them with money, if Alcibiades were restored, and the democracy abolished. The multitude, if at first irritated by these intrigues, were nevertheless kept quiet by the advantageous prospect of the pay from the king; and the oligarchical conspirators, after making this communication to the peo-

---

*Peloponnesian morale declined with delay just as the Athenian fleet's had evaporated at Syracuse. Thucydides admits that he does not know what Tissaphernes had in mind but conjectures from what happened.

†The Greek three-word phrase *hoper kai egeneto* ("which in fact happened"—translated by Crawley as "the event proved him to be right") is a Thucydidean favorite, for a plan or prediction that (unexpectedly) plays out as hoped or expected. Alcibiades wanted a recall, and Tissaphernes' friendship was to be his ticket back to Athens.

‡Alcibiades intrigued with the politically prominent and with the "best men," Hellenic code language for the aristocratic wealthy.

§The views (such as "rascally") are those of Alcibiades, presented in indirect statement. Many in the wealthy classes grew tired of demagogues and of this war, as did many of the poor. By their superior position in the military (the army was organized on plutocratic principles) they were in position to participate in a change of regime.

ple, now re-examined the proposals of Alcibiades among themselves, with most of their associates.

Unlike the rest, who thought them advantageous and trustworthy, Phrynichus, who was still general, by no means approved of the proposals.* Alcibiades, he rightly thought, cared no more for an oligarchy than for a democracy, and only sought to change the institutions of his country in order to get himself recalled by his associates; while for themselves their one object should be to avoid civil discord. It was not the king's interest, when the Peloponnesians were now their equals at sea, and in possession of some of the chief cities in his empire, to go out of his way to side with the Athenians whom he did not trust, when he might make friends of the Peloponnesians who had never injured him.

And as for the allied states to whom oligarchy was now offered, because the democracy was to be put down at Athens, he well knew that this would not make the rebels come in any the sooner, or confirm the loyal in their allegiance; as the allies would never prefer servitude with an oligarchy or democracy to freedom with the constitution which they actually enjoyed, to whichever type it belonged. Besides, the cities thought that the so-called better classes† would prove just as oppressive as the commons, as being those who originated, proposed, and for the most part benefited from the acts of the commons injurious to the confederates. Indeed, if it depended on the better classes, the confederates would be put to death without trial and with violence; while the commons were their refuge and the chastiser of these men. This he positively knew that the cities had learned by experience, and that such was their opinion.‡ The propositions of Al-

---

*Phrynichus the *strategos*, perhaps by native intelligence, but certainly because of his poor relationship with Alcibiades, analyzed the situation differently. He observed (and Thucydides endorses the view) that Alcibiades was interested in his own recall, not the form of the constitution. Further, he realized and said that the Persian king had no strategic reason to cooperate with the Athenians, competitors with his own empire for the same territories.

†This reported opinion of Phrynichus is important evidence that the subject cities, or at least their commoners (*hoi polloi*), considered a democratic constitution under Athenian control of foreign policy more congenial than a potential autonomy under their own oligarchs. Phrynichus also argues that the wealthier classes have reaped the principal profits of membership in the Athenian empire. "So-called" refers to the social catchword label "noble and good" (*kaloi k'agathoi*), the Athenian elite's name for themselves.

‡Phrynichus also recognizes that the Athenian popular courts were more merciful to malefactors than oligarchic cabals, a point that will be ratified by the behavior of the government of the Four Hundred in the near future. Here, with Thucydides' implicit agreement, we find a different opinion of the stability and law-abidingness of the democracy and its imperial administration.

cibiades, and the intrigues now in progress, could therefore never meet with his approval.

49. However, the members of the conspiratorial association assembled, agreeably to their original determination, accepted what was proposed, and prepared to send Pisander and others on an embassy to Athens to treat for the restoration of Alcibiades and the abolition of the democracy in the city, and thus to make Tissaphernes the friend of the Athenians.

50. Phrynichus now saw that there would be a proposal to restore Alcibiades, and that the Athenians would consent to it; and fearing after what he had said against it that Alcibiades, if restored, would revenge himself upon him for his opposition, had recourse to the following expedient.* He sent a secret letter to the Lacedæmonian admiral, Astyochus, who was still in the neighbourhood of Miletus; to tell him that Alcibiades was ruining their cause by making Tissaphernes the friend of the Athenians, and containing an express revelation of the rest of the intrigue, desiring to be excused if he sought to harm his enemy even at the expense of the interests of his country. However, Astyochus, instead of thinking of punishing Alcibiades, who, besides, no longer ventured within his reach as formerly, went up to him and Tissaphernes at Magnesia, communicated to them the letter from Samos, and turned informer, and if report may be trusted, became the paid creature of Tissaphernes, undertaking to inform him as to this and all other matters; which was also the reason why he did not remonstrate more strongly against the pay not being given in full.

Upon this Alcibiades instantly sent to the authorities at Samos a letter against Phrynichus, stating what he had done, and requiring that he should be put to death. Phrynichus distracted, and placed in the utmost peril by the denunciation, sent again to Astyochus, reproaching him with having so ill kept the secret of his previous letter, and saying that he was now prepared to give them an opportunity of destroying the whole Athenian armament at Samos; giving a detailed account of the means which he should employ, Samos being unfortified, and pleading that being in danger of his life on their account, he could not now be blamed by his mortal enemies. This also Astyochus revealed to Alcibiades.

51. Meanwhile Phrynichus having had timely notice that he was playing him false, and that a letter on the subject was on the point of arriving from Alcibiades, himself anticipated the news, and told the army that the enemy, seeing that Samos was unfortified and the fleet not all stationed within the harbour, meant to attack the camp; that

---

*We know Pisander only from this pivotal moment in Athenian history. Phrynichus schemes mightily to save his skin and to keep Alcibiades at a distance.

he could be certain of this intelligence, and that they must fortify Samos as quickly as possible, and generally look to their defences. He was general, and had himself authority to carry out these measures. Accordingly they addressed themselves to the work of fortification, and Samos was thus fortified sooner than it would otherwise have been. Not long afterwards came the letter from Alcibiades, saying that the army was betrayed by Phrynichus, and the enemy about to attack it. Alcibiades, however, gained no credit, it being thought that he was in the secret of the enemy's designs, and had tried to fasten them upon Phrynichus, and to make out that he was their accomplice, out of hatred; and consequently far from hurting him he rather bore witness to what he had said by this intelligence.

52. After this Alcibiades set to work to persuade Tissaphernes to become the friend of the Athenians. Tissaphernes, although afraid of the Peloponnesians because they had more ships in Asia than the Athenians, was yet disposed to be persuaded if he could, especially after his quarrel with the Peloponnesians at Cnidus about the treaty of Therimenes. The quarrel had already taken place, as the Peloponnesians were by this time actually at Rhodes; and in it the original argument of Alcibiades touching the liberation of all the towns by the Lacedæmonians had been verified by the declaration of Lichas, that it was impossible to submit to a convention which made the king master of all the states at any former time ruled by himself or by his fathers.

53. While Alcibiades was besieging the favour of Tissaphernes with an earnestness proportioned to the greatness of the issue, the Athenian envoys who had been despatched from Samos with Pisander arrived at Athens, and made a speech before the people, giving a brief summary of their views, and particularly insisting that if Alcibiades were recalled and the democratic constitution changed, they could have the king as their ally, and would be able to overcome the Peloponnesians. A number of speakers opposed them on the question of the democracy, the enemies of Alcibiades cried out against the scandal of a restoration to be effected by a violation of the constitution, and the Eumolpidæ and Ceryces protested in behalf of the Mysteries, the cause of his banishment, and called upon the gods to avert his recall. Pisander, in the midst of much opposition and abuse, came forward, and taking each of his opponents aside asked him the following question:—In the face of the fact that the Peloponnesians had as many ships as their own confronting them at sea, more cities in alliance with them, and the king and Tissaphernes to supply them with money, of which the Athenians had none left, had he any hope of saving the state, unless some one could induce the king to come over to their side? Upon their replying that they had not, he then plainly said to them: 'This we cannot have unless we have a more moderate form of government, and put the offices into fewer hands, and so gain the king's confidence, and forthwith restore Alcibiades, who is the only man living that can bring this about. The safety of the state, not the form of its government, is for the moment the most pressing question, as we can always change afterwards whatever we do not like.'*

54. The people were at first highly irritated at the mention of an oligarchy, but upon understanding clearly from Pisander that this was the only resource left, they took counsel of their fears, and promised themselves some day to change the government again, and gave way. They accordingly voted that Pisander should sail with ten others and make the best arrangement that they could with Tissaphernes and Alcibidas. At the same time the people, upon a false accusation of Pisander, dismissed Phrynichus from his post together with his colleague Scironides, sending Diomedon and Leon to replace them in the command of the fleet. The accusation was that Phrynichus had betrayed Iasus and Amorges; and Pisander brought it because he thought him a man unfit for the business now in hand with Alcibiades. Pisander also went the round of all the associations already existing in the city for help in lawsuits and elections,† and urged them to draw together and to unite their efforts for the overthrow of the democracy; and after taking all other measures required by the circumstances, so that no time might be lost, set off with his ten companions on his voyage to Tissaphernes.

55. In the same winter Leon and Diomedon, who had by this time joined the fleet, made an attack upon Rhodes. The ships of the Peloponnesians they found hauled up on shore, and after making a descent upon the coast and defeating the Rhodians who appeared in the field against them, withdrew to Chalce and made that place their base of operations instead of Cos, as they could better observe from thence if the Peloponnesian fleet put out to sea. Meanwhile Xenophantes, a Laconian, came to Rhodes from Pedaritus at Chios, with the news that the fortification of the Athenians was now finished, and that, unless the whole Peloponnesian fleet came to the rescue, the cause in Chios must be lost. Upon this they resolved to go to his relief. In the meantime Pedaritus, with the mercenaries that he had with

---

*Pisander presents a dilemma in direct speech that is brief but dramatic. He persuades the *demos* to allow an oligarchy in order to obtain both the help of Alcibiades and the military or financial support of the King. Phrynichus was dismissed.

†The associations for political and legal assistance (*synomosia* or "groups sworn together"), like modern fraternal organizations, were self-help clubs that would also contribute to funeral arrangements, if need be. (There was no social security safety net, little in the way of insurance associations.) The associations of the rich here, and in other cities, were natural bases for political subversion of the despised democratic governments.

him and the whole force of the Chians, made an assault upon the work round the Athenian ships and took a portion of it, and got possession of some vessels that were hauled up on shore, when the Athenians sallied out to the rescue, and first routing the Chians, next defeated the remainder of the force round Pedaritus, who was himself killed, with many of the Chians, a great number of arms being also taken.

56. After this the Chians were besieged even more straitly than before by land and sea, and the famine in the place was great. Meanwhile the Athenian envoys with Pisander arrived at the court of Tissaphernes, and conferred with him about the proposed agreement. However, Alcibiades, not being altogether sure of Tissaphernes (who feared the Peloponnesians more than the Athenians, and besides wished to wear out both parties, as Alcibiades himself had recommended), had recourse to the following stratagem to make the treaty between the Athenians and Tissaphernes miscarry by reason of the magnitude of his demands.

In my opinion Tissaphernes desired this result, fear being his motive; while Alcibiades, who now saw that Tissaphernes was determined not to treat on any terms, wished the Athenians to think, not that he was unable to persuade Tissaphernes, but that after the latter had been persuaded and was willing to join them, they had not conceded enough to him.* For the demands of Alcibiades, speaking for Tissaphernes, who was present, were so extravagant that the Athenians, although for a long while they agreed to whatever he asked, yet had to bear the blame of failure: he required the cession of the whole of Ionia, next of the islands adjacent, besides other concessions, and these passed without opposition; at last, in the third interview, Alcibiades, who now feared a complete discovery of his inability, required them to allow the king to build ships and sail along his own coast wherever and with as many as he pleased.† Upon this the Athenians would yield no further, and concluding that there was nothing to be done, but that they had been deceived by Alcibiades, went away in a passion and proceeded to Samos.

---

*Alcibiades' stratagems are nearly played out. The Athenians have accepted his instigation of revolutionary change to bring about Tissaphernes' assistance by treaty, but Tissaphernes is following his best advice, to wear down both sides. To avoid exposure as an impotent middleman, he raises the demands made of the Athenians.

†One puzzles over the damaging Athenian cessions of Ionia and adjacent islands, including Samos, the center of Athenian tribute and current operations. The ultimatum would negate all the Athenian achievements after the Persian Wars and more than symbolically acknowledge the King's superiority in eastern waters. The envoys of the Athenian oligarchs must depart with nothing accomplished. Tissaphernes' bluff has been called.

57. Tissaphernes immediately after this, in the same winter, proceeded along shore to Caunus, desiring to bring the Peloponnesian fleet back to Miletus, and to supply them with pay, making a fresh convention upon such terms as he could get, in order not to bring matters to an absolute breach between them. He was afraid that if many of their ships were left without pay they would be compelled to engage and be defeated, or that their vessels being left without hands, the Athenians would attain their objects without his assistance. Still more he feared that the Peloponnesians might ravage the continent in search of supplies. Having calculated and considered all this, agreeably to his plan of keeping the two sides equal,* he now sent for the Peloponnesians and gave them pay, and concluded with them a third treaty in words following:—

58. *In the thirteenth year of the reign of Darius, while Alexippidas was Ephor at Lacedæmon, a convention was concluded in the plain of the Mæander by the Lacedæmonians and their allies with Tissaphernes, Hieramenes, and the sons of Pharnaces, concerning the affairs of the king and of the Lacedæmonians and their allies.†*

1. *The country of the king in Asia shall be the king's, and the king shall treat his own country as he pleases.*

2. *The Lacedæmonians and their allies shall not invade or injure the king's country; neither shall the king invade or injure that of the Lacedæmonians or of their allies. If any of the Lacedæmonians or of their allies invade or injure the king's country, the Lacedæmonians and their allies shall prevent it; and if any from the king's country invade or injure the country of the Lacedæmonians or of their allies, the king shall prevent it.*

3. *Tissaphernes shall provide pay for the ships now present, according to the agreement, until the arrival of the king's vessels; but after the arrival of the king's vessels the Lacedæmonians and their allies may pay their own ships if they wish it. If, however, they choose to receive the pay from Tissaphernes, Tissaphernes shall furnish it; and the Lacedæmonians and their allies shall repay him at the end of the war such monies as they shall have received.*

4. *After the king's vessels have arrived, the ships of the Lacedæmonians and of their allies and those of the king shall carry on the war*

---

*Tissaphernes' strategy called for changing sides as the two Hellenic powers rose alternately to momentary supremacy. At this time, although the Peloponnesians had more ships, their fleets were nearer to the breaking point, so he joined their side.

†The third agreement in 411 has a formal heading; it may be the first that both parties ratified. Darius had become king in early 423. The agreement looks forward to the arrival of the Phoenician fleet (compare 8.46: preparation; 8.87: analysis of its non-use), but meanwhile provides pay (only as a loan) for the Lacedaemonians and their allies until that blessed day of Phoenician naval presence (which never came).

jointly, according as Tissaphernes and the Lacedæmonians and their allies shall think best. If they wish to make peace with the Athenians, they shall make peace also jointly.

59. This was the treaty. After this Tissaphernes prepared to bring up the Phœnician fleet according to agreement, and to make good his other promises, or at all events wished to make it appear that he was so preparing.*

60. Winter was now drawing towards its close, when the Bœotians took Oropus by treachery, though held by an Athenian garrison. Their accomplices in this were some of the Eretrians and of the Oropians themselves, who were plotting the revolt of Eubœa, as the place was exactly opposite Eretria, and while in Athenian hands was necessarily a source of great annoyance to Eretria and the rest of Eubœa. Oropus being in their hands, the Eretrians now came to Rhodes to invite the Peloponnesians into Eubœa. The latter, however, were rather bent on the relief of the distressed Chians, and accordingly put out to sea and sailed with all their ships from Rhodes. Off Triopium they sighted the Athenian fleet out at sea sailing from Chalce, and neither attacking the other, arrived, the latter at Samos, the Peloponnesians at Miletus, seeing that it was no longer possible to relieve Chios without a battle. And this winter ended, and with it ended the twentieth year of this war of which Thucydides is the historian.[†]

61. Early in the spring of the summer following Dercyllidas, a Spartan, was sent with a small force by land to the Hellespont to effect the revolt of Abydos, which is a Milesian colony; and the Chians, while Astyochus was at a loss how to help them, were compelled to fight at sea by the pressure of the siege. While Astyochus was still at Rhodes they had received from Miletus, as their commander after the death of Pedaritus, a Spartan named Leon, who had come out with Antisthenes, and twelve vessels which had been on guard at Miletus, five of which were Thurian, four Syracusan, one from Anaia, one Milesian, and one Leon's own. Accordingly the Chians marched out in mass and took up a strong position, while thirty-six of their ships put out and engaged thirty-two of the Athenians; and after a tough fight, in which the Chians and their allies had rather the best of it, as it was now late, retired to their city.

---

*Thucydides anticipates the fact that the Phoenician fleet never materialized in Aegean waters.

†Twenty years is already longer than almost all ancient wars. There had been years and seasons without warfare, but no secure peace. The year 412 yields to 411.

62. Immediately after this Dercyllidas arrived by land from Miletus; and Abydos in the Hellespont revolted to him and Pharnabazus, and Lampsacus two days later. Upon receipt of this news Strombichides hastily sailed from Chios with twenty-four Athenian ships, some transports carrying heavy infantry being of the number, and defeating the Lampsacenes who came out against him, took Lampsacus, which was unfortified, at the first assault, and making prize of the slaves and goods, restored the freemen to their homes, and went on to Abydos. The inhabitants, however, refusing to capitulate, and his assaults failing to take the place, he sailed over to the coast opposite, and appointed Sestos, the town in the Chersonese held by the Medes at a former period in this history, as the centre for the defence of the whole Hellespont.*

63. In the meantime the Chians commanded the sea more than before; and the Peloponnesians at Miletus and Astyochus, hearing of the sea-fight and of the departure of the squadron with Strombichides, took fresh courage. Coasting along with two vessels to Chios, Astyochus took the ships from that place, and now moved with the whole fleet upon Samos, from whence, however, he sailed back to Miletus, as the Athenians did not put out against him, owing to their suspicions of one another. For it was about this time, or even before, that the democracy was put down at Athens. When Pisander and the envoys returned from Tissaphernes to Samos they at once strengthened still further their interest in the army itself, and instigated the upper class in Samos to join them in establishing an oligarchy, the very form of government which a party of them had lately risen to avoid. At the same time the Athenians at Samos, after a consultation among themselves, determined to let Alcibiades alone, since he refused to join them, and besides was not the man for an oligarchy;† and now that they were once embarked, to see for themselves how they could best prevent the ruin of their cause, and meanwhile to sustain the war, and to contribute without stint money and all else that might be required from their own private estates, as they would henceforth labour for themselves alone.

---

*Lampsacus, on the Asian Hellespont (map 10), possessed no fortifications. With Abydos to the southwest, it had revolted, but the Athenians quickly recovered it. Sestos lies on the other, European side of the Hellespont, at its narrowest point. It had been the site of one anchored end of Xerxes' pontoon bridge. The Athenians started their empire from this vicinity (see 1.89).

†The Samians are whipsawed by the internal politics of the master city. Pisander has to admit defeat with the Persians, and they now abandon hopes of Alcibiades' assistance (as Phrynichus had advised long since). This account of the oligarchy continues from 8.63 to 72. One cannot say whether this unprecedented focus on Athenian internal politics reflects a change in Thucydides' priorities or the importance of Athenian internal struggle for the conduct of the external war.

64. After encouraging each other in these resolutions, they now at once sent off half the envoys and Pisander to do what was necessary at Athens (with instructions to establish oligarchies on their way in all the subject cities which they might touch at), and despatched the other half in different directions to the other dependencies. Diitrephes also, who was in the neighbourhood of Chios, and had been elected to the command of the Thracian towns, was sent off to his government, and arriving at Thasos abolished the democracy there. Two months, however, had not elapsed after his departure before the Thasians began to fortify their town, being already tired of an aristocracy with Athens, and in daily expectation of freedom from Lacedæmon. Indeed there was a party of them (whom the Athenians had banished), with the Peloponnesians, who with their friends in the town were already making every exertion to bring a squadron, and to effect the revolt of Thasos; and this party thus saw exactly what they most wanted done, that is to say, the reformation of the government without risk, and the abolition of the democracy which would have opposed them.* Things at Thasos thus turned out just the contrary to what the oligarchical conspirators at Athens expected; and the same in my opinion was the case in many of the other dependencies; as the cities no sooner got a moderate government and liberty of action, than they went on to absolute freedom without being at all seduced by the show of reform offered by the Athenians.†

65. Pisander and his colleagues on their voyage along shore abolished, as had been determined, the democracies in the cities, and also took some heavy infantry from certain places as their allies, and so came to Athens. Here they found most of the work already done by their associates. Some of the younger men had banded together, and secretly assassinated one Androcles, the chief leader of the commons, and mainly responsible for the banishment of Alcibiades; Androcles being singled out both because he was a popular leader, and because they sought by his death to recommend themselves to Alcibiades, who was, as they supposed, to be recalled, and to make Tissaphernes their friend. There were also some other inconvenient persons whom they secretly did away with in the same manner. Meanwhile their cry in public was that no pay should be given except to persons serving in the war, and that not more than five thousand should share in the

---

*The Thasian rebellion and revolution confirms Phrynichus' analysis of subject states' inclinations. They lost their fortifications when they revolted early, in 462 (1.101), against Athenian domination.

†Thucydides endorses this realistic analysis of subjects' hostile inclinations and the errors of the oligarchs.

government, and those such as were most able to serve the state in person and in purse.*

66. But this was propaganda for the multitude, as the authors of the revolution were really to govern. However, the Assembly and the Council chosen by lot still met notwithstanding, although they discussed nothing that was not approved of by the conspirators, who both supplied the speakers, and reviewed in advance what they were to say. Fear, and the sight of the numbers of the conspirators, closed the mouths of the rest; or if any ventured to rise in opposition, he was presently put to death in some convenient way, and there was neither search for the murderers nor justice to be had against them if suspected; but the people remained motionless, being so thoroughly cowed that men thought themselves lucky to escape violence, even when they held their tongues.† An exaggerated belief in the numbers of the conspirators also demoralised the people, rendered helpless by the magnitude of the city, and by their want of intelligence with each other, and being without means of finding out what those numbers really were. For the same reason it was impossible for any one to open his grief to a neighbour and to concert measures to defend himself, as he would have had to speak either to one whom he did not know, or whom he knew but did not trust. Indeed all the popular party approached each other with suspicion, each thinking his neighbour concerned in what was going on, the conspirators having in their ranks persons whom no one could ever have believed capable of joining an oligarchy;‡ and these it was who made the many so suspicious, and so

---

*Pisander's associates did not hesitate to overthrow long-established governments and to assassinate their enemies at home. The killers of Androcles the demagogue either acted before the failure with Alcibiades occurred or this information had been kept from them. Murder of fellow inhabitants was a Spartan and oligarchic (see 3.70), not an Athenian democratic, habit. Indeed, ostracism (see Hyperbolus, the last man to suffer it, at 8.73; Fornara #41 and #145) was an institution designed to forestall the need to murder your political opponents. The dominant propaganda was that only those who served with purse and person should determine policy and that a moderate oligarchy (of the hoplite class and above) should replace the existing democracy.

†Thucydides clearly describes the platform as merely expedient propaganda. Some moderate intentions and claims come to pass (8.97), but this outcome seems not to have been the oligarchs' plan. They were forced to form a government more moderate than the one they had planned. For the moment, the assembly and council continued to meet, but under the oligarchs' supervision.

‡The oligarchs had created a climate of mutual and mass suspicion and distrust. This random fear promoted their ends, since no one could be sure his neighbor was not connected to the plot. The catchwords about a ruling body of 5,000 reasonably led to a belief that 5,000 supported the inner core—but, like the phantom "Phoenician fleet," this group never came into play. (See Fornara #148–#150 for documents related to the regime of the Four Hundred that lasted eight months.)

helped to procure impunity for the few, by confirming the commons in their mistrust of one another.

67. At this juncture arrived Pisander and his colleagues, who lost no time in doing the rest. First they assembled the people, and moved to elect ten commissioners with full powers to frame a constitution, and that when this was done they should on an appointed day lay before the people their opinion as to the best mode of governing the city. Afterwards, when the day arrived, the conspirators enclosed the assembly in Colonus, a temple of Poseidon, a little more than a mile outside the city. The commissioners simply brought forward this single motion, that any Athenian might propose with impunity whatever measure he pleased, heavy penalties being imposed upon any who should indict for illegality, or otherwise molest him for so doing.* The way thus cleared, it was now plainly declared, that all tenure of office and receipt of pay under the existing institutions were at an end, and that five men must be elected as presidents, who should in their turn elect one hundred, and each of the hundred three apiece; and that this body thus made up to four hundred should enter the council chamber with full powers and govern as they judged best, and should convene the five thousand whenever they pleased.†

68. The man who moved this resolution was Pisander, who was throughout the chief ostensible agent in putting down the democracy. But he who concerted the whole affair, and prepared the way for the catastrophe, and who had given the greatest thought to the matter, was Antiphon, one of the best men of his day in Athens.‡ With a head to contrive measures and a tongue to recommend them, he did not willingly come forward in the assembly or upon any public scene,

---

*An accusation of unconstitutionality (*graphe paranomon*) would table an allegedly illegal proposal. The proposer then had to demonstrate that his measure offended no existing law or custom before the assembly could vote on it. This constitutional indictment, a bulwark of the democratic government, had priority over all other interventions. If a citizen brought several of them without success, he lost his political rights. The cancellation of this safeguard permitted the abrogation of the institutions of the democratic government—first of all, the election of the Four Hundred through a group originally consisting of only five eminently respectable men. Colonus was a suburb north-northwest of the Acropolis.

†They would convene the Five Thousand only when it was convenient, probably never. No one ever published their names.

‡Pisander, ostensibly a loyal Athenian democrat, pushed the revolution along. Behind the scenes was Antiphon, a writer of speeches for the assembly and the law courts. He is probably the same Antiphon as the sophist who enjoyed constructing opposing arguments on legal issues. We have examples of both kinds of compositions. Some evidence suggests that he had been Thucydides' teacher. Certainly the historian gives him high praise, although the oligarchic undertaking soon foundered and does not seem to have met with Thucydides' approval. Despite the quality of his oratory, he was tried (see Fornara #151), convicted, and executed after the fall of the Four Hundred.

being ill-looked upon by the multitude owing to his reputation for talent; and who yet was the one man best able to aid in the courts, or before the assembly, the suitors who required his opinion.

Indeed, when he was afterwards himself tried for his life on the charge of having been concerned in setting up this very government, when the Four Hundred were overthrown and dealt with severely by the commons, he made what would seem to be the best defence of any known up to my time.

Phrynichus also went beyond all others in his zeal for the oligarchy. Afraid of Alcibiades, and assured that he was no stranger to his intrigues with Astyochus at Samos, he held that no oligarchy was ever likely to restore him, and once embarked in the enterprise, proved, where danger was to be faced, by far the staunchest of them all. Theramenes, son of Hagnon, was also one of the foremost of the subverters of the democracy—a man as able in council as in debate. Conducted by so many and by such sagacious heads, the enterprise, great as it was, not unnaturally went forward; although it was no light matter to deprive the Athenian people of its freedom, almost a hundred years after the deposition of the tyrants, when it had been not only not subject to any during the whole of that period, but accustomed during more than half of it to rule over subjects of its own.*

69. The assembly ratified the proposed constitution, without a single opposing voice, and was then dissolved; after which the Four Hundred were brought into the council chamber in the following way.

On account of the enemy at Decelea, all the Athenians were constantly on the wall or in the ranks at the various military posts. On that day the persons not in the secret were allowed to go home as usual, while orders were given to the accomplices of the conspirators to hang about, without making any demonstration, at some little distance from the posts, and in case of any opposition to what was being done, to seize the arms and put it down. There were also some Andrians and Tenians, three hundred Carystians, and some of the settlers in Ægina come with their own arms for this very purpose, who had received similar instructions. These dispositions completed, the Four Hundred went, each with a dagger concealed about his person, accompanied by one hundred and twenty Hellenic youths, whom they employed wherever violence was needed, and appeared before

---

*Phrynichus had personal reasons for promoting the oligarchy—first of all, confidence that it would never welcome back his enemy Alcibiades. Theramenes would play a leading role in the later Athenian oligarchy, the Thirty, established after Athens' defeat in 404/403. His father had been the founder of Amphipolis (4.103) and a colleague of Pericles (1.117; 2.58), and one of the ten *probouloi* (senior statesmen) appointed after the Sicilian disaster (8.1). Thucydides supplies a brief epitaph for a long-lived government that would soon be restored.

the Councillors chosen by lot in the council chamber, and told them to take their pay and be gone; themselves bringing it for the whole of the residue of their term of office, and giving it to them as they went out.*

70. Upon the Council withdrawing in this way without venturing any objection, and the rest of the citizens making no movement, the Four Hundred entered the council chamber, and for the present contented themselves with drawing lots for their Prytanes,† and making their prayers and sacrifices to the gods upon entering office, but afterwards departed widely from the democratic system of government, and except that on account of Alcibiades they did not recall the exiles, ruled the city by force; putting to death some men, though not many, whom they thought it convenient to remove, and imprisoning and banishing others. They also sent to Agis, the Lacedæmonian king, at Decelea, to say that they desired to make peace, and that he might reasonably be more disposed to treat now that he had them to deal with instead of the inconstant commons.‡

71. Agis, however, did not believe in the tranquillity of the city, or that the commons would thus in a moment give up their ancient liberty, but thought that the sight of a large Lacedæmonian force would be sufficient to excite them if they were not already in commotion, of which he was by no means certain. He accordingly gave to the envoys of the Four Hundred an answer which held out no hopes of an accommodation, and sending for large reinforcements from Peloponnese, not long afterwards, with these and his garrison from Decelea, descended to the very walls of Athens; hoping either that civil disturbances might help to subdue them to his terms, or that, in the confusion to be expected within and without the city, they might even surrender without a blow being struck; at all events he thought he would succeed in seizing the Long Walls, bared of their defenders.

---

*The Four Hundred carefully planned their momentous revolution. Terror and violence were common oligarchical tools. The provision of the democracy's remaining, stipulated yearly pay to the members of the council (*boule*) is an ideological slap, as if the members served for the money, not from patriotic motives.

†The revolution in June required the new government to take over immediate functions. The *prytanes* were the individuals under both governments required to remain at all times in the *tholos*, or *prytaneion*, in the agora (see Camp, p. 69; illustration 66) to conduct both ordinary and emergency public business. The lot is an essential democratic institution, but any group of peers can find it convenient.

‡Democratic procedures were abolished only when and if they became inconvenient. Thucydides records the oligarchic murders, imprisonments, and banishment of enemies. The revolutionaries imagined that the Spartans would make peace with them, now that they had established a more congenial government. Agis did not believe the reports about developments in Athens.

However, the Athenians saw him come close up, without making the least disturbance within the city; and sending out their cavalry, and a number of their heavy infantry, light troops, and archers, shot down some of his soldiers who approached too near, and got possession of some arms and dead. Upon this Agis, at last convinced, led his army back again, and remaining with his own troops in the old position at Decelea, sent the reinforcement back home, after a few days' stay in Attica. After this the Four Hundred persevering sent another embassy to Agis, and now meeting with a better reception, at his suggestion despatched envoys to Lacedæmon to negotiate a treaty, being desirous of making peace.

72. They also sent ten men to Samos to reassure the army, and to explain that the oligarchy was not established for the hurt of the city or the citizens, but for the salvation of the country at large; and that there were five thousand, not four hundred only, concerned; although, what with their expeditions and employments abroad, the Athenians had never yet assembled to discuss a question important enough to bring five thousand of them together.* The emissaries were also told what to say upon all other points, and were so sent off immediately after the establishment of the new government, which feared, as it turned out justly, that the mass of seamen would not be willing to remain under the oligarchical constitution, and, the evil beginning there, might be the means of their overthrow.†

73. Indeed at Samos the question of the oligarchy had already entered upon a new phase, the following events having taken place just at the time that the Four Hundred were conspiring. That part of the Samian population which has been mentioned as rising against the upper class, and as being the democratic party, had now turned round, and yielding to the solicitations of Pisander during his visit, and of the Athenians in the conspiracy at Samos, had bound themselves by oaths to the number of three hundred, and were about to fall upon the rest of their fellow-citizens, whom they now in their turn regarded as the democratic party.

Meanwhile they put to death one Hyperbolus, an Athenian, a pestilent fellow that had been ostracised, not from fear of his influence or position, but because he was a rascal and a disgrace to the city; being aided in this by Charminus, one of the generals, and by

---

*The oligarchs in Athens wanted the cooperation of the fleet and army at Samos, the armed *demos* that had not been cowed by their thuglike machinations. They continued their propaganda about the government of the Five Thousand. Such a number was less than the quorum required to conduct an Athenian ostracism (6,000).

†The sailors in particular were not impressed with the oligarchic embassy's case, a predictable reaction from the class of *thetes* (poorest of the four Athenian property classes).

some of the Athenians with them, to whom they had sworn friendship, and with whom they perpetrated other acts of the kind, and now determined to attack the people.*

The latter got wind of what was coming, and told two of the generals, Leon and Diomedon, who, on account of the credit which they enjoyed with the commons, were unwilling supporters of the oligarchy; and also Thrasybulus and Thrasyllus, the former a captain of a trireme, the latter serving with the heavy infantry, besides certain others who had ever been thought most opposed to the conspirators, entreating them not to look on and see them destroyed, and Samos, the sole remaining stay of their empire, lost to the Athenians.

Upon hearing this, the persons whom they addressed now went round the soldiers one by one, and urged them to resist, especially the crew of the Paralus, which was made up entirely of Athenians and freemen, and had from time out of mind been enemies of oligarchy, even when there was no such thing existing; and Leon and Diomedon left behind some ships for their protection in case of their sailing away anywhere themselves. Accordingly, when the Three Hundred attacked the people, all these came to the rescue, and foremost of all the crew of the Paralus; and the Samian commons gained the victory, and putting to death some thirty of the Three Hundred, and banishing three others of the ringleaders, accorded an amnesty to the rest, and lived together under a democratic government for the future.†

74. The ship Paralus, with Chæreas, son of Archestratus, on board, an Athenian who had taken an active part in the revolution, was now without loss of time sent off by the Samians and the army to Athens to report what had occurred; the fact that the Four Hundred were in power not being yet known. When they sailed into harbour the Four Hundred immediately arrested two or three of the Parali, and taking the vessel from the rest, shifted them into a troopship and set them to keep guard round Eubœa. Chæreas, however, managed to secrete himself as soon as he saw how things stood, and returning to Samos, drew a picture to the soldiers of the horrors enacting at Athens, in which

---

*Thucydides pedals backward (a rare move) to correlate events in Athens with those in Samos. Pisander had convinced some of the Samian population to cooperate with the oligarchical conspirators. Cleon-like Hyperbolus and others of his sentiments (for whom Thucydides has no sympathy; compare Fornara #145) had been killed in Samos. The Athenian *demos* had merely ostracized him, a ten-year banishment without confiscation of property or harm to family members.

†Leon and Diomedon were popularly elected generals. Thrasybulus, a wealthy man and a leader of the restoration of the democracy in 404, commanded a trireme, and Thrasyllus was to hold several Ionian commands. The Samians and their Athenian allies foil the Samian oligarchic revolution with minimal bloodshed.

everything was exaggerated;* saying that all were punished with whippings, that no one could say a word against the holders of power, that the soldiers' wives and children were outraged, and that it was intended to seize and shut up the relatives of all in the army at Samos who were not of the government's way of thinking, to be put to death in case of their disobedience; besides a host of other injurious inventions.

75. On hearing this the first thought of the army was to fall upon the chief authors of the oligarchy and upon all the rest concerned. Eventually, however, they desisted from this idea upon the men of moderate views opposing it and warning them against ruining their cause, with the enemy close at hand and ready for battle. After this Thrasybulus, son of Lycus, and Thrasyllus, the chief leaders in the revolution, now wishing in the most public manner to change the government at Samos to a democracy, bound all the soldiers by the most tremendous oaths, and those of the oligarchical party more than any, to accept a democratic government, to be united, to prosecute actively the war with the Peloponnesians, and to be enemies of the Four Hundred, and to hold no communication with them. The same oath was also taken by all the Samians of full age; and the soldiers associated the Samians in all their affairs and in the fruits of their dangers, having the conviction that there was no way of escape for themselves or for them, but that the success of the Four Hundred or of the enemy at Miletus must be their ruin.†

76. The struggle now was between the army trying to force a democracy upon the city, and the Four Hundred an oligarchy upon the camp. Meanwhile the soldiers forthwith held an assembly, in which they deposed the former generals and any of the captains whom they suspected, and chose new captains and generals to replace them, besides Thrasybulus and Thrasyllus, whom they had already. They also stood up and encouraged one another, and among other things urged that they ought not to lose heart because the city had revolted from them, as the party seceding was smaller and in every way poorer in resources than themselves.‡ They had the whole fleet with

---

*The Athenians on Samos could not know of the simultaneous successful revolution of the Four Hundred in Athens. Chaereas, on his arrival in Piraeus (map 3; Camp, pp. 294–299), astutely realized that he should elude the officers of the new, oligarchic government. Returning to Samos, he painted a lurid picture. Thucydides did not admire the Four Hundred, but Chaereas' hyperbolic misrepresentations offended him.

†Thrasybulus and Thrasyllus confirm their troops' and hosts' loyalties to the democracy. The government of the Four Hundred is equated with the Spartan enemy headquartered at Miletus.

‡The army at Samos takes upon itself to be the true Athens, a government in exile or at least overseas. In orderly fashion they elect new commanders at the top level and captains for their ships. Envoys from the Four Hundred realize that they are safer remaining in Delos than coming to Samos.

which to compel the other cities in their empire to give them money
just as if they had their base in the capital, having a city in Samos
which, so far from wanting strength, had when at war been within an
ace of depriving the Athenians of the command of the sea, while as
far as the enemy was concerned they had the same base of operations
as before.

Indeed, with the fleet in their hands, they were better able to provide themselves with supplies than the government at home. It was
their advanced position at Samos which had throughout enabled the
home authorities to command the entrance into Piræus; and if they
refused to give them back the constitution, they would now find that
the army was more in a position to exclude them from the sea than
they were to exclude the army. Besides, the city was of little or no use
towards enabling them to overcome the enemy; and they had lost
nothing in losing those who had no longer either money to send them
(the soldiers having to find this for themselves), or good counsel,
which entitles cities to direct armies. On the contrary, even in this the
home government had done wrong in abolishing the institutions of
their ancestors, while the army maintained the said institutions, and
would try to force the home government to do so likewise. So that
even in point of good counsel the camp had as good counsellors as
the city. Moreover, they had but to grant him security for his person
and his recall, and Alcibiades would be only too glad to procure them
the alliance of the king. And above all, if they failed altogether, with
the navy which they possessed, they had numbers of places to retire
to in which they would find cities and lands.

77. Debating together and comforting themselves after this manner, they pushed on their war measures as actively as ever; and the ten
envoys sent to Samoa by the Four Hundred, learning how matters
stood while they were still at Delos, stayed quiet there.

78. About this time a cry arose among the soldiers in the Peloponnesian fleet at Miletus that Astyochus and Tissaphernes were ruining
their cause. Astyochus had not been willing to fight at sea—either before, while they were still in full vigour and the fleet of the Athenians
small, or now, when the enemy was, as they were informed, in a state
of sedition and his ships not yet united—but kept them waiting for the
Phœnician fleet from Tissaphernes, which had only a nominal existence, at the risk of wasting away in inactivity.* Tissaphernes not only

---

*The Peloponnesians do not capitalize on Athenian internal divisions, which are in-
deed made known to them. It is unclear whether the fault is that of Tissaphernes or
Astyochus, or both. Thucydides does not doubt the reality of the Phoenician fleet
(compare 8.87), but the Peloponnesian sailors had reason to doubt their existence, and
they focus on this point about their ally's ships. They did not wish to remain as a standing army and wanted to fight the war to a prompt conclusion.

did not bring up the fleet in question, but was ruining their navy by payments made irregularly, and even then not made in full. They must therefore, they insisted, delay no longer, but fight a decisive naval engagement. The Syracusans were the most urgent of any.

79. The confederates and Astyochus, aware of these murmurs, had already decided in council to fight a decisive battle; and when the news reached them of the disturbance at Samos, they put to sea with all their ships, one hundred and ten in number, and ordering the Milesians to move by land upon Mycale, set sail thither. The Athenians with the eighty-two ships from Samos were at the moment lying at Glauce in Mycale, a point where Samos approaches near to the continent; and seeing the Peloponnesian fleet sailing against them, retired into Samos, not thinking themselves numerically strong enough to stake their all upon a battle. Besides, they had notice from Miletus of the wish of the enemy to engage, and were expecting to be joined from the Hellespont by Strombichides, to whom a messenger had been already despatched, with the ships that had gone from Chios to Abydos. The Athenians accordingly withdrew to Samos, and the Peloponnesians put in at Mycale, and encamped with the land forces of the Milesians and the people of the neighbourhood. The next day they were about to sail against Samos, when tidings reached them of the arrival of Strombichides with the squadron from the Hellespont, upon which they immediately sailed back to Miletus. The Athenians, thus reinforced, now in their turn sailed against Miletus with a hundred and eight ships, wishing to fight a decisive battle, but as no one put out to meet them, sailed back to Samos.

Twenty-first Year of the War — Recall of Alcibiades
to Samos — Revolt of Eubœa and Downfall of the Four
Hundred — Battle of Cynossema

80. In the same summer, immediately after this, the Peloponnesians having refused to fight with their fleet united, through not thinking themselves a match for the enemy, and being at a loss where to look for money for such a number of ships, especially as Tissaphernes proved so bad a paymaster, sent off Clearchus, son of Ramphias, with forty ships to Pharnabazus, agreeably to the original instructions from Peloponnese; Pharnabazus inviting them and being prepared to furnish pay, and Byzantium besides sending offers to revolt to them. These Peloponnesian ships accordingly put out into the open sea, in order to escape the observation of the Athenians, and being overtaken by a storm, the majority with Clearchus got into Delos, and afterwards returned to Miletus, whence Clearchus proceeded by land to the Hellespont to take the command: ten, however, of their number, under the Megarian Helixus, made good their passage to the Hellespont, and effected the revolt of Byzantium. After this, the commanders at Samos were informed of it, and sent a squadron against them to guard the Hellespont; and an encounter took place before Byzantium between eight vessels on either side.

81. Meanwhile the chiefs at Samos, and especially Thrasybulus, who from the moment that he had changed the government had remained firmly resolved to recall Alcibiades, at last in an assembly brought over the mass of the soldiery, and upon their voting for his recall and amnesty, sailed over to Tissaphernes and brought Alcibiades to Samos, being convinced that their only chance of salvation lay in his bringing over Tissaphernes from the Peloponnesians to themselves.

An assembly was then held in which Alcibiades complained of and deplored his private misfortune in having been banished, and speaking at great length upon public affairs, highly incited their hopes for the future, and extravagantly magnified his own influence with Tissaphernes. His object in this was to make the oligarchical government at Athens afraid of him, to hasten the dissolution of the associations, to increase his credit with the army at Samos and heighten their own confidence, and lastly to prejudice the enemy as strongly as possible against Tissaphernes, and blast the hopes which they entertained.

Alcibiades accordingly held out to the army such extravagant promises as the following: that Tissaphernes had solemnly assured him that if he could only trust the Athenians they should never want for supplies while he had anything left, no, not even if he should have to coin his own silver couch, and that he would bring the Phœnician fleet now at Aspendus to the Athenians instead of to the Peloponnesians; but that he could only trust the Athenians if Alcibiades were recalled to be his security for them.*

82. Upon hearing this and much more besides, the Athenians at once elected him general together with the former ones, and put all their affairs into his hands.† There was now not a man in the

---

*Alcibiades rejoins his countrymen and their democracy. They voted his recall and an amnesty, although the state priests had formally cursed him for his alleged role in the profanation of the Mysteries. He hopes to destroy any cooperation between the Peloponnesians and Tissaphernes, and to return to prominence in his native land. This would not be his last abandonment of allies. His promises deceive the Athenians as they had the Peloponnesians—alarming the oligarchs and impressing the Athenian democrats. The comment on Tissaphernes' willingness to melt down and coin his silver couch, if more money were needed, represents either Alcibiades' portrait of the Satrap, a barbarian "Other," or the hyperbolic language of Persian diplomacy. Tissaphernes would imprison his dear friend Alcibiades in the winter following.

†He is elected general, in part to secure Tissaphernes' assets, and the new generals of 8.76 are confirmed.

army who would have exchanged his present hopes of safety and vengeance upon the Four Hundred for any consideration whatever; and, after what they had been told they were now inclined to disdain the enemy before them, and to sail at once for Piræus. To the plan of sailing for Piræus, leaving their more immediate enemies behind them, Alcibiades opposed the most positive refusal, in spite of the numbers that insisted upon it, saying that now that he had been elected general he would first sail to Tissaphernes and concert with him measures for carrying on the war. Accordingly, upon leaving this assembly, he immediately took his departure in order to have it thought that there was an entire confidence between them, and also wishing to increase his consideration with Tissaphernes, and to show that he had now been elected general and was in a position to do him good or evil as he chose; thus managing to frighten the Athenians with Tissaphernes and Tissaphernes with the Athenians.*

83. Meanwhile the Peloponnesians at Miletus heard of the recall of Alcibiades, and already distrustful of Tissaphernes, now became far more disgusted with him than ever. Indeed after their refusal to go out and give battle to the Athenians when they appeared before Miletus, Tissaphernes had grown slacker than ever in his payments; and even before this, on account of Alcibiades, his unpopularity had been on the increase. Gathering together, just as before, the soldiers and some persons of consideration besides the soldiery, began to reckon up how they had never yet received their pay in full; that what they did receive was small in quantity, and even that paid irregularly, and that unless they fought a decisive battle or removed to some station where they could get supplies, the ships' crews would desert; and that it was all the fault of Astyochus, who humoured Tissaphernes for his own private advantage.†

84. The army was engaged in these reflexions, when the following disturbance took place about the person of Astyochus. Most of the Syracusan and Thurian sailors were freemen, and these the freest crews in the armament were likewise the boldest in setting upon Astyochus and demanding their pay. The latter answered somewhat stiffly and threatened them, and when Dorieus spoke up for his own sailors even went so far as to lift his baton against him; upon seeing which the mass of the men, in sailor fashion, rushed in a fury to strike

---

*Thucydides finds amusement in Alcibiades' success in impressing various parties (including both the Athenian oligarchs and the democrats) with his allegedly vast influence over other parties.

†The Peloponnesians and their allies find Alcibiades' recall to Athenian command the last straw in their dealings with Tissaphernes and the greedy Astyochus.

Astyochus.* He, however, saw them in time and fled for refuge to an altar; and they were thus parted without his being struck. Meanwhile the fort built by Tissaphernes in Miletus was surprised and taken by the Milesians, and the garrison in it turned out,—an act which met with the approval of the rest of the allies, and in particular of the Syracusans, but which found no favour with Lichas, who said moreover that the Milesians and the rest in the king's country ought to show a reasonable submission to Tissaphernes and to pay him court, until the war should be happily settled.† The Milesians were angry with him for this and for other things of the kind, and upon his afterwards dying of sickness, would not allow him to be buried where the Lacedæmonians with the army desired.

85. The discontent of the army with Astyochus and Tissaphernes had reached this pitch, when Mindarus arrived from Lacedæmon to succeed Astyochus as admiral, and assumed the command. Astyochus now set sail for home; and Tissaphernes sent with him one of his confidants, Gaulites, a Carian, who spoke the two languages, to complain of the Milesians for the affair of the fort, and at the same time to defend himself against the Milesians, who were, as he was aware, on their way to Sparta chiefly to denounce his conduct, and had with them Hermocrates, who was to accuse Tissaphernes of joining with Alcibiades to ruin the Peloponnesian cause and of playing a double game. Indeed Hermocrates had always been at enmity with him about the pay not being restored in full; and eventually when he was banished from Syracuse,‡ and new commanders, Potamis, Myscon, and Demarchus, had come out to Miletus to the ships of the Syracusans, Tissaphernes pressed harder than ever upon him in his exile, and

---

*Dorieus, originally from Rhodes (map 1) but an emigrant to the Panhellenic foundation of Thurii on the boot of Italy, was an Olympic victor as well as a naval contingent commander (8.35). The Spartan commander's swagger stick was both a symbol of authority and a very real tool of punishment—not only for helots. Spartans used them on other recalcitrant subordinates. They did not expect concerted outrage from oarsmen. Astyochus, by unsheathing his weapon, lost his authority with the mass of the allied sailors. A telling vignette of Spartan failure in leadership emerged.

†The lack of trust between Peloponnesian allies and Tissaphernes leads to the former seizing a prized, recovered possession of the latter. Lichas the Spartan recognizes the breach of their recent treaty and tries to regain the Ionians' submission with an intimation that freedom may come after the war. One looks in vain for this concept, however, in the treaty. He thus wins only their animosity.

‡Mindarus replaces Astyochus, and various bickering allied delegations sail for Sparta to discuss Astyochus' and Tissaphernes' unbellicose conduct. Hermocrates the Syracusan commander joins the accusers of the dilatory Astyochus and Tissaphernes. Despite his great services in the defense of Syracuse and on the Ionian front, he suffered banishment the following year, when there was a change of regime at home. Tissaphernes also found Hermocrates' objections to Persian policy inconvenient and invented charges against him.

among other charges against him accused him of having once asked him for money, and then given himself out as his enemy because he failed to obtain it.

While Astyochus and the Milesians and Hermocrates made sail for Lacedæmon, Alcibiades had now crossed back from Tissaphernes to Samos.

86. After his return the envoys of the Four Hundred sent, as has been mentioned above, to pacify and explain matters to the forces at Samos, arrived from Delos; and an assembly was held in which they attempted to speak. The soldiers at first would not hear them, and cried out to put to death the subverters of the democracy, but at last, after some difficulty, calmed down and gave them a hearing.

Upon this the envoys proceeded to inform them that the recent change had been made to save the city, and not to ruin it or to deliver it over to the enemy, for they had already had an opportunity of doing this when he invaded the country during their government; that all the Five Thousand would have their proper share in the government; and that their hearers' relatives had neither outrage, as Chæreas had slanderously reported, nor other ill-treatment to complain of, but were all in undisturbed enjoyment of their property just as they had left them. Besides these they made a number of other statements which had no better success with their angry auditors; and amid a host of different opinions the one which found most favour was that of sailing to Piræus.

Now it was that Alcibiades for the first time did the state a service, and one of the most signal kind.* For when the Athenians at Samos were bent upon sailing against their countrymen, in which case Ionia and the Hellespont would most certainly at once have passed into possession of the enemy, Alcibiades it was who prevented them. At that moment, when no other man would have been able to hold back the multitude, he put a stop to the intended expedition, and rebuked and turned aside the resentment felt, on personal grounds, against the envoys; he dismissed them with an answer from himself, to the effect that he did not object to the government of the Five Thousand, but insisted that the Four Hundred should be deposed and the Council of Five Hundred reinstated in power: meanwhile any retrenchments for economy, by which pay might be better found for the armament, met with his entire approval.

---

*The oligarchic envoys are not in a strong position, since the Athenian military currently is based preponderantly at Samos. The angry assembled forces came just short of attacking the revolutionary, reactionary government at Athens and thus destroying what remained of their empire, when Alcibiades saved the situation. Thucydides' praise is ambivalent (compare 6.15). Samos was to become the failing Athenians' last loyal ally (see Fornara #166, a treaty of 405/404).

Generally, he bade them hold out and show a bold face to the enemy, since if the city were saved there was good hope that the two parties might some day be reconciled, whereas if either were once destroyed, that at Samos, or that at Athens, there would no longer be any one to be reconciled to. Meanwhile arrived envoys from the Argives, with offers of support to the Athenian commons at Samos: these were thanked by Alcibiades, and dismissed with a request to come when called upon. The Argives were accompanied by the crew of the Paralus, previously placed in a troopship by the Four Hundred with orders to cruise round Euboea, and who being employed to carry to Lacedæmon some Athenian envoys sent by the Four Hundred, Læspodias, Aristophon, and Melesias, as they sailed by Argos laid hands upon the envoys, and delivering them over to the Argives as the chief subverters of the democracy, themselves, instead of returning to Athens, took the Argive envoys on board, and came to Samos in the galley which had been confided to them.*

87. The same summer at the time that the return of Alcibiades coupled with the general conduct of Tissaphernes had carried to its height the discontent of the Peloponnesians, who no longer entertained any doubt of his having joined the Athenians, Tissaphernes wishing, it would seem, to clear himself to them of these charges, prepared to go after the Phœnician fleet to Aspendus, and invited Lichas to go with him; saying that he would appoint Tamos as his lieutenant to provide pay for the armament during his own absence. Accounts differ, and it is not easy to ascertain with what intention he went to Aspendus, and did not bring the fleet after all.† That one hundred and forty-seven Phœnician ships came as far as Aspendus is certain; but why they did not come on has been variously accounted for. Some think that he went away in pursuance of his plan of wasting the Peloponnesian resources, since at any rate Tamos, his lieutenant, far from being any better, proved a worse paymaster than himself: others that he brought the Phœnicians to Aspendus to exact money from them

---

*The *Paralus'* crew were determined democrats. Argive cooperation with the democratic government abroad could be expected since Argos, like Athens, had a democratic government.

†Tissaphernes wished to remain on good terms with the Peloponnesian forces: After making clear commitments, the satrap again, as always, did not bring forward the Phoenician fleet. One hundred and forty-seven ships reached Aspendus in the middle of the southern coast of Asia Minor (beyond Lycia and the east edge of map 12). Thucydides offers four explanations of their failure to join the war. Tissaphernes wanted to continue to diminish Peloponnesian power; he was trying to extort money from the Phoenician sailors; he brought them thus far to prove that they existed; and finally— Thucydides' preferred analysis—he was wearing down both sides by keeping them evenly balanced. This hypothesis seems supported by Tissaphernes' illogical excuse, that the King wanted him to provide his allies with yet more ships than he already had.

for their discharge, having never intended to employ them: others again that it was in view of the outcry against him at Lacedæmon, in order that it might be said that he was not in fault, but that the ships were really manned and that he had certainly gone to fetch them. To myself it seems only too evident that he did not bring up the fleet because he wished to wear out and paralyse the Hellenic forces, that is, to waste their strength by the time lost during his journey to Aspendus, and to keep them evenly balanced by not throwing his weight into either scale. Had he wished to finish the war, he could have done so, assuming of course that he made his appearance in a way which left no room for doubt; as by bringing up the fleet he would in all probability have given the victory to the Lacedæmonians, whose navy, even as it was, faced the Athenian more as an equal than as an inferior. But what convicts him most clearly, is the excuse which he put forward for not bringing the ships. He said that the number assembled was less than the king had ordered; but surely it would only have enhanced his credit if he spent little of the king's money and effected the same end at less cost.* In any case, whatever was his intention, Tissaphernes went to Aspendus and saw the Phœnicians; and the Peloponnesians at his desire sent a Lacedæmonian called Philip with two triremes to fetch the fleet.

88. Alcibiades finding that Tissaphernes had gone to Aspendus, himself sailed thither with thirteen ships, promising to do a great and certain service to the Athenians at Samos, as he would either bring the Phœnician fleet to the Athenians, or at all events prevent its joining the Peloponnesians. In all probability he had long known that Tissaphernes never meant to bring the fleet at all, and wished to compromise him as much as possible in the eyes of the Peloponnesians through his apparent friendship for himself and the Athenians, and thus in a manner to oblige him to join their side.†

While Alcibiades weighed anchor and sailed eastward straight for Phaselis and Caunus,

89. the envoys sent by the Four Hundred to Samos arrived at Athens. Upon their delivering the message from Alcibiades, telling them to hold out and to show a firm front to the enemy, and saying that he had great hopes of reconciling them with the army and of overcoming the Peloponnesians, the majority of the members of the oligarchy, who were already discontented and only too much inclined to be quit of the business in any safe way that they could, were at once

---

*If Tissaphernes could win the war, as he could have, with a smaller number of ships, why would he not, if ending the war was his wish?

†Alcibiades now hoped to drive another wedge between the Peloponnesians and the satrap. Since the dispute between Tissaphernes and the Athenians (8.56), such help was unlikely, but it was rarely wise to underestimate Alcibiades.

greatly strengthened in their resolve. These now banded together and strongly criticised the administration, their leaders being some of the principal generals and men in office under the oligarchy, such as Theramenes, son of Hagnon, Aristocrates, son of Scellias, and others; who, although among the most prominent members of the government (being afraid, as they said, of the army at Samos, and most especially of Alcibiades, and also lest the envoys whom they had sent to Lacedæmon, might do the state some harm without the authority of the people). Without insisting on objections to the excessive concentration of power in a few hands, they yet urged that the Five Thousand must be shown to exist not merely in name but in reality, and the constitution placed upon a fairer basis.* But this was merely their political cry; most of them being driven by private ambition into the line of conduct so surely fatal to oligarchies that arise out of democracies.† For all at once deem it right not to be equals but each the chief and master of his fellows; while under a democracy a disappointed candidate accepts his defeat more easily, because he has not the humiliation of being beaten by his equals. But what most clearly encouraged the malcontents was the power of Alcibiades at Samos, and their own disbelief in the stability of the oligarchy; and it was now a race between them as to which should first become the leader of the commons.

90. Meanwhile the leaders and members of the Four Hundred most opposed to a democratic form of government—Phrynichus who had had the quarrel with Alcibiades during his command at Samos, Aristarchus the bitter and inveterate enemy of the commons, and Pisander and Antiphon and others of the chiefs who already as soon as they entered upon power, and again when the army at Samos seceded from them and declared for a democracy, had sent envoys from their own body to Lacedæmon and made every effort for peace, and had built the wall in Eetionia,‡—now redoubled their exertions when

---

*The oligarchy of Four Hundred split apart once it was clear that they would have neither the support of the army at Samos nor that of Alcibiades with Tissaphernes' resources. Some were ready to come to terms with Sparta on any basis that left them in power and with their lives. Others, such as Theramenes and Aristocrates, pressed for the constitution and publication of the Five Thousand (disingenuously, as Thucydides indicates?).

†Thucydides (at 2.65; compare 8.66) perceived that personal ambition sometimes outweighs patriotic fervor. The charisma and authority of Alcibiades at Samos also rendered the home Athenian government's situation precarious.

‡The extreme oligarchs constructed a wall in Piraeus on the northern promontory and mole of Cantharus (map 3), Greece's most important harbor. It was to serve as a refuge for them, should the commons and/or their own confederates turn against them. The "moderate" oligarchs such as Theramenes and Aristocrates now tried to distance themselves from the "extremists"—Antiphon, Phrynichus, Pisander, Aristarchus, and their ilk. They suggested that this construction might facilitate a treasonous surrender to the enemy's fleet. The later surrender of Oenoe supports the possibility of such a move.

their envoys returned from Samos, and they saw not only the people but their own most trusted associates turning against them.

Alarmed at the state of things at Athens as at Samos, they now sent off in haste Antiphon and Phrynichus and ten others with injunctions to make peace with Lacedæmon upon any terms, no matter what, that should be at all tolerable. Meanwhile they pushed on more actively than ever with the wall in Eetionia. Now the meaning of this wall, according to Theramenes and his supporters, was not so much to keep out the army of Samos in case of its trying to force its way into Piræus as to be able to let in, at pleasure, the fleet and army of the enemy. For Eetionia is a mole of Piræus, close alongside of the entrance of the harbour, and was now fortified in connexion with the wall already existing on the land side, so that a few men placed in it be able to command the entrance; the old wall on the land side and the new one now being built within on the side of the sea, both ending in one of the two towers standing at the narrow mouth of the harbour. They also walled off the largest covered portico in Piræus which was in immediate connexion with this wall, and kept it in their own hands, compelling all to unload there the grain that came into the harbour, and what they had in stock, and to take it out from thence when they sold it.

91. These measures had long provoked the murmurs of Theramenes, and when the envoys returned from Lacedæmon without having effected any general pacification, he affirmed that this wall was like to prove the ruin of the state. At this moment forty-two ships from Peloponnese, including some Siceliot and Italiot vessels from Locri and Tarentum, had been invited over by the Eubœans and were already riding off Las in Laconia preparing for the voyage to Eubœa, under the command of Agesandridas, son of Agesander, a Spartan.

Theramenes now affirmed that this squadron was destined not so much to aid Eubœa as the party fortifying Eetionia, and that unless precautions were speedily taken the city would be surprised and lost. This was no mere calumny, there being really some such plan entertained by the accused. Their first wish was to have the oligarchy without giving up the empire; failing this to keep their ships and walls and be independent; while, if this also were denied them, sooner than be the first victims of the restored democracy, they were resolved to call in the enemy and make peace, give up their walls and ships, and at all costs retain possession of the government, if their lives were only assured to them.*

92. For this reason they pushed forward the construction of their

---

*Thucydides, without denying the oligarchs' original patriotism, affirms that they were ready to surrender the city and empire to the Peloponnesians, if that capitulation would keep them in power.

work with postern gates and entrances and means of introducing the
enemy, being eager to have it finished in time. Meanwhile the murmurs against them were at first confined to a few persons and went
on in secret, until Phrynichus, after his return from the embassy to
Lacedæmon, was laid wait for and stabbed in full market by one of
the *Peripoli*, falling down dead before he had gone far from the council chamber.* The assassin escaped; but his accomplice, an Argive, was
taken and put to the torture by the Four Hundred, without their
being able to extract from him the name of his employer, or anything
further than that he knew of many men who used to assemble at the
house of the commander of the *Peripoli* and at other houses.

Here the matter was allowed to drop. This so emboldened
Theramenes and Aristocrates and the rest of their partisans in the Four
Hundred and sympathizers beyond the Four Hundred, that they now
resolved to act. For by this time the ships had sailed round from Las,
and anchoring at Epidaurus had overrun Ægina; and Theramenes asserted that, being bound for Eubœa, they would never have sailed in to
Ægina and come back to anchor at Epidaurus, unless they had been invited to come to aid in the designs of which he had always accused the
government. Further inaction had therefore now become impossible.

In the end, after a great many seditious harangues and suspicions,
the government's opponents set to work in real earnest. The heavy infantry in Piræus building the wall in Eetionia, among whom was Aristocrates, a colonel, with his own tribe, laid hands upon Alexicles, a
general under the oligarchy and the devoted adherent of the political
associations, and took him into a house and confined him there. In
this they were assisted by one Hermon, commander of the *Peripoli* in
Munychia, and others, and above all had with them the great bulk of
the heavy infantry. As soon as the news reached the Four Hundred,
who happened to be sitting in the council chamber, all except the disaffected wished at once to go to the posts where the arms were, and
menaced Theramenes and his party. Theramenes defended himself,
and said that he was ready immediately to go and help to rescue
Alexicles; and taking with him one of the generals belonging to his
party, went down to Piræus, followed by Aristarchus† and some young
men of the cavalry.

---

*Phrynichus, the firmest of the oligarchs, was assassinated. Members of the govern-
ment of the Four Hundred in the council (*boule*) threatened with death another associate, the general Theramenes. Fast thinking allows him to go down to Piraeus and
rescue the threatened oligarch Alexicles, but also to escape the clutches of the diehard
and disappointed oligarchs.

†Theramenes' self-preservation demanded a bold move to extricate himself from the
proponents of the narrow oligarchy. Theramenes claimed to support the wider oligarchy of the Five Thousand, but his politics remain obscure.

All was now panic and confusion. Those in the city imagined that Piræus was already taken and the prisoner put to death, while those in Piræus expected every moment to be attacked by the party in the city. The older men, however, stopped the persons running up and down the town and making for the stands of arms; and Thucydides the Pharsalian, *Proxenus* of the city, came forward and threw himself in the way of the rival factions, and appealed to them not to ruin the state, while the enemy was still at hand waiting for his opportunity, and so at length succeeded in quieting them and in keeping their hands off each other.

Meanwhile Theramenes came down to Piræus, being himself one of the generals, and raged and stormed against the heavy infantry, while Aristarchus and the adversaries of the people were angry in right earnest. Most of the heavy infantry, however, went on with the business without faltering, and asked Theramenes if he thought the wall had been constructed for any good purpose, and whether it would not be better that it should be pulled down. To this he answered that if they thought it best to pull it down, he for his part agreed with them.

Upon this the heavy infantry and a number of the people in Piræus immediately got up on the fortification and began to demolish it. Now their cry to the multitude was that all should join in the work who wished the Five Thousand to govern instead of the Four Hundred. For instead of saying in so many words 'all who wished the commons to govern,' they still disguised themselves under the name of the Five Thousand; being afraid that these might really exist, and that they might be speaking to one of their number and get into trouble through ignorance. Indeed this was why the Four Hundred neither wished the Five Thousand to exist, nor to have it known that they did not exist; being of opinion that to give themselves so many partners in empire would be downright democracy, while the mystery in question would make the people afraid of one another.*

93. The next day the Four Hundred, although alarmed, nevertheless assembled in the council chamber, while the heavy infantry in Piræus, after having released their prisoner Alexicles and pulled down the fortification, went with their arms to the theatre of Dionysus, close to Munychia, and there held an assembly in which they decided to march into the city, and setting forth accordingly halted in the Anaceum.† Here they were joined by some delegates from the Four Hundred, who reasoned with them one by one, and persuaded

---

*Joining the rallying cry for establishment of the moderately oligarchical government of the Five Thousand served Theramenes well again, since that call stopped short of demanding an unwelcome restoration of the full democracy.

†Munychia is the northwestern region of Piraeus (map 3). In the theater the men decided to march on Athens, 8 miles inland. The Anaceum was a mustering ground for infantry and cavalry located on the northern slope of the Athenian acropolis.

those whom they saw to be the most moderate to remain quiet themselves, and to keep in the rest; saying that they would make known the Five Thousand, and have the Four Hundred chosen from them in rotation, as should be decided by the Five Thousand, and meanwhile entreated them not to ruin the state or drive it into the arms of the enemy. After a great many had spoken and had been spoken to, the whole body of heavy infantry became calmer than before, absorbed by their fears for the country at large, and now agreed to hold upon an appointed day an assembly in the theatre of Dionysus for the restoration of concord.

94. When the day came for the assembly in the theatre, and they were upon the point of assembling, news arrived that the forty-two ships under Agesandridas were sailing from Megara along the coast of Salamis. The people to a man now thought that it was just what Theramenes and his party had so often said, that the ships were sailing to the fortification, and concluded that they had done well to demolish it. But though it may possibly have been by appointment that Agesandridas hovered about Epidaurus and the neighbourhood, he would also naturally be kept there by the hope of an opportunity arising out of the troubles in the town. In any case the Athenians, on receipt of the news, immediately ran down in mass to Piræus, seeing themselves threatened by the enemy with a worse war than their war among themselves, not at a distance, but close to the harbour of Athens. Some went on board the ships already afloat, while others launched fresh vessels, or ran to defend the walls and the mouth of the harbour.

95. Meanwhile the Peloponnesian vessels sailed by, and rounding Sunium anchored between Thoricus and Prasiæ, and afterwards arrived at Oropus. The Athenians, with revolution in the city, and unwilling to lose a moment in going to the relief of their most important possession (for Eubœa was everything to them now that they were shut out from Attica),* were compelled to put to sea in haste and with untrained crews, and sent Thymochares with some vessels to Eretria. These upon their arrival, with the ships already in Eubœa, made up a total of thirty-six vessels, and were immediately forced to engage. For Agesandridas, after his crews had dined, put out from Oropus, which is about seven miles from Eretria by sea; and the Athenians, seeing him sailing up, immediately began to man their vessels. The sailors, however, instead of being by their ships, as they supposed, were gone away to purchase provisions for their dinner in the houses in the outskirts of the town; the Eretrians having so arranged that there should

---

*Since Attica was under siege and attack by the Spartan outpost at Deceleia, the island of Euboea furnished the Athenians with their everyday necessities.

be nothing on sale in the market-place, in order that the Athenians might be a long time in manning their ships, and the enemy's attack taking them by surprise, might be compelled to put to sea just as they were.* A signal also was raised in Eretria to give them notice in Oropus when to put to sea.

The Athenians, forced to put out so poorly prepared, engaged off the harbour of Eretria, and after holding their own for some little while notwithstanding, were at length put to flight and chased to the shore. Such of their number as took refuge in Eretria, which they presumed to be friendly to them, found their fate in that city, being butchered by the inhabitants; while those who fled to the Athenian fort in the Eretrian territory, and the vessels which got to Chalcis, were saved.†

The Peloponnesians, after taking twenty-two Athenian ships, and killing or making prisoners of the crews, set up a trophy, and not long afterwards effected the revolt of the whole of Eubœa (except Oreus, which was held by the Athenians themselves), and made a general settlement of the affairs of the island.

96. When the news of what had happened in Eubœa reached Athens a panic ensued such as they had never before known.

Neither the disaster in Sicily, great as it seemed at the time, nor any other had ever so much alarmed them. The camp at Samos was in revolt; they had no more ships or men to man them; they were at discord among themselves and might at any moment come to blows; and a disaster of this magnitude coming on the top of all, by which they lost their fleet, and worst of all Eubœa, which was of more value to them than Attica, could not occur without throwing them into the deepest despondency.

Meanwhile their greatest and most immediate trouble was the possibility that the enemy, emboldened by his victory, might make straight for them and sail against Piræus, which they had no longer ships to defend; and every moment they expected him to arrive. This, with a little more courage, he might easily have done,‡ in which case he would either have increased the dissensions of the city by his presence, or if he had stayed to besiege it have compelled the fleet from Ionia, although

---

*The people of Eretria in Euboea, like the other native islanders, were eager to rid themselves of their Athenian occupiers (see their decree, Fornara #152).

†The defeated Athenians were put to death by their subjects, if they managed to reach land. The Athenians in the city panicked again (compare 2.94; 8.1). Invasion was imminent.

‡Thucydides ratifies the special and unutilized Spartan opportunity. A Spartan fleet could have either magnified internal turmoil by its threatening presence or forced the Samian forces to return home to defend the homeland and give up their overseas territories.

the enemy of the oligarchy, to come to the rescue of their country and of their relatives, and in the meantime would have become master of the Hellespont, Ionia, the islands, and of everything as far as Eubœa, or, to speak roundly, of the whole Athenian empire.

But here, as on so many other occasions, the Lacedæmonians proved the most convenient people in the world for the Athenians to be at war with. The wide difference between the two characters, the slowness and want of energy of the Lacedæmonians as contrasted with the dash and enterprise of their opponents, proved of the greatest service, especially to a maritime empire like Athens. Indeed this was shown by the Syracusans, who were most like the Athenians in character, and also most successful in combating them.*

97. Nevertheless, upon receipt of the news, the Athenians manned twenty ships and called immediately a first assembly in the Pnyx, where they had been used to meet formerly, and deposed the Four Hundred and voted to hand over the government to the Five Thousand, of which body all who furnished a suit of armour were to be members, decreeing also that no one should receive pay for the discharge of any office, or if he did should be held accursed.† Many other assemblies were held afterwards, in which law-makers were elected and all other measures taken to form a constitution. It was during the first period of this constitution that the Athenians appear to have enjoyed the best government that they ever did, at least in my time. For the fusion of the high and the low was effected with judgment, and this was what first enabled the state to raise up her head after her manifold disasters. They also voted for the recall of Alcibiades and of other exiles, and sent to him and to the camp at Samos, and urged them to devote themselves vigorously to the war.‡

98. Upon this revolution taking place, the party of Pisander and Alexicles, and the chiefs of the oligarchs immediately withdrew to Decelea, with the single exception of Aristarchus, one of the generals,

---

*The Spartans were as different as could be, usually cautious to a fault rather than speculative or foolhardy. The Syracusans showed Athenian aggressiveness and enterprise, as described in the invasion of Sicily (books 6 and 7) and thereby anticipated their enemy's moves more effectively. But Thucydides indulges in more generalization here than he can justify.

†In the extremity of anxiety, the Athenians in the city met on the democratic Pnyx, a hill just southwest of the Acropolis suitably modified for meetings of the democratic assembly. The government of the Five Thousand drew Thucydides' admiration, but he offers few particulars except for their moderation. The refusal to provide pay for offices is a vestige of oligarchic, or rather, plutocratic ideology.

‡The oligarchy did not recall Alcibiades, realizing that his adhesion would do them no good. Those speaking for the Five Thousand recalled him and still others (but not Thucydides) in an effort to restore the war-worthiness of the state. Alcibiades did not return until 407, when an achieved victory or two seemed to insure his safety.

who hastily took some of the most barbarian of the archers and marched to Œnoe. This was a fort of the Athenians upon the Bœotian border, at that moment besieged by the Corinthians, irritated by the loss of a party returning from Decelea, who had been cut off by the garrison. The Corinthians had volunteered for this service, and had called upon the Bœotians to assist them. After communicating with them, Aristarchus deceived the garrison in Œnoe by telling them that their countrymen in the city had compounded with the Lacedæmonians, and that one of the terms of the capitulation was that they must surrender the place to the Bœotians. The garrison believed him as he was general, and besides knew nothing of what had occurred owing to the siege, and so evacuated the fort under truce.* In this way the Bœotians gained possession of Œnoe, and the oligarchy and the troubles at Athens ended.

99. At the same time of this summer, for the Peloponnesians in Miletus, no pay was forthcoming from any of the agents deputed by Tissaphernes for that purpose upon his departure for Aspendus. Neither the Phœnician fleet nor Tissaphernes showed any signs of appearing, and Philip, who had been sent with him, and another Spartan, Hippocrates, who was at Phaselis, wrote word to Mindarus, the admiral, that the ships were not coming at all, and that they were being grossly abused by Tissaphernes. Meanwhile Pharnabazus was inviting them to come, and making every effort to get the fleet and, like Tissaphernes, to cause the revolt of the cities in his government still subject to Athens, founding great hopes on his success. At length, at about this period of the summer, Mindarus yielded to his importunities, and, with great order and at a moment's notice, in order to elude the enemy at Samos, weighed anchor with seventy-three ships from Miletus and set sail for the Hellespont.† Thither sixteen vessels had already preceded him in the same summer, and had overrun part of the Chersonese. Being caught in a storm, Mindarus was compelled to run in to Icarus, and after being detained five or six days there by stress of weather, arrived at Chios.

100. Meanwhile Thrasyllus had heard of his having put out from Miletus, and immediately set sail with fifty-five ships from Samos, in haste to arrive before him in the Hellespont. But learning that he was at Chios, and expecting that he would stay there, he posted scouts in

---

*Aristarchus hands over Oenoe, a fortified Athenian outpost on the Boeotian frontier (map 2), to the enemy. This act of treachery further dooms the subsequent reputation of the Four Hundred. The other oligarchs run for safety at Decelea—except Antiphon, who stayed. He was tried and executed.

†Tissaphernes repeatedly proved his feckless or clever unwillingness to fight with and for the Peloponnesians. Those tired warriors turned to Pharnabazus to the north in the Hellespont, hoping for cooperative attacks on the Athenian empire.

Lesbos and on the continent opposite to prevent the fleet moving without his knowing it, and himself coasted along to Methymna, and gave orders to prepare barley-meal and other necessities, in order to attack them from Lesbos in the event of their remaining for any length of time at Chios. Meanwhile he resolved to sail against Eresus, a town in Lesbos which had revolted, and, if he could, to take it. For some of the principal Methymnian exiles had carried over about fifty heavy infantry, their sworn associates, from Cuma, and hiring others from the continent, so as to make up three hundred in all, chose Anaxander, a Theban, to command them, on account of the community of blood existing between the Thebans and the Lesbians, and first attacked Methymna.

Baulked in this attempt by the advance of the Athenian guards from Mitylene, and repulsed a second time in a battle outside the city, they then crossed the mountain and effected the revolt of Eresus. Thrasyllus accordingly determined to go there with all his ships and to attack the place. Meanwhile Thrasybulus had preceded him thither with five ships from Samos, as soon as he heard that the exiles had crossed over, and coming too late to save Eresus, went on and anchored before the town. Here they were joined also by two vessels on their way home from the Hellespont, and by the ships of the Methymnians, making a grand total of sixty-seven vessels; and the forces on board now made ready with engines and every other means available to do their utmost to storm Eresus.

101. In the meantime Mindarus and the Peloponnesian fleet at Chios, after taking provisions for two days and receiving three Chian coins for each man from the Chians, on the third day put out in haste from the island; in order to avoid falling in with the ships at Eresus, they did not make for the open sea, but keeping Lesbos on their left, sailed for the continent. After touching at the port of Carteria, in the Phocæid, and dining, they went on along the Cumæan coast and supped at Arginusæ, on the continent over against Mitylene. From thence they continued their voyage along the coast, although it was late in the night, and arriving at Harmatus on the continent opposite Methymna, dined there; and swiftly passing Lectum, Larisa, Hamaxitus, and the neighbouring towns, arrived a little before midnight at Rhœteum. Here they were now in the Hellespont. Some of the ships also put in at Sigeum and at other places in the neighbourhood.*

102. Meanwhile the warnings of the fire-signals and the sudden increase in the number of fires on the enemy's shore informed the eighteen Athenian ships at Sestos of the approach of the Peloponnesian fleet. That very night they set sail in haste just as they were,

---

*The Peloponnesians travel north along the coast from Ionia toward the Hellespont. The fleet made very good time in a day.

and hugging the shore of the Chersonese, coasted along to Elæus, in order to sail out into the open sea away from the fleet of the enemy. After passing unobserved the sixteen ships at Abydos, which had nevertheless been warned by their approaching friends to be on the alert to prevent their sailing out, at dawn they sighted the fleet of Mindarus, which immediately gave chase. All had not time to get away; the greater number however escaped to Imbros and Lemnos, while four of the hindmost were overtaken off Elæus. One of these was stranded opposite to the temple of Protesilaus and taken with its crew, two others without their crews; the fourth was abandoned on the shore of Imbros and burned by the enemy.

103. After this the Peloponnesians were joined by the squadron from Abydos, which made up their fleet to a grand total of eighty-six vessels; they spent the day in unsuccessfully besieging Elæus, and then sailed back to Abydos. Meanwhile the Athenians, deceived by their scouts, and never dreaming of the enemy's fleet getting by undetected, were tranquilly besieging Eresus. As soon as they heard the news they instantly abandoned Eresus, and made with all speed for the Hellespont, and after taking two of the Peloponnesian ships which had been carried out too far into the open sea in the ardour of the pursuit and now fell in their way, the next day dropped anchor at Elæus, and bringing back the ships that had taken refuge at Imbros, during five days prepared for the coming engagement.

104. After this they engaged in the following way.* The Athenians formed in column and sailed close along shore to Sestos; upon perceiving which the Peloponnesians put out from Abydos to meet them. Realising that a battle was now imminent, both combatants extended their flank; the Athenians along the Chersonese from Idacus to Arrhiani with seventy-six ships; the Peloponnesians from Abydos to Dardanus with eighty-six. The Peloponnesian right wing was occupied by the Syracusans, their left by Mindarus in person with the best sailers in the navy; the Athenian left by Thrasyllus, their right by Thrasybulus, the other commanders being in different parts of the fleet. The Peloponnesians hastened to engage first, and outflanking with their left the Athenian right sought to cut them off, if possible, from sailing out of the straits, and to drive their centre upon the shore, which was not far off. The Athenians perceiving their intention extended their own wing and outsailed them, while their left had by this time passed the point of Cynossema. This, however, obliged them to thin and weaken their centre, especially as they had fewer ships than the enemy, and as the

---

*The Athenian ships massed up to follow the enemy from their siege and port in Eresus on the western coast of Lesbos. The engagement near Sestos pitted 76 Athenian ships facing east against 86 Peloponnesians facing west. The battle eventually extended beyond the southern tip of the Chersonnesus (map 12).

coast round Point Cynossema formed a sharp angle which prevented their seeing what was going on on the other side of it.

105. The Peloponnesians now attacked their centre and drove ashore the ships of the Athenians, and disembarked to follow up their victory. No help could be given to the centre either by the squadron of Thrasybulus on the right, on account of the number of ships attacking him, or by that of Thrasyllus on the left, from whom the point of Cynossema hid what was going on, and who was also hindered by his Syracusan and other opponents, whose numbers were fully equal to his own. At length, however, the Peloponnesians in the confidence of victory began to scatter in pursuit of the ships of the enemy, and allowed a considerable part of their fleet to get into disorder. On seeing this the squadron of Thrasybulus discontinued their lateral movement and, facing about,* attacked and routed the ships opposed to them, and next fell roughly upon the scattered vessels of the victorious Peloponnesian division, and put most of them to flight without a blow. The Syracusans also had by this time given way before the squadron of Thrasyllus, and now openly took to flight upon seeing the flight of their comrades.

106. The rout was now complete. Most of the Peloponnesians fled for refuge first to the river Midius, and afterwards to Abydos. Only a few ships were taken by the Athenians; as owing to the narrowness of the Hellespont the enemy had not far to go to be in safety. Nevertheless nothing could have been more opportune for them than this victory. Up to this time they had feared the Peloponnesian fleet, owing to a number of petty losses and to the disaster in Sicily; but they now ceased to mistrust themselves or any longer to think their enemies good for anything at sea. Meanwhile they took from the enemy eight Chian vessels, five Corinthian, two Ambraciot, two Bœotian, one Leucadian, Lacedæmonian, Syracusan, and Pellenian, losing fifteen of their own. After setting up a trophy upon Point Cynossema, securing the wrecks, and restoring to the enemy his dead under truce, they sent off a galley to Athens with the news of their victory. The arrival of this vessel with its unhoped-for good news, after the recent disasters of Eubœa, and in the revolution at Athens, gave fresh courage to the Athenians, and caused them to believe that if they fought on resolutely, their cause might yet prevail.†

---

*The Athenian weakened center led to Peloponnesian advantage, but their overconfidence led to a decisive Athenian victory and Peloponnesian rout.

†The Athenian victory at Cynossema gave fresh heart to the seriously discouraged Athenians. The Peloponnesian forces had recently routed them off Euboea (8.96) and they still faced internal political divisions of a murderous sort, but now they once again had some hope of prevailing, if the Persians lent their forces to their cause. They retook rebellious Cyzicus on the Asiatic Hellespont. (Fornara #154 records an inscription with Athenian war expenses of the next year.)

107. On the fourth day after the sea-fight the Athenians in Sestos having hastily refitted their ships sailed against Cyzicus, which had revolted. Off Harpagium and Priapus they sighted at anchor the eight vessels from Byzantium, and sailing up and routing the troops on shore, took the ships, and then went on and recovered the town of Cyzicus, which was unfortified, and levied money from the citizens. In the meantime the Peloponnesians sailed from Abydos to Elæus, and recovered such of their captured galleys as were still uninjured, the rest having been burned by the Elæusians, and sent Hippocrates and Epicles to Eubœa to fetch the squadron from that island.

108. About the same time Alcibiades returned with his thirteen ships from Caunus and Phaselis to Samos, bringing word that he had prevented the Phœnician fleet from joining the Peloponnesians, and had made Tissaphernes more friendly to the Athenians than before.* Alcibiades now manned nine more ships, and levied large sums of money from the Halicarnassians, and fortified Cos. After doing this and placing a governor in Cos, he sailed back to Samos, autumn being now at hand. Meanwhile Tissaphernes, upon hearing that the Peloponnesian fleet had sailed from Miletus to the Hellespont, set off again back from Aspendus, and made all sail for Ionia. While the Peloponnesians were in the Hellespont, the Antandrians, a people of Æolic extraction, conveyed by land across Mount Ida some heavy infantry from Abydos, and introduced them into the town, having been ill-treated by Arsaces, the Persian lieutenant of Tissaphernes. This same Arsaces had, upon pretence of a secret quarrel, invited the chief men of the Delians to undertake military service (these were Delians who had settled at Atramyttium after having been driven from their homes by the Athenians for the sake of purifying Delos); and after drawing them out from their town as his friends and allies, had laid wait for them at dinner, and surrounded them and caused them to be shot down by his soldiers. This deed made the Antandrians fear that he might some day do them some mischief; and as he also laid upon them burdens too heavy for them to bear, they expelled his garrison from their citadel.†

109. Tissaphernes upon hearing of this act of the Peloponnesians in addition to what had occurred at Miletus and Cnidus, where his garrisons had been also expelled, now saw that the breach between them was serious; and fearing further injury from them, and being also vexed to think that Pharnabazus should receive them, and in less time

---

*Alcibiades re-enters the picture, still making false claims. His untrustworthiness did not mean he never did significant services for his friends of the moment.

†Tissaphernes' lieutenants, Tamos and Arsaces, matched their boss's profile. The Delian episode occurred in 421, the last year of the Ten Years' War (5.1 and 32). The Persians do not try hard to gain the goodwill of their erstwhile subjects.

and at less cost perhaps succeed better against Athens than he had done, determined to rejoin them in the Hellespont, in order to complain of the events at Antandros and excuse himself as best he could in the matter of the Phœnician fleet and of the other charges against him. Accordingly he went first to Ephesus and offered sacrifice to Artemis. . . .*

[When the winter after this summer is over the twenty-first year of this war will be completed.]†

---

*Tissaphernes cannot prevail without Peloponnesian help. Pharnabazus is his rival, and indeed enemy, so the satrap of Ionia returns to try to heal the breach with his former allies. Thucydides does not elsewhere record any sacrifice of an individual to a divinity. Tissaphernes may be sacrificing to the more Asiatic Artemis worshiped at Ephesus. The Greek breaks off not only in the middle of events but probably in the middle of a sentence. Perhaps Tissaphernes was about to make an important policy announcement. If so, we do not find it in the immediate continuation of events written by Xenophon, the *Hellenica*, a weakly Thucydidean history that carries the story of Greek internecine warfare down to 362.

†The bracketed sentence is probably an ancient editorial addition to Thucydides' incomplete manuscript or a later scribal note to provide some kind of closure, however inadequate. There is no evidence that Thucydides wrote more of his history, which extends only to 411, than we have. Several extant or reported ancient continuations, which begin from this insignificant point and extend to the end of this war in 404 (compare 2.65 and 5.26), support the belief that the Athenian historian never wrote another page.

INSPIRED BY THE *HISTORY OF THE PELOPONNESIAN WAR*

It was Quintilian or Mr. Max Beerbohm who said, "History repeats itself: historians repeat each other." The saying is full of the mellow wisdom of either writer, and stamped with the peculiar veracity of the Silver Age of Roman or British epigram. One might have added, if the aphorist had stayed for an answer, that history is rather interesting when it repeats itself: historians are not.

—PHILIP GUEDALLA, *SUPERS AND SUPERMEN* (1920)

The most obvious legacy of Thucydides is nearly all modern knowledge of the series of conflicts known as the Peloponnesian War. Scattered Athenian literary sources, inscriptions, and archaeological evidence from throughout the region provide additional insights into the conflict and the life of the age, but none of these artifacts approach the comprehensiveness of the record left by Thucydides. And the Spartans not only did not keep written records of political events but held this as a point of pride. For these reasons, broad accounts of the war throughout history have been drawn almost entirely from the work of the Athenian Thucydides. He had not completed his narrative at the time of his death, and a number of contemporary histories—including one by Xenophon, the only surviving example—began where Thucydides' book 8 abruptly ends.

Only a handful of ancient literary borrowings from *History of the Peloponnesian War* have survived the passage of time. The description by Thucydides of the plague at Athens inspired a number of ancient writers composing on similar topics, most notably Lucretius (94–55 B.C.E) in his didactic Epicurean epic *On the Nature of Things* and Ovid (43 B.C.E–17 C.E.), whose account in the *Metamorphoses* of the plague at Aegina owes much to the earlier author. Plutarch (c.45–120 C.E.) used Thucydides as a major source for his *Lives*, which chronicles a number of the most interesting personalities of the Peloponnesian War, including the Athenians Pericles, Nicias, and Alcibiades, and the Spartan Lysander. In addition to these established links to Thucydides' work is the legend that, in an effort to increase his rhetorical powers, Demosthenes (384–322 B.C.E.), Greece's greatest orator, copied out the whole of *History of the Peloponnesian War* eight times.

As with most Greek writers, Thucydides was ignored almost entirely in the centuries following the fall of the Roman Empire, then was rediscovered during the Renaissance in Europe. One step in his fortunate rediscovery was made by the Italian humanist Lorenzo Valla, who published a Latin translation of *History of the Peloponnesian War* in the 1450s. French and English translations from Valla's Latin appeared in the early- and mid-sixteenth century, and because of the burgeoning interest in antiquity, Thucydides became regular reading for students in Western Europe. In 1628 British political philosopher Thomas Hobbes, best known for the tract *Leviathan* (1651), published his English translation of *History of the Peloponnesian War* from the ancient Greek.

Nineteenth-century scholars and writers perpetuated the deep respect for classical learning, including the work of Thucydides, that had developed in the Renaissance. In the 1830s Thomas Arnold, father of great English poet and critic Matthew Arnold, published a monumental commentary on *History of the Peloponnesian War*. Matthew Arnold's "Dover Beach" (1867), one of the preeminent poems of the nineteenth century, is thought to have been inspired in part by Thucydides' description of the moonlit battle at Epipolae. During the conflict, the opposing forces couldn't distinguish their allies from their enemies in the dim night's light, and the result was utter chaos. After invoking "the turbid ebb and flow / Of human misery" that Sophocles perceived on the Aegean Sea, Arnold's melancholy lyric describes the aimlessness and terror that besets man in general. The poem closes with these lines: "And we are here as on a darkling plain / Swept with confused alarms of struggle and flight, / Where ignorant armies clash by night."

Events of the twentieth and twenty-first centuries have given new relevance to the *History of the Peloponnesian War*. Great thinkers in all disciplines have seen parallels between the record of Thucydides and the large-scale conflicts, complicated global politics, and genocides of the modern era. As a testament to the aphorism "History repeats itself," the Peloponnesian War as described by Thucydides has been compared by politicians and writers to every major war of the twentieth century. Anglo-American poet W. H. Auden did so notably in the poem "September 1, 1939" (1940), named for the day Germany invaded Poland, giving rise to World War II. Describing the fear, anger, and revulsion engendered by the invasion, the poem asserts that Thucydides had already recorded everything that could be said about dictators and democracies; it goes on to remark that the Greek historian, with regard to war, "analysed all in his book," including flight from reason, pain that builds upon itself, and the capacity for "mismanagement and grief." The stanza continues ominously, "We must suffer them all again." Philip Guedalla, Matthew Arnold, W. H. Auden, and Thucydides all warn that as long as mankind continues to indulge its impulse for armed conflict, the horrors of the Peloponnesian War will recur and its lessons will remain unlearned.

COMMENTS & QUESTIONS

In this section, we aim to provide the reader with an array of perspectives on the text, as well as questions that challenge those perspectives. The commentary has been culled from sources as diverse as comments contemporaneous with the work, literary criticism of later generations, and appreciations written throughout the work's history. Following the commentaries, a series of questions seeks to filter Thucydides's History of the Peloponnesian War *through a variety of points of view and bring about a richer understanding of this enduring work.*

Comments

DIONYSIUS OF HALICARNASSUS

Philosophers and rhetoricians, if not all of them, yet most of them, bear witness to Thucydides that he has been most careful of the truth, the high-priestess of which we desire history to be. He adds nothing to the facts that should not be added, and takes nothing therefrom, nor does he take advantage of his position as a writer, but he adheres to his purpose without wavering, leaving no room for criticism, and abstaining from envy and flattery of every kind, particularly in his appreciation of men of merit. . . .

The defects of Thucydidean workmanship and the features that are criticized by some persons relate to the more technical side of his subject matter, what is called the economy of the discourse, something that is desirable in all kinds of writing, whether one chooses philosophical or oratorical subjects. The matter in question has to do with the division (diairesis), order (taxis) and development (exergasia).

—as translated by W. Kendrick Pritchett,
from *On Thucydides* (late first century B.C.E.)

PLUTARCH

Thucydides aimeth always at this; to make his auditor a spectator, and to cast his reader into the same passions that they were in that were beholders. The manner how Demosthenes arranged the Athenians on the rugged shore before Pylus; how Brasidas urged the steersman to run his galley aground; how he went to the ladder or place in the galley for descent; how he was hurt, and swooned, and fell down on the ledges of the galley; how the Spartans fought after the manner of a land-fight upon the sea, and the Athenians of a sea-fight upon land: again, in the Sicilian war, how a battle was fought by sea and land with equal fortune: these things, I say, are so described and so evidently set before our eyes, that the mind of the reader is no less affected therewith than if he had been present in the actions.

—as translated by Thomas Hobbes,
from *De gloria Atheniensium* (late first century C.E.)

THOMAS HOBBES

It hath been noted by divers, that Homer in poesy, Aristotle in philosophy, Demosthenes in eloquence, and others of the ancients in other knowledge, do still maintain their primacy: none of them exceeded, some not approached, by any in these later ages. And in the number of these is justly ranked also our Thucydides; a workman no less perfect in his work, than any of the former; and in whom (I believe with many others) the faculty of writing history is at the highest. . . . He filleth his narrations with that choice of matter, and ordereth them with that judgment, and with such perspicuity and efficacy expresseth himself, that, as Plutarch saith, he maketh his auditor a spectator. For he setteth his reader in the assemblies of the people and in the senate, at their debating; in the streets, at their seditions; and in the field, at their battles. So that look how much a man of understanding might have added to his experience, if he had then lived a beholder of their proceedings, and familiar with the men and business of the time: so much almost may he profit now, by attentive reading of the same here written. He may from the narrations draw out lessons to himself, and of himself be able to trace the drifts and counsels of the actors to their seat. . . .

For the principal and proper work of history being to instruct and enable men, by the knowledge of actions past, to bear themselves prudently in the present and providently towards the future: there is not extant any other (merely human) that doth more naturally and fully perform it, than this of my author. . . . Thucydides is one who, though he never digress to read a lecture, moral or political, upon his own text, nor enter into men's hearts further than the acts themselves evidently guide him: is yet accounted the most politic historiographer that ever writ.

—from "To the Readers,"
in *Eight Bookes of the Peloponnesian Warre* (1629)

DAVID HUME

The first page of THUCYDIDES is, in my opinion, the commencement of real history. All preceding narrations are so intermixed with fable, that philosophers ought to abandon them, in a great measure, to the embellishment of poets and orators.

—from *Essays Moral, Political, and Literary* (1741–1742)

MATTHEW ARNOLD

Let us pass to what we said was the supreme characteristic of a highly developed, a modern age—the manifestation of a critical spirit, the endeavour after a rational arrangement and appreciation of facts. Let us consider one or two of the passages in the masterly introduction which Thucydides, the contemporary of Pericles, has prefixed to his history. What was his motive in choosing the Peloponnesian War for his subject? Because it was, in his opinion, the most important, the most instructive event which had, up to that time, happened in the history of mankind. What is his effort in the first twenty-three chapters of his history? To place in their correct point of view all the facts which had brought Grecian society to the point at which that dominant event found it; to strip these facts of their exaggeration, to examine them critically. . . . No doubt Thucydides' criticism of the Trojan War is not perfect; but observe how in these and many other points he labours to correct popular errors, to assign their true character to facts, complaining, as he does so, of men's habit of *uncritical* reception of current stories. . . .

What language shall we properly call this? It is *modern* language; it is the language of a thoughtful philosophic man of our own days; it is the language of Burke or Niebuhr assigning the true aim of history. And yet Thucydides is no mere literary man; no isolated thinker, speaking far over the heads of his hearers to a future age—no: he was a man of action, a man of the world, a man of his time. He represents, at its best indeed, but he represents, the general intelligence of his age and nation; of a nation the meanest citizens of which could follow with comprehension the profoundly thoughtful speeches of Pericles.

—from *Macmillan's Magazine* (February 1869)

GEORGE GROTE

Of this conversation [the Melian dialogue] Thucydides professes to give a detailed and elaborate account, at surprising length, considering his general brevity. . . . What we here read in Thucydides is in far larger proportion his own and in smaller proportion authentic report, than any of the other speeches which he professes to set down.

—from *History of Greece* (1871)

GILBERT MURRAY

THUCYDIDES determined to watch that war from the start, mark every step, trace every cause, hide nothing and exaggerate nothing—do all that Herodotus had not done or tried to do. . . .

It is characteristic both of the man and of a certain side of Athenian culture, that he turned away from his main task of narrative to develop the style of his work as pure literature. Instead of finishing the chronicle of the war, he worked over his reports of the arguments people had used, or the policies various parties had followed, into elaborate and direct speeches. Prose style at the time had its highest development in the form of rhetoric; and that turn of mind, always characteristic of Greece, which delighted in understanding both sides of a question, and would not rest till it knew every seeming wrong-doer's apology, was especially strong. The speeches are Thucydides's highest literary efforts. . . .

He seeks truth as diligently and relentlessly as a modern antiquary who has no object for concealment or exaggeration. But his aim is a different one. He is not going to provide material for his readers to work upon. He is going to do the whole work himself—to be the one judge of truth, and as such to give his results in artistic and final form, no evidence produced and no source quoted. A significant point, perhaps, is his use of documents on the one hand and speeches on the other. Speaking roughly, one may say that in the finished parts of his work there are no documents; in the unfinished there are no speeches. With regard to the speeches the case is clear. Nearly all bear the marks of being written after the end of the war. The unfinished Eighth Book has not a single speech; the unfinished part of Book V only the Melian Dialogue. . . .

Thucydides's style as it stands in our texts is an extraordinary phenomenon. Undeniably a great style, terse, restrained, vivid, and leaving the impression of a powerful intellect. Undeniably also an artificial style, obscure amid its vividness, archaistic and poetic in vocabulary, and apt to run into verbal flourishes which seem to have little thought behind them. Part of this is explicable enough. He writes an artificial semi-Ionic dialect, *xun* for *meta*, *hên* for *ean*, *prassô* for *prattô*. The literary tradition explains that. Literature in Greek has always a tendency to shape itself a language of its own. He is overladen with antitheses, he instinctively sees things in pairs; so do Gorgias and Antiphon. He is fond of distinguishing between synonyms; that is the effect of Prodicus. He is always inverting the order of his words, throwing separate details into violent relief, which makes it hard to see the whole chain of thought. This is evidently part of the man's peculiar nature. He does it far more than Antiphon and Gorgias, more even than Sophocles. His own nature, too, is responsible for the crowding of matter and thought that one feels in reading him— the new idea, the new logical distinction, pressing in before the old one is comfortably disposed of. He is by nature '*Semper instans sibi*' (Quintilian). A certain freedom in grammar is common to all Greek, probably to all really thoughtful and vivid writers: abstract singular nouns with plural verbs, slight anacolutha [shifts in syntax], intelligible compressions of speech. But what is not explicable in Thucydides is that he should have fallen into the absolute hodge-podge of ungrammatical and unnatural language, the disconcerting trails of comment and explanation, which occur on every third page. . . .

To return from this inevitable digression, we see easily how Thucydides was naturally in some antagonism to Herodotus's whole method of viewing things. Thucydides had no supernatural actors in his narrative. He sees no suggestion—how could he in the wrecked world that lay before him?—of the working of a Divine Providence. His spirit is *positif*; he does not speak of things he knows nothing about. He is a little sardonic about oracles, which of course filled the air at the time. He instances their safe ambiguity (2.17, 54), and mentions as a curiosity the only one he had ever known to come definitely true (5.26). He speaks little of persons. He realises the influence of a great man such as Pericles, a mere demagogue such as Cleon, an unscrupulous genius such as Alcibiades. Living in a psychological age, he studies these men's characters and modes of thought, studies them sometimes with vivid dramatic personation, in the speeches and elsewhere; but it is only the mind, never the manner or the matter, that he cares for, and he never condescends to gossip. He cares for big movements and organised forces. He believes above all things in reason, brain-power, intelligence.

—from *A History of Ancient Greek Literature* (1897)

JOHN B. BURY

But it was part of his artistic method to cover up all the traces of his procedure, in his finished narrative. [Thucydides'] principle is to mention only effective policies, and to mention them for the first time when they begin to become effective.

—from *The Ancient Greek Historians* (1909)

HENRY BRADLEY

There is a real problem, no doubt, in Thuc.'s queer gibberish. . . . The art of prose requires a long development, and although for straightforward tale-telling it had got a good way on, Thucydides was putting it to a new strain in his reflective passages, and he had been I suppose rather a man of action than of letters.

—from a letter to Robert Bridges (March 13, 1912)

THEODORE ROOSEVELT

We could better afford to lose every Greek inscription that has ever been found than the chapter in which Thucydides tells of the Athenian failure before Syracuse.   —from *History as Literature* (1913)

HAROLD LASKI

I read Thucydides I–IV with immense humility. There is something simply beyond even one's wildest dreams of creativeness. You read Thucydides line by line and each word is as vivid as a drop of blood. He has Tacitus beaten by miles for dramatic power.

—from a letter to Oliver Wendell Holmes (August 14, 1921)

ROBIN COLLINGWOOD

Herodotus had no successors. . . . The difference between the scientific outlook of Herodotus and that of Thucydides is hardly less remarkable than the difference between their literary styles. The style of Herodotus is easy, spontaneous, convincing. That of Thucydides is harsh, artificial, repellent. In reading Thucydides I ask myself, What is the matter with the man, that he writes like that? I answer: he has a bad conscience. He is trying to justify himself for writing history at all by turning it into something that is not history. . . . Thucydides is the father of psychological history. Now what is psychological history? It is not history at all. . . . Its chief purpose is to affirm laws, psychological laws.   —from *The Idea of History* (1946)

THORLEIF BOMAN

Thucydides wrote his history because what happened would, according to human ways, surely happen again in the future in the same or a similar way. This was conceived in a genuinely Greek way, for history is an eternal repetition; nothing new happens under the sun. Even in the stream of eternally changing events the Greeks sought the unalterable, the regular occurrence.

—as translated by Jules L. Moreau,
from *Hebrew Thought Compared with Greek* (1954)

ARNALDO MOMIGLIANO

Thucydides did not believe that there was a future in Herodotus' attempt to describe events he had not witnessed and to tell the story of men whose language he could not understand. . . . He was setting up stricter standards of historical reliability, even at the risk of confining history to a narrow patch of contemporary events.

—from *Studies in Historiography* (1954)

WALTER KARP

Around the time Republicans were vowing to "roll back Communism," a wise old college professor of mine suggested that his Humanities 1 class might get more out of Thucydides if it compared the Peloponnesian War to the ongoing struggle between America and Russia, then only recently named the Cold War. . . .

The combatants we identified readily. Authoritarian Sparta, ruling over a mass of terrified helots, was plainly the Soviet Union. Democratic Athens was America, of course. . . .

Two things struck me as I read: that the Cold War, now so long protracted, had come to resemble the Peloponnesian War more than ever and that in this resemblance lay a wholly unexpected vindication of political history, created by Thucydides.

—from *Harper's Magazine* (March 1981)

Questions

1. Is Pericles' funeral oration still relevant?

2. Was democracy the ultimate cause of the Athenian disaster—whether or not it was also the cause of Athenian greatness?

3. Select one episode from the *History of the Peloponnesian War* and explain how a modern historian might evaluate the situation differently.

4. Does the *History of the Peloponnesian War* give one a perspective on the recent American wars in Korea, Vietnam, and Iraq?

5. What do you think of Alcibiades? Was he a clever egoist or a man too large for the small people who controlled his destiny?

FOR FURTHER READING

The five titles marked with an asterisk are essential works of reference and interpretation.

Historical Contexts: The Early Classical Age of Greece
(c.479–400 B.C.E.)

Boardman, J. N., N. G. L. Hammond, D. M. Lewis, and M. Ostwald, eds. *Persia, Greece, and the Western Mediterranean c.525 to 479 B.C.* Vol. 4 of *The Cambridge Ancient History*. Second edition. Cambridge: Cambridge University Press, 1988. Recent, thorough historical survey that includes archaeological research.

Carradice, Ian. *Greek Coins*. Austin: University of Texas Press, 1995. Introduction to the development and role of coinage in Greek life and to numismatics as evidence for the historian.

Connolly, Peter, and Hazel Dodge. *The Ancient City*. Oxford: Oxford University Press, 1998. Useful, well-illustrated introduction to daily life in ancient (classical) Athens and Rome.

Dillon, Matthew, and Lynda Garland, eds. *Ancient Greece: Social and Historical Documents from Archaic Times to the Death of Socrates (c.800–399 B.C.)*. Second edition. London and New York: Routledge, 2000. Fuller selection than Fornara's *Archaic Times to the End of the Peloponnesian War* (see below), with elementary commentary.

* Fornara, Charles. *Archaic Times to the End of the Peloponnesian War.* Vol. 1 in *Translated Documents of Greece and Rome*. Second edition. Cambridge: Cambridge University Press, 1983. Translates and annotates documentary, nonliterary sources, chiefly inscriptions; in this edition of Thucydides' *History*, references to "Fornara" in the notes refer to document numbers in *Archaic Times*.

Garland, Robert. *The Greek Way of Life: From Conception to Old Age*. Ithaca, NY: Cornell University Press, 1990. Informed introduction to secular and sacred rituals and attitudes toward stages in human development.

Grote, George. *A History of Greece*. 1846–1856. New York: Harper, 1871 (12 vols.) and later edition in London: Murray, 1888 (10 vols.). The first historian to present democratic Athens sympathetically and to read Thucydides critically.

* Hornblower, Simon, and Antony Spawforth, eds. *The Oxford Classical Dictionary.* Third edition, revised. Oxford and New York: Oxford University Press, 2003. Excellent first resource for locating people, places, and institutions.

Kallett-Marx, L. *Money, Expense and Naval Power in Thucydides' History 1–5.24.* Berkeley: University of California Press, 1993. Traces of economic history in the most politic of historians.

Levi, Peter, ed. *The Greek World*. Oxford: Phaidon, 1980. Useful atlas with essays and maps on special topics, such as raw materials and manufacturing.

Osborne, Robin. *Archaic and Classical Greek Art*. Oxford: Oxford University Press, 1998. A historical consideration of matter and manner in Greek art in centuries extending to Thucydides' epoch.

Talbert, Richard, and Roger Bagnall, eds. *Barrington Atlas of the Greek and Roman World*. Princeton, NJ: Princeton University Press, 2000. The best modern atlas of the ancient world, although large and unwieldy.

Politics, Cities, and Leaders

Andrewes, Antony. *The Greek Tyrants*. London: Hutchinson's University Library, 1956. Good brief introduction to the era that produced the wealth and attitudes of Thucydides' powerful city-states.

Camp, John M. *Archaeology of Athens*. New Haven, CT: Yale University Press, 2001. Well-illustrated introduction to the topography, architecture, and artifacts of the richest and aesthetically leading city of the classical age.

Connor, Robert. *New Politicians of Fifth-century Athens*. Princeton, NJ: Princeton University Press, 1971. Clash of traditional and innovative political methods in the developed Athenian democracy.

Forrest, William George Grieve. *A History of Sparta 950–192 B.C.* London: Hutchinson, 1968. Sober introduction to a poorly documented but essential community.

Ober, Josiah. *Mass and Elite in Democratic Athens*. Princeton, NJ: Princeton University Press, 1989. The ideology and rhetoric of popular rule, especially in the surviving orators.

Ostwald, Martin. *From Popular Sovereignty to the Sovereignty of Law*. Berkeley: University of California Press, 1986. The evolution of legal concepts and controls on the power of the people.

Powell, Anton, ed. *Classical Sparta: Techniques Behind Her Success*. Norman, OK: University of Oklahoma Press, 1989. Essays on an esoteric, xenophobic, and fascinating culture.

Raaflaub, Kurt. *The Discovery of Freedom in Ancient Greece*. English edition updated from the German edition of 1985, translated by R. Franciscono. Chicago: University of Chicago Press, 2004. An analysis of the nuanced Hellenic vocabulary for freedom, including the extensive Athenian evidence.

Roberts, Jennifer Tolbert. *Accountability in Athenian Government*. Madison: University of Wisconsin Press, 1982. Path-breaking study of the limitations placed on executive, judicial, and legislative bodies.

———. *Athens on Trial*. Princeton, NJ: Princeton University Press, 1994. A historical analysis of opinions of the democracy through the ages, from antiquity to nearly the present.

Salmon, J. B. *Wealthy Corinth: A History of the City to 338 B.C.* Oxford: Clarendon Press, 1984. Study of the most important colonizing city-state in ancient Greece and its economic development.

Zimmern, A. E. *The Greek Commonwealth*. Oxford: Clarendon Press, 1911, last edition 1931. Excellent introduction, now somewhat outdated, into the essentials of the city-state for the Greeks.

Imperialism and Warfare

Hanson, Victor Davis, ed. *Hoplites: The Classical Greek Battle Experience*. London and New York: Routledge, 1991. Nine essays on men and equipment, organization (phalanx), environment of battle, and rules of warfare.

Kagan, Donald. *The Outbreak of the Peloponnesian War*. 4 vols. Ithaca, NY: Cornell

University Press, 1969–1987. A blow-by-blow summary of the war, following Thucydides. A "fundamentalist's" sober approach in contrast to Badian's revisionist attitude (see below under "Style, Organization, Themes, and Historical Thought . . .").

* Meiggs, Russell. *The Athenian Empire*. Oxford: Clarendon Press, 1972. Essential introduction to the imperial power's development, finance, military campaigns, and other foreign relations.

Morrison, J. S., and J. F. Coates. *The Athenian Trireme*. Cambridge: Cambridge University Press, 1986. Essential introduction to classical naval warfare and the unusual warships.

Pritchett, W. Kendrick. *The Greek State at War*. 5 vols. Berkeley: University of California Press, 1971–1991. Essential examination of many aspects of Greek hoplite and other forms of warfare and skirmishing.

Ste. Croix, Geoffrey de. "The Character of the Athenian Empire." *Historia* 3 (1954/1955), pp. 1–41. Polemical defense of an unpopular imperial institution from a Marxian perspective.

———. *The Origins of the Peloponnesian War*. London: Duckworth, 1972. Brilliant analysis in meticulous detail of international politics before the outbreak of the war. He finds that the Spartans are to blame for the twenty-seven-year conflict.

Sealey, Raphael. "The Causes of the Peloponnesian War." *Classical Philology* 70 (1975), pp. 89–109. Athenian truculence forced the Spartans to fight.

Wees, Hans van, ed. *War and Violence in Ancient Greece*. London: Duckworth, 2000. Thirteen essays on personal and organized military and political force employed against individuals and groups.

Thucydides: The Man and His Life

Delebecque, Eduard. *Thucydide et Alcibiade*. Aix-en-Provence, France: Ophrys, 1965. Discusses connections between the author and one of his protagonists, perhaps a source. In French.

Grundy, G. B. *Thucydides and the History of His Age*. 1911. 2 vols. Oxford: Blackwell, 1948. Sober study of the material and military worlds (including battlefields) of the late fifth century.

Luschnat, Otto. "Thukydides der Historiker." *Real Encyclopaedie*, Supplement-Band 12, cols. 1085–1354. Stuttgart, Germany: Druckenmüller, 1970. A thorough evaluation of the life, thought, and historiography of the Athenian. In German.

Woodhead, A. G. "Thucydides' Portrait of Cleon." *Mnemosyne* 4:13 (1960), pp. 289–317. Personal grievance and class prejudice explain Thucydides' strong negative bias toward a masterful political presence.

Detailed Commentaries

Cartwright, David. *A Historical Commentary on Thucydides: A Companion*. Ann Arbor: University of Michigan Press, 1997. A handy reference tool for beginners, based on the Warner (Penguin) translation, but using the same established book and chapter numbers as Crawley.

*Gomme, Arnold W., A. Andrewes, and K. J. Dover. *A Historical Commentary on Thucydides*. 5 vols. Oxford: Clarendon Press, 1945–1981. Fullest recent commentary in English, clause by clause.

Hornblower, Simon. *A Commentary on Thucydides*. 2 vols. to date. Oxford: Clarendon

Press, 1991, corrected (lightly modified) in 2003; 1996. A perceptive phrase-by-phrase complement to Gomme et al.'s five volumes, with recent discoveries in epigraphy, topography, etc., and new historiographic approaches.

Rhodes, Peter J. *Thucydides, History III.* Warminster: Aris and Phillips, 1994. One of several detailed volumes in a philological series with facing translations.

Historiographic Antecedents and Contemporary Social, Intellectual, Artistic, and Literary Trends

Bury, John Bagnall. *The Ancient Greek Historians.* 1909. New York: Dover, 1958. Useful and classic introductory survey with a chapter devoted to Thucydides.

Cochrane, Charles. *Thucydides and the Science of History.* 1929. New York: Russell and Russell, 1965. A discussion of the relationship of the historian to the Hippocratic and other scientific traditions of early classical Greece.

Fornara, Charles. *The Nature of History in Ancient Greece and Rome.* Berkeley: University of California Press, 1983. Survey of the genre over a period of a thousand years.

Gomme, Arnold W. *The Greek Attitude to Poetry and History.* Berkeley: University of California Press, 1954. Essays on the status of inspired verse and unphilosophical fact-finding in the archaic and classical periods.

Hunter, Virginia. *Past and Process in Herodotus and Thucydides.* Princeton, NJ: Princeton University Press, 1982. Comparative study of myth, cause, explanation, etc. in the two historians.

Loraux, Nicole. *The Invention of Athens.* 1981. Translated from the French by Alan Sheridan. Cambridge, MA: Harvard University Press, 1986. The ideology of ancient Hellenic democracy and its imagined history.

Marincola, John. *Authority and Tradition in Ancient Historiography.* Cambridge: Cambridge University Press, 1997. Comparison of the attitudes of Thucydides and other historians toward the past and its recorders.

Momigliano, Arnaldo. "Some Observations on Causes of War in Ancient Historiography." 1954. In *Studies in Historiography*, New York: Harper and Row, 1966, pp. 112–126. Comparison of immediate, long-range, and trivial causes in classical historiography.

Munn, Mark. *The School of History: Athens in the Age of Socrates.* Berkeley: University of California Press, 2000. Intellectual and popular Athenian attitudes toward the past before and after 400 B.C.E.

Parke, H. W. "Citation and Recitation: A Convention in Early Greek Historians." *Hermathena* 67 (1946), pp. 80–92. Explanation of where and when the first ancient historians mention predecessors and competitors.

Pearson, Lionel I. C. "Thucydides and the Geographical Tradition." 1939. In *Selected Papers of Lionel Pearson*, edited by D. Lateiner and S. Stephens. Chico, CA: Scholars Press, 1983, pp. 28–34. Examination of Thucydidean passages describing places and peoples.

Solmsen, Friedrich. *Intellectual Experiments of the Greek Enlightenment.* Princeton, NJ: Princeton University Press, 1975. Thucydides' and other intellectuals' responses to sophistic and scientific trends.

Style, Organization, Themes, and Historical Thought
in the History of Thucydides

Adcock, Frank. *Thucydides and His History.* Cambridge: Cambridge University Press, 1963. Well-written introduction that utilizes the work of several significant German studies.

Badian, Ernst. *From Plataea to Potidaea: Studies in the History and Historiography of the Pentacontaetia.* Baltimore, MD: Johns Hopkins University Press, 1993. A disbeliever's approach to a historian who appears here as more a journalist than a political thinker.

Canfora, Luigi. *Tucidide continuato.* Padua, Italy: Antenore, 1970. The end of the *History* and Xenophon's connection to it. In Italian.

Cogan, Mark. *The Human Thing: The Speeches and Principles of Thucydides' History.* Chicago: University of Chicago Press, 1981. A philosophical approach to Thucydides' conception of humanity, starting from an odd Thucydidean phrase.

Collingwood, Robin. *The Idea of History.* Oxford: Clarendon Press, 1946, especially pp. 28–31. A philosopher and Roman archaeologist examines the emergence and problems of the historical discipline with a famous swipe at Thucydides' "bad conscience."

Connor, W. Robert. "A Post-Modernist Thucydides?" *Classical Journal* 72 (1977), pp. 289–298. A seminal article for drawing attention to nonobjective elements in the historian.

———. *Thucydides.* Princeton, NJ: Princeton University Press, 1984. Sympathetic approach to the man and his subject presented in a format that follows the *History* itself.

———. "Narrative Discourse in Thucydides." In *The Greek Historians: Papers Presented to A. E. Raubitschek*, edited by M. H. Jameson. Saratoga, CA: ANMA Libri, 1985, pp. 1–17. The relation of authorial descriptions of events to speeches and editorial analysis.

Cornford, Francis. *Thucydides Mythistoricus.* London: E. Arnold, 1907. A revolutionary consideration of the historian's work as shaped by contemporary tragedy, with less-convincing Marxian analysis of the Athenian capitalist war-party.

Crane, G. *The Blinded Eye.* Lanham, MD: Rowman and Littlefield, 1996. Examines a tension between traditional, personal aristocratic values and the new objective study of the public and the state through the two competing types of rhetoric.

Debnar, Paula. *Speaking the Same Language: Speech and Audience in Thucydides' Spartan Debates.* Ann Arbor: University of Michigan Press, 2001. The presentation of the Spartans and their policies.

Denniston, John D. *Greek Prose Style.* Oxford: Clarendon Press, 1965. A master of Greek literary nuance briefly dissects the achievement of Thucydides on pp. 8–13.

De Romilly, Jacqueline. *Thucydides and Athenian Imperialism.* 1951. Translated from the French by Philip Thody. Oxford: Blackwell, 1963. Influential reexamination of the problem of composition, as well as a study of what Thucydides writes about imperialism.

Dewald, Carolyn. *Thucydides' War Narrative: A Structural Study.* Berkeley: University of California Press, 2005. Revised Berkeley thesis on the larger compositional units of the *History*.

Eckstein, Arthur M. "Thucydides: The Outbreak of the Peloponnesian War, and the Foundation of International Systems Theory." *International Historical Review* 25 (2003), pp. 757–774. Reconsiders Thucydides' introductory account of the causes of the war and misunderstandings by modern analysts who do not read ancient Greek.

Edmunds, Lowell. *Chance and Intelligence in Thucydides.* Cambridge, MA: Harvard University Press, 1975. Perceptive analysis of planning and its frequent disruption in the narrative.

Finley, John. *Thucydides.* Second edition. Cambridge, MA: Harvard University Press, 1942. Influential survey of the historian's literary qualities.

Hornblower, Simon. *Thucydides.* Baltimore, MD: Johns Hopkins University Press, 1987; corrected (lightly modified) in 1994. Advanced introduction to historiographical issues of dating, methods, and many fascinating problems.

Hunter, Virginia. *Thucydides: The Artful Reporter.* Toronto: Hakkert, 1973. A critical brief argument for the fictional nature of Thucydides' speeches and even his reports of historical events.

Lateiner, Donald. "Tissaphernes and the Phoenician Fleet." *Transactions of the American Philological Association* 106 (1976), pp. 267–290. An examination of a threat to Athens in book 8 that never materialized.

———. "Pathos in Thucydides." *Antichthon* 11 (1977), pp. 42–51. Thucydides' vital interest in human suffering and emotion, and their expression in the *History.*

———. "Nicias' Inadequate Encouragement." *Classical Philology* 80 (1985), pp. 201–213. Study of one important character: his predicaments, failures, and Thucydides' judgments.

Macleod, Colin. "Form and Meaning in the Melian Dialogue." 1974. In *Collected Essays*, Oxford: Oxford University Press, 1983, pp. 52–67. The relationship of content to presentation in a unique interchange.

Mahaffy, J. P. *A History of Classical Greek Literature.* Third edition. London: Macmillan, 1890–1891. Mahaffy taught Oscar Wilde a love of things Greek, and toured Italy and Greece with him. They shared Irish intellectual penchants for iconoclasm and wit. Mahaffy's independent judgments deserve—if not agreement—the respect of careful rebuttal.

Orwin, Clifford. *The Humanity of Thucydides.* Princeton, NJ: Princeton University Press, 1994. Thucydides' view of human nature, piety, and justice (from the perspective of Leo Strauss's conservative and German idealist readings of ancient philosophy and the Peloponnesian War's horrifying traumas.

Ostwald, Martin. *Ananke in Thucydides.* Atlanta, GA: Scholars Press, 1988. In Greek, *ananke* means "necessity." A monograph that examines concepts of forces not subject to individual or group redirection.

Parry, Adam. *Logos and Ergon in Thucydides.* New York: Arno Press, 1981. Dissertation on this organizing antithesis in Thucydides' thought and his speakers' rhetoric.

———. "Herodotus and Thucydides." 1968. In *Language of Achilles and Other Papers*, Oxford: Clarendon Press, 1989. Unsympathetic evaluation of two translations, Warner's and de Sélincourt's unrevised version, in an enlightening comparison to Crawley's masterpiece.

Patwell, Joseph. *Grammar, Discourse, and Style in Thucydides Book 8.* Ph.D. diss., University of Pennsylvania, 1978. The last book's deployment of abstract verbal nouns and authorial comments.

Pearson, Lionel I. C. "Thucydides as Reporter and Critic." 1947. In *Selected Papers of Lionel Pearson*, edited by D. Lateiner and S. Stephens, Chico, CA: Scholars Press, 1983, pp. 67–90. The nature of Thucydides' engagements with other authorities.

Pouncey, Peter. *The Necessities of War: A Study of Thucydides' Pessimism.* New York: Columbia University Press, 1980. A dark view of the historian responding to the United States' war with Vietnam.

Pritchett, W. K. *Dionysius of Halicarnassus: On Thucydides.* Berkeley: University of California Press, 1975. Essential exposition of the only detailed ancient essay on Thucydides' style.

Rawlings, Hunter. *The Structure of Thucydides' History.* Princeton, NJ: Princeton University Press, 1981. Analysis of the nature of the sections of this intricate construct.

Rood, Timothy. *Thucydides: Narrative and Explanation.* Oxford: Clarendon Press, 1998. Insightful consideration of the relation of reported events and Thucydides' accounts of their genesis.

Stadter, Philip, ed. *The Speeches in Thucydides.* Chapel Hill: University of North Carolina Press, 1973. Essays discussing different speeches and their relation to what might actually have been said; includes a thorough catalogue.

———. "The Form and Content of Thucydides' Pentacontaetia." *Greek, Roman and Byzantine Studies* 34 (1993), pp. 35–72. Analysis of the crucial survey describing the fifty-year period leading to war.

Stahl, Hans-Peter. *Thucydides: Man's Place in History.* 1966. Translated from the German by Stahl. Swansea: Classical Press of Wales, 2003. A path-breaking study of the role of chance and error, and the limits of human control, in Thucydides' thought.

Strasburger, Herman. "Thukydides und die politische Selbstdarstellung der Athener." *Hermes* 86 (1958), pp. 17–40. A dissection of what Athenians in Thucydides say about the Athenian form of government. In German.

Tompkins, Daniel. "Stylistic Characterization in Thucydides: Nicas and Alcibiades." *Yale Classical Studies* 22 (1972), pp. 181–214. Technical analysis of the degree of syntactical complication and subordination in two speakers.

Wasserman, Felix. "The Speeches of King Archidamus in Thucydides." *Classical Journal* 48 (1952/1953), pp. 193–200. Three speeches in the text and the narrative both portray a person of intelligence and political virtue.

* Westlake, H. D. *Individuals in Thucydides.* Cambridge: Cambridge University Press, 1968. Depictions of eleven principal figures and the nature of Thucydides' explicit and implicit judgments about protagonists.

———. *Essays on the Greek Historians and Greek History.* Manchester, UK: University of Manchester Press, 1969. Studies on historiography by perhaps the closest student of Thucydides in the twentieth century.

———. "Personal Motives, Aims, and Feelings in Thucydides." In his *Studies in Thucydides and Greek History*, Bristol, UK: Bristol Classical Press, 1989, pp. 201–223. Perceptive summary of a once-neglected facet of Thucydides' concerns.

Wilson, John. "What Does Thucydides Claim for His Speeches?" *Phoenix* 36 (1982), pp. 95–103. Defense of the historicity of the substance and of all the major points reported by Thucydides.

Other Works Cited in the Introduction

Edmunds, Lowell. Bibliographical website: http://www.rci.rutgers.edu/~edmunds/thuc.html

Nietzsche, Friedrich. *Wir Philologen* (*We Classicists*). Translated by William Arrowsmith. In *Unmodern Observations*, New Haven, CT: Yale University Press, 1990, pp. 321–387. Caustic portrait of classics professors with an appreciation of Thucydides' uniquely convoluted modes of expression.

HISTORICAL INDEX

The following index has been adapted from Thucydides, second revised edition *(two volumes), translated into English by Benjamin Jowett, published in 1900 by Clarendon Press, Oxford.*

Athenians (*continued*)

ades is accused of profaning the mysteries, but sent to Sicily untried, 6. 28, 29; the expedition starts for Sicily, 6. 30–32; review of the troops at Corcyra, 6. 42; the Athenians arrive at Rhegium, 6. 43, 44; deceived by the Egestæans, 6. 46; the generals hold a council of war, 6. 47–49; Alcibiades' opinion prevails, 6. 50; the Athenians sail to Syracuse, 6. 50; obtain possession of Catana, 6. 51; not received at Camarina, 6. 52; the excitement about the mutilation of the Hermæ continues, 6. 53, 60; the Athenians send to arrest Alcibiades, 6. 53, 61; condemn him to death, 6. 61; proceedings of, in Sicily, 6. 62, 63; capture Hyccara, 6. 62; sail to Syracuse, 6. 64, 65; defeat the Syracusans, 6. 66–71; fail in an attempt on Messene, which Alcibiades betrays, 6. 74; send home for money and cavalry, 6. 74 [cp. 93–94]; send an embassy to Camarina, 6. 94, 75; Euphemus' speech, 6. 81–87; fail to win over the Camarinæans, 6. 88; negotiate with the Sicels, 6. 88; winter at Catana and prepare for a spring campaign, 6. 88; receive aid from home, 6. 93, 94; prosecute the campaign, 6. 94; capture Epipolæ and fortify Labdalum, 6. 96, 97; receive Sicilian reinforcements, 6. 98; begin to build a wall of circumvallation, and defeat the Syracusans in various engagements, 6. 98–101; repulse the Syracusans from Epipolæ, 6. 102; begin a double wall from Epipolæ to the sea, 6. 103, 7. 2; openly violate the peace with the Lacedæmonians, 6. 105; Athenian ships arrive at Rhegium too late to stop Gylippus, 7. 1; return no answer to Gylippus' demand that they shall quit Sicily, 7. 3; are driven out of Labdalum, 7. 3; repulse an attack on their lines, 7. 4; fortify Plemmyrium, 7. 4; defeat the Syracusans, 7. 5; defeated by the Syracusans, 7. 6; the Athenians, aided by Perdiccas, make an attempt upon Amphipolis, 7. 9; the Athenians at home receive the despatch of Nicias, 7. 10–15; send a second expedition to Sicily under Demosthenes, 7. 16; send a fleet round Peloponnese, 7. 20; conquer the Syracusans at sea, but lose Plemmyrium, 7. 22,

23; skirmish with the Syracusans in the harbour, 7. 25; ravage the Laconian coast, and fortify an isthmus there, 7. 26; resolve to send back some Thracians who have come too late to join the reinforcements to Sicily, 7. 27 [who sack Mycalessus on their way, 29, 30]; suffer terribly from the occupation of Decelea by the Lacedæmonians, 7. 27, 28; Demosthenes meets Eurymedon with news from Sicily, 7. 31; Demosthenes and Eurymedon collect troops in Acarnania and Corcyra, 7. 31; the Athenians in Sicily induce the Sicels to destroy reinforcements on their way to Syracuse, 7. 32; Demosthenes arrives at Thurii, 7. 33; the Athenians at Naupactus fight an indecisive engagement at sea with the Corinthians, 7. 34; consider themselves defeated because not signally the victors, 7. 34; defeated at sea by the Syracusans, 7. 37–41; repulsed in a night attack on Epipolæ, 7. 43–45; the Athenian generals hold a council, 7. 47–49; Nicias wishes to delay and Demosthenes yields, 7. 49; Nicias at last consents to move, but terrified by an eclipse remains another 27 days, 7. 50; the Athenians are again defeated at sea by the Syracusans, 7. 52; gain a slight advantage by land, 7. 53; why they failed to conquer Syracuse, 7. 55; the list of their allies before Syracuse, 7. 57; determine to fight their way out, 7. 60; Nicias addresses the troops, 7. 61–64; and the trierarchs, 7. 69; the Athenians are completely defeated at sea, 7. 70, 71; overwhelmed by misery, refuse to renew the struggle, 7. 72; are misled by false information and delay their retreat three days, 7. 73, 74; their misery and terror when commencing the retreat, 7. 75; encouraged and consoled by Nicias, 7. 76, 77; during four days are harassed and at length confronted by the enemy, 7. 78, 79; fall back, 7. 79; recommence retreat, changing their route, 7. 80; seized with a panic, 7. 80; the second division is overtaken and compelled to surrender, 7. 81, 82; the first meets the same fate on the Assinarus, 7. 83–85; three hundred escape, 7. 83; but are captured, 7. 85; Nicias and Demosthenes are put to

Chalcidice (*continued*)

pursue the retreating Athenians, 5. 10; provisions respecting the Chalcidian cities in the Treaty of Peace, 5. 18; the Chalcidians refuse to accept the Treaty, 5. 21; join the Argive alliance, 5. 31; renew the alliance with Lacedæmon, 5. 80; receive the Dians who had revolted from the Athenians, 5. 82; maintain a ten days' armistice with the Athenians, 6. 7.

Chalcis, in Ætolia, taken by the Athenians, 1. 108, 2. 83.

Chalcis, in Eubœa, 7. 29; the mother city of the Chalcidian cities in Sicily, 6. 3–5; of Cyme in Italy, 6. 4; war between Chalcis and Eretria, 1. 15; Chalcis subject to the Athenians, 6. 76, 7. 57; the Athenians retreat to Chalcis after the sea-fight off Eretria, 8. 95.

Chance, to chance men ascribe whatever belies their calculation, 1. 140.

Chaones, a people in Epirus, are barbarians, 2. 68; have no king, 2. 80; their military reputation, 2. 81; assist in the invasion of Acarnania, 2. 80; defeated by the Stratians, 2. 81.

Charadrus, scene of military trials at Argos, 5. 60.

Charicles, an Athenian commander, 7. 20, 26.

Charminus, an Athenian commander, 8. 30, 41; defeated by the Lacedæmonians, 8. 42; abets the murder of Hyperbolus, 8. 73.

Charœades, an Athenian commander in Sicily, 3. 86; killed in action, 3. 90.

Charybdis, the whirlpool of, 4. 24.

Chersonesus, in Corinthian territory, 4. 42, 43.

Chersonese, the Thracian, cultivated by the Greek armament at Troy, 1. 11; ravaged by the Lacedæmonians, 8. 99; naval operations off its coast, 8. 102–105.

Children, a man without children has no stake in the country, 2. 44.

Children of the fallen, maintained at the public charge in Athens, 2. 46.

Chimerium, in Thesprotia, 1. 30; situation of, 1. 46; Corinthian fleet anchors there, 1. 46.

Chionis, a Lacedæmonian, swears to the Treaty of Peace and the Alliance, 5. 19, 24.

Chios, its moderate and stable government, 8. 24; its naval power, 8. 6 [cp. 1. 19, 2. 9, 56]; its riches, 8. 24; great number of slaves there, 8. 40; Chios and Lesbos the only free allies of Athens, 3. 10, 6. 85, 7. 57; Homer at Chios, 3. 104; the Chians assist the Athenians against the Samians, 1. 116, 117; furnish ships in the siege of Potidæa, 2. 56, 6. 31; Alcidas puts some Chian prisoners to death, 3. 32; releases the remainder on a remonstrance from the Samian exiles, 3. 32; Chians aid the Athenians at Pylos, 4. 13; ordered by the Athenians to dismantle their walls, 4. 51; furnish ships against Mende and Scione, 4. 129; against Melos, 5. 84; aid the Athenians at Syracuse, 6. 43, 85, 7. 20, 57; negotiate with the Lacedæmonians about revolting, 8. 5; received into alliance, 8. 6; send the Athenians ships as a pledge of fidelity, 8. 9; revolt, 8. 14; employed by Alcibiades to raise revolt in Ionia, beginning with Miletus, 8. 17; four of their ships are taken by the Athenians, 8. 19; induce Lebedos and Eræ to revolt, 8. 19; then Methymna and Mitylene, 8. 22; lose a few ships off Lesbos, 8. 23; defeated in three battles by the Athenians, 8. 24; their sufferings lead some to negotiate with the Athenians, 8. 24, 31, 38; aid in the capture of Iasus, 8. 28; the Athenians prepare to attack them, 8. 30; the Chians refuse to assist Astyochus in procuring the revolt of Lesbos, 8. 32; three Chian ships are chased by the Athenians into Chios, 8. 34; have their government changed by the Lacedæmonians, 8. 38; completely blockaded, 8. 40; implore the aid of Astyochus, 8. 38, 40; defeated by the Athenians and more closely blockaded, 8. 55, 56; gain an advantage at sea over the Athenians, 8. 61; regain the command of the sea, on the withdrawal of a part of the Athenian fleet, 8. 62, 63; the Athenians plan a fresh attack on Chios, on the arrival of a Lacedæmonian fleet under Mindarus, 8. 100; the Lacedæmonians slip away, 8. 101; the Chians lose

attack Methymna, 3. 18; Mitylene is blockaded by land, 3. 18; Salæthus is sent from Lacedæmon to Mitylene, 3. 25; Salæthus arms the people, who insist on surrendering the city, 3. 27, 28; the news reaching the Peloponnesian fleet, Teutiaplus advises an immediate attack on Mitylene, 3. 29, 30; Paches sends Salæthus, and the most guilty of the Mitylenians to Athens, 3. 35; all the grown up citizens condemned to death by the Athenians, 3. 36; feeling at Athens changes, 3. 36; speech of Cleon against the recall of the decree, 3. 37–40; of Diodotus in favour of recalling it, 3. 41–48; the decree is recalled, 3. 49; the second ship sent to stay the slaughter arrives in time by great exertions, 3. 49; the captives at Athens put to death, their fleet and dependencies taken away, the walls of Mitylene razed, 3. 50; Lesbian refugees take Rhœteum and Antandrus, 4. 52; driven out again by the Athenians, 4. 75; Mitylene revolts a second time, 8. 22; recaptured by the Athenians, 8. 23; garrisoned by the Athenians, 8. 100.

Molobrus, father of Epitadas, a Lacedæmonian, 4. 8.

Molossians, Admetus, king of the Molossians, shelters Themistocles, 1. 136, 137; the Molossians assist in the Lacedæmonian invasion of Acarnania, 2. 80.

Molycrium, a Corinthian colony, subject to Athens, 2. 84, 3. 102; taken by the Peloponnesians, 3. 102; the Molycrian Rhium, 2. 86.

Morgantine, handed over to the Camarinæans, 4. 65.

Motye, a Phœnician settlement in Sicily, 6. 2.

Munychia, a harbour of Athens, 2. 13; Peripoli stationed at Munychia, 8. 92; a Dionysiac Theatre near, 8. 93.

Mycale, battle of, 1. 89; Athenian and Peloponnesian fleets at Mycale, 8. 79.

Mycalessus, in Bœotia, 7. 29; sacked by Thracians in Athenian service, 7. 29, 30.

Mycenæ, kingdom of, 1. 9; the small remains of Mycenæ do not disprove its former greatness, 1. 10.

Myconus, one of the Cyclades, 3. 29.

Mygdonia, part of, assigned to the Chalcidians by Perdiccas, 1. 58; once inhabited by the Edonians, 2. 99; ravaged by Sitalces, 2. 100.

Mylæ, a town of the Messenians in Sicily, 3. 90; captured by the Athenians, 3. 90.

Myletidæ, Syracusan exiles, take part in colonising Himera, 6. 5.

Myoneans, an Ozolian Locrian tribe, 3. 101.

Myonnesus, near Teos, 3. 32.

Myrcinus, an Edonian town, joins Brasidas, 4. 107; Myrcinian targeteers at the battle of Amphipolis, 5. 6; Myrcinian cavalry there, 5. 10; Cleon killed by a Myrcinian targeteer, 5. 10.

Myronides, an Athenian, defeats the Corinthians in Megaris, 1. 105; defeats the Bœotians at Œnophyta, 1. 108 [cp. 4. 95].

Myrrhine, wife of Hippias, the tyrant of Athens, 6. 55.

Myrtilus, an Athenian, swears to the Treaty of Peace and the Alliance, 5. 19, 24.

Myscon, a Syracusan general, 8. 85.

Mysteries, profanation of the mysteries at Athens, 6. 28; Alcibiades accused, 6. 28; supposed to be part of a plot against the democracy, 6. 28, 60, 61; Alcibiades and some of his comrades summoned home from Sicily, 6. 53, 61.

Myus, a city in Caria (Ionia), 3. 19; given by the King to Themistocles, 1. 138.

N

Nature, human, 'always ready to transgress the laws,' 3. 84; 'prone to domineer over the subservient,' 4. 61, 5. 105; prompts men to accept a proffered empire, 1. 76; ever credulous, 1. 20; jealous, 2. 35; changes with the changes of fortune, 1. 84, 140, 2. 61, 3. 39, 4. 17; prone to error, 3. 45, 4. 18; misled in its judgments by hope, 3. 39, 4. 108; yields when met in a yielding spirit, 4. 19; inherent vanity of, 5. 68; sameness of, 1. 21, 76, 3. 45, 82.

Naucleides, a Platæan, invites the Thebans to Platæa, 2. 2.

Naucrates, father of Damotimus, a Sicyonian, 4. 119.

Naupactus, settled by the Helots from Ithome, 1. 103; allied to the Athenians, 2. 9; becomes the headquarters of an Athenian fleet, 2. 69, 84, 92, 3. 114, 4. 13; the Peloponnesians hope to take it, 2.

appointed one of the generals in Sicily, 6. 8; speech of, 6. 9–14; second speech of, 6. 20–23; gives an estimate of the forces required, 6. 25; argues in a council of war for an attack on Selinus, 6. 47; goes to Egesta, 6. 62; defeats the Syracusans, 6. 67–70; saves Epipolæ, 6. 102; becomes sole commander after the death of Lamachus, 6. 103; negotiates with the Syracusans, 6. 103 [cp. 7. 48, 49, 73, 86]; fails to prevent the coming of Gylippus, 7. 1, 2; fortifies Plemmyrium, 7. 4; defeated by the Syracusans, 7. 6; sends a dispatch to Athens, 7. 8, 10, 11–15; destroys by an ambush the Syracusan reinforcements, 7. 32; left in the Athenian lines while Demosthenes attacks Epipolæ, 7. 43; swayed by information from Syracuse and fear of public opinion at home, he refuses to abandon the siege, 7. 48, 49; yields at last, 7. 50; but, an eclipse of the moon occurring, decides in accordance with the general feeling to remain thrice nine days, 7. 50; exhorts the army before the last battle, 7. 61–64; addresses the trierarchs, 7. 69; encourages his retreating soldiers, 7. 76, 77; commands one division in the retreat, 7. 78; overtaken and compelled to surrender, 7. 83–85; put to death by the Syracusans, 7. 86.

Nicolaus, a Lacedæmonian ambassador to Persia, 2. 67.

Nicomachus, a Phocian, betrays to the Lacedæmonians the Athenian plan for the conquest of Bœotia, 4. 89.

Nicomedes, a Lacedæmonian, general in place of King Pleistoanax, 1. 107.

Nicon, a Bœotian, commands the reinforcements to Syracuse, 7. 19.

Niconidas, a Thessalian, escorts Brasidas through Thessaly, 4. 78.

Nicostratus, an Athenian general, sails to Corcyra; his humane conduct there, 3. 75; colleague of Nicias, 4. 53; assists in the capture of Cythera, 4. 53, 54; of Mende, 4. 129, 130; and in the blockade of Scione, 4. 131; swears to the one year's Truce, 4. 119; brings with Laches an expedition to Argos, 5. 61; falls at Mantinea, 5. 74.

Nightingale, called by the poets the "Daulian bird," 2. 29.

Nile, 1. 104, 110.

Nine Ways, old name of Amphipolis, 1. 100, 4. 102.

Nisæa, the harbour of Megara, 2. 93, 4. 66; connected with the city by the Long Walls, 1. 103; occupied by the Athenians, 1. 103, 1. 114; restored under the thirty years' Peace, 1. 115; Cleon demands its surrender with other places after the blockade of Sphacteria, 4. 21; garrisoned by Peloponnesian forces, 4. 66; captured by the Athenians, 4. 69; Brasidas arrives too late to save it, 4. 70; cavalry engagement before Nisæa, 4. 72; the Athenians at Nisæa refuse battle with Brasidas, 4. 73 [cp. Brasidas' account, 4. 85, 108]; not given up under the treaty, 5. 17.

Nisus, Temple of, at Nisæa, 4. 118. 3.

Nomothetæ, appointed at Athens after the deposition of the Four Hundred, 8. 97.

Notium, seditions there, Paches gains the city by a trick, 3. 34; handed over to the Colophonians by the Athenians, 3. 34.

Nymphodorus, of Abdera, negotiates an alliance between his brother-in-law Sitalces and the Athenians, 2. 29.

O

Obols, Æginetan, 5. 47. 4.

Ocytus, father of Æneas, a Corinthian, 4. 119.

Odomantians, a people in Thrace, 2. 101; Polles, their king, 5. 6.

Odrysians, a people in Thrace, their empire founded by Teres, 2. 29; Sitalces, their king, becomes the ally of the Athenians, 2. 29; his campaign against Perdiccas, 2. 95, 98–101; the greatness and wealth of his kingdom, 2. 96, 97.

Odysseus, his passage through Charybdis, 4. 24.

Œantheans, an Ozolian Locrian tribe, 3. 101.

Œneon, a town in Ozolian Locris, 3. 68, 95, 102.

Œniadæ, in Acarnania, its situation, 2. 102; hostile to the Athenians, 2. 82, 102, 3. 94; besieged by Pericles, 1. 111; attacked by Asopius, 3. 7; the fugitives from Olpæ find refuge there, 3. 114; compelled to enter the Athenian alliance, 4. 77.

V

W

Look for the following titles, available now and forthcoming from
BARNES & NOBLE CLASSICS.

Visit your local bookstore for these and more fine titles.
Or to order online go to: WWW.BN.COM/CLASSICS

Title	Author	ISBN	Price
Aesop's Fables	Aesop	1-59308-062-X	$5.95
The Age of Innocence	Edith Wharton	1-59308-143-X	$5.95
Agnes Grey	Anne Brontë	1-59308-323-8	$5.95
Alice's Adventures in Wonderland and Through the Looking-Glass	Lewis Carroll	1-59308-015-8	$5.95
Anna Karenina	Leo Tolstoy	1-59308-027-1	$8.95
The Art of War	Sun Tzu	1-59308-017-4	$7.95
The Awakening and Selected Short Fiction	Kate Chopin	1-59308-113-8	$6.95
Babbitt	Sinclair Lewis	1-59308-267-3	$7.95
Barchester Towers	Anthony Trollope	1-59308-337-8	$7.95
The Beautiful and Damned	F. Scott Fitzgerald	1-59308-245-2	$7.95
Beowulf	Anonymous	1-59308-266-5	$4.95
Bleak House	Charles Dickens	1-59308-311-4	$9.95
The Bostonians	Henry James	1-59308-297-5	$7.95
The Brothers Karamazov	Fyodor Dostoevsky	1-59308-045-X	$9.95
The Call of the Wild and White Fang	Jack London	1-59308-200-2	$5.95
Candide	Voltaire	1-59308-028-X	$4.95
A Christmas Carol, The Chimes and The Cricket on the Hearth	Charles Dickens	1-59308-033-6	$5.95
The Collected Poems of Emily Dickinson	Emily Dickinson	1-59308-050-6	$5.95
Common Sense and Other Writings	Thomas Paine	1-59308-209-6	$6.95
The Communist Manifesto and Other Writings	Karl Marx and Friedrich Engels	1-59308-100-6	$5.95
The Complete Sherlock Holmes, Vol. I	Sir Arthur Conan Doyle	1-59308-034-4	$7.95
The Complete Sherlock Holmes, Vol. II	Sir Arthur Conan Doyle	1-59308-040-9	$7.95
A Connecticut Yankee in King Arthur's Court	Mark Twain	1-59308-210-X	$7.95
The Count of Monte Cristo	Alexandre Dumas	1-59308-151-0	$7.95
The Country of the Pointed Firs and Selected Short Fiction	Sarah Orne Jewett	1-59308-262-2	$6.95
Daisy Miller and Washington Square	Henry James	1-59308-105-7	$4.95
Daniel Deronda	George Eliot	1-59308-290-8	$8.95
David Copperfield	Charles Dickens	1-59308-063-8	$7.95
Dead Souls	Nikolai Gogol	1-59308-092-1	$7.95
The Death of Ivan Ilych and Other Stories	Leo Tolstoy	1-59308-069-7	$7.95
The Deerslayer	James Fenimore Cooper	1-59308-211-8	$7.95
Don Quixote	Miguel de Cervantes	1-59308-046-8	$9.95
Dracula	Bram Stoker	1-59308-114-6	$6.95
Emma	Jane Austen	1-59308-152-9	$6.95
The Enchanted Castle and Five Children and It	Edith Nesbit	1-59308-274-6	$6.95
Essays and Poems by Ralph Waldo Emerson		1-59308-076-X	$6.95
Essential Dialogues of Plato		1-59308-269-X	$9.95
The Essential Tales and Poems of Edgar Allan Poe		1-59308-064-6	$7.95
Ethan Frome and Selected Stories	Edith Wharton	1-59308-090-5	$5.95

(continued)

Middlemarch	George Eliot	1-59308-023-9	$8.95
Moby-Dick	Herman Melville	1-59308-018-2	$9.95
Moll Flanders	Daniel Defoe	1-59308-216-9	$5.95
The Moonstone	Wilkie Collins	1-59308-322-X	$7.95
My Ántonia	Willa Cather	1-59308-202-9	$5.95
My Bondage and My Freedom	Frederick Douglass	1-59308-301-7	$6.95
Nana	Émile Zola	1-59308-292-4	$6.95
Narrative of Sojourner Truth		1-59308-293-2	$6.95
Narrative of the Life of Frederick Douglass, an American Slave		1-59308-041-7	$4.95
Nicholas Nickleby	Charles Dickens	1-59308-300-9	$8.95
Night and Day	Virginia Woolf	1-59308-212-6	$7.95
Northanger Abbey	Jane Austen	1-59308-264-9	$5.95
Nostromo	Joseph Conrad	1-59308-193-6	$7.95
O Pioneers!	Willa Cather	1-59308-205-3	$5.95
The Odyssey	Homer	1-59308-009-3	$5.95
Oliver Twist	Charles Dickens	1-59308-206-1	$6.95
The Origin of Species	Charles Darwin	1-59308-077-8	$7.95
Paradise Lost	John Milton	1-59308-095-6	$7.95
Père Goriot	Honoré de Balzac	1-59308-285-1	$7.95
Persuasion	Jane Austen	1-59308-130-8	$5.95
Peter Pan	J. M. Barrie	1-59308-213-4	$4.95
The Picture of Dorian Gray	Oscar Wilde	1-59308-025-5	$4.95
The Pilgrim's Progress	John Bunyan	1-59308-254-1	$7.95
Poetics and Rhetoric	Aristotle	1-59308-307-6	$9.95
The Portrait of a Lady	Henry James	1-59308-096-4	$7.95
A Portrait of the Artist as a Young Man and Dubliners	James Joyce	1-59308-031-X	$6.95
The Possessed	Fyodor Dostoevsky	1-59308-250-9	$9.95
Pride and Prejudice	Jane Austen	1-59308-201-0	$5.95
The Prince and Other Writings	Niccolò Machiavelli	1-59308-060-3	$5.95
The Prince and the Pauper	Mark Twain	1-59308-218-5	$4.95
Pudd'nhead Wilson and Those Extraordinary Twins	Mark Twain	1-59308-255-X	$5.95
The Purgatorio	Dante Alighieri	1-59308-219-3	$7.95
Pygmalion and Three Other Plays	George Bernard Shaw	1-59308-078-6	$7.95
The Red and the Black	Stendhal	1-59308-286-X	$7.95
The Red Badge of Courage and Selected Short Fiction	Stephen Crane	1-59308-119-7	$4.95
Republic	Plato	1-59308-097-2	$6.95
The Return of the Native	Thomas Hardy	1-59308-220-7	$7.95
Robinson Crusoe	Daniel Defoe	1-59308-360-2	$5.95
A Room with a View	E. M. Forster	1-59308-288-6	$5.95
Sailing Alone Around the World	Joshua Slocum	1-59308-303-3	$6.95
Scaramouche	Rafael Sabatini	1-59308-242-8	$6.95
The Scarlet Letter	Nathaniel Hawthorne	1-59308-207-X	$4.95
The Scarlet Pimpernel	Baroness Orczy	1-59308-234-7	$5.95
The Secret Garden	Frances Hodgson Burnett	1-59308-277-0	$5.95
Selected Stories of O. Henry		1-59308-042-5	$5.95
Sense and Sensibility	Jane Austen	1-59308-125-1	$5.95
Sentimental Education	Gustave Flaubert	1-59308-306-8	$6.95
Silas Marner and Two Short Stories	George Eliot	1-59308-251-7	$6.95

(continued)

Sister Carrie	Theodore Dreiser	1-59308-226-6	$7.95
Six Plays by Henrik Ibsen		1-59308-061-1	$8.95
Sons and Lovers	D. H. Lawrence	1-59308-013-1	$7.95
The Souls of Black Folk	W. E. B. Du Bois	1-59308-014-X	$5.95
The Strange Case of Dr. Jekyll and Mr. Hyde and Other Stories	Robert Louis Stevenson	1-59308-131-6	$4.95
Swann's Way	Marcel Proust	1-59308-295-9	$8.95
A Tale of Two Cities	Charles Dickens	1-59308-138-3	$5.95
Tao Te Ching	Lao Tzu	1-59308-256-8	$5.95
Tess of d'Urbervilles	Thomas Hardy	1-59308-228-2	$7.95
This Side of Paradise	F. Scott Fitzgerald	1-59308-243-6	$6.95
Three Lives	Gertrude Stein	1-59308-320-3	$6.95
The Three Musketeers	Alexandre Dumas	1-59308-148-0	$8.95
Thus Spoke Zarathustra	Friedrich Nietzsche	1-59308-278-9	$7.95
Tom Jones	Henry Fielding	1-59308-070-0	$8.95
Treasure Island	Robert Louis Stevenson	1-59308-247-9	$4.95
The Turn of the Screw, The Aspern Papers and Two Stories	Henry James	1-59308-043-3	$5.95
Twenty Thousand Leagues Under the Sea	Jules Verne	1-59308-302-5	$5.95
Uncle Tom's Cabin	Harriet Beecher Stowe	1-59308-121-9	$7.95
Utopia	Sir Thomas More	1-59308-244-4	$5.95
Vanity Fair	William Makepeace Thackeray	1-59308-071-9	$7.95
The Varieties of Religious Experience	William James	1-59308-072-7	$7.95
Villette	Charlotte Brontë	1-59308-316-5	$7.95
The Virginian	Owen Wister	1-59308-236-3	$7.95
The Voyage Out	Virginia Woolf	1-59308-229-0	$6.95
Walden and Civil Disobedience	Henry David Thoreau	1-59308-208-8	$5.95
War and Peace	Leo Tolstoy	1-59308-073-5	$12.95
Ward No. 6 and Other Stories	Anton Chekhov	1-59308-003-4	$7.95
The Waste Land and Other Poems	T. S. Eliot	1-59308-279-7	$4.95
The Way We Live Now	Anthony Trollope	1-59308-304-1	$9.95
The Wind in the Willows	Kenneth Grahame	1-59308-265-7	$4.95
The Wings of the Dove	Henry James	1-59308-296-7	$7.95
Wives and Daughters	Elizabeth Gaskell	1-59308-257-6	$7.95
The Woman in White	Wilkie Collins	1-59308-280-0	$7.95
Women in Love	D. H. Lawrence	1-59308-258-4	$8.95
The Wonderful Wizard of Oz	L. Frank Baum	1-59308-221-5	$6.95
Wuthering Heights	Emily Brontë	1-59308-128-6	$5.95

JB

BARNES & NOBLE CLASSICS

If you are an educator and would like to receive an
Examination or Desk Copy of a Barnes & Noble Classic edition,
please refer to Academic Resources on our website at
WWW.BN.COM/CLASSICS
or contact us at
B&NCLASSICS@BN.COM.

All prices are subject to change.